THE EXERCISE OF VITAL POWERS

LEGENDS OF THE ORDER, BOOK 1

IAN GREGOIRE

Revised 2nd Edition Published 2018

by

Lucid Dream

The Fantasy & Science Fiction Imprint Of Ian Gregoire

DEDICATION

This book is dedicated to you, Kaitlin Gray. Most writers will tell you that the biggest obstacle they had to over come was their own self-doubt. Your support and encouragement has really helped me to get the better of mine, for which I am very grateful. So, if you keep on reading, I'll keep on writing.

ACKNOWLEDGEMENTS

Writing a novel may be a solitary endeavour but getting it published certainly isn't. A number of people contributed to getting this second edition of The Exercise Of Vital Powers into your hands, and that deserves recognition. I would like to thank the following people for their hard work.

First, I'd like to thank my editor, Elizabeth M. Hurst, for agreeing to take on the task and doing such a diligent job, giving my manuscript the extra editorial polish it needed. The blame for any issues readers have with the story should be laid at my door. Next, I have to thank the design team at Damonza.com who are responsible for the excellent artwork gracing this new edition of the book. They took onboard my ideas and produced a cover even better than I hoped for. Finally, thank you to cartographer, Soraya Corcoran, for the beautiful new map that now graces this revised edition of the book.

To conclude, I want to confess that not so long ago I believed that the hardest aspect of being an author is to write and finish a novel. I have since come to realise there is something even harder than that: getting people to read your book. With that in mind, I am very grateful to those bloggers/reviewers who took a chance on reading the first edition of The Exercise Of Vital Powers in 2017 when so many others wouldn't. There are six people in particular I'd like to thank, and they are: Angelica Ross, Brittany Hay, Kristen McDowell, Rachel Green and Lukasz Przywoski. And last but by no means least, a special thank you to Kim Missen; book two, if and when it arrives will be dedicated to you.

FOREWORD

This second edition of The Exercise Of Vital Powers, exists for a number of reasons, each of them amounting to the same thing: necessity.

I originally wrote the book intending for it to be a standalone story, and it was subsequently published as such. Being a debut self-published novel, I had no expectation that it would sell well, and I didn't. In fact, sales were even more disastrous than I had anticipated and there was nothing I could do to reverse that. But there was no imperative to do so; I had no reason to view the low sales as a problem to be overcome. At least, not while The Exercise Of Vital Powers remained a standalone novel.

Once I began writing a sequel I realised I had a dilemma on my hands. Did it make sense to write a book for a potential readership of two dozen people? Probably not. However, not only was I fully committed to the sequel, I also planned to write an additional three instalments after that. It was then necessary to do something to drastically increase the number of people who have read The Exercise Of Vital Powers by the time the second book is published. The only feasible means at my disposal to accomplish that objective was to release a revised second edition, addressing all the issues preventing the first edition from selling well, particularly the external appearance of the book.

The end result of this endeavour is the book you now have in your hands. While there is no guarantee of sales success, it is my hope that The Exercise Of Vital Powers will find the audience it deserves second time around.

Ian Gregoire (London, June 2018)

THE NINE KINGDOMS
NORTHEAST KARLANDRIA

Continent of VAIDASOVIA

Continent of YANTASHA

The FAR WEST

ZENOSHA

Shali
Beltraris Campus

ASTANA

LIRANTANA

Tulido

Sharadi Forest

Jendaris Campus
Mendierta

FARINTANA

Durenis Campus

Belona

MIRTANA

Lamara

Antartis Campus
Timarto

BALINTANA

SHINTANA

Damaris Campus

Krindari Forest

Saldanina

Panacena

Runare

Merla Campus

Lilac Valley

YARISTANA

Beltraris Campus

JIBALTA

Sevantis Campus

Petilanta

Urraris Campus

LESHEK

DARMITANA

Sanlarella

Fantabelis

Ludurona

Naldashian River

Agunean River

SIRATHANIA

RANDISSAR

Bandar

Lake Anzar

Neretan

ANZARMENIA

Asderan

Sevdunor

Barzu

Nagotnorak

THE NINE KINGDOMS
NORTHEAST KARLANDRIA

◉ Capital City
◎ Major City
• Town
◈ Campus of the Order

✗ Place of Interest
‑ ‑ ‑ Agreed Border
• • • Disputed Border

CHAPTER ONE

Follow The Leader

The moment they had all been awaiting since nightfall was close at hand. The dark, billowing cloud languidly traversed the night sky, gradually eclipsing the full moon, and plunging the abandoned fort below into darkness.

Now!

Kayden was the first to emerge from the trees, breaking into a sprint up the shallow incline towards the dilapidated south wall of the fort, her five companions in close pursuit. The black hooded cloak she wore—invisible in the dark—fluttered audibly as she ran with composed, steady strides. Her calm, economic running belied her intense determination. It was imperative they crossed the three hundred yard distance between the woods and the old fortress before the moon re-emerged from behind the cloud cover. If even a single person saw them, the mission was over.

Eyes fixedly ahead, Kayden could just about make out the stone masonry of the wall towards which they were charging. She and her fellow apprentices were almost halfway there.

Just as Sinton, and then Lazar—two of the contingent's four male members—passed on either side of her, a glowing orb shot up into the air before erupting, its silent detonation illuminating the sky like a lightning strike. It had originated from the north side of the fort, allowing the would-be infiltrators to remain cloaked by darkness as they approached from the south.

1

"Keep moving!" Lazar urged, barely above a whisper.

It didn't need to be said. Kayden was just as aware, as they all were, that simply being seen by one of the patrolling sentries meant failure. Though there was no reason to suspect the King's Guard on duty that night had specific foreknowledge of an imminent infiltration, they were sure to be in a state of heightened alert given the three failed attempts that week. Their use of *Zarantar* was a good precautionary countermeasure against the darkness; the invocation of *Kiraydan* would have the same effect as a real lightning strike in lighting up the night sky. It was also a disturbing development. But there was no time to dwell upon it further; it was probably only a matter of time before someone much closer to their position sent up an orb that lit them up like a lantern.

A second, and then a third and a fourth orb erupted in the sky in quick succession...getting closer.

Kayden reached the wall moments after Sinton and Lazar, just ahead of Bartis and Vartan—the other two male members of the group—with Neryssa, the only other female, arriving shortly after.

They all crouched down low, pressed up against the wall.

"We can use that as our point of entry," Kayden whispered, pointing to a breach in the wall about eighteen feet above and a little to the right. "Sinton, go up ahead and make sure there are no surprises waiting for us on the other side of this wall."

"Hey! I was put in charge of this assignment, Kayden," snapped Lazar. "Don't you start issuing orders. I lead, you follow."

"Whatever you say, oh fearless leader," retorted Kayden with barely disguised disdain. "Go ahead and order him to make sure the coast is clear, if it makes you feel better. Just be quick about it, the cloud cover won't last forever and there's a patrol approaching our position from the west."

"I think she's right," Vartan whispered over Lazar's shoulder.

Grudgingly, Lazar glanced at Sinton to give him an affirmative nod of the head indicating he should proceed.

They all watched as their colleague shuffled to the right to stand directly below the breach in the wall, before invoking *Makfayshulat* to levitate into the air then disappear through the gaping hole in the wall. Seconds later his head peered back out and he signalled down that the way was clear.

One by one the rest of the party levitated to enter through the breach in the wall to join Sinton with Lazar bringing up the rear.

Inside, Kayden stood motionless waiting for her eyes to adjust to the dark interior. She felt an all too familiar sensation nearby then her eyes were assailed by a pale blue light that lit the room they had entered. She spun around to pinpoint the source of the light, and saw the illumination orb floating in the palm of Lazar's hand. Without hesitation she thrust out her hand, invoking *Yuksaydan* to neutralise Lazar's invocation of *Sinjaydan*, darkening the room once more as the orb was extinguished instantly.

"What the—" Lazar began.

"Are you trying to give us away, you idiot?" hissed Kayden, cutting him off mid-sentence. "If any of the perimeter patrols see a light coming from that gaping hole in the wall, they'll know we're here."

"It can't be helped. I need to take a quick look at the plans for the fort."

"Was there some reason why you couldn't memorise the layout, like I did?" There was no immediate reply. "It's all right, fearless leader, I know where in the fortress we are." She made no effort to hide the condescension in her tone. "If you like, how about I lead and you follow?"

Moonlight began to filter into the room as the cloud cover outside dissipated. Kayden could now see the rest of the group more clearly. Vartan was standing a few paces to her left—tall and stocky, with the olive complexion common to most of the people of The Nine Kingdoms, and short dark hair. Unsurprisingly, he was wearing his customary grim expression.

Standing together a few paces to her right were Bartis, decidedly average in height, build and looks, and Neryssa, slightly shorter than the young man beside her, with a svelte physique, expressive hazel eyes and straight, dark hair flowing down to her shoulders. Standing just behind her right shoulder was Sinton—tall and athletic with the swarthy complexion and thick, tightly curled hair indicative of his Yantashan ethnic heritage. His

3

usually warm, friendly demeanour was now characterised by a no-nonsense, steely determination. Which, of course, left Lazar, the unusually fair-complexioned 'pretty boy', standing directly in front of the breach in the wall ahead of her.

Kayden stood her ground as Lazar closed the distance between them in three languid strides to stand almost on her toes, aggressively infringing her personal space. At five foot ten inches she was taller than most women, but Lazar had four inches on her, and she absolutely hated that he was able to look down on her—in physical terms at least.

"I appreciate the offer," said Lazar with mock sincerity as he reached into his pouch. "But I'm just going to take a quick look at the layout to get our bearings." He pulled out a rolled up scroll and waved it under Kayden's nose. "Then, I will continue to lead the group to the successful completion of this assignment, following the plan I devised."

He walked past her, ensuring that he shoulder barged her in the process, before gesturing for the others to gather around him.

Kayden remained where she stood as the others discussed in hushed tones that they were presently situated on the second floor of the south wing of the old, abandoned fort. Their objective was located within the central keep of the fortress, on the uppermost floor of the four-storey structure, in the office where a military commander would have administered his forces two centuries ago. They would make their way to the centre of the fort to access the central stairwell within the keep, which was the only way to reach the top storey of the building.

The discussion quickly came to a conclusion.

Lazar instructed his five companions to form up in a line behind him. Both he and Vartan seemed to take undue pleasure in the announcement that Kayden should walk at the back of the line. She refrained from initiating an altercation with the pair, despite the temptation to do so. She duly brought up the rear of the party once Lazar had invoked *Sinjaydan* to create another illumination orb that he sent floating ahead of the procession as he led them out of the room into a corridor.

As the group navigated through dusty, deserted corridors

replete with stone walls haphazardly decorated by patches of mould, ceilings littered with cobwebs, and a musty smell lingering in the air, Kayden thought bitterly to herself how much quicker and easier it would be to complete the mission alone. Being compelled to work with others would only hold her back. Her cohorts simply weren't her equals, despite being two to three years older than herself. They were not as gifted, powerful or knowledgeable in *Zarantar*, nor were they as skilled and accomplished in martial combat. If the mission ended in failure she would be incandescent, to say the least.

Kayden was already certain that Lazar's plan—born of simple-minded, conventional thinking—was doomed to fail. But she would continue to feign going along with it until the opportunity to assume command of the group presented itself, which it would, sooner rather than later. In the meantime, she would console herself with her thoughts of how the successful completion of the assignment would bring her one step closer to becoming a full-fledged Sanatsai of *The Order Of The Pledge At Kassani River*. And with her nineteenth birthday only a matter of weeks away, she was well on course to becoming the youngest inductee into the Order. If she could maintain her current rate of progress it was entirely feasible for her to condense the mandatory ten years of training into seven, or maybe six years. Possibly less.

After several minutes of silent, uneventful progress through darkened corridors, the first sign of trouble materialised. Lazar led the group cautiously to a turning that brought them to a wide, enclosed walkway connecting the southern wing of the fort to the four-storey keep at the centre of the location. Right down the entire length of the walkway several lanterns hung from wall brackets, lighting the path ahead. Lazar halted abruptly bringing his fellow apprentices to a standstill.

"No, no, no!" he muttered under his breath before extinguishing his illumination orb.

"Lights mean patrols inside the fort," said Vartan, anticipating Lazar's concern.

Kayden began to chuckle knowingly.

Everyone spun around to face her. Sinton was the first to

speak.

"Are you going to fill the rest of us in on the joke?" he whispered.

"I just find it somewhat amusing that our fearless leader is surprised to discover that the King's Guard patrols the interior of the ruins as well as the outside." She locked eyes with Lazar, quietly directing her next words at him. "But it's actually worse than you realise."

"How so?" he asked, doubtfully.

"The intelligence we were provided with in preparation for this assignment was incomplete—therefore unreliable. Your stupid plan never took this into account, or even the possibility that anything could go wrong, at all." The opportunity to assume leadership of the mission had arrived. "If we continue to follow his lead we will fail the assignment, just like the other three groups did earlier this week," she added, in a thinly veiled appeal to Neryssa, Sinton and Bartis; Vartan would never side with her against Lazar.

"Oh, that's what this is about!" Lazar said in exasperation. "You just want—"

Reflexively, Kayden raised a hand in a gesture to silence Lazar while simultaneously turning her head to look back down the corridor they had just walked through.

"What now?"

"Shhhhh!"

Kayden continued to stare toward the left hand turn at the end of the corridor; they were not alone. Her almond-shaped eyes widened and her face blanched at the sight of pale blue light emanating from around the corner. It was growing brighter, getting closer... *Sinjaydan*; the light was coming from an illumination orb. She rushed immediately towards the nearest doorway still having a door set in its frame. Gently, she pushed it open, wide enough to allow her to slip through, then frantically beckoned for the others to follow her, before disappearing inside.

Sinton was the first to follow suit without hesitation. Neryssa was the next to move, closely followed by Bartis. Though seemingly reluctant to do likewise, Lazar offered no resistance when Vartan grabbed hold of his arm and dragged him towards the doorway. As they entered the room Kayden shut the door slowly behind them.

"You don't think someone else from campus followed us here, do you?" inquired Neryssa in a whisper.

"Quiet!" hissed Kayden. "No talking...and no *Zarantar* until I give the all clear." Her authoritative tone brooked no disobedience.

For the next few anxious moments, it felt as though everyone in the room was holding their breath while Kayden stood with an ear pressed against the oak door, listening. She heard the muffled footsteps of what sounded like two people walking the corridor. Her impression was quickly confirmed by two distinct voices. Eventually, the sounds subsided then faded away; the corridor fell silent once more. She pulled away from the door, satisfied that they remained undetected, then turned to face her companions. She created a small illumination orb in her hand, casting a pale blue glow across the dilapidated room. "I think we're in the clear for now," she said, her voice a little above a whisper.

"But clear from whom?" asked Neryssa. "Whoever that was out there must be from the Order, which doesn't make sense. Or we have a rogue Sanatsai on our hands, which makes even less sense."

"That's what you meant when you said things are worse than I realised." Lazar's statement was muttered more to himself, in a moment of perceived realisation, rather than a response to Kayden.

"Oh, for crying out loud!" There was nothing feigned about Kayden's exasperation. "Hasn't anyone else been paying attention tonight? Did I not mention, moments ago, that we cannot trust the accuracy of the intelligence we were provided with to plan the mission?"

"Just because someone decided to light a few poxy lanterns?" challenged Vartan.

Ignoring him, Kayden continued. "The information stated there would be no more than a dozen men patrolling the perimeter of the fort; I counted almost thirty while we waited in the trees for nightfall. But that was hardly a surprise; the figure of twelve men was never plausible to begin with. The whole reason for soldiers from the King's Guard being deployed to guard a fort that was abandoned two centuries ago is to prevent bandits from using the ruins as a staging area to launch raids against the nearby towns and villages in the neighbouring province.

"Given the reputation some of these bandits have earned for themselves, it is doubtful they would be deterred by a dozen soldiers. Besides, the structure is simply too large for twelve men to prevent anyone from sneaking in unseen. You would need at least five to six times that number to adequately secure the location. So my guess would be the actual number of guards present tonight is closer to eighty, with most of them inside the fort."

Kayden noted from the expressions on the faces of her five colleagues that their confidence in the success of the assignment had been dented.

"If that wasn't bad enough, not only was the number of guards on duty inaccurate, it's now obvious that so too is the composition of the guards. The intelligence we were given led us to believe that only soldiers from the King's Guard would be involved."

"Well, how do you know that's not the case?" queried Bartis.

She frowned at the stupidity of her fellow apprentice. "Are you seriously suggesting that you failed to notice the invoking of *Kiraydan* to light up the sky when we began our approach?" It was a rhetorical question; everyone had seen the lightning flash orbs erupting in the night sky. "Wielders of *Zarantar* are not permitted to serve in the armies of The Nine Kingdoms; neither the Sanatsai, nor the Jaymidari, and certainly not the Saharbashi—if they still exist."

"And, by law, anyone who is born imbued with *Zarantar* is required to join the Order or have their *Zarantar* bound," interjected Sinton in understanding. "So how can there be soldiers among the King's Guard who are able to invoke *Kiraydan*?"

"Exactly!" Kayden was pleasantly surprised that someone else also got it. "We should assume there are several Sanatsai present.

8

At one point during our infiltration five orbs went up simultaneously. So, at the very least, there are five of them outside, plus whoever that was we nearly crossed paths with moments ago, inside.

"Whether it's routine for the Order to provide personnel to assist the King's Guard or if they are here specifically to hinder our attempt to complete the assignment, it should be clear, now, that following Lazar's plan is no longer viable."

"Hey! There's nothing wrong with the plan," protested Lazar, with little conviction.

"No, Kayden's right," rebutted Sinton. "Your plan made sense when we believed the interior of the fort would be empty. But now? Come on! There's no way we can stroll through brightly-lit corridors to reach the central stairwell of the keep if there are patrols inside. And according to the layout of the fort, that central stairwell is the only way to reach the top floor."

"That's...not exactly true." Kayden's voice was thick with smugness.

Sinton glanced sideways at her. "Kayden, if you know something the rest of us don't know, now is the time to share."

"Before I fill you all in on what our next move is, I want consensus, right now, that I am to assume leadership of the mission from this point on."

"That's not going to happen," objected Lazar.

Kayden ignored Lazar's protestation, and looked expectantly at Sinton, Neryssa then Bartis, in turn. She knew it was only necessary to get the trio to side with her in order to overrule the objections of Lazar; it was safe to assume Vartan would support his friend, regardless. "The three of you know I'm right. Persevering with Lazar's redundant plan will see this assignment end in failure. You may be fine with that, but I'm not."

The tension increased as she waited on the silent ruminations of her cohorts.

"Oh, all right," piped up Bartis, finally. "If you have an alternative to the agreed upon plan, then yes, I think you should lead the mission from here."

"I'm with you too." Sinton's decision provoked the faintest

flutter of a smile to touch Kayden's lips. She never doubted his support; Sinton was one of the very few apprentices of the Order who truly appreciated both her abilities and her single-minded determination to succeed.

"What about you, Neryssa?" she pressed the other young woman.

Vartan placed a hand upon Neryssa's shoulder, gripping tightly. "Don't even think about it." His raspy voice was almost a growl. "The last thing we need is 'girls sticking together' shenanigans derailing this mission."

Neryssa shrugged off his hand, irritation written all over her face. "If it wasn't for Kayden this mission would be over already. We would have been caught, out in that corridor, a short while ago." She turned her head to address Lazar. "Whether you like it or not, even you must admit this entitles her to an opportunity to pursue another course of action."

As far as Kayden was concerned Lazar didn't have reasonable grounds for prolonging his opposition. With only Vartan prepared to stand up for him it would be churlish not to acquiesce to the wishes of the majority. They all wanted the same thing, after all—to successfully complete the assignment—though it would no doubt irk Lazar if he was compelled into acceding to her wishes. He clearly didn't enjoy having to deal with someone who didn't simply fall into line, letting him have his way. Or maybe he just found her abrasive, headstrong, and downright overbearing; but that was his problem, not hers.

Kayden noticed the subtle change in Lazar's expression, and she had a pretty good idea what he was thinking. If he reluctantly agreed to the change of leadership, at least he would have the satisfaction of knowing that when the mission inevitably failed, he could lay the blame entirely at her door.

"All right! Fine! I guess the majority has spoken. I relinquish leadership to Kayden." He flashed Kayden an insincere smile to go with his begrudging tone. "Good luck coming up with a new plan in the time we have left. Not only do you need to guide us to the top floor of the keep, *unseen*, to acquire the mission objective; you need to get us back out of the fort again, *unseen*. Then we'll need to make our way to the rendezvous point before sunrise." He appeared rather confident she wouldn't be able to pull it off.

"You needn't concern yourself with that," she quipped with a wry smile. "I already devised a superior plan a week ago." She caused the illumination orb in her hand to float up and over her head as she turned around to face the door behind her. "Sinton! Bartis! Form up close behind me. Neryssa, you're in the middle. Lazar and Vartan, bring up the rear."

Neryssa took up her position behind Sinton and Bartis. "Aren't you going to tell us your plan?" she inquired. "We've just established we can't risk walking through lit corridors, and you implied there was another means for us to get to the top of the keep."

Without looking back over her shoulder, Kayden replied. "There is a network of hidden passageways throughout the fort. We'll use them to forgo the need to access the central stairwell to reach the top floor, thereby avoiding any risk of bumping into a patrol."

"Wait a minute!" blurted Lazar. "There were no secret passages marked on the layout of the fort."

Kayden peered over her shoulder. "They wouldn't *be* secret if they were etched on a map for any idiot to look at." There was no attempt to conceal the condescension in her voice. "Now," she continued, turning her attention back to the door in front of her, "if there are no more pointless questions, let's get moving."

"Kayden! One more thing before we go," said Sinton. "The Sanatsai we almost ran into earlier, how did you know they were approaching? You reacted before the light from the invocation of *Sinjaydan* became visible."

Kayden didn't immediately respond.

"I just knew," she conceded, evasively. "That's all that matters. Now it's time to go." She opened the door, her illumination orb floated ahead of her as she led the group back out into the corridor.

After several minutes spent retracing the steps they had taken through the south wing, Kayden finally began to lead the group through areas they had not previously been through. It wasn't long before she eventually brought the party to a halt at the turning into a long corridor. She stared intently, straight ahead, at the T-junction at the opposite end of the corridor.

Something was wrong.

Around the right hand turn of the junction, someone—a Sanatsai from the Order she assumed—was present. But there was no reason for anybody to be lurking there, at all. She knew that particular turn led into a short, dead-end corridor with a couple of ramshackle storage rooms leading off it.

"Why have we stopped?" Sinton whispered over her shoulder. "Is there a problem?"

Looking back over her shoulder, Kayden pressed a finger to her lips then returned her gaze to the corridor ahead. After a moment of deliberation she whispered, "Stick close to me," then deftly tiptoed forward, down the corridor, towards the nearest open doorway. The rest of the group followed close behind.

Inside the empty room Kayden casually waved her hand up at the illumination orb floating overhead, her invocation of *Yuksaydan* neutralising *Sinjaydan*, darkening the room as the orb winked out of existence. Without preamble she began to explain, in a hushed tone, the situation. "There is an access to the hidden passageways around the right hand turn at the end of the corridor. I have reason to believe there might be someone lying in wait for us there. I need the rest of you to remain here while I go ahead to investigate."

"Do you really think we're going to fall for that?" retorted Vartan. "We stay here twiddling our thumbs while you take off without us to complete the mission alone?"

"Don't be silly, Kayden wouldn't do that," protested Neryssa.

"Of course I would," she said. "But it's too late for that now. If I wanted to give you all the slip I should have done it before we even entered the fort. As things currently stand, I'm going to need you if I want to successfully complete the assignment from here. So you needn't worry about me ditching you all, as tempting as that idea may be." She took a resigned breath. "Anyway, as I was saying, I need to be absolutely certain someone is waiting around that corner before I decide our next move. I'm just going to take a quick look then I'll come straight back."

Without waiting for agreement, she quickly and quietly exited the room.

Out in the corridor once more, Kayden crept stealthily towards the end, keeping close to the wall at her right hand side. As she inched further along the corridor, her certainty increased that a wielder of *Zarantar* was nearby, vindicated by the faint traces of a pale blue glow around the corner. The illumination wasn't growing brighter, meaning it wasn't moving closer, nor was it getting fainter, indicating it wasn't moving away. Whoever was around the corner was stationary.

Kayden reached the end of the corridor, stopped, held her breath and listened. She could hear noises coming from around the corner, but those sounds couldn't possibly be what she was imagining them to be. But she would have to risk peering round the corner for a quick look, just to be sure, one way or the other.

She pulled the hood of her cloak over her head, pressed her back against the wall then slowly squatted down onto her haunches. She mentally counted to three then cautiously peeked her head round the corner.

Drat! You have got to be kidding me!

Halfway along the dead-end corridor an illumination orb floated close to the ceiling, casting pale blue light upon two figures standing below. The couple were engaged in a session of increasingly heavy petting. From the uniforms they were wearing Kayden knew at once they were Sanatsai from the Order. But she did not recognise either of them, which meant it was unlikely they were instructors from her campus. Wherever they were from, they were now being incredibly amorous between her and the concealed access to the hidden passageways set in the wall at the end of the corridor, and it didn't appear as though the couple had any plans to vacate the area any time soon. The woman had just released her partner's straining erection from the confines of his garments, giving it a playful tug as they continued kissing. It wasn't long before she slowly sank to her knees to...

Kayden looked away then stood back up. She remained where

she was, unmoving, giving thought to how best to draw the lovers out of the corridor. A solution to the problem came to mind rather quickly; she knew exactly what needed to be done. She nonchalantly walked straight back to the room where her fellow apprentices awaited her return.

"So what's the situation?" asked Sinton.

"An unexpected obstacle stands between us and access to the passageways," she answered with a sigh. "Two Sanatsai have decided that this is the appropriate time and place to be intimate with one another."

"You're telling us two members of the Order are fucking around that corner?" Vartan inquired incredulously.

"Watch your language, you pig," she hissed. "And, no, they aren't. But if we don't draw them out right away it probably won't be long before they are, and we don't have time for that."

"Can we assume you have a plan to get us past them?" Neryssa asked.

Kayden flashed her counterpart a habitual smug look that likely went unnoticed in the dark. "What do you think?" The condescending tone made it abundantly clear that, yes, of course she had a plan. "But I'm going to need a volunteer to come with me to make it work."

"Count me in," said Sinton.

"Not you, Sinton." Kayden's retort was very matter-of-fact. "Vartan will be my volunteer."

"What?" blurted the surprised apprentice.

"You seemed so concerned that I might try to ditch you all, earlier on." She hadn't forgotten about that. "So you get to come along this time, to keep an eye on me. Besides, I think it's for the best that I keep you and Lazar apart before either of you get any stupid ideas about him reclaiming leadership of the mission while my back is turned."

She couldn't be absolutely certain in the dark, but it looked as though Lazar and Vartan exchanged guilty looks as they glanced at each other.

"So what's the plan?" asked Neryssa.

"Vartan and I will head back the way we came, to create a

noisy diversion that should draw out our amorous friends from around the corner," Kayden replied. "Chances are it may also attract the attention of any nearby patrols, so the moment the Sanatsai rush past this doorway to investigate the disturbance, you make your way around the corner then wait for me to rejoin you."

She glanced at each of her colleagues, awaiting further questions but none were forthcoming.

"Very well, if there are no more questions," she created an illumination orb, "Vartan, you're with me." She sent the orb floating out of the door then marched swiftly out of the room after it. Hesitating briefly, Vartan dubiously followed in her wake.

With her reluctant assistant in tow Kayden did not stray too far from the room where they had left the rest of the group. She led Vartan back through half a dozen deserted corridors then stopped outside the open double doorway of a large room she guessed had once been a communal room. She glanced at a single doorway on the opposite side of the corridor, about thirty yards back the way they had just come. She gauged that she would have more than enough time to exit the communal room then dart into the other room, once she had created her diversion. There she would wait until the Sanatsai passed by to investigate the commotion, before making her way back to the rest of the group.

"What are we waiting for?" Vartan whispered irritably at her side.

"Nothing! Follow me."

She trailed behind her illumination orb as she sent it floating into the room ahead of her. The pale blue glow highlighted the sparse surroundings of the room. There was only one piece of furniture in the room—a badly damaged oak table with one of its legs missing, against one wall. Presumably the room had been stripped bare when the fort was abandoned, or in the intervening years. She halted in the centre of the room then sent her orb floating straight up to the ceiling and silently stared upwards.

"What are we supposed to be looking at?" queried Vartan.

Kayden tore her eyes away from the ceiling to stare vacantly at Vartan. "I'm going to assume that as a level seven apprentice you have successfully mastered all the applications of *Zarantar* taught as part of the level four syllabus."

"Of course I have." He appeared somewhat confused by her question, or perhaps her tone of voice. "What's that got to do with the price of milk?"

"So you have complete control of your invoking of *Inkansaylar*? You can form a barrier sphere around yourself, and maintain it?"

"Yes," he replied impatiently.

"And for how long are able to sustain it?"

The frown marring Vartan's face made it clear how thrown off he was by Kayden's line of questioning. "Five hours was the longest time I kept one up during training," he replied. Far from impressive but more than enough for her needs. "Why?"

Kayden slowly backed away from Vartan, taking small measured steps. "For my diversion to work I need you to form a barrier sphere around yourself, now. And no matter what happens next don't let it down until it's safe for you to do so."

"You had better start making sense," he rasped threateningly, "because if you're messing me around—"

"Protect yourself, now!" It was a command that brooked no dissent, an order that would not be repeated a second time. She observed with relief as a translucent, spherical shield— reminiscent of a large, soapy bubble—enveloped Vartan. A smirk tugged the corner of Kayden's lips, and then she extinguished her illumination orb, plunging the room into darkness.

Without hesitation she thrust a hand upwards at the ceiling above where Vartan stood, invoking *Yuksaydan*. Simultaneously, she turned on her heels and darted toward the exit as the invisible blast she had unleashed struck with ferocious force, obliterating a section of the ceiling. With the thunderous cacophony of masonry falling upon the shielded apprentice assaulting her ears, Kayden created another illumination orb to aid her rapid departure from the room. Out in the corridor, she dashed towards the doorway of the room where she planned to hide and wait for the arrival of the two randy Sanatsai.

Giving no thought as to whether Vartan was as good as his word, she reached the room without incident, disappeared inside and extinguished her orb. Standing to one side of the open doorway—her back pressed against the wall—the sound of her own heartbeat thudded in Kayden's ears for what felt like an eternity. But barely a minute elapsed by the time she heard running footsteps go past her hiding place. She carefully peered out into the corridor to observe.

Success!

The two Sanatsai had been lured away to investigate the disturbance; they were both standing at the threshold of the communal room. The female Sanatsai sent the illumination orb floating before them straight into the room. Immediately, both she and her male counterpart rushed forward swiftly into the room after it.

That was Kayden's cue to move. She created an illumination orb then exited her temporary hiding place and ran. She retraced her steps back the way she had come, through deserted corridors lit by the orb racing ahead of her, to rendezvous with the remainder of the group. When she finally breezed around the corner into the dead-end corridor, a part of her was almost disappointed to find her fellow apprentices anxiously waiting for her. She quickly shrugged off that feeling; she might need another sacrificial lamb to complete the mission, so she would tolerate Lazar's presence for a while longer.

"What the heck just happened?" said Sinton. "We heard a loud crashing sound."

"No time to discuss it," replied Kayden. "We have to get going, now."

"Where's Vartan?" demanded Lazar.

Kayden brushed by Lazar as she walked towards the end of the corridor. "The idiot got himself caught." Assuming he had survived. "Which is why we need to move quickly, before he gives us away."

"There's no need for Vartan to do that. Our instructions for what to do in the event we are caught are clear: we remain silent and wait for one of the Masters to retrieve us."

"I wouldn't put your faith in Vartan's willingness to keep his mouth shut on this occasion." Kayden halted at the dead-end wall

17

at the corridor's end. "Fortunately, he doesn't know how to access the passageways. So, even if he does tell them our plans and they believe him, we still have an advantage." She grabbed hold of a metal bracket on the wall and twisted it ninety degrees, then back. There was an audible click before she pushed against the wall, revealing a door-shaped section that slowly opened inwards.

"You were right!" gasped Neryssa.

Kayden peered back over her shoulder. "Was that ever in doubt?" Her incredulous tone was simultaneously dismissive.

"How could you possibly have known about this?" Bartis wondered aloud.

She turned around to address the remainder of the group.

"No time for questions. The patrols will be aware of our infiltration into the fort; they'll be actively searching for us now. Just follow my lead." She made a move to turn back around, but stopped herself. "And those of you unable to stop asking questions, please at least keep your voices to a whisper. While we're making our way through the passageways it might be possible to hear talking through the walls in certain places."

Finally, Kayden turned to face the dark entrance to the secret passages. The illumination orb floating overhead she sent forward before her, into the opening, then followed after it. The rest of the party followed behind her in single file.

CHAPTER TWO

Failure Is Not An Option

For a good quarter of an hour, Kayden led her cohorts through a maze of dusty, narrow passageways. The decidedly roundabout course she took—going up floors, then down again; navigating, at various times, east, north, west and south—elicited the occasional complaint from Bartis. Where was she going, and why was it taking so long to get there? Lazar, too, contributed a gloating quip that she should admit she was lost. But Kayden paid them no mind. It was water off a duck's back. She knew exactly where she was going.

Eventually she brought the group to halt then turned to face the wall on her right side. She had finally reached the access point leading out of the passageways that would admit them to their mission objective—the office once used by the fort's commanding officer. The section of wall she was standing in front of was just as nondescript as the rest of the wall except for one notable difference: a short metal bar attached vertically to the wall like a handle, plus the bracket allowing the access point to be opened.

"The office we're looking for is on the other side of this wall," Kayden whispered, as she gently patted the wall. "Once I'm certain there's no one in there, we can go in and retrieve the box."

Pressing an ear against the wall, she listened for any indication the room on the other side was not empty. She could hear no voices or sounds of movement. She was satisfied the room would be clear when they entered. A glance at her accomplices let her know they were waiting expectantly.

"Are we good to go?" asked Sinton.

Kayden nodded before reaching up for the bracket on the wall. She gently twisted it ninety degrees, then back. Once again there was a discernible click. She grabbed hold of the metal handle then slowly pulled a door-shaped section of the wall inwards. Peering into the room beyond, she was pleased to see that it was bathed in moonlight pouring in from the Palladian windows dominating one side of the office. There was no longer any need to sustain her invocation of *Sinjaydan*, potentially alerting anyone to their presence with the tell-tale pale blue glow of her orb. She extinguished it then signalled for her colleagues to enter the room—before she did...just in case.

She took a moment to close the access panel behind herself then looked around the office. The few remaining furnishings were in reasonably good condition, though, oddly, nothing in the room was as dusty as it should have been. Somebody had recently gone to the trouble of doing a little cleaning, presumably after having concealed the box she and her fellow apprentices were tasked with recovering.

While the other apprentices began rummaging in search of their quarry, Kayden found her attention being drawn to the entrance. The oak door looked innocuous enough, but she was perturbed by what she could feel emanating from the doorway. She was sensing *Zarantar*—but not the familiar *Zarantar* wielded by all Sanatsai. What she was picking up, now, was the much less familiar *Zarantar* wielded by the Jaymidari. It was an unexpected surprise, though perhaps it shouldn't have been. The *Sisterhood Of The Covens* and the Order went together like horse and cart. To all intents and purposes, though the Sisterhood was officially a separate and independent entity, it was still an integral part of the Order; or vice versa, as the case may be.

According to the women of the Sisterhood, *Zarantar*—a word from a long dead language preserved by them, meaning 'the arts'—was of three types: *Zarantar Jist*, *Zarantar Shayd*, and *Zarantar Najist*; three similar, but very distinct expressions of a preternatural force emanating from the same source.

The branch of *Zarantar* wielded by the Sisterhood was *Zarantar Jist*, meaning 'the pure arts'. It could only be wielded by women who pursued the calling of the Jaymidari, allowing them to channel the power of the ley-lines that crisscrossed the world, and were believed to be the source of all *Zarantar*. The Sisters deemed their expression of *Zarantar* untainted because it could only be used for beneficial purposes: to heal and preserve life. It wasn't possible to kill with *Zarantar Jist*, nor was it necessary to cause harm in order to wield it.

The opposing expression of *Zarantar*, however, known as *Zarantar Najist*, meaning 'the impure arts', was its antithesis. Its primary purpose was to inflict harm. It was wielded by those who sought to oppress people, to cause death and destruction: the Saharbashi. The word roughly translated as 'he who corrupts', with reference to men who used blood sacrifice to overcome the obstacle that ordinarily prevented them from channelling ley-lines. This corruption subsequently allowed them to taint the power drawn from a ley-line in order to wield it for ill purposes.

The most recent manifestation of *Zarantar* known as *Zarantar Shayd*, meaning 'the grey arts', emerged little more than three centuries ago with the initial appearance of the children who would later be dubbed as Sanatsai by the Jaymidari who first discovered them. It was an appropriate word—literally meaning 'living weapon'—for in the years before the founding of the Order, the Sanatsai were taught to master their power by the Sisterhood who then co-opted them as weapons to combat the activities of the Saharbashi. Unlike the *Zarantar* of the Saharbashi and the Jaymidari, the power of the Sanatsai wasn't channelled directly from ley-lines. Though it was not fully understood how they came to be born, it was known that all Sanatsai were inherently imbued with *Zarantar*, so their power was invoked from within themselves. The Sisterhood deemed this third expression of *Zarantar* as 'grey', for though no Sanatsai required blood sacrifice to wield their power, *Zarantar Shayd* could be used for both good and ill.

"Any idea what the box looks like?"

Kayden's musing was disturbed by Sinton who approached

her from behind.

"Presumably like a box," she replied, not tearing her eyes away from the door. "We were told we'd recognise it if we find it."

She remained preoccupied with the office door as Sinton inquired, "Is something wrong?"

Offering no reply, Kayden instead marched towards the door, prompting Sinton to quickly fall into step behind her. As they stood together before the closed door Kayden stared all along the door frame—up the left hand side, across the arch-shaped top, then back down the right hand side.

"Are you going to let me in on what's so interesting about this door?" pressed Sinton.

By way of reply, Kayden nonchalantly waved her right hand across the doorway, invoking *Yuksaydan*. A series of glowing red glyphs began to appear along the frame.

There was a sharp intake of breath from Sinton. "The door has been warded."

"No doubt intended to keep us from entering the room, rather than preventing us from leaving with the box."

"Then it can't just be Sanatsai who are helping the guards. This ward could only have been set by a Sister."

"Something we should have anticipated," Kayden said matter-of-factly. "Sanatsai and Jaymidari have always worked hand in hand, even before the founding of the Order." She glanced at her fellow apprentice. "Just one more surprise the Masters neglected to give us advance warning of." A knowing smile curled her lips. "No matter, this could work to our advantage. Should any guards decide to investigate the room while we're here, they won't be able to enter. They'll need to call someone to break the ward for them."

Bartis trundled over, joining Kayden and Sinton at the door. "We've searched the entire room," he announced. "The box isn't here. It looks like the Masters have sent us on a wild goose chase."

"That would explain why nobody has ever successfully completed the 'capture the box' assignment," said Sinton, exasperated. "We can't capture something that was never here in the first place."

"No!" rebutted Kayden, turning her back on the door to cast

an eye around the room. "Some of the intelligence we were given may have been inaccurate or outright lies, but you can be certain the box is here...somewhere." She looked at Neryssa perched on the edge of the mahogany desk before the windows, her feet dangling off the floor. "There's a small bedchamber through there," she said pointing at a door set in the recess of the wall to Neryssa's left. "Did you check inside?"

Neryssa slid off the edge of the desk to stand on her feet. She peered at the door she somehow hadn't noticed before. "No," she said. "We didn't."

Kayden sighed. "Well, what were you waiting for, an invitation?" She said, marching to the door.

The other apprentices crowded behind her as she pushed it open. The bedchamber was empty save for the remnants of a bed along one wall. From the small window in the opposite wall, moonlight diffused into the room, casting light on a dark metallic box on the floor in the centre of the room. The rectangular-shaped box appeared to be made of lead, adorned with silver-coloured engravings.

A jewellery box from the Underworld, Kayden thought to herself.

"What are you waiting for?" asked Lazar impatiently. "Let's grab the box and get out of here."

"Do you really think it's that easy?"

It was probably a stupid question. If Lazar was unable to sense the *Zarantar* permeating the room, he surely thought it *was* that easy; but Kayden knew better. Once again she could feel the *Zarantar* of the Sisterhood. It would be unwise to simply rush forward to pick up the box.

"Oh, stop being such drama queen!" Lazar barged past Kayden into the room, intent on snatching the box.

She grabbed his cloak to yank him to a halt.

"Wait!" she snapped.

Lazar spun around —fists clenched—glaring at Kayden, but he made no further attempt to reach the box. "I get it," he said. "You think *you* deserve all the credit for retrieving the damned box. You want all the glory by personally delivering it yourself."

"Would you stop being so petty," said Neryssa. "Kayden has

been one step ahead all night. If she says 'wait', then you need to listen."

Kayden skirted past Lazar to return her attention to the box on the floor. She slowly paced in a half circle around the box, like a predator stalking its prey. She paused, then stared up at the ceiling directly above the box, before looking back down at the floor.

"I knew it!" she muttered to herself, before waving a hand over the box. Instantly, another series of glowing red glyphs began to appear in a circle on the floor around the box. "It's been booby-trapped."

"Ha! Is that what you're worried about?" asked Lazar. "I guess you're not as all-powerful as you thought. Even I can break a simple ward. Stand aside."

Kayden stared at the cocksure apprentice then flashed him a subtle, knowing smile. "Very well, genius. Please! Go ahead and break this *simple ward* for us." She slowly backed away from the box, inviting him to move closer.

"Stand back everyone. Let's watch an amateur at work."

Apparently heedless of the fact he was being goaded, Lazar stepped confidently to the box then held out both his hands in front. At first nothing appeared to be happening. Suddenly, the glowing glyphs briefly flared, before seemingly changing to a gaseous state and dissipating out of existence with a fizzing sound.

Kayden looked on as Lazar crouched down to retrieve the metal box. As he reached to pick it up she closed her eyes and covered her ears. The moment his hand met the surface of the box there was a blinding flash of white light, followed by a loud noise like the rumble of thunder. Lazar was sent hurtling backwards through the air, out of the bedchamber, back into the office, where he landed at the foot of the mahogany desk.

"What the fuck?" barked Bartis, rubbing his eyes.

"Like I said," Kayden said. "The box has been booby-trapped."

"But we saw Lazar break the ward," said Sinton, eyes blinking rapidly, trying to regain focus once more.

"A harmless decoy. The real ward is up there."

She waved a hand up at the ceiling. This time, her invocation of *Yuksaydan* revealed a larger, more intricately patterned circle of glyphs that glowed a brighter, fiery hue of crimson.

"You will note the more intense glow coming from this one. It means—" She noticed Neryssa had left the bedchamber and was now checking on Lazar's condition in the office. "Neryssa! Forget Lazar. He's going to remain unconscious for a little while."

"But—"

"Don't argue! Because of his stupidity we're going to have company, sooner rather than later. Get back in here!" Kayden resumed her explanation for Sinton and Bartis. "As I was saying, the intensity of the glow means that whoever set the ward has linked it to a nearby ley-line from which it is drawing additional strength. The ward cannot be broken without first severing its link to that ley-line."

"And how are we supposed to do that?" asked Sinton

The question, highlighting the groups reliance upon her, provoked feelings of smug satisfaction within Kayden before she looked up at the glowing red ward. A translucent, half-spherical shield materialised on the ceiling, courtesy of her invocation of *Inkansaylar*, to contain the circular pattern of glyphs.

"A barrier sphere?" queried Neryssa. "Is that it?"

Kayden nodded. "Now we wait."

"How will we know if it worked?" Bartis inquired. "I'm certainly not going to risk picking that box up."

"When the intensity of the glow has dimmed, it means the connection to the ley-line has been severed. Then I can break the ward. Then we can take the box and get out of here."

"Kayden?" said Sinton. "How is it you know so much about *Zarantar Jist*? I don't recall learning any of this stuff from the Masters."

There was no opportunity for her to respond. In unison, they all turned their heads towards the sound of someone attempting to open the door to the office. She darted to the open doorway of the bedchamber and peered out to investigate. The glyphs on the doorframe were still glowing red; the ward remained unbroken. Her three companions were quickly at her back to also hear the conversation of two male voices coming from the antechamber beyond the locked door.

"See? I told you!" said the first voice. "The door is obviously still warded. Even if anyone had managed to slip past us, they couldn't have gone inside."

"I'm telling you, whatever that noise was it came from in there," insisted the second voice. "I'm going to fetch Terio. He can break the ward so we can go inside to take a look."

The four apprentices stepped away from the doorway.

Kayden promptly checked on the state of the ward protecting the box. The intensity of the glow remained undimmed.

"How much longer, Kayden?" asked Sinton quietly.

"Any moment now."

An increasingly agitated Bartis paced haphazardly back and forth. "We can't afford to wait," he complained, "they're going to catch us."

"Cool your boots!" Kayden demanded. "They're sending for one of the Sanatsai; we still have enough time."

"No we don't." His rebuttal was more urgent this time. "Let's just hide in the secret passage and wait for them to finish checking the room. Once they leave we can come back for the box."

Kayden glared at her panic-stricken cohort with contempt. "Are you an idiot? With all the rummaging around, not to mention Lazar lying unconscious right over there, they will know we were here." It was impossible not to sound condescending while explaining simple things to an idiot. "They won't vacate the room until Lazar regains consciousness, and even if he keeps his mouth shut about the hidden passageways, there's no reason to think the guards will leave until they can figure out how we got in here without coming in through the front door."

"Kayden!" interrupted Sinton. "I think you did it."

She looked away from Bartis back to Sinton who was staring up at the ceiling. She did likewise to see that the glowing red glyphs of the ward had, indeed, dimmed. Casually, she brought down her barrier sphere then raised both hands upwards. With the link to the ley-line severed it was a simple matter invoking *Yuksaydan* to now break the ward. Moments later, the glowing glyphs briefly flared, appeared to change to a gaseous state, then dissipated out of existence with a fizzing sound.

"You see?" she crowed triumphantly, for Bartis' benefit. He said nothing in return. "All right, Sinton, grab the box and let's get out of here."

Sinton hesitated; the look of apprehension on his face clear for all to see.

"Oh, for crying out loud!" huffed Kayden. She bent down to pick up the box. Nothing untoward happened as she grabbed the box then tucked it into a pouch beneath her tabard. She was inclined to chastise her fellow apprentice for having the nerve to doubt her, but something more pressing diverted her attention. Her head turned sharply toward the open doorway.

"Drat! They're about to come in."

Bartis reacted first, darting to the doorway to peer out into the office. The glowing glyphs on the doorframe had flared and were now becoming gaseous in appearance. "That's it, I'm out of here!"

He bounded out of the bedchamber in a futile dash to reach the hidden passageway. Neryssa attempted to follow suit but the door slammed shut in her face before a translucent barrier formed across the doorway, preventing it from being opened again. She looked back over her shoulder to see Kayden—left hand outstretched in front of her, right hand pressing a finger to her lips.

"Hold it right there, apprentice!" came the voice of one of the guards on the other side of the door. "We've got you. This assignment is over for you."

Kayden lowered her outstretched left arm, and pulled her right index finger away from her lips to beckon Neryssa to walk towards her and Sinton.

"How long has your colleague been unconscious for?" asked a previously unheard third male voice—presumably that of the Sanatsai named Terio. "And how did the two of you even manage to get in here in the first place?"

An annoyed looking Neryssa stood in front of Kayden. "You've trapped us in here," she whispered.

"Would you rather be out there having failed the mission?" Kayden whispered back.

The bedchamber door rattled as someone outside tried to

open it.

"We're as good as caught anyway," whispered Sinton. "Even if you could sustain your *Inkansaylar* indefinitely, to keep them out, we can't leave to deliver the box to the rendezvous point, can we?"

The rattling stopped.

"The door's locked," came the voice of one of the guards.

"It shouldn't be," came the response from the third male voice. "There are three more apprentices unaccounted for. They must have barricaded themselves inside. Tell them to come out; the game is up."

The man's knowledge of their numbers effectively confirmed Kayden's assumption that he was the Sanatsai called Terio whom the guards had fetched to break the ward to permit them to enter the office.

Neryssa's shoulders slumped in resignation. "You may as well let them in, Kayden, we're out of options."

"All right, apprentices, it's time to come out," the voice of first guard called out to them.

"She's right, Kayden," sighed Sinton. "It's over."

"It's not over yet," hissed Kayden defiantly. "Over here!" She marched to the wall where the remnants of the room's bed still lay. Neryssa and Sinton followed, and stood on either side of her. "The hidden passage that brought us into the office terminates behind this wall." She gently patted the stonework in front of her.

"If there's an access to the hidden passages in here," whispered Neryssa, standing at Kayden's side, "why didn't you just say so?"

"There isn't one."

From beyond the door the guard barked out a second order for whoever was inside to come out immediately.

"If the passageway cannot be accessed from inside this room," continued Neryssa, "then how are we supposed to enter?"

"We go through the wall."

"Kayden, if we blast a big hole in the wall to escape," whispered Sinton, "they'll know for certain we were here, then they can simply pursue us through the passageways."

"I didn't say anything about blasting a hole in the wall," replied Kayden cryptically. "I said, go *through* the wall."

Neryssa and Sinton exchanged wide-eyed looks.

There was heavy thudding on the bedchamber door indicating that the guards were attempting to shoulder charge the door open.

"Have you been drinking, Kayden?" blurted Neryssa, in a hushed tone. "We're still just level seven apprentices. We can't pass through solid objects."

"Exactly," agreed Sinton. "We won't be trained to master the invoking of *Naymutandushay* until we become level ten apprentices." He could barely keep the exasperation from his hushed voice. "Besides, to invoke it safely requires the wearing of a siphon cloak, like all the Sanatsai of the Order wear."

"What you say is correct. And it just so happens," Kayden tugged at the hooded cloak she was wearing. "I created a cloak of my own a few months ago, though I didn't anticipate needing to use it tonight."

The pounding against the door grew louder, but the *Zarantar* induced barrier keeping it closed did not yield.

"Kayden, even if you *could* do what you're proposing," whispered Sinton dubiously. "How does that help me and Neryssa? We're wearing these ordinary cloaks, and lack the ability to pass through a wall, anyway."

"Doesn't matter. All you have to do is take my hand; anything I am holding will pass through the wall with me."

"You've done this before?" queried Neryssa.

Kayden conspicuously hesitated before responding. "Not through an *actual* stone wall," she conceded. "But the principle is the same irrespective of the composition of the material you intend to pass through."

"In that case, you can definitely count me out."

Kayden looked expectantly at Sinton. Surely he would have more faith in her? But he silently shook his head at her, demonstrating that he didn't.

"This is the second time in quick succession you've doubted me today."

"No one could ever doubt your self-belief, Kayden. But I'm not going to stake my life on your ability to take us safely through a stone wall." He looked guilt-ridden by the admission. "You do understand, if you mess up, you could die in the attempt?"

"I'd rather die than fail this assignment!"

The exchange of dismayed glances made it clear that both Sinton and Neryssa understood Kayden's words were not bravado. She really did intend to avoid capture by passing through the wall, even if it killed her.

"Kayden, would you listen to yourself." There was genuine concern in Neryssa's plea.

"Failure maybe acceptable for the two of you," Kayden retorted. "For me, it's not an option."

The thudding against the door stopped abruptly, drawing the gazes of the three apprentices towards the doorway.

"They must be using *Zarantar* to keep you out," came the voice of the Sanatsai from the other side of the door. "Stand aside!"

Suddenly, the barrier shield Kayden created across the doorway began to slowly deteriorate. It appeared as though it was being eaten away by a corrosive substance. It was only a matter of time, now, before the guards could enter the room and the mission would be over.

"That's my cue to leave." Kayden returned her focus to the wall that stood between her and escape from the bedchamber. "I'll see you both back at campus." She pulled the hood of her cloak over her head. The air around her appeared to ripple gently, like water. Then she calmly stepped forward towards the stone wall and...

Kayden walked right through the wall.

For several minutes Kayden navigated swiftly through a maze of passageways—her path lit by an illumination orb racing ahead of her. She had no way of knowing whether any of her fellow apprentices would reveal the existence of the hidden passages. Nonetheless, she was glad she hadn't let slip how she intended for the group to exit the fort undetected.

Thankfully, her uneventful course eventually brought her to the access point she was looking for; she had made it safely to the east wing of the fort, and down to ground level. Pressing her ear against the concealed opening set in the wall, she listened for sounds on the other side. But it was a mere formality; she knew there would be no one there. She proceeded to twist the metal bracket on the wall. There was a perceptible click then she grabbed hold of the metal handle that allowed her to pull open a door-shaped section of the wall inwards. Her illumination orb floated into the dark opening and she followed in its wake, closing the access door behind her.

Kayden was standing in what had once been a large kitchen area. She wasted no time in heading straight for the nearby walk-in pantry; she was eager to be out of the old fortress right away. On the wall, just to the right side of the open entrance to the pantry, there was metal bracket that she twisted ninety degrees, then back. Inside, a trapdoor hatch popped up slightly in the centre of the floor. The orb floated into the pantry to hover over the trapdoor while Kayden moved to squat down and pull the hatch open. She sent her orb down into the dark opening, watching as its steady descent down the shaft lit up the underground tunnel approximately sixty feet below. As she prepared to drop down into the shaft the presence of *Zarantar* nearby made her pause. Before she could gather her thoughts, she was startled by a pale blue illumination followed immediately by a chorus of slow handclapping coming from behind her.

Kayden froze.

She hadn't heard anybody entering the kitchen. That could only mean whoever was behind her must have been lying in wait before she even arrived.

"You did exceptionally well to make it this far, apprentice," said a female voice. "I'm very impressed."

Kayden turned around slowly to see a woman standing just outside the entrance to the walk-in pantry, an illumination orb floating above her head. She recognised the other woman immediately—it was the female Sanatsai who had been getting rather intimate with a male counterpart in a corridor, earlier that night.

"You know," said the Sanatsai, with a smile. "I've volunteered for guard duty during the 'capture the box' exercise on at least half a dozen occasions, and I had no idea about any secret passages in the fort, let alone underground tunnels leading out of it."

"It's a wonder you notice anything," Kayden quipped, "if you spend all your time lurking in dark corridors, down on your knees with a dick in your mouth."

She had come far too close to success to accept failure now. Goading the other woman was her only hope of recovering the situation.

The Sanatsai flushed; the smile vanishing from her face.

"Oh, it looks like I need to have words with your instructors at the Antaris campus about your appalling lack of manners." It was clear from her tone she was more affronted than embarrassed. "In the meantime, follow me. I'll take you back to rejoin the rest of your group. You have failed, too." She turned around to lead the apprentice away.

Behind Kayden, the orb she had sent down into the underground tunnel slowly began to rise back up the shaft, its pale blue glow gradually morphing into a brilliant white fluorescence in response to Kayden's surreptitious invocation of *Kiraydan*.

Affecting her sweetest, most insincere voice, Kayden said, "Excuse me, Master. May I be so bold as to correct you?" The Sanatsai turned back around, frowning. Kayden quickly sized her up and down. She appeared to be in her early thirties, lithe and athletic. Kayden had at least four inches in height on the other woman, with a notable weight advantage, too. This was going to be easy. "*Technically*, the assignment only ends in failure if I am seen by anyone on guard duty tonight." She dropped the put on voice, adopting an aggressive, hostile tone to match the similar expression on her face. "And by the time I've finished with you, not only will you not remember having seen me, you won't remember how I beat you senseless, either."

The Sanatsai appeared too stunned for words. That brief moment of hesitation was all the time Kayden required. A smirk curled one corner of her mouth then she closed her eyes. The lightning flash orb shot up through the hatch, back into the pantry, flew over her shoulder towards the other woman, then silently erupted with a flash of blinding white light. Opening her eyes she saw the Sanatsai stumbling backwards, rubbing her eyes. She charged forward out of the pantry, launching a flying kick at the woman that sent her hurtling backwards onto the floor. Kayden continued her forward momentum, diving forward to pounce upon her fallen opponent.

The Sanatsai regained her wits quickly enough to raise a leg up between herself and Kayden in order to flip the apprentice up and over her own prone body.

Kayden landed painfully on her back but scrambled swiftly back onto her feet to face the Sanatsai who was back on her feet, also.

"Have you lost your mind?" screamed the woman.

Wasting no time with a verbal response, Kayden darted forward, unleashing a flurry of punches and kicks. The Sanatsai successfully evaded, parried and blocked the initial barrage but the intensity and ferocity of the attack increased, forcing her onto the back foot. Kayden's confidence in her close quarters, hand-to-hand martial training was quickly vindicated as she rapidly gained the advantage. Her fierce blows began to find their target with increasing ease, prompting a desperate counter-attack from her opponent who threw a succession of wild punches that Kayden parried easily before sweeping the legs out from under the woman.

The Sanatsai made a valiant attempt to regain her feet to prevent the apprentice from capitalising on the successful attack... but not quickly enough.

Kayden landed another kick square in the middle of the Sanatsai's chest, just as she was rising to her feet, knocking her violently back against the wall behind her. The heavy collision clearly knocked the wind out of the woman, yet she bravely managed to throw a couple of half-hearted punches in a futile attempt to fend off Kayden as she continued her brutal assault. Kayden ducked beneath the first punch, then in one fluid motion caught hold of the flailing arm of the second, throwing the Sanatsai over her shoulder on to the ground. This time, her adversary was given no opportunity to defend herself, as she lay sprawled on her back. Pouncing on the woman's torso, pinning her to the ground, Kayden rained down a succession of savage blows to the head.

In seconds, the bloodied and bruised Sanatsai was completely subdued. She lay beneath Kayden, unmoving, while her illumination orb—that had been casting light upon the pair during the confrontation—slowly dissipated from existence as she lost consciousness. Kayden invoked one of her own to chase away the resulting darkness, sending it floating up above her head. She returned her attention to the job at hand, placing the fingers of both hands on either side of the unconscious woman's head, then closed her eyes in concentration.

She'd had little opportunity to practice her invoking of *Barmityanzak*; being a level seven apprentice meant she wasn't yet supposed to have practical knowledge of this particular application of *Zarantar*. But it was now necessary to employ her illicit know-how before she could continue the assignment.

Finally, Kayden rose to her feet and looked down at her handiwork. She smiled in satisfaction, content that she must have successfully raided the mind of the defeated Santasai and destroyed her short-term memory of their violent encounter. This would *technically* mean she *had* avoided being seen by anyone during the completion of the mission.

She stepped away from the prone figure on the floor and followed her illumination orb back into the walk-in pantry. She sent the orb back down the open hatch, then clambered down the first few metal rungs descending the shaft, before stopping to reach up and close the trapdoor hatch over her head. Looking down the shaft, she saw that her orb had made it all the way down to the underground tunnel. She decided to waste no further time following suit so she released her grip of the metal rungs to drop down the shaft. Invoking *Makfayshulat* to slow down her descent, she landed gently in the tunnel. With the hard part over, Kayden was ready to complete the final stage of the mission. Deliver the box to the rendezvous point.

The underground tunnel ran eastward, and it was considerably wider than the network of passageways within the fort; there was no reason why a horse-drawn cart could not traverse the length of it. Kayden imagined that rather than being built solely as a means of escape, the tunnel was intended to smuggle in supplies in the event of a siege, also. Whichever the case, she began walking briskly through the tunnel, her illumination orb lighting the way.

Kayden couldn't be sure how much time had elapsed when she finally reached the end of the tunnel. What she did know was that the tunnel was approximately a mile long. Set into the dead-end wall before her, metal rungs ascended up into a narrow shaft that wasn't even half as long as the one that brought her into the tunnel. It went up approximately sixteen feet—give or take—and terminated at a wooden hatch. Kayden decided against the short climb in favour of levitating up the shaft, leaving her illumination orb floating in the tunnel below.

She briefly floated in the air beneath the hatch, listening out for any indications that someone was lurking on the other side. The only sound she could hear was the steady beat of her own heart; the only thing she could feel was the cool draught seeping into the shaft. Then she realised she didn't care if anybody was lying in wait for her beyond the hatch. She would simply handle the situation in the exact same manner as she had dealt with the Sanatsai who ambushed her prior to her exit from the fort.

Without further delay, Kayden pushed the hatch open as she levitated up through the opening to emerge into what had once been the tack room of a stable. Alighting on the lip of the opening in the floor, she allowed the hatch to drop shut behind her. She had successfully arrived in the stables of the abandoned farm located a mile east of the old fort.

Taking a few steps out of the room, she took a quick glance up and down the stables then smiled triumphantly; there was not another living soul present to cause her concern.

The ramshackle structure was still in relatively good condition—only a few sections of roofing were missing, exposing the night sky above. As she stared up at the moon, Kayden estimated she had at least three hours before dawn; more than enough time to deliver the box to the rendezvous point. She shifted her gaze to the far end of the stables—at the open entrance there—while idly patting the pouch at her waist, hidden beneath her tabard, feeling the metallic box within. She began jogging towards the gaping double doorway but hadn't taken more than a dozen strides before being brought to an abrupt halt by the sudden appearance of a silhouette blocking her exit. She couldn't discern who the interloper was, though she did have the impression the figure was female. But it wasn't until the tall silhouette spoke she knew for certain her instincts were correct.

"Just what do you think you have been playing at?"

Kayden recognised the stern voice immediately. It belonged to the last person she wanted to bump in to that night.

CHAPTER THREE

A Problem Searching For A Solution

Fay Annis stood motionless in the entrance to the stable, glaring at the young apprentice before her, with piercing hazel eyes. She wore the black and three shades of grey uniform of a Sanatsai of the Order. The only concession to colour amid the dark attire was the eye-catching lapis lazuli pendant pinned below her right collarbone, it's ultramarine pigmentation mottled with white and brassy yellow marking her as a senior figure within the institution, though few outside the Order would be aware of the significance of the little trinket. Beneath the hood of her black cloak, her face was the flawless olive complexion so commonly found among the people of the Nine Kingdoms, though the burgundy of a few strands of hair escaping from under the hood was a decidedly unusual sight.

She waited to hear what Kayden had to say for herself in response to the question of what she had been playing at during the successful escape from the fort.

"I don't know what you mean," the apprentice barked in reply.

Fay duly noted the irritation in Kayden's voice.

"I'm completing the assignment," she continued, "so why don't you just stand aside so I can make my way to the rendezvous point in time?" Fay noted the unspoken threat: *or else*.

Fay marched slowly into the stables to confront Kayden, up close and personal; she had no intention of being drawn into a shouting match from several feet away. She closed the gap between herself and Kayden to a reasonable three feet—the younger woman holding her ground as they stared unblinkingly into each other's eyes. Both master and apprentice stood five feet, ten inches tall. It was something Fay was not really accustomed to—speaking to another female who stood at eye-level with herself.

"The actual purpose of the 'capture the box' exercise," she began tersely, "is to task small groups of apprentices with devising, then executing, a plan to infiltrate a secure location to recover a mission objective, *unseen*, then extricate themselves, *unseen*."

"That's what I—"

"I'm not finished!" She raised a hand, and her voice, unceremoniously cutting off the apprentice mid-sentence. "At no point were you instructed to undermine the authority of the designated group leader. At no point were you instructed to deliberately sacrifice other members of your group. And, *you most certainly weren't, at any point, instructed to attack a member of the Order and invoke a potentially dangerous application of Zarantar, that you've not been trained to use, to rob her of her memory of the assault*."

"How did you—?" Kayden was visibly rattled for the first time.

"Did you imagine I would not be observing this assignment tonight?"

The awkward silence that followed stretched for several heartbeats. It was the first time Fay had ever known Kayden to be at a loss for words; the troublesome young woman usually had such a quick, sharp tongue.

Fay tensed in anticipation when the apprentice took an aggressive, single stride towards her.

"I only did what I had to," Kayden's expression was hostile, her stance determined, "once it became apparent the mission had been set up to fail from the get-go."

"What are you talking about?"

"We were given dud intelligence to prep for the assignment. Not *everyone* on guard duty tonight was from the King's Guard. It turns out they were being assisted by a number of Sanatsai from the Order. Not to mention there were considerably more than a dozen men patrolling the perimeter, in addition to several more within the fort itself. And, if that wasn't bad enough, the useless intelligence also neglected to mention that the damn box was being protected by a ward invoked by a Jaymidari."

"Yes," Fay conceded, finally. "Some of the information provided was incomplete, while some of it was deliberately misleading. The whole purpose of the exercise is to test for initiative and adaptability. During a real mission, no matter how well planned, things can and do go wrong. There are always variables that cannot be anticipated ahead of time, that is why it is essential for every Sanatsai to have the wherewithal to overcome such eventualities, should they arise."

"Well, I did overcome all the obstacles set up to ensure this assignment ended in failure, that's the real reason why you're annoyed with me." A flash of realisation seemed to pass over Kayden's face. "I'm just recalling something said to me by the Sanatsai I encountered in the fort. She let slip that she had no knowledge of the hidden passageways inside the fort nor of the underground tunnels beneath it. And yet, she just happened to be lying in wait for me near the access to one of those tunnels?" She added more accusingly, "It's almost as if someone who *was* aware of them told her where to go, so she could lie in wait to ambush me."

Fay ignored the less than subtle accusation; that it was true was not at all relevant. She did not flinch as Kayden swiftly stepped toward her, completely closing the gap between them, standing toe-to-toe with her, their faces inches from touching. The indignation burning in the apprentice's eyes was all too clear to see.

"Don't think for one moment I don't know what you're doing," Kayden snarled. "You're doing everything you can to prevent me from being inducted into the Order. From the moment you arrived at Antaris campus you have been singling me out, unfairly, for reasons I can only speculate on. As if you are hoping to sabotage my training, to justify having me forced out. Forced to have my *Zarantar* bound, before being sent back to the worthless life I had before it manifested..."

Kayden paused for a moment. It appeared to Fay as though she was considering her next words carefully. They arrived moments later, uttered in a quieter, more even tone.

"Let me assure you of this... *You. Will. Fail!*"

Fay felt the air all around them begin to bristle with *Zarantar* emanating from right under her nose. *The nerve of this girl!* The thought popped into her head as she fought off the urge to mock the young upstart's attempt at intimidation. However, if Kayden developed any silly ideas about attacking her as she had attacked Zalayna, inside the fort, she would disabuse the apprentice of such a foolish notion, very swiftly.

"Kayden. Step back, *now!*"

"Why don't you make me, you uptight bitch!"

It wasn't just a direct challenge to her authority; it was outright defiance and unacceptable disrespect.

Fay slowly moved her hands behind her back, clenching her fists beneath her hooded cloak. She could feel something dark and dangerous begin to stir deep within herself. It was a sensation she had not succumbed to for so very long, nor ever wanted to again. It had lain dormant inside her for such a long time she sometimes allowed herself to forget that it was once an integral part of who she was. But, increasingly, her interactions with Kayden were giving it new life, threatening to bring it to the surface. She pushed it down into the pit of her stomach as she stood her ground before the apprentice. Things wouldn't end well if she allowed it to overwhelm her.

"That's what I thought," crowed Kayden triumphantly after a prolonged silence. A carefree smirk curled the lips of her smug face. Evidently she had mistaken Fay's strained expression as a sign of apprehension, or perhaps even outright fear.

Fay was unmoved when Kayden turned her back on her, walking half a dozen paces away before turning back around to wave a finger in her direction.

"I think I've finally worked out why you're so tightly wound." The apprentice made no effort to disguise the amusement in her voice. "You really need to lay down with a man as soon as possible. I imagine it's been quite some time since you last had a good seeing to…if ever." That quick, sharp tongue was back. "Might I suggest Master Darrian for the task? I can't help but notice he has great difficulty in hiding his arousal when he's around you." Kayden stifled a chuckle as she continued. "I'm sure he'd love to bend you over and stick it to you real—"

Suddenly, Kayden was sent hurtling backwards through the air, landing almost forty feet away in a dishevelled heap. Fay paced forward, taking quick, menacing strides towards the younger woman as she scrambled back to her feet.

"You crazy bitch!" cried Kayden. "You're going to regret—"

Invoking *Yuksaydan* for a second time, Fay unleashed it against Kayden once again. How appropriate that the Sisterhood had named this particular application of *Zarantar* with a word that translated roughly into 'the unseen hand', for Kayden was instantly seized tight by an invisible, vice-like grip that lifted her right off her feet. Fay continued to stalk towards the apprentice who remained suspended several feet off the ground as she wriggled about in a futile struggle to break free of the *Zarantar*-induced hold on her.

You foolish little girl! thought Fay. There wasn't a single Sanatsai within the Order whose *Zarantar* was strong enough to resist her without considerable help. What hope did this insolent apprentice have in opposing her?

Fay came to a stop, just short of where Kayden hung in the air. Staring up intently at the incapacitated apprentice, she felt completely at ease—almost indifferent—about what she was going to do to the pathetic creature before her.

"I should have done this the day I first laid eyes upon you."

Fay barely recognised her own voice; it was cold, monotone.

"I can have no rival. I can have no equal."

She raised a hand up at Kayden. A stream of air, distorted, as if by a heat haze on a sweltering day, charted a course from her to the apprentice. The invocation of *Shakbarilsan* caused the clothing Kayden was wearing to erupt in flames that engulfed her in mere seconds. An amused smile curled Fay's lips while the inhuman screams of the burning apprentice echoed through the stables.

It wasn't long before the screaming ceased, completely; the

stables fell silent once more. Satisfied with her ruthless work, Fay put out the flames with a wave of the hand that released her invisible hold on Kayden's floating body. The charred form that dropped at her feet, with a heavy thud, no longer resembled the arrogant young upstart who stood before her only moments earlier. In some ways that was actually a pity. It was hard to fathom how such a beautiful girl could make for such a hideously grotesque corpse.

Gazing down at the body of the apprentice, Fay's satisfaction was short-lived. First, she saw Kayden's chest rise and fall; then she heard the ragged gasps for breath. Cold rage swept over her face like a dark cloud eclipsing a full moon. Fay was furious that the young woman had the indecency to cling on to life. She unsheathed the dagger at her hip then squatted down to straddle Kayden's prone form. Raising the blade high over her head, she let out a blood-curdling scream as she thrust the weapon down with both hands, plunging her dagger repeatedly into Kayden's torso. She paid no attention to the blood that spattered across her own face as she continued her ferocious mutilation of the corpse lying beneath her.

"Fay?" A familiar voice called out to her from nearby, though it sounded much farther away.

"Fay?" The voice sounded closer this time. "Fay!"

Fay snapped out of her thoughts, and quickly glanced back over her shoulder.

Fellow Sanatsai, Darrian Lanza, had entered the dilapidated stables and was walking sedately towards her. His tall, lanky frame was clothed in the monochromatic garb of the Order, and he too wore the hood of his cloak over his head. She noted the concerned look on his clean-shaven face as he halted by her side.

"Is everything all right?" asked Darrian.

"Yes. Everything is fine." She returned her gaze to Kayden—alive and well—still standing before her, looking slightly confused and perhaps a little disturbed. "Young Kayden, here, was just leaving to complete the assignment." Addressing the apprentice, she added, "Please don't let me hold you up any longer, apprentice. You still have time to deliver the box to Master

Pedrano at the rendezvous point."

Kayden seemed happy to receive her cue to leave. She tipped her head at Darrian, in acknowledgement. "If you'll excuse me Master," she said, pointedly ignoring Fay, before stepping away from the two Sanatsai to hurriedly exit the stables.

Fay remained where she stood, staring blankly straight ahead as Darrian gazed expectantly at her. "Is something troubling you Darrian?" she inquired. "I'm sure I asked you to wait outside for me."

"No. I'm not troubled, Fay, I'm just surprised," he replied. "You were so incensed by the assault on Zalayna I assumed you would come in here to give Kayden a severe tongue lashing, before letting her know she had failed the assignment."

Fay sighed. "Nothing good would come from failing her."

The words were muttered more to herself than as a response to Darrian. She fell silent for a moment, thinking. Finally, she broke her reverie, turning to face her friend and colleague directly. "Besides, would it not be a shame to deny her the honour of completing the assignment, having made it this far? In the twenty-four years since this current 'capture the box' exercise was first instituted, no apprentice has come even remotely close to success." In fact, no previous variant of 'capture the box' had gone longer than three years without being successfully completed.

The anticipated challenge to her reasoning failed to materialise, so Fay elaborated further. "Although her methods are not to be condoned, Kayden's resourcefulness and dedication are to be...admired."

"I suppose we should be impressed by her determination to succeed," Darrian conceded. "But electing not to fail her will likely only be a temporary stay of execution. I imagine the Council will insist upon Kayden's expulsion and the immediate binding of her *Zarantar*, once they learn of the savage attack on Zalayna."

"I will personally smooth things over with the Council to avoid that outcome."

Darrian raised his eyebrows, seemingly surprised she would go out on a limb for Kayden's benefit. "I don't doubt for a moment you could get the Council to accede to your wishes," he said. "But should Zalayna push the matter and insist upon Kayden's expulsion..." He trailed off, leaving it to Fay to fill in the blank herself.

"Zalayna has no memory of the attack. She remembers nothing that has happened since she sat down for dinner earlier today." The rebuttal was very matter-of-fact. "Besides, when she is told the truth there's little chance of her taking the matter to the Council. No Sanatsai would willingly acknowledge, let alone publicise the fact they had been comprehensively bested by a mere apprentice."

"You're probably right."

All of a sudden, Fay became conscious of the nagging urge to look down at Darrian's groin. *Damn Kayden for putting such absurd notions into my head!* She purged the thought from her mind as she concentrated on maintaining eye contact with her counterpart. If Darrian did harbour any romantic or sexual inclinations towards her, she would have noticed. And even if she hadn't, she knew him well enough to be certain he was one of the few members of the Order who wouldn't be too intimidated to make known his interest.

"Well, there's nothing more to be done here," she said casually. "Shall we get going?"

"All right. But before we leave, there is one thing about Kayden's exploits tonight that I can't help but wonder about."

"What's that?"

"I had no idea about a network of secret passages inside the old fort, nor underground tunnels beneath it, until you mentioned them as we made our way here. So how could Kayden possibly have known about them?"

"Simple. She cheated."

Evidently, Darrian was taken aback if the look upon his face was anything to go by. "How so?" His tone strengthened the impression that Fay had just given him an answer he hadn't expected, or even contemplated.

"The apprentices are assigned into their respective groups a week before the exercise is scheduled to take place. They are afforded that time to devise a plan to complete it successfully. It would have been easy enough for Kayden to abscond from campus for a few hours each night to extensively explore the fort. I'm actually very impressed she discovered the passageways and tunnels. Though there are subtle, tell-tale signs indicating their existence, few people would ever notice."

"How can you be certain that's what Kayden did?"

Fay smiled knowingly and patted Darrian on the shoulder. "Because it's what I would have done."

She began walking towards the exit, her colleague quickly falling into step beside her.

"And that's why you didn't fail her?" It wasn't clear if Darrian intended for his words to be a question but they came out sounding like one.

"No, of course not," she rebutted. "It's one thing to know about the passageways and tunnels, it's another to actually complete the assignment. Kayden couldn't have anticipated there would be five times more King's Guard on duty than is normal. She certainly couldn't have predicted volunteers from the Order among their number. And I know the Jaymidari wards protecting the box were an unexpected surprise to her. Yet, in spite of that, she was still able to overcome these obstacles, and that's why I won't deprive her of this victory." They exited the stables together, side-by-side. "But tonight's events have made it painfully apparent to me that Kayden has the potential to become a very serious problem—one that I must take care of as soon as possible."

"That sounds ominous," said Darrian. "What exactly are you planning to do about her?"

Fay contemplated her response for a moment. "I will need to give that some thought. But for now, I shall return to campus. I want to contact the Council, tell them about tonight's events before they can hear about it from someone else. The problem that is Kayden Jayta can wait until tomorrow."

They rounded the corner of the stables to walk along the side of the building where their horses were waiting...or should have been waiting. One horse was conspicuous by its absence. Only a single horse remained tethered in its place—the grey mare belonging to Fay.

"She stole my horse!" cried Darrian. "Can you believe the nerve of that girl? She took my horse!"

Fay made a half-hearted effort to stifle her laughter. "I told you she was trouble," she managed to say as she approached her horse.

"Why couldn't she take yours?"

"I expect she probably tried," Fay said, stroking the mare's nose. "But Shadow knows better than to allow anyone but me ride her—don't you my darling?" The horse whinnied, as if in acknowledgement.

After untying Shadow, she clambered up into the saddle.

"I would offer you a ride," she said, smiling down at Darrian, "but you're not going my way."

"You're not coming to the rendezvous point?"

"Like I said, I'm returning to campus right away. I'll leave the conclusion of the exercise in your capable hands. It's not far to walk from here, and I doubt Terio and the other Sanatsai have arrived there with the rest of Kayden's group yet."

She urged Shadow into a trot then pulled up almost immediately.

"One more thing. When you get there, could you please ensure all of tonight's participants are gathered together before returning to campus. I don't want anyone being left behind like last night."

"Will do!"

Fay urged her grey mare into a canter this time, leaving Darrian alone to begin the short walk to the designated rendezvous point.

"I'll see you back on campus!" she called out into the night.

Fay had been riding for almost an hour, and finally the Antaris campus loomed into view in the distance, getting ever closer as her grey mare moved onwards at a gentle trot. She would arrive within the next quarter-hour at her current speed, though she was in no real hurry to do so; she still had a lot on her mind.

Named after the province in the Kingdom of Mirtana—the easternmost realm of the Nine Kingdoms, in which it was located—the sprawling Antaris campus was one of nine campuses run by the Order. Along with the other eight sites dotted around the Nine Kingdoms, it served as the public face of The Order—as much as that was possible. Each location was deliberately situated far enough away from major population centres to minimise contact, though never too far from the small towns and villages of the surrounding countryside.

The network of campuses was established for the purpose of locating, identifying and taking in those adolescents born imbued with the *Zarantar* of the Sanatsai—an attribute that always manifested during the early teens. Once found, these individuals were presented with two options: to have their nascent power bound immediately—to prevent its use—so they may resume their lives uninterrupted or alternatively, undertake the ten years apprenticeship required to gain mastery of their *Zarantar*. Those who failed the training would likewise have their power bound, before being allowed to return to their former lives. But those who were successful were inducted into the Order as fully-fledged Sanatsai, to dedicate the rest of their lives to fulfilling the mission for which the Order was founded: to prevent the misuse and abuse of *Zarantar*.

In essence, the nine campuses run by the Order were simultaneously a boarding school, university and military academy, among other things.

For the past three years Fay had been serving as the administrator of the Antaris campus, overseeing the education and training of over three hundred apprentices. Three years on, her assignment to the post was still the subject of much speculation. Why would the Council waste the talents of one of the most powerful, renowned Sanatsai of the Order? Why turn Fay Annis into a glorified headmistress? This is essentially what had been done, people had argued. Many such voices viewed the awarding of a campus teaching position as the equivalent of being put out to pasture. Their credulity would no doubt be tested if they were to learn the truth: that Fay herself had requested to take on the role. But she had good reasons for doing so. Reasons that had been brought back into sharp focus by the events of that night.

As she continued her approach to the campus, Fay had spent the best part of the hour-long journey mulling over how to tackle the problem that was Kayden Jayta. The course of action she had settled upon basically amounted to passing the problem on to someone else, which didn't sit well with her. But the truth of the matter was, she only knew one person whom she felt confident could turn the wayward apprentice away from the path she was heading down. He had done so, successfully, once before with someone who had gone well beyond being just the potentially serious problem that Kayden currently was. The moment she arrived back at Antaris Fay intended to contact the Council to set things in motion, right away.

The campus grounds were illuminated by the muted glow of a network of hanging lanterns containing orbs as Fay entered via the south entrance. She was greeted first by two Sanatsai sentries, then a couple of ground staff on night duty, ready and waiting to help her dismount. As Shadow was led away to be stabled, she made her own way, on foot, towards the administrative building situated close to the north entrance at the other end of the campus. Given the late hour—or more precisely, the early hour—she only encountered one other person walking the grounds. The elderly Zando Morna, fellow Sanatsai and campus instructor, was exiting the mess hall just as she was passing the building. The portly, bearded man flushed upon seeing her, and looked more than a little guilty. He immediately fell into step beside Fay as he began his return journey towards the staff accommodation buildings.

"Administrator Annis, you've returned from the exercise alone?" he asked quickly, no doubt hoping to head off any potential questions about his nocturnal visit to the closed mess hall.

"Yes, I needed to return early," replied Fay.

She was more than happy to ignore the matter of the mess hall; Zando's late night, after hours snacking, was common knowledge among all the campus staff.

"One of the apprentices among tonight's group successfully completed the 'capture the box' exercise. It's fair to say I'm rather eager to pass on the news to the Council."

"Well, don't keep me in suspense," pleaded Zando, when she failed to identify the individual. "Who was the industrious apprentice?"

"Kayden Jayta."

"Oh!" he exclaimed. "Miss Jayta." After a brief pause, he added, "I guess I shouldn't be entirely surprised by the news. Despite the attitude problem, Kayden is certainly a dedicated pupil."

"Yes. Kayden is a very gifted young woman," she agreed, pensively.

"Of course, it probably helps that the administrator has taken a special interest in her development." Zando's tone wasn't accusatory, but the inflection was enough to convey his awareness that no other apprentice invited the same degree of attention from Fay.

The mirth in her voice was unintended when she replied, "I'm not sure Kayden would agree with that assessment."

"Yes, well, she is rather full of herself, isn't she?" Zando chuckled at the observation.

The two Sanatsai shortly parted ways upon nearing the administration building. Zando made known his intention to return to his bed to get two or three hours more sleep in preparation for the morning lessons he would be teaching. He bid farewell to Fay as he departed towards the residential building for the campus' male staff, leaving her to continue the short walk back to the administration building alone.

It was a large rectangular building, three storeys tall, its rows of Palladian windows all dark as she approached. Atop the structure, beyond the parapet—though not readily visible from the ground—were generous living quarters with a roof garden intended for use by the serving administrator. The ground floor of the building was given over, almost entirely, to the campus archives: records pertaining to various things such as progress reports, visitor logs, inventories, employment records and details of business transactions. There were also two lobbies within. The main one, which faced the north entrance of the campus, was for receiving visitors from outside the campus. The smaller lobby was used by staff and apprentices alike. The next floor up housed a spacious staff common room, a private library, and several staff offices. The top floor featured a large reception hall for visiting dignitaries, guest quarters for said VIPs, and offices for senior staff members, as well as the administrator's office.

Fay entered the building via the south entrance. Unsurprisingly, no one was on reception duty, though the lobby was bathed in the natural light of burning candles within wall-mounted lanterns. Proceeding immediately to the staircase to her left, she began the climb up to her office, making it as far as the first floor landing where she detected bright light coming from beneath the closed double doors of the common room at the far end of the dim central corridor. With a resigned sigh, she decided to quickly investigate.

She entered the common room without ceremony and was somewhat surprised to find Elsa Renzi lounging on one of the sofas with a hot beverage in one hand, a vellum document in the other, reading. Light seemed to emanate from everywhere and nowhere, though none of the room's obvious light sources were lit.

Ah, the wonders of Zarantar Jist, thought Fay.

The middle-aged woman wasn't just a history teacher at the campus, she was first and foremost a Jaymidari—as evidenced by her cream and beige attire. It was common practice for women from the Sisterhood to serve as teachers and teaching assistants within the Order's campuses; Jaymidari had been guides and teachers of Sanatsai even before the founding of the Order.

Elsa rose up in acknowledgement of the administrator's entrance, setting down her porcelain cup and document upon the tea table in front of her.

"Forgive the interruption, Sister," said Fay, motioning for Elsa to retake her seat. "I didn't expect anyone to be up and about at this hour." She ambled sedately to the sofa. "Why are you still here so late?"

Tucking her grey tinged, brunette hair behind her ears, Elsa sat back down before replying, "I woke a short while ago. And as there's only a couple of hours until dawn, I thought I may as well get a head start on my preparations for this morning's lessons."

"That's right, it's not long until sunrise." Fay perched on the arm of the sofa. "I've been so preoccupied I'd forgotten the time."

"Are you only just returning from tonight's training exercise?" inquired Elsa. "The apprentices usually fail much sooner; yesterday's group returned before midnight."

"Well, things went very differently tonight. One of the apprentices beat the odds to complete the assignment."

"That can't be right!" exclaimed Elsa, appearing genuinely astonished. "I'd always assumed the exercise was devised in such a way as to make it impossible for a level seven apprentice to accomplish."

"Well, that's not entirely correct. The goal was to make it impossible to complete by *conventional* planning; the idea being to encourage the apprentices to think outside the box, as it were."

"So who was the bright spark who thought outside the box?"

"I'll give you three guesses."

Elsa contemplated briefly. "Of the six apprentices in tonight's group, Kayden would seem the most obvious candidate. But you don't look or sound particularly pleased. Perhaps it was one of the others?"

"No, you're right, it was Kayden. And I wouldn't say I was displeased about it."

"I'd love to hear how she accomplished the feat."

I have several unanswered questions I'd like to ask about that myself, thought Fay. "A story for another day, I think," she said evasively, before rising to her feet from her perched position on the arm of the sofa. "For now, I really should be going. I was on my way up to my office, I have matters I need to discuss with the Council about tonight's events."

"Oh, yes, of course." Elsa rose to her feet, also. "Please don't let me delay you further." She added, "I guess it will be necessary for the Order to devise a new 'capture the box' exercise, now. And, presumably, the rest of the week's training nights for the remaining two groups of apprentices will have to be postponed."

"I hadn't thought of that," admitted Fay. "But, yes, you're right. News of Kayden's exploits will spread around the campus

51

pretty quickly in the coming hours. It could give the other apprentices an unfair advantage should they learn how she was able to complete the assignment. Although, truth be told, I don't believe any other level seven apprentice—either here or at any of the other campuses—would be capable of pulling it off, even then." She smiled, then said, "Goodnight, Elsa."

"Goodnight Fay."

With that, she exited the common room to resume climbing the staircase to the top floor. The subsequent walk through the corridors leading to her office was lit by the glow of an illumination orb floating ahead of her, lighting the way.

Upon entering her office, Fay closed the door silently behind her, then spent a few moments lighting the wall-mounted lanterns in the room, as well as the hanging chandelier. With the warm glow of candles now casting light throughout the office, she extinguished her illumination orb and walked to her desk. She removed her black cloak, placing it over the back of her chair, then proceeded to the west-facing wall where the sole ornamentation was a large rectangular mirror, hung in landscape orientation. Only it wasn't a mirror...at least, not just a mirror.

Standing in front of the mirror, Fay casually waved a hand across it. At once, a series of glyphs began to glow red along its frame, while her reflection gradually disappeared as the glass seemingly transmuted into a liquefied screen with swirling lavender mists contained within. The 'mirror' served as part of a *Zarantar* based visual communication system pioneered by the Sisterhood, allowing members of both the Order and the Sisterhood to communicate with each other from various secure locations, across great distances, throughout the Nine Kingdoms—and even further afield.

Fay stood motionless as a statue, waiting for the call she had sent out to the Council to be answered. The members were based at a location that was three hours ahead of the Antaris campus. It would be morning there already so she should get through to someone pretty quickly. Which proved to be the case. Within just a minute the swirling mists of the mirror dissipated, replaced by the image of a hooded middle-aged man dressed in the garb of a

52

Sanatsai of the Order; the amethyst pendant pinned below his right collarbone marked him as a serving member of the Council. Just behind him and to his left stood a diminutive older woman with long, greying locks. She too possessed an amethyst pendant that hung from a chain around her neck, though her cream and beige clothing was unmistakably that of a Jaymidari. But she wasn't just any Jaymidari. She was Idelle Silavas, a serving member of the Council, and global head of the *Sisterhood Of The Covens*.

"Good morning, honoured friend," greeted the Sanatsai, with genuine warmth. "To what do we owe this unexpected call?"

Fay's communication with the Council lasted no longer than five minutes; it was long enough to inform them of her intention to arrive there, in person, that very day. Regrettably, the Sanatsai whom she wanted to speak with was unavailable so the details of her visit would have to wait until her arrival. All she was prepared to convey was that she had a problem with one of the apprentices at Antaris campus; a problem that required a significant breach of protocol, on her part, to address.

The mirror once again held her reflection, and that of the office around her. She stepped away from it, heading immediately to the open entryway to the spiral stairwell in the corner leading up to the rooftop living quarters. She went up to her quarters where she stripped out of her uniform, put on a bathrobe, then spent several minutes manually pumping water to fill the tub in the bathroom. Though she could have employed *Zarantar* to draw the water, Fay needed a little distraction—no matter how brief. Her mind was preoccupied with thoughts of a precocious apprentice called Kayden Jayta.

Once the bath was sufficiently full, Fay poured in some bath salts then held a hand over the water. Her invocation of *Shakbarilsan* had steam wafting up from the water in seconds, whereupon she disrobed then languidly got into the tub and laid back, allowing the hot water to submerge her body up to her bare shoulders. As she relaxed, her thoughts drifted back to Kayden. Was she overreacting to the events that played out during the training exercise? Was it really Kayden's attitude and conduct that was giving her cause for concern? Was it, instead, the adverse effect the apprentice was on having on her own state of mind, with that uncanny ability to get under people's skin?

Or was it simply that Kayden reminded her so much of someone else?

Whatever the case may be, things would be coming to a head very soon. Kayden's stint as an apprentice of the Order could be brought to an abrupt, unceremonious end if Fay's gambit didn't go as she wanted. If Kayden couldn't be turned away from the path she was surely heading down, the Council, in response, would almost certainly pursue a course of action more extreme than the mandated expulsion and binding of *Zarantar*.

Fay did not wish to dwell on that idea at all, hoping instead it could be averted by her intervention. All the same, she knew only too well that if the unruly apprentice proved to be a lost cause, the alternative could be worse...so much worse.

CHAPTER FOUR

Accepting The Challenge

Kayden tied her long raven hair back into a ponytail. She was dressed in the dark blue cotton garb she favoured for exercising and ready to commence her regular morning workout, though several hours later than usual on this occasion. She, along with the failing participants from the group on last night's assignment, had only arrived back on campus an hour or so before dawn. As a result of their late night exertions the six apprentices were given permission not to attend their morning classes, allowing them to sleep in. Kayden managed to get four hours shut-eye, enough to feel completely refreshed and ready to tackle a brand new day.

Upon waking, she visited the campus library, spending an hour doing some research for her own gratification. With little more than an hour before the lunch hour commenced, she had returned to the women's dormitory wing on the western side of campus, back to her dorm room. She intended to spend the remainder of the time before lunch going through her habitual exercise routine before running three circuits around the perimeter of the campus.

Kayden glanced casually around the dorm room she shared with nine other level seven apprentices. Of the ten beds evenly spread around the room, only one was currently occupied. Neryssa, who had been a participant during last night's assignment, was seemingly still sound asleep in her bed on the opposite side of the room; the other apprentices were attending their morning lessons, as normal. After a short deliberation, Kayden determined that Neryssa had slept for long enough so it didn't matter if her roommate was disturbed by her belated morning workout.

She spent a few minutes doing some stretching exercises before lying down on the floor beside her bed to do some sit-ups. Her movements were executed in a smooth, relaxed fashion: exhaling as she rose up, inhaling as she went down. In short order, she completed a hundred sit-ups without breaking a sweat. Without pausing for breath she turned over onto her front to do some push-ups. As before, her execution of each repetition was smooth and relaxed: exhaling as she pushed up, inhaling as she went back down. Once more, she completed a full set of a hundred repetitions, in short order. The only signs of physical exertion were the few beads of perspiration on her brow.

Rising to her feet, Kayden quickly recovered a rope from the draw at the base of the wardrobe beside her bed. With the rope in hand, she stepped away from her bed—and any other potential obstructions—giving herself plenty of room to jump the rope unhindered. She swiftly attained a steady rhythm, eventually waking Neryssa in the process.

"What time is it?" groaned the apprentice as she sat up in bed.

"Must be about...quarter past...Eleventh Hour...by now," Kayden panted in reply.

Neryssa groaned again, then slumped back in her bed.

A further quarter-hour elapsed as Kayden jumped the rope; her skipping rhythm never once faltered, her breathing remained steady and controlled. Her skin positively glowed with the sheen of perspiration on her face, a few strands of hair sticking to her forehead. She could have sustained the effort for a considerable time, if she wanted, but she stopped abruptly when the dorm room door swung open, and in walked a willowy female apprentice with shoulder-length, wavy chestnut hair. Kayden recognised the interloper as a level eight apprentice by the name of Danya Shaylanis. She was supposedly the daughter or niece of a nobleman from an influential Mirtanese family, though she was more commonly known as the campus gossip. The books carried in her arms seemed to indicate she had either just finished a class rather early, or was incredibly late in attending one. Whatever the case, it wasn't her dorm room so she had no obvious reason to be intruding.

"Ever heard of knocking?" snapped Kayden.

Danya ignored the question as she closed the door behind her.

"Which one of you is Kayden?" she asked, casting her gaze between the sweat drenched apprentice and Neryssa, now sitting up in bed having been roused again by the intrusion.

"Who wants to know?" demanded Kayden, making no effort to disguise her irritation.

Casually, Danya leaned back against the dorm room door. "If that bad attitude is any indicator, you must be Kayden." She looked her counterpart up and down, appraisingly. "So, you're the apprentice who's been the talk of the campus all morning?" she drawled. "They said it couldn't be done; that nobody would ever successfully complete the 'capture the box' exercise. But somehow you managed to accomplish it."

"And yet, I'm just not getting the impression you're here to congratulate me." Kayden folded her arms across her chest. "Are you jealous?"

Danya giggled. She looked genuinely amused by Kayden's front. "I'd heard you were full of yourself. That must be why no one has a good word to say about you."

Kayden glared at Danya. "If there is a reason for you being here, I suggest you spit it out now...while you still can."

The casual threat wiped the smile from Danya's face. She pushed herself away from the door, and calmly walked towards Kayden. If she was intending to intimidate the other apprentice, being four inches shorter didn't help her cause.

"Don't you go getting your panties in a bunch, *Missy!* I'm here to deliver a message." When Kayden failed to ask from whom, Danya smiled again, before continuing. "It turns out that two of your classmates—I believe their names are Lazar and Vartan—aren't terribly happy about your success last night; not to mention they both hold you responsible for their own failure."

"So what's the message?" Kayden asked testily.

"They...*request* your presence at the start of the lunch hour in the old training arena. They would very much like the opportunity to..." Danya paused for dramatic effect, "in their words, teach you a lesson you'll never forget."

Kayden couldn't help but laugh. "They want to fight me?"

From her bed, Neryssa threw off the linen sheets and sprang out of bed. "Kayden! Don't even think about it."

"Would you cool your boots, Neryssa," retorted Kayden, berating her fellow apprentice. "If Lazar and Vartan are so eager for a beating, I'm more than happy to oblige them."

Neryssa stood at her roommate's side. "What's the matter with you?" she asked, exasperated. "Can't you go a single day without looking for trouble? Why must you needlessly get yourself into bother with other people?"

"Interesting," mused Danya. "The way people speak about you, Kayden, led me to assume you had no friends on campus."

"She's not my friend, *Straw For Brains*," Kayden snapped, dismissively. "I don't need friends."

If Neryssa was stung by the words, she did not let it show.

"Fine, whatever you say, *Missy!*" said Danya, raising both hands in mock surrender, while invoking *Yuksaydan* to prevent the books she had been holding from tumbling to the floor. "Anyway, I've delivered the message, now. I'll return when the bell sounds for Twelfth Hour." She grabbed hold of the floating books before her, cradling them in her arms once more.

"What for?"

"To escort you to the old arena."

"Why would I need you to escort me?"

"To make sure you show up, of course." Danya smiled when Kayden scowled at the not-so-subtle insinuation she could ever be guilty of cowardice. Mischievously she added, "I do love a good punch-up, and I wouldn't miss this one for all the mango juice in Jedeen."

Kayden took a threatening step towards the unwelcome guest. "I suggest you leave now or you won't have to wait to witness punches being thrown."

Danya promptly turned on her heels, and quickly exited the dorm room without another word. Alone with Neryssa once more, Kayden huffed as she began aggressively peeling off her sweat drenched clothing.

"Kayden, I realise you think you're invincible, and that the rest of us are beneath you." Another annoying lecture was under way. "But surely you can see…" Neryssa trailed off, falling silent as Kayden stood naked in front of her.

An amused smirk curled Kayden's lips upon noticing Neryssa averting her eyes. She fought off the temptation to make a caustic quip at the other young woman's expense. Instead, she stepped away to grab a grey cotton robe from her wardrobe. "Surely I can see…what?" she prompted, while putting the robe on.

"That Lazar and Vartan's challenge is obviously a trap." Neryssa looked comfortable again, with Kayden no longer nude. "After what you did yesterday it wouldn't surprise me if they intend to do more than just send you to the infirmary. You goaded Lazar into walking into that booby-trap, and the way Vartan tells it, you knowingly set him up to get caught by the Sanatsai who captured him, almost killing him in the process."

Kayden walked around to the other side of her bed. She pulled out a large towel from the bedside chest of drawers, flinging it onto her shoulder. "Neryssa, you worry far too much for a twenty-one-year-old."

"You don't worry enough."

Kayden didn't respond. She slipped on a pair of sandals then moved towards the exit.

"You're not going for your usual run?" Neryssa inquired.

"No. I may as well save my vigour for Lazar and Vartan. I'm going to the bathhouse to soak in a hot tub for a little bit."

"Oh, all right. Wait for me!"

Kayden slouched her shoulders as she stopped abruptly in her tracks, sighing with obvious irritation. Nonetheless, she waited while Neryssa quickly readied herself. Once her roommate had put on her own bathrobe and grabbed a towel, the pair exited the dorm room together, then leisurely made their way to the women's bathhouse.

The two apprentices returned to their dorm room shortly before the midday bell signalling the arrival of Twelfth Hour was due to ring out. They were now both fully dressed in their matching apprentice apparel—the black and three shades of grey uniform—similar in design to that worn by full-fledged Sanatsai of the Order. Neryssa sat perched on the edge of Kayden's bed, while Kayden stood several feet away at one of the windows, staring out at the campus clock tower in the distance, easily visible from the second storey of the dormitory building.

"Nothing I say is going to make you change your mind, is it?" opined Neryssa.

Kayden turned round to regard her roommate. "Change my mind about what?"

"Taking the bait laid out for you by Lazar and Vartan. Sneaking off to the old arena to meet them."

"No, of course not."

"But, why?" demanded Neryssa, clearly trying to understand her roommate's reasoning. "Just what is so terrible about keeping yourself out of trouble?"

Kayden marched indignantly back to her bed to stand over her sitting colleague. "Neryssa," she said, "people who are foolish enough to allow others to view them as weak and vulnerable, only increase their misfortune."

"What are you talking about?" The expression on Neryssa's face made plain her befuddlement wasn't feigned. "What does that even mean?"

"The strong prey on the weak, secure in the knowledge that there are no consequences for doing so. Those who don't wish to be victimised must avoid showing weakness, at all cost. It is the way of the world."

"No, it is the way of animals in the wilderness."

Kayden threw her hands up in frustration. Neryssa just didn't *get it*.

Turning on her heels, Kayden walked three paces from her roommate, stopped, turned on her heels again, then walked three paces back.

"I shouldn't expect you to understand," she declared. "You were born and raised in a small, insignificant Mirtanese farming town. Had you grown up in a large Astanese city, like Shali, and walked streets where people can and do behave like animals, you'd realise that a man will knife another man on the pretext that his victim looked at him wrong, just to prove himself a big man who should be feared." Kayden raised her voice. "Another man will beat to death an elderly couple, in their own home, because he feels entitled to deprive them of all their worldly possessions." Her voice rose even higher, still. "While another man will drag a woman kicking and screaming into a darkened alley to have his way with her, simply because he can."

She fell silent to regain her composure, and eliminate the rising anger in her voice.

When she broke the brief silence, Kayden spoke in a more measured, even tone. "The bottom line is, if I were to ignore their challenge it would only encourage Lazar and Vartan—or anyone else with a mind to do so, for that matter—to see me as weak and frightened. Someone who can be victimised without consequence. I can't allow that. I *won't* allow that. So, yes, I will meet them at the old arena, and once I am done with them, neither Lazar nor Vartan will look at me the wrong way again, much less cause me trouble in future." Kayden frowned at her roommate. "Unless, of course, you doubt my ability to defeat them in a fair fight."

Neryssa sighed; it was her turn to vent her frustration.

"Kayden, you're not understanding my concerns here," she said. "I'm well aware of what you are capable of, so too are Lazar and Vartan. Believe me when I tell you, they are not going to walk into this situation intending to have a fair fight with the possibility they could come off second best. This whole thing is a set-up. You could end up getting seriously hurt, or worse. And if not, all of you could get into big trouble if the Masters find out."

Kayden had no time to respond to her roommate. The campus clock tower began to chime. Twelfth Hour was upon them, and lunch hour was under way.

Moments after the final chime rang out across campus, there was excited knocking on the dorm room door.

"Come in!" called out Kayden and Neryssa, simultaneously.

The door swung open and Danya Shaylanis breezed back into the room. "Ah, good! You're ready, I see," she said cheerfully, closing the door behind her.

"Ah, good! You've learned how to knock before entering, I see," said Kayden in mock imitation of the willowy apprentice.

"Although two or three times would have sufficed," Neryssa appended. "Knocking twenty times in quick succession wasn't really necessary."

Ignoring them, Danya strutted to the nearest bed and leapt, back first, onto it. She stretched out upon the mattress, hands behind her head, legs crossed at the ankles.

"What are you doing?" asked Kayden. "I thought you wanted to escort me to the old arena."

Danya rolled onto her side, one arm propping up her head. "Hold your horses, *Missy*," she barked. "The bell has just rung. People are leaving classes; returning to dorm rooms; exiting dorm rooms; heading to the mess hall for lunch; leaving campus to go into town on errands." She spoke as if explaining things to youngsters. "Far too many eyes about campus that might catch us sneaking away towards the arena." She lay out on her back once more, hands behind her head, legs crossed at the ankles. "We'll just wait here for a little while until things have quieted down."

"You're just loving this, aren't you?" said Neryssa.

"Of course," Danya replied cheerfully. "I did arrange this fight, after all."

"You?" blurted Kayden, incredulously.

"Yes, me." She turned onto her side again, head propped up on one arm. "Did I not mention that before?" Without waiting for a reply, she continued, "Well, you see, at the end of my first class this morning I decided to pop into the mess hall for a quick snack before my second class. I just love those little lemon curd tartlets they served this morning. There were only a handful of people present, having late breakfasts, but I couldn't help overhearing two apprentices having some less than complimentary things to say about the hero of the hour who completed the 'capture the box' assignment. It turns out they had been part of your group last night, and from what they were saying, your success was entirely down to their selfless sacrifices, whereas their own failure was actually the result of your gross incompetence and rank stupidity."

Kayden scowled at Danya, but held her tongue.

"Anyway, my ears really pricked up when they mentioned how much they would love a few minutes alone in a room with you, though I'm not sure the human body could endure half the things they had in mind. So, being the helpful soul that I am, I walked over to let them know that if they happened to be at the old arena at the start of the lunch hour, I would arrange for you to be there so the three of you may thrash out your differences with your fists."

Neryssa vacated her seat on the edge of Kayden's bed, standing up to glare at Danya. "Oh, how considerate of you," she sarcastically. "What would we do without you?" Without waiting for a response she stomped purposefully towards the exit, obviously displeased.

"Aren't you coming to the arena to support your roommate?" asked Danya.

"No. I'm going to lunch." Neryssa stopped at the door to glance back at Kayden. "Are you coming, Kayden?"

"You know the answer to that," was her response.

Neryssa looked none too thrilled as she exited the dorm room, leaving Kayden alone with the organiser of the upcoming fight.

The old training arena was situated on the north western outskirts of the campus. The building was circular in shape with a shallow domed roof. Its design was completely at odds with the rectangular buildings that comprised the rest of Antaris campus—a discrepancy explained by the arena pre-dating the campus by two centuries. When it had been in use, the arena was where all the apprentices trained to master the invoking of the offensive applications of their *Zarantar*. It had now been disused for over two years, having been rendered obsolete by the construction of a new, larger training arena on the eastern outskirts of the campus.

Ten minutes after Neryssa left them alone in the dorm room, Kayden and Danya exited the women's dormitory, cautiously sneaking away from campus grounds to begin the four hundred yard march to the old arena. Preferring to walk there in silence, Kayden ignored the senior apprentice's attempts to strike up a conversation; she was even able to turn a deaf ear to several verbal jabs clearly intended to provoke a reaction.

Before long they reached the old arena unseen and without incident. They entered the building through a large double door entrance that should have been chained up, but wasn't. They navigated the outer ring of the interior then turned into the first corridor leading to the training area that lay at the heart of the building. As they approached the twin doors at the end of the short corridor, Kayden's swift, confident stride began to falter. She was apprehensive for the first time, noticing that *something* wasn't quite right. Naturally enough, she had assumed it would be just Lazar and Vartan waiting for her, but judging from the noise emanating from the other side of the doors there was obviously several more people inside.

"I hope you're not getting cold feet," said Danya when they stopped at the twin doors. "It would be a shame for you to chicken out now."

Kayden glanced to her right, giving Danya a dirty look; cowardice and fear were the last things she would ever be guilty of. It didn't matter how many people were lying in wait for her on the other side of those doors, she wasn't going to back out now. She marched forward with purpose, shoving the doors inwards to enter the fray.

Inside the training hall, Kayden's assessment of the situation proved to be correct—there was, indeed, several people present. There had to be close to a hundred and twenty apprentices, she estimated, all chatting and laughing as they loitered. Upon witnessing her arrival they instantly fell silent, as one. If each of them intended to harm her, Kayden knew she was in big trouble.

Stiffening her resolve, to ward off the possibility of apprehension marring her countenance, she proceeded to march confidently towards the middle of the arena. She noted that very few of the gathered apprentices she and Danya walked by had hostility etched upon their faces. Presumably, most of them—just like Danya—were hoping to see a good punch-up. Whatever the case may be, with over a quarter of the campus' apprentices not in the mess hall sitting down for lunch, it was only a matter of time before a member of staff noticed, and one of the Masters decided to investigate the absences.

This will need to end quickly, thought Kayden.

Now standing at the centre of the arena, Danya threw an arm around Kayden's shoulder. "My fellow apprentices," she called out, "please gather round for the event you have all been waiting for."

With military precision the assembled apprentices swiftly formed a big circle around the two young women. Glancing around the ring, Kayden finally spotted Lazar and Vartan staring fixedly at her. Judging by the expressions on both their faces, Neryssa was right, they did intend to do worse than just send her to the infirmary. At least, Vartan certainly did; he appeared to have murder in mind if the savage look upon his face was any indication.

He's going to be bitterly disappointed.

Danya stepped away from Kayden to casually saunter around the circle like the master of ceremonies at a circus. "We are gathered here today because some of our fellow apprentices have been aggrieved by Kayden... Kayden..." It seemed she had neglected to learn Kayden's family name before commencing her announcement.

"Jayta!" came a cry from the audience.

"By Kayden Jayta," Danya continued. "They now seek redress by way of unarmed combat." She paused to take in the rapturous applause of the crowd. Once the rowdy apprentices had settled down again, she resumed her address. "Will the injured parties please enter the circle?"

Kayden was unsurprised to see both Lazar and Vartan step forward immediately. She was caught completely unawares, however, when a further five apprentices—two of them female—stepped into the circle after them. She recognised the additional three male apprentices, having had previous run-ins with each of them at various times in the not-too-distant past. But she'd had no such run-ins with either of the two young women.

Racking her brain, she tried to ascertain possible motivations for the two female apprentices. The shorter of the two was completely unknown to her. In fact, she couldn't actually recall ever having seen the young woman on campus before, and she was certain she would remember an apprentice who couldn't be more than five feet tall. Kayden could only conclude that ethnic bias was the motivating factor; it certainly wouldn't be the first time. Although she had been born and raised a subject of the Kingdom of Astana, it was impossible to conceal her Vaidasovian origins. Her porcelain skin was at odds with the olive and tan complexions that were the norm for most of the people of the Nine Kingdoms, while her almond shaped eyes—a feature unique to the peoples of the continent of Vaidasovia—meant she could never hope to pass for a native of the Nine Kingdoms, or any of the lands comprising the continent of Karlandria, for that matter.

As for the taller apprentice standing beside the one she now thought of as *Little Miss Shorty*, Kayden had seen her frequently around campus. She was not the type of woman anyone would likely forget having seen: attractive features coupled with a curvaceous figure, attributes guaranteed to cause excessive blood flow to a certain part of the male anatomy. Yet, in spite of this recognition, Kayden still couldn't put a name to the pretty face. She had heard other people referring to her would-be opponent by a number of different names—not all of them flattering—but she had never spoken so much as two words to the woman before.

While the other apprentice stared daggers at her with cold dark eyes, Kayden found herself secretly hoping the gossip circulating around the campus some three months earlier was actually true—that *Miss Voluptuous Vixen* had acrimoniously ended an illicit relationship with a level ten apprentice after he allegedly called out 'Kayden' while they were fucking.

Whatever the reasons for it, Kayden was now faced with seven hostile opponents instead of two, which even for her was probably too many to fend off if they attacked simultaneously.

"To all participants," said Danya, "there is only rule you must adhere to during this trial by combat: the use of *Zarantar* is strictly prohibited. As the arena is no longer shielded to prevent structural damage, we can't risk alerting the Masters to this gathering by having holes blown into the roof."

Kayden noted how her seven would-be assailants were all fidgeting, no doubt eager to go on the offensive.

"Once started," Danya continued, clearly enjoying her role, "the fight will only be concluded when Kayden has been beaten unconscious."

A frown appeared on Kayden's face in response to that pronouncement, though she readily accepted there was a distinct possibility of the showdown ending with her lying face down, unconscious, in a puddle of her own blood. So, before that could happen she needed to do something to even up the odds, a little. She had to prevent her adversaries from rushing her as a group, otherwise she would have to resort to wielding *Zarantar*, and hoping one of the Masters came to her rescue in time.

She removed her cloak and nonchalantly tossed it at Danya. "I guess I shouldn't be surprised that the two of you were too cowardly to face me alone." She addressed Lazar and Vartan with the most mocking tone she could muster. "You just had to bring backup in your futile attempts to prove yourselves my equals, didn't you?"

"I don't need any help to fuck you up, bitch!" snarled Vartan. "Everyone, hang back until I've finished rearranging her face." Nobody protested as he advanced towards Kayden.

"Let the fight begin!" yelled Danya, before hurriedly leaving the circle to join the ranks of the spectators.

Kayden was quietly pleased. Vartan attacked alone while his six cohorts dutifully stood their ground, watching and waiting. If she could face each of the apprentices one-on-one, this would be so much easier.

He was on to her quickly, launching a barrage of kicks and punches that she parried and evaded easily. Kayden smirked in condescension as she danced around the circle on the tips of her toes, keeping well out of range of her opponent's attacks. She was about the same height as Vartan, though he was the heavier set and stronger of the two. But she was confident that her superior speed and athleticism would prove decisive. She even briefly contemplated toying with him, just to aggravate him further, but decided the better course of action was to put him down quickly then prepare for the next assailant.

Vartan was becoming increasingly flustered as his blows were failing to land. Sidestepping another punch, causing an opening to present itself, Kayden initiated her first attack, moving inside Vartan's defences to land a punch to the throat, followed instantly by a kick to his groin. The apprentice dropped like a stone, gagging—one hand clutching his neck, the other gripped between his legs.

An appreciative cheer from the watching crowd resounded through the arena in response.

Kayden spun around sharply to face the remaining six apprentices, her arms outstretched in challenge. "Who's next?" she yelled triumphantly.

Lazar sprang forward, as did one of the other male apprentices. Kayden was familiar with the second assailant: Gordo had been a classmate of hers when she was a level four apprentice. They had never been friends, but nor had they been outright enemies. The only source of antagonism between them was that he was always irked by her ability to best him into second place in any given discipline, whether it was archery or something more academic, such as geography. His pathetic inability to contain his jealousy, his frequent bickering with her—in addition to the constant sniping insults behind her back—had been a source of great amusement to Kayden, at the time. Well, if playing second fiddle to her upset Gordo that much, she thought, he was going to have to get used to it. She was about to beat him, *yet again*, not just figuratively this time.

Lazar and Gordo lurched on to the offensive, unleashing a succession of punches and kicks that Kayden was able to parry and evade. Her two attackers were pretty much cut from the same cloth. Both stood a little over six feet tall, both had unusually fair complexions and mousey hair. Even their features were similar. The notable point of departure was in their builds. Lazar had the toned, athletic physique of a man in his early twenties. Gordo, on the other hand—still only nineteen years old, not much older than Kayden—hadn't fully developed into his adulthood. They were both quick and agile adversaries; overcoming them both would be more difficult than facing Vartan had been. Fortunately, the ease with which she had dealt with that repugnant dunderhead had made Lazar and Gordo wary of her. Their attacks thus far had been more cautious than they might otherwise have been.

The fight continued for several more seconds; Lazar and Gordo were unable to capitalise on their numerical advantage. Kayden was comfortably able to keep them at bay, all the while biding her time, waiting for the opportunity to land a decisive blow on either of the two apprentices.

Without warning, Kayden felt a kick land between her shoulder blades, sending her hurtling forward. She reacted instantly, executing a forward roll, rising to her feet then spinning around to face her new attacker in one fluid movement. It was *Little Miss Shorty* who'd cowardly attacked her from behind. Kayden was not amused. Her first instinct was to rush forward to teach the good for nothing bitch a harsh lesson, but both Lazar and Gordo were on to her again; she was on the defensive, once more.

Things had been relatively comfortable for her while facing just two opponents, but now that a third fighter had entered the fray, Kayden knew it was time to change tack. Before the fight began she had intended to hold back as much as was feasibly possible, in order to avoid seriously hurting anyone. If several apprentices were to arrive at the infirmary with broken bones it would be next to impossible to keep the Masters from learning of the fight. But that was no longer a consideration. The only way she was going to walk away from the arena relatively unscathed was to inflict serious injuries on her foes.

Consequences be damned! The gloves are coming off!

Kayden blocked a punch from Gordo then countered quickly with a rapid combination of punches to the sternum then the head, culminating with an uppercut to the jaw that felled him like a tree. She followed up, immediately, with a fierce kick to *Little Miss Shorty*'s torso, connecting with enough force to send the apprentice stumbling back half a dozen paces before falling on her petite behind.

The violent display was met with joyful cheers from the crowd.

Her attention was drawn back to Lazar, just in time to duck beneath a high kick aimed at her head. In response she swept his standing leg out from underneath him, putting him to the ground. She followed him down, dropping to one knee to rain down five rapid punches to his 'pretty boy' face, before rising up in time to react to *Little Miss Shorty* launching a flying kick at her. She narrowly evaded the attack by sidestepping out of the way, but walked straight into a punch thrown by Vartan. The glancing blow caught her on the side of the face, cutting her above the left eye. Kayden was momentarily stunned as she staggered backwards and fell to the floor on her hands and knees.

Son of a bitch!

Her indignation brought her quickly back to her senses. Vartan was back in the fight and he looked furious. But now, so was she.

Kayden rose to her feet then gently brought the fingers of her left hand up to her head. She looked at the tips of her fingers. They were stained red. Vartan had drawn first blood, and in that moment she resolved that hers would not be the only blood spilled that day. As she prepared to initiate an attack on her advancing opponent, someone grabbed her ponytail from behind, yanking her head back. Before Kayden could react, an arm snaked around her neck to secure her in a choke hold.

"Only blind men will want to fuck you once we've finished messing up your pretty face," hissed *Miss Voluptuous Vixen* in her ear.

Vulnerable now, Kayden knew she had to break free of the hold on her, right away, but she was given no time to take any action. *Little Miss Shorty* dashed past Vartan to beat him to the punch—literally. The scrappy apprentice jumped upward to land a vicious right hook to Kayden's face. It was followed swiftly by a straight kick to the body. And just for good measure, she followed that up by thrusting herself forward to savagely drive a knee into

Kayden's gut.

Feeling nauseous, Kayden was saved from what should have been a prolonged beating when Vartan inadvertently came to her rescue. He started to jostle with *Little Miss Shorty* for the right to inflict even more violence upon the object of their mutual rancour.

"Get the fuck out of my way," Vartan demanded. "This smug bitch is all mine."

Kayden took full advantage of the temporary reprieve. She thrust her right elbow as hard as she could into *Miss Voluptuous Vixen*'s ribs, causing the apprentice to loosen her grip, just a little. The left elbow that followed weakened the choke hold on her sufficiently to break free. She spun around to face the curvy apprentice who lashed out at her with a straight right. Kayden parried the punch then retaliated with a swift, five punch combination, followed by a low kick that took her opponent's legs right out from under her.

She turned her back on the fallen apprentice to witness Vartan shoving *Little Miss Shorty* to the floor. She dashed towards him, leaping into the air with a flying kick. Vartan attempted to step backwards out of range but she successfully connected with three kicks to the chest, knocking him off balance to fall on his back. This time she had no intention of letting him off the hook to continue fighting. As he quickly scrambled back onto his feet she rushed forward again, kicking out with her left leg. She caught Vartan between the legs, causing him to double over. *That had to hurt*, she thought, then promptly capitalised on his vulnerability, thrusting her right knee up into his face as forcefully as possible. She felt, more than heard, the unmistakable crunch of Vartan's nose breaking. The belligerent apprentice finally crumpled to the ground—much to the delight of the cheering onlookers—clutching both hands to his face in a vain attempt to staunch the flow of blood, now seeping between his fingers.

Kayden stood over Vartan, her own blood streaking the left side of her face, and from a cut to her lower lip. "Now it's your turn to bleed," she taunted.

Anger at her words seemed to chase away Vartan's shock and pain. He struggled back on to his feet to resume hostilities, with a force of will that left Kayden exasperated.

This numbskull just doesn't know when to call it a day!

She nonchalantly swayed out of the way of a laboured right hook. When it was followed by an equally futile straight left, she caught hold of Vartan's arm, restraining him in an arm lock. As he struggled feebly against her hold on him, she caught sight of the two remaining male apprentices who had not yet attacked her. They appeared to be slowly inching forward, seemingly trying to coax one another into entering the fray against her. She decided to nix that idea right away. With all the strength she could muster, Kayden twisted the arm in her grip and was instantly rewarded with the satisfying sound of Vartan's arm dislocating at the shoulder.

The anguished scream of the apprentice vied with the renewed cheers of the raucous crowd. Vartan fell to his knees as soon as Kayden relinquished her hold on him. He settled into a prone position with his forehead pressed to the ground, in obvious agony.

Kayden took a single threatening stride towards her two potential foes. "Come on!" she yelled, her arms outstretched in challenge, daring the hesitant pair to attack.

The two apprentices—both formerly classmates of Kayden—exchanged dubious glances with each other. It didn't need to be said that they were both slightly smaller than Kayden. Nor could it have escaped their notice she clearly had no fear of them. The only question was whether their hostility towards her was significant enough to risk serious injury. The answer was obviously no, so they both hurriedly exited the circle, forcing their way past spectators trying to keep them within the circle, prompting a chorus of derisory booing from the disdainful crowd.

Kayden quickly glanced around the circle to assess her situation: Gordo was still lying unconscious where he fell; Lazar was sat on the ground with a hand pressed to the right side of his face, the pained look of dismay he was wearing indicated he knew better than to continue the fight; Vartan remained on his knees, injured, nearby, and though his screams had ceased he was in no condition to cause her any further harm. Which left only *Little*

Miss Shorty and *Miss Voluptuous Vixen* as active adversaries. The two young women were now standing side-by-side having seemingly decided to team up to take her on in a co-ordinated effort.

Standing in her fighting stance, Kayden's body twitched with anticipation, waiting for one of her opponents to make the first move. Her focus on the pair was so acute it prevented her from noticing Vartan rising to his feet behind her. Nor did she notice as he used his uninjured right arm to unsheathe the dagger at his back, concealed beneath his tabard. As a result, she failed to see him throwing the weapon with intent, aimed squarely between her shoulder blades.

Her first indication that anything was amiss was hearing the loud gasp that issued simultaneously from everyone inside the arena, followed by the low murmuring of dozens of voices. She realised at once that the eyes of all the apprentices in her field of view, including *Little Miss Shorty* and *Miss Voluptuous Vixen*, were focussed on something happening behind her. She spun around and was startled to see, right under her nose, a small dagger suspended in mid-air, its sharp blade no more than a couple of inches from her chest.

The dagger flew rapidly away from Kayden, and her gaze followed its path out of the circle towards one of the entrances to the arena, right into the hand of a waiting Sanatsai.

CHAPTER FIVE

The Exception That Proves The Rule

Fay nonchalantly caught the dagger in her left hand. In an instant there was complete silence. The eyes of everyone in the old arena were fixed upon her and the anxious looking apprentice standing at her side.

When Neryssa had sought her out to inform her of an illicit fight involving Kayden, Fay did not expect to enter the scene she was now witnessing. At a guess, there were at least a hundred apprentices present as spectators to a fight that had not only resulted in injuries, but had also, very nearly, ended in tragedy. Had she not been there to intervene, Kayden would now be lying on the floor dead or dying with a dagger protruding from her back.

She marched slowly towards the gathered apprentices, and the group parted to allow both herself and Neryssa to enter the circle. Fay was acutely aware of the awe she inspired within the ranks of the apprentices. She walked with the calm assurance of a woman fully cognisant of her own power; her body language inherently majestic. She glanced briefly at Kayden who was glaring at Neryssa—presumably unhappy with her fellow apprentice for turning informer—then cast her gaze around the circle.

"Those of you who were not active participants in this egregious breach of discipline," she began, "your lunches are getting cold. I suggest you make your way to the mess hall. Now!"

The apprentices began to disperse, vacating the arena as

quickly as they could.

"Not you, Danya!" Fay called out, as she spotted the willowy instigator of proceedings trying to sneak away unnoticed.

"But I wasn't an active participant in—" Danya began to protest. She was quickly silenced by a look from Fay.

Once the last of the excused apprentices had left the scene, only ten remained behind: five young men and five young women. Fay suppressed a sigh. She had another matter she wanted to attend to. She really didn't need this unwanted distraction. But this incident had to be addressed, even if it meant delaying her plans for Kayden. She cast her eyes upon the bloodied apprentice once again.

"I know what you're thinking—" Kayden blurted, pre-emptively.

Fay raised a hand to cut the apprentice off.

"I very much doubt that." She looked to Neryssa at her side. "Neryssa, please take Kayden back to the dormitory. Help her get cleaned up, then wait for my arrival. I will be joining you just as soon as I have dealt with this." She could tell Kayden wanted to object but was prevented from doing so. Neryssa quickly grabbed hold of her arm and, eventually, managed to pull her away—once she had retrieved her cloak from Danya.

Fay waited silently for the two young women to exit the arena before returning her full attention to the remaining apprentices. She noticed that Gordo—still laid out on the ground—was beginning to stir.

"Zorin! Rayshio!" she said, addressing the two male apprentices who had backed out of fighting Kayden. "Could you rouse Gordo and help him to his feet."

They rushed to obey.

"Danya! This is not the first time you have instigated a fight between apprentices." She spoke in a very matter-of-fact manner; there was no anger or harshness in her voice. "However, it is the last time. If not, you will find that being the daughter of a nobleman will not shield you from the consequences."

Adopting the most shamefaced expression she could pull off, the apprentice stared down at her feet.

"Yes, Master," she uttered, in convincingly contrite fashion.

"And for the record, how is it you came to set seven people against Kayden? I was led to believe she would be facing just two."

Danya looked up. It was difficult for Fay to determine if it was embarrassment on the apprentice's face or something else.

"It was supposed to be just Lazar and Vartan beating her up," she said awkwardly. "But things kind of got out of hand after I invited a small group of friends to come watch the fight. Word got out. Suddenly, not only were there dozens of apprentices wanting to attend, some wanted to participate in putting the boot in." She tried, but failed, to suppress a smile. "I guess Kayden isn't the most popular person on campus."

Fay was confident that Danya's observation was a major understatement, but she kept the thought to herself. She gazed at the seven apprentices who had faced Kayden.

"So, seven of you were insufficient to get the better of Kayden?"

It was a rhetorical question, requiring no response. Even if it hadn't been, none of the seven were prepared to offer up an answer.

She noticed that Gordo was looking unsteady on his feet, even with the assistance of Zorin and Rayshio on either side of him. He also appeared to have suffered a broken jaw during the fight.

"Zorin and Rayshio," she called. "As the two of you, wisely it seems, refrained from attacking Kayden, I will not be taking further action against either of you. So, if you would kindly escort Gordo to the infirmary, you are free to leave."

The two apprentices took their cue to leave, helping their injured cohort towards the exit.

"And Gordo," Fay called out without looking back, "I'll be having words with you once your injury has been treated." Returning her attention back to Danya, she added, "Danya, you may leave also. But remember what I said."

Grateful for the reprieve, the apprentice smiled a silent thank you then rushed for the exit as quickly as she could.

Fay turned to face the two female apprentices who had fought

Kayden; both women appeared nervous. "Janessa! What were you thinking?" she asked the shorter of the two women. "I cannot begin to tell you how disappointed I am to find you involved in this. Both you and Ella, get yourselves to the administration building. You are to wait outside my office until I arrive."

"But what about Kayden?" blurted the curvaceous apprentice, Ella. "She gets to go back to her dorm room while we get sent to your office?"

Fay glowered at the apprentice. "Ella, maybe if you worried less about Kayden, and more about your own conduct you would not be here. Now, do not make me repeat myself." Her tone made it abundantly clear that further protestation would be ill-advised.

The two young women silently trudged away towards the exit.

Fay stared at both Lazar and Vartan until the two female apprentices had vacated the arena. Vartan stood with his left arm hanging limply at his side as he held a bloody rag to his nose with his right hand. Lazar was considerably better off than his colleague, though he was obviously in some discomfort on account of the fractured cheekbone he had suffered.

"What is the matter with you both?" barked Fay. "I do not doubt for one moment that you each have reason to be holding a grudge against Kayden. But this?" She held up the dagger thrown by Vartan. "What were you planning on doing if you killed her? Did you imagine you could just bury her somewhere then hope no one would notice or care that she was missing?"

"Master Fay," pleaded Lazar. "I had no intention of killing Kayden. I... I just wanted to bring her down a notch, to wipe that condescending smirk from her stupid, smug face."

"I have no interest in petty justifications." She noted Vartan didn't try to offer any defence for his own actions. "My only concern, now, is what happens next. But first, you are both injured. Get yourselves to the infirmary and have those injuries seen to. The moment you are both patched up come to my office. I will be waiting for you."

"Master. What's going to happen to us?" asked Vartan nervously.

"Lazar's punishment I've not yet determined," she said. "As

for what happens to you: do you really need to ask? Now get going, both of you! I have other, more pressing matters I would rather be taking care of."

The two marched dutifully towards the exit.

As Fay observed them departing, it hadn't escaped her notice that while Lazar had seemed genuinely contrite about his involvement in the fight, Vartan, on the other hand, had looked altogether unrepentant. Not that it would have changed anything if he had expressed any regret; his fate was sealed.

Finally alone in the arena, Fay remained where she stood for a while, contemplating. In spite of herself, she could not help but be impressed at how Kayden was able to hold her own against seven other apprentices—without the use of *Zarantar*, no less.

At last, she let out an exasperated sigh then turned on her heels, marching swiftly for the exit. It was time to vacate the old arena and return to her office to discipline some unruly apprentices. Then would come the much greater challenge. Kayden Jayta.

Kayden was sitting, perched on the edge of her bed, with Neryssa seated beside her attempting to tend to her facial injuries. Three of their roommates had also returned to the dorm having finished their lunches, two perched on the adjacent bed, while the third, Yanina—the bed's usual occupant—stood over Kayden and Neryssa, eager to hear the latest gossip.

Yanina was as tall as Kayden, her swarthy complexion and thick hair, braided into plaited pigtails, highlighted her obvious Yantashan origins.

"Oh, come on!" she urged. "Are you seriously not going to tell us what happened?"

Kayden attempted to swat Neryssa's hand away as she pressed a clean cloth to the gash above her left eye. "Would you just stop that!" she snapped irritably. "If you can't stem the bleeding I'll just have to go to the infirmary."

"The bleeding has mostly stopped, but you still need to keep this wound clean so it doesn't get infected," retorted Neryssa. "And you cannot leave yet, anyway. Master Fay explicitly told us to wait here. Besides, what would you tell the Sisters in the infirmary? That you walked into a door?"

"I don't think it's any longer necessary to conceal that I was in a fight," she said, snatching the cloth from Neryssa's grasp, "since you already told on me."

Yanina's ears pricked up at the retort. "You've been fighting?" she exclaimed excitedly. "I just assumed someone jumped you, given the way your face is cut up and bruised like it is."

Kayden looked up at the standing apprentice. "You should see the state I left the others in." There was a degree of smug satisfaction in her voice. She had well and truly taught Lazar and Vartan a lesson they would be unwise to forget in a hurry.

"You got into it with more than one person?"

Neryssa explained. "A level eight apprentice roped Kayden into a fight with Lazar and Vartan in the old arena. They were both still angry about some of the things that happened last night, so they wanted to get back at her." She returned her gaze to Kayden. "But Kayden being Kayden couldn't be the bigger person and stay out of trouble."

Kayden scowled at her roommate.

"Why in the world would you want to fight 'pretty boy' Lazar?" Yanina asked Kayden, in surprise. "I can think of much more pleasurable physical activities to engage in with him."

The expression that swept over Kayden's face in that instant made a verbal response completely redundant. She was clearly repulsed by the mere suggestion. "Don't be so disgusting," she replied. "Besides, he'd be far too afraid to be left alone in a room with me for anything like that." The dubious look from Yanina prompted her to add, "If you don't believe me, why was he too cowardly to face me with just Vartan for backup? When I arrived at the old arena it wasn't just the two of them waiting. In total, I had seven apprentices to contend with."

"Just seven?" The quiet voice came from the other bed.

Kayden glanced at the olive skinned Malorini twins sitting across from her. It was Vida who had spoken, addressing her sister Aida who was sitting beside her. "You'd think there'd be a lot more than that queuing up to give her good a kicking," she quipped.

The twins began to chuckle to themselves before stopping abruptly upon noticing Kayden's gaze upon them.

"What?" challenged Aida. "You know she's right. You're not exactly popular around here."

Kayden had no trouble accepting there was truth in the jibes. She would never win a popularity contest on campus. And, in all likelihood, the Malorini twins would also be standing in a queue of apprentices who would happily give her a beating. But she didn't care; they would all be welcome to try, if they dared.

"Kayden, if you were in a fight with seven other apprentices who had it in for you," observed Yanina, drawing Kayden's attention away from the twins, "you'd be in much worse shape than you are."

"I was actually winning until *Miss Goody Two Shoes* decided to intervene." She gestured with her head towards Neryssa. "You should have seen it. Only two of them were still standing by the time she walked in, except she's not alone. She's accompanied by the administrator. Of all the Sanatsai in the world, she has to bring the only one I cannot stand."

"You got caught fighting by Master Fay?"

"Unfortunately." Kayden diverted her gaze away from Yanina to direct her ire at Neryssa. "I still can't believe you went to *that woman*; you said you were going to lunch. Did you really think I couldn't take care of myself?"

"Hey," barked Neryssa, "*that woman*, is the reason you aren't seriously hurt, or worse." The apprentice's voice rose in obvious anger. "We could be burying your corpse right now if not for Master Fay; why don't you show some respect?"

Kayden was vexed by her roommate's sudden outburst. "If you expect me to idolise her, and revere the ground she walks upon like the rest of you. Don't hold your breath."

"Ladies! Ladies!" interrupted Yanina. "Could we just go back a moment, please? First Kayden says she was winning the fight, now you're saying she could have died. Well, which is it?"

"Kayden might have had the upper hand," conceded Neryssa, "but that was before Vartan tried to kill her with a dagger in the back." The revelation caused Yanina to stare at her in wide-eyed disbelief. "It was Master Fay who saved her ungrateful life."

An outbreak of laughter from the other bed intruded upon the conversation.

Neryssa glared across at the Malorini twins. "Does that amuse you?" she snapped angrily.

Vida stopped laughing first. "How could it not?" she replied. "Not only does she get caught fighting by Master Fay, of all people, it's a fight in which the participants were actually trying to kill each other. I would hate to have been in the shoes of any of the apprentices involved."

"Exactly!" agreed Aida. "So how severe was the punishment meted out by Master Fay?"

"We don't know, yet," admitted Neryssa. "Master Fay instructed me to bring Kayden back to the dorm then wait for her to arrive."

"She's coming here?" gasped Yanina. "Why didn't you say so from the start?" Immediately, she sprang into action, making a fuss around the dorm room—smoothing bed sheets and clearing clutter from the floor.

"Yanina, would you cool your boots," said Vida. "Since when does the administrator visit an apprentice in their dorm?"

"Exactly!" concurred Aida. "When Master Fay wants to see you, you must go to her, she doesn't come to you."

"And yet," said Kayden. "I don't have to go to her, she has to come to me." The trademark smug condescension was back in her voice. "How jealous are you, both, right now?" she concluded, mockingly.

Aida looked for all the world as if she was about to spring forward from the other bed to attack Kayden. But her attention was diverted back to Yanina when she returned to stand in the space between the two beds.

"You may not like it, but if you believe the gossip about Master Fay," she said to the twins, "Kayden is the one apprentice on campus she'd go out of her way for."

"What gossip?" the Malorini twins asked, in unison.

"Apparently," began Yanina, "in recent months several of the Masters have been overheard complaining about having to tolerate

Kayden's frequent misconduct because she is Master Fay's favourite apprentice."

"*You have got to be joking!*" Kayden was unable to keep the incredulity from her voice.

"Not only that," Yanina turned to address Kayden directly. "There also seems to be a great deal of speculation about why Master Fay has taken special interest in your training and development."

"Now you're just being ridiculous," said Kayden in irritation. "You need to stop giving an ear to absurd rumour-mongers. The truth is, *that woman* has it in for me."

"All right, don't bite my head off," retorted Yanina, holding her hands up in a placating gesture. "I'm only repeating what more and more people are beginning to say."

"Well, I for one don't believe a word of it," said Aida unreservedly. "Why would Kayden be Master Fay's favourite anything?"

"Look, I'm not saying I'm entirely convinced myself," Yanina conceded. "But if Kayden escapes punishment for her involvement in the fight, it'll give the rumours some credence."

There were three solid knocks on the door.

Neryssa rose swiftly to her feet. "That must be Master Fay, now."

The urgency in her voice prompted Vida and Aida to to rise to their feet, joining herself and Yanina in standing to attention for their expected visitor. Kayden nonchalantly remained seated.

"Please, enter," Neryssa called out.

Peering back over her shoulder, Kayden saw the door swing open. It was, indeed, the campus administrator who entered the dorm, closing the door behind her. As Fay approached the beds that they were standing between, Kayden was startled by a kick to the shin from Neryssa; it was presumably an effort to make her stand to attention.

"There's no need to stand, Kayden," said Fay.

Kayden glanced up at her roommate, to smirk.

"The rest of you, please continue with whatever it is you were doing. If you will excuse my intrusion I need to have a word with

Kayden."

Vida and Aida quickly went to their respective beds to sit down. They each grabbed a book from their bedside drawer and pretended to read—all the while keeping an eye and ear on whatever was about to transpire next. Neryssa and Yanina, for their part, both sat down on the edge of Yanina's bed—newly vacated by the twins—making no effort to conceal the fact they had every intention of listening in on the coming conversation between master and apprentice.

Kayden was surprised when Fay sat down beside her on the bed. She visibly flinched when the Sanatsai reached for the bloody cloth she was still pressing to her head.

"Here, let me take a look at that," said Fay, prising the rag from her grasp. She grimaced slightly as she examined the laceration above Kayden's eye. "For most people, such a wound would require stitches and leave a nice little scar." She dropped the bloodstained cloth then placed her hand against the side of Kayden's face. "Fortunately for you, that won't be necessary."

Kayden felt a warm, tingling sensation spread all over her face from Fay's touch. The sharp, stinging pain from the cut above her eye, dissipated, as did the numbness of her mouth. She knew right away from the awed expressions on the faces of both Neryssa and Yanina that her facial injuries must have healed instantaneously. If that was the case, they certainly had every reason to be impressed. Kayden was unaware of Sanatsai having this aptitude in their repertoire. By contrast, the healing capabilities of the Sisters who manned the infirmary would have simply accelerated the natural healing process, allowing her injuries to heal in minutes, rather than hours or days. It was by no means the instantaneous process just demonstrated by the administrator.

Kayden mentally added another entry to her rapidly dwindling list of applications of *Zarantar* she intended to gain mastery of.

Gently, Fay withdrew her hand from Kayden's face. "Though it should be noted that your injuries were minor compared to those suffered by Vartan, Lazar and Gordo." The look upon her face mirrored the reproach in her voice.

Now we're getting to it, thought Kayden. "If you plan to use the incident in the old arena as a pretext for my expulsion, I won't allow you to do that." Her words were blunt; but now was the time for candour. "I will vigorously appeal such a decision before the other Sanatsai, if I have to."

"Do not concern yourself about what happened earlier. That matter has now been dealt with." It was Fay's turn to be forthright. "But, be that as it may, the incident could easily have been averted if you had refrained from getting involved in the first place. Once you became aware of the intentions of Lazar and Vartan, you should have come to myself or another member of staff to report the matter."

Although she felt laughter was the only appropriate response to that suggestion, Kayden remained silent.

"Having said that, I will not be taking any action against you. I accept you were the intended victim today, not the instigator, so there is no need for us to discuss the matter any further."

Kayden noted the expression on Yanina's face, directed at her from the adjacent bed. It seemed the apprentice was starting to buy into the rumours she had relayed earlier. And though she didn't share that sentiment herself, Kayden was just as surprised to hear that there would be no repercussions for her involvement in the fight.

"I was actually preparing to pay you a visit, about another matter, when Neryssa came to inform me of the trouble you were walking into."

"Another matter?" asked Kayden. It could only be about the 'capture the box' exercise the previous night.

"I have some urgent business with the Council to attend to," said Fay in explanation. "I will be leaving campus for Temis Rulan, shortly, and I will be taking you with me."

"What?" Kayden gasped. "Why?"

Fay ignored the questions and continued. "I had intended to leave at Thirteenth Hour, on the dot. It's almost that time now. But, obviously, dealing with the aftermath of the misbehaviour at the old arena has delayed me." She rose to her feet, staring down at Kayden. "You have half an hour to get yourself ready to join me.

You should dress in full ceremonial attire, and be sure to collect your weapons from the armoury."

Kayden felt her anxiety begin to grow. If Fay truly intended for the two of them to travel to the headquarters of the Order, why was it necessary to be armed? "I don't understand," she conceded.

Again, Fay continued speaking as though she hadn't heard Kayden. "Once you are ready, proceed immediately to the administration building. I will await your arrival."

Fay stepped away from the bed and began marching towards the door. She hadn't taken half a dozen steps before she was stopped in her tracks by one of the apprentices.

"Master Fay?" called out Neryssa.

Peering back over her shoulder, Fay saw Neryssa standing a couple of paces behind her. "What is it, apprentice?"

"If I may ask," said Neryssa, nervously. "Can you tell us what's going to happen to Vartan?"

Fay turned round to face the apprentice. "Vartan has been expelled with immediate effect; he is having his *Zarantar* bound as we speak. He will shortly, thereafter, begin his journey home—to resume the life he had before coming here to Antaris."

Kayden glanced silently around the dorm room to see the reactions of the other apprentices to the news. She saw stunned surprise etched on all their faces. She was certain that if she could see her own face in that moment she would observe a similar expression upon it. She rose swiftly to her feet to address Fay. She was unexpectedly experiencing some feelings of regret at the news of Vartan's expulsion, and the role she no doubt played in it.

"Administrator Annis! It was not my intention to get Vartan expelled," Kayden blurted. "I would never want another apprentice kicked out on my account."

"For the record, Vartan was not expelled because of anything you did, Kayden. His punishment is the result of his own actions. The Order cannot have would-be murderers in its ranks." Fay spoke in that characteristically matter-of-fact tone that Kayden invariably found so irksome. "Think no more upon it, any of you."

Kayden looked on in silence as Fay turned on her heels then resumed her exit from the dorm, without another word. The instant the door closed behind the Sanatsai the other apprentices hurriedly gathered around Kayden with disbelieving expressions on their faces.

"Hey! Stop crowding me," she grumbled, before slowly sitting down on her bed again.

Neryssa promptly sat down beside her. "Kayden, this is unbelievable." Evidently, she was excited about something. But she was an excitable young woman.

"I know. I *almost* feel bad for Vartan."

"I'm not talking about Vartan, silly; he got what he deserved," replied Neryssa, dismissively. "I'm talking about *you*—going to the headquarters of the Order. And in the company of Fay Annis, no less."

"You're right not to believe it," said Kayden. "I know I don't believe it. The location of Temis Rulan is a closely guarded secret, known only to the members of the Order, and the Sisterhood; not even the royal families of the Nine Kingdoms know. There's no feasible way that a mere apprentice would be permitted to know where it is, much less be allowed to go there."

"You're probably in so much trouble that an exception had to be made just for you," said Aida, with a chuckle. "I would hate to be in your shoes right about now."

"Exactly!" agreed Vida, before joining her twin sister in a fit of giggles.

Kayden didn't say anything; the same thought had already crossed her mind. But she had never read or heard of an expulsion of any apprentice that required a journey to Temis Rulan.

"Don't listen to them, Kayden." Neryssa gave the Malorini siblings a reproachful glare before returning her gaze to Kayden. "I imagine Master Fay is taking you to Temis Rulan to receive some kind of special commendation—for being the first apprentice to best the 'capture the box' exercise, last night."

"I suspect that's not nearly as silly as it would have sounded yesterday," said Yanina. "For one thing, Master Fay just let you escape punishment for your involvement in the fight earlier. If we add that to the rumours you're her favourite apprentice, it's actually plausible that you *are* going to be honoured in some way.

Why else would she make an exception to the rule so you can accompany her to Temis Rulan?"

Kayden thought back to her confrontation with Fay in the abandoned stables the previous night, how she had insulted the Sanatsai in an attempt to provoke a response from the stoic woman. If the expression that briefly passed over her face, and the look in her eyes was indicative of Fay's true intentions, then wherever it was she was planning on taking Kayden, one of them surely wouldn't be coming back.

The campus clock tower sounded, announcing the arrival of Thirteenth Hour, the end of lunch, and the beginning of the first afternoon classes of the day. The twins and Yanina took this as their cue to start gathering their things for their next lesson.

Noting that Neryssa had made no effort to get off the bed to gather her own stuff, Kayden frowned at her. "Aren't you planning to go to class?"

"I will," replied Neryssa. "Just as soon as I've finished helping you to get ready for your journey."

"You'll be late."

"Who cares? This is so much more important." There was no hiding Neryssa's excitement. "I am witnessing history being made today. You will be the first apprentice to travel to Temis Rulan *before* actually being inducted into the Order. I don't imagine that's likely to happen again any time soon...if ever." She smiled then added, "In light of that, I'm quite sure Master Darrian will forgive my tardiness on this occasion."

Yanina, Vida and Aida headed quickly for the door—books and other paraphernalia in hand. Neryssa called out to the trio before they could leave. "Could you let Master Darrian know I'm running late. I'm helping Kayden get ready for her big moment."

"All right," replied Yanina. "We'll see you in class."

As Yanina and the twins exited the dorm room, five more apprentices entered, in quick succession. They each hurriedly went to their respective beds and drawers to collect their own things for their upcoming classes.

"Don't the two of you have to go to class?" asked one of the latecomers as she noticed both Kayden and Neryssa sitting idly on the former's bed.

"I have a class to get to," admitted Neryssa. "Kayden, on the other hand, is preparing to embark upon a journey to Temis Rulan with Master Fay."

"Uh huh, of course she is." The response was uttered sarcastically, but the apprentice's initial incredulity quickly evaporated once she realised Neryssa wasn't being facetious. "Oh, wait, you're not joking, are you?" Without waiting for an answer, she addressed Kayden, "What kind of trouble have you got yourself into this time? There's a rumour going around that you sent three apprentices to the infirmary, but you must have done something much more serious than that for Master Fay to take you to Temis Rulan."

"There's no reason to believe that Kayden's in any kind of trouble," said Neryssa.

"But it's a safe assumption." quipped Kayden.

"Well, Neryssa, you'll have to tell me all about it later this afternoon, I need to get to class. Kayden, if I don't see you again... well, goodbye and best of luck with whatever you do in future."

Moments later, the last of the apprentices had vacated the dorm leaving Kayden and Neryssa alone. It was Neryssa who rose to her feet first. She looked down at Kayden, smiling. "Let's not keep Master Fay waiting any longer than necessary," she said, cheerfully. "It's time to get you ready."

Fay stood at the reception desk of the lobby in the south of the administration building. She spoke briefly to Marla—the receptionist on duty that afternoon—to inform her that an apprentice would be arriving some time around half past the hour to see her. The apprentice was called Kayden Jayta, and as soon as she arrived, Marla should instruct her to go immediately to the staff common room on the floor above, where Fay would be waiting.

Having conveyed the message, Fay made her way up the stairs to the top floor. She proceeded swiftly to her office then headed up to her rooftop living quarters where she spent a few moments retrieving her weapons—a sword and twin daggers—from where they were displayed on the wall above the mantelpiece. She fitted the sword into place, secured in the black leather baldric she wore, its hilt within easy reach behind her right shoulder. The twin daggers she fixed into place, one on either hip.

Without further delay, Fay left her quarters and vacated the office to go to the staff common room where she had requested Isko Nardini to meet with her and Sister Elsa. All the while, her thoughts were preoccupied with her upcoming excursion with Kayden. Although she was unaccustomed to feeling nervous, her trepidation about what she had set in motion was undeniable.

Fay entered the staff common room through its double doors, without ceremony. She was pleased to see that both Isko and Elsa were already present. They were both seated on one of the couches at the centre of the room, being served tea by another Sister, Alina Grinello, one of the infirmary staff. Fay approached the couch with a smile for her colleagues; they duly reciprocated. She perched on the arm of the couch to join the seated pair.

"Would you care for some peppermint tea?" Alina inquired, cordially.

"No thank you, Sister."

Alina poured herself a cup of tea then withdrew to sit alone at a table in the corner, several feet away, so the trio may speak freely.

Fay looked toward the middle-aged Sanatsai, Isko Nardini. He was still an imposing figure, in spite of his advancing years. He remained a fine physical specimen—trim and athletic, with just a few flecks of grey in his hair and beard, and even fewer wrinkles on his face. She'd got to know him well during the Leshek campaign. They had both served on the front line after the forces of Sirathania had launched a surprise invasion of Leshek in an ill-fated attempt to annex the island from the dominion of the Kingdom of Darmitana. Upon taking up the administrator's post at Antaris, Fay was gratified to have Isko on her staff; his experience made him an exceptional instructor to the level eight, nine, and ten apprentices. It also made him the ideal person to act in her stead while she was away from campus.

"Thank you for your time, Isko," she started. "I apologise for the short notice, but I'll be departing for Temis Rulan shortly and

I've decided to leave you in charge of overseeing the campus until I return."

"Of course," replied Isko, somewhat surprised. "Is there some kind of emergency? This will be the first time you've returned to Temis Rulan since you were assigned here."

"No emergency," she assured him. "Though it is an urgent matter. I'm not sure how long I'll be away for, that's why I've asked Elsa to join us." Addressing the Sister, she said, "I would like for you to be at Isko's service should he need to delegate any tasks while I'm away."

"Certainly," replied Elsa, with a nod of the head.

Addressing Isko, again, Fay said, "Ideally, I don't want my absence to distract you from your teaching duties, as you are the best instructor here. So, please, don't hesitate to make use of Elsa's assistance. She has always been a great help to me."

"Will do," agreed Isko. "Anything else I should know?"

"Um..." Fay hesitated for a moment. "There is one more thing I should probably mention. I'll be taking one of the apprentices with me."

Both Isko and Elsa looked surprised by the announcement, Isko more so. "The Council agreed to that?" he asked, clearly astonished.

"Yes, so if anyone should inquire about the absence of Kayden Jayta, she will be with me."

Elsa inquired, "Does this have anything to do with the training exercise last night?"

"You could say that," Fay said. "But more than that, no one needs to know."

An awkward expression appeared on Isko's face. Fay realised he wanted to question her about something, but he was always such a tactful person—reticent to say or do anything inconsiderate or impertinent, unless he had no choice.

"If you have something to say Isko," said Fay, "please do so."

"Well," he began awkwardly. "What should I tell Kayden's instructors if they should ask about your *reasons* for taking her to Temis Rulan? If I can't provide an answer it will only lead to even more rumours about you and your, uh... Well, your *attitude* to this particular apprentice."

"As I said, no one needs to know," Fay reiterated. "Rumours are of no consequence." There was a finality to the response that discouraged further questioning.

Fay rose from her position on the arm of the couch, then casually walked to the other sofa opposite her two colleagues. She promptly sat back down to resume the conversation across the tea table between herself and them. "Kayden should be arriving here, soon, but in the meanwhile I'd just like to go over my schedule for the rest of today, and tomorrow. You shouldn't have any difficulty keeping on top of things while I'm gone."

CHAPTER SIX

Suspicious Mind

Kayden stood in front of the dorm room's only tall mirror, looking at her own reflection. The ceremonial attire she was wearing was certainly very fetching—much more so than the everyday uniform she and the other apprentices were accustomed to. The clothing wasn't just made from finer quality fabrics; its design was more elaborate, too, though not to the same extent as the uniform worn by full-fledged Sanatsai. Nonetheless, it was certainly a step above the garb she usually had to wear.

While she admired her reflection, Kayden couldn't help but lament that there were so few opportunities for her to wear the ceremonial outfit. It was usually only worn for graduation ceremonies at the end of each training level, or during visits by dignitaries—either government officials or members of the Order. Wearing it made her feel like a bona fide Sanatsai, not just an apprentice.

All the while, Neryssa stood behind her continuing to diligently brush her long raven hair for her. Kayden was rather bemused to witness her counterpart fussing over her like a proud mother would her daughter. She was only two years her senior, after all.

"You really should be wearing your hair down all the time," said Neryssa, wistfully. "You have such great hair. It's a shame you insist on keeping it in a ponytail or that dreadful braided bun at the nape of your neck."

"It's easier to fight when you don't have to worry about hair getting in your face," replied Kayden.

Neryssa finished brushing Kayden's flowing locks, then gazed over her roommate's shoulder to evaluate her own handiwork. "I suppose," she said absent-mindedly, admiring Kayden's reflection.

Kayden frowned as she noticed the weight of Neryssa's scrutiny. "Why are you looking at me like that?"

"I'm just remembering the first time I ever saw you on campus." Neryssa had that wistful cadence to her voice again. "Being born and raised in Mirtana, and never having been outside the kingdom before, I had never seen anyone of Vaidasovian descent until I saw you. But I had frequently heard it said, by many people, that Vaidasovia is home to the most beautiful women in all the world, so when I was told you are a Vaidasovian girl, I knew immediately the saying had to be true."

"What are you talking about?"

"Oh, come off it, Kayden! I don't believe for a moment you're oblivious to just how beautiful you are," replied Neryssa. "Your hair is as black as the sky on a moonless night, yet shines like the stars. It's softer than silk to the touch, and smells like a warm summer day. Your skin is so flawless I have to resist the urge to touch it, just to be certain you are real. And those stunning, almond shaped eyes...they're simply captivating. You could make people throw themselves to their death with just a look."

Kayden began to feel uneasy about where the flattery might be heading.

"And your lips are a shade of pink so delicate, they draw eyes to them as a naked flame draws moths."

Kayden turned away from the reflections in the mirror to face Neryssa directly. "If this is an attempt at seduction, I suggest you stop, now." There was more than a hint of threat in her voice. "I cannot be taken advantage of. No matter how much you flatter me, you won't get what you want because you have nothing that I want."

Neryssa was visibly taken aback. "You really don't make it easy to be friends with you. Sometimes I wonder why I even bother."

"Well, we're not here to make friends," said Kayden irritably. "At least, that's not why I'm here. Besides, why are you so eager to be my friend?"

Neryssa didn't reply right away. Her face took on a contemplative air; she appeared to be reminiscing.

"My father always says," she began finally, "it is better to make friends than to acquire enemies. I realise you probably feel differently, but you cannot tell me, in all seriousness, you want to go through life shunning friendships entirely."

Kayden was unable or unwilling to offer a response. After a drawn-out, awkward silence she turned back round to face the mirror, before sweeping her hair back to tie it into a ponytail as Neryssa looked on.

"If I misinterpreted your intentions," she said. "I'm... I'll try not to repeat that mistake." She turned around again to face Neryssa. "For what it's worth, I appreciate your help in getting ready."

Neryssa smiled; it was probably as close as she would ever get to hearing Kayden say she was sorry. "Apology accepted," she said. "And think nothing of the assistance, I'm probably more excited about your trip than you are."

That was certainly true, Kayden realised, though not difficult under the circumstances. She wasn't at all convinced by Neryssa or Yanina's assessment that she was being taken to Temis Rulan to be honoured in some fashion because of her exploits the previous night. On the contrary, she suspected a far more sinister motive for the alleged journey.

"Now that you're ready, it wouldn't do to keep Master Fay waiting any longer," prompted Neryssa. "And I need to get going myself."

Making the first move, she headed towards the door.

"I'm right behind you."

Kayden followed behind Neryssa as they made their way out of the dormitory building on to campus grounds, walking side-by-side on the way to their respective destinations.

"So, how long do you reckon it takes to get to Temis Rulan?" asked Neryssa.

"Without knowing where it is, I cannot even guess," Kayden conceded. "There are numerous locations throughout the Nine Kingdoms where it could have been established."

"I guess you'll know soon enough," offered Neryssa. "I wonder how long you'll be gone for?"

If that woman has her way it will be permanently.

Kayden didn't give voice to the thought. If Fay Annis was intending to get rid of her, and the alleged journey to Temis Rulan was just a smokescreen to get her away from campus, she would cross that bridge when she came to it. "You seem so certain I'll be coming back," she muttered under her breath, louder than she meant to.

"Why wouldn't you?" asked Neryssa.

Kayden didn't answer. How could she explain her suspicion that the administrator was luring her away from campus to murder her, based solely on a look that briefly passed over the Sanatsai's face the night before? Neryssa would never believe such a thing. She—like many others—idolised the woman. It was better to keep her suspicions to herself, to minimise the likelihood of inadvertently letting Fay Annis know that she was wise to her machinations.

Unfortunately, Neryssa was too perceptive not to notice her reticence to answer the question. "What is it you're not telling me?"

"Neryssa, there are many things I don't tell you."

"Stop being so flippant, I'm asking you a serious question. Is there some reason why you think you won't be coming back?"

"Of course I'll be back, Neryssa. So you needn't concern yourself with how long I'll be gone for." The reassurance was uttered in Kayden's most unaffected tone. "You will see me again before you've even noticed I've been away, and that's a promise." She felt as confident of that as she sounded; she would not allow Fay to make a liar of her. "But for now, this is where we part ways." She stopped in her tracks to gesture at the lecture building on their left, where Neryssa had a class to attend, while her own destination—the armoury—lay directly ahead. "You have a class to get to."

Neryssa came to a halt, likewise, to face her counterpart.

"All right," she said. "You can tell me all about your adventures with Master Fay once you've returned." She held out her right hand to Kayden who offered her own in response. They clasped each other firmly by the forearm. "But before you go, though you may not like or respect her, please try to keep in mind the reason for this honour Master Fay has seen fit to bestow upon you. She obviously sees something in you that she doesn't see in any other apprentice, something that sets you apart from the rest of us. You're a very special person, Kayden. I knew it the day I first met you."

Kayden didn't know what to say to that. Neryssa's words were heartfelt, but they were nonsense, all the same. At some unspecified point after leaving campus with Fay Annis, either she would die at Fay's hand, or Fay would die at her hand; that much was certain.

She released her grip of her roommate's forearm. "Farewell, Neryssa."

Kayden stepped away to continue her walk to the armoury, leaving her fellow apprentice outside the lecture building.

"Good luck," Neryssa called out. "And try to keep out of trouble."

Moments later, Kayden was approaching the armoury where she was to collect her weaponry for the journey, but her attention was drawn away from the building by something else—or more to the point, by someone else. She saw Vartan being escorted by four Sanatsai. His arm appeared to have healed completely, while the minor bruising on his face indicated the broken nose she had given him, only an hour or so ago, was well on the mend, if not already healed. Their eyes locked instantly as he caught sight of her. Although she had, on occasion, witnessed disdainful looks on people's faces aimed at her—usually because of her background—what she saw, now, on Vartan's face was something else entirely. It was unrestrained hatred, and not because of any ethnic bias. This was personal.

"You!" shouted Vartan. "This is all your fault!" Two of the Sanatsai escorts had to grab him by each arm as he attempted to dash towards her. "I get kicked out while you escape any punishment. It's not right! It should be you being expelled! You're the one who doesn't deserve to be here!" He continued struggling futilely against the hold of the Sanatsai.

Kayden was of a mind to ignore the outburst—to simply continue on her way into the armoury. But she just couldn't resist getting in one last dig at Vartan's expense. "Oh, what are you crying about, you big baby?" she taunted. "I've done you a favour. You would have failed the training sooner or later; you're just not Sanatsai material. At least now you get to go home to spend the rest of your days tending pigs on a farm. You'll be much more in your element there."

"Apprentice!" snapped one of the Sanatsai not busy restraining Vartan. "If you have somewhere to be, I suggest you go there, now."

She smirked then proceeded towards the entrance to the armoury.

"Kayden!" shrieked Vartan. "You think you've won, but this isn't over. I don't care how long it takes; someday, soon, I'm going to kill you. You're going to die screaming, you slant-eyed bitch! Do you hear me?"

It appeared several people could hear his vitriolic tirade.

While Vartan was dragged away by his Sanatsai escorts, Kayden noticed more than a few faces peering out from a number of windows of the nearest lecture building, observing the commotion.

"You know where to find me," Kayden shouted back, smirking.

Her gaze remained on Vartan until he finally accepted his fate, allowing the Sanatsai to lead him away without further resistance. Her smirk disappeared as she muttered under her breath, "And if you are stupid enough to ever come looking for me... I'll be waiting for you."

Kayden eventually tore her gaze away from the departing dunderhead, to complete the rest of her short walk to the armoury.

Inside the armoury, the array of weaponry the apprentices were trained to use was stored away in the vast storage space behind the sturdy oak counter. There were two Sanatsai on guard duty, one standing on either side of the entrance, both of whom fell silent when Kayden entered the building. As they fixed intent glances on her, she couldn't shake the feeling they had just been talking about her, though she didn't dwell upon it. She headed directly to the counter where she was pleased to see Master Solen on duty.

The ever-genial Sanatsai was of mixed heritage: a father of Yantashan descent, hence the tightly curled, kinky hair, and a Karlandrian mother. Though principally the campus armourer, Solen, in his capacity as a weapons master, frequently acted as an assistant instructor in various martial disciplines, including swordsmanship. Kayden had benefited greatly from his instruction, and he was one of the very few instructors whom she had never fallen out with.

"Kayden, I've been expecting you," he said jovially as he walked out from behind the counter to greet her.

She noted that her sword was laid out upon the counter along with her two daggers. "Greetings, Master Solen."

"Quickly!" Solen held a baldric in one hand then picked up Kayden's sword in the other. The two-handed, straight, single-edged blade, known as a Shilla, was the weapon of choice given to all Sanatsai of the Order. "Let's get you kitted out, right away. You don't want to be late for Master Fay."

Kayden quickly removed her black hooded cloak in order to put on the baldric that would allow her to wear the sword at her back. Once done, she sheathed the sword into place—its hilt peering up over her right shoulder in easy reach, so the weapon could be drawn at a moments notice. She put the cloak back on while Solen retrieved the two daggers to hand them over to her. The two blades she neatly put into place; one on either hip.

"Now you're good to go," Solen said with a smile.

"Master Solen?" She wasn't quite ready to enter the lion's den, not while several questions remained unanswered. This would be the last opportunity to acquire those answers. "I take it you're aware of where I'm going?"

"Master Fay did mention it when she was here earlier."

"As I understand it, it's not the norm for an apprentice to go to Temis Rulan before being inducted into the Order."

"It's unprecedented," Solen amended. "It has never happened before."

"So, why am I being taken there?"

"That is a very good question." Kayden was not at all thrilled by that response. It could only mean Solen didn't know himself. "But if Master Fay has persuaded the Council to make an exception for you, then, rest assured, she has very good reason for wanting to take you."

Kayden was more than a little alarmed by the notion Fay could induce the Council into violating its own rules. "Are you saying she has the power to influence the decisions of the Council?"

"She certainly holds a lot of sway with the members," Solen confirmed. "Not to mention she is a close friend of Ari Shinadu."

Kayden wasn't really getting the answers she wanted, but she did just learn a few things about Fay that were unknown to her previously. Master Ari Shinadu was the founder of the Order, as well as the ostensible head of its ruling body, the Council. If what Solen had said was correct—that Fay was a close friend of Ari, and held a lot of sway with the other members—then it was likely Fay could do just about anything she wanted and get away with it; like making an apprentice disappear without trace.

"Then it is possible I could be in trouble?" She tried her best to avoid sounding as concerned as she felt.

"Have you done anything to get in trouble for?"

She hesitated. "Possibly."

"Well, I wouldn't worry about it," said Solen, reassuringly. "If you were in trouble I can assure you Master Fay would not be rewarding you with a trip to Temis Rulan. Now, no more questions, you need to go and meet her right away." He placed a hand on the small of Kayden's back to gently usher her towards the door.

Before exiting the armoury, Kayden thanked Master Solen for his kind assistance then bade him farewell. He in turn requested that she tell him all about her trip once she returned, so she promised him that she would, further increasing her resolve to thwart whatever plans Fay Annis had for her.

Kayden made her way swiftly to the administration building without further delay. At the reception desk she informed the civilian receptionist on duty that she had arrived to meet the administrator, who was expecting her. The woman, who appeared to be in her mid-forties, must have been a newcomer as Kayden had never seen her before, despite having been sent to the administrator's office on more occasions than she could remember. If she had to hazard a guess she would say the new receptionist was from the nearby town of Timaris. The Order generally favoured employing locals for most of the non-teaching positions at its campuses; it was good for public relations.

"Oh, you must be Kayden Jayta," said the receptionist. She was unabashedly affable.

"Yes, that's right."

"My, aren't you a pretty thing!"

Kayden fought off the urge to roll her eyes, the woman was just being amiable, after all.

"Administrator Annis is in the staff common room waiting for you, just go on up." She gestured toward the staircase.

Kayden left the reception desk to amble up the stairs to the next floor. She made her way through the corridor to the double doors of the staff common room and announced her arrival with three raps, then waited. Moments later, one of the doors swung inwards to reveal a young Jaymidari with a friendly smile. Kayden recognised the woman. It was Sister Alina from the infirmary who sometimes doubled as an assistant instructor, teaching first aid to the level two apprentices.

"Your guest has arrived," Alina called over her shoulder. "Please come in, Kayden, Master Fay is expecting you." She stepped aside, gesturing with an outstretched arm for the apprentice to enter.

Strolling into the common room, Kayden saw Fay seated on a couch speaking with Master Isko and the Sister, Elsa Renzi, who were both seated on another couch, opposite Fay, drinking hot beverages from porcelain cups. All three stood up as she approached. She noted that Fay was also armed with sword and twin daggers.

"I'm ready to go when you are, Administrator," she said, indifferently.

"Very well, Kayden." Fay turned to address her two colleagues. "Thank you, both, for your time and understanding. As I said, I shouldn't be gone too long, though it pleases me to be leaving matters here in capable hands."

It didn't escape Kayden's notice that Fay had said, '*I shouldn't be gone too long*', not '*we shouldn't be gone too long*'.

Elsa walked around the tea table embrace the Sanatsai, kissing her on both cheeks. "May your journey be a fruitful one," she said, cordially, "and please convey my greetings to Idelle when you see her."

"Thank you, Sister, consider it done." Fay acknowledged Isko with a nod of her head then turned to address Kayden. "Follow me."

Kayden fell into step a couple of paces behind Fay, following her as she marched to the double doors set in the east wall of the common room. When the doors were pushed open she saw that the room beyond was a library—not nearly as vast as the dedicated campus library building, but the interior was certainly more attractive. The library was adorned with polished wood panel walls, several rows of book shelving made from similarly burnished wood, and three chandeliers holding illumination orbs, evenly spaced along the ceiling.

"Close the doors behind you," said Fay as she stepped into the library.

Kayden did as instructed, then followed Fay through a number of aisles separating the consummately arranged shelves until they came to the north wall of the library. There were no shelves lining this wall, just two large tapestries hanging down to the floor. She observed impassively as Fay stood directly in front of the wide space between the two tapestries. A sudden spike of anxiety hit her with the realisation she could sense *Zarantar* emanating from the wall, right in front of where Fay stood. Kayden hadn't considered the possibility of the Sanatsai making a move against her while they were both still on campus, but why wouldn't she? After all, Fay wasn't just the administrator of Antaris, she had significant influence over the Council, in addition to being a close friend of the founder of the Order. She could practically do whatever she wanted, whenever she wanted, to whomever she wanted.

Kayden's anxiety increased further, still, when Fay peered back over her shoulder to cast a strange, appraising look toward her.

"Come, stand beside me, Kayden," Fay instructed.

Reluctantly, Kayden obeyed, moving forward to stand beside her nemesis, showing neither fear nor overt signs that she was alert to whatever the woman planned to do next. And Kayden most certainly was prepared. If Fay attempted something now, she would respond accordingly.

"Is there anything out of the ordinary about this section of the wall?" Fay asked. "If so, can you tell me what?"

"A Sister has hidden something in or behind the wall," she said in reply.

Without waiting for confirmation from Fay she waved a hand across the wall; invoking *Yuksaydan* would reveal whether she was correct or not. And so it did. Instantly, a series of glowing red glyphs began to appear on the wall, forming the shape of a doorway. Once the glyphs faded from view, an actual door materialised in the wood panel wall in front of them.

"Very good," said Fay in her usual matter-of-fact fashion.

She opened the newly formed door to reveal a landing at the top of a spiral stairwell in a confined space on the other side.

Kayden stared at the stairwell. It was lit by a descending series of illumination orbs contained within wall-mounted lanterns. "What is this?" She hoped she had successfully kept the apprehension from her voice.

"Something you should not really be seeing." Fay's voice took on an authoritative edge. "So I will have to insist that you do not speak of anything you see or hear from this point onwards to any of the other apprentices." She proceeded through the door, onto the landing, to descend the stairs. "Now, follow me."

"Wait!" Kayden's exclamation halted Fay at the first step.

"Where do these stairs go? I thought we were going to Temis Rulan."

"We'll be on our way, soon enough." Fay resumed her descent, making it obvious there would be no further elaboration.

Kayden did not want to follow Fay down those stairs. Subconsciously, she was urging herself to refuse to do so, but her curiosity had been piqued. The part of herself that had to know everything demanded that she proceed, to find out where exactly the Sanatsai was leading her. There could only be one winner between those two vying instincts. Kayden marched through the door, closing it behind her, then quickly caught up with Fay, falling into step right behind her.

Minutes later, Kayden could only guess at how far below the campus they had descended by the time she and Fay reached the bottom of the stairwell, arriving into a vast underground cavern. As she gawked at the cavernous expanse, she estimated it had to cover up to two thirds of the area covered by the campus above ground. Possibly more. It was brightly lit by a network of orb filled lanterns much like those that lit up the campus grounds at night, except the glow lighting up the cavern was not at all muted like it was above. She could see scores of Sanatsai milling about, in addition to several Jaymidari.

Kayden kept pace with Fay when she started advancing further into the cavern. "This can't be..." she began in a disbelieving tone, "this can't be Temis Rulan, can it?"

Fay stifled a chuckle. "No, of course not; we're still on campus," she said. "This place you are seeing now, it serves a few functions, but for our purposes you can consider it a shortcut." To elaborate the point, she added, "It would take us weeks to travel to Temis Rulan by conventional means, plus the same amount of time to get back here. For obvious reasons, I cannot be away from campus that long."

Kayden was intrigued by Fay's revelation. A journey of weeks suggested Temis Rulan was located somewhere in one of the western realms of the Nine Kingdoms; the Kingdom of Yaristana in all likelihood, though Balintana and Jibaltana were both possibilities.

As the pair continued walking, side-by-side, further into the cavern, they were approached by another Sanatsai. He reminded Kayden of a male version of Neryssa, only taller with shorter hair. She wondered if her roommate had an older brother who had already been inducted into the Order. If so, why would she neglect to mention having such an attractive sibling? She looked him up and down: those rugged good looks; the dark hair just begging to have her hands run through it; those sparkling, expressive eyes; those full lips; *that body*. She could just visualise his strong muscular physique straining beneath the uniform. Oh, the things she could do with him; the things she'd let him do to her...

Kayden mentally berated herself. This was hardly an appropriate time to be distracted, to lose focus. She tore her gaze away from the man to casually cast her gaze around the cavern.

It was impossible not to view her surroundings as akin to a small village swallowed by the earth. There were several buildings dotted throughout the cavern, some of which were obviously barracks. When coupled with the large numbers of Sanatsai present—none of whom Kayden recognised—it quickly dawned on her that there was, essentially, a small army stationed beneath the Antaris campus. That being the case, the other eight campuses must surely have the same, she thought.

"Mirai Santelis," said Fay in salutation of her counterpart as they both came to a halt. "I trust all the necessary preparations have been made."

"Yes, Danai Annis." The Sanatsai addressed Fay in a very formal tone. "Everything is set for your departure." He glanced at Kayden standing at Fay's side. "This is the apprentice who will be accompanying you?"

"Correct."

Addressing Kayden directly, the Sanatsai said, "You are the subject of much speculation, apprentice."

Kayden wasn't listening. She was still trying to decide if she'd correctly heard the Sanatsai address Fay by the title 'Danai'. *Surely not!* She must have misheard him; it was more or less the highest rank any Sanatsai could attain within the hierarchy of the Order. The only individuals with greater seniority were the thirteen

104

members of the Council. It was inconceivable for somebody of such rank to be serving as a campus administrator, not to mention the fact Fay was clearly too young to have achieved the rank, anyway.

"Kayden! You're being spoken to."

Fay's reproachful voice snapped her out of her ruminations. "What? Oh, I...uh... I was distra..." she rambled. "What was that?"

"What is the matter with you, Kayden," said Fay, sounding displeased. "Master Dionardo was speaking to you; must you be so discourteous?"

Realising she was staring at Fay, in wide-eyed disbelief, Kayden turned her attention to the male Sanatsai. "I'm afraid I didn't catch what was said. I wasn't ignoring you, Master."

"That's quite all right. It's perfectly understandable for you to be a little overawed. No other apprentice has been in your position before," remarked Dionardo Santelis. "Anyway, I was just wondering what you had done to earn your master's favour."

Suppressing a groan, Kayden wished that people would stop suggesting she was in any way favoured by Fay Annis, the ridiculous notion was driving her crazy. "I'm not sure I'm the best person to ask, Master," she conceded.

"Well, whatever the reason, I assume you've been told you cannot speak about what you are seeing right now, or what you will see once you leave here."

"Kayden won't be speaking to anyone about this," interjected Fay.

Though Fay's words were apparently intended to reassure the other Sanatsai, Kayden couldn't help but hear a threat directed her way.

Fay resumed walking, prompting Dionardo to fall into step at her right side, while Kayden paced on her left. For the next few minutes the Sanatsai pair made small talk about things of no interest to Kayden, causing her to mentally switch off while idly observing what was happening all around her.

Suddenly, her attention was drawn away from everything else by a sight in the distance, at the furthest reaches of the cavern; it was an object resembling what could only be described as a giant illumination orb. She was staggered by the sheer strength of *Zarantar* emanating from it, even from such a distance away. Realisation quickly set in; the underground cavern must be a significant depth beneath Antaris campus, otherwise she couldn't fathom how such a powerful manifestation of *Zarantar* could ever have escaped her senses.

"What is it, Kayden?"

She broke her reverie to peer at Fay. Once again the woman had that same strange, appraising look on her face that she wore earlier, back in the administration building's library. "Nothing," she replied, evasively. "I'm...just surprised to learn that the Order has been able to conceal the existence of this place. And, presumably, all the other campuses have been built above similar caverns?"

Fay neither confirmed nor denied the query. She tore her studious gaze away from Kayden. "Tell me, what do you make of that?" She pointed toward the spherical light source up ahead.

"I don't know. I have no idea what it is."

The remainder of their walk to the end of the cavern was completed in silence. Upon arrival, Kayden saw that what had appeared to be spherical from a distance, was in fact flat. Whatever the object was, it was more like the opening of a tunnel; no, more like a hole in the world, filled with swirling mists of varying shades of blue and purple, approximately seven feet high and seven feet wide, situated on a raised stone platform with three steps leading up to it. Nearby there was a group of six Jaymidari whom she assumed were responsible for the creation of the object on the raised platform.

One of the Sisters approached the trio as they stopped at the foot of the steps. "Greetings, administrator," she said in welcome. "Your destination is set. You may proceed as soon as you are ready."

"Thank you, Sister." She turned to face Dionardo, offering her hand. "This is where we part ways, Mirai Santelis." He gripped her by the forearm. "I hope to not be away for too long, but should anything occur here that I need to know about, don't hesitate to send a message."

"As you wish, Danai," Dionardo affirmed. "Good journey to you both." He released his grip of Fay's forearm then stood aside to allow master and apprentice to ascend the three steps.

"Follow me, Kayden," instructed Fay as she proceeded to climb.

Kayden reluctantly followed the administrator's lead up onto the raised platform. Still not knowing or understanding what was really going on, she couldn't shake the feeling of apprehension growing within her. But she followed behind Fay towards the unknown object before halting abruptly in her tracks.

"Wait!"

Fay halted, and peered back over her shoulder to see the uneasy apprentice. "Is there a problem, Kayden?"

"I'm not going another step until you tell me what's going on," Kayden said, keeping her voice low. "What is that?" She pointed at the mysterious opening ahead of them.

Turning around to face Kayden directly, Fay replied, "As I alluded to, earlier, we will be taking a shortcut to Temis Rulan. This is a portal opening; it is part of a network of portals created by the Sisterhood, connecting various locations used by the Order throughout the Nine Kingdoms. When travel between these places by conventional means is not an option—like when time is of the essence, as it is now—the portals allow us to complete those journeys almost instantaneously. Needless to say, this is more knowledge you are not permitted to share with anyone else. Now, come along. Just follow me into the portal, there's nothing to fear."

Kayden resented the implication she was afraid of entering the portal, but she restrained her tongue. She watched Fay turn back around and march purposefully into the portal, disappearing from view in the blink of an eye. Though she had no real justification to doubt the veracity of what she'd just been told, Kayden remained incredibly reluctant to enter the portal after Fay. But what choice did she really have? If she tried to remain behind, to explain to the other Sanatsai and the Jaymidari that Fay was planning on killing her, who among them would believe that? And what if they were all in on it? There would be little she could do to prevent them from forcing her through the portal, to wherever her would-be murderer was lying in wait.

But none of these concerns ultimately mattered. Nothing about what was happening that day was making any sense. She still had several unresolved mysteries plaguing her thoughts; unanswered questions that she couldn't get answers to without entering the portal. So stiffening her resolve, Kayden marched forward into the portal of swirling mists, and her eyes were assailed by a flash of brilliant light.

CHAPTER SEVEN

Questions And Answers

The blinding light subsided as Kayden emerged from the portal shortly after Fay. Her eyes adjusted to take in the sights of their brand new surroundings; they were not in the cavern beneath the Antaris campus any more. But as the portal opening blinked out of existence behind her, it was abundantly clear the tall cylindrical structure they were standing in was not Temis Rulan either. Though she had never been inside a windmill before—had never seen an actual windmill at all, for that matter—Kayden knew the portal had brought them into one, and she very much doubted that the leadership of the Order would be found here.

Kayden's suspicion that Fay had brought her to this place under false pretences was now vindicated. She grabbed the hilt of her sword, unsheathing it in one swift motion, to point it at the Sanatsai's back. Did *that woman* really think she was gullible enough to believe that decades' worth of protocol would be discarded just for her benefit? Everyone knew apprentices were never told the location of Temis Rulan, much less actually taken there. The idea that Fay Annis would insist on having any apprentice—never mind one she had it in for—accompanying her to the headquarters of the Order was absurd.

Fay spun round to see Kayden with drawn sword tightly gripped in both hands. "At ease, Kayden," she said, calmly. "There is no danger here, we are perfectly safe. You can put your weapon away."

"Do you take me for some kind of idiot?" The vehemence of Kayden's tone signalled she had no intention of disarming. "This is *not* Temis Rulan."

Frowning at the apprentice, Fay retorted, "Of course it's not."

The lack of denial threw Kayden off, momentarily.

"For security reasons," Fay began to elaborate. "No portals open directly inside Temis Rulan. In the event that any of our locations are compromised or infiltrated by a hostile force, the portals cannot be used to launch an attack."

Kayden reluctantly conceded that the explanation made perfect sense. And the way Fay spoke didn't appear to be in any way evasive or calculating. "Why didn't you tell me this before?"

"Well, I'm telling you now."

It was another matter-of-fact response that Kayden found so irritating. Almost as vexing as the woman's obliviousness, or unconcern that she was being threatened with a deadly weapon.

"But you need not fret, Temis Rulan isn't far from here. We'll be travelling most of the way by horse." She turned her back on Kayden then calmly walked towards the open exit of the windmill. "Now, come along!"

"No, wait!" Still in a fighting stance with her unsheathed blade, Kayden's demand prompted Fay to halt in the doorway and turn back around to face her. "Who are you?"

Fay looked at the apprentice quizzically. "That is a rather odd question to ask me, Kayden."

"Before we arrived, Master Dionardo addressed you as 'Danai' more than once." There was an accusatory note in Kayden's voice. "I know enough about the hierarchy of the Order to realise that any Sanatsai who holds the rank of Danai would never be assigned to a position on campus, not even as the administrator. Not to mention you're far too young to have attained that rank. So why would he address you as Danai?"

Fay sighed, evidently aggravated by yet another delay.

"Technically, you are correct," she said. "The Council would not assign a high-ranking member of the Order to the position of campus administrator. However, there is no prohibition preventing such a person from volunteering to assume that role."

"You asked to be the administrator of Antaris campus?" Kayden was dubious, to say the least. It didn't seem credible. "Why would you do that?"

"Kayden, my reasons are my own, that is all you need to know," said Fay. "Now, if you are coming with me to Temis Rulan, then follow." With that she exited the windmill, walking to the right and out of Kayden's view.

Remaining where she stood, her sword still drawn, it suddenly dawned on Kayden that Fay was no longer behaving like a woman who wanted to kill her. In fact, she was becoming increasingly uncertain as to whether or not Fay ever had been. Aside from the disturbing expression that briefly masked her face, coupled with the even more disturbing look in her eyes during their confrontation the night before, Fay had never actually said or done anything genuinely threatening during her tenure as administrator. Perhaps they really were going to Temis Rulan together after all.

But, why?

Kayden still couldn't buy into the idea she was somehow Fay's favourite apprentice; the Sanatsai had never once given her reason to believe that. And yet, by the same token, if Fay's true intent was expulsion, why go to the trouble of dragging her all the way to Temis Rulan? She could expel an apprentice just as easily on campus, like the expulsion of Vartan that very day.

Whatever the reasons for their journey to Temis Rulan, the only way Kayden could learn the truth was to go along with the Sanatsai. She quickly sheathed her sword then dashed out of the disused windmill after Fay.

Outside, Kayden caught sight of the burgundy-haired woman, already several yards away, striding down the shallow incline of a hill, towards a cluster of farmhouses in the distance. She also noted with interest the position of the sun in the cloudless, blue sky. It was further west and lower than it had been just a short while ago back at Antaris campus. The temperature was noticeably warmer, too. She surmised that either the journey through the portal that seemed to have taken no more than two or three seconds had actually taken two or three hours, or they had travelled so far east of Antaris they were now some place where it was two or three hours later in the day.

Kayden swiftly caught up with Fay and fell into step alongside her. While they drew closer to the farming village ahead—for that's what it was, Kayden now realised—she could make out a small group of people gathered together outside one of the buildings.

"It looks like we have company," she said to Fay. "Do you know who they are?"

"Friends."

Glancing at the woman, Kayden promptly decided it was a waste of time to ask for elaboration.

For the next few minutes the duo trudged towards the farmhouse in silence. As they made their approach, Kayden could see there were numerous people milling about the village and the surrounding fields. While most of them were presumably just civilians, she did notice a small number of women wearing the cream and beige garb of the Sisterhood, including a tall woman standing amid the group gathered outside the building they were nearing.

The group was comprised of eight people, and they made to welcome the newcomers, or rather Fay, with enthusiasm. There were two adult men standing to one side of the gathering, each gripping the reins of a horse. At the centre of the group was an older man holding the hand of the elegant Jaymidari beside him. In front of the couple was a young girl with pigtails, no older than seven, squeezing a ragdoll in her little arms, and standing nearby were an adolescent boy and girl who were evidently brother and sister. Further behind the group, leaning against the farmhouse, was a young man, maybe a year or two older than Kayden, armed with a short bow and a quiver of arrows on his back.

Once Fay's warm welcome had abated, she introduced her travelling companion to the Sister, Larinda, and her husband, Miro.

"You're married?" Kayden blurted.

"Yes, my dear," replied Larinda. "Why does that surprise

you?"

"Pardon my ignorance. It never occurred to me that a Jaymidari could, or even would, get married."

"Well, duh!" muttered the young teenage boy, rolling his eyes.

Kayden glowered at him. *That's right, I heard you, pip-squeak.*

"Fenrik! Could you not be so rude to our guest?" Larinda chastised the boy. "Please forgive my son, Kayden, he's at that awkward age."

"Oh, no harm done," she managed to utter, grudgingly. "So, you have children too?"

"Yes. That's our eldest, Arlo, lurking in the background." Larinda gestured towards the archer leaning against the farmhouse. He casually inclined his head in acknowledgement. Kayden did the same. "This is Fenrik and his twin sister Faynara."

"Nice to meet you," chirped the girl.

"Likewise," said Kayden.

"And this little bundle of joy, right here," continued Larinda, placing her free hand on the shoulder of the young girl standing in front of her and Miro, "is our youngest, Lara."

"Hello," said the little girl, smiling up at Kayden. "You're so pretty!"

Kayden squatted down on her haunches in front of Lara. Compliments for her looks were usually unwelcome but not on this occasion. "Thank you, Lara, I think you're adorable yourself."

"This is Bess," Lara said, holding out her ragdoll. "She thinks you are pretty too. And she says she likes your eyes."

"It's a doll, stupid," said Fenrik. "It doesn't think or say anything."

Kayden glowered at the adolescent dunderhead. "Don't call her stupid." Her voice carried just enough threat to warn the boy not to test her patience.

"Ma! Are you going to let her speak to me like that?"

Larinda seemed to sense the situation could turn ugly, prompting swift intervention to diffuse the tension.

"Fenrik, you have chores you can be getting on with, now run along." His sullen expression prompted her to add, "Don't make me tell you twice."

Kayden smirked at Fenrik before he reluctantly skulked off back into the farmhouse.

"Your uniform is unfamiliar, Kayden," observed Miro. "Has the Order instituted new uniforms for the Sanatsai?"

"No," replied Kayden, rising up from her haunches. "I'm still just an apprentice. This is our ceremonial outfit; we don't get to wear it often."

Miro flashed a confounded look at Fay.

"I thought apprentices weren't permitted to go to Temis Rulan."

"That still remains the case." Fay glanced at the apprentice beside her, adding, "But Kayden isn't like the others."

Kayden wasn't sure she liked the way those words were just uttered. The comment sounded more negative than positive, no doubt intended as a veiled criticism. She was distracted from that line of thought when she felt something tugging at her leg. Looking down she saw Lara trying to get her attention.

"Can you make me float?" asked the little girl.

"Uh..." Kayden glanced at Larinda, seeking guidance. The Sister smiled back, giving a silent nod of the head. "Do you mean like this?"

Lara was lifted gently off her feet and floated up to eye level with the apprentice. Slowly, she began to spin around in the air, causing her to laugh out loud in unconstrained delight. *Yuksaydan* had so many destructive applications Kayden never contemplated the idea of 'the unseen hand' being a source of joy and wonder to a young child. As she continued to enthral Lara with the simple demonstration of *Zarantar* she kept an ear on the conversation between Fay and the young girl's parents.

"As you see, horses for you and your apprentice are ready when you are," she heard Miro say. "Though we hope you don't need to depart right away."

"Yes," said Larinda. "We've missed your company these past three years. Please stay for tea, I've just baked some apple turnovers."

"Thank you, both," replied Fay. "But we really need to leave at once, we are already running a little late as it is."

"As you wish," said Miro.

"Just promise we won't have to wait another three years for your next visit," added Larinda. "You're always welcome in our home."

"I promise," agreed Fay.

Kayden peered at the couple. It was surprising how they both looked even more disappointed than they sounded. Though why anyone would miss Fay's company was beyond her comprehension.

Fay turned to address the little girl bobbing up and down in the air, orbiting the apprentice. "I'm sorry to have to steal your new friend from you, Lara," she said, "but Kayden and I have an important appointment elsewhere."

Lara stopped laughing. "Oh, all right." The disappointment in the child's voice was palpable. "Can she come back with you later?"

"Maybe, one day," Fay replied.

"Wild horses couldn't keep me away," added Kayden, setting Lara down gently at her mother's feet. "As long as your parents say it's all right."

"Well, Lara has taken quite a liking to you Kayden," said Larinda. "You are more than welcome to return."

"Any friend of Fay is a friend of ours," said Miro in agreement.

Kayden found she didn't have the heart to shatter the illusions of the couple by pointing out that she and Fay were not friends. They didn't need to know she actually disliked the woman a great deal, so she simply said, "Thank you!"

"We should get going," Fay prompted Kayden. Addressing the couple, she added, "I apologise for the brevity of this visit. I will make it up to you as soon as I can. But for now, farewell."

Miro, Larinda and their children bid Fay and Kayden farewell as they ambled towards the two men holding their waiting horses. Accepting them, first Fay, then Kayden, mounted their respective geldings.

Fay gently urged her mount forward into a slow trot, and Kayden did likewise, pulling alongside her and following her lead. For the next few minutes she and Fay proceeded onward towards the woodlands in the distance without exchanging a word. Once some distance had been put between themselves and the village, Kayden noticed, from the corner of her eye, that her travelling companion was sneaking the occasional look in her direction. She resisted the urge to look back and challenge Fay as to what she was staring at, choosing instead to maintain their silence.

Unfortunately, it wasn't long before Kayden's hopes that the journey would be completed in silence were thwarted. Moments after reaching the first trees of the woodlands they had to travel through, Fay finally decided to speak.

"It will take about a half-hour to reach our next stop," she announced. "We should use that time to talk."

"Talk about what?" Kayden replied with disinterest.

"There are several personal questions I've been meaning to ask you, and it is long past time that I asked them."

Kayden peered to her left to look at Fay; her curiosity was piqued, in spite of herself. What questions had the administrator been wanting to ask? And, just how personal?

"You can ask me anything you like," she said. "As for whether or not I give you any answers, or if you like the answers you are given if I do..." She left the rest of the statement unsaid.

"Very well." The acknowledgement seemed to indicate Fay was satisfied with that response. "First question: how long have you been able to sense *Zarantar*?"

Well, now! thought Kayden. That was not the kind of question she'd been anticipating. It was trivial. Not to mention the distinct lack of judgement, disapproval or reproach in Fay's voice when she asked the question. She sounded genuinely curious to know. Kayden decided there was no harm in answering truthfully.

"I guess I've been able to pretty much since my *Zarantar* first manifested when I was fourteen." She spied no discernible reaction on Fay's face. "But it wasn't until I had been at Antaris for a few months that I finally understood what it was I was sensing."

"I see."

Kayden couldn't tell if the Sanatsai was impressed or disappointed by her answer.

"Why?"

"Apprentices are never taught how to sense the presence of *Zarantar*, because it's not something that can be learned. A Sanatsai's senses simply aren't attuned to *Zarantar*. Under normal circumstances, it is an attribute that only develops in the women who pursue the calling of a Jaymidari."

It was an eye-opening revelation, shedding light on a mystery that had been gnawing away at the back of Kayden's mind for much of her five years at Antaris. She had frequently wondered why no other apprentice had ever mentioned sensing the presence or wielding of *Zarantar*. None of her instructors had done so, either.

"However," Fay continued, "a small number of Sanatsai do develop this ability naturally. But it is an *extremely* rare occurrence."

A feeling of smug satisfaction swept over Kayden.

"So, I'm one of the chosen few." It wasn't a question, merely a statement of fact.

"Perhaps."

The less than enthusiastic response didn't quell Kayden's desire to crow about her gift. But the discovery would be so much sweeter if she possessed this attribute, while Fay didn't; then she could rub it in the woman's face.

"Can you sense *Zarantar*?" she asked innocently.

"Perhaps." Fay's response was noticeably more guarded this time. "But I'm more interested in how many people you've told about your ability."

"I... I haven't told anyone, actually." Though there had been no hint of accusation in Fay's voice, Kayden felt a little defensive, nonetheless. "It never escaped my notice that no one else ever mentioned having the ability to sense *Zarantar*, so I thought it prudent not to draw attention to myself by claiming I that could."

Was that a wry smile that briefly touched Fay's lips? Kayden wondered.

"Clever girl!" Fay murmured to herself. She then glanced to her right to address Kayden, directly. "It would be wise to continue keeping it to yourself," she said earnestly. "You may find that having this ability in your repertoire will be advantageous in the future. For one thing, as I said a moment ago, it is not an attribute inherent to Sanatsai. As a result, when the time comes for you to face adversaries who also wield *Zarantar*, the ability to sense your foes' attacks before they are invoked will allow you to defend yourself more effectively."

The conversation paused momentarily as they both fell silent once more. The only sounds were the trotting of their horses mingling with the myriad sounds of the woodlands they were traversing.

Kayden began to ponder the purpose of the conversation started by the administrator. She had now completely ruled out the notion that Fay intended to murder her; even the idea of expulsion from campus after the binding of her *Zarantar* was looking increasingly unlikely. After all, why would Fay bother to reveal the things she just had, or speak about what may be advantageous in the future, if she was intending to expel Kayden once they reached Temis Rulan?

"I don't understand why you're telling me any of this," she said.

"There's no reason to conceal this knowledge from you."

"But how did you know I was able to sense *Zarantar* if Sanatsai are not supposed to possess this ability."

"During the three years I've been serving as the administrator of Antaris campus, you have frequently given me reason to suspect you of possessing the ability," admitted Fay, taking another sideways glance at Kayden. "But I could never be entirely certain. There was always the possibility it was simply a case of you having good instincts or intuition. However, the 'capture the box' exercise last night proved that you can sense *Zarantar*. That's why I tested you earlier—to confirm it."

Kayden began searching her memory of everything that had happened that day. When had Fay tested...? *Oh, of course,* she realised. Back at the administration building, in the library; before going down to the underground cavern beneath the campus. *Sneaky woman!*

The administrator's revelation led to another question.

"This is the second time you've implied you know exactly

what occurred during last night's assignment. I don't see how that's possible," said Kayden. "If you had been using *Zarantar* to follow and spy on us, I would have known."

Fay glanced at the apprentice once more.

"Are you certain about that?" There was a mischief in her voice.

Glancing at the rider alongside her, Kayden met Fay's eyes. The mischief was also present in her gaze. That all too familiar, inscrutable expression on her face seemed to be saying, *I know something that you don't know.* Kayden resisted the urge to demand that Fay explain herself, knowing there was little chance of her doing so if she didn't wish to. Instead, she made a mental note: discover other applications of *Zarantar* a Sanatsai isn't supposed to possess that she might develop in future. She returned her gaze straight ahead, looking between the ears of her horse.

"Well, I was sure," she said in response to Fay's question, "until a moment ago."

Again, there was another lengthy silence; almost long enough to make Kayden suspect the conversation was over.

"Since we've touched upon the matter of last night's training exercise," said Fay, breaking the silence, "the most pressing questions I have for you are in relation to some of your feats during the challenge."

Kayden had a good idea where this line of questioning was going.

"Let's begin with what you did after your assault of Master Zalayna. Not content with just physically harming a member of the Order, you stripped Zalayna of her memories of the attack, demonstrating your knowledge of *Barmityanzak*, an application of *Zarantar* that you won't be trained to master until you are a level nine apprentice. Given what a skilled job you did—causing no damage to her mind—it is all too obvious you have done it before. So, the question now is: when and how did you learn to invoke *Barmityanzak*?"

Now *this* was a question Kayden didn't particularly want to answer.

She couldn't think of a convincing lie to tell but, did she really need to fabricate a plausible answer? There was always the option of prevaricating, or simply refusing to respond—though neither choice was likely to be acceptable to Fay. However, the woman would dislike the truth even more. So why not just give it to her? There was a good chance that the circumstances that led to her learning to invoke *Barmityanzak* would get the Sanatsai who taught her into much more trouble than herself.

"I'm not sure you really want me to answer that question," she said, in her most carefree manner.

"But you are going to tell me anyway," retorted Fay. "And that's not a request."

"Suit yourself!"

There was a hint of smug satisfaction in Kayden's voice. She knew that once she told the story in full, Fay would find it difficult to justify penalising her.

"It was last year, during the annual campus inspection, that I first started learning to master *Barmityanzak*. On the second day of the inspection, a member of the delegation, Master Turan, approached me while I was studying in the library. He said he needed help to carry some books to the archives in the administration building. I could tell from the look in his eyes what he *really* wanted, but I didn't want to cause a scene so I agreed.

"Once we were alone in the archives he lived up to my expectations and made a pass at me. So predictable! At first he wasn't willing to take no for an answer, but let's just say I demonstrated that I was more trouble than I was worth, which only served to amuse him—much to my annoyance. I told him he wouldn't be laughing after I reported him, yet he calmly responded by saying that I wouldn't be reporting him to anyone because I wouldn't remember what had happened. The way he said it threw me off, distracting me momentarily. Enough to let him to grab me by the head with both hands. I felt his *Zarantar* but nothing seemed to happen. When I pushed him away I saw the confusion on his face then confusion quickly gave way to fear. Whatever he tried to do to me didn't work, and he didn't know or understand why.

"I can't begin to tell you how angry I was: at myself for

walking into a situation I saw coming; but also with him, for thinking he could *victimise* me. I demanded to know what he did to me or I would rat him out to anyone who would listen. He said he invoked *Barmityanzak* against me to eradicate my memory of his inappropriate advances but something went wrong: he couldn't enter my mind. As he spoke, I could see in his eyes he was terrified of me, and not because I might expose his misconduct.

"Fortunately, for Turan, I decided there was more benefit to be derived in not reporting what happened. As long as I kept the incident to myself I had leverage over him. I could make him do whatever I wanted. And what I wanted was for him to teach me how to invoke *Barmityanzak*. Initially, he baulked at the idea, so I reminded him to think about what would happen if his superiors were to learn that after failing in an attempt to force himself upon a young apprentice, he then tried to violate her mind in order to cover his tracks. Although this made him slightly more amenable, he was adamant there wasn't enough time to teach me; he would be leaving Antaris in three days once the inspection was over. To him it wasn't feasible for me to learn in three days something level nine apprentices are taught over a three-month period. I told him not to doubt my ability to learn quickly, while also making it clear I wasn't giving him a choice in the matter.

"To cut a long story short, I arranged for Turan and I to sneak away from campus that evening—and the following two evenings—to Timaris. We stayed at an inn where he spent each night teaching me the fundamental principles of invoking *Barmityanzak*. I think he was more frightened than impressed at how quickly I was able to master it, and the level of control I had.

"I hope that answers the question to your satisfaction, Administrator Annis."

She peered to her left with a smirk on her face to gauge Fay's reaction. The stoic Sanatsai was staring straight ahead, sitting rigidly in her saddle, the grip on the reins of her horse noticeably tighter. Clearly, Fay was not amused by what she had just heard.

"You look a little miffed, Administrator." Kayden made no effort to keep the sarcasm from her voice. "Maybe you shouldn't ask questions that lead to answers you don't like."

Fay looked at the apprentice.

"Why would I be angry, Kayden?" She didn't wait for a response to her rhetorical question. "That you would stoop so low as to blackmail someone is bad enough. But given the nature of Master Turan's misconduct, the fact you chose not report the matter to me is simply *inexcusable*."

"Why?" She was confused by the second criticism. "No harm was done. That reprobate didn't hurt me, nor did he have his wicked way with me."

"Did it never occur to you that Turan may have done this before?" Fay's exasperated tone was as close as Kayden had ever come to hearing the placid woman speak in anger. "He may very well have abused his power to violate other girls and women in the past who were not as fortunate as you. And how many more victims have there been since you failed to turn him in?"

Kayden couldn't speak. She had not thought of that, and she realised she should have done. She would have been even more disgusted with herself—for only thinking of how she could use the situation to her advantage—if not for her indignation at having Fay Annis be the person to confront her with the gravity of her lack of judgement.

"I'm not the person who permitted a man like Turan to be inducted into the Order!" snapped Kayden.

She looked away from Fay, finding she could no longer meet the woman's gaze. "If I had my way," Kayden continued in a muted voice, "men like Turan would forfeit their lives for what they do."

"You needn't concern yourself with Master Turan," said Fay. "Now that I know what has happened I will have him dealt with in due course."

Kayden was more than happy to forgo any further discussion about her indiscretion with regard to Master Turan.

"What else did you want to question me about?" she asked sullenly. Any question would have to be better than dwelling on Turan's potential victims.

"Last night," began Fay, "it became apparent that your knowledge and understanding of *Zarantar Jist* is more advanced than it should be. As a general rule, we Sanatsai are not exponents of this branch of *Zarantar*. Consequently, every apprentice's education in this area is rather rudimentary. You are only taught the basics of what it is, how the Jaymidari use it and why. In addition, you are also taught to recognise when it has been used and how to counter or neutralise it, should the need ever arise.

"While your ability to sense *Zarantar* does give you an advantage, I was still impressed that you were able to identify, then neutralise, the booby-trapped ward Lazar so carelessly walked into. Which begs the question: who's been teaching you outside of classes?"

Unlike the previous question, Kayden decided this question was mostly harmless so she gave a *mostly* truthful answer.

"I spend a great deal of my free time in the campus library." Any of the librarians could vouch for that, she calculated. "There are numerous volumes on the subject of *Zarantar Jist*, and I have read most of them. In the process I've learned many interesting and helpful things." It wasn't the whole truth, but it wasn't a lie, either.

"So...you're saying that *nobody* has helped you increase your knowledge beyond what it should be."

The manner in which the question was asked seemed to imply Fay knew, or at least suspected, that Kayden wasn't being entirely forthcoming. It would probably be a waste of time to concoct an outright lie so Kayden decided to reveal just enough to allay Fay's suspicions. She could then, hopefully, steer the conversation in another direction; the Sanatsai was getting perilously close to asking her questions she had no desire to answer.

"If you are asking me if a member of staff has been informally teaching me, outside of class, things that I wouldn't be taught in class, then the answer is no," said Kayden. "However, on those occasions when I read something in a book that I either didn't understand, or just wanted to gain a deeper insight into, I would ask the first Sister I came across to enlighten me." If Fay asked around campus there were at least half a dozen Jaymidari who could confirm that they'd been approached by her with questions pertaining to *Zarantar Jist*, including Sister Elsa. "Not one of the Sisters I approached took issue with me asking questions. They were all more than happy to address any queries I had."

"So, why don't you tell me about the cloak you are wearing?" asked Fay, in a decidedly leading fashion. "It is the same one you were wearing last night when you invoked *Naymutandushay* to walk through the wall to avoid capture after trapping yourself in the bedchamber with Sinton and Neryssa."

How does she know that?

"What about it?" Kayden replied as nonchalantly as she could. She didn't want to to betray the anxious thought that had just flashed through her mind.

"Who gave it to you?"

"I made it myself."

"Kayden, I don't care how many books you may have read, you could not have created a siphon cloak by yourself. Certainly, not one that actually works. Someone else made it for you, or at the very least, assisted you in doing so."

"You underestimate me if you doubt my ability to accomplish anything I set my mind to."

The retort was abrasive. Any insinuation she was incapable of doing something irked Kayden greatly.

"I'm not interested in obfuscation or evasion, Kayden. I want the name of the person or persons responsible for you possessing that cloak."

Kayden realised the Sanatsai wasn't going to let the matter go; Fay was behaving like a dog with a bone.

"What difference does it make?"

"I am the administrator of Antaris campus. I need to know if and when instructors, or other staff members serving under me, are breaching protocols or otherwise engaged in unbecoming conduct. That way I can put an end to it and, if necessary, discipline those responsible." She added, more forcefully, "I hope you're not going to make me ask again."

"All right, fine!" she said in a huff. "If it will stop you badgering me, it was Sister Daria who told me what I needed to know. In fact, she's taught me many things she probably wasn't supposed to. Happy now?"

Surprised by the absence of an immediate response to her

revelation, the pregnant silence prompted Kayden to glance to her left to see Fay staring disbelievingly at her. Presumably, Sister Daria was the last person Fay suspected given she was the Jaymidari in charge of running the campus infirmary, and had little day-to-day contact with the apprentices. Kayden felt an odd sense of smug satisfaction knowing she had caught Fay off guard, leaving her speechless in the process.

"Sister Daria would never be so irresponsible or foolish," Fay proclaimed emphatically, breaking her silence. "If you are playing games, hoping to get someone else into trouble…"

Kayden gave the Sanatsai her trademark condescending smirk.

"Haven't you been paying attention? Do you still not realise I know how to get what I want, when I want, from whomever I want?" She gazed fixedly into Fay's eyes to drive home her point. "And I always get what I want."

"Why would Daria risk her position, not to mention her integrity, for you? What could she possibly have to gain by it?"

Sighing, Kayden gazed straight ahead once again.

"Do you want the short version or the long version?"

She took Fay's silence as her cue to narrate the full story.

"About three years ago, shortly before you replaced our previous administrator, I found myself needing to visit the infirmary for the first time since I arrived at Antaris. It was the morning after the week-long survival excursion to Krindari Forest to test our woodcraft. I had woken with a stiff neck and lower back pain. It was nothing serious. Not particularly painful or debilitating, but it did hamper my mobility.

"While I was being tended to by Sister Alina I couldn't help but notice Sister Daria observing us, or, more precisely, me. The way she would stare at me whenever she thought I couldn't see her amused me. She was ogling me the way a fat child eyes a piece of chocolate cake. I knew right away what her predilection was, if you know what I mean.

"My suspicion about her was confirmed a short while later. Sister Alina wanted to administer a concoction for the pain but Daria intervened, kindly mentioning that while the cordial would ease my discomfort it wouldn't loosen the stiffness of my neck and back. She suggested that I stay awhile, let her give me a massage to loosen me up a bit. There was an hour to go before my first class that morning so I agreed.

"Of course, nothing inappropriate happened between us then as there were other people in the infirmary. But let's just say it was clear from the way Daria was touching me she was enjoying the task a lot more than she should.

"When I eventually left the infirmary I made a mental note that one day, should the need arise, I could take advantage of the fact Daria desired me."

Kayden peeked at her silent companion. Fay was staring impassively at the trail ahead, though her posture indicated she didn't like what she was hearing. Kayden returned her own gaze forward and continued her narration.

"That day arrived about a year and a half ago. I was becoming increasingly frustrated by the pace of progress in my studies. Although I'd already been granted permission to advance one level early, I still felt as though I was being held back in certain aspects of my education and training. I was spending more and more of my free time in the library, reading about the things that I wasn't being taught yet in class—not just in terms of *Zarantar Jist*, but more generally about the various abilities and attributes of a Sanatsai.

"What provoked my interest most were advanced subject matters I knew I wouldn't be taught for a few years. But I'm not the most patient person; I wanted to delve into those things, and I wasn't prepared to wait. The problem was, I couldn't exactly approach any of my instructors to insist they teach me things that—from their point of view, at least—I had no business asking them to instruct me in. And that's when I remembered Daria.

"I orchestrated a chance encounter between us, early one evening, just as she was preparing to leave campus and head home to Timaris. I not-so-subtly indicated I was in need of some private tuition to learn my way around the female anatomy, so to speak, and that I believed her to be the most qualified person on campus to teach me. You should have seen the look on her face. She thought it was her lucky day, and I knew I had her right where I wanted her. I finally had access to someone I hoped could teach me anything I wanted, whenever I wanted. Though it must be said, given Daria's appetite, it's a miracle she had the time or energy to teach me anything."

She took another quick peek at Fay to gauge the woman's reaction to this revelation. It wasn't necessary to be a mind reader to discern just how distasteful Fay found her willingness to use sex to get what she wanted.

The amusement she felt at seeing the disapproving gaze staring right back at her, prompted her to add, "Please don't tell me you thought I was a virgin."

Fay ignored the latter comment. "Do you not understand how problematic it is to allow yourself to believe that a woman's only recourse for accomplishing anything is to trade her body?"

Kayden disliked the sympathetic tone; she didn't need or want Fay's pity. "I've done nothing to be ashamed of," she offered in response to the question.

"You're freely admitting to conducting an illicit relationship with a member of staff for the past year and a half." Her voice was full of reproach. "Trading carnal pleasures for knowledge you had no entitlement to receive."

"You make it sound easy," quipped Kayden, returning her gaze to the woodland trail ahead. "It was anything but. Daria was a hard nut to crack...initially. First of all, she's such a talented woman, if you get my meaning, I often found it difficult to keep in mind my reasons for letting her have her way with me to begin with. But once I was able to focus on what I really wanted from her, she wouldn't even entertain the idea of teaching me anything that I hadn't already learned in class—at least, not at first. However, I quickly learned how to break down her defences, until I could end all resistance at will. I could get her to tell me anything I wanted to know. Not that she was particularly helpful much of the time, at least, not when it came to matters of *Zarantar Shayd*. I mean, of course, Daria could explain to me in detail the various applications of *Zarantar* I would eventually learn to master in class, but not being a Sanatsai herself meant she was never able to demonstrate how I could invoke those abilities.

"Daria's usefulness to me was limited to increasing my understanding and knowledge of *Zarantar Jist*. She was always willing and able to teach me anything I wanted to learn—except on one occasion, about four months ago."

"Why? What was so different four months ago?"

"It was the first time I brought up the subject of the siphon cloaks worn by all the Sanatsai of the Order. I asked Daria to tell me how they are created so I could make one for myself. She refused. So I asked her to make one for me. She refused, again. In fact, she was so adamant in her unwillingness to oblige, my usual methods of persuasion weren't enough to make her compliant. Fortunately, I'm not the kind of person who gives up when things become difficult; I prefer to overcome the obstacles I encounter. So I decided to change tack, to use a different approach to persuade Daria to give me what I wanted. I told her that my days of sneaking away from campus in the evenings so she could enjoy the pleasure of my company, in the privacy of her home, were over. I made it clear I never wanted to see or speak to her ever again, then I left.

"After a week of pointedly ignoring her on campus I began to suspect that I'd miscalculated just how addicted to me she was. By the tenth day I had more or less resigned myself to the idea I had irreparably harmed my chances of learning anything from her again. But that was when she finally approached me to tell me she was missing me, that she would teach me anything in her power to teach if I would agree to see her once more.

"And so it was I learned from Daria how the Sisterhood creates siphon cloaks for the Order, though she still wouldn't go as far as to help me make one. You see, she let herself believe there was no harm in me knowing, on the basis that I wouldn't be able to successfully create one for myself without her assistance. So imagine her surprise when I showed up at her door three nights later with a cloak I had made without her help. Actually, surprise is not the right word, horrified is more like it."

"Horrified?" The concern in Fay's voice was evident. "Why?"

"For one thing, the realisation that my cloak would work if I knew how to use it. For another, she had finally become worried about the prospect of getting into trouble because of me. She pleaded with me not to show the cloak to anyone else or ever wear it while I was still an apprentice. She also said I shouldn't reveal that it was her who taught me how to create it, much less pass on the knowledge to someone else. But for all her concern about getting into trouble herself, I think she was actually more afraid for my wellbeing. As she couldn't instruct me in how to use the cloak safely, she made me promise never to attempt to use it before being trained to do so, once I've become a level ten apprentice.

"I guess I don't need to tell you I lied when I made that promise. And that, Administrator Annis, concludes the long version of the story you were so eager to hear."

Fay was clearly displeased by what she'd heard, Kayden realised as she glanced at her Sanatsai companion once more. *Too bad*, she thought. After all, it was Fay who insisted on being told.

"Who else?" demanded Fay.

"Excuse me!"

"Which other members of staff have you been laying with?"

The question, as well as the accusatory tone of voice, infuriated Kayden. She wasn't some filthy whore who spread her legs for anybody prepared to compensate her with whatever she wanted from them in return. She hated the implication that she was; it was demeaning.

"Oh, don't worry Administrator," she snapped back. "Master Darrian only has eyes for you, if that's what you're concerned about."

"Don't make me ask a second time, Kayden."

"I'm not a whore!" Her voice rose, almost to a shout. "I'm not laying with any of my instructors, and even if I was it would be no concern of yours."

Kayden tore her eyes away from her interrogator to stare straight ahead. She needed to recompose herself. She always prided herself on her self-control but Fay was now threatening that control.

After a brief silence she muttered under her breath, "We can't all be uptight, frigid bitches, like you."

From the corner of her eye Kayden noticed Fay's grip on the reins of her horse tighten, as did her posture. Fortunately, she didn't say anything in reply. With any luck Fay would continue to hold her tongue. Kayden didn't want to be drawn into a needlessly heated exchange; she already wanted to slap the woman's face as it was. A little time for them both to regain their composure would probably be better than escalation; she didn't want to give Fay the satisfaction of knowing she had got under her skin.

They continued to ride through sparse woodlands in silence. Neither woman looked at the other, much less exchanged any words. Eventually, it was Fay who took the risk of resuming her questioning of the apprentice.

"Kayden, if my question insulted you," she began in a conciliatory tone, "that was not my intent." No response or acknowledgement was offered. "While there is no requisite for apprentices to be celibate, there are very good reasons why the Order has rules prohibiting intimate relations between apprentices and members of staff, the principal one being to protect you from being taken advantage of. This rule also protects staff members. An instructor who crosses the line with an apprentice leaves themselves open to blackmail. And a compromised individual on campus is a potential security risk."

Kayden hadn't given that possibility any consideration. But security wasn't an issue in this instance. She'd always been very diligent about concealing her nocturnal activities with Daria. No one knew about it, ergo there was no risk.

"But, if you are saying Sister Daria is the only staff member you have had relations with, I will take you at your word," continued Fay. "However, as you have already acknowledged, Daria could not have trained you to use the cloak you made, even if she wanted to. Yet, last night, you demonstrated your mastery of one application of *Zarantar* associated with the wearing of a siphon cloak when you passed through the bedchamber wall to re-enter the hidden passages. Even if I accept there were no intimate favours involved, only a Sanatsai could have instructed you in how to invoke *Naymutandushay*."

"And once again you underestimate me."

Kayden's rebuke of the flawed assumption was as decisive as she could make it.

"Enlighten me!"

"You're correct to say I required guidance," Kayden conceded. "But as I already stated, I couldn't take the chance of approaching any of the Sanatsai instructors; I didn't want to risk revealing that I possessed a siphon cloak of my own making. My only other option was to acquire what I needed to know from someone who'd already received instruction in how to use the cloaks, which meant lots of flirting with several level ten apprentices. And before you ask, no, I did not lay down with any of them.

"From the answers I was able to tease from the apprentices I approached, it was apparent that *Naymutandushay* was the only application of *Zarantar* they had received instruction in by this point. But the ability to pass through solid objects was more than enough to be getting on with, so I took what I'd learned and embarked upon a few weeks worth of trial and error, to master the ability."

"Trial and error?" Fay's incredulity was unmistakeable. "Are you telling me you spent weeks walking through walls on campus without formal training or supervision? Do you have any idea how foolish you were being? You could have killed yourself."

"I'm not an idiot!" Kayden retorted. "Until last night I had never attempted to pass through a wall. When I first began testing my invoking of *Naymutandushay*, I only did small, simple things—like pass my fingers through sheets, then my whole hand. It was only after I felt confident enough about my mastery of this ability did I risk passing my whole body through something, and when I did so it was just a bed sheet I hung up in a doorway. Once I had accomplished the feat numerous times without a hitch, I was satisfied I didn't need to bother experimenting with objects more substantial than a bed sheet."

Fay sighed. "At the risk of my words falling on deaf ears..." There was more than a hint of exasperation in her voice. "...the ten-year training regimen that all apprentices must undergo is structured in such a way that with each level you progress, the more potent the applications of *Zarantar* you are trained to wield. And by more potent, I mean more powerful, hence, more dangerous—not just to those around you but also to yourselves."

Kayden didn't say anything. What could she say? Was she even expected to say anything to that? Eventually she managed a glib, "What's done is done."

"Quite!" Fay concurred. "Now, why don't you tell me why the Sanatsai of the Order wear siphon cloaks? And how do the cloaks work?"

"You're supposed to be a Sanatsai," quipped Kayden. "Don't you already know?"

"Kayden, I'm giving you the chance to persuade me not to confiscate your cloak and destroy it. Are you going to take it?"

Reluctantly, Kayden decided to humour the woman. "Very well, wearing a siphon cloak enables Sanatsai to wield the most powerful applications of their *Zarantar*."

"Our *Zarantar* comes from within, not from what we are wearing." Fay's sharp response came back instantly, as if rehearsed. "So what is the purpose of the siphon cloak?"

"When a Sanatsai wields *Zarantar* it's like using any muscle of the body. The longer and greater the exertion the more worn down and fatigued he or she will become, until they must stop in order to recuperate. During this recovery period they would be vulnerable to attacks from other wielders of *Zarantar*. The cloak mitigates this possibility as it saves a Sanatsai from depletion."

"And why is the use of a siphon cloak limited to such a small subset of a Sanatsai's abilities?"

"Most applications of *Zarantar* are not very taxing. The invoking of these abilities can be sustained continuously for several hours, if necessary, without significantly weakening a Sanatsai. Though, in practice there is rarely cause for prolonged use. However, invoking the more powerful applications of *Zarantar*, even for a brief period, will quickly drain a Sanatsai, and attempting to sustain that invocation for a prolonged time would result in death."

"So how do siphon cloaks work to prevent that outcome?"

"When a Sanatsai invokes one of the high-level applications of *Zarantar* their siphon cloak establishes a link to the nearest ley-line, allowing them to draw strength from an external source rather than from within. This, in turn, means he or she can sustain their invocation for as long as necessary."

Fay was silent for a long moment. Kayden knew it couldn't be because she'd answered incorrectly. It was more likely the duplicitous bitch was trying to think of a way to renege on letting her keep the cloak without losing face.

"Have you been experimenting with any other applications of *Zarantar* associated with the cloak?"

"No." she replied. "As I said earlier, the level ten apprentices I sought out had only mastered *Naymutandushay* at the time. My efforts to research the other applications of *Zarantar* that require Sanatsai to wear siphon cloaks were unproductive. The library back at Antaris only has a three volume set of books on the subject, but..."

"But, what?"

"But when I saw that those books had been authored by you..." Kayden looked across at Fay. "I decided not to read them."

If the woman was offended by the admission there was no sign of it on her face.

"No matter," said Fay after a brief pause. "You are still just a level seven apprentice, Kayden. You have not yet earned the right to study and develop the higher level applications of *Zarantar* that those above you are learning."

"And yet," began Kayden, "I have mastered one such ability without the instruction of any Sanatsai, as you yourself have said."

"Indeed!"

Kayden couldn't tell from the muttered concession whether Fay was impressed or displeased by that fact.

"And how many other people do you plan to get into trouble in pursuit of your ambition?"

"What?"

"I was forced to discipline several apprentices today on your account, including ordering the expulsion of Vartan, and the binding of his *Zarantar*," said Fay. "In addition to this, though I have no sympathy for him, I will have to report Master Turan to the Council. They will take a dim view of his conduct, and should their subsequent investigation uncover the wrongdoings I suspect him of, you can be sure he will be cast out from the Order.

"As for Sister Daria, though I do not have the authority to discipline members of the Sisterhood myself, if I should report her to Sister Idelle once we reach Temis Rulan, which I am more than a little inclined to do at the moment, it is likely she will be in a world of trouble, too. All because of you."

Kayden managed to stifle a laugh. "Am I supposed to feel guilty?" she asked. "Because I don't! I'm not responsible for other people's actions. I didn't hold a blade to anyone's throat and force them to do anything they didn't want to do. If their choices have got them into trouble, that is on them, not me."

"So you're completely blameless in all this?"

"Finally, something we both agree upon!" exclaimed Kayden, mockingly. "Will wonders never cease?"

There was silence between them once more as Fay failed to respond.

Kayden expected the pause in conversation to be a momentary respite, and another question would be cast her way any moment, until the protracted silence extended for so long she finally realised Fay was done with questioning. She glanced at the Sanatsai just in time to catch the woman staring at her, only to quickly avert her gaze back to the path ahead.

What was that look on her face?

Kayden initially took the expression for disappointment, but no, it was more than that. There was a sense of resignation about it, almost as though Fay had just lost all hope and given up. She felt more than a little unnerved by the look, but thought it best not to dwell upon it.

CHAPTER EIGHT

Kayden Is A Special Case

It was beginning to bother Kayden that Fay had been silent for several minutes as they continued their journey on horseback through the woodlands; she did not like being ignored—not that she would ever admit to it.

"I thought you said you had many questions you wanted to ask me," she said, breaking the silence.

"I did." Fay didn't take her eyes off the trail ahead of them.

"But not any more?" She received no answer from the Sanatsai.

"I take it you weren't enjoying my answers then," she added with amusement, moments later.

Once again Fay ignored her.

"Administrator, if you've decided to give me the silent treatment, you should know I'm more than happy to continue this journey without saying another word to you."

"There will be time enough for you to answer more questions later," said Fay. "But not now, we will be dismounting shortly."

Kayden diverted her attention away from Fay back to the trail ahead. They were passing beyond a final line of trees as they exited the woodlands. Some distance further on she could see the bank of a...was it a lake? It was certainly a large body of water. If it was a lake it was the largest she had ever seen. The opposite bank was not visible, though looking to the left, then the right, she could just about discern the shorelines. And if she and Fay were about to dismount, it probably meant they would be crossing the lake to reach Temis Rulan, assuming the large wooden cabins grouped along the waterfront weren't their final destination, which seemed highly unlikely in light of Fay ignoring the buildings and heading straight for the bank.

Minutes later, Kayden was surprised when Fay abruptly pulled her horse up several yards short of the lake. Doing likewise, she glanced at the Sanatsai, awaiting instructions. She was puzzled when Fay stared silently back at her with a questioning look upon her face. Suddenly, Kayden could sense *Zarantar*, lots of it, circling all around them. Instinctively, she reached back over her shoulder for the hilt of her sword.

"What's going on?" she demanded, in a low, urgent tone as she drew her weapon.

Whether or not Fay intended to answer the question there was no time for her to do so. More than a dozen hooded Sanatsai appeared out of thin air, forming a circle around the two horses and their respective riders.

Kayden knew that invisibility was one of those applications of *Zarantar* that required the wearing of a siphon cloak in order to be invoked safely for a prolonged period, but this was the first time she had witnessed *Raytandushay* in action. She was impressed by the demonstration; she had a strong desire to master this ability herself.

The surrounding Sanatsai pulled back the hoods of their cloaks. One of them stepped forward towards Fay's horse. He stood well over six feet tall, had short dark hair, a neatly trimmed beard, twinkling eyes, and appeared to be in his early forties.

"Is your young friend expecting trouble, Fay?" he asked with a chuckle.

"Perhaps," Fay replied with a coy smile. "She certainly has the knack for finding it."

Kayden would have taken issue with the jibe but she was too taken aback by the coquettish tone of voice Fay had affected.

"Or maybe, just like you, Sebasio, trouble just seeks her out."

Although she had noticed how Fay's demeanour and speech

136

had become less formal since they left Antaris, Kayden had never before heard the woman speak in such an informal, familiar manner.

"Or maybe you've been filling her head with the ghost stories that keep people away from the bay," said Sebasio, "and that's why she's so jumpy."

"If ghosts were real they'd have more cause to fear her, than vice versa." Fay turned to address Kayden. "You can put your weapon away, we are among friends here."

She then dismounted with a graceful flourish, handing the reins of her horse to one of her fellow Sanatsai.

Kayden sheathed her sword then dismounted her ride. She watched as the two horses that had brought herself and Fay to the lake—or the bay as the Sanatsai Sebasio had referred to it—were led away in the direction of the nearby wooden buildings. The following few moments were spent silently observing as the remaining Sanatsai crowded around to warmly greet Fay like a long lost sister. There was an abundance of smiles, gripping of forearms, several fierce hugs, and a kiss on both cheeks from one of the female contingent.

Curiosity fell upon the apprentice accompanying Fay on her first return visit to Temis Rulan in three years. Fay casually introduced her to the other Sanatsai as Kayden Jayta, an over-achieving apprentice, originally hailing from the Kingdom of Astana, who had successfully completed the 'capture the box' exercise the previous night. Kayden felt a deep sense of gratification when everyone seemed so impressed by her accomplishment. It also served to make the unprecedented decision to bring an apprentice to Temis Rulan seem more reasonable—which was just as well because she could see that Fay didn't wish to dwell on the matter for too long.

Once the introductions were concluded the gathering of Sanatsai began to disperse, most of them heading towards the largest of the nearby wooden buildings: a two-storey structure resembling an inn with white smoke drifting up into the air from its chimney. A few made their way towards the other buildings that looked more like barracks, where Kayden now noted several more Sanatsai appearing from indoors, while the rest took up sentry positions. She and Fay were left alone in the company of Master Sebasio.

"You know," said Sebasio, addressing Fay, "a great many of us are out of pocket because of you."

"Me?" said Fay, surprised. "How so?"

"When the Council assigned you to Antaris as campus administrator, we started taking bets on how long it would be before they realised their error and recalled you."

Kayden was intrigued. The way Fay told it, she had requested to take on the administrator's post at Antaris campus. Yet Master Sebasio was indicating it was a decision made by the Council, which meant Fay had either lied about wanting the position, or she had concealed her desire to have the job from her colleagues.

"Most of us thought you'd be back within a month. Others wagered two months. Some, myself included, wagered three. There were even a handful who thought you'd be gone a full year before coming back." Sebasio sounded exasperated when he added, "It's been over three years, and *still* the Council has you playing the role of glorified headmistress...it's madness!"

"Now, now, Seb. You're not questioning the wisdom of the Council, are you?" teased Fay, playfully.

"No...of course not," he replied in a more conciliatory in tone. "But can you tell me in all seriousness that being a campus administrator is a productive use of your time? You can't possibly have enjoyed the last three years."

Fay seemed to choose her words carefully when she replied, "It has been a challenging experience thus far, and while I realise I may not necessarily be the ideal person for the role, right now it's where I need to be."

Kayden silently wondered what exactly Fay meant by *needing* to be at Antaris campus. Why not one of the other campuses?

"So, how much longer do you think you'll be stuck in the post?" pressed Sebasio.

"That is a better question than you might realise, Seb," replied Fay. "I suspect I'll have a clearer idea by the end of my visit. But I certainly don't plan to leave the post while I have unfinished business."

"There's a boat approaching," interjected Kayden. "There looks to be half a dozen Sanatsai on board."

"That will be our ride," Fay said matter-of-factly, staring out at the water.

"If you're in no hurry to get to the island," said Sebasio, "we'll be sitting down for tea shortly. Both you and Kayden are more than welcome to join us."

"Thank you, Seb. But we're already running late, I'd rather not delay any further."

Fay began to amble towards the bank.

Sebasio kept pace at her side. "As you wish," he replied.

Kayden trailed behind the two Sanatsai as they meandered to the bank to await the arrival of the incoming boat. *So, Temis Rulan is on an island, or is an island*, Kayden mused to herself. She had not considered that possibility while contemplating the location of the Order's home.

Before long, the incoming boat lurched to a halt as it landed on the bank. There were five Sanatsai aboard the rowing boat, four of them serving as oarsmen. When the fifth jumped from the vessel, landing on the muddy ground to greet the waiting trio, Kayden was surprised to find she recognised him.

Nando Benidas had been an apprentice at Antaris campus until he was inducted into the Order two years ago. Unfortunately, the only two occasions Kayden's path had crossed his on campus had both been negative encounters, to say the least.

The first time was in the mess hall during the breakfast period one morning. She was sitting by herself at a table when a group of level eight apprentices sat themselves down on the unoccupied spaces of the benches at her table. There wasn't enough space for Nando to have a seat at the table so he asked if she would vacate her place and find another table to sit at. Her far from polite refusal ruffled his feathers prompting him to advise her that she needed to learn to respect her elders. She in turn told him he should learn to respect his superiors. A Sanatsai sitting at a nearby table walked over to instruct her to sit elsewhere and not cause a scene. Kayden subsequently picked up her bowl of semolina and poured it all over Nando's head, to rapturous cheers, earning her yet another visit to the administrator's office.

The second incident occurred in the library, one afternoon. They were both in the same aisle searching the same bookshelf. As Kayden reached up for the book she was looking for, Nando grabbed it first. The ensuing commotion led to the defacement of the book resulting in them both being banned from the library for a month.

If Nando was the type to hold a grudge, this reunion could prove to be awkward.

"How goes it, Seb?" said Nando gripping the forearm of the bearded Sanatsai. "It's really good to see you again, Master Fay." He clasped Fay by the forearm with a bright smile.

"You're not an apprentice any more, Kai Benidas," Fay replied warmly. "There's no need to address me as Master, my rank will suffice."

"Of course...Danai Annis," he managed, sheepishly. "Though it will take some time to get used to not calling you Master."

Kayden rolled her eyes. *What a suck up!* He'd only known the woman for a year back at Antaris.

Nando turned his attention to her, and Kayden saw the recognition in his eyes when his smile quickly evaporated. He glared at her then looked her up and down, taking in the sight of her uniform. Looking puzzled, he turned back to Fay.

"We were told you would be travelling with a guest," he said. "But surely you're not bringing *her?* I thought it was forbidden for an apprentice to come to Temis Rulan."

"That still remains so. But Kayden is a special case."

As Nando glanced back at her, Kayden duly gave him a smirk. The corner of her mouth curved up just enough to say, *that's right! Special Case. Now stew on that for a while.*

"In that case," he said addressing Fay, "why don't we get going?"

Kayden joined Fay and Nando in bidding Master Sebasio farewell before getting aboard the waiting boat. Moments later they were pulling away from the muddy bank.

Next stop, Temis Rulan.

Kayden sat on the bench in the rear of the boat, alongside Fay. In front of them, four Sanatsai were maintaining a swift, steady rhythm on the oars, while Nando sat at the front of the boat staring out over the water.

While Fay was engaged in idle chit-chat with the oarsmen, catching up on three years worth of gossip within the Order, Kayden was doing her best to mentally block it all out. She wanted to keep her focus on looking out for Temis Rulan, plus she was hoping to identify distinguishing landmarks that might help her pinpoint where in the world they were. It was a thankless task thus far, as was trying to block out the conversation and banter of the Sanatsai. She couldn't fathom how Fay was seemingly so popular and well regarded by everyone. Not to mention her easygoing manner and laughter were completely at odds with the woman Kayden knew back at Antaris campus.

All of a sudden, Kayden felt her senses struck by *Zarantar* emanating from directly in front of the boat, though she could see nothing but clear blue, calm waters ahead. Ordinarily, it would not be cause for such heightened alarm but what she was feeling now was more *Zarantar* than she had ever felt in her life. She had never encountered anything so powerful before. Instinctively, she stood up to stare straight ahead hoping to identify the source of the disturbance.

"Apprentice! Sit back down," cried one of the Sanatsai, "before we have to fish you out of the bay."

Fish her out of the bay? There was no need for exaggeration, thought Kayden. Even if she didn't already know how to swim, if she did fall overboard she would simply levitate back out of the water. She glanced imploringly down at Fay who was looking up at her.

"But there's something—"

Reaching up, Fay gave Kayden's hand a gentle squeeze.

"I know what you're going to say," she said cutting the apprentice off.

Her eyes conveyed the message that Kayden shouldn't give voice to her feelings. "I feel it, too. Sit back down, your concern will be alleviated soon enough."

Kayden reluctantly sat back down beside Fay. She remained tense; the *Zarantar* she sensed was coming closer—or more to the point, they were drawing nearer to its source. Moments later, she was taken by surprise when the front of the boat began to disappear, along with Nando. It was as though the boat had come into contact with some unseen force that was now rapidly consuming it and its passengers.

More of the boat disappeared, taking the first two oarsmen also.

Before Kayden could react Fay placed a reassuring hand on her thigh. "Don't be alarmed," she said gently.

Kayden had little choice but to trust that everything would be all right. She watched and waited for herself and Fay to disappear just as the rest of the boat and its occupants had done. Suddenly, she could see the whole boat again, including its passengers—all present and accounted for. She released the breath she didn't realise she was holding, then marvelled at the sight before her. There was a large island looming a short distance away.

"Temis Rulan?" she asked breathlessly.

"No," replied Fay. "But Temis Rulan is located on the island."

"Concealing an entire island from view must require an unbelievable amount of *Zarantar*." Kayden was awed. "How in the world did anyone manage to accomplish such a feat?"

"The island is the ancestral home of the Sisterhood—the centre of their power. It is said that the island is situated at a nexus point, a place where over a hundred ley-lines intersect. Keeping the island permanently cloaked from view is easy enough for the Jaymidari—their *Zarantar* is strongest here. That's why you won't find this island on any map less than two thousand years old."

Kayden could feel her excitement and anticipation growing. When she had originally been told she was to accompany Fay to Temis Rulan, she hadn't truly believed it. She was so certain the journey was just a ruse to get her away from Antaris, a malicious plot hatched by Fay to end her life and dispose of her body. But now there was no reason to doubt where she was going. She would be arriving at Temis Rulan, soon, though the purpose of the visit remained shrouded in mystery.

The boat was moored at the docks of a small port town on the southern shore of the island. Though the waterfront couldn't be described as a hive of activity, there were several people present, many dressed in the garb of the Order. Some were helping to unload cargo from docked barges, while others transported goods to storage buildings. A small number of vessels could be seen departing and approaching the island to and from both the east and from the west, across the placid bay.

Kayden disembarked with Fay and the other occupants. She glanced quickly around the waterfront, but before she could wonder what their next move might be, Nando pointed Fay in the direction of a female Sanatsai standing outside a nearby storage building. At least Kayden assumed it was a woman, she couldn't be absolutely certain from a distance. The Sanatsai waved enthusiastically in their direction once Fay caught sight of her, prompting Fay to duly raise a hand in acknowledgement with a big smile on her face.

"I appreciate the ride," said Fay, turning to her colleagues. "It was good to see you all again. But for now, Kayden and I must get going."

The gathered Sanatsai bid a fond farewell to Fay, declaring their hopes to catch up with her back at Temis Rulan during her stay. Kayden was, likewise, given a warm departure, though only from the four Sanatsai who had manned the oars of the boat. Nando pointedly ignored her.

"Follow me," Fay instructed Kayden, as she set off briskly towards her awaiting counterpart.

Kayden found herself needing to walk more quickly than before to keep pace. If she didn't know better, she would think Fay was actually excited to see the other Sanatsai, whom she could now clearly discern was a woman. She was of medium height, slender frame, average looks with dark hair tightly braided into rows. The moment they reached the storage building Kayden looked on in astonishment as Fay and her colleague embraced each other fiercely—neither seemingly inclined to release the other.

Will wonders never cease? Kayden mused to herself. Fay was genuinely pleased to see the other woman.

"Dora! It's so good to see you again," said Fay.

"You too, Red." The unrestrained glee in Dora's reply made it apparent just how happy she was to see Fay. Though why did she just call her Red? Fay's unusual hair colouring, perhaps? "You've been gone too long; I've missed you so much."

Eventually, the two Sanatsai released each other, stepping back an arms length to smile warmly at the other.

"You are the last person I expected to greet us here," said Fay, cheerily. "The last I heard, you were among the contingent the Council deployed to Yaristana to assist the kingdom in a border dispute with Randissar."

"I still am. But as luck would have it I arrived at the Beltranis campus first thing this morning to send a progress report back to the Council. When I was informed of your visit to Temis Rulan today, I immediately requested a couple of days leave, so here I am!"

"I'm pleased. So how has the mission been progressing?"

"We can discuss that later." Dora smiled while waving a dismissive hand. "First, why don't you introduce me to your companion. I heard you would be bringing an apprentice with you; I wasn't sure I believed it until now."

Finally! Kayden was beginning to feel as though her presence had been forgotten during the nausea-inducing reunion.

"Of course," replied Fay. "Dora, this is Kayden Jayta, currently a level seven apprentice at Antaris campus. Kayden, meet Master Dora Bendatis."

Kayden accepted Dora's outstretched hand, gripping the Sanatsai firmly by the forearm in greeting.

"Pleased to make your acquaintance, Master Dora."

"And you, Kayden." said Dora. She affected a serious tone of voice when she added, "You must have made quite an impression on your master for her to breach protocol bringing you here. You must be in a great deal of trouble."

That was unexpected. But Kayden didn't allow the words to faze her. "You're not the first person to suggest that today,

Master," she replied, evenly.

Dora didn't immediately reply. Slowly, a smile began to curl her lips then she started laughing.

"I'm so sorry, Kayden," she managed to say, stifling her fit of laughter, "I'm just pulling your leg."

"Don't tease her like that," Fay chided her friend.

"Oh, don't mind me, Kayden." Dora stopped laughing. "Knowing your master like I do, the mere fact she has taken you under her wing and brought you here can only mean you are one exceptional individual." She glanced at Fay; admiration for her friend positively beamed from her face. "Take it from me, you are most fortunate to have someone like her take a special interest in your ongoing development."

Wanting to roll her eyes, Kayden, instead, managed a simple, "So I've been hearing."

"Perhaps we should get going," prompted Fay.

"Right you are," said Dora, cheerily. "Tobin is waiting on the outskirts of town with our horses. Follow me."

Kayden fell into step behind the two Sanatsai as they departed, Dora placing a friendly arm around Fay's shoulder. She followed a few paces back while the pair made small talk. It was disconcerting just how different a person Fay seemed to be away from campus. Over the course of the last half hour or more, in the presence of fellow Sanatsai, Fay had transformed from a cold, standoffish, taciturn woman—who frequently aroused Kayden's ire back at Antaris—into a warm and friendly, approachable person.

In spite of herself, Kayden started feeling better disposed towards the woman. She didn't like that one bit. She tried to keep in mind her conviction that Fay was resolutely sabotaging her training to prevent her induction into the Order. The woman was without question the bane of her life. Who cared if she showed a different side of herself to the rest of the world?

A short while later they reached the outskirts of the port town. Waiting to meet them was a male Sanatsai alongside two tethered chestnut geldings. Looking at him, Kayden instantly saw a forty-something version of Lazar. Not that they looked alike, it was more a case of them being of the same archetype. He was over six feet tall. His uniform accentuated the toned, athletic physique beneath, his mousey hair was neatly trimmed, and a week's worth of facial hair embellished his strong jaw. He was the archetypal rugged 'pretty-boy' that so many women seemed to fantasise about. And the glint in his brown eyes gave away his awareness of the effect he had on such women.

"Well, aren't you a sight for sore eyes," he exclaimed heartily, seizing Fay in a bear hug.

Kayden was astonished by the way the Sanatsai was holding on just a little tighter than was necessary or appropriate. The 'mmmmm!' that emanated from deep within him as he squeezed Fay's body against his, suggested he was excited to see Fay in more ways than one, an observation quickly confirmed by one of his hands gliding slowly down Fay's back to...

"Tobin, if your hand wanders any lower," said Fay, a hint of coy threat in her voice, "you will lose it...for good."

Tobin released Fay from his enthusiastic embrace, grinning.

"My humble apologies," he said with mock sincerity, one hand placed over his heart. "But it *has* been three years. You can't blame me for being happy to see you and your shapely be—"

He cut off as he caught sight of Kayden standing behind the two female Sanatsai. The cheeky grin vanished instantly from his face. He slowly looked Kayden up and down, his eyes devouring her as though she were a sumptuous desert.

Realising she was being mentally undressed, Kayden scowled at him. But the intensity of Tobin's gaze did not falter until Fay snapped her fingers under his nose.

"Hey!" she barked, clearly unimpressed by the leering. "Put your eyes back inside your head."

Gazing at Fay with innocent eyes, Tobin said, "I was just inspecting the next generation." His tone was affectedly meek. He returned his attention back to Kayden. "And who might you be, apprentice?"

"She is Kayden Jayta," Fay offered. "More than that, you do not need to know."

Tobin took a step towards Kayden, extending an arm to her in

146

greeting. "Allow me to introduce myself; Tobin Rinaldi."

Kayden reached for Tobin's outstretched limb. Before she could grip his forearm he took hold of her fingers then leaned forward to plant a delicate kiss upon the back of her hand.

"It's an honour to make your acquaintance, Kayden Jayta. I hope you will permit me to say that they certainly didn't make apprentices half as beautiful as yourself during my tenure as an apprentice." Tobin's voice was velvety charm personified. "You must be a real heartbreaker back at Antaris."

Kayden yanked her hand back from his grasp. "Well, I don't know about that, Master Toby." He did not react to the deliberate mispronunciation of his name. "However, I have been known to break other body parts when the need arises."

Dora, who had remained silent until now, tried and failed to suppress an outbreak of laughter at the expense of her colleague.

Tobin was left speechless by the quip. He quickly recovered his wit, smiling as he turned to address Fay. "I see your three years at Antaris has been spent moulding the apprentices in your image."

"I assure you, Kayden requires no guidance from me when it comes to putting a lecherous Sanatsai in his place." A sardonic smile curled Fay's lips. "You'd probably do well to remember that. Now, I suggest we head out before I'm tempted to break something."

"Very well." Tobin untethered one of the horses, handing the reins over to Dora. "Presumably, you and Fay will want to ride together, so to speak." He began to untether the second horse. "So, I guess Kayden will have the pleasure of riding with me." He raised his eyebrows suggestively at the apprentice.

"I don't think so!" Fay snatched the reins of the second horse away from Tobin. "I'd prefer to reach Temis Rulan without incident, if you don't mind, so Kayden will ride with me."

"Why are we not getting horses of our own to ride?" Kayden demanded to know, indignant.

"Oh my, she's not just a pretty face, is she?" Tobin uttered to Fay, with a cheeky smile. "Likes to ride too, it seems." He fixed his lustful gaze on Kayden. "Let me guess," he continued. "It's the sensation you get having something big and powerful between your legs that does it, am I right?"

Both Dora and Fay simultaneously rewarded Tobin with a smack to the back of the head.

"Tobin, if one more inappropriate word comes out of your mouth..." Fay did not finish her stern warning. Tobin would know he had crossed a line she wasn't prepared to overlook just from her glowering countenance.

"All right! I was just joking."

Moments later Tobin was mounting his ride, then pulling Dora up to sit behind him. Likewise, Fay mounted the other horse, giving Kayden a helping hand up, to sit behind her. Without further ado the grey and black clad quartet rode away from the port at a gentle canter.

Kayden's arms were wrapped tightly around Fay's waist, her head resting gently against the Sanatsai's back. In the hour or so since riding out of the port, she had contented herself with wistfully breathing in the scent of Fay's burgundy hair. The combination of jasmine and sandalwood brought to mind her beloved mother, and it had a soothing, calming effect. The warm summer air, coupled with the sights and sounds of the unspoilt countryside all around them, with its rolling fields of dandelions and daisies, lavender covered hills, and fleet rabbits scampering through the long grass only served to relax her further.

The journey thus far had seen them pass through two farming villages, both inhabited by communities comprised of Sanatsai and Jaymidari. The observation provoked a new appreciation for the Order in Kayden. She had always viewed it as a shadowy organisation of powerful warriors, but there was obviously more to it than that.

The horses were now moving at a languid trot across open fields rather than a brisk canter. Since passing through the second village, the conversation between the Sanatsai trio had thankfully moved away from Tobin's tiresome repartee, and his testing of Fay's patience with his unabated sexual innuendos. At Fay's request, Dora was giving a brief rundown of the mission in

Yaristana to bring an end to the border dispute between the kingdom and its neighbour, Randissar; Kayden was listening with interest.

The so-called border dispute was in fact a full-scale insurrection in the restive province of Mattis. About six weeks previously a long-gestating secessionist movement in Mattis had taken up arms to break away from the kingdom with the aim of merging with Randissar. As more than two thirds of the province's population was of Randissari descent the rebellion had considerable internal support, not to mention the rebels were unofficially receiving help from within Randissar, in the shape of weapons and volunteers smuggled across the border.

Despite assurances from the Randissari ambassador that his government were not in any way providing support to the rebels, King Santando and his advisers held firm to their conviction that the rebellion wasn't possible without outside interference, an assertion that had been seemingly confirmed two weeks ago when *Zarantar*-wielding fighters first began to appear among the ranks of the separatists. At this point the Yaristanese king had no option but to formally request assistance from the Order to quell the insurrection.

A five-hundred strong cadre of Sanatsai was deployed in Yaristana by the Council in response to the request. For over a week, what was ostensibly intended to be a brief intervention to restore peace in Mattis province was nothing of the sort. The Sanatsai were engaged in fierce fighting, side-by-side with Yaristanese soldiers against the rebels.

"Three days ago we helped to push the separatists out of the provincial capital, after recapturing and securing all the major towns in the eastern half of the province," proclaimed Dora. "We were subsequently able to negotiate a truce with the rebel leaders. For the time being they still hold the western areas of Mattis where support for the rebellion is strongest.

"Our Yaristanese friends did not welcome the ceasefire, to say the least. But the truce is holding...for now."

"I can't say that I blame them," said Tobin. "Why didn't we continue our momentum and push west towards the border? As long as their supply lines to Randissar remain intact the rebels have no reason to lay down their arms."

"Because our orders were to bring an end to the fighting, which we've done. Besides, we don't currently have the manpower in Mattis to fight an all-out war if Randissar should enter the fray on the side of the separatists." Dora sighed in frustration. "We're having a difficult enough time as it is preventing the Yaristanese soldiers from exacting retribution against their fellow subjects of Randissari descent, even those not involved with the rebels."

"Is that likely to happen?" Fay inquired. "Randissar entering the conflict, I mean."

"Despite the lull in fighting, Danai Rentis is concerned that intervention by the Order all but guarantees an escalation in the conflict."

"Pouring oil on to fires never seems to put them out," mused Fay. "But knowing Larko Rentis, as I do, his mind does tend to favour the worst possible scenario."

"While I was at Beltranis campus this morning, updating the Council on our progress, he had me request that the size of our contingent in Mattis be increased tenfold, to five thousand. He believes it's only a matter of time before an incursion from Randissar to annex the province."

"Have we ascertained whether or not the government of Randissar really is behind the supply of weapons and men to the rebels? Knowing that will make it easier to predict how they may react to our involvement."

"Covert operations inside Randissar have confirmed that support for the rebellion is being orchestrated by three high-ranking military officers," Dora said. "However, there's no evidence to suggest the ruling body is aware of this, let alone actually sanctioned it."

"It's possible that if presented with proof of the unauthorised actions of these three officers, the government could put an end to it." Fay didn't sound particularly hopeful. "It would go some way to taking the wind out of the sails of the rebels."

"Or..." interrupted Tobin. "They've been in on it from the word go, and having their secret exposed would simply force them

150

into openly pursuing the annexation of Mattis province. If that happens, we'll have no choice but to go to war on the side of Yaristana."

"The Order won't be drawn into open warfare so easily," warned Fay. "The Council will pursue any and every avenue available to avoid that."

Kayden, who had been listening attentively to the discussion until now, decided it was time to speak her mind.

"If the Order truly wants to end the conflict without going to war, the Council should be demanding that the king and queen of Yaristana rectify the poor treatment of their subjects who are of Randissari descent."

The conversation came to an abrupt halt. Both Dora and Tobin peered across towards the other horse, looking quizzically at the apprentice.

"Why are you staring at me like I just said something crazy?" Kayden challenged the two Sanatsai. "It is well known that those of Randissari heritage are treated worse than dirt throughout Yaristana. As far as I'm concerned, the separatists are more than justified in taking up arms against their oppressors. The interests of their people would be better served by breaking away from the kingdom, and for Mattis to be absorbed into Randissar."

Tobin began to laugh heartily. "Oh, Fay," he managed to say between fits of laughter. "Only you would have the testicular fortitude to bring a separatist sympathiser to Temis Rulan."

"Be quiet, Tobin," said Fay, irritably. "And stop laughing." He promptly obeyed her command. "Kayden, there is undoubtedly truth in your assertion that the poor treatment of the Randissari population has been a contributing factor in the current crisis. That being said, the Order cannot tell the rulers of Yaristana how to govern their kingdom."

"Why not?"

Dora answered on Fay's behalf. "The Order was founded to prevent the misuse of *Zarantar* in the Nine Kingdoms. We do not interfere in the internal politics of any of the kingdoms."

"Well, maybe it is time you started." There was an unmistakable edge to Kayden's voice.

"You seem to be taking this personally, Kayden," observed Fay.

"I have no stake in what's happening in Mattis province, if that's what you're wondering," she replied. "But I know what it's like to belong to a visible minority living in the Nine Kingdoms. Assumptions are made about us based on fanciful tales that people carelessly spread. The wrongful actions of a single individual are used as a pretext for smearing the rest of us with the same brush, and if the fortunes of the land take a turn for the worse, we become convenient scapegoats for people to point the finger of blame.

"The Order should be taking advantage of the current truce to insist on the rulers of Yaristana taking steps to address the terrible mistreatment of their Randissari subjects. Why should they be treated less favourably than everyone else simply because of what they look like? It's not as though they can conceal their pallid complexions, their freckles, or their ginger hair.

"It may not be enough, initially, to quell separatist sympathies entirely. But acknowledgement that there is a problem is a necessary first step."

"Your suggestion has merit, Kayden," conceded Fay. "The Council, too, would see the wisdom in advising King Santando to act accordingly. However, as I already stated, the Order cannot compel the rulers of the Nine Kingdoms to adopt policies they do not wish to adopt."

Kayden was becoming exasperated. "What is the point of having all this power if you can't force people to do what you want?"

From the corner of her eye, Kayden noticed that neither Dora nor Tobin reacted well to her words; they were both directing concerned glances at Fay sitting in front of her. Fay, for her part, seemingly feeling the weight of her companions' gazes upon her, glanced wordlessly at them for a moment before returning her attention straight ahead; the two horses were starting to ascend a steep hill.

"Is that what you would do, Kayden?" queried Fay. "Use your power to impose your will on others."

"If that's what it takes."

The reply was decidedly blasé.

Her words appeared to mark the end of the discussion. Fay offered no response to her answer, though glancing at the other two Sanatsai it certainly seemed to Kayden as though Dora really wanted to take issue with it. Instead, the woman directed her address to her friend and counterpart.

"Red? If I may ask—"

"No, you may not," said Fay abruptly, cutting Dora off in mid-sentence. "This conversation is over."

The affable woman who had emerged during the journey to Temis Rulan was gone; the stoic administrator of Antaris campus had returned. "Any questions can wait until we reach Temis Rulan."

"How much further to go?" Kayden asked no one in particular.

"The other side of this hill," said Fay.

Minutes later the two horses reached the top of the hill, ready to begin the descent down the gently sloping, grassy incline.

"Oh, my..." gasped the apprentice.

In her mind, Kayden had always envisioned Temis Rulan as a larger-scale version of the Antaris campus that had been her home for the past five years. The reality that now lay before her dwarfed those preconceived notions. She marvelled at the sight of the sprawling cityscape in the distance, at the centre of which she could clearly see the complex of buildings that could only be the headquarters of the Order, surrounded by a circular perimeter wall. From her vantage point it was difficult to accurately gauge the size of the headquarters but she estimated that it must cover five times the area of the Antaris campus.

Radiating outwards from the perimeter wall, myriad buildings and habitations stretched out in every direction. Kayden guessed that it would take at least two hours to walk from one end of the city to the other.

"I had no idea Temis Rulan was a city in it's own right," she exclaimed.

"I'm not sure that it qualifies as such, at the moment," Fay replied in her customary matter-of-fact fashion, "but it continues to grow over time. When it was first established, Temis Rulan was contained entirely within the perimeter wall you can see at the centre. Over time, as more Sanatsai were inducted into the Order, and people began having families, it became necessary to expand beyond the wall in order to accommodate the increasing population."

Given how much it had expanded, Kayden could only imagine the size of population, currently.

"Just how many people live here?" she wondered aloud.

"Well, there are over a hundred thousand people on the island, most of whom live here in Temis Rulan."

"A hundred thousand!" Kayden was flabbergasted. "Surely they can't all be members of the Order?" She found it inconceivable that there could be so many Sanatsai in the world, let alone just on the island.

"No," acknowledged Fay. "At the last count, the number of Sanatsai in our ranks was just north of the thirty thousand mark. At any given time, you'll find at least three quarters of us living here. The rest of the population is made up of Jaymidari and the offspring of those who have started families here."

Kayden was astonished to discover the number of Sanatsai in the Order exceeded thirty thousand; that was considerably larger than any single army of the Nine Kingdoms. She could not say for certain, but she suspected their combined armies did not total thirty thousand men. "Are you telling me that the Order has more manpower at its disposal than the Nine Kingdoms has soldiers?"

Fay chuckled, slightly, at that. "Only if you underestimate the number of men-at-arms the kingdoms can call upon," she said. "But you are right to point out that the Order is a sizeable force; one to be reckoned with."

The two horses began the steady descent downhill towards Temis Rulan. What awaited them once they got there, Kayden could only guess at.

CHAPTER NINE

What The Future May Hold

As the group made their approach to the southern gate, Kayden was still awestruck by the sheer numbers of Sanatsai she had observed while traversing the streets of Temis Rulan. She never imagined ever seeing so many in one location, and someday soon, she would be rubbing shoulders with them—as one of their number—calling the city her home, too.

The journey through the city also highlighted just how well known a figure Fay Annis was. Numerous men and women had given warm salutations as they witnessed her passing by. She wasn't just a highly regarded Sanatsai of the Order; evidently, she was also a genuinely much-loved person.

They were admitted through the gate without hindrance, allowing Kayden her first real look at the grounds of the Order. It was like a grand rural estate—usually the preserve of the nobility of the Nine Kingdoms. She could see well manicured lawns crisscrossed by grey brick pathways leading to and from several imposing buildings. The most impressive structure lay at the heart of the complex several hundred yards in the distance. She concluded that the building must be where the Council was to be found. As a young child back in Astana she had seen the royal palace in the capital, Shali, on more than one occasion, and while the building she could see ahead of her wasn't nearly as ostentatious, it was certainly similar in scale. It was five storeys of beautifully constructed, palatial manor house built from grey masonry.

Dora then Tobin dismounted their horse in quick succession.

Fay peered back over her shoulder at Kayden. "You can dismount now," she said.

Doing as instructed, Kayden dismounted the horse, quickly followed by Fay herself who handed the reins to one of the Sanatsai sentries on duty at the gate. She watched as both horses were led away in the direction of the stables situated to the east of the grounds.

The group proceeded a short distance on foot along the grey brick path, coming to a halt when met by a dozen Sanatsai accompanying an elderly Jaymidari standing at the forefront of the welcoming party.

"Welcome back," the Sister greeted Fay with affection.

She was a short, old woman with long, grey-white hair, a warm smile upon her wrinkled face, and a fetching amethyst pendant hanging from the chain around her neck. Kayden guessed her to be in her eighties, possibly even older.

"Thank you, it feels good to be back," said Fay, embracing the Jaymidari.

Dora said, "Tobin and I will be stopping in at the communal hall for a while. I presume you'll be taking care of whatever business you have here, right away." Fay nodded in the affirmative. "In that case, if you are free this evening maybe you can join us in the mess hall for dinner; we can catch up some more."

"I would like that."

Fay gripped Dora by the forearm, then bid both her and Tobin farewell before they departed, making their way to the communal hall.

The Jaymidari turned to address her Sanatsai escort.

"You may leave us," she told them.

They dispersed in compliance, leaving her alone with Fay and Kayden. She turned around to face the direction she had arrived from then held out her left arm, silently gesturing for Fay to take hold of it. Without hesitation Fay looped her own arm through the offered limb.

To Kayden's surprise the woman indicated that she should take hold of her right arm, now held out to her. She flashed a quick glance towards Fay, looking for guidance.

"Come, child," said the Sister, with no hint of condescension, "let us be on our way."

Kayden looped her arm through the woman's waiting arm then the three of them walked leisurely along the grey brick path leading to the main building at the centre of the sprawling complex. She supposed they must look like an odd spectacle to any onlookers, given the disparity in height of the trio. Both she and Fay had eight or nine inches on the short Jaymidari confidently guiding them onwards.

The Sister glanced up at Kayden. "Forgive me, my dear," she said, "I'm afraid your master has neglected to give your name." There was a note of mild amusement in her voice.

"Idelle, this is Kayden Jayta," Fay offered succinctly.

Kayden almost stumbled at the name. She was aware that Idelle was the name of the head of the Sisterhood, and if this Jaymidari was the same person, she was also a serving member of the Council, the ruling body of the Order.

"And she is the reason for your visit, yes?"

"She is."

"But you still don't wish to tell myself or the rest of the Council why."

That's strange, thought Kayden. She had been led to believe that Fay had important business to discuss with the Council.

"For the moment the problem does not require the immediate attention of the Council," replied Fay, guardedly, "and I would prefer not to burden you with it before absolutely necessary."

Kayden realised that if Fay was describing her as 'the problem', then the notion that she had been brought to Temis Rulan to receive some kind of special commendation had just flown right out of the window.

"I take it you plan to burden Ari with your problem?" Idelle's question was obviously leading. "And that's why you requested to see him?"

Again, Kayden almost stumbled, this time at the mention of

yet another familiar name. Ari Shinadu was the Sanatsai who founded the Order in the aftermath of the Great War seven decades ago. He, too, was a serving member of the Council. Had Fay brought her here to meet Master Ari?

"Yes," Fay conceded. "He has prior experience that I hope will negate the need to formally bring the matter to the Council."

"As you wish." There was no disappointment or annoyance in Idelle's voice. "I know he'll be thrilled to see you. Your absence these past three years has been greatly felt by many, myself included."

They walked in silence for a brief spell until Idelle, once again, glanced to her right to address the apprentice. "So, Kayden," she began warmly, "how has your training been progressing?"

Kayden briefly contemplated giving a humble answer, but false humility wasn't in her make-up.

"The pace of my progress is barely satisfactory, Sister. Despite everything I have learned thus far, I do not feel as though I am being adequately challenged. As of this moment I'm already a level seven apprentice, though only into the fifth year of my apprenticeship, yet I feel like I'm being held back unnecessarily; a situation I believe isn't helped by my having no peer among my fellow apprentices."

Kayden noted how Idelle cast a quick glance at Fay—presumably none to impressed by the immodest response—before returning her gaze back, to reply.

"Well, you've certainly made quite an impression on your master, she wouldn't have brought you here otherwise. I don't imagine another apprentice will ever be brought to Temis Rulan—certainly not during my lifetime."

"I imagine not." It was the only thing Kayden could think to say.

Smiling up at the apprentice, Idelle's eyes were searching. "I hope you will not object to my saying so, Kayden," she said, "but if you should prove to be as beautiful on the inside as you are on the outside, you will be a great asset once you are inducted into the Order."

Kayden flushed in spite of herself. She was accustomed to

being told she was beautiful—usually by people who wanted something in return for such compliments. But she knew Idelle neither wanted or expected anything from her in return. In fact, Kayden had the odd sense that the Sister had just imparted some sage advice.

She hesitated before responding.

"I appreciate your kind words, Sister," she said, in an uncharacteristic, self-effacing manner. "I will do all I can to make them true."

For the next few minutes Kayden walked silently, taking in the sights of the grounds while listening to Fay and Idelle making small talk about Fay's duties as the administrator of Antaris campus.

"As it happens," Fay was saying, "I have recently become aware that I have a problem with one of the Sisters serving under me at Antaris." Kayden knew she was referring to Sister Daria. "I've not yet had the opportunity to speak with the Sister, to hear her side of the story, so I won't go into details now. However, once I return to Antaris and discuss the matter with her, it is likely I will have to report it to you so that you may take whatever action you deem appropriate."

Idelle signalled her assent with a muted 'hmm' before bringing the two younger women, on either arm, to a halt outside the main building of the complex that she informed Kayden was Kassani House—named after the river where the Order was founded. They were a few paces short of the stone steps leading up to the main entrance, its large oak doors wide open. Kayden could see a smattering of Sanatsai and Jaymidari congregated on the steps as well as a few more loitering near the doors at the top. At ground level there were a number of wooden benches lined up along the wall of the building. She took particular interest in a male Sanatsai sitting beside a young Sister on one of the benches to the right. He was whispering something in her ear, she was blushing with a demure smile on her face.

"I do have a more serious matter that I wish to bring to the attention of the Council," said Fay, drawing Kayden's focus away from the flirting couple nearby. "It concerns deeply troubling allegations of misconduct made against a fellow Sanatsai. Given the nature of the allegations, the sooner the Council can investigate the veracity of the accusations the better." She was referring to the revelations about Master Turan, Kayden realised. "I'd like to get Kayden settled in first, if that's all right, but I shall seek you out later this evening to present you with full details of the alleged offences."

"As you wish," replied Idelle, simultaneously releasing her hold on both Fay and Kayden. "Will you be wanting to see Ari immediately?" She raised a hand to signal the nearest Sanatsai, gesturing for him to approach. "I can have a message sent to him right away."

"If you could just let him know I've arrived, and that I would be grateful for a few minutes of his time whenever he is ready, that will be fine."

The Sanatsai signalled over by Idelle stopped in front of the trio of women. "How may I be of service, Sister?"

"Would you kindly convey a message to Rendai Shinadu? I believe he's in the orchards." The Sanatsai nodded in the affirmative. "Please inform him that Danai Annis has arrived," Idelle continued, "and she wishes to see him at his earliest convenience." Addressing Fay, she added, "Would you like Ari's return message sent to your quarters? I assume you'll want to go there now."

Kayden's stomach growled audibly, intruding on the conversation. She looked down, self-consciously, at her feet as Fays eye's turned to her.

"No," Fay said in reply to Idelle, "I'm going to take Kayden to the mess hall." To the Sanatsai messenger she added, "You may bring Ari's response to me there."

"As you wish, Danai."

He nodded in acknowledgement then marched purposefully away, following the path leading around the west wing of Kassani House, en route to the orchards and gardens located in the northwest of the grounds.

"Now that you're here, please don't let me keep you both from a meal," said Idelle cheerily. "I shall return to the Council's chamber." Addressing Fay, she added, "If you should require anything from us during your stay, please don't hesitate to ask."

She shifted her focus to Kayden, affecting a more sober tone as she took hold of the apprentice by both hands. "Heed well the lesson you will learn here, Kayden. Do so, and your lovely face will grace Temis Rulan for many years to come." She released her grip on Kayden's hands then took her leave of master and apprentice.

Kayden watched the elderly Jaymidari float up the stone steps towards the entrance of the building. Her stomach growled noticeably once again.

"Can I assume," began Fay, "that not only did you miss lunch, but you also skipped breakfast too?"

"That would be a safe assumption."

"Follow me."

Falling into step alongside the Sanatsai, Kayden followed Fay as she led them away from the front of Kassani House. The mess hall catering to members of the Order was situated about a hundred yards east of the building, in easy walking distance. They made their way around the corner and Kayden was treated to her first glimpse of the mess hall. She was amazed at the size of it. Not only was it considerably larger than the one back at Antaris campus in terms of the area it covered, it was also three storeys tall.

"That is the mess hall?" she exclaimed in wonder. "It's huge!" She noted there were four separate entrances in total—that she could see.

"About half a century ago the dining hall inside Kassani House was no longer able to accommodate the number of people present during mealtimes. It became necessary to build a dedicated mess hall big enough to cater for the ever-increasing population. These days the dining hall is used exclusively by the members of the Council, their attendants, and other senior figures within the Order."

They entered the mess hall together via the nearest entrance. Kayden was quietly impressed by the understated beauty of the interior. She imagined it to be akin to the dining halls of the nobility throughout the Nine Kingdoms. Silently she followed Fay's lead down one aisle, observing as the woman nodded the occasional greeting to the small number of Sanatsai and Jaymidari they passed.

"The evening meal is still a couple of hours away from being dished up," Fay informed Kayden. "But I will ask the kitchen to rustle up a light meal for us." She came to a halt at one of the tables nearest the serving counter outside the kitchen. She instructed Kayden to take a seat, before departing towards the counter.

The two middle-aged women behind the counter wore plain clothing beneath their aprons. Kayden was unable to determine if they were Sanatsai or Jaymidari, though it was possible they were neither. She was now aware that not everyone living on the island was a wielder of *Zarantar*. A part of her was fleetingly disappointed when she noticed how the two women's faces lit up radiantly as Fay came to speak with them. *Even the kitchen staff are thrilled to see her?* The observation was enough to cause Kayden to grudgingly question if she had badly misjudged the administrator. Surely a woman as beloved as Fay apparently was couldn't be the horrid bitch she deemed her to be.

A short while later Fay returned to the table carrying a tray laden with a steaming pot of tea, a jar of honey, a bowl of cane sugar, and two porcelain cups. She set it down upon the table then sat opposite Kayden.

"Rina will bring some food out to us shortly." She began to pour some tea into one of the cups. "Help yourself to some tea in the meantime."

Kayden inhaled the aroma wafting from the herbal infusion. "Camomile and spiced apple," she exclaimed.

"There's nothing wrong with your sense of smell." There was a joviality in Fay's quip that Kayden was unaccustomed to hearing.

"It's my favourite blend." Kayden took the teapot from Fay and poured herself some tea into the second cup.

Fay fixed a penetrating gaze upon the apprentice. "It's my favourite, too." She proceeded to add a teaspoon of cane sugar followed by two teaspoons of honey. Kayden stared intently back at her while she stirred her hot beverage. "What is it?"

The cadence of Kayden's spoken words indicated surprise. "That's how I have mine, too."

It had never occurred to Kayden that she and Fay might have anything in common. She'd certainly never contemplated the possibility of sharing similar tastes. But she was beginning to suspect that maybe she and the administrator were more alike than she realised. She also began to speculate that Fay was already aware of such likenesses—that perhaps she reminded Fay of herself in some way. And maybe that was ultimately why the woman seemed to take an instant dislike to her.

She refrained from voicing those thoughts as she finished stirring her tea. She raised the cup to her lips then took a sip. *Mmmmmm!* Liquid paradise in a cup.

One of the two women manning the serving counter, whom Fay had spoken with earlier, arrived at the table a short while later carrying a tray of food. Kayden guessed she must be Rina. The matronly woman promptly laid a plate of fish fritters with a side serving of creamy potato salad in front of Fay, then did the same for Kayden.

"It's not much," said Rina, modestly, "but it should tide you over until the evening meal is served."

"That's fine, Rina," replied Fay. "Thank you."

"If you'd like I can bring you both a slice of apple and pear pie, with cream, in a little while."

"Yes please," piped up Kayden through a mouthful of fish fritter.

"That would be wonderful, Rina," said Fay with a smile.

With that, Rina trotted off back towards the kitchen, and Fay slowly began to eat her meal in silence while Kayden gobbled her own, hungrily.

Eventually, Kayden looked up from her plate to question the Sanatsai.

"Sister Idelle mentioned that I would be learning some kind of lesson while I'm here." She took another sip of tea from her cup. "What kind of lesson are we talking about?"

"That is a very good question." Fay looked thoughtful for a moment. "I suspect you will know the answer before I do."

Kayden was puzzled by Fay's admission that she didn't know. Surely the woman had to know why she had brought an

163

apprentice to Temis Rulan?

"Well, what did she mean when she asked if I was the reason for your visit?" Kayden pressed. "Did you bring me here to have someone else make the decision to expel me and bind my *Zarantar* for you?"

Fay sipped some more tea then set down her cup. "Listen to me carefully, Kayden." Her tone was gravely serious, as was the look on her face. "What the future may hold for you is entirely out of my hands. I've done all I can for you; your fate rests in your own hands now."

"What's that supposed to mean?" asked Kayden in evident frustration.

Rina returned to the table, causing the suspension of the conversation. She placed two small bowls on the table, each one laden with a warm slice of apple and pear pie, and a generous dollop of whipped cream. "Enjoy," she said with a smile, before ambling away and leaving the two diners to continue their meals.

"Thank you, Rina," said Fay, to the departing woman.

As Fay bit into another fish fritter, Kayden attempted to resume their unfinished conversation. "You didn't answer my question."

"Kayden, try to enjoy your meal." Fay began refilling her cup. "All your questions will be answered, one way or another, soon enough. Just be patient."

Feeling as though she had just been unceremoniously dismissed, Kayden quietly ate the last remaining fritter on her plate, before wolfing down what little remained of the potato salad. She set the empty plate aside then set about devouring the apple and pear pie.

"May I ask you a personal question?" Kayden asked finally, through a mouthful of her glorious dessert.

"I doubt I could stop you."

Kayden hesitated momentarily. "What did I do to make you hate me?" She tried but failed to conceal the hurt in her voice.

Looking visibly disquieted, Fay set her teacup down. "Why in the world would you think that I hate you?"

"It's true, isn't it?"

Before Kayden could receive a reply, someone approached the table with purpose, stopping at Fay's side. It was the same Sanatsai who had been tasked with conveying a message to the leader of the Order, announcing Fay's arrival. Kayden didn't hear what was said when he bent forward to whisper in Fay's ear, though it was obviously the return message. Whatever was said, Fay stood up promptly, wiping her hands with a napkin.

"Thank you," Fay said to her Sanatsai counterpart, who silently nodded in acknowledgement then marched away just as swiftly as he had arrived.

"Are we leaving?" asked Kayden, rising up from her seat.

Fay gestured for the apprentice to sit back down. "I'm going to meet with Master Ari now," she said. "You stay here and finish your meal." She stepped away from her chair then pushed it back in towards the table. "I'm not sure how long I will be, but if you finish eating before I return, go back to Kassani House and ask someone to direct you to the third floor common room. I will find you there. On the off-chance anyone should question your presence, just let it be known you are here with me."

Kayden was only half paying attention; her eyes were on Fay's untouched dessert. "So you won't be wanting your pie?" she asked sheepishly.

"Help yourself, Kayden."

She reached across the table, pulling the apple and pear pie closer, while Fay casually departed towards the nearest exit. As Kayden peered back over her shoulder to watch the Sanatsai leave, the woman's words returned to her, reverberating in her mind:

What the future may hold for you is entirely out of my hands. I've done all I can for you; your fate rests in your own hands now.

Fay languidly approached the orchards located in the northwestern quarter of the complex. It was a glorious late afternoon. The sky was clear and blue, the sun was shining, and birds were chirping; summer had well and truly arrived on the island. She inhaled the sweet fragrance of Bramley apples, and pears, carried upon the air by a cool, gentle breeze. The scent made her wonder why she had not visited Temis Rulan, even once, during the past three years. Casting her gaze around the orchard she could see several Sisters picking fruit, enjoying the sunshine. But the person she had come to see was the mixed heritage Sanatsai seated on a wooden bench, casually plucking pears from a tree courtesy of his invocation of *Yuksaydan*, sending them floating into the basket of a nearby quintet of Jaymidari. A smile threatened to break out on Fay's face at the sight of it as she headed towards him.

The Sanatsai stood up in anticipation as he caught sight of her silent approach.

Ari Shinadu wasn't just a Sanatsai, and serving member of the Council. He was the visionary who had founded the Order at the tail end of the Great War, seven decades ago. It was a moment in history that forever altered the political landscape of the Nine Kingdoms. And though, officially, each of the thirteen members who comprised the Council were of equal rank and status, Ari was undeniably the leader of the institution he founded. Fay was proud to have the distinction of calling him, not only a friend, but her best friend—though their relationship hadn't always been so cordial. No one would ever guess that once upon a time they had been bitter rivals. It wouldn't have been an exaggeration to call them avowed enemies. But that was a lifetime ago. Since then Ari had saved her life, become a trusted friend, and more than that, she credited him for helping her to develop into the woman she now was.

Fay came to a halt in front of Ari and reciprocated his welcoming smile with one of her own. She gave him a derisory look when he tentatively offered her his hand. He swiftly withdrew the offered limb to open both arms wide, inviting a hug. Fay was more than happy to accept this time, stepping into his embrace, wrapping her arms tightly around him while his wrapped around her.

"It's good to see you, old friend," said Ari, holding her close. "I've missed you these past three years."

They released each other from the fervent hug. "Let's have a little less of the *old*, thank you," Fay said with a smile. "You have a few years on me, old timer."

Ari chuckled. "Yes, thank you for reminding me." He paused briefly, the mirth slowly vanishing from his face. His next words were uttered in a more serious tone. "Your visit today is most unexpected, Fay—the first since you took on the administrator's position at Antaris campus three years ago."

"I never intended to stay away for so long." Her words were tinged with regret; she had missed the place.

"And now...here you are." Ari's eyes searched hers. "Though you weren't prepared to tell the Council the reason for your visit, only that it concerned one of your apprentices whom I understand you've brought here with you." There was no disapproval in his tone or demeanour, just curiosity. "I have to confess, Fay, you have me rather intrigued."

"In a nutshell, I have an urgent but delicate matter I need to discuss with you," she glanced discreetly at the nearby quintet of Sisters, "*and only you.*"

Ari had no difficulty taking the hint. "Very well," he replied. "Walk with me to the flower garden. You can fill me in on this urgent but delicate matter, there. In the meantime, tell me how life as a campus administrator has been treating you."

They set off together, walking side-by-side along a grey brick pathway en route to the nearby flower garden. Fay gave her counterpart a summary of what her three years at Antaris had entailed, thus far, culminating with the fight in the old arena earlier that day. Her usual, mundane routine at Antaris was a far cry from the hazardous missions she had undertaken on behalf of the Order in years gone by. But being the campus administrator had been a rewarding experience, nonetheless.

A short while later the pair were entering the flower gardens; it was a breathtaking sight to behold. In every direction there was a dazzling array of floral arrangements. Flowerbeds of assorted blossoms: roses, bluebells, tulips, lavenders, daffodils and more, all immaculately maintained and in full bloom. The concomitant shrubs, hedgerows and trees were likewise well tended, the flawless lawns trimmed. All around, the air carried the sound of birdsong and a dizzying blend of floral fragrances, while, here and there, squirrels scampered, to and fro. The flower garden was a decidedly picturesque venue for a most unpleasant conversation.

There were several people scattered about the flower garden. Fay and Ari sought out a nice secluded spot away from potential prying eyes and ears. They eventually stopped at her favourite spot—a bench in the shade of a willow tree.

Sitting down, Ari invited Fay to take a seat beside him. "So, old friend," he began, "what is it that troubles you to the extent you cannot discuss it with the other members of the Council?"

"I have grave concerns about the future of the apprentice I have brought with me from Antaris." Fay replied soberly. "Things finally came to a head last night, making me realise I'm not the right person to address the matter."

"Tell me about this apprentice."

"Her name is Kayden Jayta—"

"Isn't that the apprentice who completed the 'capture the box' exercise?" Ari interrupted. "And assaulted a Sanatsai in the process, as I understand it."

"That's correct."

"I don't believe I heard the full story of how she accomplished the feat," Ari mused.

"All you really need to know is that Kayden is more advanced than any other level seven apprentice."

"Very well. Do go on. Her name is Kayden Jayta..."

"Yes," continued Fay. "Born and raised in the Kingdom of Astana, but of Vaidasovian descent. I assume her forebears were migrants from Zenosha. Interestingly, when she was located after her *Zarantar* manifested at fourteen years of age, Kayden was living in the Kingdom of Mirtana."

"A long way from home," Ari noted.

Fay murmured in agreement before continuing. "She... She is... From the moment I first laid eyes upon her..." She was at a loss as to how best to broach what she wanted to reveal about Kayden. What needed to be said would cast the apprentice in a very negative light; there was no getting around that.

"Fay?" Ari cut in. "I know I never questioned you about it at the time—I figured you had your reasons—but can I assume Kayden was the reason why you requested the administrator's position at Antaris?"

"Oh, yes," she affirmed. "If you recall, it happened upon my return from being part of the delegation that carried out the annual inspection at Antaris campus that year.

"Kayden had my attention the moment I first laid eyes on her. She was clearly very gifted, and I was impressed with the speed at which she absorbed instruction, not to mention her exemplary control and mastery of her *Zarantar*. But I also had concerns. Kayden was so driven and focussed, so determined to excel and be the best at everything she did. I have never seen such dedication in an apprentice before."

"Why would that be cause for concern?" queried Ari. "Kayden sounds like the model apprentice; if only they could all be so driven."

"It's not her drive, in and of itself, that troubles me. It's what's driving her that has me worried."

"And what is it that's driving her?"

"I don't know, I've never asked her," admitted Fay. "Not that I would get an honest answer from her even if I did. Nonetheless, though she covers it up well, when I look at Kayden I can see it: a traumatic event from her past that she hasn't come to terms with yet. Something she is unable to let go of."

"If you are correct, I can understand why that might elicit sympathy. But I fail to see why it would trouble you enough to break protocol by bringing Kayden here."

"Ari, a person can only bottle up their pain and anger for so long," reasoned Fay. "Sooner or later it will come out. In Kayden's case, when it does come out it could have profoundly tragic consequences."

The conversation paused for a moment. Ari was evidently attempting to parse the point Fay was trying to make. He finally broke the silence to admit, "I'm still not sure I get what you're asking of me, Fay. From where I sit you are the ideal person to guide a troubled apprentice."

"Regrettably, in this instance, I'm not," she conceded. "Truth be told, Kayden and I have never got on well with each other. We have butted heads numerous times since I took the administrator's position, and our clashes have been increasing in frequency and severity over the past year. Last night things actually threatened to turn violent. If one of my staff hadn't walked in on us... I don't know what would have happened."

"My dear friend. I realise there's a larger point you're trying to convey to me, but I'm just not seeing it," said Ari. "Kayden is by no means the first unruly apprentice to be trained by the Order, and she surely won't be the last. So what is so different about her that you refuse to speak of it with the Council?"

Letting out a half-hearted laugh, born of frustration, Fay rose to her feet and turned away from Ari who remained seated on the bench. "You call her an unruly apprentice, and that may be who and what she is today. But it's who and what she may become in the future that should worry you, as it worries me. She is so wilful and sure of herself—"

"Confidence is a virtue," Ari interrupted.

Fay spun around to gaze at her friend. "Ari, there is a fine line between self-assurance and arrogance. Kayden has crossed far beyond that point." Her speech was becoming more fervent, her agitation more apparent. "She shows no humility. She is so certain of her own superiority and, by implication, the inferiority of everyone else around her. She is manipulative, willing to use and exploit other people for her own ends, with no regard for the consequences. She is confrontational, believing power should be employed to cow people—to impose her will upon them."

Fay paused for a moment. When she spoke again her voice was subdued.

"Kayden is such an angry and bitter young woman. Doesn't that remind you of—?"

She couldn't bring herself to finish the sentence. But she didn't have to. She saw realisation appearing on Ari's face. He finally understood.

"I see," he said, gravely. "All the more reason for your concerns to be presented to the Council."

Fay sat back down on the bench, searching Ari's face with forlorn eyes. Kayden's future would be decided by whatever she said next.

"In just two years, the Great War claimed the lives of at least a million people," she began. "That unprecedented loss of life is greater than the combined death tolls of every other conflict in the history of the Nine Kingdoms. Any intimation that history could repeat itself, with Kayden at the centre of it—the catalyst for it... I fear the Council would deem expulsion and the binding of *Zarantar* insufficient sanction."

"You're almost certainly right," agreed Ari. "I'm sure most members of the Council would insist on the ultimate sanction in that case. But if your apprentice is as potentially dangerous as you fear, why shouldn't we eliminate the threat by ending Kayden's life this very day?"

Fay rose to her feet again, Ari following suit this time. She turned away from him then shuffled a couple of paces away from the bench, contemplating.

"I would consider such a course of action as an admission of failure," she said, without looking back, "particularly on my part."

"That's not a reason," said Ari. "Not one the Council will accept."

"Kayden is the most exceptionally gifted apprentice I have ever seen. Her *Zarantar* is very powerful. As strong as yours, maybe even mine. She would be a tremendous asset once inducted into the Order."

"Not good enough!" Again Ari's retort was swift and matter-of-fact. "The same could be said of any other apprentice."

Fay couldn't help but spin around at that. "Oh, come now, Ari," she said incredulously. "For several years, many within the Order, including certain members of the Council, have been bemoaning the quality—or lack thereof—of the graduates being inducted into the Order. Yet now, having identified an apprentice with the potential to be one of the greatest Sanatsai to ever join our ranks, I am expected to provide the Council with justification for not executing her because that isn't deemed good enough."

"Fay, the Council will simply argue that the risk represented by your apprentice outweighs the possible rewards, and right now I'd have a hard time arguing against that. You still haven't given me a reason to allow Kayden to live."

Slowly, Fay closed the gap between herself and Ari. She stared down at her feet for a moment before looking up imploringly into his eyes.

"Dearest friend, I realise my dispraise of Kayden may have already condemned her. But let me tell you this, unequivocally. In spite of the worrisome traits I see in her, hidden beneath it all I also see a compassionate heart belonging to someone who genuinely cares about redressing injustices, and confronting those who prey on the weak. She just needs somebody who is prepared to look beyond her faults, someone who can help her to let go of the pain and anger that is hindering her. Only then will she see the error of her ways and how it is leading her astray.

"Ari, I brought Kayden here because you're the only person I know who is capable of bringing to the surface the great woman I believe she can be, if only you're willing to take that chance—if not for her, then for me."

Placing a hand on Fay's shoulder, Ari gave it a gentle squeeze. "I will see what I can do for your apprentice," he said, gently. "But you must understand, if Kayden demonstrates an unwillingness to mend her ways, she will not be leaving Temis Rulan with you when you go back to Antaris."

"Thank you, that's all I ask."

Ari smiled affectionately. "There's little I wouldn't do for you, old friend. Now, I will go make the necessary preparations immediately. I will be sending for Kayden this evening. But please come see me in my quarters in about...half an hour? Your arrival today is rather fortuitous. While you may have a cocksure apprentice in need of my help, the Council has a demoralised Sanatsai whom I feel could benefit from your assistance."

"As you wish."

Fay remained rooted to the spot as Ari stepped away to walk alone back along the grey brick pathway that would lead him out of the flower garden. She was relieved to have secured a reprieve for Kayden, even if only a temporary one. Although she couldn't be certain what he had planned for the apprentice, there was no doubt Ari was the best person to get through to her.

After a protracted moment in which her thoughts dwelt on

her young charge, Fay remembered that she should probably return to the mess hall to check up on Kayden, if she was still there. After that, she would visit Ari in his quarters to discuss this supposedly demoralised Sanatsai he had mentioned. Like her counterpart, moments earlier, she stepped away from the bench in the shade of the willow tree, and began the walk back to the mess hall, following the grey brick footpath. As she did so, she couldn't help but wonder about the identity of the Sanatsai to whom Ari had been referring.

CHAPTER TEN

Wild Speculation

Kayden thanked Rina for the meal as the matronly woman cleared away her empty dishes. She glanced around the mess hall contemplating whether she should sit and wait for Fay's return, or if she should just make her own way to Kassani House and go to the common room where Fay said she would come find her. She estimated that the Sanatsai had been gone for at least a quarter of an hour by this point, if not longer. There was no telling how long the woman would be gone, or if she even intended to come back, at all. That was reason enough to head to the main building forthwith. Kayden stood up and, without ceremony, headed straight for the nearest exit.

Back outside, Kayden glanced this way and that, taking in the sights of the grounds as she made her way to the front of Kassani House. She wondered what it would be like to call Temis Rulan 'home'. She wondered if she would actually get the opportunity to call it home. She still didn't know the reason for her being there, after all. What she did know was that when Fay departed the mess hall, the woman had looked troubled. It was as though she was dreading having to impart some bad news. But whatever the reason for her still unexplained presence, it couldn't be to expel her and bind her *Zarantar*. There was no real justification for it, not to mention that it could have been done back at Antaris campus.

Kayden shook the negative thoughts from her head as she approached the front of Kassani House. She had attracted a few cursory glances from people while walking to the building, but no one attempted to interfere with her so she paid them no mind. She went up the steps leading up to the main entrance as though she belonged there, and had walked those steps innumerable times before. She proceeded to enter the building in the exact same fashion.

The interior of Kassani House was even more impressive than Kayden imagined. The grandiose foyer was immaculate; she doubted she could successfully locate even a single speck of dust, no matter how hard she looked. She stopped to cast an admiring eye around the place. There was an elaborate chandelier hanging from above, and two large, intricately detailed tapestries on either side of the foyer, adorning the walls. There were a number of abstract sculptures sitting upon marble pedestals and, on the floor just ahead of her, a large mosaic crafted into the insignia of the Order, complete with the inscription: *To Wield Great Power Is To Carry Greater Responsibility.*

Kayden turned her attention to the staircase on her far left, then to the other on her far right. She wasn't sure which one to take, though presumably they both led to the same floors of the building, making a decision between the two redundant.

"You look a little lost, sweetheart." The female voice at her side caught Kayden by surprise. She mentally berated herself for being distracted enough to allow someone to come upon her undetected. "Do you need some help?"

Kayden glanced to see who the voice belonged to. Standing beside her was an unusually tall woman bedecked in the cream and beige garb of a Jaymidari. The Sister had two or three inches on her in height, her blonde wavy hair cascaded down almost to her waist, and her pale, pretty face was welcoming, with sparkling blue eyes and a warm smile. The woman couldn't possibly hail from the Nine Kingdoms; her complexion was all wrong, as was the colour of her hair and eyes. Though she couldn't place the accent, Kayden was able to deduce that her new companion was from one of the lands in the southwest of Karlandria.

"I'm supposed to go to the common room on the third floor," answered Kayden, "but this is my first time here, I'm not really sure where I'm going."

"In that case, why don't you follow me?" offered the Sister. "I can show you the way."

Kayden fell into step beside the statuesque Jaymidari who promptly led her towards the staircase to their left. As they proceeded up the stairs Kayden noticed the Sister staring intently at her.

"My name is Nelda Barinsdattar," said the woman, introducing herself. "And what do they call you, my love?"

"Kayden. Kayden Jayta."

"It's nice to meet you Kayden. And, I must say, you are something of a curiosity...in more ways than one, I suspect."

Uncertain as to whether she had just been complimented or insulted, Kayden simply replied, "What makes you say that, Sister?"

"For one thing," began Nelda, "your uniform indicates that you are still just an apprentice, yet apprentices are never permitted to visit Temis Rulan. So how is it you came to be here?"

"The administrator of the Antaris campus brought me with her today. I don't really know why. But she was called away a short while ago to meet with the leader of the Order. She said that I should go to the third floor common room and wait for her there."

"Interesting!" Judging from the expression on Nelda's face she certainly did find the revelation interesting. "If Fay Annis, of all people, has brought you to Temis Rulan, then you must be a very special young woman indeed. In any event, your master has certainly honoured you with her favour."

Kayden was growing weary of repeatedly hearing that sentiment, though she refrained from objecting.

"Another curiosity is your heritage, if you don't mind my saying so. You are clearly of Vaidasovian extraction," stated Nelda, pointing out the obvious, "but your accent is unmistakably Astanese. While I realise merchants from the empire of Zenosha regularly make the arduous journey across the mountains into Astana and Lirantana, for trading purposes, it's unusual for any to settle down in either kingdom permanently—or long enough to pick up an accent. Consequently, it is extremely rare for the Order to find Astanese subjects of full Vaidasovian descent who manifest the *Zarantar* of the Sanatsai. Prior to you, I was aware of only seven such individuals in the entire history of the Order. And do you know what's even more unusual than that?"

Kayden didn't respond. She had no idea what the correct answer was, though she was certain Nelda would tell her whether she wanted to know or not. And the Sister did not disappoint her.

"You consenting to undertake the ten years apprenticeship to become a full-fledged Sanatsai of the Order," said Nelda answering her own question, leaving Kayden to wonder how and why that was deemed so unusual. "It is unprecedented, in fact. When the previous seven individuals were found and presented with the choice to have their *Zarantar* bound or train to master it, each of them adamantly insisted on having it bound.

"The peoples of Vaidasovia view *Zarantar*, and those who have mastery over it, as evil. The rulers of the continent go to great lengths to kill those believed to be tainted by it, which would explain the choice made by your predecessors. It's also the reason why the Sisterhood has always had to function clandestinely in Vaidasovian territories, and why there has never been a Vaidasovian Sanatsai inducted into the Order. You will become the very first should you successfully complete your training."

They continued their ascent of the staircase making small talk—or more precisely, Nelda spoke while Kayden listened. Upon reaching the third floor, Nelda guided Kayden directly to the common room—its double door entrance wide open. The Sister gave Kayden the go-ahead to enter, before bidding her farewell and departing to resume her duties.

Kayden wandered slowly into the common room and felt the eyes of everyone present upon her. The room stilled and conversations paused abruptly. There were at least two dozen Sanatsai throughout the room, most lounging on couches, some seated on chairs around tables, while one or two were standing idly about. Nobody made an effort to address or confront her, so she sauntered to the row of bookshelves that caught her attention

177

at the far end of the room, and the conversations quickly resumed.

Kayden was curious to know whether Temis Rulan housed volumes that were not available to her in the library back at Antaris campus. A cursory examination of the books on display revealed most of them to be works of fiction. Perhaps not so surprising since the common room was intended for rest and relaxation, rather than being a place for quiet study. The final shelf she checked proved to be an exception. Here she noted that the volumes were principally comprised of history books. There were also biographical works about various historical figures within the Order—Fay Annis was notably the subject of many of these books—as well as the diaries of a number of less well known Sanatsai.

None of the titles on display really jumped out her, but Kayden decided she may as well pick out one book to read, just to pass the time; there was no way of knowing how long she would be waiting for Fay to come and find her. She eventually settled for a memoir entitled, *Dawn of a New Day: The Pledge at Kassani River*, by Ari Shinadu. Though she already knew the story of how the Order was founded, having learned about it during history lessons back at Antaris, it would still be interesting to read about it in Master Ari's own words. She grabbed the book from the shelf then began to look around the room for a secluded spot where she could sit down. The unoccupied small table in the corner, overlooked by an east-facing window, would do just fine—despite being in rather close proximity to a group of six Sanatsai seated on two couches, facing each other across a tea table.

Casually, Kayden made her way to the table with book in hand. She set the volume down upon it then moved one of the chairs around so she could sit facing the window, her back to the rest of the room.

She had not been reading for more than a couple of minutes when her attention was drawn away from the memoir to the conversation taking place between the six Sanatsai sitting nearby. Under normal circumstances Kayden wouldn't deign to eavesdrop on other people. But on this occasion—though the group had lowered their voices—her hearing was acute enough to hear that she was the topic of conversation for the four men and two women, especially the male Sanatsai whom she gathered was called Kassano. For some reason, he in particular seemed to have a bee in his bonnet about her.

"I'm telling you Larita, what other plausible reason could there be for her to bring an apprentice here?" she heard Kassano say.

"Certainly not for the reason you seem to be suggesting," said a female voice Kayden assumed belonged to Larita. "You see, unlike you, Fay Annis is a Sanatsai of impeccable character. She would never abuse her position for her own gratification."

"You might think that," continued Kassano, "but I find it just a little too coincidental that Fay was made the administrator of Antaris campus only days after she led the yearly inspection of the campus. And in the three years since taking up the post she hasn't returned to Temis Rulan once, not even to visit Ari himself. But now she's finally back and she has brought an apprentice with her, in contravention of decades' worth of protocol.

"What about you, Niko? You were part of the inspection team that went to Antaris earlier *this* year. Did you hear any gossip about Fay from members of staff there?"

"There might have been some...rumblings from a few of the instructors," admitted a male voice Kayden had to presume was Niko. "And I did pick up on the general impression, whether it was justified or not, that an ill-disciplined apprentice called Kayden has gained Fay's favour to the point where she is able to escape adequate punishment for her misconduct. But as I said, it was only a small number of instructors who made mention of this. And it's by no means conclusive proof of an inappropriate relationship, as you seem to be implying. Besides, we don't even know if the named apprentice is the same person sitting over there."

Kayden heard an exasperated sigh. It had to be Kassano, frustrated by his inability to get his fellow Sanatsai to buy into his theory—although twisted, juvenile fantasy was probably a far better term for what he was insinuating. To Kayden's mind the very idea was absurd.

179

"Am I really the only person here who can put two and two together?" asked Kassano. "When have any of you ever seen Fay with a man? And now, after three years slumming it as a campus administrator she pays a visit with an attractive female apprentice in tow. None of you can deny the girl is a looker, arguably more beautiful than Fay herself. It seems pretty clear to me that Fay and this apprentice are lovers."

"You idiot!" snapped the other female Sanatsai who wasn't Larita. "Fay is not that way inclined. And the only reason you want to believe otherwise is because your own laughable attempts to charm your way into her bed failed so spectacularly."

There was a brief chorus of laughter at Kassano's expense.

"Belen, if my charm is good enough to get you out of your clothes and into my bed," retorted Kassano, "on more than one occasion I might add, then it's good enough for Fay."

Kayden heard what sounded like a cushion being thrown and finding its target.

"Just because I took pity on you a few times," said Belen, "doesn't mean Fay would give you the time of day."

"Oh, I don't care what you say. And don't act like I'm the only man in the Order who wants to fuck Fay Annis. Even Zanti Alberino failed to get under her cloak when he attempted to seduce her."

"Keep your voices down," urged Larita in a hushed tone, though not quiet enough to prevent Kayden from hearing. "Do you want the apprentice to hear you then report back to Fay?"

Kassano resumed his spiel in a quieter voice. "The point I'm trying to make is, Zanti is a man who has no trouble wooing women. Sometimes it seems as though he's laying down with a different one each day. He surely must have bedded every unmarried female Sanatasai in Temis Rulan by now. It wouldn't surprise me if he's had his way with a few married ones too, probably some of the Sisters as well for that matter. The bottom line is, any woman who passes up the opportunity to get fucked senseless by Zanti, obviously has no interest in men whatsoever."

Kayden hoped the sound that preceded Kassano's yelp was a thump from one of the other Sanatsai. She also quietly lamented that being inducted into the Order wasn't sufficient to prevent some men from being pigs. Belen was right to call Kassano an idiot—he most certainly was. But Kayden resisted the urge to issue some stinging barbs of her own. She didn't want the Sanatsai to know she was eavesdropping on their conversation.

"Kassano, would you give it a rest," said Larita, clearly getting annoyed. "Fay would never take an apprentice as a lover, it is prohibited. And, as Belen mentioned, there's no grounds for believing she is inclined towards women in that way. Besides, to answer your earlier question: have we ever seen her with a man? Before you were inducted into the Order, Fay was married to a Sanatsai from Shintana called, Renik Katarnian—Marit's older brother."

Kayden's ears pricked up at that titbit of information. Fay was married? *Who in the world would marry such a cold, detached, and quite possibly frigid woman?* she wondered. But Larita had used the past tense, so whoever this Renik Katarnian was had obviously cut his losses and divorced her.

"As for why you never see her with a man today...some people just never get over the death of a spouse."

Fay's husband was dead? Kayden almost felt a little pang of guilt for assuming the marriage had ended in divorce.

"Or maybe Fay simply hasn't met another man worthy of her affections." Larita concluded.

"Or..." drawled Kassano. *What inanities is he going to utter now?* thought Kayden in annoyance. "Maybe Fay has recently acquired an appreciation for the gentler sex, courtesy of her nubile young apprentice." He affected a decidedly lecherous tone of voice to add, "It can't have escaped your notice she's Vaidasovian. And you know what they say about Vaidasovian women."

"Actually, no we haven't heard what they say." Belen's tone suggested she had heard what was said about Vaidasovian women but gave such tales no credence, not to mention she clearly thought Kassano a fool for even bringing it up. "Why don't you enlighten us?"

"Well, not only is it said that Vaidasovian women have insatiable needs, they are also said to be so skilled in carnal pleasures they can literally drive a person to insanity. I've even heard stories of men dying from sheer ecstasy between the sheets. If true, no one could really blame Fay for succumbing to temptation."

"Oh! In that case, you must be right," said Belen with mock sincerity. "But there is only one way for us to be certain." Kayden could tell from the woman's tone that she was baiting Kassano. "You'll have to go over and work your charm on the apprentice, right now. If she responds favourably to your overtures, then presumably you're mistaken. But if she spurns your advances, we can safely assume that she and Fay truly are lovers."

Well played. Kayden was beginning to like Belen. As for Kassano, he would have to be an even bigger fool than she thought if he took the bait.

"That's not a bad idea." He had taken the bait. "And if it turns out that I am wrong about them being lovers, it may still present me with the chance to learn just how accurate those stories about Vaidasovian women are."

Kayden mentally prepared herself for what to do if Kassano did try to approach her as suggested.

The conversation between the six Sanatsai ceased. She heard someone get up from one the couches behind her—if it was Kassano he was making a big mistake. She listened to footsteps make the short journey from the couch to her table, halting on her right hand side. She didn't look up from her book; she may as well keep up the pretence of reading.

"Greetings, apprentice. I—"

"No!" said Kayden, without looking up.

"I'm sorry?"

Turning her head to the right, Kayden looked up at Kassano. The Sanatsai was over six feet tall, with a muscular physique, rugged features, short dark hair, and an immaculately groomed goatee. He was a surprisingly well put together specimen of a man; she could certainly see why Belen would lay with him. Besides, in all likelihood it was the only thing he was good for.

"Whatever it is, the answer is no."

"But you don't even know what I want," Kassano replied

182

awkwardly.

Kayden frowned. "Of course I know what you want, you're a man."

Folding his arms across his chest, Kassano inquired, "Meaning what, exactly?" He appeared displeased that his charm offensive was off to a bad start.

"Meaning that—like all men—you want what you cannot have."

In response to the stifled laughter of his cohorts close by, Kassano leaned down towards Kayden, placing both hands on the table, glaring into her eyes.

"That's quite a tongue you have," he said in a hushed tone. "I assume when you're alone with your master it gets put to more productive use, though I can think of better ways for you to make use of that pretty mouth of yours."

Kayden rose sharply to her feet, causing Kassano to flinch and take half a step backward as he stood upright. She glared up at the Sanatsai, not caring that he stood four inches taller than she did.

"Would you care to repeat that?" She matched her tone to that of Kassano.

"Is everything all right?"

Kayden was bemused by the speed with which Kassano's head spun around at the sound of Fay's voice. The woman had surreptitiously joined them, unseen and unheard, standing within touching distance. Kassano was obviously worried about how much Fay had overheard, though he swiftly composed himself to eliminate the guilty expression he wore, replacing it with a casual, welcoming smile.

"Fay, I heard you were back. I was just introducing myself to your lovely apprentice."

"Is that right, Kayden?"

Kayden refused to tear her simmering gaze away from the poor excuse for a Sanatsai while she answered Fay. "Actually, your colleague wanted to know if my insatiable Vaidasovian needs, coupled with my insanity-inducing carnal skills had tempted you into taking me as your lover."

Judging from the way Kassano's countenance blanched,

Kayden knew that Fay was glowering at him. She peered back over her shoulder for confirmation. She was right. Fay's face was like thunder.

"Oh come on, Fay..." began Kassano, before a withering look from the senior Sanatsai prompted him to adopt a more formal address. "Danai Annis, I'm afraid there's been some kind of misunderstanding. I was just—"

"Kassano, would you excuse us, please?" Fay's tone was neutral; her face was not. "I would like to speak with my apprentice, alone."

He didn't have to be asked twice. Kassano quickly withdrew, taking leave of the two women, though he did not return to his spot on the nearby couch. Instead he headed straight for the exit. As he passed the two couches where his colleagues were now looking as innocent as new born babies, he glared at one of the female Sanatsai—Kayden didn't need to guess that she must be Belen—whom he no doubt blamed for his own indiscretion.

"So you found your way here all right?" Fay asked rhetorically, as she pulled a second chair out from the table. "Please, have a seat. We have a few things to discuss." She waited for Kayden to sit back down before doing so herself. "First of all, let me apologise for any offence caused just now. As you are no doubt already aware, beauty can be a disadvantage to a woman, even within the Order. Although we may be more egalitarian than the world outside, you may still find that there are times when you will have to work twice as hard as you should to earn the respect of certain people."

Kayden merely offered a nod of the head, indicating she understood.

"Now, let us get down to business," Fay continued. "I spoke with Master Ari a short while ago, and he would like to meet you."

Kayden's eyes widened in surprise. The founder of the Order wanted to meet her? "Meet me? When? Why?" It was all she could think to say, her heart was suddenly racing.

"When he is ready to see you, he will send for you," replied Fay. "As for why... I hope that becomes clear once you've spent some time with him."

So, she was going to meet with Ari Shinadu, the man who founded the Order at the end of the Great War. Was that the reason why Fay brought her to Temis Rulan? Should she ask and find out? she wondered.

"So...will it be just Master Ari?" she inquired, trying not to sound too enthusiastic. "Will I not be meeting the rest of the Council?"

"Today would not be a good day for you to stand before the Council." There was something odd in Fay's voice that Kayden couldn't help picking up on; she was holding something back. But, what? "In the meantime, while you're waiting for Master Ari's summons perhaps I could arrange for someone to give you a guided tour of the grounds and the facilities here."

"Someone else?" She added, suspiciously, "Where will you be?"

"I will be meeting Master Ari again in a little while, to discuss a problem he'd like me to deal with during my visit.

"Alternatively, if you'd like to forgo the tour, I can take you up to my quarters, now, so you can get some rest, and relax in peace."

Kayden was glad Kassano was no longer in the common room, sitting with his nattering Sanatsai cohorts nearby. She could imagine how the invitation to Fay's quarters would be interpreted. Nonetheless, it was the more appealing of the two options. She really could not face walking around the grounds, potentially having to put up with people gawking and gossiping—wildly speculating that she'd slept her way into Fay's good graces, thereby earning a trip to Temis Rulan.

"I think it would probably be best if I waited in your quarters," she said. "There will be time enough to get to know my way around this place once I've been inducted into the Order."

"Very well." Fay rose to her feet. "Follow me."

Rising up from her chair, Kayden fell into step behind Fay, but they weren't able to leave the common room immediately. As the pair tried to make their way to the exit they were repeatedly stopped by Sanatsai who wished to convey their greetings to Fay, starting with Larita, who also apologised for not preventing Kassano from bothering her young apprentice. This was followed by several more firmly gripped forearms, embraces, and kisses on the cheek for Fay, making it even more evident to Kayden just how revered the burgundy-haired Sanatsai was.

Once all the salutations were concluded, they were eventually able to extricate themselves from the common room.

Having followed Fay up two more flights of stairs to the fifth floor, and then through a maze of corridors, Kayden was grateful when they finally halted outside the door to Fay's quarters. When she wasn't admitted into the room right away she suspected her assumption that Fay's quarters lay on the other side of the door must be incorrect. She glanced quickly at the other woman to see what she was waiting for. Fay had a faraway look on her face as she stared blankly at the door. It was as though she was reminiscing about something. Kayden couldn't help but wonder what the Sanatsai was thinking at that exact moment.

Was Fay having second thoughts about the wisdom of bringing Kayden to Temis Rulan? Was she harbouring regret about something she had done, or was going to do? Fay certainly hadn't been completely forthcoming about the reasons for their trip away from Antaris. Or perhaps it was something much more mundane. Fay might just be embarrassed about the messy state in which she left her quarters when she left three years ago.

Kayden's pondering was cut short when Fay finally pushed the unlocked door open and stood aside, gesturing an invitation for Kayden to enter first.

"You didn't lock your door before you left for Antaris?" queried Kayden as she stepped across the threshold into Fay's quarters.

Fay's brief chuckle was barely audible. "This is the last place in the world where I need to worry about theft." The amusement in her voice was plain as day. "Nobody here would ever steal, even if they could get away with it." Fay followed Kayden through the door then closed it behind herself. "Besides, the only two people who would have entered my quarters during my absence are Sister Bettina, whom I requested to dust the place once a week while I'm gone, and Master Ari."

Interesting, thought Kayden. *Master Ari has permission to come and go from her quarters as he pleases? Maybe he and Fay are more than just friends and colleagues. Maybe they...* Kayden quickly abandoned that line of thought. Since Master Ari had founded the Order seven decades ago he would be old enough to be Fay's grandfather; great grandfather, even.

Kayden paced further into Fay's quarters, glancing here and there. The spacious main interior was divided into three distinct spaces. The smallest area was intended for dining; there was a small dining table adorned with a chequered dining cloth. The second area was clearly set up to be Fay's study, complete with a mahogany desk strewn with assorted writing paraphernalia and sheets of vellum, in addition to the three bookcases lining the nearby wall, holding several volumes.

As she ambled around the largest of the three areas—which accounted for over half the available space—the world plush entered Kayden's mind. It was the perfect word to summarise her surroundings. She would describe it as a regal living room, furnished with an upholstered sofa and two matching upholstered armchairs, between which was a polished tea table, all set atop a beautiful, intricately patterned Zenoshanese rug. To the right of this seating arrangement was a small table upon which were the ornate board and pieces of an unfinished game of chess. Hanging on the wall, overlooking the board game, were three paintings. Each work of art depicted a beautiful scenic landscape, three locations that were, presumably, all real places in the Nine Kingdoms. Kayden recognised the middle picture, it was a painting of the Lilac Valley in the Kingdom of Shintana. Though she had never been there herself, it was famously the location of the decisive battle that had brought an end to the Great War. If she had to guess, she would say the other two paintings were also places in Shintana, which would make sense, for though she didn't know with certainty where Fay was born and raised, the administrator's accent was Shintanese, so it was likely the paintings reminded her of home.

"Do you play?" Fay asked Kayden from behind as she lingered before the chessboard, admiring the paintings.

"Chess?" Kayden tore her attention away from the paintings to glance at Fay, now standing beside her. "Someone taught me how to play, once upon a time. I never enjoyed it. I would always lose...and I hate losing. Apparently, I lack the patience to ever be a good chess player."

"Well, chess is a game of strategy," mused Fay, "so patience is a beneficial attribute to possess if you wish to win." She gestured at the unfinished game before them. "Master Ari and I had been playing this particular game for three days before I departed for Antaris to take on the administrator's position."

Kayden glanced back at Fay, fixing her with an incredulous stare. "You actually sat here for three days playing a single game, yet couldn't finish in that time?" She stepped away from the table and the unfinished game of chess. "Rather you than me," she muttered, casually walking to the sofa with Fay trailing behind. She halted in front of one of the armchairs but remained standing. For reasons she could not explain, she felt obliged to wait for permission to sit.

"Please, have a seat," offered Fay. Kayden did so, after removing her cloak and then her sword, and Fay did likewise, sitting down in the armchair opposite the apprentice. "I realise you ate a short while ago but if you would like something to drink I can have some fresh water or fruit juice brought up to my quarters."

"No...thank you."

Kayden was having difficulty interacting with the new, unfamiliar version of the administrator. Over the course of the past three years their relationship had consistently been antagonistic, even adversarial. It was hard to reconcile the recent change in the woman. Only a few hours ago she was utterly convinced Fay wanted to kill her. Now, she didn't know what to think.

"I'll be leaving you on your own again, in a little while," continued Fay. "In the meantime, are there any questions you'd like to ask?"

Kayden glanced idly around Fay's quarters. "As it happens," she began, "it just occurred to me that in my five years as an apprentice I never once thought to ask about something that has been staring me in the face the whole time."

"Go on," prompted Fay.

"Where does the Order get its money from, to be able to live like this?" She gestured at her surroundings. "To establish a city to rival many in the Nine Kingdoms, not to mention the financing of nine campuses to train hundreds of apprentice Sanatsai. It can't all be coming from the royal treasuries."

"As a matter of fact, the Order doesn't receive funding from any of the kingdoms. It was deemed vital, from the outset, that financial independence be ensured in order to avoid becoming pawns for whomever might hold our purse strings. We are able to remain self-sufficient through the earnings of ourselves and the Sisterhood, selling goods and services to the public." Fay smiled wryly at Kayden. "I realise that many of you apprentices do not fully understand or appreciate having to learn vocations such as carpentry, masonry or pottery, but it's how you will generate revenue for the Order when you're not on active duty."

That made perfect sense Kayden had to concede. But truthfully, though her curiosity about the Order's finances had genuinely been piqued, the answer to the question wasn't that important to her in the scheme of things. There was a more serious question she wanted to ask of the Sanatsai sitting across from her, but something was preventing her from doing so. Whether it was embarrassment or fear of what the answer might be, she couldn't say for certain. So she just stared silently at Fay, mulling over the appropriateness of asking the question.

"If there is something else you wish to ask..." Fay prompted, once again.

Kayden leaned forward in her chair. "Before we arrived in Temis Rulan you told me that you volunteered to take the administrator's post at Antaris campus."

"Correct."

"But when I pressed you about why, you said that your reasons were your own."

"Correct, again."

"Well, it seems clear to me now that I'm the reason for your presence at Antaris. From the day you first took the position I was constantly the focus of your undue attention. Others may not have noticed it, but you always made me feel singled out. The way looked at me was different, the way you spoke to me was different, the way you treated me was different. Initially, I just thought you disliked Vaidasovians. Eventually, I thought it must be jealousy, or maybe you felt threatened by me somehow. I didn't care to know the actual reason, I just knew I hated you for it.

"But now? I don't even think it's any of those things. With everything that has happened over the last few hours, the things I've heard said about you. It's obvious, now, that your fixation with me is personal. So, I have to ask... Are you in love with me?"

Fay offered no response. In fact, Kayden could see how the woman was trying her hardest to contain an outburst of laughter—a struggle she quickly lost. The placement of a hand over her mouth proved a futile gesture as she started laughing uncontrollably.

"This isn't a laughing matter," Kayden blurted out in exasperation. "If you're in love with me, I need to know, because whatever feelings you have for me, they're having a negative impact on my life."

It took a little while, but the laughter ended once Fay managed to recompose herself. "Please forgive my inconsiderate reaction to your question, Kayden." She sounded genuinely contrite. "In all honesty, a part of me wishes that I was in love with you—at least then I'd know how to deal with the matter. The truth is, you are the reason I requested the administrator's post at Antaris, but not for any of the reasons you have speculated."

"Then, why?"

"Because..." Fay's protracted pause was fraught with hidden meaning that eluded Kayden. "Because...you remind me so much of someone I knew many years ago."

The revelation required tremendous effort on Fay's part, Kayden realised.

"Someone who made many terrible, costly choices. Horrendous mistakes that harmed more people than you can imagine. And though it is not in my power to alter what occurred in the past, I feel an obligation to prevent you from making similar mistakes, to do whatever I must to prevent history from repeating."

Finally, Kayden knew the truth—or as much of it as Fay was prepared to reveal. But the answer wasn't enough to mollify her. It simply wasn't fair of Fay to use the actions of an acquaintance from her past to influence and justify her mistreatment of someone else, today. She was her own person. It didn't matter if she reminded Fay of someone she once knew. Being made to pay the price for somebody else's mistakes, just to make Fay feel better about herself, was unacceptable.

"Who exactly is this person you're referring to?" Kayden demanded to know. "And why should I allow you to continue taking your unresolved issues with this person out on me?"

Fay rose to her feet. "I think that's enough questions for now," she said, "I really must get going. In the meantime, make yourself at home. If you need to lie down for a while, my bedchamber is right through there." She pointed to an open door several feet away. "And if you would like to freshen up, the bathroom is over there." She pointed at the closed door further away. "I'm not sure if I will see you again before Master Ari summons you. But I hope I don't need to remind you to afford him all the respect he deserves."

"No, of course not."

"There's one more thing I should show you before I leave." Fay headed towards her study. "Follow me." Kayden trailed behind to join her standing at the mahogany desk. "If you should need anything while I am gone, you can signal for one of the Sisters to attend you, with this." Fay tapped the small glass sphere set upon a small wooden stand on her desk. "It's a beacon. Activate it by invoking *Yuksaydan*, then someone will arrive for you shortly after."

"All right, fine," said Kayden. "Anything else?"

"That's everything. Now, I really should be going."

Kayden was a little unsettled by Fay's hesitation before she walked away, but it was the expression on her face and the look in her eyes, more than anything else, that unnerved her. It appeared as though the woman wanted to say one final goodbye, almost as if she was concerned she might not get another opportunity to do so. If there was a possibility the two of them would never see each other again, Kayden knew it was pointless to ask why, so she simply stood and watched as Fay exited her quarters.

Once the door shut she let out an audible sigh. She remained frustrated by the Sanatsai, as well as the situation she found herself in. Notwithstanding everything else she had learned since arriving in Temis Rulan, Kayden still did not have a clear idea of why she was even there, though she suspected that would change once she met Master Ari.

Kayden diverted her attention to the nearby bookcases. There was no telling how long she would be waiting for the summons to meet the head of the Order, but if she had to remain in Fay's quarters until then, what better way to spend that time than reading a good book? She began to peruse Fay's collection, which seemed to consist entirely of fictional works and poetry. A few of the books were even in foreign languages, including—much to Kayden's surprise—Zenoshanese, the mother tongue of her parents. She quickly settled for the novel, *The Last Of The Saharbashi*, by famed Shintanese author, Delano Tarelis—a story she had read twice previously, but was well worth reading for a third time. She grabbed it from the shelf then went back to the armchair she had vacated moments earlier, to sit and read.

CHAPTER ELEVEN

First Impressions

Fay didn't have a long walk ahead of her. Ari's quarters were situated on the same floor as her own, though in the north wing of Kassani House. She slowly navigated through several quiet corridors, encountering only a one fellow Sanatsai and a couple of Jaymidari, each of whom acknowledged her with a warm, welcoming smile.

Making her way to the appointment with Ari, Fay's thoughts lingered on two matters, though one was more pressing than the other. She wondered about the identity of the Sanatsai having the crisis of confidence Ari briefly touched upon in the flower garden. But more importantly, she wondered how Ari intended to get Kayden to open up to him, how he planned to help her come to terms with the source of the pain and anger she was bottling up inside. If he was unsuccessful, that pain and anger would lead Kayden inexorably to an ignominious end.

Fay entered the corridor leading to Ari's quarters, at the same moment Ari strolled into view from the opposite end. She guessed he had only just finished finalising the arrangements for whatever it was he had planned for Kayden that evening.

"You're early," said Ari as he joined Fay outside the door to his quarters.

"My troublesome apprentice began to ask some awkward questions," she replied ruefully. "I had to leave her in my quarters, then I came straight here. The sooner you can meet with her the better I will feel."

Opening the door, Ari stood aside to allow Fay inside. "You're assuming your apprentice can be reformed, and that I can help to bring that about."

"You've done it once before." She heard the door closing behind them. "With someone unspeakably worse than Kayden, I might add."

"I had more time and more leeway before." Ari indicated with a hand for Fay to have a seat on the upholstered sofa to their left, while he headed straight ahead to the desk set in front of the large Palladian window. "I too have had to fend off some awkward questions in the last few minutes."

Taking a seat on the sofa, Fay watched Ari gather up some documents from his cluttered desk.

"Already three other members of the Council have inquired about why you have brought an apprentice here with you," continued Ari as he ambled towards the sofa, documents in hand. "The longer she remains here the more questions will be asked. Eventually, I'll have no choice but to bring the rest of the Council up to speed, although you can be sure Idelle is already fully aware of what is going on; she's always been an incredibly perceptive woman." He sat down beside Fay. "The bottom line is, Kayden only has the rest of today, and maybe some of tomorrow, to save herself."

"Why so soon?" asked Fay in dismay.

"Because, if she can't persuade me, before midday tomorrow that your worries about her aren't fully justified, I will have no option but to convene a meeting of the Council. And while most of my colleagues won't understand the significance of *you* bringing these concerns, once they are informed of the nature of the concerns about your apprentice..." Ari trailed off, finishing his sentence wasn't necessary.

Fay was crestfallen. Ari's pronouncement cut her like a knife. Though she wasn't a woman given to admitting defeat, her hope of saving Kayden had been severely dented. The likelihood of Ari successfully getting through to the apprentice during the remaining hours of the day was so remote as to be non-existent.

"I know it's not what you wanted to hear." Ari reached for her hand to give it a comforting squeeze. "But don't be disheartened, old friend. There is always hope, until there isn't."

Looking into her friend's eyes, Fay smiled affectionately. If anyone could pull off the impossible, it was Ari.

"For now, let us table this discussion about your apprentice," he said. "I have a task that you are eminently qualified to tackle. But first... I need to tell you something."

There was a drawn-out pause while Ari fidgeted with the documents in his hand. Fay knew him well enough to know the look on his face; he was about to impart some bad news.

"I regret to have to inform you like this," he began, "but while you were away, Marit Katarnian was killed during a mission."

Fay's heart seemed to skip a beat. Her breath caught in her throat. Marit was the younger brother of her late husband who had also lost his life while on duty. She had subsequently always felt a sense of responsibility towards him after the passing of his sibling, she felt duty-bound to ensure that he didn't meet the same fate. Hearing of his death was a crushing blow, especially as it had occurred while she was away.

"When did it happen? How?"

"A little over five months ago. He was—"

"Five months!" Fay gasped in shock. "Why am I only hearing about this now, Ari?"

"For one thing, I felt an obligation to let you know, personally—face-to-face," said Ari in a placating tone. "I didn't want you to learn of it via a long distance message. Secondly, the mission was in Anzarmenia and, as you know, the Order has no jurisdiction outside the Nine Kingdoms. We weren't able to acknowledge that Marit had been on a sanctioned mission. We had to deny even being aware of his presence in the realm altogether.

"As it is, the incident caused some diplomatic tension, not just between Anzarmenia and Darmitana, but also between ourselves and Darmitana. We had to pressure King Orinoso into interceding on behalf of the Order to have Marit's body recovered and returned for burial. As a result, he had to agree to make certain concessions to the queen of Anzarmenia, and believe me, he and his advisers were far from happy about it. It's fair to say our standing with the Darmitanese has taken a bit of a knock."

After a prolonged silence, during which Fay took stock of what she had just been told, she finally inquired, "What was the nature of the mission?"

"This is the report detailing the mission and outcome." Ari dropped the documents he was holding, down on the tea table in front of them. "Anything you want to know will be in there."

"I want to hear it from you," pressed Fay.

He knows me well enough to realise I'm not going to take no for an answer, thought Fay, and sure enough he reluctantly began to narrate, in full, the mission in Anzarmenia, and the reason for it.

Almost a year ago the Order became aware of a cult movement that had become active in rural areas of southern Anzarmenia. Under normal circumstances someone starting a cult abroad would be of no concern. This occasion, however, couldn't be described as normal. What made this cult so worrisome was the type of people it was drawing into its ranks. Among the followers of the group were a disproportionately large number of *Zarantar* wielders.

Anzarmenia did not have an equivalent of the Order to control those of its population who manifested the *Zarantar* of the Sanatsai. While such people were highly sought after by the military, there was no obligation to enlist. The unaffiliated Sanatsai of the realm were left entirely to their own devices, to live their lives in any way they wished, provided they broke no laws. If that wasn't disturbing enough, the authorities did not even deem it necessary to outlaw learning the ways of the Saharbashi—on that same basis: as long as no laws were being violated, there was no harm. It was a naive position to take, to be sure. Nonetheless, the Order had yet to uncover evidence of the cult recruiting any Saharbashi into its ranks.

It was the increasing number of reports coming from the Sisterhood in Anzarmenia—of a small but steady flow of Jaymidari abandoning their calling, to join the cult—that prompted greater scrutiny of the group. It was troubling enough that the cult had free rein to recruit unaffiliated Sanatsai in Anzarmenia. They could even recruit Saharbashi if they wished. But it was the ability to attract followers from the ranks of the Sisterhood that made its activities that much more concerning. Although the cult had not done anything that could be construed as threatening or dangerous, the Order couldn't ignore the most obvious motivation for starting a movement that assembled large numbers of individuals who wielded *Zarantar*.

Six months ago the Council authorised a clandestine mission inside Anzarmenia, to investigate.

On account of his not too distant Anzarmenian ancestry—giving him some knowledge of the realm, its people, history, culture and language—Marit Katarnian was tasked with carrying out the assignment to infiltrate the cult, to identify its leader, and conclusively establish the aims and objectives of the group. Marit decided to take a young, inexperienced Sanatsai with him to play the role of potential recruit for the cult, while he oversaw the mission from a distance. His eventual choice, Kenit Darbandian, was born and raised in Anzarmenia before his parents migrated north to the Kingdom of Darmitana when he was eleven years of age. In theory, this made Kenit an ideal candidate for the mission as he spoke the language fluently and would have no difficulty passing for a local.

Ordinarily, an inexperienced Sanatsai as new to the Order as Kenit was wouldn't be thrust to the forefront of a mission, particularly one abroad. The decision was the result of Marit's concern that the large numbers of former Sisters in the cult increased the likelihood he would be recognised as being from the Order, if he played the role of potential recruit himself. Besides, the mission was deemed to be low risk.

From the progress reports being sent back to the Order by Marit, the mission was seemingly going according to plan–Kenit had been recruited and was going through an indoctrination period at one of the cult's communes, all the while trying to learn more about the goals of the group. The final message received from Marit, two days before his death, provided some deeper insights into how the cult operated, but still very little about the identity of the group's mysterious leader. However, Marit was pleased to report that Kenit was due to leave the commune in the next few days to meet the unidentified man with a group of fellow recruits. It was his intention to shadow Kenit to this meeting in order to see for himself the man who could persuade scores of committed Jaymidari to abandon their calling.

That meeting did not go as planned.

"From what Kenit was subsequently able to tell us," said Ari, "the cult suspected him of being a spy almost from the start. What they didn't know was whom he was spying for. The proposed meeting with the leader of the group was actually a trap intended to draw out any accomplices.

"That evening, Kenit was among a dozen-strong party that journeyed to a woodland a few miles from the commune. Come nightfall he was taken by surprise when the rest of the group turned on him. They subdued him, with little difficulty, before threatening him with decapitation if he did not reveal who sent him to spy on the group. At this point Marit, who was tailing them, entered the fray to rescue his charge. But his adversaries were well prepared; it was an ambush. Up to a dozen more cult members emerged from hiding places and Marit was eventually overpowered and captured."

Fay did not like what she was hearing. "How is that Marit ended up dead while this *Kenit* is still alive?" she interrupted.

"Upon the arrival of the additional ambushers, Kenit apparently froze, forcing Marit to fight them off alone. Initially, it seems he was able to fend off his attackers easily enough until the leader of the cult appeared from nowhere to single-handedly overcome him. Whoever this man is, his *Zarantar* was too powerful for Marit to defeat him alone. Regrettably, Kenit attempted to flee. In doing so, not only did he not get far before being apprehended, his decision perhaps contributed to Marit's capture."

"If they were both taken alive," Fay interjected, "why is Marit dead and Kenit not?"

Fay could read Ari's expressions and mannerisms like a book;

what he was about to tell her next was going to anger her.

"Kenit says the leader of the cult was more enraged that the Order was aware of the existence of the cult than he was about spies being dispatched to infiltrate them. In response, he announced his intention to release Kenit so he could deliver a message back to us.

"For the next hour Kenit was forced to watch as Marit was sadistically tortured before his eyes. At the end of that hour Marit was killed. Eviscerated. His guts spilled on the ground." Ari paused for moment, probably anticipating a comment from Fay. She said nothing, so he continued. "Next, Kenit was gagged and had his hands bound behind his back. Then a rope was tied around his waist while the other end was tied around the ankles of Marit's body. He was instructed to walk back to the Order, dragging Marit's body behind him, with the message that we are not welcome.

"While making his way back to the Sisterhood seminary where Marit had based himself to oversee the mission, Kenit encountered an Anzarmenian army patrol that promptly detained him, which in turn led to the diplomatic ructions I mentioned earlier."

Once it was clear Ari had completed his narration, Fay rose to her feet, turning her back on him as she stepped a few paces away from the sofa. She placed her hands behind her back, clenching her fists beneath her cloak. It wasn't just anger consuming her at that moment; her indignation was coupled with a burning desire for vengeance.

"Sanatsai trained by the Order are incredibly hard to kill, Ari," she said through gritted teeth. "There are few wielders of *Zarantar* outside the Nine Kingdoms who could go up against an experienced Sanatsai of Marit's ability, and prevail." She turned back around to see that Ari had risen to his feet also. "Have you identified the leader of this cult? And what has been done to avenge the death of one of our own?"

"As is to be expected, some of my colleagues on the Council advocated immediate retaliatory action against this group."

Fay could tell by Ari's hesitation there was a 'but' coming.

"But...?" she prompted with consternation.

"Wiser heads prevailed," Ari responded. "Politically, we can't just march openly into a foreign land to exact retribution for a fallen comrade. Besides, we cannot take appropriate action before we fully know what we are up against. We still know too little about the cult, in terms of its numbers, capabilities and objectives. Not to mention we have yet to positively identify the leader of the group, though in light of what we learned from Marit and Kenit, I have certain suspicions about that."

"So Marit's blood remains to be avenged!" It was meant to be a question, but it came out like an accusation. "Have the Council send me to Anzarmenia and I will swiftly rectify that."

"Fay, I can see you're angry and upset. But I don't want to be side-tracked by a discussion about how the Order intends to address the issue of the cult in Anzarmenia. My purpose in telling you the circumstances of Marit's death lies in how it relates to the impact it has had on Kenit; he is the Sanatsai I want you to help."

"I don't know Kenit." The way she was feeling at that moment, she did not want to know him. "But why should I concern myself with someone who would abandon a fellow Sanatsai in a moment of dire need just to save his own neck? I cannot cure cowardice, Ari."

Fay was shamed by the look of disappointment on Ari's face. He almost certainly read the unspoken thought that flashed briefly through her mind as she said those words—that Kenit should have been the one to die, not Marit.

"As you said, Fay, you don't know Kenit," said Ari, sombrely. "He is not long past being a novitiate. He was inducted into the Order the year after you left for Antaris, so he's only been a full fledged Sanatsai for two years, now. The assignment to Anzarmenia was his first covert mission abroad, hence his inexperience."

"Forgive me, Ari." She stared shamefaced at her feet. "I didn't mean to imply that I'm unsympathetic." She looked back up at Ari. "I realise what Kenit went through must have been incredibly traumatic for him. Through no fault of his own he was placed in a situation far more dangerous than anticipated, and he was unprepared for it. I'm sure if Marit knew what was awaiting them in Anzarmenia he would not have risked placing Kenit in harm's way."

There was understanding on Ari's face. "There's nothing to forgive, old friend." he said. "I know how much Marit's death has hurt you. And I promise you, when the time comes to mete out retribution against his murderers, you will be there. But you should know, Kenit has also been deeply affected by Marit's death. He blames himself. Consequently, he has consistently refused to leave Temis Rulan to carry out any duty for the Order—no matter how innocuous. He's a broken young man, of no use to anyone in his current state, which has left the Council with a dilemma.

"Attempts to permanently purge the memory of events in Anzarmenia from Kenit's mind have proven unsuccessful; the memories keep resurfacing. Some members of the Council feel that it would be best to bind his *Zarantar* and release him from the Order, while others feel he should be given an instructor's position at one of the campuses. I consider the former option to be premature, whereas the latter is not really an option, given Kenit lacks the necessary experience to be an instructor of young apprentices.

"It is my hope that while we have you here in Temis Rulan you can do something to set him right again. So, do you think you're up to the challenge?"

A smile threatened to breakout on Fay's sullen face. "Would you have asked me if I wasn't?" she asked rhetorically. After a brief silence she continued. "Perhaps the best way to help Kenit is to force him to confront both his actions and his inactions on the night Marit was killed. It is likely he's been torturing himself about what he could and should have done differently; he probably wishes he could go back and change what happened. So, I'm going to give him the chance to do things over. I might even get it done tonight."

Ari smiled appreciatively. "Thank you, old friend." He placed a hand on her shoulder, giving it a gentle squeeze. "And once again, my condolences for the death of Marit. And my apologies for not letting you know sooner."

Fay leaned into Ari, wrapping her arms around him, giving him a fervent hug that he reciprocated. Eventually, she reluctantly released him from her embrace.

"Now," said Ari. "Why don't we sit back down? I'd like to discuss your apprentice."

Fay followed in Ari's wake as he led her back to the sofa. They sat down together and she waited for him to speak once more.

"I plan to take Kayden on a hike this evening," he said, "just the two of us, ostensibly to get to know her better. But before I meet her I need you to tell me everything there is to know about her—and don't leave anything out."

"Yes, of course," Fay replied. "But there is only so much I can tell you. Kayden is not an open book."

Kayden sat in Fay's quarters trying, but failing, to become engrossed in the book she had loved on the two previous occasions she had read it. But it wasn't boredom derailing her reading pleasure; it was restlessness. Fay had been gone a while with no guarantee she would be back, though the real problem was that Kayden was growing impatient, not to mention anxious, about meeting Master Ari Shinadu. She glanced over her shoulder to look at the grandfather clock; the time was fast approaching half past Eighteenth Hour.

With a sigh Kayden closed the book, set it down on the tea table in front of her, then stood up. She cast her gaze around Fay's quarters and her eyes eventually settled on the open doorway to the bedchamber. Maybe lying down for a little while wasn't such a bad idea. She ambled into Fay's bedchamber, heading straight for the four-poster bed—she had never slept in one before. She clambered onto the bed then rolled onto her back to lay down, her hands beneath her head, staring up at the canopy.

It was only a matter of minutes before Kayden's restlessness forced her off the bed. It was pointless trying to relax, she was simply too anxious. So she stood, glancing around the room. There was no other option. She would have to while away the time by rummaging through Fay's room. It's not as though she would likely have another opportunity to do so. And what better way to gain more insight into Fay, and what makes her tick, than going through all her personal belongings?

Kayden moved first to the closets lining the far wall of the bedchamber. She slid open one of the doors to reveal several identical, three shades of grey and black uniforms. She slid the door shut then opened the door of the next closet along. Contained within was an assortment of plain, casual attire in muted colours, equally as dull as the uniforms. *Boring,* she thought. Though what was she really expecting to find? Fay didn't strike her as the type to be interested in the frivolous fashions favoured by the nobility of the Nine Kingdoms. She slid the door shut then opened the door of the next closet along. This time she was surprised at the contents of the closet. Hanging inside were scores of dresses. They weren't excessively lavish garments by any means; nonetheless, Kayden had never seen Fay wearing a dress before. She could just about picture the woman wearing one of the long, flowing formal dresses at a social gathering, but those frilly, floral-patterned summer dresses...? She tried to imagine Fay skipping barefoot through a field of buttercups while wearing one. She almost laughed out loud; it was a ridiculous image.

As she slid the door shut, Kayden considered not bothering with the final closet; she was unlikely to find anything interesting. But she slid the door open anyway. What she saw provoked a sharp, audible intake of breath. "Oh my—" she gasped. Her assumption that Fay was not the type of woman who would be interested in the expensive fashions of the Nine Kingdoms' nobility was misplaced. Before her eyes were several stunning dresses and gowns made from the finest fabrics, fit for a noblewoman. And, unlike the dresses hanging inside the previous closet, these garments were surely not intended to be worn in public—the designs were too risqué, to say the least.

One dress in particular grabbed Kayden's attention. She reached for it and gently pulled it out. The sheer black dress, made from silk and lace, felt exquisite to the touch; its elaborate, provocative design was decidedly elegant. How and why did Fay come to own such a creation? Kayden wondered. This was the kind of head-turning garment a noblewoman would wear for an intimate evening indoors while entertaining close friends; or a 'close friend'.

Kayden carried the dress slowly to the nearby tall mirror. As she held the dress up against herself to observe her reflection, she realised the garment was a little more revealing than she initially thought. It had a backless design that required lacing up, and the sleeves were translucent, as was the triangular panel at the front of the dress at chest height. Then there was the slit along the left side, going up almost to the waist, entailing the exposure of one leg up to the thigh while walking. So, wearing the dress basically meant showing off one's arms, back, cleavage and leg, leaving little to the imagination—the latter two being too much for Kayden to even contemplate; she didn't need or want the kind of attention that would inevitably come as a result.

Once again, she briefly pondered why Fay would own such a garment, though the answer was obvious. Kayden grudgingly had to acknowledge that Fay was a very attractive woman. Beautiful, in fact. She could pull off wearing such a dress just as well as any highborn lady of the Nine Kingdoms, probably better. If not for her long-lived dislike of the woman, Fay was someone Kayden could happily entertain inappropriate thoughts about while lying in bed at night, relieving her 'tension'.

She stepped away from the mirror to return the dress to its place in the closet. As interesting as Fay's wardrobe eventually proved to be, Kayden knew she wasn't going to learn anything of true import about the woman from her choice of clothing. It was time to rummage about elsewhere. She proceeded to go through all of Fay's drawers. After several minutes the only thing out of the ordinary she had discovered was a phallic-shaped sculpture made from marble. Kayden had occasionally heard other female apprentices speaking facetiously of such objects; they were allegedly used by women from the southern lands of Karlandria to pleasure themselves. But she had always dismissed the gossip as a tall tale of the variety people were prone to making up about foreigners from strange and distant lands. It now appeared she needed to revise her stance; there seemed to be a kernel of truth in this particular story, after all.

Kayden did her best to rearrange the drawers as they had been, so Fay wouldn't know she had been snooping. She then perched on the edge of the bed with a sigh, frustrated at not finding anything worthwhile. She was ready to give up and leave the bedchamber when it dawned on her she hadn't yet looked under the bed. She sank to her knees to rectify the oversight.

Peering beneath the bed she spied a lone, small chest, which she promptly pulled out from below. She set it upon the bed then tried to flip open the lid. It was locked. *No matter!* She casually waved a hand over the box; the invocation of *Yuksaydan* caused the lock to tumble with an audible click, allowing her to open the chest. A cursory examination of the contents revealed a few inexpensive trinkets, in addition to several finely handwritten letters. *What a complete waste of time!*

But, wait. Surely there must be something of significance in the letters; why else would they be kept locked away inside a box hidden under the bed?

Kayden snatched up all the letters then sat on the edge of Fay's bed to peruse each one. The correspondence appeared to be nothing more than love letters and poetry to Fay—presumably from her late husband. Judging from the sappy poetic compositions, he was either hopelessly in love with her when he wrote them, or he was desperate to get between her legs. Whatever the case, Kayden was only prepared to read so many declarations of love, or deferential claims to being unworthy of Fay's affections, or comparisons of Fay's beauty to this, that or the other. If she didn't come across something that was actually worth reading, soon, she'd be tempted to gouge out her own eyes.

As Kayden placed another vomit-inducing ditty about Fay's sweet kisses back in the chest, ready to call it a day, the next letter she picked up instantly re-ignited her interest.

Dearest Fay,

I deeply regret leaving Temis Rulan in the manner that I did, without so much as a word of explanation, my actions no doubt confirming your fears as to how I would react to your candour. I hope you understand that given the nature of your revelation it was necessary to have some time and space to process everything you told me, that is why I requested the assignment to Shintana. To say that I was a shocked to hear about your past would be a significant understatement on my part. While we all may have skeletons in our closet, I could never have guessed at yours. No one could.

These past few days may have caused you to conclude that I wish to break our engagement and bring an end to our courtship. Please allow me to allay those fears, my love. Knowing what I now know about you has not in any way changed how I feel about you. On the contrary, your willingness to risk sharing your darkest secret with me has only deepened my affection for you. That you would trust me to such an extent, knowing the scandal that would ensue if I were to betray that trust only vindicates my desire to be your husband, if you still wish to be my wife.

I shall be returning to Temis Rulan a fortnight after this letter reaches you. I anxiously await seeing your beautiful face once more, and holding you in my arms. Being so far away from you has become more than I can bear.

Yours always,

Ren

Well, well, well. *Miss I'm So Perfect, You Will Idolise Me*, is not so perfect after all, thought Kayden, feeling a perverse sense of gratification at the discovery. She was concealing a scandalous skeleton in her closet, one she feared revealing to the man she eventually married.

Kayden briefly wondered what Fay's dark secret could be, then realised she couldn't imagine the administrator doing anything improper. The woman was such a straight arrow. Her idea of wrongdoing probably amounted to no more than purchasing a cake from a bakery and being given too much change in return, so choosing to pocket it.

Three knocks at the door of Fay's quarters broke Kayden's ruminations. She hastily began putting the contents of the chest back where they belonged, then stopped. It obviously couldn't be Fay at the door; she wouldn't need to knock. She sat stock still on the bed, waiting. Hopefully, whoever it was would just go away when no one opened the door.

Three knocks were repeated.

Maybe not.

She finished returning the letters to the chest, locked it then slid it back under the bed. She dashed out of the bedchamber, through the sitting area to find out who was at the door. With any luck it was someone to escort her to see Master Ari. If not, Kayden would quickly send whoever it was on their way. She yanked the door open to reveal a tall, middle-aged Sanatsai standing at the threshold. He wore an amethyst pendant, pinned below his collarbone—its significance lost on her—and carried a knapsack on his back, while holding a second one in his left hand, dangling about his ankles. Whoever he was, his complexion and tightly curled hair betrayed his mixed ethnic heritage; one of his parents originally hailed from somewhere in Yantasha.

"Greetings, my young friend," said the Sanatsai, with a smile. "I—"

"If you're here to see Fay Annis," Kayden interjected, "she's not in at the moment. And I don't know when she'll be back."

"That's quite all right," he replied jovially. "I'm here to see you actually, assuming you're Kayden Jayta—Fay's apprentice." He made a small movement forward, as if to enter Fay's quarters. "May I come in?"

Kayden pointedly refused to stand aside to allow him inside. "Well, that depends."

"Depends on what?"

"Who you are."

"Well, who do I need to be in order to come in?"

Kayden suppressed a groan. Whoever this person was she just knew he was going to be one of those awkward people who effortlessly got on her last nerve. "For a start, you could try not being someone who answers questions with questions."

"What makes you think I am such a person?"

She raised her eyebrows at the interloper as if to say, 'are you serious?'

"Oh, did I just do it again?" the Sanatsai said with a chuckle.

"Look," began Kayden, "unless you are here to escort me to see Master Ari Shinadu, you need to leave...*now*."

"Temis Rulan is the safest place I know, why would you need an escort?"

"Hey! Now you're doing it on purpose." Kayden was becoming tetchy. "I don't have the time or patience for your personality quirk, so if you don't tell me what you want I'm going to close this door."

"Did I not already mention that I wanted to see Fay's apprentice, Kayden Jayta?" He had to be trying to get a rise out of her "And that is you, is it not?"

It suddenly dawned on Kayden who her tormentor was, and what he was *really* after. "Hold on a moment! I see what this is," she said. "You're a friend of that poor excuse for a Sanatsai, Kassano Whatever-His-Name-Is.

"Did you figure you could come up here and succeed where he failed, is that it? Prove that I am Fay's secret lover, maybe even catch us in the act? Or maybe...you knew she wasn't in. Perhaps you thought you could try your luck with me, too; find out just how insatiable and skilled a lover I really am, all for yourself. Have a thing for younger women do you?"

The startled expression on the stranger's face made Kayden realise her accusations were not only ill conceived, they were also wildly off the mark. *No matter!* It was time to slam the door in his face irrespective of who he was and why he wished to see her.

Before Kayden could do any such thing, the elderly Jaymidari, Idelle, appeared in the doorway to stand alongside the unwelcome visitor.

"Sister Idelle," said the Sanatsai in greeting.

"I see you've met Kayden," observed Idelle.

"Yes, we were just getting acquainted."

208

"Well I'm glad I caught you before you departed. Fay has just been to see me to make some serious allegations about the conduct of Turan Kodi."

Kayden blanched at the mention of Master Turan's name. What exactly had Fay told Idelle about Turan? Did the Sister know she had blackmailed the lowlife Sanatsai after his failed attempt to assault her?

"Given the nature of these allegations I would like to convene a meeting of the Council at Tenth Hour, tomorrow morning, to discuss the matter. I just wanted to know if you would be back by then."

"If things go as I hope," replied the Sanatsai, "I should be back in time. So, please, go ahead and convene the members of the Council."

Oh no! Kayden had a sinking feeling in the pit of her stomach concerning the identity of the mystery Sanatsai. *Please don't let him be who I think he is.*

"Very well, we shall see you tomorrow." Idelle placed her hand on the Sanatsai's arm. "And good luck for tonight, Ari," she added, before departing with a silent smile for Kayden.

Kayden's world seemed to move in slow motion. It was probably too much to hope that her Sanatsai visitor was not Master Ari. She was mortified and couldn't keep it from showing on her face. It was typical of her luck that she would get off on the wrong foot with the leader of the Order. She hoped against hope that this was a different Ari, altogether; it was a common enough boys name in both Mirtana and Darmitana. Then she hoped she would wake up, and the poor first impression she had just made was just a bad dream.

No such luck.

"Master Ari!" Kayden exclaimed. "Please, do come in." She stood aside to allow the Sanatsai to enter Fay's quarters. "I hope you'll forgive my rudeness just now, I... I..." What excuse could she use?

"Oh, think nothing of it, my young friend," said Ari in placation, as he entered through the door. "So, you are Fay's apprentice then?"

Kayden closed the door. "Yes, Master Ari," she said deferentially. "And if I'd known who you are I would never have been so discourteous, or levelled such awful accusations against you." She followed Ari to the sitting area. "It's just that...well, in the short time I have been here I've already had to endure inappropriate behaviour from two people, as well as listen to insulting gossip about myself from others."

Ari dropped the knapsack he was carrying in his left hand beside one of Fay's upholstered armchairs. "I'm sorry to hear that." He removed the second knapsack from his back and placed it on the chair.

"And at the risk of causing further offence, Master..." Kayden trailed off. She decided it was more prudent to avoid putting her foot in her mouth again.

"At the risk of causing further offence?" queried Ari as he turned around to face the apprentice.

"Well... Um... Truth be told..." She might as well just say it, she realised. "You don't look anything like I expected, Master."

"Oh, I see." Ari didn't look offended, that was a good sign. "I guess I should probably explain. I'm only half Karlandrian; my father was Yantashan. He was one of the lucky few who made it across the ocean after the fall of the Ajunti Empire, settling in the Kingdom of Darmitana where he eventually met and married my mother."

If she hadn't already made a hash of her initial introduction to Master Ari, Kayden would have questioned how his father could possibly have been one of the refugees who escaped the notorious pogroms that followed the fall of the Ajunti Empire. It had been over a century since the Jurundi Empire had conquered the Ajunti Empire—once hailed as the greatest civilisation in the known world, encompassing almost two thirds of the continent of Yantasha, at its peak—prompting an exodus of the nobility and royalty of the fallen empire as they tried desperately to flee the massacres targeting the former holders of the reins of power.

"You misunderstand me, Master," said Kayden. "It's not your heritage that took me by surprise. It's just that I assumed... Well, I expected you to be older...much older, in fact."

Laughing heartily at that, Ari replied, "Why, thank you, Kayden. I will take that as a compliment. But don't let my seemingly youthful appearance deceive you, I can assure you I'm a lot older than I look." He clasped his two hands together. "Now, before you make an old man blush any more with your flattery, perhaps I should explain why I am here."

Yes. That would certainly be appreciated, thought Kayden, though she was still more concerned with why she was there.

"I am about to embark upon a hike to the north of the island," continued Ari, cheerily, "and I would very much like for you to accompany me."

"Yes, Master," Kayden replied. It wasn't the explanation she had anticipated hearing, but then, she didn't know what she had expected to hear. She frowned slightly. "If I may ask, Master. Why?"

"Truthfully, your master has told me some very interesting things about you, Kayden." *Oh no! That can't be good.* The thought came to her unbidden. "So, now, I would like to take this opportunity to spend some time getting to know the apprentice who has made such a profound impression on Fay."

"Just the two of us, Master?" What had she done to warrant the personal attention of the leader of the Order? she wondered. Or more to the point, what had Fay been telling him about her?

"Yes, just the two of us."

Kayden's excitement at the prospect of spending time alone with Master Ari was tinged with trepidation. She couldn't help but be concerned about what 'interesting things' Fay had imparted to her counterpart. "When do we leave?" she asked.

"I'd like for us to be on our way immediately." Ari turned away, heading straight for Fay's bedchamber. "But first, let's get you into the bedchamber and out of those clothes."

Kayden's eyes widened—aghast. This couldn't be happening. Surely the legendary Ari Shinadu hadn't come to Fay's quarters hoping to take advantage of her; there was no way Fay would have approved of that. She was relieved when Master Ari halted abruptly in his tracks, turning back around to face her. His face was the picture of embarrassment—certainly not the look of a lecherous old man wanting to lay with her.

"I just realised how wildly inappropriate that must have sounded," said Ari. "What I meant to say was, you shouldn't be hiking across the island in your ceremonial uniform." He gestured at her garb with a casual wave of the hand. "You and Master Fay are pretty much the same height, similar build. You should change into one of her spare uniforms. I know she won't mind."

Kayden's relief was complete. She didn't know what she would have done if Master Ari had proved to be another Kassano. As it was, she followed him into the bedchamber and watched him open one of the closets she had rummaged through earlier, pulling out a Sanatsai uniform from within.

"Here you go," he said, handing the attire to Kayden. "I will wait outside while you get changed. Once you're ready we'll be on our way."

Kayden watched Master Ari vacate the room, closing the door behind himself. She ambled to the four-poster bed, laid Fay's uniform upon it then quickly began to undress. Standing in her undergarments, Kayden hesitated as she reached for the black and three shades of grey garb. The past five years of her life had been devoted to earning the right to wear the uniform of the Order. Now that an opportunity to do so had been presented to her, early, it somehow didn't seem right. But she pushed her misgivings aside; there was no doubt in her mind she was worthy of donning Fay's clothes, and before she returned to Antaris campus she was going to prove it.

Picking the outfit up off the bed, Kayden walked purposefully to the tall mirror. She proceeded to get dressed in a slow, measured manner, all the while her gaze shifting constantly to her reflection in the mirror. Her languid demeanour in getting dressed as a Sanatsai was in stark contrast to the haste in which she got undressed as an apprentice.

CHAPTER TWELVE

Set In Motion

Standing in a quiet alcove of a deserted third floor corridor, Fay awaited the arrival of Sister Nelda whom she had arranged to meet there. She had made her way there shortly after a brief meeting with Idelle to relay the details of Turan Kodi's misconduct towards Kayden, and her suspicions that numerous other girls and women had likely been victimised. She had chosen not to share the specifics of how Kayden had blackmailed the unscrupulous Sanatsai after his attempted assault on the apprentice had ended in failure. Idelle promised to convene a meeting of the Council the following day to discuss the allegations.

Fay had been waiting several minutes for Nelda by the time her thoughts drifted to Ari, and how he would fare upon meeting Kayden for the first time. After the conclusion of their meeting in his quarters, Ari had announced his intention to go to her quarters to introduce himself to her apprentice. While she would have preferred to accompany him to make the initial introduction, Ari insisted that he needed to make Kayden's acquaintance before she knew who he was.

Alone in the alcove, Fay couldn't help but worry about all the ways in which Kayden could have made a terrible first impression on the head of the Order. But there was nothing she could do about it now.

The sound of approaching sandal footsteps finally snapped

Fay out of her reverie. Looking down the corridor she saw Sister Nelda drawing near, the statuesque Jaymidari was walking in her characteristically graceful fashion. As soon as she arrived at the alcove she immediately embraced Fay, planting a kiss on both cheeks.

"Greetings, Fay. I received your summons."

"Nelda, thank you for coming," said Fay, looking up at the taller woman. "I apologise for the secrecy but I require some assistance for which discretion is of utmost importance."

"Understood. So how may I be of assistance?"

Fay spent the next few minutes outlining what she needed from Nelda. She would be leaving Temis Rulan that night to complete an assignment, the successful completion of which required certain things to be put in place first—arrangements she would not be able to see to herself. It was up to Nelda to make them, and ensure knowledge of Fay's plans went no further than the individuals involved. It was imperative no other Sanatsai learned of them, as it could jeopardise the outcome of her endeavour, and failure was an unacceptable outcome.

"Consider it done," said Nelda, once Fay had finished explaining. "I will take care of things right away." She fell into step beside Fay as they left the alcove together, walking slowly down the corridor. "I hope you realise you'll still need a healthy dose of luck to pull this off. There is a lot that can go wrong with a scheme as elaborate as the one you are proposing."

"If your Sisters do their part, I will take care of mine." The only variable completely out of her control was Kenit.

"I had the opportunity to meet your apprentice earlier today," said Nelda, changing the subject. "She is an intriguing young woman."

"That's certainly one way to describe Kayden," replied Fay with a hint of mirth.

"I must confess to being more than a little curious about her presence here." Nelda was obviously hoping to tease an explanation out of her.

"You're by no means the only one, I'm sure." There was little doubt that Kayden was certain to be the main topic of conversation within the Order for the next few days. "But if you must know, I brought her here to meet Ari."

Nelda looked sideways at Fay. "Is it really that simple?"

"There's nothing simple about Kayden, I'm afraid."

The pair continued their slow walk, making small talk for a while longer, until they went their separate ways, Nelda departing to make the arrangements for Fay's plan, while Fay decided to head back up to her quarters.

Fay hoped she still had time to catch Ari before he left Temis Rulan with Kayden. She just needed one final moment to speak to the apprentice, to press home the importance and seriousness of the excursion with Ari. Whether or not she could do so without actually giving away that Kayden's life depended on it, remained to be seen.

Upon entering her quarters, she was disappointed to discover Ari and Kayden had already left. It couldn't have been long ago so it was probably worth making a dash to the northern gate to catch up with the pair before they were out on to the streets of Temis Rulan. She hurried down to the ground floor, then exited Kassani House via the north entrance. Outside on the grounds she fixed her gaze on the path leading to the north gate of the perimeter wall of the complex. Half way along the grey brick pathway she could see two figures making their way towards the gate. Even from behind, she knew that the taller, hooded Sanatsai was Ari, while his companion—despite the recent change of uniform—was obviously Kayden, if the distinctive long, raven ponytail was any indication.

"Ari!" said Fay, materialising behind the pair in the blink of an eye. Both Ari and Kayden peered back over their shoulders at her. They halted in their tracks and turned around. "I'm glad I caught you before you left."

"Is there a problem, old friend?" inquired Ari.

"No," she replied. "I was hoping to have a moment alone with Kayden."

"Of course." Ari glanced at Kayden. "I will wait for you at the gate. Meet me there once you're done here."

"Yes, Master."

Ari shifted his gaze back to Fay. "Do let me know how things work out with the young Kai when we return," he said. "And good luck."

"And to you," Fay replied earnestly, as Ari departed down the grey brick pathway, leaving her alone with Kayden.

"What is this about?" asked the apprentice.

"I don't want you to leave," began Fay, "without knowing my reason for bringing you here." Kayden silently stared back at her, expectantly. "I wanted you to meet Master Ari, as I have recently come to realise he is better equipped to guide you than I am. I can't say that I know exactly what he has planned for you today, but I do know his purpose in taking you away with him is to get to know you—to discover who Kayden Jayta really is." Fay hesitated. "Maybe even help you learn some things about yourself."

"That's it?" queried Kayden, seemingly nonplussed by the revelation.

"I strongly advise you to be open with Master Ari. Whatever questions he may put to you, do not hide anything from him. Answer him as truthfully as possible."

The clock tower bell began to chime, promptly joined by the distant sound of other bells from the city beyond the perimeter wall. The din signified the arrival of Nineteenth Hour, which meant the evening meal was ready for those who resided within the walls of the Order's headquarters.

"I should get going," said Fay. "So should you. Best not to keep Master Ari waiting. Farewell, Kayden." She turned around to walk away.

"Wait!"

Kayden's call stopped Fay in her tracks. She immediately turned back to face the apprentice who appeared hesitant.

"You've been acting strangely ever since you intervened in the fight this afternoon," said Kayden, warily. "And right now, it feels a lot like you're saying goodbye. Is this goodbye?"

Fay was unsure how best to answer Kayden's question. That moment, standing there on the grey brick path, could very well be the last time she saw Kayden if Ari decided the apprentice was a lost cause. And if the worst did come to the worst, she would not be able to bring herself to see Kayden one final time before the end.

"I'll be leaving Temis Rulan tonight," began Fay, "I—"

"What do you mean you're leaving?" Kayden interrupted. Was that a hint of alarm Fay detected in her voice? "Where are you going?"

"That's not important." Fay realised immediately it probably wasn't the most reassuring response. "But if you must know, I have a small assignment to complete. If things go according to plan I should be back early, tomorrow morning. Whether I will still be the administrator of Antaris campus upon my return... I do not know."

Fay had no idea if the answer was to Kayden's satisfaction, nor did she wish to hang around to find out. She immediately turned on her heels and briskly walked away. She couldn't face the prospect of being asked why she might not still be the administrator in the morning. The truth was, she would relinquish the position if the Council decided to condemn the apprentice to death, and she had no desire to burden Kayden with that awful truth.

She did not look back. She was just relieved that Kayden refrained from calling out to her. She set a course straight for the mess hall where, hopefully, she would make the acquaintance of Kenit Darbandian.

In the wake of Fay's rather abrupt departure, Kayden quickly rejoined Ari at the north gate. He displayed no inclination to know what had passed between herself and Fay, choosing instead to silently lead her through the gate, out of the grounds into the city. She noticed how he adjusted the hood of his cloak, further obscuring much of his face, as if he didn't wish to be recognised.

"Are you worried about bumping into someone you know, Master?" Kayden inquired.

Glancing at her sideways, Ari replied with a smile, "No. I'd just like us to reach our destination before sunset. Being recognised walking the streets would not be conducive to that end; we'd likely be delayed, repeatedly, by people wanting to offer their greetings."

"Sunset is about two hours away, surely that's more than enough time to get there." It suddenly occurred to Kayden that Ari hadn't actually mentioned where he was taking her. "Where exactly are we going, Master?"

"To a place few people know about, and even fewer people ever go."

It was a frustratingly cryptic reply. She considered pressing Ari further but figured she would be wasting her time. Wherever it was they were going, she would know in due course. She remained silent and switched her focus to the city streets they were traversing. The hustle and bustle she experienced during her arrival in Temis Rulan was greatly reduced—presumably most of the populace were now indoors sitting down for dinner, much like the inhabitants within the Order's headquarters.

Ari adopted a swift walking pace that Kayden matched as she was guided steadily northward through the city. While she cast cursory glances at the buildings and structures they passed by, it suddenly dawned on Kayden that she had failed to notice, during her initial arrival, something that was now glaringly obvious. The architecture of Temis Rulan was not typical of any city she had ever been to before, which she thought very odd. Though her travels had been rather limited, it was well known that the Nine Kingdoms shared a monoculture; the people spoke the same language, Shintanese—although those not born and raised in Shintana insisted on calling it 'the common tongue' instead. They upheld compatible social mores, pursued identical pastimes, and enjoyed similar cuisine. It also meant the architecture of one kingdom was more or less interchangeable with another—to the extent that it was frequently said, 'the unvisited places of the Nine Kingdoms are as familiar as the visited.' There was only one thing Kayden could infer from the observation, something she had already speculated upon since she first emerged from the portal that transported herself and Fay from Antaris campus. Temis Rulan was located outside the Nine Kingdoms.

After several minutes walking, Master Ari still hadn't said so much as a word to Kayden. For a man who supposedly wanted to get to know her better his efforts thus far left a lot to be desired. Apparently, he was in too much of a hurry to leave the city to talk.

"Master?" Kayden decided she might as well be the one to initiate discussion if Ari wasn't going to. "I was under the impression the purpose of our excursion was to allow you to get to know me." He glanced at her but said nothing. "How do you propose to do that if we do not speak to each other?"

"Patience, my young friend," replied Ari. "We will speak soon enough, once we are beyond the outskirts of the city."

Kayden's anxiety spiked. The continued evasiveness—first Fay, and now Ari—was making her very wary once more. If their intentions toward her were benign, why all the secrecy? Why the cloak and dagger? She decided to suppress her concerns for the time being. She'd have to trust that Master Ari would be as good as his word.

"As you wish, Master."

Fay sauntered into the mess hall. It was quickly beginning to fill with scores of Sanatsai and Jaymidari. She scanned the faces of those present on the ground floor, hoping to catch sight of Dora who, she recalled, had extended an offer to join her and Tobin for the evening meal. Once she was satisfied Dora and Tobin weren't among those present on the ground floor of the building she proceeded to the staircase in order to seek them out on the next floor. She casually went up the stairs to discover the first floor was more crowded than the floor below. In spite of the throng, she had little difficulty spotting Dora with Tobin at a table by a window. The moment she emerged at the top of the stairs her counterpart rose immediately to her feet, enthusiastically waving an invitation to join the pair. Fay promptly marched to the table to take a seat opposite her two colleagues.

Dora beamed as she sat back down. "I wasn't sure we'd see you here this evening." Her relief was palpable. "Glad you could make it."

"Where is your precocious young protégée?" chimed in Tobin through a mouthful of savoury meat pie.

"Kayden is Ari's concern now." Fay was not inclined to

219

elaborate.

"But you're not going to tell us why, are you?" said Dora, scooping up a spoonful of soup from her bowl. "Or the real reason for your visit with Kayden in tow."

"You know me too well, friend." The smile on Fay's face complimented the mirth in her voice. "Though some people here would have you believe that Kayden and I are secret lovers."

Tobin's eyes lit up as he lowered his fork from his wide-open mouth; the skewered piece of meat pie received a temporary reprieve. "Now that I'd love to see," he blurted.

Fay kicked out at Tobin under the table. The silent grimace on his face let her know she had struck her intended target.

"Would you give it a rest, Tobin?" Dora lambasted her colleague. "Why don't you make yourself useful? Go up to the counter and get Fay something to eat." She looked to Fay questioningly. "What would you like to eat, Red? I can recommend the pumpkin soup." She held up a spoonful of soup to illustrate.

"Nothing for me, thank you." Fay gestured with her hand for Tobin to remain seated. She returned her focus to Dora and continued, "If you really must know about Kayden, I brought her here specifically to meet Ari. He will ultimately decide whether or not she has a future with the Order."

"Oh, I see," said Dora, frowning. "I assumed Kayden had impressed you greatly these past three years. Now it seems you're saying that's not the case, that she's actually a problem apprentice."

"Don't misunderstand me, Dora. Kayden Jayta is an exceptionally gifted apprentice. Of that there is no doubt. But that's not the sole criteria for determining her suitability to be inducted into the Order." Fay didn't wish to waste any further time elaborating, she wanted to steer the conversation away from Kayden to the task Ari had given her. "Anyway, that's enough about my apprentice. I actually wanted to ask if either of you is familiar with a young Kai by the name of Kenit Darbandian? I believe he's originally from Anzarmenia."

Recognition appeared, instantly, on the faces of Tobin and Dora at the mention of the name. The expression on Tobin's face in particular indicated a deep antipathy on his part.

"I know to whom you are referring," replied Dora, "though I've had little in the way of personal interaction with him. He's still relatively new to the Order—inducted not long after you left for Antaris." Concern for her friend swept over Dora's face. "Why do you ask?"

"I need one of you to point him out to me, assuming he's present."

"I hope this means you plan on having him cast out from the Order for getting Marit killed." Tobin made no attempt to conceal his disdain for Kenit. "It's a fucking outrage that the Council has refused to sanction him for his unforgivable cowardice."

Gazing at Tobin for a moment, Fay refrained from censuring him for the sentiment or the coarse language. Now probably wasn't a good time to ask him to have some empathy for a fellow Sanatsai. She was well aware that Tobin and Marit had been good friends. "Actually, I'd like to make his acquaintance this evening, in as informal a manner as possible." She returned her gaze to Dora. "So if you are able to point him out to me, I'll make my approach at the appropriate time."

"I don't believe what I'm hearing," huffed Tobin. "Is this a joke? Instead of pushing for the removal of this worthless miscreant who got Marit killed, you're hunting for a young plaything to keep your bed warm, is that it?" Tobin was walking on thin ice. "What would Renik think if he were alive to see you going soft on the man responsible for the death of his beloved little brother?"

Fay leaned across the table glowering at Tobin. "I will let that comment pass," she said coolly, "because I know how close you and Marit were. But do not presume to tell me how Ren would feel about anything. I knew him better than you or anyone else ever could." She could see that Tobin wanted to retort but wisely thought better of it. "As for Marit's death, his blood is on the hands of those who murdered him, not Kenit's. You seem to forget he was also a victim in this—as such, he's entitled to the support and understanding of all his fellow Sanatsai."

"You keep telling yourself that, if you must," said Tobin

dismissively. "Maybe if you repeat it often enough you'll actually believe it."

Leaning back back in her chair, Fay glared at her counterpart "You know what, Tobin? I would like something to eat now. Go up to the counter and get me a bowl of the pumpkin soup Dora recommended, and a buttered bread roll. And while you're up there be sure to ask that a pot of camomile and spiced apple tea be brewed for me. And don't forget the cane sugar and honey too."

Tobin rose to his feet, his chair screeching on the floor as it was pushed back. "As you wish...Danai Annis." He marched away from their table, his displeasure all too clear to see.

"Don't take it personally, Fay," assuaged Dora. "I don't need to tell you Tobin didn't take the news of Marit's death well. He still hasn't fully come to terms with it yet."

"Believe me, I understand. Ari didn't tell me about Marit's passing until a short while ago and my initial reaction wasn't too different," Fay admitted. "But I have to be better than that, for Kenit's sake."

"So what's the real reason for your interest in Kenit?" inquired Dora. "If you don't mind my asking."

"The Council is still undecided about what to do with him. While they can excuse his failings during the fateful mission, his subsequent poor mental state cannot be ignored indefinitely. Ari has tasked me with determining if he still has a future with the Order, hence my need to meet him this evening.

"Before I return to Antaris, Kenit will have the chance to demonstrate to me that he can get past what happened in Anzarmenia."

A short while later a contrite Tobin returned to the table carrying a tray laden with Fay's food and drink. After setting the items down in front of her, Tobin remained standing while he issued an apology for his earlier behaviour. He then informed Fay that if she had no luck in finding Kenit in the mess hall, she would be able to locate him in the flower garden at sunset, as he habitually went there, alone, after the evening meal. Fay thanked him for the tip before he excused himself citing tiredness for his premature departure.

After finishing their respective meals Fay and Dora spent the next hour sitting contentedly at their table, enjoying pleasant conversation over several cups of tea. Eventually, Dora drew Fay's attention to the staircase. There was a young Sanatsai descending from the floor above, heading to the ground floor.

"There's your man now, Red."

Finally, Fay had a face to put to the name. It dawned on her that Kenit would be rather handsome if he weren't so melancholy-looking. She wondered if he was always that way or if it was the result of his experience five months previously.

"I guess that's my cue to leave, then," she replied to Dora. "But there's something I need you to do for me when I go."

"Name it."

"Deliver a message to Sister Nelda for me. Tell her she can find me in the flower garden at sunset. She'll know what it's concerning." Fay rose to her feet and promptly made her way towards the staircase to discreetly follow Kenit.

CHAPTER THIRTEEN

The Ulterior Motive

Kayden continued to trudge silently half a dozen paces behind her guide. She and Ari were now trekking north across open country—rolling fields of long grass, dotted with daisies and dandelions. It had been a while since they left Temis Rulan in the distance, yet Ari still hadn't made good on his promise that they would talk once clear of the city. What was he waiting for? she wondered. Maybe he was too absorbed in the beauty of their environs to remember she was trailing in his wake. If that was the case, she could hardly blame him. With the sun hanging low in the sky, the sights and sounds of the island were captivating. Even she could appreciate tulip-covered hills, woodlands graced with magnolia trees, a babbling brook lined with fragrant lilies. Nonetheless, with sunset fast approaching Kayden found the continued silence intolerable. It was time to test Ari's taciturnity.

"Master Ari!" she called out. He peered back over his shoulder at her but did not stop walking. "I don't wish to appear impatient or pushy, Master. But it's been at least an hour since we cleared the outskirts of Temis Rulan and you haven't said so much as a word to me. Are we going to talk or not?"

"I was actually waiting for you," said Ari, returning his gaze to the way ahead. "But if you're ready now, let us talk."

Quickening her stride, Kayden closed the gap between herself and the Sanatsai. Moments later they were walking side-by-side.

"As you are no doubt aware," began Ari, "no apprentice before you has ever set foot in Temis Rulan. But have you given any thought as to why Master Fay brought you along with her?"

"Apparently, to meet you, Master."

"And was that the reason you imagined when you were first told? What was your initial reaction to the news?"

"I didn't believe it."

Kayden debated whether or not to provide a more comprehensive answer. She was disinclined to do so since Master Ari would more than likely be bemused by the thoughts that had gone through her mind after being told about the visit to Temis Rulan. Then she remembered Fay's advice—to be open with Ari, not hide anything from him, and to answer his questions as truthfully as possible.

"At first I was certain that..." she trailed off. Perhaps the whole truth wasn't necessary after all.

"At first you were certain that...?" pressed Ari.

"Well, Master..." There was no reason to hold back, Kayden decided. She had nothing to be ashamed or embarrassed about. "The truth is, Master Ari, I was certain the administrator intended to lure me away from campus in order to kill me and dispose of my body."

Ari chortled, much to her chagrin. "You have strange thought processes, my young friend." Kayden told herself Master Ari wasn't purposely trying to be patronising, though she felt it. "As I understand it, Master Fay saved your life earlier today when a fellow apprentice tried to kill you during an illicit fight." *Fay told him about that?* "But you believed she only prevented this person from taking your life so she could take it herself, later on, after luring you away from campus?"

When put like that it did sound laughable. But Kayden held on to the conviction that her concern was more than justified at the time.

"With all due respect, Master," she said, glancing sideways at Ari, "I had very good cause for believing she meant me harm. Last night, while I was in the final stages of completing the 'capture the box' exercise, she confronted me in a right huff; she ranted and

225

raved about..." Kayden paused for a moment. How could she narrate this story without making herself look bad? "I... I may have spoken a little out of turn in response, at which point this strange look passed over her face. If only you could have seen the look in her eyes, it was as though she were thinking how easy it would be to murder me, right there and then, and be done with it."

Ari returned her sideways glance. "Fay would never hurt you, Kayden." His voice took on a more serious bent when he appended, "And for that, you should be very grateful indeed. If Fay wished you harm, believe me when I say there would be nothing you or anyone else could do to prevent it—not even me."

If those words were meant to be reassuring... It was fortunate Kayden had already dismissed the notion of Fay wanting to kill her.

"Now, returning to why your master brought you to see me," continued Ari, "Fay has some concerns about your development. Do you have any idea as to why that might be?"

Was he asking because he didn't know? Kayden wondered. Or had Fay already fed him a litany of stories detailing the questionable things she'd done?

"Well, from my point of view, Master," she replied. "The administrator has no grounds for concern. However, from what she has said to me, I gather I remind her of someone from her past." She glimpsed a flash of understanding on Ari's face. "You know to whom she's referring, don't you, Master?"

"Oh, yes," came the sober response.

"Do I remind you of this person? Because Administrator Annis made it sound like a bad thing."

"I've only just met you, Kayden," conceded Ari. "But before the night is through I intend to find out if your master's concerns about you are justified."

"And if they are...?"

Kayden did not like the pregnant pause that preceded Ari's reply.

"We'll cross that bridge if we come to it."

She liked the response even less.

The trek was taking them slowly uphill once more, Kayden

comfortably keeping pace with her older travelling companion, awaiting his next question with a little less enthusiasm than before. But she needed to get something off her chest before she was questioned further.

"If I may speak freely, Master," she began.

"Of course you may."

"I don't think it's right or fair for the administrator to use the fact that I remind her of someone from her past, as a pretext for undermining me and my training as an apprentice of the Order."

"And on what basis do you claim this to be the case, Kayden?" Ari asked dubiously.

"From the moment she arrived at Antaris she's been on my case. I am constantly being scrutinised by her in a way that no other apprentice is. And there are times when it actually feels like she is trying to sabotage me. It's almost as if she's determined to prevent me from being inducted into the Order because I'm somehow unworthy in her eyes."

"Tell me something, my young friend." Ari's tone suggested he remained unconvinced of the veracity of her assertions. "You are currently a level seven apprentice though you're only into the fifth year of your apprenticeship, is that correct?"

"That's right, Master," she replied tentatively, wondering where Master Ari was going with this.

"But each level requires a full year to complete," said Ari. "No apprentice before you has ever been permitted to take the end of level tests early in order to advance to the next level. So how is it you were allowed to do so?"

Kayden had an inkling the question was intended to trip her up, though she couldn't be sure of how. There was nothing about the circumstances of her progression that could be used against her. "I twice demanded to be allowed to advance to the next level, and twice I was permitted to undergo the tests early." It wasn't as simple as that, of course, but that was the gist of it—from her point of view.

"You demanded?"

"Yes!"

"And why did you do that?"

"Because I grew tired of being held back." Kayden was becoming testy; she failed to see the point of Ari's line of questioning.

"Explain."

She took a deep breath to compose herself.

"None of my instructors ever push me hard enough," she said. "It's a problem that's further compounded by the strange insistence that all apprentices must progress at the same rate. But how does it benefit me having to wait a month for my classmates to master things I only need a week to learn?" Kayden didn't wait for a reply. "Things first came to a head early on during level four training. At the end of the first month I approached Master Darrian to inform him that there was no part of the level four syllabus I didn't already have a firm grasp of, at least in terms of our education as it pertains to the applications of *Zarantar*. Although he was dubious of the claim, I requested to be allowed to undertake the level four tests immediately so I could join the level five apprentices for the remainder of the year. His response was that this wasn't possible, and even if it was, he didn't have the authority to grant my request.

"To my surprise, that wasn't the end of the matter; my disappointment was short-lived. The following day Master Darrian came to me to let me know I would be taking the tests during the spring term holiday, and if I successfully passed them all I would then have to spend the rest of the holiday on campus, catching up on everything taught to the level five apprentices during the first term, before joining them for the start of the second term.

"It was a similar story once I progressed to level six. By the end of the first term I was confident there was nothing on the syllabus I didn't already have mastery of. This time, it was Master Briselda I approached to arrange for me to take the end of level tests during the holiday. Presumably, I didn't ask politely enough for her liking because she said she would do no such thing, and that I should never have been allowed to advance to the next level on the previous occasion. She was adamant that if I were permitted to do so, for a second time, it would only encourage the other apprentices to expect the same consideration. In her words, I would just have to accept that I am not special, that the rules will no longer be bent for me, and that I must complete the level six syllabus over the course of the year just like everyone else."

Kayden allowed herself a smug little snicker.

"I guess Master Darrian had a word in Master Briselda's ear, because the next morning she accosted me on my way to the mess hall for breakfast. She was none too pleased when she told me I would be taking the tests during the holiday, and advancing to level seven at the start of the second term if I passed.

"So there you have it, Master. That's how I came to be a level seven apprentice two years ahead of time." What could he say to question that?

Flashing her a knowing smile, Ari said, "Would it interest you to learn it was Master Fay who, on both occasions, authorised your advancement—breaking several decades' worth of convention despite the objections of a number of her colleagues?" Kayden's surprised expression prompted him to add, "Surely you can't have believed Darrian Lanza was responsible for your early progression, did you?"

"Why would she do that?"

"That is the question," Ari answered jovially. "Hardly the actions of a woman intent on sabotaging you, wouldn't you say?"

Kayden didn't say anything. She had no grounds for contradicting Ari's words. On some level she realised it was unlikely her advancement could have occurred without Fay's consent. That would explain why she convinced herself Master Darrian had played a crucial role in forcing the administrator's hand.

The more she learned about Fay Annis, the more enigmatic the woman became.

"So...what is your hurry, Kayden?"

On the surface, Ari's question should have been innocuous, yet it sounded anything but to Kayden's ear. "I'm sorry, Master. I'm not sure what you mean." She was suddenly feeling discomfited by his prying.

"I'm curious to know why you are in such a rush to be

inducted into the Order. Do you have some time-sensitive plans I'm not aware of?"

Master Ari was clearly digging now. Did he suspect her true motivation? How could he have any suspicions about her hidden agenda? It didn't matter. She simply couldn't afford to tell Ari what he wanted to know. Honesty in this instance would guarantee her expulsion and the binding of her *Zarantar*, quite possibly jeopardising her very reason for living. And though she could feasibly still achieve her aim without joining the Order—using skills she had acquired that couldn't be stripped from her—becoming a Sanatsai was too important a component of how she sought to accomplish her ultimate objective, so under no circumstances was she prepared to sacrifice that.

With barely a second thought, Kayden decided to provide Ari with an answer that was tangential to the reason for her determination to complete her training as swiftly as possible. At least that way she could avoid telling an outright lie.

"I have no time-sensitive plans, Master," she began forthrightly. "I just have a strong desire to protect people who cannot defend themselves. Being a Sanatsai will allow me to that in ways I could only have dreamed of before my *Zarantar* manifested."

"I see," replied Ari. Was that acceptance of her answer? "That is certainly a worthy goal, Kayden. So, would I be right to assume you were neither upset nor fearful on the day your *Zarantar* manifested?"

"Upset or fearful?" Kayden blurted, incredulously. "You must be joking. Why would I have been?"

"Because that is the universal reaction of people who discover they were born imbued with the *Zarantar* of the Sanatsai," he claimed. "Which is only natural. The gift always manifests in adolescence, between the ages of thirteen and fifteen, and for people of such tender years the implications of that change are difficult to cope with. It is well known throughout the Nine Kingdoms that once *Zarantar* manifests in any individual, the Order will arrive soon after. Young people are understandably upset by the prospect of being taken away from their family for ten years. Not to mention many of them invariably find the weight of possessing such great power a tremendous burden to carry.

"So...if you felt none of those things, Kayden, how *did* you feel when your *Zarantar* manifested?"

There was no need to think about her answer to that question. Kayden remembered the moment as if it occurred only yesterday.

"I was absolutely elated, Master," she said, trying but failing to keep the glee out of her voice. "I couldn't wait for the Order to show up and take me away. Nothing was more important than learning to control my new found power."

Master Ari glanced sideways at her. "Interesting."

There was something about the way Ari uttered that single word that let Kayden know she had answered his question in a manner that displeased him. If that was the case she found the reaction incomprehensible. Surely excitement and enthusiasm for becoming an apprentice of the Order was actually a good thing?

"Meaning no disrespect, Master," she began, "but your underwhelming response suggests I've answered your question incorrectly."

"The truth is never the wrong answer, Kayden," Ari replied sagely. "But if you ask any Sanatsai of the Order how they felt in the aftermath of their *Zarantar* manifesting for the first time, elation will not be among the answers."

"You make it sound as though my being pleased was a bad thing, Master; I don't understand why."

There was a prolonged silence before Ari answered. "During your history lessons you learned how Sanatsai were trained in the days before the founding of the Order, yes?"

"Yes, Master," said Kayden, unsure what that had to do with anything. "When a young Sanatsai's *Zarantar* manifested, a single Jaymidari would arrive a few days later to take that person under her wing. They would then disappear into the wilderness together until the Sister had taught her new charge how to control his or her *Zarantar*. Once accomplished, they would live out their days wandering the lands together, hunting down practitioners of *Zarantar Najist* wherever they were to be found. In those days, we Sanatsai were the weapons used by the Sisterhood to kill the

Saharbashi." Kayden realised a simple yes would have sufficed, but there was no harm in demonstrating she had paid attention during history lessons. "Having said that, I fail to see how this is in any way relevant to what we're discussing, Master."

"Well, bear with me a little longer," Ari said. "This collaboration between Sanatsai and Jaymidari was, for the most part, a successful venture. However, there were occasions when a very small minority of Sanatsai became problematic to their Jaymidari guides. It was for this reason the Sisterhood would eventually adopt the practice of binding a Sanatsai's *Zarantar*."

The revelation was not something Kayden had learned in history class. "When you say 'problematic', Master, what exactly do you mean?"

"Some Sanatsai enjoyed the killing they were tasked with, took pleasure in it. For a small number of these individuals it ceased to matter who they were actually killing. In their warped view not only was their *Zarantar* something to be exploited for their own amusement and benefit; it also made them better than everyone else. Superior. It's fair to say they failed to grasp the weight of responsibility they carried in wielding such great power."

Was Master Ari actually insinuating she was like these people? I certainly seemed that way to Kayden.

"Master, why are you telling me all this?" she asked, failing to keep the indignation from her voice. "Surely you don't believe I'm anything like the people you've just described."

"It is a sad truth that those who crave and seek power, invariably abuse that power once they obtain it."

Kayden resented Ari's implicit accusation.

"I didn't ask for my *Zarantar*," she retorted, stopping in her tracks, prompting Ari to do likewise. "Nor did I seek to obtain it."

"But you're glad you possess it."

She couldn't deny that given what she had already said.

"You believe it makes you superior to others."

She reluctantly held her tongue.

"You would never willingly give it up."

Still she maintained her silence.

"And, you would resist any attempt to bind your *Zarantar*."

Kayden's heart began to race. Why was Master Ari pressing her so forcefully?

"Master!" she snapped, barely keeping her anger in check. "Why are you trying to get me to incriminate myself? I would never kill..."

Kayden trailed off; she couldn't risk being caught in a lie. She took a breath to compose herself—to speak more evenly.

"If I should ever have cause to take a life in the future," she continued, "I would derive no pleasure from doing so."

She looked away from Ari, turning her gaze towards the hills to the west.

"I've upset you. I apologise," said Ari. He waited for Kayden to glance back at him. "Let's keep walking. We can discuss something else."

Ari resumed the trek northward and Kayden fell into step beside him, hoping she had the forbearance to resist any further attempts he might make to test her patience. Clearly his behaviour was all Fay's doing. The administrator had no doubt orchestrated this whole situation because she was too much of a coward to take responsibility for the decision to bind Kayden's *Zarantar*. Why do it herself when she could just as easily engineer a scenario that would lead to Master Ari making the decision instead? Well, Kayden had no intention of providing either of them with justification for pursuing that course of action.

"Earlier, you stated that your instructors don't push you hard enough," said Ari, conversationally. "But other than that, why don't you tell me how you feel you are progressing at Antaris campus,"

"Truthfully, I don't see how I could be doing much better, Master. I'm on course to complete the ten years of training in just seven, maybe even six years—which has never been done before. It would also make me the youngest person to be inducted into the Order. I'm already the most accomplished apprentice on campus, and not just in terms of the strength of my *Zarantar*. Both academically and vocationally I learn more quickly than anyone else, I study longer than anyone else, I train harder than anyone else. I don't say this to boast."

"Interesting," Ari mused.

It was the second time Master Ari had uttered that word in a manner Kayden found indecipherable.

"That doesn't sound like a compliment, Master," quipped Kayden, her tone decidedly accusatory.

"It wasn't a criticism," Ari retorted. "I just meant... Well, if what you say is true, shouldn't you be happy about it? You don't look particularly happy."

She glanced quizzically at Ari. "What do you mean, Master?"

"Well, I hope you won't take this the wrong way but I don't believe I've ever met a more miserable looking person in all my years."

Kayden halted in her tracks yet again, pursing her lips.

"You're trying to provoke me! Why?" she demanded.

"I'm sorry you feel that way, Kayden," said Ari, attempting to placate her. "But I assure you, it is not my intention to antagonise you or cause you offence, I'm just trying to understand you better. Unfortunately, time is not on our side. As a result, not only do I need to ask questions you might find impertinent, I'll also have to forgo tactfulness in some of the things I say."

"In that case, Master Ari," Kayden struggled to suppress her simmering anger, "might I suggest you get to the point and just ask me whatever it is you want to know without further barbed insults, as nothing good will come of it."

"As you wish." He glanced up at the sky; the sun hung low in the west, turning the sky several shades of red and orange. "But let us keep moving, we have less than an hour's daylight left." He set off once more, continuing the trek northward.

Kayden stood her ground for a moment while Ari departed. She was no longer enjoying the excursion; she was feeling put upon. She was beginning to wish she hadn't left Antaris campus, and was looking forward to going back. After a brief spell of contemplation she set off swiftly to catch up with Master Ari, falling into step alongside him.

"Master Fay wasn't able to tell me a great deal about your background or history," said Ari out of the blue after several minutes of silence. "I know you were living in Mirtana when you consented to the ten years apprenticeship, though you were born and raised in the Kingdom of Astana—which is obvious from your accent. I can also see you are of Vaidasovian extraction, so I assume your parents are migrants from Zenosha, is that correct?"

"Yes, Master."

"How and why did your family come to settle in Astana?"

Kayden was taken aback. In her five years as an apprentice not one person had ever asked about her family. Even before then very few had inquired. She hesitated. "I can only tell you what my mother told me, Master." Ari glanced at her expectantly so she continued. "My parents were forced to leave Zenosha before I was born, that's why they travelled to Astana."

"What do you mean, they were 'forced to leave'?"

"Well..." Kayden realised she would have to provide some background detail for the story to make any sense. "Though I've never been to the empire myself, I was always taught that social mores in Zenosha—and throughout Vaidasovia generally—are stricter than those held by the people of the Nine Kingdoms. Intimate relations between unmarried couples are frowned upon, for example, so bearing a child out of wedlock is considered scandalous. It's also the case that marriages are commonly arranged in Zenosha.

"To cut a long story short, my parents were not much older than I am now when they fell in love. But they were prohibited from marrying by their respective families. My father's parents opposed their union on the grounds that they did not want their son marrying a woman of lesser social standing, while my mother's parents objected on the grounds they had already arranged a suitable marriage for their daughter.

"In spite of these objections, my mother and father continued their illicit relationship, believing that in time their respective families could be persuaded to accept a union between them. However, before that time arrived my mother fell pregnant with me. In order to avoid the inevitable scandal that would have ensued if the pregnancy was discovered, my parents did the only thing they could do—they eloped. They married in secret before embarking on the journey across the mountains into Astana, to start a new life together. And that's how my parents came to settle in the kingdom."

Kayden glanced at Ari to gauge his reaction. He was staring directly ahead with a subtle smile on his face. She guessed he liked the story of how she came to be born and raised a subject of the Kingdom of Astana. If so, hopefully he wouldn't ask how the tale ultimately ended. Why spoil the story?

"The cultures of Vaidasovia have traditionally been universal in their hostility to the existence of *Zarantar*, and those who wield it," Ari commented. "I'm curious to know how your family reacted to the manifestation of your *Zarantar*. But more importantly, what was their response when you decided to become an apprentice rather than have your *Zarantar* bound."

"The issue never arose. I no longer had any family." Kayden ensured her reply was as matter-of-fact as she could manage. She didn't wish to tip Ari off that the loss of her family was a sore subject for her. The last thing she wanted was for him to start prying deeper into the matter.

"Oh, I'm so sorry." The note of surprise in Ari's voice was obvious as he glanced sideways at Kayden. "Fay never mentioned you're an orphan."

"I don't know for certain that I am, Master. I lost my mother when I was eleven years old, but my father abandoned my mother while I was still a baby. I have no idea if he's dead or alive. I don't know if I care either way—I have no memory of him."

"So how did you come to be living in Mirtana without any family?"

The direction the conversation was moving in was beginning to make Kayden uncomfortable. "There was nothing keeping me in Astana after I lost my mother," she said evasively. "As for how I ended up in Mirtana...it wasn't by design, it's just how circumstances transpired. There's no sense in boring you with the story, Master—it's of no consequence."

"But Mirtana is over six hundred miles away from Astana. That's a long journey for someone so young to undertake."

"As I said, it's not important." The edge that accompanied Kayden's words spoke volumes. She wanted Ari to drop the subject immediately.

"Very well."

Ari fell silent for a while. But it was a brief respite. Moments later he resumed the conversation, broaching the subject Kayden least wanted to discuss.

"Tell me about your mother, what was she like?"

The pregnant silence that followed the question was palpable. Kayden glanced to the west, staring blankly at nothing in particular.

"Mama was my whole world," she murmured wistfully. "I could not have wished for a more loving, gentle, patient and selfless person to be my mother." The strain in her voice betrayed how painful a topic it was for her to discuss. "I was truly blessed to be her daughter."

"You mentioned your mother passed away when you were eleven years old." Kayden instantly became fearful Master Ari would pry where he wasn't welcome. "How did she die?" Her fear was justified. "If you don't mind my asking."

Shifting her gaze to Ari, she said, "I'd rather not talk about it, Master." The tone she affected reinforced the point.

"I respect that, Kayden," replied Ari gently. "But I believe it would be tremendously beneficial for you to answer the question."

"I said I don't want to talk about it!"

"You need to tell me Kayden."

Kayden stopped abruptly in her tracks once more, glaring at Ari as he halted alongside her. "What part of *I don't want to talk about it* do you not understand?" she snapped, raising her voice.

"Tell me how your mother died."

Ari continued to press her, seemingly oblivious to her state of agitation.

"No!"

"How did she die?"

"Shut up!"

"Tell me how she died."

"No!"

Taking a swift step towards her, Ari stood almost on her toes. "Kayden, how did your mother die?" he barked, staring down at her. "Tell me, now!"

"The piece of human garbage that is my stepfather killed her," Kayden snarled, her voice rising further. "Is that what you wanted to hear?"

She was visibly trembling with rage.

Kayden could feel her eyes sting as she fought to keep her tears at bay while Ari stared silently at her. She was determined not to give him the satisfaction of making her cry. It was bad enough she had let him provoke her into speaking of the most painful experience of her life, but she wasn't going to compound the lapse by crying in front of him.

She back-pedalled a couple of paces away from Ari.

"How dare you," she uttered in a low, monotone voice. "This is over."

She dropped the knapsack from her shoulder, letting it fall at her feet, then stormed away from the Sanatsai—stomping back the way they had come, intending to return to Temis Rulan. So what if she was blowing her chances of being inducted into the Order? It didn't matter. She wouldn't allow them to rob her of her power. Anyone stupid enough to attempt to bind her *Zarantar* would have an almighty fight on their hands.

She hadn't gone more than a dozen yards when Master Ari called out to her. "Tell me about your stepfather."

What?

Kayden shuffled to a stop, frowning. She took a calming breath, then slowly turned around to stare back at him. He remained standing in the same spot she had left him in, staring fixedly at her. What was he hoping to gain by goading her further?

Fuelled by indignation, Kayden marched purposefully back towards Ari.

"My stepfather is a worthless waste of breath," she said coldly, halting a couple of paces in front of Ari. "What else do you want to know about him?"

"Why did he kill your mother?" Ari asked gently.

"What do you mean, why?" she griped incredulously. "Because he could. Because he is a spineless, gutless bully and abuser who knew my mother would take whatever he dished out.

He was wholly incapable of appreciating her. He would always find fault with her—some excuse or other to beat her—and she let him, over and over again. He would beat her down and she would just get up again, never willing to rock the boat as long as he never laid a finger on me."

Kayden paused. She was trembling again, still fighting to keep back her tears. "But the last time he beat her down... Mama never got up again."

There was sympathy in Ari's eyes. "Were you there when it happened?" he asked. "Did you see your stepfather kill your mother?"

Kayden didn't reply. But she didn't need to, she knew the answer was written all over her face.

"Tell me how it happened," Ari prompted, softly.

There was a protracted silence while Kayden dithered as to whether she should oblige the request. But some part of her, however reluctantly, needed to get it off her chest. She took a breath to compose herself.

"I was in the kitchen helping my mother prepare the evening meal when my stepfather came home in a foul mood. He began ranting and raving about why his supper wasn't ready yet, and how many times did he have to tell her to let the kitchen staff handle all the cooking—that's what they were there for.

"Mama told me to go to my room. She knew what was coming. But she said it in Zenoshanese, and he hated hearing me and Mama speak her mother tongue. So he grabbed her by the hair. 'Don't think I don't know when you're insulting me to your good for nothing sprog!' he shouted. Then he started hitting her, and she just let him." Her toes clenched inside her boots as she recalled the harrowing incident. "I tried to help her. I screamed at him to stop. 'Shut up, you little shit stain!' he shouted, pointing a finger at me—a warning that I would get the same treatment as my mother if I didn't stop. But I wasn't afraid of him. I was never afraid of him."

Pausing briefly, she pursed her lips while grinding her teeth. She felt as though she were reliving the moment, making it hard to suppress the impulse to lash out at someone or something.

"I grabbed a bowl from the table and I threw it at him as hard as I could. It struck him in the face. He was furious. He let go of Mama and came for me instead, but she rushed to put herself between us. And as she had done on many previous occasions, she willingly offered herself up for a beating just so he wouldn't lay a finger on me. She never *ever* let him hurt me."

The throbbing at her temples, and the quickening of her heartbeat, prompted Kayden to concentrate on steadying her breathing.

"But there was nothing I could do as he knocked Mama to the floor. He started kicking and stamping on her, over and over again. He wouldn't stop. I tried to stop him but I wasn't strong enough, he just tossed me aside like I was a piece of rubbish. So I rushed out of the house, into the street, screaming for help. I eventually came upon a two-man patrol of the City Guard, but by the time I persuaded them to come back to the house with me...it was too late.

"When we entered the kitchen, Mama was on the lying on the floor and my stepfather was kneeling over her, crying, trying to rouse her. One of the Guard asked him to explain what happened to my mother, and he responded by blaming me. He told them that I'd had a wild tantrum, and that my mother fell and hit her head while chasing me out of the kitchen. Of course, the Guard knew he was lying and they promptly arrested him. But being who he is, my stepfather was able to bribe them. He paid them to take my mother's body away for interment the next morning."

Kayden could feel her lips quivering but she was determined to keep her emotions bottled up.

"I didn't know what to do. I was crying for Mama and I started begging the Guard to arrest my stepfather, but he just called for one of the servants to drag me away and lock me in my room. It wasn't until later, when my mother's body had been removed from the house by the Guard, that my stepfather came to my bedroom. He was so angry. He grabbed hold of me, lifting me off my feet saying it was bad enough I killed his wife, but I had crossed a line by trying to get him into trouble with the City Guard. He said he was finally going to give me what I deserved—that he was going to teach me a lesson I would never forget. He started beating me, and I thought he was going to kill me, too. But I wanted to die. I didn't want to live without Mama. But I wasn't granted death."

Fists clenched at her side, Kayden's fingernails bit into the palm of her hands.

"Once my stepfather had exhausted his anger on me I was still alive, lying curled up on the floor as he stood over me. He told me that as soon as my bruises had cleared up he would start shopping me around the bordellos of the courtesan district; he was going to sell me to whomever made the highest bid. He took great pleasure in stating that all the madams of Shali were sure to offer exorbitant sums of money for the opportunity to acquire a piece of young and tender Vaidasovian meat.

"As he was leaving my room he stopped in the doorway and looked back at me. He said I should be grateful I was worth more money unbroken, otherwise he would have tested my merchandise first and fucked me senseless, right there and then, on the bedroom floor." She scowled unwittingly. "But I didn't care what plans he had for me. I'd already decided he wouldn't live to see another day; I was going to kill him that very night.

"I waited up most of the night, until I was certain he was sleeping. I left my room with an oil lamp in hand then made my way to the kitchen to grab a knife before creeping to my stepfather's room. As I stood outside the door, I still hadn't made up my mind as to whether I was going to set his room ablaze or stab him to death—so I decided to do both."

A wry smile curled her lips before a hollow laugh escaped her mouth moments later. There was no mirth in the outburst, but laughing kept her anger in check and her tears at bay. At least for a moment.

"I burst into the room, threw the oil lamp against the wall then rushed straight to the bed where he was sleeping. I jumped onto it and thrust the knife down as hard as I could. He woke up with a shocked gasp, and looked stunned to see me above him with a knife in my hand. I thrust the knife down again, this time he raised his arms to protect himself. The blade stuck deep in his forearm and he screamed. But before I could pull it back out to stab him a third time his thrashing movement beneath me caused me to tumble off the bed onto the floor. I started to scramble towards the door on my hands and knees then I heard him yell behind me, 'I'm going to skin you alive!' I looked back to see he had clambered out of bed and stood with the knife in his hand. I'll never forget the look on his face in that moment. He meant what he said, and would have done what he said, if not for the curtains being engulfed in flames. Once he noticed the fire started by my broken oil lamp, he had a choice to make: punish me or save his home.

"His hesitation allowed me to get to my feet, and I ran. I ran out of the bedroom, out of the house, into the night, and I never looked back."

Kayden hoped that was the end of her narration, that it would be enough to satisfy Master Ari, and put an end to his prying into her past. *Damn him!* But he dashed those hopes immediately.

"You feel guilty about your mother's death," he said gently, "don't you, Kayden?"

"How can I not?" she lamented in reply. "Mama married my stepfather for my sake. And she only stayed with him because of me."

Ari looked confused. "Explain."

"I said earlier that my father abandoned my mother when I was still a baby. But the truth is he did not want to leave her; he wanted to leave Astana. He had difficulty adjusting to life there, and he never could get to grips with the language, that's why he wanted us to return to Zenosha to seek forgiveness from their families. However, there was an obstacle in the way of that goal... Me. My parents had married without the consent and blessing of their families so their marriage would be deemed illegitimate back in Zenosha. Returning home with a two-year-old baby girl would have scandalised them and their families even further.

"My father proposed that they leave me behind in Astana—give me up to an adoptive family to raise as their own. Mama refused this. She wouldn't abandon me for anything or anyone. I was her baby girl, her pride and joy.

"The next morning Mama awoke to find my father had gone,

leaving a goodbye note. It was just me and Mama then, and for the next three years she struggled on as best she could to take care of us both. Eventually she decided it was in my best interest that she remarry.

"Mama was a beautiful woman, inside and out, so she was never short of admirers and suitors, though none were ever prepared to raise another man's child—not until she came to the attention of my stepfather. It didn't bother Mama that she would be a trophy for him, just an exotic novelty. He was, in most ways, exactly what she was looking for. Although not nobility himself, my stepfather is the accountant for an Astanese Baron, Beniro Raytano, so he is a wealthy man in his own right. That's why mama married him. She never loved him. She just wanted the financial security that being his wife could provide for me, that's why she tolerated his all too frequent mistreatment of her.

"So yes, Master," Kayden said bitterly, "of course I feel guilty about my mother's death. Mama's love for me ultimately led to her murder. If only she had abandoned me as a baby and returned home with my father, she might still be alive today."

"Kayden, I realise witnessing your mother's tragic death must have been deeply traumatic for you, but you cannot blame yourself."

"*I don't*," she retorted. "One person, and one person alone is responsible for murdering my mother."

Kayden was finding it increasingly difficult to keep her emotions in check and her tears at bay. She had to end the conversation before the floodgates opened. She hadn't cried in years and she'd be damned before allowing Master Ari to reduce her to tears now. She looked imploringly into his eyes, and murmured, "Why are you doing this to me?" Her forlorn voice was barely above a whisper.

"You have never spoken about your mother's death before, have you?" There was no response from Kayden. "Getting you to open up about it, now, is a crucial first step in helping you to come to terms with it, because until you do you will never be able to let it go."

Ari's words were the final straw. Kayden took a step towards him, glaring furiously.

"I will never let it go!" she yelled. "I don't want to come to terms with it."

"Then what do you want?" Ari challenged.

"I want to kill the son-of-a-bitch who took my mother away from me!" Kayden's raised tone was as manic as the look she knew was in her eyes. "And I will kill him. But it won't be quick. He is going to suffer. I'm going to make him experience the terror and the helplessness of facing someone stronger and more powerful. When I stand before him as a Sanatsai of the Order I want to see the fear in his eyes when realisation finally sets in that he is a dead man walking, and that nothing and no one can in this world can protect him from what is coming next. I'm going to torment him the way a cat toys with a mouse. I will use my *Zarantar* to slowly shatter every bone in his body, then I'm going to make him beg for his life." Kayden paused briefly, but she wasn't finished yet. When she spoke again her voice was low and deliberate. "And when he does... Once he pleads for mercy... He will find none forthcoming from me—just vengeance for my mother as I end his worthless life."

"Murderers are not welcome in the Order, Kayden" said Ari in a very matter-of-fact fashion.

Backing away slowly from the Sanatsai, Kayden shrugged. "But they are welcome everywhere else." As she spoke she sounded utterly defeated. "Welcome to terrorise and brutalise a beautiful, gentle soul who never harmed anyone. Welcome to snuff out the radiant light that made my world a brighter place. Welcome to rob me of the person I loved most in this life." A single tear trickled down Kayden's cheek. "It's not fair. It's not fair. It's not fair."

Kayden finally broke down, and the floodgates opened. She bent at the waist—her hands on her knees, tears streaming down her face as she wept uncontrollably. Her whole body racked with her heart-rending sobs.

The apprentice barely noticed the hand that slowly, gently stroked her back. But she heard Master Ari's soft voice intone the words, "That's it. Let it go, Kayden. Let it go. Let it go."

CHAPTER FOURTEEN

In The Company Of Living Legends

Kenit enjoyed going to the flower gardens in the evening after finishing his dinner at the mess hall. It wasn't just that the gardens seemed to grow more beautiful in the fading light at the end of a day. Nor was it his fondness for sitting down to observe the stars emerge in the heavens as evening gave way to night. His principal reason for being there most evenings was the solitude it afforded him. Although there would invariably be a few Jaymidari wandering about now and then, few—if any—of his fellow Sanatsai ever came to the gardens at that time of day. After the evening meal some would just loiter in the mess hall well into the night, enjoying conversation. Many would return to Kassani House to gather in one of the common rooms to put their feet up and socialise; others would leave the grounds entirely, to visit colleagues living in other locations in Temis Rulan, while a few hurried off to their accommodations in the barracks, either alone, or with an amorous partner, eager to indulge in carnal pleasures.

Not so long ago Kenit enjoyed doing all of those things...but not any more.

These days he found it difficult to be in the company of other Sanatsai; he resented the way everyone stared at him. A small number would look at him with pity or sympathy in their eyes. But most eyes simply held antipathy and contempt, maybe even hatred. Though nobody had ever voiced the assertion—at least not within earshot—many people in the Order deemed him culpable for the violent death of Marit Katarnian. It was a viewpoint he understood and shared because he blamed himself for Marit's demise. Nonetheless, it hurt him that so many people seemingly failed to see that he, too, was deeply affected by what happened. He was just as upset, if not more so.

Upon being inducted into the Order two years ago, Kenit—as with all new additions—inherited the status of novitiate. This designation entailed being taken under the wing of an established Sanatsai for a year, shadowing them, and learning the ins and outs of the duties of a member of the Order. It was Marit who had been assigned to be Kenit's mentor during his first year, and Kenit had come to appreciate and respect the man a great deal. When Marit had approached him six months ago to enlist him for a clandestine mission outside the Nine Kingdoms, not only did he jump at the opportunity to participate in his first real mission for the Order, he also felt honoured and gratified by the confidence Marit showed in him.

If Kenit had known then what he knew now—that Marit's confidence in his suitability for the mission was misplaced—he would surely have refused the assignment. What was assumed to be a simple, low risk mission proved to be nothing of the kind. He had no idea what he'd said or done to tip off the cult that he was a spy for the Order. He would probably never know. But what wasn't in doubt was that when placed in a life or death situation he had frozen. Worse than that, when Marit came to his aid, not realising it was a trap, Kenit had attempted to flee. In the weeks and months since then, he had frequently tried to convince himself that if only he held his nerve and assisted Marit to fight off the cult members involved in the ambush, Marit would still be alive. In truth, such a belief was wishful thinking, and he knew it. Once the leader of the cult appeared—seemingly from nowhere—nothing he could have done would have altered the outcome of events.

Kenit had never encountered a Saharbashi before that night. He'd even doubted that such people still existed. Yet the cult leader surely had to be one; that was the only possible explanation, as he told the Council. Whoever the man was, his *Zarantar* was incredibly powerful—stronger than Marit and Kenit combined, without a doubt. So even if he had held his nerve and helped Marit face the Saharbashi, it would have been a futile gesture. Marit Katarnian would still be dead and he would still be racked by guilt, seeking the solace of being alone in the flower gardens in the evenings.

But at that moment, sitting on a wooden bench in front of a hedgerow, Kenit wasn't quite as alone as he would have liked. Several yards along the grey brick path, sitting on a bench beneath the hanging tendrils of a willow tree was the most beautiful woman he had ever seen. The Sanatsai beauty sat languidly on the bench with her legs outstretched, crossed at the ankles, and her arms resting on the back of the bench as she gazed up at the reddening sky above. She had been sitting there for the best part of half an hour, and Kenit couldn't shake the suspicion that not only had she followed him to the garden, she was also surreptitiously spying on him.

Although he'd never seen or met the woman before, Kenit was certain he knew who she was, nonetheless. If her stunning looks alone were not a give away, her burgundy hair was—it was known to be the distinguishing feature of Danai Fay Annis. And assuming she was who he suspected, Kenit was perturbed by her presence in the garden, only yards away. He was vaguely aware that she was once the sister-in-law of Marit Katarnian. Now that she was back in Temis Rulan, after a three-year absence, she was sure to know about Marit's death and the role he had played in it. And, unlike most other Sanatsai, her status as a living legend of the Order meant she would have little to fear from exacting retribution if she held him responsible for the death of her former brother-in-law.

Danai Annis must have felt the weight of his gaze upon her because she slowly turned her head towards him. In an instant, her eyes were locked on his, and suddenly his breath seemed to catch in his throat. Then, much to his surprise, she flashed him a warm, close-lipped smile, causing his heart to skip a beat. He returned a half-hearted smile before quickly looking away.

For the next few minutes Kenit avoided looking in Fay's direction. As pleasant as she was to look at, he didn't want to run the risk of encouraging her to approach him. But his attention was eventually drawn back to her position by the sound of oncoming footsteps. Slowly, he turned his head, dreading the prospect of seeing Fay walking towards him. But, much to his relief, Fay was still seated on the bench beneath the willow tree; the footsteps were coming from a statuesque Jaymidari approaching Fay. Kenit had seen the Sister many times before though they'd never formally been introduced, nor did he know what her name was. But he could discern that she was of southern Karlandrian stock, given her pale complexion and fair hair. It also appeared as though Fay was acquainted with the Sister for she quickly sat up straight when she spotted the other woman walking to meet her.

Kenit looked on with interest as the Jaymidari stopped in front of Fay and bent down to say something into her ear. Whatever was said prompted Fay to stand up to issue her response. He couldn't hear the words exchanged by the pair but the conversation was brief, and ended with the Sister departing the way she had come. Then, to his horror, Fay turned around to look in his direction.

"You!" Fay called out, beckoning Kenit with a hand. "Come with me."

Kenit rose swiftly to his feet. "Me?" he yelped.

"Yes, you. Get over here."

In spite of himself, Kenit quickly scampered away from his bench to join the senior Sanatsai. "How may I assist you, Danai?" he asked cautiously.

"I have an errand to complete in Lirantana. You're coming with me."

"But—"

His protestation was cut abruptly short as Fay turned on her heels and began marching away. He darted after her, falling into step on her left side.

"Uh... Danai," he said, flustered. "Could you not get someone else to accompany you?"

Without looking at him, Fay replied, "I probably could, but you're the first person I saw so it's your lucky day."

Kenit blanched. The prospect of leaving Temis Rulan on any kind of assignment made him feel ill. And though she had described whatever it was she had to do as an errand, he very much doubted Fay Annis was journeying to Lirantana to deliver milk. He was going to have to insist that he be excused from joining her.

"Meaning no disrespect, Danai," he said diffidently, "but you have to take someone else with you, not me."

Fay glanced sideways at him. *"I have to?"* Her tone made Kenit instantly regret his choice of words. "Is that an order?"

"No, of course not, Danai. It's just that... Don't you know who I am?"

"Should I?"

"Well..." This was going to be more difficult than it needed to be, he realised. "If I told who I am you wouldn't be asking me to accompany you."

"Why don't you tell me who you are?" said Fay. "So I can be the judge of that."

Taking a breath to compose himself, Kenit said, "My name is Kenit Darbandian."

The moment the words passed his lips he braced himself for the inevitable vitriolic reaction.

"And...?"

Fay seemed genuinely nonplussed by the utterance of his name. Could it be she was unaware of the part he played in the death of Marit Katarnian? If so, he knew that now was not a good time to anger her by letting her know. Nonetheless, he had to say something to dissuade her from compelling him to go to Lirantana.

"Danai," he began, breaking the silence. "You are Fay Annis, correct?"

"That is correct."

"Well, please believe me when I tell you I'm the last Sanatsai you want watching your back in a life or death situation."

Fay halted abruptly, causing Kenit to stop as well. She looked at him pointedly and said, "Kai Darbandian, is something wrong with you? I'm not asking you to march into battle with me. I've been asked to complete a simple errand, and for the sake of protocol I need you to be present with me."

"What exactly does this errand entail, Danai Annis?"

Fay resumed walking, and Kenit fell into step beside her.

"The Sisterhood has a seminary about three miles outside the town of Relona in Lirantana. A few hours ago the Sisters there sensed the manifestation of a Sanatsai-to-be in the town. While under normal circumstances they would be required to send two people into town to locate the individual, at the moment the seminary is in quarantine due to a suspected outbreak of violet fever.

"As a favour, I've been asked to assign a couple of people to go to Relona to find the young boy or girl as it could be a week or two before the quarantine is lifted. And since I have nothing better to do at present I've decided to go myself, and I'm taking you with me."

Kenit thought it odd that someone of Danai Annis' status would deign to undertake such a trivial task.

"Can't you assign others to go?" he queried, "this hardly seems worthy of your personal attention."

"Kai Darbandian, if I didn't know any better I would think you were trying to get out of coming with me," Fay replied. "I realise it's by no means an exciting task, but someone has to go to Relona to present the child in question, and their anxious parents, with the choice of ten years apprenticeship or the binding of *Zarantar*. Are you trying to tell me you aren't up to the task?"

"Yes. I mean, no. I mean...yes, of course I'm up to the task," he stammered.

"Or maybe you think such a mundane assignment is beneath you?"

"No, I don't think that at all, Danai." Kenit reluctantly gave up hope of worming his way out of it. "I apologise if I appeared less than enthusiastic. I'm ready to leave when you are."

He suppressed his annoyance at his superior for not allowing him to refuse a duty as readily as the Council had done. He also berated himself for not attempting to force the issue. If only Danai Annis wasn't so damn beautiful, he thought, he would have offered more resistance. As it was, he was going to the Kingdom of Lirantana whether he liked it or not. He just hoped this supposedly simple assignment would not end as disastrously as the previous one.

"I'm pleased to hear it," said Fay.

For a brief moment, Kenit thought he spied a subtle, satisfied smile on Fay's lips as he glanced sideways at her. But he didn't dwell on it; he simply followed her lead out of the flower garden.

Kayden wiped her runny nose on the right sleeve of her borrowed uniform then wiped the tears from her cheeks with her hands. It had taken a while, but she had finally stopped weeping. Ari stood close by but she was unwilling to meet his gaze—partly because of embarrassment. It had been years since she last cried, and she couldn't recall ever doing so in front of anyone other than her mother.

"Please don't tell anyone, Master Ari," she murmured, keeping her eyes focussed on the ground between herself and Ari.

"About your mother, or that I saw you crying?"

"Either." She sniffled then wiped her nose again. "Both."

"Anything you tell me today will remain between the two of us," said Ari, seeking to reassure her. "No one will hear of it from me."

With a sigh, Kayden turned her gaze westward where the sun hung low in the evening sky, slowly disappearing below the horizon. She silently took stock of what had just transpired. She had bared her soul completely to Master Ari, revealing the hidden agenda driving her on to become the most powerful Sanatsai she could be, as quickly as possible, and the secret heartache behind it. Now that she had announced her intention to torture and kill the man who had hurt her so profoundly, there was sure to be a price to pay.

She finally turned back to Ari, meeting his gaze.

"Master, what's going to happen to me now?"

"That still remains to be seen." He bent down to pick up the knapsack Kayden had discarded earlier. "For now, let's keep moving. Our destination is not far from here, if we pick up the pace we can be there within the next half hour." He handed the knapsack to Kayden.

"We're not going back to Temis Rulan?" she asked in surprise. "You still want to continue this excursion even though I just told you I plan to kill someone?"

Ari offered no response; he simply resumed the march northward. Kayden remained rooted to the spot, perplexed, as he walked away. She pondered what to infer from his silence, then she remembered the promise he just made: *Anything you tell me today will remain between the two of us.* Maybe Master Ari also intended to turn a blind eye if and when she killed her erstwhile stepfather. Maybe he actually approved of her quest for revenge, and would do nothing to deny her of it. Maybe she hadn't blown her chances of becoming a Sanatsai of the Order—as she had feared—after all.

Kayden slung the knapsack over her shoulder then rushed to catch up with Ari. She fell into step beside him, and for several minutes the pair marched onward together without exchanging a word.

Eventually, it was Ari who broke the silence when he looked sideways at Kayden to say, "Master Fay informed me that you and she have never got on particularly well." To Kayden's mind that was a major understatement. "And I've noticed a certain degree of antipathy on your part towards her today. While I realise you believed she had it in for you when she became the administrator of Antaris campus, I find it difficult to accept this is the sole reason for your dislike of her. Surely there is a bit more to it than that?"

"Why does it matter, Master?"

"Maybe it doesn't," conceded Ari. "But Fay is my closest, dearest friend, and though I've only known you for a couple of hours it's becoming readily apparent that you and she have a great deal in common. It would be a shame if the two of you were unable to establish some kind of rapport with each other. So again, I'm curious as to your ill-feeling towards her."

Kayden struggled with how best to respond to the query. It wasn't so much she didn't know the reasons for her issues with Fay—of course she knew. It was more a case of not knowing how she could give voice to those reasons without it being interpreted as jealousy on her part. But in light of everything she had already revealed to Master Ari there seemed little reason to withhold anything now.

"Truthfully, Master, there isn't one specific reason I can point to," she admitted. "It's more an accumulation of different things. For a start, the way she conducts herself on campus—she is always so standoffish and impersonal. None of the other instructors are like this. They make the effort to be relatable and approachable which makes it easier to interact with them.

"And why is it anytime I get sent to her office to be reprimanded, she never displays any emotion? Why can't she lose her temper and get angry with me like a normal person? At the very least she could raise her voice to indicate her displeasure.

"But the thing that aggravates me the most," Kayden was on a roll now, "I just can't stand the way everybody idolises her, especially as the adulation is based on nothing but absurd folk-tales of her supposed exploits."

"I'm not sure I understand what folk-tales you are referring to," said Ari. "Would you care to elaborate?"

"I mean the silly tales taught as historical fact during history lessons. She features so prominently, and so frequently, throughout the entire history of the Order, it's just not plausible—yet nobody ever thinks to question it. For example, we're supposed to believe she was an escort for the Darmitanese trade delegation that set sail for Bantujura only to end up shipwrecked in Nanjasutu during the civil war there, and that she subsequently prevented the survivors, including Prince Tonio, from being captured and held for ransom, by single-handedly wiping out a three hundred strong brigade of anti-monarchist rebel fighters, before leading everyone on a sixty mile walk along the coast to safety in Bantujura." For good measure Kayden added, "I mean, really?"

"You doubt Fay's ability to defeat three hundred powerless soldiers?"

"Master, whether or not she is capable of accomplishing such a feat is beside the point."

"Then what is the point?"

"Master Ari!" exclaimed Kayden. She couldn't believe she needed to point out the bleeding obvious. "The shipwrecking of the Darmitanese trade delegation happened almost forty years ago. If Administrator Annis had really been there she would have to be in her sixties today; the woman doesn't look a day over thirty-five." In response to Ari raising his eyebrows at her, Kayden amended, sheepishly, "All right, thirty."

"Would it interest you to know your master is ninety-six years old?"

"That's impossible!" Kayden blurted, in obvious disbelief.

Ari began laughing, which raised her hackles. She hated being laughed at—being the butt of the joke.

"I fail to see what's so funny," she said pointedly.

"Forgive me, Kayden," said Ari cheerfully. "I just find it amusing that someone born with the power to do things that are impossible for most people in this world, can be so reluctant to believe Fay is older than she appears. As I recall, you had no trouble accepting that I am older than I look."

"With all due respect, Master," replied Kayden. "While you look younger than I expected, you still look old enough to be somebody's grandfather. But Administrator Annis, on the other hand... She doesn't even look old enough to be *my* mother, so how can she possibly be as old as you say?"

"The same way I have over forty years on her." Ari smiled upon seeing Kayden's disbelieving expression. "Perhaps I should explain," he continued. "You are aware that not all Sanatsai are born equal in terms of the strength of our *Zarantar*?"

"Yes, Master."

"So you've already been taught that in centuries past, when the Sisterhood first became aware of the emergence of the Sanatsai, they developed a grading system to measure and determine the strength of *Zarantar* possessed by any given Sanatsai?"

"Yes," Kayden confirmed. "They designated three grades: foundational, intermediate and advanced."

"Very good!" Master Ari was easily pleased, thought Kayden.

"Initially, this grading system was considered definitive, and to this very day more than ninety-nine per cent of all Sanatsai in recorded history have fallen into one of these three classifications. That is why you apprentices aren't taught about any other grade. However..." Ari trailed off, presumably for dramatic effect. "Every once in a blue moon, the Sisterhood would find a Sanatsai whose *Zarantar* was far greater than that of those who were advanced grade Sanatsai. These people were incredibly rare, but they possessed attributes no other Sanatsai, Jaymidari or Saharbashi possessed, attributes responsible for them developing abilities their peers found very difficult, if not impossible to master. As a result, the Sisterhood had to come up with a fourth category: the elite grade Sanatsai.

"If it's not already obvious to you, my reason for mentioning all this is because myself and your master are both elite grade Sanatsai—two of only three currently within the ranks of the Order today. One of the attributes we share, separating us from other Sanatsai is that we age more slowly than is normal. Consequently, our life expectancy is more than double that of ordinary people, hence why I am a hundred and thirty-nine years old, while Fay is ninety-six years old."

Kayden was awed by the revelation. She knew with certainty Master Ari was speaking truthfully.

"That's incredible, Master."

A flash of memory from earlier in the day came to her. Back in the dormitory Fay gently placed a hand on her face, and moments later the facial injuries she sustained during the illicit fight in the old arena healed completely, leaving no trace at all. "So that would explain how she was able to heal some minor injuries I had earlier today just by touching me."

"Indeed," Ari affirmed cheerily. "And though I myself was never able to master the ability to the same extent, Fay's healing power is actually the reason why she's able to remain even more youthful looking than me." He chuckled to himself. "Come to think of it, by the time your master passes away, she will doubtless be the youngest looking old corpse the world has ever known."

"I can't imagine what it must be like to live for so long yet remain so young, while all the people around you grow old and die." Kayden's tone was tinged with sympathy.

"It might surprise you then," replied Ari, "to hear that one of the reasons for your Master's interest in you is her belief that you, too, are an elite grade Sanatsai. Though you cannot be tested before being inducted into the Order, if her suspicion proves true you would be the first new elite Sanatsai to emerge since I founded the institution seventy-three years ago."

Silently, Kayden mulled the speculation in her mind. It would certainly explain why she was patently more gifted than her fellow apprentices. But she wouldn't know for sure until she was formally inducted into the Order. That was when all new inductees were tested to officially determine which of the three grades they belong to—or, potentially, in Kayden's case, which of the four. But given recent events, her admission into the Order was still very much in doubt.

She and Ari began walking down a grassy incline into a wide valley. To the west the sun had sunk below the horizon, to the east the sky had darkened significantly.

"Haradeen Bay!" announced Kayden out of the blue.

"I'm sorry?" queried Ari, glancing at the apprentice.

"This island, it's located in Haradeen Bay."

"And how exactly did you arrive at that conclusion?" said Ari, neither confirming nor denying her assertion.

"First of all," began Kayden, "when I emerged from the portal that transported me from Antaris campus, the position of the sun indicated it was about three hours later in the day, even though the journey through the portal took no more than two or three seconds, if that. This let me know that not only had I travelled a significant distance east, I had actually left the continent entirely. Logically, I had to be somewhere in Yantasha.

"Next, the length of time I've been walking with you, and the distance we've covered since leaving Temis Rulan, in addition to the distance I covered when travelling from the south coast of the island to reach Temis Rulan in the first place, has given me a rough idea of the size of the island. While there are half a dozen inland bodies of water in Yantasha large enough to contain an island this size, all of them are in regions much further east, so it would be even later in the day if we were there. Plus, those regions are populated entirely by native Yantashan people, which also rules them out because the settlement I briefly passed through with Administrator Annis was populated by ethnic Karlandrians who spoke the common tongue of the Nine Kingdoms."

Kayden sounded mightily pleased with herself when she concluded her reasoning. "It is a well known fact that the northwestern region of Yantasha is the only region of the continent inhabited predominantly by Karlandrians, while also being the location of Haradeen Bay. And as I noticed the island is enclosed by land to the west, south and the east, it makes sense to conclude it is situated in Haradeen Bay, despite not appearing on any map."

Ari smiled at her, and she was gratified by the admiration written on his face. "You are clearly a very perceptive young woman," he said. "That is a very good sign."

Kayden wondered what Ari meant by 'good sign,' but as it sounded like a compliment she kept the question to herself.

"We don't have much farther to go," announced Ari as he led Kayden further into the valley, little knowing how relieved she was to hear that.

Kenit was standing in the portal chamber beneath Kassani House, observing as Fay Annis conversed with a pair of Jaymidari several yards to his right. He had a bad feeling about this whole situation. If the assignment was so innocuous, why had she ordered him to return to his barracks to collect his weapons before coming to the portal chamber? Obviously, he knew that all Sanatsai of the Order were expected to be armed as a matter of course while on active duty, but was it really necessary on this particular occasion if there was no expectation of trouble occurring?

He watched impassively as Fay said her farewells to the Sisters before approaching him, standing alone at the foot of the steps of the raised platform where an open portal awaited them. When she inquired if he was ready to leave he didn't bother to reply. It was a rhetorical question; Fay wasn't going to give him the option of refusing to go. He silently trailed behind her up the steps and followed her as she marched into the portal, disappearing from view.

The bright light that assailed Kenit's eyes dissipated the instant he emerged from the portal. He found himself standing beside Fay in a large wooden building containing crates of fruits and vegetables, sacks of grain, and an assortment of other foodstuffs. The portal opening had transported the pair into the food store used by the Sisterhood seminary they had come to visit. He noted that the light of day, diffusing through the windows, was in stark contrast to the duskiness of approaching nightfall back in Temis Rulan. They were now hundreds of miles away in the Kingdom of Lirantana.

Without preamble Fay headed straight for the exit and Kenit followed her outside. It was late afternoon. The temperature was notably cooler than it was back in Temis Rulan—though by no means cold—and there was a gentle breeze blowing from the east. Fay walked left, and doing likewise Kenit saw the main building of the seminary about sixty yards or so away. The building looked very much like a school, and standing at its main entrance was a single, middle-aged Jaymidari.

"Kenit, you'll have to remain here," said Fay. "Although violet fever is rarely fatal it is an unpleasant affliction, nonetheless. I'll go ahead and speak briefly with the Sister."

Did she just address him by his first name? "Wait," he called out as Fay strolled towards the seminary. "What happens if you become infected?"

"Don't worry, I'm immune," Fay replied.

Kenit doubted the claim but he wasn't going to argue the point; it was Fay's life, if she wished to gamble with it, who was he to interfere.

He observed the conversation between Fay and the Jaymidari before boredom prompted him to cast his gaze around the grounds. Having had the opportunity to visit two other seminaries run by the Sisterhood, Kenit thought it noteworthy just how quiet and deserted this one was. The place should have been a hive of activity with scores of Sisters milling around the grounds, yet he couldn't see or hear another living person. The outbreak of violet fever had to be severe, he concluded, hence the decision to quarantine the seminary.

He almost jumped out of his skin when a hand gripped him by the shoulder.

"Come along," said Fay at his side. "A couple of horses have been made available to us at the stable, we'll head into town right away."

Kenit followed Fay's lead to the nearby stable where two chestnut mares waited, tethered outside—bridled, saddled and ready to ride. He looked on bemused as she untethered one of the horses then began speaking to it with a motherly voice.

"Oh my, aren't you a pretty girl," she said, stroking it's nose. "Yes you are. Yes you are."

Why did women do that? Kenit wondered. It's a horse, not a baby. Of course, he didn't dare say it out loud. He untethered the other mare then promptly climbed up into the saddle and waited for Fay to do the same. Once she did so, then urged her mount into a trot, Kenit followed her lead once more. Together the pair departed the grounds of the seminary moments later, setting off at a canter in a northwesterly direction.

A quarter of an hour later they had slowed to a trot, with the town of Relona looming a short distance ahead. In the time since leaving the seminary Fay hadn't said so much as two words to Kenit, though, by the same token, he hadn't spoken to her, either. He simply didn't have the confidence to strike up a conversation. During his decade-long apprenticeship he had heard and read so many fantastical accounts of the many exploits of Fay Annis, she had become a larger than life figure in his mind. Yet here he was riding alongside her, a real life, flesh and blood woman—a stunningly beautiful one at that—and the awkwardness he was experiencing, courtesy of all the lustful thoughts he was having, ensured that he kept his mouth shut. He could do nothing but stare at her. She was perfection personified. He started to wonder what she looked like out of her uniform, so his mind duly formed images of intimate scenarios that allowed him to find out.

Without turning her head to look sideways at him, Fay casually asked, "Kai Darbandian, is there a problem with my uniform I should be aware of?"

"What!" Kenit gasped as he was snapped out of his thoughts. "Uh, no...no of course not, Danai Annis."

"Then why are you staring at me?"

Feeling flustered, Kenit retorted, "I don't know what you mean."

"You have been staring at me since we left the seminary," Fay reiterated. "Is there a problem?"

Kenit realised Fay was unlikely to drop the matter, which perturbed him. He would have to tell her something.

"I... I... I was..." he stammered. "I was just wondering..."

"Yes?" Fay prompted.

"How old, exactly, are you?"

Fay finally tore her eyes away from the town ahead, glancing sideways to fix her gaze on him. *Oh no!* Kenit assumed from the look on her face he must have offended her.

"Kai Darbandian," began Fay, "did your mother not teach you never to ask a woman her age?"

He had no idea what to say. It was probably best to keep quiet. Anything he said was likely to make things worse. But much to his relief Fay looked away from him, returning her gaze to the way ahead.

"To answer your question," Fay continued, moments later. "I am far too old for you. Now, perhaps you could keep your mind on the task at hand?"

"Yes, Danai!"

They continued to ride in silence for the remainder of the journey to Relona—Kenit taking extra care to ensure his eyes didn't wander to his riding companion once again.

It wasn't long before they arrived at the outskirts of the town, and Fay informed Kenit there was an inn nearby where they could have their horses stabled, so that was where they headed first. Upon dismounting, their horses were attended to by a couple of stablemen while they set off, on foot, into town as late afternoon gave way to early evening.

Walking through the streets of Relona, Kenit noted with keen interest the awed expressions upon the faces of the town's inhabitants. He initially assumed Fay was the cause of their reverence, but that would only make sense if they knew who she was. It was more likely the case that he, too, was inspiring the reaction of the townsfolk he and Fay passed by. That realisation made him feel rather proud.

"Danai Annis?" he said, to gain Fay's attention. "This may seem like a silly question but it just occurred to me. How are Sanatsai-to-be located after their *Zarantar* manifests? As I understand it, Relona has a population of almost fourteen thousand people, we could search all evening for the child we're after and still not find them."

"Do you not recall what happened to you on the day your *Zarantar* manifested?"

"Yes," he replied. "I was escorted home from school by the City Guard after I somehow caused a chair to fly through a window. For the rest of the day, and the following morning, my parents said I wasn't allowed to leave the house because I'd been born imbued with *Zarantar*, and the Order would be arriving soon to see me. Sure enough a Sanatsai and Jaymidari came to our home to give me the choice of apprenticeship or the binding of my *Zarantar*.

"That, however, doesn't tell me how they knew how and where to find me as quickly as they did, especially as I was resident in Fantabelis at the time; a city of over a hundred thousand people."

"The established protocol throughout the Nine Kingdoms, in the event of the manifestation of an adolescent's *Zarantar*, is for it to be reported to the local authorities, immediately, and the child in question confined to home. The personnel subsequently sent to find the child—in this particular instance, you and I—need only report to a Guard station and request to be taken to the family home, which is what we are doing now."

"I see."

Continuing to follow Fay's lead through busy streets, Kenit noted how they were still attracting reverent glances from passersby. He spotted a group of young boys congregated on a corner—one of their number excitedly pointing a finger in his and Fay's direction. He waved at the kids, prompting them to dash away with excited looks on their faces. His ego began to inflate at the prospect of the boys rushing off to tell their family, friends, and anyone else who would listen, that they had just seen a Sanatsai who waved at them. Moments later he caught sight of a pretty young woman wearing a dark blue dress standing in the doorway of a bakery, smiling demurely at him as he and Fay walked by. If he weren't already so enamoured of Fay he would have found his admirer rather beautiful. He might even have halted briefly to speak with her. As it was, all he could do was simply smile back.

"Master Sanatsai!" screamed a female voice. "Master Sanatsai!"

Kenit tore his gaze away from his attractive admirer to see an agitated woman rushing towards them. She appeared to be in her mid-to-late thirties with shoulder-length, dishevelled brunette hair. The beige dress she was wearing had a torn sleeve, and there was noticeable bruising around her throat. The woman stopped Fay in her tracks, gripping her by both arms.

"Master Sanatsai, help me!" cried the woman frantically. "They've taken my son and trapped my husband in some kind of bubble."

"Calm down, calm down," said Fay, trying to soothe the panic-stricken woman. "First of all, take us to your husband."

"Danai Annis," Kenit interjected. "Shouldn't we leave this for the local Guard?" The withering look Fay gave him made him wish he'd refrained from talking. "I just mean—"

Fay ignored him. "Go on," she coaxed, "lead the way, we'll follow."

The woman turned on her heels and darted away in the direction she'd arrived from. Fay immediately gave chase leaving Kenit no option but to do the same. They were led on a short, winding course through the town until their distressed guide slowed to a walk, peering back over her shoulder at Fay.

"It's this way," she said as she headed down a narrow alleyway separating a couple of three-storey residential buildings. She proceeded to lead the pair around the back of the building on their right-hand side where she ran up a staircase leading up to a first floor landing that gave access to a back entrance.

Upon entering the residence, Kenit witnessed a large living room with several pieces of damaged furniture tossed about, and the broken shards of a porcelain vase—obvious signs that a struggle of some kind had taken place. In the centre of the room was a tall middle-aged man standing inside a barrier sphere, pounding away with his fists in a futile effort to escape his translucent confinement.

"That's my husband," said the woman. "Please, help him."

Kenit watched while Fay approached the barrier sphere with one hand outstretched. Her invocation of *Yuksaydan* neutralised the bubble, causing it to dissipate as if consumed by fire or a corrosive substance. Once the man within was free his wife rushed into his arms.

"Thank you," she said in gratitude to Fay. "Thank you."

"My name is Fay Annis, this is my colleague, Kenit Darbandian. Could you tell us who you are and what happened here," said Fay, getting straight down to business. "Who did this to you?"

"My name is Sedona," said the woman. "This is my husband, Radmilio. I don't know who the men were, but they forced their way into our home and did this."

"You mentioned your son was taken," Fay prompted.

The husband responded first. "I arrived home from work a short while ago to find Sedona lying unconscious on the floor while our son, Tylo, was being dragged outside by six hooded men," said Radmilio. "I went to his aid, immediately. One moment I was tackling one of the men to the floor, the next moment I was literally being thrown around the living room by nobody as the intruders looked on in laughter.

"Once they'd managed to get Tylo out of the house, two of the intruders remained inside. I picked myself up off the floor then charged at them both, but one of them just waved his hand and I found myself trapped inside that...bubble. There was nothing I

263

could do to free myself, and when the second man asked, 'shall we kill the parents?' I thought it was over. I was sure Sedona and I were both going to die. But the first man said in reply, 'that won't be necessary, we've got what we came for', then they left. I heard their horses leave in a hurry.

"I must have been trapped for at least a quarter-hour by the time Sedona regained consciousness. I told her to run, to get help...and here you are."

"So neither of you know who these men are," asked Fay, "or why they would want to abduct you son?"

"I have no idea," admitted Radmilio. "On either count."

"I suspect I might know," offered Sedona. "At least the reason why they took Tylo, if not who they are." She looked away from Fay to lock eyes with her husband. "Sweetheart, I'm sorry I didn't have the opportunity to tell you until now, but while you were at work our son... Tylo, he has... he has developed the power of the Sanatsai." She diverted her gaze from her incredulous husband back to Fay. "A few hours ago Tylo accompanied me to the market to help me buy some things for this evening's meal. While I was picking out some fruit from a stall Tylo was messing around, juggling three peaches, when suddenly those three peaches started floating haphazardly in the air in front of him. At first we didn't realise it was him doing it but more fruits began floating up from the stall and they started whirling around him—faster and faster. There must have been five or six dozen fruits spinning round Tylo by the time they all just stopped and fell to the ground around his feet.

"I couldn't believe what I had just seen, but I knew what it meant—and what the law requires in such an event. So, I apologised to the grocer for the damage then I took Tylo to the main Guard station right away to report the incident. After giving our names and address, I was instructed to confine my son to home and ensure he doesn't leave because the Order would be sending someone to see him within the next couple of days."

It finally dawned on Kenit that the couple's son had to be the child he and Fay were looking for. What were the odds that the boy would be abducted shortly before they arrived, by a mysterious group of *Zarantar* wielders?

"About half an hour ago there was a knock at the backdoor—six hooded men wearing matching uniforms, gathered on the landing. The leader of the group claimed they were from the Order, and that they had come to take the new Sanatsai away to be trained. But I knew he was lying. Something about those men made my skin crawl, not to mention I've seen the uniforms worn by the Order before, and theirs was nothing like yours. Although they had the black hooded cloaks, the rest of their uniform was mostly a dark shade of red with black trim and black stitching."

Kenit noted the very subtle change in Fay's demeanour when Sedona described the uniforms worn by her son's kidnappers. Did she know who this group was? he wondered.

"I told the men they had made a mistake—that they'd come to the wrong address," Sedona continued. "I said I was unmarried and had no children, and then I closed the door. I don't know why but I was scared. I just knew I had to get Tylo out of the house, quickly. As I was heading for his room the door burst open behind me. I spun around, and as I feared, the six men marched into our home. The head of the group said that I was a terrible liar, and without even laying a hand on me, he started to strangle me. I could feel the invisible hand around my throat, squeezing. I must have passed out, because the next thing I remember is waking up on the floor to find Radmilio trapped inside that bubble."

Kenit couldn't believe what he was hearing. This supposedly simple little errand was fast turning into a potential nightmare, and worse than that, it was only just beginning.

"All right," said Fay. "It appears that it is your son my colleague and I have come to Relona to find. I realise you must both be worried sick about him, but I assure we will do everything we can to rescue him." She turned her attention to Kenit. "First, we should notify the local Guard, at once. We need to ask them to set up checkpoints at all the exits out of town, and provide men to help us conduct a thorough sweep."

"I think it might be too late for that," Radmilio interrupted, "I heard the men say they were leaving town straight away. And the haste in which they left makes me doubt they'll still be here for you to find."

"In that case," replied Fay, "we'll try to pick up their trail right away. They don't have too great a head start on us. Nonetheless, once we leave I'd still like for you to go to the local Guard to request the setting up of checkpoints and the initiation of a sweep of the town. In all likelihood you're probably correct in your assessment that the men have already left. But they won't be able to evade us for long. You'll see your son again, I promise."

Fay sounded so convincing Kenit almost believed her—wanted to believe her. But he wasn't nearly as confident they could track down the boy let alone rescue him. The men who took Tylo had at least a half-hour head start, but worse than that, they were demonstrably wielders of *Zarantar*, a prospect that filled him with dread because these men couldn't possibly be from the Order.

"Danai Annis, what if the Guard should come upon this group while we're trying to pick up their trail outside town?" Kenit asked. "They would be powerless to prevent them from escaping."

"The Guard will know to give a wide berth to misusers of *Zarantar*. All they need do is to keep watch until we arrive to take care of the situation. Now, let us move out."

"Thank you, Master Sanatsai." Though clearly anxious, Sedona seemed to be holding it together well. "Please bring our son back."

Turning on her heels, Fay marched purposefully towards the backdoor, and Kenit fell into step behind her, following her out of the house. As they descended the staircase at the back of the building he wondered just how his counterpart was planning to pick up the trail of the men who'd abducted Tylo. They could be heading anywhere, assuming they had left the town already. He refrained from voicing any such query, content to just follow Fay's lead while she retraced their steps back the way they had come.

Several minutes later they arrived back at the inn where their horses were stabled. The two stablemen were surprised to see them return so early but they were pleased when Fay tossed them each a gold ranid.

"So, I take it we're heading back to the seminary to send a message to the Council?" said Kenit questioningly, as they led their mounts outside.

"Why would we do that?" Fay's tone made him feel as though he'd just posed the most stupid question imaginable.

"To request reinforcements to help us recover the boy."

"There's no time for that," said Fay, dismissively. "Besides, what purpose would it serve to call reinforcements?"

"Well, whoever these men who took the boy are, there's at least six of them and just two of us." And rescuing Tylo from the clutches of his *Zarantar* wielding abductors almost certainly meant a confrontation: a fight he would be ill equipped to participate in. And while he had grounds to believe Fay could handle six adversaries by herself—if all the stories about her were true—Kenit was all too conscious of the fact that he'd believed similarly about Marit Katarnian, five months earlier.

"And your point is?" asked Fay, as she brought them to a halt outside on the street in front of the inn.

"The point is..." Kenit didn't wish to appear cowardly but he had to tell Fay the truth, or something resembling the truth. "The point is," he said, "if it becomes necessary to fight in order to rescue the boy, you might want someone other than myself as backup. Somebody with actual combat experience."

"You're probably right. But you're all I've got right now, so I'll just have to make do."

"But—" Kenit's protestation was cut short when Fay sighed, pointedly locking her eyes on his. Whether she was angry or just exasperated he couldn't say for certain but there was no doubt she was displeased.

"Kenit." It was the second time Fay had addressed him by his first name, not by his rank and family name. "When you were given the two choices, why did you choose to become an apprentice?" Given her demeanour Kenit hadn't anticipated the gentleness in her tone; she sounded like a concerned mother.

"Because..." It dawned on him that he didn't really have an answer. "Because I... Well..."

"It's all right, there isn't a right answer," interjected Fay, "so

267

you don't need to tell me what you think I want to hear."

It was a relief for him to hear those words. "The truth is I don't really know why I accepted the apprenticeship," Kenit conceded. "I guess I saw the opportunity as a chance for a little adventure. Plus, I assumed I would be sent back home to my family sooner rather than later."

"And yet you completed the ten years training and were inducted into the Order. You succeeded where many fail, and others choose to quit. You have earned the right to wear that uniform," Fay gestured at his clothing, "so never doubt yourself in that regard. But you must also remember that having embraced the tremendous gift you've been bestowed with, you now have a responsibility to use it whenever the need arises."

Kenit began to feel somewhat guilty about his reticence to attempt a rescue of the kidnapped boy. Fay was right, he did have a responsibility to use his power to help others. Whether or not he was up to the task was another matter entirely. "All right, what's the plan?" he asked. "The abductors could be anywhere by now."

Fay elegantly climbed up into the saddle of her horse. "We'll head north out of town, see if we can pick up a trail."

"How can you be sure they went north?" asked Kenit, looking up at Fay.

"I can't be certain. But the balance of probability favours going north. If the group had fled south we would have encountered them on our way here. Heading east would take them towards the border with Mirtana. There's a large military presence in the area: three major garrison towns, not to mention the border patrols. And assuming the group wants to avoid a confrontation with the Order, they wouldn't travel westward as we have a training camp a few miles west of here, and of course, the Duranis campus is to the northwest.

"It would make the most sense for our quarry to head north, taking them into the Sharadi Forest. It's a vast wilderness spanning both sides of the border, going there would make it easy for them to conceal their crossing into Mirtana. For all we know, they could very well be based in the Sharadi. The forest contains several ruins of an ancient civilisation that could be used as a base."

Kenit had to trust in Fay's judgement. She obviously knew what she was doing, she was the experienced one and following her lead was the prudent course of action. So, in spite of his misgivings about the potential dangers that lay ahead of them, he mounted his horse.

"Very well, Danai. Lead the way."

Fay urged her horse into a brisk trot and Kenit did likewise. The hunt was on for the mysterious kidnappers of a young Sanatsai-to-be.

CHAPTER FIFTEEN

The Calm Before The Storm

Kayden and Master Ari were not yet out of the valley, so she was taken by surprise when he halted in his tracks to proudly declare that they had finally reached their destination. Confused, Kayden slowly spun around, three hundred and sixty degrees, to cast her dubious eyes over their surroundings. Straight ahead, to the north, were deserted flatlands, just grass as far as the eye could see. To her left she saw the western ridge of the valley, the skies behind it tinged with the orange-red glow of the dying light from the sun, disappearing below the horizon. Behind her was the southern pass that had brought them into the valley, while to her right she could just about see the eastern ridge of the valley being encroached upon by the darkness of rapidly approaching nightfall.

She and Ari had just a handful of small and medium sized white rocks for company, haphazardly scattered about, protruding from the earth. She very much doubted she'd been brought all that way just to stare at some rocks.

"Master Ari," she exclaimed. "We're in the middle of nowhere."

"That's a matter of perspective."

Kayden looked on as Ari invoked *Sinjaydan* to create a large illumination orb that he sent floating several feet above their heads. Next he removed the knapsack from his shoulder, crouched down, and began to unpack it. First came out a large red and white check tablecloth that he spread out upon the grass before him. Though she was growing accustomed to Ari's unorthodox manner, Kayden had a hard time believing he'd brought her on a two-hour trek for the sole purpose of having a picnic.

Ari looked up at her. "Have a seat, Kayden." He gestured for her to sit opposite him on the other side of the tablecloth.

Kayden removed the knapsack from her shoulder, placing it gently on the ground, then duly sat down across from Ari. She watched as he removed a number of cloth bundles from his own knapsack that he proceeded to unwrap. The respective bundles contained stoned dates, an assortment of nuts and dried fruit, slices of cold meat, and some vegetable fritters. They were going to have a picnic, it seemed.

"If you look inside your knapsack you'll find a canteen and two mugs, plus a few treats for desert," said Ari. "The canteen contains honeyed mint tea, why don't you pour us both a cup?"

Kayden reached for the knapsack and proceeded to empty its contents. First she pulled out the canteen—still very warm to the touch—then two ceramic mugs. Next she removed three cloth bundles and set them down on the tablecloth. As she began pouring the tea, Ari stood up and turned his back to her. She observed with interest as he thrust a hand forward at one of the larger rocks before him. A stream of shimmering air, resembling a heat haze, extended from him to the white rock; Ari was invoking *Shakbarilsan* to rapidly heat up the rock. Within moments it was so hot the rock was radiating heat back towards them. He repeated this process with a few of the smaller rocks that circled their picnic spot before sitting back down.

"Summer nights here on the island tend to be rather mild," announced Ari, "but once you reach my age a little extra warmth is always very welcome, nonetheless."

Kayden handed Ari a cup of mint tea, for which he thanked her, then she set about unwrapping the three remaining cloth bundles. The first bundle contained a selection of jam tarts, the second an assortment of flapjacks, and the third contained several oatmeal biscuits.

"Master Ari, you didn't bring me all the way out here to eat," she said. "What are we really doing here?"

"The answer to that question shall reveal itself to you soon," Ari replied cryptically. "In the meantime, tuck in. We'll be here a while yet." With that he began to help himself to some dates.

Grasping her mug of tea, Kayden held it up to her nose. She had never tasted mint tea before, honeyed or otherwise, but it sure did smell good. She took a cautious sip of the beverage and swallowed.

"Mmmmm!" she sounded. "That tastes so good."

Smiling back at her, Ari replied, "Yes, it does."

Kayden proceeded to help herself to the food on offer. For the next few minutes she and Ari ate and drank in contented silence.

The lull in conversation eventually came to an end when Ari said, "On our way here you brought up the topic of your history lessons, which is rather fortuitous because the weight of history is one of the reasons for your presence here today." He took another sip of mint tea then set down his mug. "Perhaps the most important historical account you would have been taught while on campus is the role played by the Rogue during The Great War; correct?"

"Yes, Master," replied Kayden as she helped herself to another fritter. "Though I don't see how the stories about a rogue Sanatsai constitute actual history."

"I'm not sure what you mean."

"Oh come on, Master! The alleged accounts of the Rogue are nothing more than tales of the kind parents tell their children in order to frighten them into behaving."

Ari fixed her with a penetrating gaze. "In some ways, Kayden, you are right," he said soberly. "The life of the Rogue is very much a cautionary tale. But I assure you, the Rogue was a real flesh and blood person just like you, and the instrument by which Josario, the Usurper King, waged war in his quest to subjugate the Nine Kingdoms and establish an empire." The intensity of his gaze eased, slightly. "I'm curious as to why you believe otherwise."

Kayden didn't have to give Ari's query much thought. "Back on campus, whenever any of the instructors mention the Rogue, it's always in such vague terms. They seem to go out of their way to avoid identifying this person: they never provide a name, never provide a place of birth, never provide a physical description... Nothing. For that matter, they also refrain from specifying the gender of the Rogue, as you've been doing. It's almost as if someone decided that the less detail provided about this alleged rogue Sanatsai the easier it will be for everyone to keep the story straight."

"You are very cynical for one so young." Ari chuckled in good nature. "But to address your point, the reason for the vagueness in the specifics of the Rogue's identity is twofold. Firstly, the purpose of teaching you apprentices about the role played the Rogue during the Great War is to warn you of the dangers of misusing and abusing the great power you've been blessed with. So in that regard the identity of the Rogue is ultimately irrelevant. And secondly, the truth of the matter is, none of your instructors know the true identity of the Rogue any more than you do.

"When Josario unleashed his weapon of choice against the Nine Kingdoms very few people who subsequently encountered the Rogue lived to tell the tale. As a result, during the Great War it was frequently whispered that to look upon the face of the Rogue was to see death itself."

"But Master Ari," said Kayden. "Even if I accept you at your word that the Rogue was a real person, surely the accounts taught to us are exaggerated."

Picking up another date, Ari asked, "What makes you say that?" He placed the sweet brown fruit in his mouth and chewed.

"According to the historical accounts, after Josario usurped the throne of Balintana and subjugated the kingdom, he was then quickly able to conquer the kingdoms of Yaristana, Jibaltana and Farintana. The rapid advancement of his forces only slowed down when the king of Shintana pre-empted Josario's inevitable invasion of his kingdom to launch a counter-offensive. Yet, in spite of this setback Josario's forces were still able to conquer two thirds of Shintana before the coalition you helped form defeated them decisively during the final battle of the Great War, at Lilac Valley.

"The problem with this simplistic account of history is the

idea that by seizing the reigns of power in Balintana—the smallest and weakest of the Nine Kingdoms—Josario could then use it as a springboard for accomplishing such incredible military successes, in under two years, because of a single Sanatsai spearheading his forces. It's just not believable."

While waiting for his response, Kayden took the opportunity to pour herself some more honeyed mint tea. She glanced at him when the reply she was anticipating did not arrive. Master Ari appeared to be locked in thought. Reminiscing about something, perhaps?

"It's not believable to you because you never witnessed with your own two eyes what the Rogue was capable of," Ari remarked, finally. "Experience would surely change your mind, make no mistake. For my part, I can tell you in no uncertain terms that the Rogue was the most powerful Sanatsai I had ever encountered—able to utilise *Zarantar* in ways I never imagined, and with a mastery and control I'd never seen the like of before.

"It might interest you to hear that some of the abilities you have learned to master as an apprentice, were first pioneered by the Rogue."

That was a very interesting revelation, Kayden realised; no wonder she'd never heard it mentioned before. Throughout the Nine Kingdoms it was a commonly held view that the Rogue was evil incarnate. If the people were to learn that all Sanatsai of the Order are trained to use abilities first mastered by the Rogue it would likely prove very controversial.

"Suffice to say," continued Ari, "you *should* believe everything you have ever been told about the Rogue. To this day no other Sanatsai has reached the heights or matched the power of the Rogue, not even me."

"Master, if that were true, how could you have single-handedly defeated the Rogue on the last day of The Great War?"

He began laughing wholeheartedly.

Kayden didn't think she had said anything even remotely funny, but clearly Master Ari felt differently.

"Oh, my young friend," sighed Ari once he had regained his composure. "As much as I might like to take all the credit for our victory that day, the truth is, it required many of us, Sanatsai and Jaymidari alike, working in unison to overcome the Rogue. And fortunately for us, it proved decisive. Once word spread across the battlefield that the Rogue had fallen it took the wind out of the sails of Josario's forces and they quickly began to surrender. It seems he made the mistake of convincing his soldiers they could not be defeated as long as they were led into battle by the Rogue. That his men believed this to be true was a blessing in disguise for our side. By the time we defeated the Rogue we had lost so many people during the battle we would surely have lost anyway if Josario's men hadn't laid down their arms."

"So how did you do it, Master?" said Kayden, reaching for a jam tart. "The accounts of how the Rogue was killed are very vague. I would love to hear the whole story from you, from the beginning, starting with the evening before the battle, when the coalition encamped along the bank of the Kassani River and the leaders of the resistance pledged to help you realise your dream of establishing the Order."

"It's a rather lengthy story," Ari warned.

"I'm not going anywhere, Master."

"Very well." Ari poured himself some more mint tea then proceeded to narrate his story as Kayden listened with intent interest.

It had taken over an hour, but finally Kenit and Fay reached the southern edge of Sharadi Forest. During the ride Kenit found it hard to countenance Fay's assertion that the six-strong group of kidnappers must have journeyed to the Sharadi. They hadn't picked up a trail, or any signs to confirm the validity of Fay's conviction. Nonetheless, he refrained from giving voice to his misgivings. As far as he was concerned he was very much the junior party of this partnership, therefore had no real option other than to trust Fay's judgement.

A quarter of an hour after entering the forest it was proving slow going on horseback. The trees were densely packed together, so the pair couldn't ride much faster than a trot. Kenit could see the sky in places through the thick canopy of branches and leaves overhead but it was darker than it should have been. Although there were still a couple of hours daylight left, ominous dark-grey rainclouds were rolling in from the north, blotting out the late evening sun entirely. Those clouds were also triggering Kenit's anxiety. While it was bad enough that he and Fay were searching Sharadi Forest without backup, it now seemed as though they were in for a drenching sooner rather than later, too.

Upon reaching the moss-covered remnants of a stone wall—the first sign they had encountered of the ancient ruins Sharadi Forest was known for—Fay brought her mount to a halt. Kenit did the same, but was caught by surprise when Fay gracefully dismounted her horse then looked up at him.

"We'll leave the horses here and continue on foot," she announced.

"Why?"

"They make too much noise," she replied. "I'd rather our quarry didn't hear us approaching when we find them."

Kenit couldn't argue with that logic so he too dismounted, though it did make him feel more vulnerable which he knew wasn't logical. He was no safer from attack on horseback than on foot, although it was certainly the case he could flee more quickly on a horse if the need arose.

After they tethered the horses to a couple of trees, Kenit was caught off guard again when Fay invoked *Dashimkuzar*, creating a thin, translucent aura that enveloped her, rather appropriately, like a second skin—the literal meaning of the word. The obvious inference to be drawn from the action was that Fay was anticipating trouble from this point onwards.

"Until we locate our men, let's err on the side of caution and maintain *Dashimkuzar*," said Fay. "It is getting dark, and we might not spot an archer lurking in the trees until it's too late."

"But we already know the men we're after are wielders of *Zarantar*, so why worry about arrows?" He knew the 'second skin' was an impenetrable barrier that would protect them against conventional projectile weapons, as well as bladed weapons, but it would still leave them vulnerable to certain *Zarantar* attacks.

Fay looked at him as though he were a simpleton. "An arrow

or crossbow bolt will kill the unsuspecting Sanatsai just as well as a *Zarantar* strike."

She had a point there, Kenit admitted to himself—not that it negated his contention that *Dashimkuzar* would be effectively useless against adversaries who also wielded *Zarantar*. For one thing, the 'second skin' could only withstand one, maybe two direct hits from a strike unleashed by a wielder of *Zarantar*. For another, the level of concentration required to sustain the protective barrier around a constantly moving body, made it near impossible to maintain while engaged in actual combat. And as powerful as she might be, not even Fay would rely upon *Dashimkuzar* for defence if they should be drawn into a fight with the kidnappers in order to rescue the abducted boy.

Nonetheless, until they did encounter their quarry—assuming they were present in Sharadi Forest—it was prudent to mitigate the risk of a silent, but deadly projectile let loose from the trees. Kenit invoked *Dashimkuzar*, forming the tell-tale translucent aura that would offer the necessary protection against such an occurrence, then followed Fay further into the forest.

He couldn't be certain just how long they had been walking when he first noticed the change in their surroundings, but they had reached an area of the forest that was much less dense and was increasingly littered with the dilapidated remains of a lost civilisation. What he could be reasonably certain of was they were now getting closer to finding what they were searching for. At least Fay seemed to think so. She ceased her invocation of *Dashimkuzar* and stopped in her tracks. Looking back over her shoulder at him, she pressed a finger to her lips before advancing forward once more, taking extra care to move as quietly as possible.

Kenit let down his protective aura and followed Fay through the trees. It wasn't long before he picked up the murmur of voices and the movement of bodies a short distance ahead. Fay brought them to a stop then crouched down at the foot of a tree. Kenit squatted down behind her, and peering over her shoulder he could see, beyond the line of trees a few yards ahead, the forest opened up into a vast clearing that was home to the ruins of what he believed must have been a temple complex. It was an educated guess. The present day people of the Nine Kingdoms held no religious beliefs so places of worship did not exist anywhere in the Nine Kingdoms, leaving Kenit with no frame of reference. But historians seemed to be in agreement that in the distant past the ancients had built temples to worship statues they had carved with their own hands; a notion Kenit found bizarre in the extreme.

Surveying the scene, he spied men dressed in dark red uniforms with black trim, and hooded black cloaks. There was considerably more than six of them—a lot more. He doubted there were less than eighty of them in total. It was entirely possible there were as many as a hundred. Any hopes of rescuing Radmilio and Sedona's son just evaporated.

"It's as I suspected," said Fay barely above a whisper, seemingly to herself rather than to Kenit. "The Conclave."

"The Conclave?" queried Kenit. He had absolutely no idea what Fay was referring to.

"It is something the Order does not like to acknowledge," she began, "so you cannot repeat what I am about to tell you."

"Understood, Danai."

Kenit's curiosity was well and truly piqued.

"There is one particular detail of the early history of the Order that has been censored at the insistence of the Council. You will find no mention of it in any records, and anyone who possesses knowledge of it will deny having any such knowledge if questioned about it.

"At the end of the Great War, when the ruling families of the Nine Kingdoms agreed to pass into law the requirement that all present and future Sanatsai born within their realms must join the Order or have their Zarantar bound, there was some...dissent against the idea. While most of those Sanatsai who opposed the creation of the Order reluctantly assented in the end, there was a significant minority who became fanatically opposed to relinquishing their autonomy. They banded together to form the Conclave—a movement dedicated to eliminating the Order in its infancy. Subsequently, the first six months of the Order's existence was spent putting down the rebellion. It was a... destructive period, but we succeeded in wiping out the renegade

Sanatsai."

If Fay's account was accurate, and the Conclave was destroyed seven decades ago, then it appeared someone had resurrected the group without the Order getting wind of it.

"Danai Annis, if you're right, how could anyone have reconstituted the group without us finding out about it?" asked Kenit. "And how were they able to recruit people? Thanks to our alliance with the Sisterhood we always know when a new Sanatsai manifests in the Nine Kingdoms, so it's not feasible that these men gathered here are people who slipped through the cracks."

"I don't have an answer," admitted Fay. "But it's possible this group is comprised of foreigners who've infiltrated the Nine Kingdoms from abroad. Sharadi Forest is a very good place to hide and remain undetected."

"Well, whether you're right or not, we still need to withdraw. We'll have to return to the seminary to report back to the Council, and to request the reinforcements I mentioned before we left Relona."

"No!" said Fay. "We stay until we can ascertain if the boy is being held here, somewhere."

"So what if he is? There's nothing we can do to help him—not without reinforcements. It looks as though there's at least a hundred of these renegade Sanatsai, and only the two of us. We should go now before we are discovered. We can return in greater numbers tomorrow."

"There's no guarantee they will still be here tomorrow, besides—" Fay's attention was drawn back to the ruins of the temple complex; there was some activity.

Two Conclave personnel emerged from behind the remnants of a stone wall, escorting an adolescent boy. It was a safe assumption he was Tylo, the abducted boy Kenit and Fay had come to rescue. His hands were bound in front of him, while a gag was tied around his mouth. As the gathered throng of uniformed men and women looked on, the boy was slowly led towards an area of the complex that had once been the interior of a large building but was now completely exposed to the elements. The roof was gone entirely, while here and there the remnants of several ruined walls remained standing—all but one no taller than waist height. A raised stone platform prominently featured, upon which stood a weather-worn stone altar.

Tylo was brought to the altar and made to stand beside it while his two escorts remained on either side of him, waiting—for someone or something.

"Things are worse than I thought," muttered Fay.

"What do you mean?"

"There is a Saharbashi present, or there will be soon."

Kenit's heart skipped a beat, his breath caught in his throat. The mere mention of the word Saharbashi made him feel nauseous. "That...that doesn't make any sense...does it?" he stammered. "Why would there be a Saharbashi among a group of Sanatsai, even if they are renegades?" He failed to keep the fear from his voice.

"An alliance of convenience actually makes a lot of sense," countered Fay. "Alone, a single Saharbashi could never hope to take on the Order—he would need to form a group. Yet the formation of a group of Saharbashi has never been possible because they simply cannot trust each other. But joining forces with a group of Sanatsai fanatically devoted to destroying the Order would be the perfect alternative. For all we know, this Saharbashi could very well be responsible for the revival of the Conclave in the first place."

Kenit couldn't understand why Fay didn't sound at all disturbed by what she was speculating; he found the whole idea terrifying, if it was true.

"How can you even be sure there is a Saharbashi here?" he asked.

"A blood letting is being prepared." Fay didn't take her eyes off the scene ahead of them. "The boy will be drained of some or all of his blood."

"I...I thought Saharbashi used blood from animals."

"Most do," Fay affirmed. "But the more knowledgeable among them favour blood from people, especially when they have no fear of being caught."

Kenit had never heard this about the Saharbashi before, but

Fay spoke so authoritatively he didn't doubt the truthfulness of the claim.

"A blood letting is usually conducted at nightfall," continued Fay, "so I don't expect our Saharbashi to make an appearance until then. We will await his arrival before we make our move to save the boy."

Was Danai Annis out of her mind? Kenit thought, in alarm. It was bad enough she was insisting on attempting a rescue of Tylo from a hundred or so hostile Sanatsai, but now she wanted to wait for a Saharbashi to join them before doing so. He knew only too well what a practitioner of *Zarantar Najist* was capable of, he had seen it first hand five months ago during the ill-fated mission in Anzarmenia. What Fay was suggesting was folly of the highest order.

"Danai Annis," he said quietly, "I don't mean to speak out of turn, but the two of us attempting to rescue the boy from a hundred renegade Sanatsai is madness. And not to put too fine a point on it, attempting to do so only *after* their Saharbashi ally has arrived would be suicide. We've done everything we can, but now it's time to leave, there's nothing to be gained by throwing our lives away on a fool's errand."

Fay slowly turned around to face Kenit; she did not look amused. "Your concern has been duly noted. But we're going to rescue the boy, nonetheless."

Kenit started to inch away from Fay, readying to leave. "You'll have to do it without me," he hissed, voice rising, "I didn't come here to die."

Grabbing Kenit by his tabard, Fay yanked him towards her—their faces inches apart. "Keep your voice down before you give us away." The indignant look in her eyes made it clear she had finally lost patience with him. "Now listen to me very carefully. You can be as afraid as you want. I don't care. But as for running away and leaving the boy to his fate? *Not happening!* We do not abandon our own...*ever!*" She released her grip on him. "In other words, we're going to rescue Tylo or we will die trying, is that understood?"

He was at a loss for words; Fay had him between a rock and a hard place. If he fled now, he was finished as a Sanatsai of the Order. He couldn't return to Temis Rulan in the event of another prominent figure being killed in the line of duty because he had abdicated his responsibility. He felt shamed by Fay's commitment to her calling, even if it meant her death. What choice did he have but to stay? Whether he liked it or not he was Fay's backup.

"Forgive me, Danai," he said finally. "You're right, we can't abandon the boy. So what do we do now?"

"Now we wait." Fay turned back around to resume her observation of the Conclave gathering amid the ruins of the temple complex.

Kayden had completely lost track of time while sitting, listening to Ari recount the final battle of the Great War. The manner of his narration was such that not only was she thoroughly engrossed, to the point where she couldn't say how long she'd been listening for, she also needed to frequently remind herself she wasn't hearing a fictional tale from a master storyteller. What she was being told was historical fact, events that had really taken place seven decades earlier. And now, finally, Master Ari had come to the part she most wanted to hear.

"Though I, too, had heard all the stories of the undefeatable Sanatsai leading Josario's forces to victory after victory, ruthlessly terrorising those who opposed the Usurper King, nothing could have prepared me for the reality I bore witness to on the battlefield that day. The Rogue was a brutal and sadistic killer, and I believe this fuelled not only the certainty of victory in Josario's men, but also their fear of defeat. As long as the Rogue lived there was no hope they would ever surrender.

"We knew from the start it was imperative that Josario's greatest weapon be removed from the battlefield if victory was to be achieved, hence the reason the resistance decided to throw all its eggs into one basket. Even though three other divisions had been mobilised to march against smaller Shintanese cities further north, we committed to engaging the division that had to pass through Lilac Valley before crossing the Kassani River to attack the capital. We knew this division would be led by the Rogue so that's where all our resources were devoted–the fate of the Nine Kingdoms would be decided at Lilac Valley.

"As the battle raged into its eighth hour many fighters had fallen, on both sides, but we were undeniably bearing the brunt of those losses, and we couldn't afford to lose. Defeat that day would have meant relinquishing the unconquered third of Shintana to Josario. If that happened there would have been no stopping him then. With Shintana being both the largest and the most powerful of the Nine Kingdoms, its fall would have been swiftly followed by the conquests of Darmitana, Mirtana, Lirantana and Astana.

"We were slowly being pushed back towards the river when I finally caught sight of the Rogue for the first time. A tall figure, clad head to toe in black, a hooded cloak billowing in the breeze, and a face inexplicably obscured by shadow, despite the bright light of day. At last we knew where to concentrate our attack. I remember it vividly, more than a dozen of us—both Sanatsai and Jaymidari—rallied together and surged forward with singularity of purpose...to kill the Rogue."

Ari briefly paused his narration and Kayden found she was holding her breath in anticipation, eagerly waiting to hear how the Rogue was ultimately defeated.

"It would be an understatement to describe the ensuing encounter as hard fought," Ari continued. "Only three of us remained standing when the Rogue was finally subdued—down on hands and knees, head bowed in defeat, staring resignedly at the ground, just yards in front of me."

Finally. The moment Kayden was longing to hear had arrived.

"With sword in hand I moved in for the kill."

"So what happened when you killed the Rogue?" she interrupted, sounding more excited than she intended.

Ari gazed fixedly at her, his face looking sombre. "I didn't."

"What do you mean you didn't kill the Rogue?" Kayden was confused. This wasn't how the story was supposed to go.

"I couldn't do it," Ari confessed. "Not until I had looked with my own eyes upon the face that had been the harbinger of death to so many. 'Look at me,' I demanded. The Rogue looked up at me, and our eyes locked. What I saw staring back at me was difficult to comprehend. I had expected to see a monster, the personification of evil, someone hideous in every conceivable way. Instead, what I saw was distress, self-loathing, a longing for death...but nothing remotely ugly. I hadn't anticipated this. Until that moment, I had lost sight of the fact that the Rogue was an actual human being."

All of a sudden, Kayden's senses were assailed by *Zarantar*. Whatever the cause, it was so close she involuntarily gasped with a discernible intake of breath.

"You can feel that, can't you?" said Ari rhetorically.

"What is it?"

Ari slowly rose to his feet. "It's the reason why you're here," he replied. "Stand up, Kayden." Despite her apprehension she duly obeyed his instruction. "Now turn around."

Turning around in obedience, Kayden unwittingly took a step backwards, on account of the sight that greeted her. When she had first sat down on the spot where she now stood, all that was behind her were rolling fields as far as the eye could see. Yet, she was now confronted by the sight of a vast forest, literally a couple of feet before her, and a dirt path winding its way through the trees into the darkness.

She peered back over her shoulder at Ari. "Master, what is this?"

"The Sisterhood call it many different names: the Forest of Revelation; the Forest of Enlightenment; the Forest of Reflection. These are just three such given names," said Ari. "It can only be seen at night, and it is the reason why I brought you out here."

"I don't understand."

"In the years before I founded the Order," Ari began in explanation, "if a Jaymidari had concerns about a Sanatsai in her charge, but those concerns did not yet warrant the binding of *Zarantar*, she would bring the Sanatsai in question to this place."

"Why?"

"The forest provided a final opportunity for troublesome Sanatsai to avoid the binding of their *Zarantar*." Kayden did not like the sound of that. The implication was obvious. "The Sister responsible for guiding such a Sanatsai would send her charge into the forest to walk the path to the other side, in order to determine if the binding of *Zarantar* was the appropriate course of action."

The explanation left Kayden confused.

"How exactly would sending somebody into the forest help a Sister make that decision?"

"Walking the path reveals the path of the walker."

Kayden wanted to roll her eyes but settled for groaning on the inside. The cryptic response made no sense whatsoever—ergo it was less than useless. She averted her eyes from Ari back to the dirt path ahead of her, disappearing into the forest.

"If I am expected to enter the forest," she said, "I would like to know what's in there waiting for me."

"I couldn't tell you," Ari conceded. "I've never entered the forest myself; it's been almost a century since anyone has. But as I understand it, what lies within is different for everyone."

Peering back over her shoulder at Ari again, Kayden asked, "So what do I do?"

"Just make your way to the end of the path. I'll be waiting for you there."

"That's it?" Surely it couldn't be that simple, she thought.

"Yes, that's it," affirmed Ari. "But I must warn you..."

Kayden listened attentively.

"It's important you don't turn back or stray from the path."

"Understood," said Kayden, though she didn't really understand. She returned her gaze to the path laid out before her and stiffened her resolve. Whatever obstacles may be lying in wait for her within the forest, she would overcome, just like she always did. She marched forward purposefully, setting one foot in front of the other, initiating her journey into the unknown. The Forest of Revelation held no fear for her.

CHAPTER SIXTEEN

To The Rescue

The thick, dark clouds made it impossible for Kenit to see the setting of the sun through the canopy of branches and leaves overhead. Nonetheless, he was still able to discern, from the increasing gloom, that night was falling. While remaining crouched behind Fay at the foot of a large tree, the only light visible was emanating from a dozen or so illumination orbs floating above the ruins of the ancient temple complex. During the wait for nightfall, there had been so little activity among the contingent of renegade Sanatsai gathered amid the ruins in the clearing beyond the trees, Kenit found himself having to suppress a prolonged bout of yawning that culminated in a whack to the arm from Fay, after he inadvertently dozed off on one occasion.

His mind wandered uneasily to thoughts of how the night would likely play out. The rescue he was preparing to pull off with Fay was dangerous, even if everything went to plan. And given his prior experience, his confidence that nothing would go wrong was pretty low. The only crumb of comfort he had to hold on to was that this time he was in the company of the legendary Fay Annis. Not only was she regarded as the most powerful Sanatsai of the Order, she was also, thankfully, going to be implementing the most dangerous part of the rescue mission.

He was jolted out of his ruminations when Fay muttered, "The guest of honour is arriving."

He peered over her shoulder to catch sight of a short, middle-aged man dressed in dark robes entering the clearing from the north with four escorts from the Conclave.

Fay peered back over her shoulder at him, staring intently into his eyes. "Are you ready for this, Kai Darbandian?" she asked.

"Ready as I'll ever be," he replied, with as much conviction as he could muster.

"Repeat the plan to me."

After a sharp intake of breath, he duly obliged. "Very well. You will move into position in the trees on the western edge of the clearing. Before the blood letting ritual commences you will create a diversion to induce the Conclave into pursuing you into the forest. Once the boy is left unguarded I will invoke *Raytandushay* in order to enter the clearing unseen. I will release Tylo, then lead him back to where we left our horses. You will rejoin us there, at which point we'll swiftly depart Sharadi Forest and head back to Relona."

"Very good," said Fay. "But keep in mind I cannot guarantee they will all follow me into the forest. It may be necessary for you to fight off any stragglers in order to rescue the boy."

That concern had already occurred to Kenit. "I know," he acknowledged.

"I don't know for certain how these people will react once we make our move. What I can tell you is that the original incarnation of the Conclave was very fanatical. Whenever the Order engaged its members, they always refused to surrender; they fought to the bitter end."

"I understand." If the worst came to the worst he would have to kill to save the boy. "I won't let you down."

Without another word Fay quickly rose from her crouching position and scampered away into the trees. Kenit slowly stood up to watch her depart until she was out of sight. He then turned his attention back to the clearing to keep an eye on events unfolding amid the temple ruins, and await Fay's initiation of their rescue plan.

As he watched proceedings, Kenit was surprised at just how calm the young boy appeared to be, standing on the dais, flanked by two hooded men. Clearly, Tylo had no idea what was in store for him. Either that or he was simply an incredibly brave kid. There was also the possibility he was already resigned to his fate.

Kenit tensed when the boy was finally forced to lay upon the weathered stone altar. Whatever Fay was planning to do to attract the attention of the Conclave was going to happen any moment now. He trembled involuntarily as he watched the Saharbashi ascend the dais while withdrawing a dagger from beneath his garments. In stark contrast to himself, the gathering of renegade Sanatsai were apparently looking forward to what they thought was coming. Every man and woman was standing uniformly, facing the raised platform, as still as a collection of statues.

He shifted his gaze from the spectacle to glance towards the trees at the western edge of the clearing. What was Danai Annis waiting for? he wondered. If she didn't make her move quickly it would be too late to save the life of the boy.

Kenit didn't have to wait long for Fay's action. When it came it happened so swiftly it took him just as much by surprise as it did the Conclave. Without warning, one of the renegade Sanatsai standing at the rear of the gathering was lifted off his feet and pulled rapidly through the air—well over a hundred yards—into the trees at the edge of the temple complex. His disappearance was immediately followed by a blood-curdling scream that caused those close by to spin around.

From the edge of the clearing the ground began to erupt and tear up, swiftly cutting a number of paths towards the gathered renegade Sanatsai; it was as though a dozen invisible, giant ploughs were hurtling across the ground, shredding the earth in their wake. Almost half the contingent of Conclave personnel was bowled over onto the ground while the remainder were able to react in time, invoking *Makfayshulat* to levitate into the air and successfully evade the unconventional attack.

Their quick thinking was punished instantly.

From her cover in the trees Fay invoked *Balatlaydan*, unleashing a rapid volley of incendiary orbs through the air directed at the multiple floating targets. No fewer than a dozen of the enemy were blown to bloody, smouldering pieces.

Kenit was awed by the display of power. Fay's diversion was devastating in its effectiveness. From start to finish the attack had taken no more than four or five seconds to throw the Conclave into disarray. Regaining some of his own composure, he returned his gaze to the dais and the stone altar. He was mightily relieved to see the Saharbashi being hurriedly escorted from the scene towards the line of trees at the eastern edge of the temple complex. During the commotion that ensued, Tylo, was forgotten and left alone upon the altar like a piece of discarded rubbish, though thankfully unharmed.

"The Order!" somebody yelled.

Turning his head, he saw that those renegade Sanatsai who'd escaped death or injury were all back on their feet, their initial disarray overcome. The Conclave was now preparing to retaliate. They stood, angrily facing the trees at the western edge of the clearing where the attack had originated. Several men and women unleashed a barrage of incendiary orbs of their own into the trees. Kenit heard the unmistakeable sound of the lethal orbs detonating as they struck against...

He couldn't see Fay from his position, but he had to assume she was either standing inside a barrier sphere or behind a barrier shield, which should protect her from the onslaught; and now that she had the attention of the Conclave she would retreat as planned, hopefully drawing most, if not all of their number away from the ruins into the forest.

"I only see one person," someone announced. "He's fleeing."

"Hurry!" yelled another voice, "We need to hunt him down before he can send for help."

There was an almighty roar as the Conclave charged forward en masse into the trees in pursuit of their attacker. Kenit observed with keen interest to see how many would remain behind. He was more than a little perturbed by all the fanatical cries of, *Death to the Order,*" coming from several of the departing renegade Sanatsai, but very relieved that nearly all the Conclave had decided to give chase into the forest. Only three of them remained amid the ruins. One was sitting down on the torn-up ground with a hand gripped around his ankle and a grimace upon his face, while a second male was hobbling on one leg, leaning against an uninjured female counterpart for support. None of the three were paying any attention, whatsoever, to the dais where Tylo had been left alone and unguarded.

The boy was obviously quick-witted, Kenit realised, for he was taking advantage of the disturbance to make an escape attempt. His hands were still bound in front of him, but he was able to remove the gag from his mouth before clambering off the weathered stone altar. He took the time to glance here and there to discern the best route for escape then cautiously descended the raised platform. Once on the ground, he began to creep forward through the ruins, while simultaneously manoeuvring his fingers to loosen the bonds around his wrists. He was heading steadily towards the trees at the eastern edge of the temple complex, which was the wrong direction as far as Kenit was concerned—in more ways than one.

Kenit pulled the hood of his cloak up over his head before invoking *Raytandushay* to make himself invisible. He dashed out of the trees into the clearing towards Tylo. If he could reach the boy before anyone noticed him trying to escape and, more importantly, before he disappeared into the trees where the Saharbashi and his escorts had fled, Kenit was certain he could pull off his part of the rescue plan without having to engage the Conclave at all.

The short length of rope binding Tylo's wrists fell away to the ground, discarded, as Kenit swiftly closed in on the boy from behind. Before he could reach the escaping, adolescent hostage, Tylo came to an abrupt halt about two dozen yards short of entering the forest. It was the emergence from the trees of two of the four renegade Sanatsai who had quickly ushered the Saharbashi away from the scene that caused the boy to freeze. It appeared Tylo's presence on the site hadn't been forgotten after all.

"Where do you think you're going, boy?" taunted the taller, stockier of the two men.

Kenit stopped right behind his quarry. "Tylo, listen very carefully," he whispered. The boy peered back over his shoulder; the confused expression that appeared on his face was to be expected—Kenit was still invisible. "Look straight ahead and remain calm. I'm from the Order." Tylo returned his gaze to the two renegade Sanatsai. "When you feel my hand on your shoulder, we'll back away from them, slowly and quietly."

As he reached forward, Kenit remembered how strange he always thought it was that while invoking *Raytandushay* he was still able to see himself while being invisible to other people. Nonetheless, he placed his hand upon Tylo's shoulder and gripped firmly. Immediately, the boy began to back-pedal slowly, so he did the same.

"Son of a bitch!" gasped the first renegade Sanatsai. "The kid shouldn't have any control of his *Zarantar* yet." It was confirmation that Tylo was now invisible, too.

"He doesn't," snapped the second renegade, angrily. "There is someone from the Order here." He thrust a hand out in front of himself, casting it from left to right, and back again.

Kenit knew it was safe to assume his opposite number was invoking *Yuksaydan* in the hope that the 'unseen hand' would locate him and the boy. It might even be an attempt to neutralise the invocation of *Raytandushay*, making him and Tylo visible. So while he continued to amble backward with the boy, he strengthened his invocation of *Raytandushay* just in case.

"What's happening?" whispered Tylo. "Can't they see us?"

"No, they can't. But we're not safe yet."

Fortunately, he was able to guide Tylo several feet away from the pair of renegade Sanatsai—back as far as the dais—without their invisibility being compromised. He paused at the base of the raised platform in order to assess their situation. The other two Conclave men, who'd escorted the Saharbashi away, were emerging from the trees to assist in the search for the absconded blood sacrifice. Kenit glanced to the western area of the ruins to check the position of the three renegade Sanatsai who hadn't joined the pursuit of Fay. They were far enough away not to pose a problem. Next he turned his focus to the line of trees at the southern edge of the clearing where he intended to lead Tylo to safety. He had a clear path back into the forest.

"Tylo, I'm going to take hold of your hand now," Kenit

announced in a whisper.

He let his grip slide from the boy's shoulder, down his arm, taking extra care not to release his hold on him. The instant his hand found Tylo's the boy's grip tightened around his. "Be ready to move when I give the word. I'm going to lead us south into the trees." He fell silent as one of their pursuers passed close by their position. He resumed his instruction once the danger had cleared. "Whatever happens, make sure you don't let go of my hand. You will only remain invisible while I have a hold on you, so I'll try not to move too quickly."

He cast his gaze across the ruins of the temple complex one more time. Several of the Conclave renegades who'd left in pursuit of Fay were returning. He had no choice but to make his move with Tylo now, while their route into the trees was still clear.

"Now!"

Slowly, Kenit began walking towards the southern edge of the clearing, guiding Tylo along with him, making every effort to move as silently as possible.

They were more than half way to reaching their destination when Kenit felt a drop of water hit the end of his nose. A second struck his forehead, and a third landed on his cheek. *Oh Shit!* Being invisible ceased to be as much of an advantage in the rain; the outline of an invisible form could be discerned if it was raining hard enough. He peered up at the sky. The dark clouds overhead made a downpour seem inevitable.

"Tylo, we're going to have to make a run for it," Kenit whispered, "or the rain will give us away."

"I'm ready when you are."

"All right. On my say, we'll sprint the rest of the way. And whatever you do, don't let go of my hand." There was a distant rumble of thunder then the heavens opened.

"Now!" hissed Kenit, dashing forward.

Seconds later they were entering the forest undetected, sheltered from the deluge by the thick canopy of branches and leaves of the trees. They advanced several yards into the forest before Kenit pulled up, bringing them both to a standstill. He ceased his invocation of *Raytandushay*, making himself and Tylo visible again, then released the boy's hand.

"It seems we weren't spotted," Kenit said in triumph, "so we can afford to walk from this point onwards."

"Wow! The Order really did come for me," blurted Tylo, his excitement obvious as he stared at his rescuer's uniform.

"Kenit Darbandian, at your service." He held out his hand to the boy. "It's nice to formally meet you, though I would have preferred it to be under better circumstances."

"I'm Tylo Solari," replied Tylo, shaking Kenit's hand enthusiastically.

"Well, Tylo, let's get moving. There are a couple of horses waiting for us further in, it's time to get you back to your parents, they're worried sick about you."

Kenit set off at a brisk walking pace that Tylo matched, falling into step alongside his Sanatsai saviour.

"All my life I have heard the stories of what the Sanatsai can do," said Tylo, awestruck. "But I never imagined the reality would be even more incredible than all of the stories. What you did back there was absolutely amazing."

Courtesy of Tylo's high praise, Kenit's ego inflated. It was the first time in his life anyone had described his actions as 'absolutely amazing'.

"The way you dealt with those people, making the earth tear up beneath their feet, knocking them to the ground, and letting loose those fireballs to kill the ones floating in the air, causing the rest of them to run away into the forest. I've never seen anything so spectacular in my life."

Instantly, Kenit's ego deflated. There was no way he could take credit for Fay's handiwork. "That wasn't my doing, actually," he confessed, awkwardly. "It was my colleague creating a diversion so I could get to you. She'll meet up with us back where we left our horses."

For the next few minutes Kenit silently led Tylo through the trees back to where he and Fay had left their mounts. Upon arrival at the remnants of the wall where the horses were tethered, Fay was nowhere to be seen. He decided there was no cause for alarm... yet. As she had already demonstrated, Fay was more than capable of taking care of herself. He instructed Tylo to climb up into the saddle of his horse while they awaited Fay's arrival. Turning away from the boy to look back the way they had come, Kenit thought his mind was playing tricks on him when Fay appeared out of nowhere and casually walked towards him. Her sudden appearance was not in any way indicative of the invocation of *Raytandushay*. When Sanatsai used *Zarantar* to become invisible, they quickly, but gradually, faded from view. Likewise, when they became visible once again, the fading back into view was gradual, also. What Kenit saw—or thought he saw—was not like that at all. One moment Fay wasn't there, the next moment she was. But he chose not to dwell on it. He was just glad to see her back in one piece.

"Any trouble recovering the boy?" Fay inquired as she joined Kenit.

Kenit shook his head. "Not really. We made it out of there unseen."

"Well done." Fay gave him an appreciative pat on the shoulder. "Now it's time for you to get our young friend, here, back to his parents. Take both horses back to Relona, and once you reach there have the local Guard place a protective detail around the family until the morning—just in case."

"What do you mean, 'take both horses'?"

"I don't know when I will return to Relona, so I don't want to potentially leave her tied up in the forest all night."

"Wait! You're not coming back with us?" asked Kenit, slightly alarmed. "So where are you going to be?"

"I cannot leave Sharadi Forest yet."

"Why not?"

"There are standing orders from the Council in regards to the presence of Saharbashi in the Nine Kingdoms: They are to be killed on sight, whenever and wherever they are found. Now that I'm satisfied the boy is in no immediate danger from his captors, I'm going back to kill the Saharbashi we encountered at the ruins."

Kenit was unnerved by the idea of separating now: it made more sense for them both to return to Relona with Tylo. While it was unlikely they would be pursued all the way back to the town, sticking together was preferable to splitting up.

"Why not return tomorrow with reinforcements?" he asked. "Why risk going after this Saharbashi alone?"

"There's no guarantee we would still find him here tomorrow. I have no choice but to take care of this tonight."

Not yet ready to just accept that, Kenit felt compelled to try to dissuade her.

"Danai Annis, I realise you have your orders, but have you forgotten about the rest of the Conclave?" he asked. "You may have killed more than a dozen of them earlier, but that still leaves at least eighty or so more you'll need to get through in order to reach your target. And even then..." He paused, recalling that fateful night five months earlier when Marit Katarnian was killed during their ill-fated mission in Anzarmenia. "I have seen first hand what a Saharbashi is capable of. What you are proposing is potentially suicidal."

Fay smiled at him "I appreciate your concern for my wellbeing, but you have your orders: get the boy safely back to Relona. If I have not returned by midday tomorrow, you should assume the worst has happened and go back to the Sisterhood seminary. Inform the Sisters of my fate and have them send a message to the Council, then await instructions."

Kenit realised it was pointless continuing to argue—not just because Fay had turned on her heels and begun walking away. It was clear to him now that she was completely committed to her obligations as a Sanatsai of the Order. She would carry out her duty or die trying, no matter what he said.

"That's it, it's time to leave," he said to Tylo who had sat silently in the saddle of his horse, listening to the brief discourse between the two Sanatsai. "Please tell me you can ride a horse," he added. "It appears I'll be riding my colleagues mount back to Relona."

Taking hold of the reins, Tylo replied, "Yes, of course I can ride,".

"Excellent," said Kenit, before swiftly clambering up into the saddle of Fay's horse. He looked across at Tylo. "We'll take it slow through the trees, but once we're clear of Sharadi Forest we can pick up the pace."

The two horses set off at a slow, cautious trot, with Kenit leading Tylo through the forest as the torrential downpour from the heavens subsided.

Half an hour later, the pair had ridden beyond the edge of the forest, out into open country, without incident; that was when they heard it. Deep within the forest came the noise of several detonations—the sound of *Zarantar* fuelled combat. Fay had presumably engaged the remnants of the Conclave in her quest to kill the Saharbashi allied with them.

Pulling his horse up, Kenit came to a halt to peer back at Sharadi Forest. In the night sky above the treetops he could see the occasional flash of coloured light accompanying the rumble of incendiary orbs detonating.

"We should go back and help your friend," said Tylo, pulling up alongside Kenit's mount.

"What?" he replied. Then, "No, I have orders to take you safely back to Relona, and that's what I'm going to do."

"But it looks and sounds like your friend might be in trouble."

"She's more than capable of taking care of herself."

"But she's just one person against dozens," insisted Tylo. "You should never have let her go off by herself."

"If you knew who she is you wouldn't think like that," Kenit retorted. "Believe me when I say she will be just fine."

The sounds of combat within Sharadi Forest ended abruptly, much quicker than anticipated. Though Kenit didn't wish to infer anything negative from the apparent cessation of hostilities, the worried look upon Tylo's face caused him to consider the possibility.

"Do you really think your friend is all right? Or is that what you have to tell yourself to make you feel better about wanting to run away?"

Kenit resented the accusatory tone, especially coming from an adolescent boy. "I'm not running away," he countered. "I'm following the orders I was given."

There was a swift resumption of the sights and sounds that indicated the fighting was not quite as over as Kenit had feared.

"You might be comfortable with that excuse," said Tylo, "but I'm not." He tugged on the reins of his mount to turn the animal around. "I'm going back to help your friend." He dug his heels into the flanks of the horse, urging it forward into a canter back towards the forest.

"Wait, damn it!" yelled Kenit.

He brought his own mount around then set off after the impetuous boy. He was quickly alongside Tylo allowing him to reach across and grab hold of the horse's bridle. He brought the brief pursuit to an end just a few yards short of re-entering the forest.

"What do you think you're playing at?" He couldn't keep the simmering anger out of his voice. "Do you think you're going to go back in there and save the day? You're just a boy who's had his *Zarantar* for a matter of hours. Don't start getting delusions of grandeur. What's the matter with you?"

Tylo pointedly stared back at him. "If a stranger risked her life to save yours, wouldn't you feel an obligation to do the same for her?" He sounded older and wiser than his tender years, Kenit noted. "So what if I don't have the ability to offer any meaningful help? That's not the point. What's important is that, regardless of what happens, no one will ever be able to say I wasn't there for her in her moment of need."

Something in the boy's voice shamed Kenit, then he remembered Fay's words to him earlier on that night, "We do not abandon our own...ever!" The vivid memory only increased his sense of shame. In that moment his mind was made up.

"You're right," he mused quietly. "I will go back to see if Danai Annis needs my assistance. But I cannot let you come with me, you'll have to make your way back to Relona by yourself."

"But—"

He cut Tylo off mid-sentence. "Don't argue. If the worst comes to the worst, the sacrifice will have been in vain if you don't get back home. Just head southwest," he indicated with his outstretched hand, "and you should reach Relona in under an hour. Be sure to report what has happened to the local Guard, and have them send someone out to the Sisterhood seminary outside town—a message will need to be sent back to the Order." Kenit was unsure if his words were getting through to the boy. "Do you think you can do that for me, Tylo?"

Tylo looked reluctant to leave, but he agreed to make the journey back to Relona if Kenit was staying to help his fellow Sanatsai. He steered his horse away from the trees of the Forest, then set off at a gallop in a southwesterly direction.

As the boy swiftly departed, Kenit watched and waited until he was far enough away to feel confident he wouldn't double back. Finally he urged his own mount forward, back into Sharadi Forest.

CHAPTER SEVENTEEN

Close Encounter Of The Eerie Kind

Kayden was still pacing the winding dirt path through the forest with purpose, but her enthusiasm was beginning to wane. She had no idea just how long she'd been walking; it felt like a lifetime. Her journey thus far had been completely uneventful, which only added to her frustration. The other source of annoyance was the unshakeable feeling she was walking round in circles. The forest surroundings were so nondescript, no matter where she cast her eye everything looked the same. Even the call of nocturnal birds and the buzzing of insects sounded repetitive. Wherever it was the path was supposed to lead her, she seemed no closer to getting there.

After passing a gnarled tree she could have sworn she'd passed at least half a dozen times already, Kayden began to wonder if she was the victim of a petty prank. It was highly suspicious she was going nowhere fast. Had Master Ari played a trick on her, sending her on a wild goose chase to see how long it took for her to get a clue and turn back? If that was the case, she would have a hard time keeping a respectful tongue in her mouth when she next saw him. She really disliked being messed around by anyone.

Kayden was so preoccupied with her ruminations she initially failed to notice the forest becoming less dense as the trees started to thin. What finally brought it to her attention was her awareness of the unnatural, deathly silence that had fallen all around her.

She could no longer hear the breeze rustling the leaves of trees, nor the sound of birds and insects. For that matter, she couldn't hear her own footsteps on the forest floor. It was like being inside a barrier sphere formed for the purpose of blocking out sound, only this was eerie by comparison. She peered upwards to glance at the night sky through the canopy of branches overhead. It was pitch black. There wasn't a single star in the heavens, nor any sign of the moon, so where was the soft luminescence emanating from? Kayden couldn't work it out, the light seemed to be coming from everywhere and nowhere.

Moments later, she emerged into a large circular clearing. She could see how the dirt path—that stopped at the beginning of the clearing—resumed on the other side, disappearing into the trees. Whatever was responsible for the lack of sound was gone; she could hear the sounds of the forest once more, though the eeriness of the scene hadn't let up. And looking up at the sky she saw that it remained an empty black canvas, devoid of all celestial bodies of light.

She proceeded to advance further into the clearing, though she did so slowly and cautiously. Something wasn't right—something she wasn't able to put her finger on. She felt threatened and vulnerable; feelings she was unaccustomed to experiencing. As she ambled forward her eyes darted from left to right and back again, hoping to catch sight of trouble before it could take her unawares. She saw nothing and no one, yet the sense of imminent danger was increasing. It dawned on her that she could hear her own heartbeat thumping in her ears—her heart was racing.

Half way across the clearing Kayden stopped. She was suddenly aware of the nearby presence of *Zarantar*, and to her surprise it wasn't just the familiar *Zarantar Shayd* wielded by all Sanatsai. She could also feel *Zarantar Jist*, the art of the Jaymidari. But what alarmed Kayden was the sensing of a third variation she had never felt before. It could only be *Zarantar Najist*, the art of the Saharbashi, and the sensation caused her to shudder. The subsequent sense of impending doom closing in on her became so oppressive, it prompted her to invoke *Inkansaylar* to create a barrier sphere around herself.

And, not a moment too soon.

Out of nowhere a volley of half a dozen incendiary orbs shot across the clearing, striking Kayden's translucent, protective bubble. The sneak attack hit with such power that despite her barrier sphere holding firm, the force of the detonation caused her to stumble slightly, and the vibration from the blast went right through her body.

Kayden realised with alarm that had she not reacted as quickly as she did the clearing would be strewn with multiple, smouldering body parts—her own. But she was given no time to dwell on how close she had come to being blown to pieces. A second volley of incendiary orbs struck her barrier sphere. This time she saw where the attack emanated from. The orbs had flown from the edge of the clearing ahead of her, about thirty feet in the air, though there was no sign of her attacker.

She braced herself for a possible third consecutive attack, but it failed to materialise, for which she was grateful.

Kayden recalled the level four test that required her to demonstrate her mastery of *Inkansaylar* by maintaining a barrier sphere for as long as possible, while under constant attack from various *Zarantar* strikes. She remembered just how effortlessly she was able to maintain her invocation for well over eighteen hours—an unprecedented feat in the history of the Order—without her defences being breached. Her sense of smug satisfaction at easily fending off scores of fellow apprentices, not to mention a small number of full-fledged Sanatsai, when some of the instructors joined in, lingered long after the event.

But that was then.

The here and the now was an entirely different proposition altogether. Whoever it was invoking *Balatlaydan* to unleash the barrage of incendiary orbs against her was so powerful, Kayden doubted her own ability to prevent her defences being breached for even a full hour. With that in mind, the respite from attack was more than welcome. Her mystery assailant would have worn her down, sooner rather than later.

When her attacker finally came into view, Kayden's eyes

widened in disbelief. Directly ahead, at the edge of the clearing, floating thirty feet in the air, a figure became visible before descending slowly towards the ground. What she was witnessing was impossible. As far as she knew, invoking *Raytandushay* to become invisible meant it wasn't possible to invoke any other application of *Zarantar* simultaneously. Yet there was no question her attacker had not only invoked *Balatlaydan* while invisible, but also *Makfayshulat*, to levitate above the ground. No Sanatsai had the power to do that.

Kayden observed intently as her assailant alighted on the ground in a crouching position several yards ahead her. The figure then slowly rose into an upright, standing pose. She couldn't discern whether the hooded attacker, dressed from head to toe in black, was male or female—a determination made even harder by the hood of the cloak concealing the upper half of the person's face, while the lower half was inexplicably obscured by shadow.

In the ensuing silence Kayden gathered her wits enough to finally realise what was happening. She furiously wondered how she could have been so stupid. During their conversation, prior to her entering the forest, Ari had essentially foretold what was to occur. She had been sent into the forest to die. At the hands of the Rogue.

Her mind racing to put the pieces together, the realisation that this situation was a setup, and that she had walked straight into the trap, made Kayden's blood boil. But it didn't make any sense. Would Fay and Ari really conspire to lure her away from Antaris campus, bring her to Temis Rulan, then take her on a two hour long trek north of the city just to have her killed? No, she couldn't believe that to be true. Yet she remembered Ari's confession that he did not kill the Rogue during the last battle of the Great War, and the truth of his admission was now standing no more than sixty yards in front of her.

Anger warred with confusion within Kayden. Her only hope for clarity lay with the black clad figure that had just tried to kill her. She terminated her invocation of *Inkansaylar*, bringing down her barrier sphere. "Who are you?" she demanded to know, though she was already certain of the answer.

"Some call me Fate. Some call me Destiny," an androgynous voice said in reply. "Whatever you choose to call me, you cannot escape me."

Kayden suppressed a groan; she really should have known better than to expect a simple, straightforward response.

"What do you want?" she called out. It would be harder for the Rogue to provide quite as useless an answer to that question.

"I seek to help you," came the androgynous reply. "I am here to prevent you straying from your path." Kayden was unsure if this was a reference to a metaphorical path or a literal one, until the Rogue added, "Your path does not lie before you, it lies behind you."

Cocking her head slightly to one side, Kayden tried to catch a glimpse of the dirt path behind the Rogue, leading into the trees. She had been tasked with following the path to its end and she wasn't about to be dissuaded from doing so, if that's what was being suggested.

"I appreciate your concern," she replied with evident insincerity, "but I am more than capable of walking my own path without your assistance. So, if you would kindly stand aside, I believe my path lies right in front of me."

"Your true path lies behind you," retorted the Rogue. "Turn back now. Return the way you came."

The subtle threat carried in the command didn't escape Kayden's notice. But it was of no consequence. The Rogue could have asked her to go back as politely as the politest person in the kingdom of politeness and it would have made no difference, at all. She wasn't about to be intimidated into turning tail for anyone.

"If I refuse?" she asked pointedly.

She sensed the Rogue's attack just before two incendiary orbs were unleashed against her. Reacting instantly, she invoked *Inkansaylar* to create a barrier shield in front of herself. The translucent, rectangular barrier did its job, protecting her from the violent, fiery death being delivered by the orbs that struck it. Nevertheless, the force of the detonation unbalanced her, causing her to stumble backward then drop to one knee. She berated herself. It would have been smarter to invoke *Yuksaydan* to divert the orbs harmlessly up into the sky, or better yet, straight back at her attacker.

As Kayden quickly stood back up, the ground beneath her feet erupted. Several clumps of grassy turf flew upwards as she was propelled five feet into the air before landing on her back. Though she had sensed the attack coming just before it was unleashed, Kayden failed to react in time. Not that it would have altered the outcome. She had never seen *Yuksaydan* used to literally rip up the ground beneath someone's feet, so she was ill prepared to defend herself against the attack. Now that she knew, she'd be better prepared if it happened a second time.

Kayden was determined not to allow the Rogue to capitalise on the successful attack. The instant she clambered back on to her feet she invoked *Kiraydan* to let loose a lightning flash orb towards her adversary. She closed her eyes and waited for the tell-tale sign, through her eyelids, of the flash of light accompanying the silent detonation that would momentarily blind the Rogue. When it came she opened her eyes and dashed towards her opponent while simultaneously invoking *Turmiraydan* to unleash two concussion orbs. The pair of fast moving, glowing spheres unexpectedly blinked out of existence just before reaching their target—completely neutralised—but she didn't stop to curse the unsuccessful attack.

Continuing her charge towards the black clad figure, the air around Kayden suddenly became so thick she found herself moving in exaggerated slow motion, as though she were trying to run through a wall of molasses. It was the first demonstration of the Rogue's mastery of *Zarantar Jist*. And while the effect was harmless in itself, as an actual Jaymidari would only use this power defensively, to slow down would-be attackers, Kayden was all too aware of how horribly exposed and vulnerable she now was. If she was unable to neutralise the inertia field, she would be a sitting duck for the Rogue who was now striding towards her at normal speed.

The distance between the pair was almost entirely closed when Kayden's invocation of *Yuksaydan* finally neutralised the inertia field. Unfortunately, her focus had been so intent she forgot that the moment she was unimpeded she would be moving at normal speed again, so she was unable to halt her sprint towards the Rogue in time to avoid running straight into the *Yuksaydan* counter-strike unleashed against her. The invisible blast lifted her off her feet, sending her hurtling backwards almost fifty feet before landing in a crumpled heap on the ground.

Badly winded, Kayden lay on her back, eyes closed, her face contorted in a grimace, and her mouth open in a silent scream. She imagined this had to be what being trampled upon by a wild horse felt like, but her pain was dimmed somewhat by her awareness that she could and should have just been killed. The fact she was still alive could only mean one thing: the Rogue was toying with her, either to prolong her suffering, or in the hopes of forcing her to abandon the attempt to reach the end of the forest path.

Slowly, she sat up to check the Rogue's current position. The black clad figure was sauntering nonchalantly towards her—forty feet and closing. The apparent casualness raised her hackles, for it implied she represented no threat whatsoever. It was time to demonstrate otherwise.

Ignoring her aching body, Kayden scrambled back to her feet and stood upright.

"You son of a bitch!" she shrieked vehemently, thrusting her right hand forward, invoking *Yuksaydan* against her foe, reaching out for its throat with the 'unseen hand'.

Immediately, her assailant responded in kind, halting and thrusting out a hand towards Kayden.

It was *Yuksaydan* against *Yuksaydan*.

Kayden slowly shuffled forward, all the while increasing the intensity of her attack. If she could just overpower the Rogue long enough to get a hold around the throat, she could end the confrontation decisively. Inching ever closer to the stationary figure ahead of her, she was utterly determined to overcome her implacable foe, but the exertion was starting to take its toll on her. Beads of perspiration began to dampen her brow. She was gritting her teeth, and her arm was noticeably trembling. Never before had she pushed herself so hard. But it still wasn't enough.

Kayden came within ten yards of the Rogue before her

concentration—and with it control of her *Zarantar*—slipped. It was only a momentary lapse, but long enough for her to be punished for it. The Rogue's invocation of *Yuksaydan* seized her around the neck, lifting her off the ground, choking her. She tried in vain to repel the counter-attack but her adversary was simply too powerful; she was completely at the mercy of the Rogue who could snap her neck like a twig, at any moment.

While her feet dangled helplessly a foot above the ground, the Rogue calmly approached Kayden, stopping just in front of her. She was perturbed when the figure in black looked up at her. Even up close she still couldn't see the face of the Rogue—the upper half of the face remained concealed by the hood, while the lower half was still obscured by a strange shadow.

"I cannot allow you to stray from your path," reiterated the Rogue, in the same androgynous monotone. "You will return the way you came, or your journey will end here. Decide now."

There was no decision to be made as far as Kayden was concerned. Not even the threat of death could compel her to do something she didn't want to do. "Go stroke yourself," she snarled.

Apparently, the Rogue didn't appreciate the use of even mild profanity. The firm grip around her neck tightened. She couldn't breathe. But the peril she was in did not provoke any panic within her. Keeping her wits about her allowed her to think clearly about the next course of action. She invoked *Balatlaydan*, creating an incendiary orb between herself and the Rogue. It was a desperate gambit on her part. Her assailant would have to cease the invocation of *Yuksaydan* that had her by the throat, or they would both be blown to flaming pieces when the orb detonated.

The invisible grip ceased. Before her feet could touch the ground she instantly invoked *Makfayshulat* to levitate and drift backwards away from the Rogue, hoping to put enough distance between herself and the blast of her incendiary orb. But the expected detonation did not occur. Looking down she saw her orb still floating harmlessly in front of the Rogue. *No matter*, she thought, it had allowed her to break free from her attacker.

Kayden alighted on the ground a good fifty yards away from

the Rogue. She glared with intent at her opponent. It appeared the Rogue had somehow assumed control of her incendiary orb—that would explain why it had failed to detonate as she intended. The fiery sphere, now rotating rapidly in the air before them, was growing noticeably larger.

She decided not to wait and see what her adversary was going to do next. She invoked *Balatlaydan*, letting loose a volley of ten more incendiary orbs. The attack was thwarted again, the orbs halted abruptly just short of their target. Once more, control of her orbs had been hijacked by the Rogue. She looked on in frustration as her ten spherical weapons of destruction began to circle around the stationary figure, half of them were moving clockwise, the others moving counter-clockwise, gathering speed with each orbit. She could do nothing as one by one each of the orbs collided with the larger orb growing in front of the Rogue, merging with it, contributing to its increasing mass. It wasn't long before the singular orb had grown large enough to conceal most of the black clad figure from Kayden's sight. She could only see the shoulders upward, plus the legs below the knees—everything in between was hidden.

Once the orb's growing mass had completely obscured the Rogue from view, Kayden unwittingly began to shuffle backwards. Creating an incendiary orb that size was overkill, to say the least, especially if it was intended to be used against her.

The fiery orb gradually stopped rotating then slowly floated upward, prompting Kayden to halt her unbidden retreat. She watched its steady ascent into the night sky, climbing higher and higher. Though she hadn't forgotten about the Rogue, still standing several yards ahead of her, Kayden couldn't tear her eyes away from the large orb rising into the air. By the time it stopped ascending, it had risen higher than the tops of the tallest trees surrounding the clearing. It was still growing but also changing shape; the incendiary orb was no longer spherical, it had elongated, with a number of appendages sprouting from it.

Is that a tail? Kayden wondered. And four legs?

As the transformation continued, Kayden's eyes widened in disbelief at the emergence of a large pair of wings, followed by the growth of a long neck and ferocious looking head. At last, she realised the orb was taking the form of a Zu'tayral—a mythological creature from ancient Zenoshanese mythology. She was utterly transfixed. Once the change was complete the fiery form flapped its wings and began circling high above the clearing.

Kayden finally averted her eyes from the winged entity overhead to stare at the Rogue, standing as still as a statue in the same spot. She couldn't understand what the point of this demonstration of *Zarantar* by her opponent was. Admittedly, she'd never before witnessed anyone manipulating the shape of an incendiary orb to resemble a mythological creature, but if it was intended to intimidate her, it would take a lot more than that.

"If you were hoping to frighten me," she barked, "I don't scare easily."

A blood-curdling sound, between a roar and a piercing shriek, issued from the sky above. Startled, Kayden looked up to spy the winged monstrosity created by the Rogue. It was no longer circling overhead; it was holding its position above the trees at the edge of the clearing. Its big, fiery red eyes locked on hers before it flapped its wings once, bringing them to rest against its sides, propelling it forward into a dive—its trajectory sending it inexorably on a collision course with her.

Oh drat!

Kayden turned on her heels and ran. She sprinted as fast as she could in the opposite direction, towards the relative safety of the trees. If she was able to escape back into the forest, the trees would take the brunt of the destruction. Several yards short of reaching the trees Kayden realised she was never going to make it. She stopped in her tracks and spun around; the Zu'tayral shaped incendiary orb was bearing down on her—so close she could the feel the heat radiating from it. Reflexively, she invoked *Inkansaylar*, forming the strongest barrier sphere she could muster to protect herself.

Just in time.

The huge, fiery projectile struck the translucent bubble around Kayden, instantly engulfing it in raging flames. The force of the blast released by the detonation shook the ground beneath

Kayden's feet, causing her to fall flat on her back.

Recovering her wits, Kayden quickly sat upright to inspect the damage done. The wall of flames surrounding her position rapidly subsided revealing the smouldering, shallow crater her barrier sphere was sitting at the centre of. She was mightily relieved that the protective bubble withstood the destructive force of the attack, but it was cold comfort for her. Not only was she certain it wouldn't withstand a second strike of similar strength, she had also reluctantly come to the conclusion she was hopelessly out of her depth. She had no hope of defeating the Rogue in a battle of *Zarantar*; her own abilities were neither as strong or well developed. As it was, she could have been killed more than once already.

Kayden's sight was drawn back to the Rogue again. Her black clad foe was floating just above the ground, slowly drifting ominously in her direction—hooded black cloak billowing dramatically behind. She scrambled back up on to her feet to face down her approaching adversary, wondering what it had in store for her. The floating figure stopped at the edge of the crater, just a dozen yards or so away from the perimeter of her barrier sphere. She remained a little unnerved that she still couldn't see the face of the person under the hood, but given her current predicament she had greater concerns.

"In your heart you realise the futility of continuing to defy me," said the androgynous voice from beneath the hood. "You know your *Zarantar* is not sufficient to overcome me. I am more powerful than you can imagine."

"Oh, you talk a good game." Kayden held both arms out to the side in challenge. "But I'm still alive—undefeated," she bellowed defiantly. If taunting was the only weapon she had left at her disposal, she was going to use it.

"This is your final chance to return the way you came. If you do not take it I will end your journey now."

Kayden knew it was no idle threat. But she was not the kind of person who responded favourably to threats. Instead, she scowled at her adversary. "Do your worst," she muttered, in a defiant undertone.

The Rogue unleashed half a dozen incendiary orbs that struck Kayden's barrier sphere, one after the other, in quick succession. It held firm, provoking an outburst of laughter from the apprentice. In response, the Rogue held out a hand, invoking *Yuksaydan* in a renewed effort to neutralise Kayden's defences. Almost instantly, several areas of the translucent bubble began to deteriorate as though consumed by fire or a corrosive substance.

The threat prompted Kayden to intensify her invocation of *Inkansaylar*. Those damaged areas of her barrier sphere rapidly healed but she continued to increase the strength of her invocation, further still—putting everything she could into the maintenance of the protective shield. It no longer mattered that her opponent was more powerful, she was going to make the Rogue work for the victory.

For several minutes Kayden was able to withstand the Rogue's efforts to breach her barrier sphere. But as beads of perspiration started to reappear on her brow, due to the intensity of her exertions, she felt her strength begin ebb. A few minutes more and she was done for. Suddenly, much to her relief, respite came when the protracted *Yuksaydan* assault ceased abruptly and the Rogue's outstretched arm lowered. It was too much to hope her assailant had given up completely, but it felt like a victory nonetheless.

Exhaling deeply, Kayden smiled at her adversary. "Is that all you've got?" she yelled, mockingly.

The Rogue's head slowly dipped in response.

As much as Kayden wanted to believe her resistance had demoralised her implacable foe, she knew better; something else was going on. She could just about hear the Rogue reciting or chanting in a low voice. She did not understand what was being uttered, but it sounded suspiciously like the dead language used by the Sisterhood for invoking the more potent applications of a Jaymidari's *Zarantar*.

Kayden sensed the surge of *Zarantar*. Once again it was the unfamiliar third variation she had felt for the first time shortly after entering the forest clearing. Though it shouldn't be possible, the Rogue, having already demonstrated unquestionable mastery of both *Zarantar Jist* and *Zarantar Shayd*, was now going to strike with *Zarantar Najist*, the forbidden art of the Saharbashi.

Nothing appeared to be happening but the observation did nothing to dampen Kayden's alarm. She knew she was under attack, she just didn't know how. Waving a hand in front of herself, she invoked *Yuksaydan*; hopefully the 'unseen hand' would reveal the hidden manifestation of the attack.

And so it did.

On the undamaged ground within her barrier sphere were four glowing, red glyphs. Another suddenly appeared, making five—they were emerging clockwise in a circle around her. Kayden didn't recognise the glyphs, so didn't know what they symbolised, but she was disturbed that they were appearing inside the perimeter of her barrier sphere. It meant the Rogue had somehow breached her defences. She knew that once the circle was complete she was in big trouble. In desperation, she held both hands out in front of her; with any luck *Zarantar Najist* could be neutralised in the same way as *Zarantar Jist*.

"Drat!" she complained in frustration. Whatever the Rogue was doing was too strong for her to repel.

The final glyph of the circle manifested and the glow of all twelve glyphs intensified. Kayden was instantly overwhelmed by the crushing sense of imminent death; she knew she was about to die. Without conscious thought, she reacted decisively, pulling the hood of her cloak over her head, invoking *Naymutandushay*. The air around her briefly appeared to ripple as she became intangible.

Suddenly, out of nowhere, multiple lightning bolts erupted inside the barrier sphere, cascading violently within the confines of Kayden's translucent bubble, ripping apart the air all around their target. Though the onslaught of lightning strikes passed harmlessly through her non-corporeal form, Kayden was forced to cover her ears and shut her eyes against the deafening rumbles of thunder and blinding flashes of light.

Eventually, she sensed the cessation of the attack, allowing her to open her eyes and pull her hands from her ears. Her heart was pounding ferociously in her chest, as though it was trying to punch its way out. She had cheated death, yet again, only this time she was genuinely rattled by what happened. The Rogue had initiated a deadly attack against her, replicating one of nature's most destructive phenomena. And if that wasn't disturbing enough, the attack was unleashed inside her barrier sphere where she should have been safe from harm. Kayden lost all focus, causing the barrier sphere to quickly dissipate, leaving her defenceless.

Involuntarily, she started to back-pedal as the Rogue began drifting across the shallow crater towards the circular island of undamaged ground she was standing on. In her moment of panic, Kayden stumbled, falling backwards into the crater. She didn't waste any time trying to get back on to her feet, frantically scrambling backwards to keep as much distance between herself and her unrelenting assailant. She made it out of the crater back on to the untouched grass of the forest clearing, though she had little hope of escape. The Rogue, floating just above the ground, was drifting closer and closer, bearing down on her like a shadowy apparition. It was an imposing spectacle.

Kayden's alarm spiked when she sensed *Zarantar*. The attack that would end her life this time was imminent, and she was powerless to prevent it. She stopped scrambling backward and held her hands up at the black figure looming over her.

"Wait!" The anguished plea came out like a yelp. "Wait! Don't kill me, don't kill me," she pleaded, in apparent desperation. "You win, you win!"

Kayden could no longer sense the impending *Zarantar* strike—she had earned herself a reprieve...for now. Watching the feet of her adversary alight on the ground just before her, she slowly, cautiously stood up. For the first time she noticed that she and her black clad foe were the same height. But that didn't detract from the disquieting realisation that even standing just a couple of yards from the Rogue, she still could not see the face of whomever was beneath the hood.

She held up both her hands in a gesture of compliant surrender.

"All right. I was a fool to oppose you," she conceded. "I should have just turned back when you told me to."

Slowly, she started to back away from the Rogue.

"It you let me live, I will go back the way I came."

The Rogue remained rooted to the spot, making no attempt to follow her or prevent her from leaving.

"But before I go," Kayden continued, "I just need to know one thing."

A fraught silence followed as Kayden waited for the Rogue to ask what it was she needed to know. The question did not come. Presumably, her taciturn tormentor was waiting for her to finish what she had to say.

"I need to know why you're forcing me to go back? What difference does it make to you if I continue to the end of the path?"

"I have a vested interest in preserving your destiny," replied the Rogue.

The admission would have intrigued Kayden had she not been so preoccupied. As it was, she had no interest in whatever was said between herself and her adversary; she was just stalling for time. If she couldn't overpower the Rogue, she would just have to outsmart her opponent instead.

"I'm curious," she responded. "In what way would my destiny be altered if I were to continue to the end of the path?"

"If I allow you to complete the journey you have been tasked with," the androgynous voice replied, "Andro Radulini will live."

Kayden halted dead in her tracks, her heart skipping a beat. How could the Rogue possibly know the name of her stepfather?

"What are you talking about?" she demanded to know.

"If you turn back now, you shall fulfil your destiny. You will kill Andro Radulini, and avenge your mother's unjust death. But if you proceed onwards and reach the end of the path, your mother's death will never be avenged."

If any words had the power to spur Kayden into abandoning her attempt to complete the task Master Ari had given her, the Rogue had just uttered them. Whether or not it was merely a deliberate ploy to unbalance her, Kayden realised she couldn't let it cloud her judgement. She needed a clear head if she was going to survive this ordeal. Closing her eyes, she tried to block out all thoughts of being denied revenge on her stepfather.

Moments later Kayden opened her eyes again; her mind was

made up. Without a word she turned on her heels then stomped purposefully away from the Rogue, heading straight back towards the dirt path that had led her into the clearing. If she had to make a choice between avenging her mother's death or proving herself to Master Ari, there was no choice to be made. However, there was no reason why she couldn't accomplish both.

Kayden slowed to a stop at the edge of the clearing just as she was about to re-enter the trees. For a protracted moment she remained stock-still, staring down the length of the dirt path. Finally, she slowly turned her body sideways on to the Rogue, turning her head the rest of the way to stare at her adversary.

"You could be lying to me," she called out casually. "For all I know, going back could be what deprives me of my revenge."

"I have no reason to deceive you."

Without taking her eyes off the Rogue, Kayden slowly ambled forward, walking counter-clockwise along the edge of the clearing.

"You would say that whether you were lying to me or not," she said, accusingly. "Why should I trust anything you tell me?"

"Because we both desire the same thing: the death of Andro Radulini."

"Why do you care if my stepfather lives or dies?" Kayden continued to slowly circle the Rogue, along the edge of the clearing.

"I care for the same reason you do."

The androgynous voice was starting to irritate Kayden. There was something intrinsically unnatural about it.

"But more importantly than that, you cannot become the person you are destined to be until you have killed Andro Radulini."

"And who am I destined to become?" asked Kayden, humouring her foe.

"The greatest Sanatsai this world has ever seen."

Under normal circumstances such a pronouncement would have gone to her head. But this occasion was not a good time to be distracted so she had little difficulty keeping her ego in check. The answers she was receiving to her questions were of no consequence; she only wanted to keep the Rogue talking for long enough for her to do what needed to be done, without giving away her true intentions. She continued the irrelevant verbal exchange back and forth for a while longer, all the while continuing to circle the black clad figure.

When Kayden finally came to a halt, she was standing on the opposite side of the clearing—her ploy proved to be so much easier than she anticipated. She turned her body to face the Rogue head on, rather than sideways on, putting the dirt path she needed to follow at her back, just a yard or two behind her. As she glared at her adversary, Kayden just couldn't help herself. She smirked smugly then promptly turned on her heels, making a dash for the path, sprinting as fast as her legs would carry her.

She re-entered the forest only to discover that the burst of *Zarantar* she felt behind her was bringing the trees around her to life. Several branches became stretching, flexible limbs—reaching for, and lashing out at her. First, she was tripped when a branch took her legs out from under her, causing her to tumble to the ground in a heap. Before she could regain her footing, another branch wrapped around her legs and threw her high up into the air where she was seized by half a dozen leafy branches. She invoked *Yuksaydan* to shatter the branches, but as she fell towards the ground, she was caught by several more wooden limbs. She repeated her countermeasure with the same result: she broke free of the living branches only to be grabbed by several more before she could hit the ground. For a third time Kayden invoked *Yuksaydan* to break free of the hold on her and was rewarded when she landed on the forest floor without being seized again.

Setting off at a sprint once more, she hoped to flee out of range of the Rogue's *Zarantar*, but her effort was in vain. The trees lashed out at her more violently and she endured three painful blows to the body before a fourth blow to the side of the head stunned her. Unwittingly, Kayden slowed down then dropped to one knee. She was granted no time to recover her equilibrium as several branches reached out for her at once. One grabbed her around the neck, a second coiled around her waist, two more wrapped themselves around her wrists, while a further two seized her round the ankles. She was immediately hoisted off the ground, several feet into the air and vigorously shaken like a ragdoll, disorienting her further.

The assault ended quickly but Kayden had lost all sense of up and down, left and right, backward and forward when the branches released their hold by tossing her through the air. She was caught in mid-air by yet another wooden limb that promptly tossed her through the air a second time, into the waiting clutches of another branch brought to life. She was being thrown all the way back towards the clearing she was trying to escape.

The final branch that caught hold of Kayden stretched unfeasibly into the clearing then slammed the hapless apprentice face down onto the ground at the feet of the Rogue. Kayden just laid there, unmoving and hurt. Her eyes were shut tight in an effort to keep the pain of her aching body at bay. In spite of the burning anger she was feeling she was ready to give up the ghost. She had little fight left in her. Reluctantly, she opened her eyes and was greeted by the sight of the Rogue's booted feet under her nose. As she prepared to force herself up from her prone position she sensed the *Zarantar* that would spare her the trouble. She was lifted up off the ground and suspended helplessly in the air before her black clad nemesis. Face to face with the Rogue, Kayden was beyond caring that she still couldn't see the face beneath the hood.

"You were warned that you cannot escape me."

"Oh, just kill me, you son of a bitch." The bitterness in Kayden's snarled response was palpable. "But know this, you will never be able to revel in my death. What glory can there be in stacking the deck in your favour?" she taunted. "You picked on a mere apprentice, safe in the knowledge I couldn't possibly match you in a battle of *Zarantar*. If you weren't such a coward you would have confronted me on a level playing field. You would have given me the option of dying by the sword."

The Rogue's invocation of *Yuksaydan* started to tighten the invisible grip around Kayden's neck, squeezing her throat, choking the life out of her.

"Struck a nerve, did I?" spluttered Kayden, taunting her assailant. "Then face me on an equal footing. No *Zarantar*. Just your blade against mine."

Kayden was certain she was about to pass out when the Rogue abruptly released the hold on her, letting her to fall to her knees, coughing and gasping for breath. Looking up, she saw her black clad adversary slowly back-pedalling away from her. She was caught off guard. The Rogue halted half a dozen yards from her and unsheathed the sword hung behind its right shoulder.

The possibility that her opponent would accept the challenge of a duel hadn't occurred to her—she simply wanted to have the last word before she died.

"As you wish," said the Rogue, adopting a two handed stance.

Kayden slowly stood upright then drew her own blade. She mirrored the two handed stance of the Rogue and stared fixedly at her opponent while she composed herself. She had never fought to the death before, but in that moment she knew—in her heart of hearts—there was no other way for the encounter to come to an end.

It was kill or be killed.

CHAPTER EIGHTEEN

To The Death

Kenit slowed his sprint through the trees to a steady walk when he realised the sounds of fighting he was rushing towards had ceased a good few minutes earlier. He had left his horse tethered in the same spot he and Fay dismounted their rides when they first arrived in Sharadi Forest, then dashed off, ostensibly to render assistance to Fay in her mission to assassinate the Saharbashi they encountered while rescuing Tylo.

Now that the fighting had seemingly reached a conclusion, Kenit wasn't sure if he should interpret the silence as Fay not actually requiring his help or, more worryingly, she was beyond help and he was heading straight into danger.

As he approached the site of the initial encounter with the Conclave and the allied Saharbashi, Kenit could hear a number of angry voices hurling profane insults. He reached the edge of the clearing to see the ancient temple complex was now strewn with scores of dead bodies. He couldn't say for certain how many of the renegade Sanatsai had been killed as few of the bodies were still in one piece, but the bloody scene was obviously Fay's handiwork.

He cast his eyes to the right and caught sight of Fay. His breath caught in his throat as he saw her limp body being held upright by a pair of Conclave men—one on either arm—holding her securely before the dagger-wielding Saharbashi. A further five renegade Sanatsai were loitering nearby, spewing obscenities at their captive. From his vantage point Kenit was unable to discern whether Fay was dead or alive—she certainty wasn't moving or struggling to break free of her captors. But he reluctantly concluded that even if she was still alive she wouldn't be for much longer, and there was nothing he could do to change that outcome.

The Saharbashi grabbed hold of Fay by her face with one hand, while he waved the dagger in his other hand under her nose. Kenit felt sick, absolutely certain he was about to witness Fay having her throat slit, or the blade of the dagger plunged into her chest. But neither happened. Instead, the Saharbashi pointed at the nearby stone altar, prompting the two men holding Fay to drag her towards the dais upon which the altar was erected.

So, there was going to be a blood letting that night, after all.

Kenit felt guilty that having come this far, he had now decided against intervening as Fay was dragged to the stone altar, though he tried to convince himself it was the correct course of action, under the circumstances. He was outnumbered, and had no confidence in his ability to overcome the remaining seven renegades, plus the Saharbashi, all by himself. That's what would be required in order to save his colleague. He looked on forlornly while Fay was laid upon the altar in preparation for the blood letting. That was his cue to leave—he had no desire to watch what was about to happen next.

Before he could depart, Kenit was startled by the sounds of movement approaching his position from behind. He spun round sharply, ready to invoke *Turmiraydan* and let loose a concussion orb at the interloper. But much to his surprise, and relief, it was young Tylo darting towards him.

"What are you doing here?" Kenit hissed in annoyance. "You should be on your way back to Relona."

"I couldn't leave without knowing you and your friend were all right." Tylo caught sight of the gruesome scene among the ruins before spotting Fay laid out on the altar.

"Oh no! She's been captured. What are you waiting for?"

"There's nothing I can do for her now," Kenit lamented. "But I can get you out of here so her death isn't in vain."

"Wait! We can't just leave," retorted Tylo, incredulously. "We have to do something."

Reacted swiftly when the boy attempted to dash into the clearing, Kenit grabbed hold of Tylo then brought him to the ground, pinning him down.

"What do you think you're playing at?" He was livid. The impetuous kid had come perilously close to bringing them unwanted attention. "If you go out there you'll die right alongside my colleague."

"I don't care!" Tylo struggled futilely beneath Kenit. "I'm not just going to run away and let the woman who saved my life be killed."

"And what exactly are you going to do about it?" hissed Kenit derisively. "You haven't been trained to wield your *Zarantar* yet."

"It doesn't matter. If you're not going to do anything, then it's up to me. Now let me go or I'll scream."

Kenit clamped a hand down over the boy's mouth just in case he tried to make good on the threat. For several seconds Tylo increased his futile struggle to break free before he gave up. An attack of conscience hit Kenit at the sight of two tears trickling down the boys face. Was he so afraid to do the right thing he would upset a young kid?

He pulled his hand away from Tylo's mouth and stopped pinning him to the ground.

"I'm sorry," he said.

He stood upright and allowed Tylo to get back to his feet.

"I don't understand how you can do this," complained Tylo. "I may not know your friend, but from what little I've seen, if your places were reversed right now, and it was you on that altar about to be slaughtered like an animal, I can't imagine she would hesitate for a moment to risk her life to save yours."

The impassioned words struck Kenit like a punch to the gut. He felt ashamed by the boy's keen insight. What's more, Tylo was right; Fay would never contemplate leaving him behind.

"You're absolutely right," he conceded, "and I'm going to do the same for her. But you need to get out of here, now."

"Fine." Tylo glanced back at the ruins. "But whatever you're planning to do, you'd better be quick about it."

Kenit cast his gaze back to the stone altar where he saw the Saharbashi standing over Fay's prone form. He couldn't hear the words being uttered by the man but his intent was easily understood as he raised his dagger overhead. There was no time to insist that Tylo resume the journey back to Relona—he had only a matter of seconds to respond to the threat to Fay's life.

Kenit stepped into the clearing with one hand outstretched in front of him as he walked calmly towards the altar. Invoking *Yuksaydan*, he reached out with the 'unseen hand' to snatch the dagger from the grasp of the Saharbashi before it could be used on Fay. The weapon flew through the air, several yards across the temple complex ruins, straight into his hand. As all eyes turned towards him in surprise, he tossed the dagger aside then dashed towards the enemy, invoking *Turmiraydan* to let loose a volley of concussion orbs at them. He could not take the risk of unleashing incendiary orbs—just in case they missed their targets, inadvertently killing Fay instead. Only one of the projectiles found its mark, rendering a single renegade unconscious, while the rest were either deflected away harmlessly or struck *Inkansaylar*-induced barrier shields.

Undeterred by the partially successful attack, Kenit continued to rush towards the dais and stone altar, noting that the Saharbashi had levitated into the air to evade the volley of orbs. Fay was safe for the time being. His immediate concern was the six remaining renegades charging towards him with swords drawn. He reached back over his shoulder, drawing his own blade in response, but just before meeting the renegades head-on he jumped up and invoked *Makfayshulat* to levitate over the heads of the onrushing group, drifting to the raised platform. He alighted beside the stone altar then instantly invoked *Inkansaylar* to create a barrier sphere encompassing himself and the altar to guard against attack.

He was relieved to see Fay's chest rise and fall as she lay, unmoving, upon the altar. She *was* still alive, thankfully, so he hadn't stranded himself in the midst of a hostile group of *Zarantar* wielders for no good reason. Suddenly, he heard and felt the detonations of a succession of incendiary orbs striking his barrier sphere—a reminder of the peril he had recklessly placed himself in, without any thought as to how to get out again. The translucent bubble held firm against the continuous onslaught, but Kenit knew his only hope of getting out of the situation unscathed was to rouse Fay.

"Danai Annis!"

He shook Fay gently.

"Danai Annis, wake up," he urged, tapping the side of her face.

There was a blinding flash of light and something struck the barrier sphere from above, followed immediately by a deafening rumble of thunder. He looked up in panic to see the Saharbashi still floating high above. A second lightning bolt, emanating from just in front of the hovering attacker, lanced downwards striking the barrier sphere again, with another deafening rumble of thunder following in its wake. Kenit's heart began to race. He knew he could sustain his invocation of *Inkansaylar* for two or three hours against the orbs unleashed by the six renegades of the Conclave, but fending off the lightning strikes of the Saharbashi as well was a different matter entirely.

He began to shake Fay more rigorously. Still she did not stir. He gave her a harsh slap to the side of the face.

"Wake up, damn it!" he yelled, before slapping her a second time.

As he attempted to make it three, Fay's hand shot up, catching hold of him by the wrist, then her eyes flashed open.

"If you hit me one more time," Fay said, evenly, "you're going to have a problem on your hands."

She released her grip on his wrist.

Kenit swiftly buried his face against Fay's chest.

"Oh, thank goodness!" he exclaimed with relief, before raising his head just as quickly, realising how inappropriate it was to have any part of his anatomy pressed against Fay's breasts.

A third lightning bolt struck the translucent bubble prompting Fay to clamber off the stone altar.

"What's our situation?" she asked, facing Kenit.

322

"I was worried about you. I came back just in case you needed my help," he replied. "But now it looks like I need your help if we're to get out of here. There's too many of them."

Fay took a cursory glance at the six renegades holding their positions a short distance from the dais. "On my order, lower your barrier sphere." She shifted her focus skyward. "I will take care of our friend in the air, while you handle the remnants of the Conclave."

"Wait!" blurted Kenit. The suggested course of action was uttered in such a matter-of-fact manner he felt guilty that he was about to put a dent in it. "I don't think I can defeat all six by myself."

"Then reduce the number you have to face."

Again, Fay's response was so matter-of-fact he felt silly for having to ask, "How am I supposed to do that?"

Another volley of incendiary orbs struck Kenit's barrier sphere, followed immediately by another lightning strike.

"Just make use of the environment to help you."

Fay looked past Kenit, focussing on the nearby renegades.

"You see the two skirting to the left? They are both close enough to the remnants of that wall. Should it collapse..." she said suggestively, "you'd be left with just four men to overcome."

Kenit was about to voice his concern about his ability to take on 'just' four renegade Sanatsai, when Fay barked out the order to bring down his barrier sphere. Without thinking, he neutralised the translucent bubble then thrust out a hand, invoking *Yuksaydan* to bring the aforementioned stone wall crashing down upon the two unsuspecting renegades. There was no hesitation or doubt when he jumped from the dais, and charged towards the remaining group of four, with sword in hand. As he closed the gap between himself and his opponents the ground beneath the renegades erupted, knocking them off their feet. He took full advantage of what he assumed was Fay's handiwork, stabbing the first assailant in the chest as he lay prone on the ground. He did likewise to a second before cutting down a third as he was rising to his feet. The fourth man was able to get up and retrieve his weapon just in time to defend himself. Kenit now had more favourable odds to contend with—it was one on one, to the death.

His initial attack was parried easily, but as he and his opponent faced off, slowly circling each other and waiting for an opening, he noticed the other man's sword arm trembling. And the look on his face made it clear the renegade Sanatsai was just as fearful as he was, if not more so. This boosted Kenit's confidence. He suddenly believed that he could, and would, prevail. Launching into another furious attack, striking high then low, he endeavoured to press home the advantage he felt he had over his opposition. The renegade was able to fend him off for a short while but wasn't able to counter-attack. All of a sudden, with a flourish, Kenit disarmed the renegade, sending his sword flying away. His opponent barely had time to look surprised as he followed up immediately with a lethal slash across the chest.

Time seemed to slow down as Kenit watched the renegade Sanatsai keel over, falling dead at his feet. Blood began to seep from the savage gash he'd inflicted, but he was given no time at all to crow about his decisive victory. His attention was drawn by the sounds of *Zarantar*-fuelled conflict in the air, some distance behind him. He spun around sharply, looking upwards just in time to catch sight of the Saharbashi dropping like a stone to the ground, while Fay descended slowly in his wake.

Kenit looked on as the Saharbashi gingerly got up off the floor. He was bemused when the man, rather than stand his ground and fight, slowly began to hobble away towards the trees at the northern edge of the ruins. Unsurprisingly, he did not get very far. The moment Fay reached the ground she thrust out a hand, invoking *Yuksaydan* to seize hold of the fleeing man and lift him off his feet. Kenit couldn't help but be amused at the sight of the enemy being comically flipped several times in the air before Fay finally brought his humiliation to an end, dumping him harshly face down on the ground.

For a moment Kenit stood rooted to the spot as he observed Fay marching towards her fallen foe, presumably to finish him off for good. As she closed the gap between herself and her prey, Kenit suddenly decided he wanted to witness the demise of the dreaded Saharbashi, up close and personal. He advanced across the ruins of the temple complex towards Fay's position as she moved in for the kill.

The defeated Saharbashi slowly rise to his feet to meet Fay, but as she stopped in front of him, he dropped to his knees. Though Kenit could see Fay had both hands clasped behind her back, he could tell from the strained grimace on the man's face he was being forcibly held down, immobile, by the strength of Fay's invocation of *Yuksaydan*. As he drew closer to the pair, Fay thrust out a hand to the side, and suddenly her sword—lying discarded some eighty yards away—flew speedily through the air, directly into her waiting grasp.

When Kenit reached Fay's side, she was holding the tip of her blade beneath the chin of the Saharbashi. The defeated man was uttering a desperate refrain.

"Have mercy! Have mercy! Have mercy!"

But the expression on Fay's face made it abundantly clear she had no intention of obliging his request.

"Kai Darbandian," said Fay, addressing Kenit without tearing her eyes from her captive, "take a look at what you were so afraid of. Do you see how he cowers before us, pleading for the mercy he would never show to others?"

He had to admit the man did look and sound pathetic. It was hard to believe this same individual had inspired such terror in him only a short while earlier.

"It was my responsibility to kill him," continued Fay, "but he would have lived had you not come back for me."

Finally she averted her eyes from the Saharbashi, to peer intently at Kenit.

"So, would you like to do the honours?"

Kenit held Fay's gaze for a moment before staring down at their mutual enemy. While this Saharbashi may not be the man responsible for the brutal death of Marit Katarnian, he was a living embodiment of the fear Kenit had for the cult leader whom he'd crossed paths with during the ill-fated mission in the land of his birth. He could not, and would not, pass up the opportunity to eliminate that fear, once and for all.

"It would be my privilege, Danai," he replied.

Standing aside, Fay allowed him to step directly in front of the condemned Saharbashi. He loomed over the man who finally fell silent. The look in his eyes showed acceptance of his fate. Kenit raised his sword, already stained with the blood of four renegades of the Conclave, gripping the hilt tightly in both hands. For Marit Katarnian, he thought. Then, with one swift, fluid swing he wielded his blade expertly to decapitate the Saharbashi. The severed head fell to the ground with a thud while the body slowly keeled over after it.

"You did it!"

Kenit spun around to see Tylo racing towards them.

"I knew you could do it," the boy cheered.

It was somewhat disconcerting that a young adolescent could seemingly be so excited at witnessing a man being beheaded.

"You're supposed to be on your way back to Relona," Kenit chided. "You shouldn't be seeing this."

"Go easy on the boy," said Fay. "He's right, you did it."

"I didn't do much. You did all the heavy lifting."

"Do not sell yourself short, Kai Darbandian." Fay was smiling warmly at him. "Before today, the number of people who could lay claim to saving my life could be counted on the finger of one hand."

Kenit's tension eased a little. He cast his gaze around the ruins of the temple complex, taking in the sight of all the dead renegades. While he was unable to take credit for most of the devastation—it was principally Fay's doing—he realised that he had made a significant contribution, saving the life of the legendary Fay Annis, and striking the killing blow against a Saharbashi.

"*We* did it," he said.

Kayden was growing increasingly frustrated and flustered as her duel with the Rogue continued unabated. Back on campus, training with wooden swords against other apprentices, it had never taken so much as five minutes for her to either land a decisive strike upon an opponent or—rather less frequently—be on the receiving end of one. But it had been at least quarter of an hour since hostilities had been initiated between herself and her black clad opponent, yet still she hadn't managed to stain her blade with the blood of her adversary—all her attacks were parried and countered effortlessly, almost as if the Rogue knew her every move before she made it.

She fended off another counter-attack, their blades clashing multiple times in quick succession, before another brief lull ensued while she and the Rogue circled each other again, waiting for an opening to exploit. With each passing second Kayden was becoming ever more conscious of the fact she couldn't keep going indefinitely, her body had already taken a battering that night so she was fighting at less than a hundred per cent. If things continued as they were, the Rogue would surely wear her down and prevail. She had to do something quickly to gain the upper hand.

The Rogue launched into another attack, striking high then low, then high again, forcing Kayden on to the back-foot. Once more, she was able to keep her adversary at bay, but it was getting harder with each new offensive. She briefly counter-attacked, without success, before another lull in the duel ensued. As she began to circle her opponent, yet again, she caught sight of a clump of turf torn up from the ground during her initial confrontation with the Rogue. Now was the right time to engineer an advantage. She invoked *Yuksaydan* to seize hold of the clump of turf and propel it towards the Rogue's head before causing it to erupt into tiny little pieces, spraying dirt into the face of the hooded figure.

Kayden charged forward seeking to take full advantage of the sneak attack. She thrust her blade at her opponent, aiming for the heart, but the Rogue promptly sidestepped out of the way, delivering a slashing cut to the top of her left arm as she breezed past. She let out an involuntary yelp then quickly spun around to face her foe, now standing motionless in a two-handed stance. Briefly, she took her eyes off her adversary to peek down at her upper arm. Though the injury was superficial, the Rogue had drawn first blood.

"Was it not you who desired a *Zarantar* free level playing

field?" said the Rogue.

Although the question was asked in the same androgynous monotone, Kayden felt certain she detected mockery in the voice of her assailant.

"I lied, you son-of-a-bitch!" she snapped, angrily. "If I have to cheat to kill you, I will."

Letting out a shrill battle cry, she dashed forward again, back on the offensive. She slashed furiously at the Rogue, her blistering attack unrelenting as she sought to overwhelm the defences of her hooded adversary. But once more, despite the ferocity of her onslaught, the Rogue was effortlessly able to parry every attack, as if possessing foreknowledge of every move she made.

As she started to tire, Kayden began to feel disheartened; there seemed to be no way through the defences of her implacable foe. She was about to ease off a little when an opening presented itself. She swung her blade at the Rogue's exposed neck, intent on separating head from shoulders.

The sword sliced through thin air as the Rogue disappeared in the blink of an eye. But there was no time to be shocked or paralysed by fear; she felt *Zarantar* behind her, and with it the sense of imminent danger. She spun around swiftly to be greeted by the sight of the Rogue's sword flashing down at her skull. She raised her own blade just in time to block the fatal blow, but there was nothing she could do about the kick that followed, landing square against her chest, knocking her to the ground.

"I can cheat too," said the Rogue, no hint of triumph in the emotionless voice.

Lying on her back, Kayden's heart was racing. Whatever her opponent had just done could not have been the invocation of *Raytandushay* to become invisible; it was something else entirely. One moment the Rogue was standing before her, about to be cut down by her blade, the next moment the hooded figure was right behind her, ready to land a killing blow upon her. If not for her ability to sense *Zarantar* she knew she would be dead. Her gamble in seeking an unfair advantage had ironically put her at a disadvantage.

She scrambled back on to her feet and stood on guard, her

sword gripped tightly in both hands.

"It seems you're no better at cheating than I am," she taunted, "I'm still alive."

"For now."

The Rogue lurched forwards, initiating hostilities once more.

Kayden evaded and parried a succession of slashing and stabbing attacks from her opponent before counter-attacking. Again, the Rogue disappeared in the blink of an eye to escape her blade, and yet again she felt the tell-tale *Zarantar* that alerted her to the imminent threat from behind. She spun around in time to deflect the thrust blade bound for her chest that would have run her through, between the shoulder blades, had she not turned around. She back-pedalled several paces to put a little distance between herself and her attacker. The brief lull in combat gave her just enough time to regret having violated the no *Zarantar* condition she had stipulated beforehand. She had needlessly made a difficult task even more difficult for herself; but was done was done.

Again, Kayden charged at the Rogue, attacking high with lethal intent. Still her adversary was able to fend her off with nonchalant ease before disappearing once more—this time reappearing, almost instantly, thirty yards ahead of her, arms outstretched to the side as if to say, 'I'm over here! What are you waiting for?'

"If you think I'm chasing after you, you've got another thing coming," Kayden yelled in annoyance.

The Rogue disappeared, yet again, and as before Kayden sensed the tell-tale *Zarantar* of her enemy behind her. She spun around to parry another series of slashing strikes, followed by another lull in the ongoing duel.

Smirking at her hooded foe, Kayden said, "You can disappear and reappear all you want. I'll always see you coming."

In response, the black clad figure disappeared again, reappearing in the blink of an eye on her right-hand side to slash her across the right thigh before vanishing again. She squealed in anguish, dropped her sword and keeled over clutching her leg. Instinctively, she invoked *Inkansaylar* to create a barrier sphere to protect herself. From her prone position on the ground she frantically looked around the clearing to see where the Rogue was. She caught sight of her assailant some twenty yards away, to her left, walking slowly towards her. She promptly created an additional barrier sphere around her first, then repeated the process until she was protected within the confines of seven translucent bubbles. The desperate measure wouldn't keep the Rogue at bay indefinitely, but hopefully long enough to allow her to tend to her injury.

Kayden tore her gaze away to examine her thigh. Blood was seeping between the fingers of her right hand as she tried in vain to staunch the flow. She slapped the ground three times with her left hand. The pain was agonising, but the petulant outburst was provoked more by anger than anything else. The Rogue was just toying with her. Somehow, the son of a bitch had the ability to prevent her from sensing the invocation of an application of *Zarantar*, and that's how she was taken by surprise. There was no forewarning of the attack that injured her.

She tore open the slash in the uniform borrowed from Fay's quarters, to better see the extent of the injury. It was little comfort to note that the gash in her leg didn't look nearly as bad as it felt. The wound inflicted upon her by the Rogue was a deep one that needed to be cauterised before she lost too much blood. If she passed out, she was as good as dead. Taking several calming breaths to prepare herself, she invoked *Shakbarilsan*—using two fingers of her left hand to guide the burning stream of hot air over the wound. Her mouth opened wide in a silent scream as the heat seared her flesh and blood, bringing tears to her eyes.

Once the wound was cauterised Kayden slumped backwards, lying flat on her back, looking up at the night sky through her multiple barrier spheres, breathing hard. She realised her amateur ministration was probably a wasted effort. She was still in no condition to defeat the Rogue—not that such a goal was feasible even if she was uninjured. But as long as she could draw breath there was still hope, so she would do her utmost to survive.

The sound of an incendiary orb, detonating against the outermost of her seven barrier spheres, did not intrude upon

Kayden's thoughts. She just lay on the ground intending to make the most of the respite afforded to her within her multiple translucent bubbles—however long that might be. When she was good and ready she would get up off the floor to face the Rogue, one last time.

Fay watched Kenit departing towards the western edge of the temple complex ruins in compliance with her order—the pretext being that she had seen one of the bodies moving, and didn't want to leave the Sharadi Forest until she was absolutely certain all the renegade Sanatsai of the Conclave were dead. In truth, she merely wished to speak to Tylo, alone.

"So, Tylo," she said, pulling her eyes away from her departing colleague, "you're Sister Inara's son, right?"

"Yes, Miss Annis."

She smiled at the boy. "You won't remember this, of course, but the last time you and I met," she said, "you were just a toddler, barely able to walk. But it appears you have grown up to be a very capable young man. Whoever picked you to play the hapless abducted child, chose well. I was unsure if Kenit could be persuaded to come back for me."

"He was certainly hard work, but I can be very persuasive when I need to be." Tylo chuckled, knowingly.

"Well, I thank you," she patted Tylo on the shoulder, "and I trust you've been told not to speak about tonight's events in the presence of anyone from the Order?" The boy nodded at her in affirmation. "Also, while travelling back to Relona you are not to do or say anything to my colleague to tip him off that this whole thing was staged for his benefit."

"Kenit won't learn of it from me, Miss Annis." Tylo mimed turning a key in a lock next to his lips.

The pair briefly made small talk, until Kenit returned to inform Fay that the corpse she had supposedly seen moving, was very much dead. She in turn instructed him to begin the journey back to Relona with Tylo. She would catch up with them a short while later.

"I don't understand," said Kenit. "Why aren't you coming

back with us now?"

"I need to stay behind to incinerate all these bodies," she replied. "Erase all evidence that the Conclave was ever here."

"Let me stay and help, then we can all go back to Relona together."

"You have already helped me enough," she insisted, "and I'd rather we didn't further delay getting Tylo back to his parents. So, it's time you took him home—that's not a request."

Kenit didn't argue the point. He told Fay that he would leave her horse tethered at the same spot so she wouldn't have to walk back to Relona—he and Tylo would ride back together on his horse. He then instructed the boy to fall into step alongside him, and follow his lead while making their departure from the ruins, back into the trees.

Fay watched the pair leave the clearing, then waited until she was certain they were gone and not coming back. Once she was satisfied they were not likely to intrude upon her, she cast her gaze around the ruins. The bodies strewn throughout the ancient temple complex, including the decapitated Saharbashi, vanished into thin air, as though they had never been there at all. Smiling, she then turned to face the trees at the northern edge of the clearing. She began clapping her hands in applause, prompting a dozen-strong group of Jaymidari to emerge from the trees to join her among the ruins.

"I cannot thank you enough, dear Sisters," she declared, clearly pleased. "Your illusion was incredibly convincing, despite the short notice—for which I apologise."

The only Sister among the group whom Fay recognised by sight, Lola Meris, stepped forward.

"Think nothing of it, Fay," she said before embracing her. "We were more than happy to help."

Upon being released from the embrace of her Jaymidari counterpart, Fay inquired, "Is Inara not with you?"

"No," replied Lola. "She plans to meet you when you return to Relona."

"Good! I'm pleased to hear it. I really must commend her on doing such a sterling job raising young Tylo; he is a credit to her."

"Yes, he's a wonderful boy," said Lola, with a smile. "It's just a shame he cannot follow in his mother's footsteps and pursue the calling. Tylo would make an exceptional Jaymidari if he'd been born female."

After a brief round of introductions with the other Sisters of the group, followed by some small talk, Fay notified the other women that she needed to get going as she didn't want to fall too far behind Kenit and Tylo.

"Will you be heading to Relona also, or returning straight back to the seminary?" she asked the Sisters.

"Actually," began the Sister introduced to Fay as Riva, "we'll be camping here for the night before returning to the seminary in the morning."

With that, it was time for Fay to take her leave and begin the return journey to Relona. She bid the Sisters farewell then left the ruins back into the trees to retrieve her horse for the ride. Soon enough she was on horseback, leaving Sharadi Forest at a gallop, hoping to catch up with Kenit and Tylo. She congratulated herself on a job well done, content that she had helped Kenit turn a corner.

Her only concern now was how well Ari was faring with the much tougher proposition presented by Kayden.

CHAPTER NINETEEN

The Unbelievable Truth

The Rogue had soon abandoned trying to breach Kayden's barrier spheres through the brute force of incendiary orbs, choosing instead to rely on the invocation of *Yuksaydan* to neutralise the impenetrable bubbles.

Still on the ground within her translucent defences, Kayden ignored the fall of the first four barrier spheres but once the fifth was neutralised—leaving just two between them—she decided it was time to get to her feet. She forced herself up off the ground, trying to mentally block out the pain of her wounded leg, then bent down to retrieve her sword off the grass. She gripped the hilt tightly in both hands, glaring at the Rogue standing on the other side of her two remaining barrier spheres.

While she had been lying on the ground, Kayden spent the time thinking of every conceivable way she could get out of the predicament she was in. Eventually, she came to the realisation that the only way she could bring an end to the confrontation with the Rogue, on her own terms, was to lose their duel...or at least appear to lose.

The sixth of the original seven barrier spheres was neutralised. The beginning of the end was close at hand.

Kayden kept her eyes on her adversary. The Rogue's sword dangled in one hand, the tip of its blade hovering just above the grass, while the other hand was outstretched as the hooded figure continued invoking *Yuksaydan* to neutralise the final barrier sphere separating the two combatants. She elected to save her black clad enemy the trouble of breaching the last impediment, bringing down the barrier sphere of her own volition.

The Rogue advanced a couple of paces, then stood on guard, sword gripped tightly in both hands, mirroring Kayden's opposing stance. But the similarities between the pair ended there. In stark contrast to the Rogue's motionless poise, Kayden's blade was shaking perceptibly, courtesy of the pronounced trembling of her arms.

"Let's put an end to this, now," she uttered without conviction.

The Rogue bound forward on the offensive, putting Kayden on the back foot. Her injured leg caused her to grimace, but worse than that it was hampering her mobility; she would not be able to hold off her assailant for very long. She evaded and parried several slashing strokes then swiftly attempted to counter-attack. Not only was the effort in vain, it proved costly. The Rogue effortlessly disarmed her, knocking the sword out from her grasp, sending it tumbling to the ground. She back-pedalled as quickly as she could, narrowly avoiding the follow up swing that would have cleaved her head from her body, while simultaneously reaching for the twin daggers at her hips. She unsheathed the blades then stood her ground, waiting for her opponent to make the next move.

Again, the Rogue advanced towards her while she slowly backed away, making no effort to steady the clearly trembling grasp she had on her weapons.

"Do not be fearful, my intransigent friend," came the androgynous voice from beneath the black hood. "Your death will be quick...if not painless."

Kayden halted in her tracks. Although she had a two-to-one numerical advantage in weaponry, there was little chance her two daggers would allow her to overcome her sword-wielding opponent. Lowering her arms, she dropped the daggers at her feet and submissively sank to her knees before the Rogue, eyes cast down at the ground. When she saw the booted feet stop under her nose, she looked up. It no longer bothered her that the face beneath the hood continued to elude her vision.

"I do not fear death," she declared, defiantly. "But I am not ready to die." Her whole world seemed to move in slow motion. The Rogue's sword rose slowly upwards, readying to be thrust down upon her skull.

Kayden invoked *Yuksaydan*, reaching first for the two discarded daggers lying on the ground on either side of her. The twin blades began to rise up, their trajectory setting them on a course to plunge into the chest of the hooded figure in front of her, though she knew the weapons would never meet their target—the Rogue would make sure of that. Simultaneously, she used the 'unseen hand' to reach several yards behind her foe to seize the sword she had purposely allowed to be knocked from her grasp. The bladed weapon rose off the floor, heading towards the black clad form of the Rogue, on a lethal course between the shoulder blades.

Eyes never leaving her assailant, she looked on as her two daggers were deflected harmlessly away by the Rogue's invocation of *Yuksaydan*—one to the left, the other to the right—just as she had anticipated. The downward stroke of the sword that should have followed, never came—the weapon fell to the ground, behind its owner. The hooded figure shuddered then froze with an audible gasp of shock; the blood-stained blade of a sword protruding from the chest was the apparent cause.

Kayden had succeeded in besting her implacable adversary, who never saw it coming.

She had snatched victory from the jaws of defeat.

The strange sense that time had slowed down came to an end as she rose from her kneeling position. She took a few steps backward to avoid the Rogue's body keeling over, falling to the ground before her. She stood silently for a moment, staring down at the body with her sword stuck in its back. There was no reason to believe the Rogue wasn't dead but Kayden cautiously circled the body of her fallen adversary, just in case. She kicked the body once, twice, three times. Only then—satisfied she had achieved her first successful kill—did she pull her sword from the corpse, wiping the blood off with the sleeve of her borrowed uniform.

Sheathing the weapon back into its scabbard, she proceeded to retrieve her twin daggers from the ground.

With both blades back in place, one on either hip, Kayden hurried off in the direction of the dirt path that would guide her through the forest, determined to complete Master Ari's task; her journey had been delayed for long enough. She walked no more than a dozen paces before slowing down, then halting in her tracks. She wasn't able to leave the clearing just yet. Something was gnawing away at the back of her mind. She needed to know who was lurking beneath the Rogue's hooded cloak.

For a drawn-out moment, pregnant with tension, Kayden stood motionless, peering back over her shoulder at her vanquished assailant. She could not shake the horrible feeling she would recognise the person in the black uniform. Finally, she decided to find out for sure. She returned to the Rogue's body and then, using her right foot, flipped the corpse over onto its back.

That's impossible!

Kayden staggered backward, then tripped over her own feet, falling flat on her back. Quickly, she sat upright to look back at the Rogue. She couldn't believe what she was seeing. It was her own face staring lifelessly back at her.

It's some kind of trick!

The sound of footsteps approaching from behind caused her head to spin around sharply. Her racing heart skipped a beat—again she couldn't believe her eyes.

"Mama?"

Her deceased mother, Tan'dee Jayta, was walking slowly towards her like an ethereal apparition. She was still so young and beautiful, just as Kayden remembered, wearing nothing but a flowing, sheer white dress that rippled like water. Her bare feet seemed to glide across the grass as she walked past her daughter, ignoring her presence completely to kneel down beside the body of the Rogue. Kayden was even more dismayed when her mother began to gently caress the face of the dead impostor.

"Oh, my sweet baby girl. Is this how you have chosen to honour me?" lamented Tan'dee, speaking Zenoshanese with the lilting voice Kayden hadn't heard in so many years. "Why would you become the very thing you despise?"

Kayden crawled quickly on her hands and knees to her mother's side, and knelt next to her.

"Mama, get away from her," she pleaded, adopting her mother tongue. "That's not me! I'm right here!"

"Why would you shame me this way?" Tan'dee continued, seemingly oblivious to her daughter's presence at her side. "Why would you make me the mother of a murderous monster?"

Seeing her mother lay her head upon the chest of the Rogue was too much for Kayden. She rose to her feet then bent down to grab Tan'dee under the arms. She was simultaneously disappointed and relieved by confirmation her mother was real—a living, flesh and blood woman she could touch. Pulling Tan'dee up on to her feet and away from the impostor, she placed her hands on either side of the beautiful face she had missed all these years, forcing her mother to meet her gaze. It was a surreal moment. The last time she gazed into her mother's loving eyes required her to look up at Tan'dee, since she was several inches taller than herself. But now, she was the one with a three-inch height advantage, so her mother had to look up at her.

"Mama, I would never do anything to shame you," Kayden protested. "How could you think otherwise?"

Finally, Tan'dee acknowledged her daughter's presence.

"Your hatred has overcome you."

Kayden was deeply perturbed by the accusatory look in her mother's eyes.

"Now you deem yourself the arbiter of who should live and who should die. And very soon, you will kill as no one before you has killed."

"No, Mama," she retorted. "I'm not a killer. I will never be a killer. You know I would never harm anyone."

"What about your stepfather?"

Slowly, Kayden's hands fell away from her mother's face.

"Mama, that's different," she said meekly, taking a step backward. "When I end his life, I will simply be meting out the justice he has escaped all these years."

"Because you are the arbiter of who lives and who dies?"

Kayden could feel herself beginning to choke up but she was determined to keep her emotions bottled up.

"He deserves to pay for what he did to you—for taking you away from me," she said. "How can I go on living knowing that he is out there enjoying the life he forfeited the day he took yours?" She was close to breaking down but she stiffened her resolve. "Mama, I have to kill him. I will kill him. Please tell me you understand and accept that. Tell me I will not shame you by this one-off action."

Tan'dee took a step toward Kayden and gently placed her hands on either side of her face.

"My baby girl, listen to me very carefully," she implored. "Once you start down that path you will not stop. Multitudes will drown in the rivers of blood you will shed." Her hands slowly fell away from her daughter's face, then she took a step back. "The mere mention of your name will shame me, forever."

The retort Kayden wanted to utter was forestalled when she noticed a red stain appear on her mother's brilliant white dress. The circular spot began to grow and spread, quickly joined by several more identical stains that she realised was blood. She was absolutely horrified when blood began to leak from her mother's eyes, ears, nose and mouth.

"Mama, what's happening?" she asked in wide-eyed panic.

There was no reply.

She heard the sound of water trickling rapidly on the ground, prompting her to look down. It wasn't water; it was blood. A steady flow dripping from the sleeves and hem of her mother's dress. Kayden was shocked to see that enough blood had already pooled beneath herself and her mother to cover the entire surface of the forest clearing, giving it the appearance of a small lake of blood. Her horror was compounded further by the sight of her mother and the body of the her doppelgänger sinking slowly into the blood, though her own feet remained upon the surface as if it was solid ground.

"Don't be alarmed," said Tan'dee. "It's not my blood. It's the blood of all the people you are going to kill."

Ignoring her mother's outrageous claim, Kayden looked on

helplessly as the lifeless body of her doppelgänger disappeared beneath the surface, with a disturbing squelching sound. If she didn't do something, quickly, her beloved mother—already sunk half way up to her shins in blood—would soon submerge.

"Mama!"

She grabbed hold of her mother by both arms in a desperate attempt to pull her free of the blood. The effort only seemed to make matters worse. The more she pulled, the quicker her mother sank. Tan'dee was now knee-deep in the blood.

Kayden cast her gaze frantically around the clearing. "Whoever's doing this," she yelled, "make it stop...now!"

"Only you can make it stop," said Tan'dee.

Kayden stared intently into her mother's eyes. "How?" she pleaded.

"You have to let me go."

"No!" She was bewildered by the request given that her mother was now waist-deep in the blood. "I won't let you go." It suddenly dawned on Kayden that her mother meant for her to 'let go' in the figurative sense. "I can't let you go," she lamented. "I don't want to lose you all over again."

"You can never lose me, Kayden," her mother said in a soothing tone. "You are my baby. You are a part of me, as I am a part of you. Wherever you go, I will always be with you." There was an expectant pause while Tan'dee looked beseechingly at Kayden. "Please...let me go."

Kayden's eyes began to water. "I don't want to," she said, choking up, trying to keep her tears at bay.

"My love, if you are to escape the terrible fate that awaits you," Tan'dee persisted, "you must let me go, now."

Tears slowly rolled down Kayden's cheeks. With a tremendous effort she reluctantly released her hold on her mother, letting Tan'dee sink chest deep in blood. She was inconsolable, standing there watching helplessly as her mother sank deeper into the blood.

"I love you so much, my baby girl," said Tan'dee with obvious pride; only her head remaining above the surface.

"I love you too, Mama," sobbed Kayden. "With all my heart."

Tan'dee was fully submerged in the blood, leaving Kayden standing alone in the clearing; she had lost her mother for the second time. Dropping to her knees, she shut her eyes and let out a long, piercing scream that reverberated around the clearing.

After what felt like an eternity, she fell silent and opened her eyes. The scene surrounding her had changed: the forest clearing was just how it was when she first entered. The lake of blood that took her mother and the body of the Rogue was gone, nor was there any indication of the titanic confrontation with her doppelgänger. Those areas of ground that had been torn up during their duel were undamaged, and there was no sign of the crater caused by the elaborate incendiary orb unleashed against her.

Kayden was disturbed by the seeming normality of the scene around her. If not for the pain of the two wounds inflicted upon her by the Rogue, she might have questioned whether or not what she had just experienced was real or imagined. But it had been real. She had fought a duel to the death against The Rogue, and triumphed—only to discover that her vanquished enemy was in fact her own self. And much worse than that, she had been reunited—albeit briefly—with her beloved mother, who warned her of the shame she would bring if she pursued her desire for revenge, thereby becoming the black clad killer she had no wish to be.

A distorted recollection of events came to her mind, unbidden.

Her mother was kneeling beside her as she lay dead on the ground wearing the black garb of the Rogue.

Is this how you have chosen to honour me? her mother was saying. *Why would you become the very thing you despise?*

The look of shame, hurt and disappointment in her mother's eyes was overpowering. Kayden couldn't bear to have her mother look at her in such a way; she had no desire to be a source of shame for the person she loved most.

Kayden rose abruptly to her feet, it was time to get out of there.

Why would you make me the mother of a murderous monster?

Her mother's accusatory voice echoed around the clearing—it

wasn't in her head. Her heart began to race in panic. She needed to get out of the cursed forest as quickly as possible, while she still had her sanity.

She darted towards the dirt path and sprinted as though her life depended on it, but still she couldn't outrun her mother's heartbreaking voice.

Why would you shame me this way?

She re-entered the trees at speed and her mother's voice followed her still.

Is this how you have chosen to honour me? Why would you make me the mother of a murderous monster?

It didn't matter how fast or how far she ran, Kayden couldn't escape the voice. Tears began streaming down her face, the hurt in her mother's voice stabbing at her like a knife.

The frantic nature of her effort to escape the forest, coupled with her stinging tears, prevented Kayden from noticing how the dirt path was leading her towards a pitch black curtain of nothingness. She continued running, oblivious. The moment she met the blackness she ran straight into strong arms that stopped her in her tracks.

"I'm sorry! I'm sorry, Mama!" Kayden cried. "Please forgive me. I never meant to shame you. I will make it right, I promise."

"Calm down, Kayden. Calm down" came Ari's soothing voice. "I don't understand a word you are saying. I don't speak Zenoshanese."

Kayden suddenly realised she was being held in Master Ari's arms, her head against his chest. She looked up at him with tears in her eyes, confused.

"Welcome back," he said.

She was back. They were standing at their picnic spot in the valley, bathed in the light of an illumination orb. The red and white check table cloth was still spread out on the ground behind Ari, with the remains of their meal upon it, and the assortment of white rocks protruding from the earth. Pulling away from Ari's embrace, she wiped her eyes with her sleeve. Slowly, she peered back over her shoulder to glance at the forest that had deeply disturbed her. There was no forest, just the rolling fields of the valley extending into the dark of night.

"What's the matter?" asked Ari when she turned back to him.

"The forest...it's—"

"Gone?" he finished for her. "Yes, it has served its purpose."

"Master Ari, while I was in the forest I saw—"

"Shhhhh!" Ari held up a finger, signalling for her to be silent. "Whatever it was you were shown was for your eyes only. You shouldn't speak of it to anyone else."

Kayden noticed that she was uninjured. There were no tell-tale slashes in her uniform where her doppelgänger had inflicted wounds to both her upper left arm and her right thigh. Nor was her body aching from the beating she received when trying to flee from her adversary.

"Was it...? Was it even real, Master?"

"I suppose that depends what you mean by real," Ari replied. "If you are asking me whether or not what you experienced really happened... Then yes, it did—that's the best answer I can give you."

He turned away from Kayden, stepping over the tablecloth to reclaim his place sitting across from her.

"Why don't you have a seat; the tea's still hot, would you like some more?"

"Thank you, Master."

Kayden sat down, cross-legged, opposite him. She reached for one of the remaining tarts as he poured more tea into her empty mug. It dawned on her that she had no idea just how long she'd spent wandering the Forest of Revelation. It had felt like ages, though she suspected otherwise.

"Master, how long was I gone for?"

Ari set Kayden's mug down in front of her.

"An hour or so, I'd say. Not much more than that."

He took a sip from his own mug then looked up at the night sky. Without the customary physical gesture, he casually invoked *Inkansaylar* to generate a large barrier sphere around the makeshift camp.

"Just in case we get some rain tonight," he said in response to Kayden's questioning look. "We wouldn't want to get drenched while we sleep."

"We're spending the night out here, Master?"

"Not unless you want to trek in the dark for a couple of hours to get back to Temis Rulan before dawn."

Kayden was in no real hurry to get back to the city. Her time with Master Ari had almost certainly put paid to her chances of ever being inducted into the Order. Returning to Temis Rulan would merely make it official.

"No, I could use the rest," she conceded. "It's been a trying day."

After a prolonged break in the conversation, punctuated by the sipping of tea, and the nibbling of food, Kayden was ready to engage Ari once more.

"Master, may I tell you something?" He silently nodded his assent. "I realise it's far too late to make any difference to what happens to me when we return to Temis Rulan, but I want you to know...it is no longer my intention to kill my stepfather for what he did to my mother."

"I see," said Ari, thoughtfully. "You seemed rather adamant about doing so, earlier. Why the change of heart?"

Kayden recalled the look in her mother's eyes, and the hurt in her voice.

"For too long I've allowed my anger and hatred towards my stepfather blind me to one simple truth: my mother would never approve of me killing anyone in cold blood, irrespective of the pretext," she said. "The mere thought of becoming someone Mama would be ashamed to call her daughter hurts me more than losing her has done. That being the case, if I cannot have justice for my mother, the least I can do is honour her memory."

"If your mother could see you now, Kayden, I'm sure she'd be immensely proud of the woman you are becoming."

A lump formed in Kayden's throat.

"Thank you, Master."

She lowered her head as a single tear trickled down her cheek. She would not allow Ari to see her cry for a third time.

Despite the darkness of nightfall, Fay could just about make out

Kenit and Tylo on horseback ahead of her, against the backdrop of the muted glow of lights coming from the town of Relona, looming further in the distance. She had more or less given up on catching the pair before arriving back in town, but now they were in view she urged her mount into a swift gallop. A short while later she was riding at a trot alongside the other horse. It amused her to note how obviously thrilled Kenit was to see her. But it was also gratifying to see that he looked so much more confident and self-assured. It appeared her elaborate charade had been an unqualified success.

As they rode into town, Fay informed Tylo that she and Kenit would be taking him home to his parents, immediately. They would return first thing in the morning to discuss the two options for his future: ten years apprenticeship, or the binding of *Zarantar*. Tylo played along like a consummate professional, earning a surreptitious wink from her when Kenit wasn't looking.

After having the two horses stabled at an inn located in the north of the town, she and Kenit escorted Tylo through the streets of Relona. In spite of the late hour, they passed several other people while navigating the main streets on their way to the residential building where Fay and Kenit had met Tylo's faux parents, Sedona and Radmilio. Before long the group reached their destination, without incident.

Fay led her two companions in single file down the narrow alleyway that separated the residential building from its neighbour. As she emerged around the back of the building on her right hand side, she was greeted by the sight of two women dressed in the cream and beige attire worn by all the Jaymidari, standing near the staircase leading up to the first floor landing. She did not recognise the younger of the two Sisters, but she knew the elder with the long, wavy hair, smiling warmly at her—it was Tylo's real mother, Sister Inara.

"Has the quarantine been lifted?" Fay asked in mock surprise, for Kenit's benefit, as they approached the two women.

"It turned out to be a false alarm. A case of misdiagnosis," replied Inara. "Sister Klara and I," she gestured at her companion, "headed into town not long after you left the seminary, to let you know. Of course, once we located your young friend's parents they told us what had happened. We've been waiting here for you ever since."

"Well, no harm was done in the end," said Fay, "thanks to my colleague here, Kenit Darbandian." There was a brief exchange of salutations after she introduced Kenit to the Sisters. "As for those responsible for Tylo's adventure, they won't be bothering anyone again," she continued. "And now that you are here I assume you can handle the discussions with Tylo and his parents about his future."

"If it's all right with you," said Inara.

"Yes, of course it is. We're more than happy to leave the matter in your capable hands."

Inara turned to her counterpart. "Klara, could you take Tylo indoors, please? I'll be up shortly."

Klara held out her hand to Tylo who dutifully stepped forward to take hold of it. He looked back at the two Sanatsai to address them one last time.

"It was an honour to meet you," he said. "Both of you."

"Likewise," replied Kenit. "I'm sorry it couldn't have been under better circumstances."

"Farewell, Tylo," added Fay.

Allowing Sister Klara to lead him away, the pair departed up the stairs heading for the back entrance of his faux parents' home. Fay noted the look of pride on Inara's face while watching the boy leave and disappear indoors with her colleague.

Inara returned her gaze to Fay. "So, what did you make of young Tylo tonight?" she asked.

Fay smiled. "He is a credit to his mother," she answered, knowingly.

"That's very nice to hear." Inara couldn't keep the gratification from her voice. "I'll be sure to let her know you said so."

"Well, we won't keep you any longer. Now that the situation has been resolved, Kenit and I should begin our journey back to Temis Rulan."

"Very well," said Inara, taking a step forward with arms open to embrace Fay. "It's just a shame we don't have time to catch up. It

346

has been too long."

"The next time I find myself in Lirantana," said Fay, releasing her hold on Inara. "I will make a point of checking in on you."

With that, the Sanatsai duo bid farewell to Inara before departing to make their way back to the inn where their horses were stabled. Upon arriving outside the establishment, minutes later, Kenit questioned the necessity of returning to Temis Rulan right away.

"It must be sometime after First Hour in the morning back there," he pointed out. "I see no reason to rush back to the seminary tonight to use their portal chamber—it will still be there at dawn. And after the night we've just had I think we've more than earned the right to spend the night here together.

"In separate rooms, of course," he added, after Fay had raised her eyebrows.

"That goes without saying," she retorted in her habitual matter-of-fact fashion.

"So...we are agreed?" queried Kenit. "We can get a few hours sleep and still be back in Temis Rulan in time for breakfast."

Fay agreed to checking into the inn for the night, though, in the end, she and Kenit did have to share a room—it was the only one vacant.

After they'd shared a pot of camomile tea, Kenit generously offered to allow her to sleep in the only bed while he slept on the floor. She graciously accepted the chivalrous gesture, not that she would have given him the option had he not offered. But Kenit didn't need to know that.

Kayden lay upon the grass with her knapsack beneath her head, wrapped in a blanket, staring up at the stars through the translucent bubble surrounding herself and Master Ari. It had been a while since she laid down to get some rest but she was unable to sleep; she had so much on her mind. On one hand, she had been given the opportunity to see her mother again—to speak to her, to touch her. Whether it was real or not didn't matter; she would cherish the memory, regardless. Yet, on the other hand, she was increasingly disturbed by the recollection of her own face staring back at her from beneath the hooded cloak of the Rogue. Obviously, she knew she wasn't the actual historical figure who had wreaked havoc across much of the Nine Kingdoms during the Great War, seven decades earlier. But her surreal experience in the Forest of Revelation strongly implied that she could, potentially, become the successor to the original rogue Sanatsai.

However, Kayden's most immediate concern was what she was going to do with her life once she was expelled from campus, after having her *Zarantar* bound. For five years the Antaris campus had been home. Being an apprentice there meant never having to worry about keeping a roof over her head, clothes on her back, and food in her belly—things she hadn't always been able to take for granted. Expulsion was going to take that away, and more. She had no idea what she would do at that point. Suddenly the future was a daunting prospect.

She rolled over onto her side to glance at Ari. He was lying on the other side of the red and white check tablecloth separating them, covered by a blanket, with his back to her. It looked as though he was sound asleep, but there was no harm in finding out for certain.

"Master Ari," she called out, tentatively. "Are you still awake?"

She heard a deep sigh in response.

"Would you believe me if I said no?" replied Ari, wearily.

"Sorry for disturbing you, Master. It's just that I can't sleep while I have so many questions running through my mind. Not until I have some answers."

Ari rolled over to face Kayden.

"What is it you need to know?"

"I was wondering..." She propped her head up with an arm. "What does it feel like to have your *Zarantar* bound? Does it hurt?"

"Well, I've never experienced it myself, of course, but to the best of my knowledge there is no pain, though I have occasionally heard it described as being like losing a limb.

"I can only speculate, but I assume that the longer someone has had their *Zarantar* the worse it would feel to lose it. For someone like myself, I imagine it would be more akin to having my very being ripped from my body, leaving an empty shell."

Kayden suddenly felt nauseous. Ari's answer was worse than the one she was anticipating. While it was true she hadn't possessed her *Zarantar* for very long, in that short period of time it had become such an integral part of who she was, the thought of having it taken away filled her with a deep regret.

"Is there a reason why you needed to know that, Kayden?"

"I... I just wanted to prepare myself—to know what to expect when the time comes."

"So, you're planning to abandon your apprenticeship?"

"No, of course not." Kayden couldn't conceal the surprise in her voice. "I'm going to be expelled...aren't I?"

"I can't think of any reason why you should be. Can you?"

Slowly, she sat upright.

"But... I thought..." Ari's response had her tongue-tied for a moment. "I just assumed the purpose of this excursion to the middle of nowhere was to confirm that I should be kicked out and have my *Zarantar* bound."

"It was never as simple as that," said Ari. "But I am satisfied that no such action will be necessary. And while, ultimately, I'll leave the final decision in your Master's hands, I can assure you if Fay wanted you gone she wouldn't have brought you to me in the first place. She has always been on your side, Kayden. As I mentioned earlier, you and Fay have much in common."

With a sense of overwhelming relief, Kayden slumped back down, laying her head on her knapsack once more. She began to giggle, in spite of herself, as she held both hands to her face to conceal her obvious delight.

"What's so amusing?" Ari inquired.

Kayden removed her hands from her face.

"Nothing, Master," she said once she had her fit of giggles under control. "It's just that...for most of the day I've been worrying about what being brought to Temis Rulan actually meant for me. At first I thought I was going to be killed, then I was certain I was going to be expelled. But now you're basically saying I was worried for no reason."

"So it would seem," affirmed Ari. Then he added, "Now, what about all the other questions keeping you awake?"

"They're no longer relevant, Master. All of them were in relation to what the future held for me once I was expelled."

"Does that mean I can now try to get some sleep?"

Kayden chuckled. "Of course, Master."

She heard him roll over and start fidgeting, attempting to get comfortable. She absent-mindedly stared up at the stars without a care in the world, hoping to doze off quickly herself. Then it suddenly dawned on her, she had one final matter gnawing away at the back of her mind.

She rolled onto her side, propping her head up with her arm.

"Master Ari, there is one more thing, actually."

Ari sighed deeply before replying.

"Yes?"

"Earlier tonight, you never quite finished telling me about the events of the final battle of the Great War. You said you couldn't bring yourself to kill the Rogue, but you didn't get any further than that. However, every account of the Great War I've ever read or heard states that the Rogue died at your hands. Now I can't help but wonder... If all the accounts are wrong, what did happen to the Rogue at the end of the war?"

Rolling over on to his side, Ari faced her again. He silently held her gaze for a moment—perhaps deciding whether he should tell her the truth—before eventually replying.

"That is a rather long tale, Kayden." Meaning, he had no intention of narrating it to her right there and then, or at all, she thought. "But if you really must know what became of the Rogue at the conclusion of the Great War, you could just ask her yourself the next time you see her."

In that moment, Kayden was sure that if she could see her own face she would surely see a picture of befuddlement. By this point she thought she had grown accustomed to Ari's cryptic, roundabout way of answering a simple question. But she was at a loss this time. What exactly was he trying to tell her?

Suddenly, she sat bolt upright, staring at him with incredulous eyes. Realisation had just set in. She knew exactly what Ari had just revealed to her.

Fay Annis was the Rogue.

CHAPTER TWENTY

Mission Accomplished

Kayden had a spring in her step as they continued their trek back to Temis Rulan. It was a brand new day and, in many ways, she felt like a new person, too. So much had changed in such a short space of time. She had unexpectedly been given a new purpose in life, and was looking forward to what the future would bring. It was as though a great weight had been lifted from her shoulders. She couldn't wait to return to Antaris campus to resume her apprenticeship without the burdens she had been carrying.

Making their way steadily across open country in the glow of the early morning sun, Kayden found she was able to appreciate all the sights and sounds of the return journey to Temis Rulan so much more than the initial journey away from the city. She had no concerns or anxieties to distract her from the beauty of the environment and its wildlife. It probably helped that she and Ari hadn't exchanged so much as a word during the hour or so they'd been hiking. And she was perfectly content to walk in silence. Everything that needed to be said had already been said at the crack of dawn.

Upon being woken by Ari at first light, Kayden felt truly invigorated, much to her surprise. She had slept peacefully and contentedly in spite of the shocking revelation about Fay Annis—a revelation that should have kept her up all night, especially because of Ari's unwillingness to elaborate.

As they were gathering up their things in preparation for the trek back to Temis Rulan, Kayden briefly contemplated broaching the matter with Ari but decided against it. She suspected he regretted revealing the unbelievable truth about Fay to her. But once their knapsacks were packed, it was he who finally brought up the previous night's revelation.

"So," he began, as he hoisted his knapsack over his shoulder, "regarding the matter we spoke of last night, concerning your master."

Kayden's ears pricked up. Was Ari going to tell her the whole story now?

"The number of people alive today who know the truth about her past can be counted on the fingers of one hand—including you. Needless to say, you cannot repeat it to anyone else."

She gathered as much, though who would believe it anyway?

"It is obviously a very sensitive subject. If it were to become common knowledge that the Rogue still lives, and is a senior member of the Order, it would be politically very damaging to us—perhaps fatally so."

"Then why did you tell me, Master Ari?" asked Kayden. "I find it hard to believe she would have asked you to reveal something like this to me."

"She didn't," Ari affirmed. "But I deemed it to be in your best interest to know. I just hope the truth doesn't further sully your feelings towards Fay."

Ari's fear was unfounded, Kayden suddenly realised. The moment she heard the truth about Fay, her opinion of the woman had immediately and irrevocably been changed...for the better.

"As strange as this might sound, Master," she said, "now that I know the truth about her, I feel like I understand her better. I can finally appreciate where her attitude and actions towards me, these past three years, have been coming from." Fay had not been persecuting her after all. "I guess when she said I reminded her of someone from her past, she was referring to herself?"

"Yes. Your master was not much older than you are now, when she went down a dark path that led to her becoming the Rogue. And I know how much she would have hated for you to make the same mistakes she made."

Hearing about Fay's past didn't make it easier to reconcile how the woman she knew could ever have been the infamous rogue Sanatsai.

"It's still difficult to believe that a woman like her could be the same person who is so reviled in our history," she confessed. "How and why did she become the Rogue?"

"That's not really my story to tell, Kayden."

"Should I ask her?"

"I'll leave that to your judgement," he said. "Now, why don't we get going? We can make it back to Temis Rulan in time for breakfast."

She hoisted her knapsack over her shoulder.

"Very well, Master," she said. "You lead, I'll follow."

They continued their silent trek across open fields until, eventually, Kayden realised how odd it was they hadn't encountered any other people, or seen any towns or villages—or habitations of any kind, for that matter. The same was true of the previous evening's hike.

"Master Ari?"

"Yes, Kayden," he replied, without looking back at her.

"I've just noticed, since leaving Temis Rulan yesterday we haven't seen any other people about, nor come across any villages. Why is that?"

"When the Sisterhood invited us to the island to establish a permanent headquarters for the Order, we were told we could not build any settlements north of where we eventually chose to found Temis Rulan."

"Why?"

"I have no idea. But I'm sure they have their reasons."

That concluded their conversation, reinstating the silence that had been briefly intruded upon. Neither made any further attempts at small talk as they continued on their way. The serene quiet was perfect for contemplation, and Kayden soon found herself preoccupied with thoughts of Fay. She couldn't wait to see the administrator again once she and Ari arrived back in Temis Rulan. She wasn't sure what she was going to say to the woman, but she knew she wanted to thank her—if nothing else.

It was just after half past Seventh Hour when she and Ari reached the outskirts of the city. She silently followed his lead while he navigated the way back to the Order's headquarters at the centre of Temis Rulan. It was somewhat surprising to her that the city was already wide awake. Although the streets couldn't be described as teeming with crowds, as they were during her two previous journeys through the city, there were certainly a lot more people roaming around than Kayden anticipated. Once again, Ari had his hood pulled up over his head to conceal his identity while he led her to their destination. It was obviously an effective measure because few people gave him a second glance as they passed by.

The pair eventually arrived at the northern gates of the perimeter wall surrounding the complex that was the headquarters of the Order, some time after Eighth Hour. They were warmly greeted by the sentries on duty who promptly permitted them to enter without fuss. Kayden strolled alongside Ari as they paced the grey brick path leading towards Kassani House, wondering if Fay had returned from her trip yet.

"Would you like to head straight to the mess hall for breakfast," began Ari, "or will you return to Master Fay's quarters to freshen up first?"

Kayden hadn't given any thought to sitting down for breakfast until that moment. She wasn't particularly hungry anyway, not to mention she had more pressing matters to attend to.

"Well, I could do with a bath right about now," she admitted. "Breakfast can probably wait until I get back to Antaris." She suddenly wondered if she would be going back to campus that day. "Assuming, I'll be going back to Antaris this morning?"

"I don't see why not," said Ari. "I imagine your master will want to take you back there as soon possible, once she returns."

"Oh, so she's not back yet?" Kayden was surprised at how disappointed she sounded.

"I don't know. I suspect you'll know before I do, if you're going up to her quarters."

"She never did say where she was going," said Kayden,

recalling the last time she spoke to Fay. "Do you know where she went?"

"I had a task for her that she believed could be completed in short order while she is here. If she hasn't returned yet, then she must still be elsewhere taking care of the matter."

Kayden contemplated asking Ari about the nature of the assignment Fay had undertaken for him, but decided it didn't matter. Now that she knew just how powerful a Sanatsai Fay truly was, it was safe to assume she was more than capable of executing whatever the task may be without difficulty. And though she was concerned by her recollection of Fay's intimation she might no longer be the administrator of Antaris campus upon her return, there was little cause to be concerned about her safety. Fay would return as she had said, and once she did, the two of them would spend some time alone together—to talk and mend fences. She was determined to ensure their relationship became a more positive one, moving forward.

While she and Ari continued their approach towards the north entrance to Kassani House, Kayden could see Sister Idelle, dressed in her cream and beige robes, standing at the threshold awaiting their return—or, more likely, Ari's return. Seeing the elderly Jaymidari's wizened old face, Kayden suddenly wondered if Idelle was one of the people who knew about Fay's infamous past. It made sense that she would be. She was a serving member of the Council, and she certainly looked old enough to have been alive during the Great War.

"Master Ari," she said, in a low voice. "When you said the number of people who know the identity of the Rogue can be counted on one hand, am I right in believing Sister Idelle is one of those people?"

"Indeed, she is."

Idelle greeted them with a warm smile once they reached Kassani House. She was the kind of person it was impossible not to like, Kayden realised.

"I'm pleased things went so well out there, last night," she said, directing her words to Ari.

How could she possibly know how things went last night?

Kayden wondered.

"Your master will be most relieved to know that," she continued, addressing the apprentice. "She won't admit it yet, but she's rather fond of you."

Somehow, Kayden knew Idelle's words to be true, though she was at a loss to understand why Fay would be fond of her, at all. It wasn't as if she had given the woman any reason to be.

"So Fay has returned, then?" Ari inquired.

"Not yet. But she'll be returning soon enough." Idelle fixed her gaze on Kayden. "If you could excuse us, Kayden, I have some matters I need to discuss with Master Ari."

Not so long ago, Kayden might have taken umbrage at being dismissed so the 'grown ups' could talk. But things were different now; she was different. Besides, how could the lovable old lady ever aggravate her?

"Of course, Sister," she replied before tipping her head at Ari. "Master Ari."

Stepping away, she crossed the threshold into the building, but didn't get far—she was halted in her tracks when Idelle called out to her.

"One more thing before you go, Kayden," said Idelle, peering over her shoulder. "If I do not see you again before you return to Antaris campus, it was an honour to meet you."

"The honour is all mine."

Kayden continued on her way, wondering why Sister Idelle would be honoured to meet a mere apprentice. Perhaps she was just being courteous? Whatever the case, Kayden didn't dwell on it as she headed swiftly back up to Fay's quarters without further delay.

She stopped outside the door and knocked first, though she knew Fay would not be in. As expected, there was no reply so she let herself in. She set her knapsack down upon one of the armchairs as she made her way through the living area en route to Fay's bedchamber. She paused in the doorway, recalling Fay telling her how to call for someone to attend her if she needed anything. Well, she needed to have a hot bath, and for the uniform she had borrowed from Fay to be cleaned; that was reason enough to take advantage of the assistance.

Kayden stepped away from the doorway of the bedchamber, and strolled to the mahogany desk in Fay's study. She waved her hand over the glass sphere sat upon the desk, invoking *Yuksaydan* to activate it, as Fay had instructed. The sphere briefly glowed, indicating she had successfully alerted someone, somewhere, that she required assistance in Fay's quarters. She had no idea how quickly this person would arrive to attend her, so she decided to take a look inside Fay's bathroom, having neglected to do so while nosing around the previous day.

She pushed the door open and ambled into the bathroom. It was rather compact in comparison to Fay's bedchamber, but Kayden was still impressed, nonetheless. Firstly, Fay had a bathroom for her own use—she had grown so accustomed to sharing the campus bathhouse with dozens of other women and girls—and, secondly, everything in the room was in such immaculate condition. She was especially impressed by the sight of the large tub that dominated the bathroom. It must surely take an age to pump up enough water to fill it.

The sound of knocking on the door to Fay's quarters intruded upon Kayden's reverie. *That was quick*, she thought. Assuming, of course, her visitor was the person summoned by the beacon she activated. She hurriedly vacated the bathroom to see who was at the door. When she pulled it open she was pleasantly surprised to see that the tall Sister standing before her was someone she recognised.

"Sister Nelda," she greeted the statuesque Jaymidari.

"Hello again, Kayden," replied Nelda. "So, what can I do for you this morning?"

Kayden stood aside to permit the fair-haired woman to enter, then shut the door after her.

"I was hoping I could have a hot bath," she said, "plus, I borrowed this uniform when I went out with Master Ari yesterday, so it will need to be laundered."

"Very well, right this way."

Nelda took charge, leading Kayden into the bedchamber.

"Go ahead and strip out of those clothes. I'll start drawing your bath immediately, then I'll bring back a bathrobe and towel for you in just a moment."

Kayden watched Nelda exit the room while she absent-mindedly wondered if all the women from the lands of southern Karlandria were as tall and fair as the Sister. She began peeling off the uniform then neatly placed each garment in a simple pile on Fay's bed. As she stood waiting for Nelda to return with a bathrobe, she casually sniffed her armpits. Oh, yeah, a hot bath was definitely in order, she concluded.

Listening to the sound of water being pumped into the bathtub, she began to wonder how long it would take Nelda to get the tub even half full. Seconds later, Nelda sauntered back into the bedchamber carrying a white bathrobe with a matching white towel, yet the sound of water being pumped continued. So who was filling the tub if...? *Of course!* she realised. Why go to the trouble of drawing water by hand when you can use *Zarantar* to do the job?

"Here's a bathrobe and towel for you," said Nelda, handing them off to her. "I'm sure your master won't mind you using them."

"Thank you."

"If you like I can have your undergarments washed, also, while you take your bath."

Kayden looked down at herself. "I guess they could do with a cleaning," she admitted, looking back up at Nelda. "But I'm not sure there's enough time for that. I expect I'll be returning to Antaris campus pretty soon."

"Your master has not returned from Lirantana," said Nelda, questioning the idea time was short. "But, if you like, I can personally have them laundered and dried before you've even finished your bath."

"In that case, please do," replied Kayden. "And thank you."

"Think nothing of it. I'll leave you to get undressed while I check on your bath."

As Nelda headed back out of the room Kayden decided she may as well inquire about Fay's mission in the Kingdom of Lirantana.

"Sister Nelda," she called out, stopping the Jaymidari in the doorway. "Do you know what was so urgent in Lirantana?"

"Nothing you need to be concerned about. Your master went there to help a colleague who's been having a hard time recently. She should return sometime this morning." With that Nelda continued on her way.

Kayden stripped out of her undergarments, letting them fall to the floor, then put on the bathrobe. The cotton fibres felt wonderfully soft against her skin. She picked up the towel and slung it over her shoulder, then waited for Nelda to finish drawing her hot bath. The wait was brief. Nelda returned moments later to let her know that her bath was ready, and to collect her undergarments and Fay's uniform for cleaning. Before leaving with the dirty laundry in her arms, Nelda reminded Kayden that if she required anything else all she had to do was activate Fay's desktop beacon again.

Kayden wasted little time vacating the bedchamber to go back into the bathroom. She was impressed by how much effort Nelda had made for her benefit. Several scented candles had been lit and placed in the four corners of the room, and the air was tinged with the fragrance of lavender. Steam was wafting up from the water filling the tub, while a bar of soap and a sponge lay on the fluffy mat laid out beside it. Testing the water with her hand to satisfy herself it wasn't too hot, she found that it wasn't; it was just right. She also realised that the scent of lavender was not just emanating from the candles, it also came from the bath salts put into the steaming water.

Once she was done admiring all the trouble Nelda had gone to for her sake, Kayden allowed her bathrobe to slide down her body and fall around her feet. She dropped the towel along with it, retrieved the bar of soap and sponge then carefully stepped into the tub.

A quarter of an hour later, Kayden slowly reclined in the water with a contented sigh, letting her arms rest on either side of the tub. It felt good to have washed away the exertions of her trek with Master Ari. Now she could just sit there and relax. She had no intention of getting out of the tub for at least another quarter-hour.

Kenit was rather irritable when Fay roused him at dawn, bright eyed and bushy tailed. She seemed highly amused by his irritation, he thought, but worse than that she wouldn't entertain his request for an extra hour's sleep. To his chagrin, he was compelled to get up from the hardwood floor. Fay was adamant they leave the inn right away and make the journey down to the Sisterhood seminary outside town.

Within a couple of minutes he was ready to check out of their room. There was no need to get dressed, having slept in his uniform. All that was required was to put his hooded cloak back on, and retrieve his weapons. Following Fay's lead out of the room, he took out a chew-stick from one of his pockets and proceeded to scrub his teeth with its bristles. As for answering the call of nature, followed by a bath and breakfast–that would have to wait until later.

Upon leaving the inn, Kenit and Fay set off on horseback through the quiet, deserted streets of Relona, heading south, by dawn's early light. Once they were beyond the outskirts of the town, Fay urged her mount into a canter, prompting Kenit to follow suit. He made no attempts to engage Fay in light conversation during the journey as she didn't seem inclined to talk, which was probably for the best, he decided. Especially as he, too, was rather distracted himself. Something about the previous night's events was nagging away at the back of his mind—something he couldn't quite put his finger on.

When they entered the grounds of the seminary some time later, the sun had chased away the last of the early morning gloom. Kenit noted, right away, that the quarantine in place the previous day had been lifted. The seminary was a hive of activity—in stark contrast to the barren sight that greeted them when they had first arrived from Temis Rulan—apparently confirming Sister Inara's assertion that the quarantine was the result of misdiagnosis. There were scores of Jaymidari beavering away doing chores, or whatever it was they did at such an early hour. Several of the women briefly stopped what they were doing to wave or smile as the Sanatsai duo passed by while guiding their borrowed horses back to the stables. There was a time, not so long ago, when Kenit's head would have been turned by some of the Sisters. But now that he had met Fay Annis, the beauty of other women paled in comparison.

He and Fay left the two horses in the care of the group of Sisters tending the stables, then made their way to the main building. The same middle-aged Sister they had encountered the day before greeted them at the entrance; Fay called her Sister Briella. Kenit's expectation that they would be led to the seminary's portal chamber right away was dashed when Briella asked if they would like to have breakfast before returning to Temis Rulan. Fay declined the offer—for both of them—but did request the use of the bathhouse.

Oh, great! he thought. Was there some reason why she couldn't wait until they were back in Temis Rulan before having a wash?

He was even more put out when, after making use of the privy, he was forbidden from using the bathhouse also. Apparently, the seminary did not have separate facilities for men. Instead, he was provided with a small bucket of lukewarm water, a bar of soap and a sponge, then left to his own devices—to find a quiet, secluded spot on the grounds where he could have a quick wash away from prying eyes.

Eventually, he settled for a space between a wall and the back of a tool shed where he stripped off his uniform. He levitated a couple of inches off the ground, then spent the next five minutes soaping himself down while bitterly wondering what was the big deal about using the bathhouse. Did they honestly think he would see anything he hadn't already seen numerous times before? He was a red-blooded male in the prime of his life; he was more than familiar with the female anatomy. But maybe that was the problem. Maybe the Sisters assumed he couldn't be trusted in a building with several naked, wet women without wanting to ravish them.

Kenit was startled out of his thoughts when a young Sister silently came around the back of the tool shed. He instinctively placed the soapy sponge over his groin with both hands, though he quickly noted she had little difficulty maintaining eye contact. In fact, the Sister displayed no interest in his body, whatsoever—her purpose for intruding upon him was to bring a towel, and ask if he had finished with the bucket, soap and sponge.

"Thank you," he said, dropping the sponge into the bucket of water and reaching for the towel with his one free hand. "And yes, I've finished with the bucket."

The bucket—with its remaining water, bar of soap and sponge—floated up off the ground and gently glided into the outstretched hand of the Sister. She departed without another word, leaving Kenit in seclusion once more. He dried himself off then put his uniform back on. The quick wash had taken no longer than ten minutes, he estimated, so it was more than likely Danai Annis would still be in the bathhouse for a little while longer. Slinging the damp towel over his shoulder, he sauntered back to the bathhouse. Outside the building he sat down on a nearby wooden bench, waiting for Fay to emerge from within.

A quarter-hour later he was growing impatient. There was no sign of Fay, *still*, yet he had seen a number of Jaymidari enter and leave the bathhouse. As he let out a sigh of frustration, the Sister who intruded upon him earlier reappeared to ask if she could take back the towel she'd given him.

"Yes, of course," he replied, handing over the damp towel. Once again, she departed without a word. "Excuse me," Kenit called out to her. "Sister...?" His voice trailed off; she hadn't given a name earlier.

Stopping in her tracks, the Sister peered back at him. "Alma," she offered with a smile. "Alma Rayis."

"Kenit Darbandian," he said, standing up to introduce himself. "I wonder if I could trouble you for a moment, Sister Alma," he said. "Would you mind checking if my colleague is still in there?" He gestured towards the entrance of the bathhouse.

"Yes, Miss Annis is still inside," said Alma. "I'm sure she won't be much longer. Would you like me to wait with you?"

He was slightly taken aback by the offer. "I... I wouldn't want to trouble you further," he managed to say. "I'm sure you have other things you'd rather be doing."

"It's no trouble at all." Alma came back to the bench to sit beside him as he sat back down again. "So, as I understand it, you and Miss Annis had quite the adventure last night."

It was funny she should mention that, Kenit thought. He couldn't stop thinking about what had transpired in Sharadi Forest, something about it just wasn't quite right.

"You could say that," he replied. "But the more I think over everything that happened, the more I..."

"The more you...?"

"I don't know," he admitted with a sigh. "Have you ever had the nagging feeling that things aren't quite what they appear to be? That somehow you're not seeing something that's right in front of you?"

Alma didn't answer. But her silence, coupled with the look in her eyes, said enough to cause Kenit to suspect she knew more about the previous night's events than she should.

"What do you know that I don't?" he said, quizzically.

"Only what I was told," Alma assured him. "But if you believe there is more to what happened, perhaps your instincts are correct. If so, maybe you'll work out what it is about yesterday's events that troubles you."

To Kenit's mind, that response more or less confirmed his suspicions. Something *was* off about last night's events, something that continued to elude him. But he would work it out eventually, that much he was sure of.

"You're rather enamoured of her, aren't you?" said Alma unexpectedly, changing the subject.

"I'm sorry?"

"Miss Annis. You're very taken with her," Alma teased.

Kenit flushed, in spite of himself. What gave the Sister that impression? he wondered. Was it that obvious?

"I... I have no idea what you're talking about," he lied. None too convincingly, at that.

"Anyone who saw the way you were looking at her when you arrived here this morning, will know what I mean." Alma seemed to be enjoying his discomfort. "There's no need to be embarrassed. I doubt you are the first man in the world to ever fall for her—you certainly won't be the last. However..."

In the blink of an eye, Kenit went from wanting Alma to shut up, to wanting her to continue speaking.

"However...what?" he pressed, eagerly. He couldn't just let her stop in mid-sentence like that.

The playful smile left Alma's face, replaced by a pensive expression.

"A wise woman once said, 'Never set yourself unattainable goals. You will spare yourself the disappointment of false hope'. I think you should take heed of those words."

It was difficult not to feel insulted. No man wants to be told he's not good enough for the object of his affections. And while he freely accepted that Fay had no interest in him, either romantically or sexually—at least at present—there was no reason to believe that couldn't change in the future.

"Is that your way of telling me Danai Annis is out of my league?"

"I wouldn't want to put it like that," replied Alma, "especially as I do not know her personally. But from the way some of the older Sisters speak about her, I have to assume a woman like Fay Annis would be out of reach for most men—including those more worthy than you."

Kenit wasn't sure how he was supposed to respond to that. Alma seemed to possess more insight into Fay's history and persona than he did—which wouldn't be too difficult given he'd only met her for the first time the previous evening.

"It's better that you know now," continued Alma, gently placing a hand on his knee, "before you become too besotted with her. Hopefully it will make it easier for you to guard your heart."

The conversation quickly moved away from matters of the heart to more mundane matters. Kenit found Alma to be very engaging company—so much so, he failed to notice a good half-hour fly by. It could have been half a day, and still he would have been oblivious to the passage of time.

"I hope I'm not interrupting."

Fay's voice took him completely by surprise. Not only had he not seen her appear, he'd almost forgotten he was waiting for her.

"Not at all," replied Alma. "I was just keeping Kenit company until you returned."

"I hope he didn't bother you too much, Sister. Likes to complain a lot, this one," Fay shifted her gaze to her colleague, "if you give him the chance."

Kenit would have taken issue with the dig if not for the twinkle in Fay's eyes, letting him know she was just teasing.

"I take it you're ready to leave now, Danai?" he asked, fidgeting on the bench in preparation to stand up.

"Yes, I've been ready for a while," said Fay. "While you were talking the poor Sister's ears off, I was indoors sending a message back to Temis Rulan to arrange for a boat to be waiting for us when we leave here."

The reply caused him to wonder how much time had elapsed while he was conversing with Alma. And how had he not noticed Fay leaving the bathhouse to go into the main building? But there was no time to dwell on either thought. Fay bid Sister Alma farewell, then instructed him to follow her as she departed towards the main building of the seminary. He paused long enough to say his own farewell.

"It was a pleasure meeting you, Alma," he said, rising up from the bench. "If I have cause to be in Lirantana again I'll be sure to pay you a visit, assuming I'd be welcome."

Alma rose to her feet, still clutching the damp towel. "It was nice to meet you, Kenit. And yes, our doors are always open to the Order; it would be a pleasure to have you visit us in future." As he departed with a smile, to catch up with Fay, she added, "Remember what I said!"

Kenit stopped and looked back at Alma, questioningly.

"Save your heart for someone who will appreciate it."

He was still for a moment, pensive, as he considered her words. Finally, he continued on his way.

"And trust your instincts!" Alma called out, one last time.

Swiftly, he rejoined Fay, and they entered the main building together. They were met by Sister Briella, once more, who guided them down to the portal chamber beneath the seminary. As he stood before the opening of the portal, he thought it odd that Fay would take the time to thank the handful of Sisters gathered nearby for their assistance. What assistance? They hadn't done anything other than allow Fay the use of the bathhouse.

When Fay returned to stand beside him in front of the portal, his heart skipped.

"Are you ready to go?" she asked.

There was a part of him that did not wish to return to Temis Rulan yet. He would welcome the chance to prolong his adventure with Fay for a while longer. He could get to know her better and, more importantly, she could get to know him. Once they returned to Temis Rulan who knew when, or even if, they'd have the opportunity to spend any time alone together again. He was aware that Fay was currently a campus administrator, and would be returning to Antaris campus sooner rather than later. It was very doubtful he had made enough of an impression on her to ensure she didn't forget all about him once they parted ways, and as the old adage warned, 'out of sight, out of mind,' although in his own case, absence was sure to make his heart grow fonder.

"Ready when you are, Danai Annis," he replied.

Kenit watched Fay march forward and enter the portal, disappearing from his view—but he didn't follow immediately in her wake. He hesitated. So much had occurred in the short space of time since Fay enlisted him to join her on her errand to the Kingdom of Lirantana. For one, the trip was by no means the uneventful one she had insisted it would be. On the contrary, it proved to be an incredibly perilous adventure that culminated in him having to save the life of his legendary counterpart.

Or had he?

Realisation set in. Kenit suddenly knew what it was about the events in Sharadi Forest that had been bothering him. Finally, he proceeded to enter the portal, feeling reassured, but also uncertain of how he would confront Fay to confirm what he suspected.

For the second time in two days, Fay stood within the confined interior of the disused windmill overlooking the village of Adara. While she waited for Kenit to emerge from the portal she began to wonder if he might have decided not to return to the Order. Just as the thought crossed her mind, he appeared in front of her, and the portal opening blinked out of existence behind him.

"Finally!" she said with mock impatience. "I was beginning to wonder if that pretty young Sister had tempted you to stay in Lirantana."

"Why would you think that?" Kenit asked, obliviously.

Fay noted he was looking at her strangely. It was as though he wanted to say something to her, but was concerned about the response he might receive.

"Come along," she said, hoping to dissuade him from getting it off his chest. "I have places to be, and people to see."

She promptly turned on her heels and strode towards the open exit of the windmill.

Turning right when she exited the disused structure, Fay was greeted by the sight of the many farmhouses of the village downhill in the distance. It was a bright sunny morning with blue skies and wispy white clouds overhead. She marched purposefully down the hill towards the village where a couple of horses would be waiting for them. Already she was able to see scores of villagers milling about, which was to be expected—the time here was three hours ahead of Lirantana. She estimated arriving back in Temis Rulan some time after half past Ninth Hour.

Fay heard and felt Kenit fall into step on her right hand side, but she did not look at him. She wanted to avoid encouraging the crush he so clearly had on her. After having successfully boosted his confidence, to allow him to walk into harm's way and fulfil his duty as a Sanatsai, it would be most unfortunate to have to dent that newfound confidence by making it clear she would never reciprocate his feelings, whether romantic or sexual.

Marching silently downhill, drawing ever nearer to Adara, she could see from the corner of her eye Kenit frequently casting glances in her direction. With an imperceptible sigh, she knew she was going to have to bring the matter to a head and just get it out of the way as quickly as possible, whether she wanted to or not. It was time to let Kenit down gently.

"Kai Darbandian!" Finally, she glanced at him. "If there is something you wish to ask me, now is the time to do so."

For a moment Kenit looked uncertain.

"I don't have a question, as such," he managed to say. "But something has been bothering me ever since I woke up this morning."

"And what might that be?"

"There was no outbreak of violet fever at The Sisterhood seminary, was there?"

What is he getting at here? Fay wondered. "I thought that much had been established already," she said, carefully, "when Sister Inara informed us that the quarantine was a case of mistaken diagnosis."

"Well...yes," Kenit acknowledged, having seemingly forgotten that little detail. "But that's not really the point I'm trying to make."

"What is the point you're trying to make?"

"I've heard many stories of your exploits on behalf of the Order," began Kenit, "and last night, in Sharadi Forest, I got a small glimpse of what you are capable of. But in the midst of all the danger, I lost sight of one simple fact."

Fay could tell from the look in Kenit's eyes that he knew—or at least had good reason to believe—he'd been duped. If so, what would that mean for her efforts to preserve his status as a member of the Order? She thought last night had been a success. Was she wrong?

"A Sanatsai as powerful as you would never require help from someone like me," Kenit continued. "I didn't really save your life yesterday, did I? You were never in any real danger, were you?"

"Kenit," she interjected, "I—"

He cut her off. "It's okay, Danai, there's no need to explain. I don't need to know what really happened in Sharadi Forest—it doesn't matter. But I guess I should be thanking you for going to so much trouble on my behalf. Even though you don't know me, you did not give up on me, nor did you allow me to give up on myself. I really appreciate that. You've helped me to realise I cannot use past failures as an excuse to shirk my responsibilities today, or in the future. I may not be as powerful as you, but I have a duty to use the power I do have to the best of my ability, for as long as I am a Sanatsai of the Order."

She looked intently at her counterpart. It appeared her plan had worked even better than she hoped. Last night was an unqualified success after all.

"In that case," she said with a smile, "the mission has been accomplished." Now her only concern was whether Ari had been equally as successful with Kayden.

She returned her focus to the village up ahead, content to walk the rest of the way in silence. But, as luck would have it, Kenit had other ideas.

"Danai Annis, there is one more thing I'd like to discuss with you."

"Go on," she replied.

"It's of a...personal nature," he said, awkwardly.

Oh, no! She had almost forgotten about Kenit's burgeoning infatuation. She glanced to her right.

"Well, spit it out," she prompted.

"I realise this may be inappropriate, so please forgive me," began Kenit, "but I need to ask. If someone such as myself wished to court you, would that be a possibility—if not today, maybe in the future?"

Fay stopped in her tracks, prompting her would-be suitor to do the same. She no longer had concerns about the fragility of Kenit's state of mind, but she still wanted to be as tactful as possible. He needed to be told, once and for all, there would never be anything between them.

"Kai Darbandian," she addressed him, formally, "you may not know this about me, but I am a widow, and I have been for many years now. Since I lost my husband, I have never been with anyone else, not even for a single night. In truth, I cannot envisage the day when I will ever want to be with someone else. And while it is possible I may feel differently, someday, I advise you not to wait for me. Who knows how many other opportunities for love would pass you by if you did?"

"I understand," Kenit replied.

"I hope you're not too disappointed."

"I suspected the odds were against me," Kenit conceded, "but if I hadn't asked the question, I would have spent the rest of my life wondering, 'what if?' and driven myself mad."

Fay smiled at that. "If it makes you feel any better," she said, "you've had a lucky escape. I come with a lot of baggage—the kind few people could cope with." She resumed the downhill march towards the village. "Come along now, let's get you back to Temis Rulan while breakfast is still being served."

CHAPTER TWENTY-ONE

Mending Fences

The journey back to Temis Rulan from Adara was wholly uneventful—in stark contrast to the same journey Fay had made with Kayden the previous day. She and Kenit were provided with horses and travelled the short distance to the banks of Haradeen Bay, where a boat manned by four fellow Sanatsai awaited them. The quarter-hour boat ride across the water brought them to the port town of Rindas on the southern coast of the hidden Haradeen Isle, where they acquired horses to take them inland to Temis Rulan.

When they were admitted through the southern gate of the perimeter wall surrounding the headquarters of the Order some time later, Kenit thanked her again for taking him to Lirantana before dashing off, citing his eagerness to return to active duty. Fay, for her part, was eager to find out if Ari had returned with Kayden. The woman most likely able to tell her was standing alone on the grey brick pathway, half way between the southern gate and Kassani House in the distance. She marched forward to meet Idelle, and inquire about Ari's whereabouts.

"Welcome back," said Idelle, greeting Fay with affection. "And yes, Ari returned with your young apprentice a couple of hours ago."

Trust Idelle to answer a question before it was asked, thought Fay.

"Thank you, Idelle. It's good to be back." She was also relieved to hear Ari was already back. But was his time with Kayden a success or not? "Did Ari happen to say anything about Kayden or the time they spent together?" she inquired.

Idelle looped an arm around Fay's arm, gently tugging her forward to commence the walk to Kassani House.

"No," she replied. "But I did not ask. However, I'm sure Ari will tell you what you're yearning to hear when you speak with him. You need not worry about the path your apprentice will walk."

Fay never ceased to be amazed by Idelle's keen insight and intuition. Her contemporary always seemed to know what was on her mind.

"Why don't you tell me about your little adventure in Lirantana," Idelle continued. "Nelda informed me of your plans for the troubled young Kai."

Fay smiled down at her shorter companion. "Do you really need to ask, Idelle?" she said. "You always seem to know more than you let on."

"Humour me."

She proceeded to give as brief a summary of events in Lirantana as she could about the elaborate ruse in Sharadi Forest made possible with the help of the Sisterhood, despite the short notice given. She noted how Idelle was highly amused upon hearing of Kenit's infatuation with her.

"Upon your gravestone, Fay, we shall surely engrave the epitaph: *The Breaker of Many Hearts*," said Idelle.

Fay understood the sentiment, though she couldn't bring herself to laugh about it. She had certainly spurned the advances of numerous men over the years—so many she had lost count.

"You think it foolish I'm not open to the possibility of finding love again with someone else." The words came out sounding like a statement rather than the question she intended.

Stopping Fay in her tracks, Idelle looked intently into her eyes.

"Fay, I would never tell you such a thing," she protested. "I remember well the love you and Renik Katarnian shared. I also remember how much it affected you to lose him. If you are unable to get over your loss, there is no foolishness in that."

"But it's been over twenty years," she reasoned. "More than enough time to let go of Ren's memory, and find love with someone new." She paused for a moment. "Sometimes I wonder if there is something wrong with me."

"Fay, do not place a time limit on your grief. It's entirely possible you will never fully get over your loss," said Idelle. "As for finding love again, there is no law requiring you to do so—try to remember that."

She gently tugged Fay's arm to prompt a resumption of their walk to Kassani House. As they set off once more, Idelle spoke again.

"While we're on the topic of love," she said in a more cheerful tone, "I'd like to remind you that love takes many other forms besides romantic love: the love between parent and child, for example. Someday, soon, you may discover that another kind of love will fulfil you in ways romantic love never will."

There was something about the way Idelle said those words that caused Fay to wonder what her friend was really trying to tell her; the elderly Sister obviously had some insight she wasn't privy to. She would have asked for an explanation, but knew the response would be a variation of, 'you'll understand soon enough,' so there was no point.

As the pair approached the southern entrance to Kassani House, Fay began to think to herself whether she should return immediately to her quarters to find Kayden, or seek out Ari first. It probably made more sense to speak to Ari first, especially if he had bad news to impart.

"So, I take it you'll be wanting to speak to Ari before you return to your quarters," said Idelle. "You can find him in the Council chamber, he said he had some matters he wants to attend to before we convene at Tenth Hour." Her ability to address questions not yet asked was uncanny. "As for myself, it appears my attention is wanted elsewhere."

Fay caught sight of the trio of Sisters a short distance ahead, standing at the foot of the steps leading up to the entrance to

Kassani House. The women did appear to be waiting for Idelle, which proved to be the case once she and her counterpart reached them.

After a brief farewell, Fay left the leader of the Sisterhood to attend to her fellow Jaymidari, while she entered the building to find Ari. She made her way up to the top floor and navigated the corridors en route to the Council chamber, hoping for the best but preparing for the worst.

She finally arrived in the circular corridor surrounding the chamber, and proceeded immediately towards the double doors of the south facing entrance where two Sanatsai sentries stood—one one either side of the doors—while a further two sentries were patrolling the corridor, walking in her direction. She acknowledged the roving patrol with a nod of her head as they passed by, before stopping outside the guarded double doors.

"Please inform Rendai Shinadu that Fay Annis is here to see him," she requested formally.

"Unnecessary, Danai Annis," replied the sentry on the right hand side of the door. "Rendai Shinadu said you should be admitted as soon as you arrive. You may enter right away."

The second sentry opened the doors to allow her to proceed inside. She acknowledged both men with a slight nod of the head then stepped across the threshold into the chamber. She waited for the doors to be closed behind her before advancing any further.

Directly ahead of Fay, at the centre of the chamber, was the area where sessions of the Council convened. There were twelve rostrums dotted in a large circle around a circular mosaic of the insignia of the Order on the floor. This central spot was where Ari would stand to chair meetings of the Council while each of the remaining twelve members of the thirteen-strong body would stand at their designated rostrum. Each of the positions was currently unoccupied, including Ari's. He was on the west side of the chamber, standing before a large screen allowing Ari to see and communicate with someone beyond the city of Temis Rulan.

Noticing her arrival, Ari briefly glanced back over his shoulder to silently beckon her forward before returning his attention to the conversation he was engaged in. As she approached, Fay recognised the man whose image appeared on the screen speaking with Ari. It was Milo Lukatoni, the administrator of the Belisaris campus in the Kingdom of Astana.

"Greetings, Fay," said Milo as she walked into his field of view to stand behind Ari. "Ari mentioned you were back in Temis Rulan."

"Only for a short while," she replied. "And please forgive the intrusion, don't stop on my account."

"It's quite all right, Ari and I have concluded our business." Milo directed his focus back to Ari. "I will make the necessary arrangements at once, and I will see you here first thing tomorrow." Addressing Ari and Fay together, he concluded, "Farewell to you both."

After bidding his counterpart farewell, Ari waved his hand across the screen, invoking *Yuksaydan* to deactivate the *Zarantar* based communication system. The image of Milo in his office quickly faded, replaced by swirling lavender mists. Moments later those mists dissipated, and the screen became a mirror, reflecting Ari and Fay standing in the chamber.

"Welcome back, old friend," Ari said, placing his hands behind his back. "How did things go with Kenit Darbandian?"

"Better than expected," she replied in her matter-of-fact manner. She gestured at the mirror behind Ari. "So, what was that about? You're going to Astana tomorrow?"

"Yes."

"Why?" she inquired.

It had to have something to do with Kayden—she was born and raised in the Kingdom.

"There was a murder in the capital several years ago that was covered up. I've asked Milo to arrange a meeting for me with the relevant authority within the City Guard as I have recently acquired new information that will ensure justice is finally done."

A murder cover-up? Fay wondered. *What does that have to do with Kayden?*

"Who was killed?" she asked.

"A story for another day, old friend," replied Ari. "Why don't we discuss what you really want to know?"

It was the moment Fay was dreading. She was about to learn Kayden's fate. Ari would either inform her that Kayden was condemned to death, or she was free to return to Antaris to resume her apprenticeship.

"What is to become of Kayden?"

"I think you'll be pleased to hear she'll be returning to Antaris with her master," Ari said with a smile.

Fay released the breath she was holding. She remained speechless for a moment, then threw her arms around Ari and held him tightly in her embrace. Eventually, she found her voice.

"Thank you" she said, with palpable relief. "I knew if anyone could get through to Kayden, it would be you."

Ari waited until she was ready to relinquish her ardent hold on him before replying. When she finally did, he gently stroked her upper arm.

"For a while the outcome was in doubt. Your concerns about where Kayden's anger and bitterness might lead her were certainly justified. However, I am satisfied there is no longer any possibility of her following in the footsteps of the Rogue. You can now stop worrying about history repeating itself on that front."

"How can you be so certain?" Fay didn't doubt Ari; she just needed to understand his certainty. "What was it that persuaded you?"

"The answer to both questions is the same: there is much about Kayden that is very reminiscent of you."

"Would not any similarities between us make it more likely she could repeat the same mistakes I made, not less?" It was the only rational conclusion to be inferred, she thought. "What guarantee is there that Kayden will never become more than just a theoretical threat?"

"You are the guarantee," said Ari. "And Kayden having you has already averted the potential danger she formerly posed."

"I don't understand."

"You cared enough about Kayden to see the pain she was in, and get her the help she needed by bringing her here. In doing so, you became the catalyst for her to finally come to terms with the source of that pain. She understands now where her anger was leading her to—somewhere she does not wish to go." Ari looked at her intently. "If someone had cared enough about you when you were Kayden's age, maybe you could have avoided walking the path you took. Instead, through no fault of your own, you found yourself in the sphere of influence of an unscrupulous man who exploited your pain for his own ends."

That was one way to interpret her history, Fay silently mused.

"I suspect Kayden has come to greatly appreciate how fortunate she is to have you on her side," Ari concluded.

Fay found that assertion very difficult to believe; it didn't sound like the Kayden Jayta she knew. But Ari was a good judge of character, with a knack for getting people to open up to him. It was a quality she knew well from personal experience.

"So, if you really did succeed in getting through to Kayden," she said, envisioning what might have transpired between Ari and her apprentice the previous night, "you must have learned what happened in the past to make her so...difficult."

"Yes, she told me, eventually," Ari affirmed. "And you were right, again, when you described it as a traumatic event she hadn't yet come to terms with."

Looking at her friend, she waited for him to elaborate.

"It's not my story to tell," he declared, disappointing her. "But I imagine Kayden will want to share it with you once the two of you are reunited."

She fought off the urge to laugh incredulously.

"I've always admired your optimism, Ari, but I just don't see Kayden wanting to share anything personal with me."

Ari smiled, knowingly. "I think you will find your apprentice's attitude towards you greatly improved, old friend," he said. "Which is just as well. She's going to need you a great deal over the next few years. I believe you are correct about how powerful Kayden is—though confirmation will have to wait until after she has been inducted into the Order. And having you to guide her will be of tremendous benefit to her."

Fay harboured doubts about her own suitability to continue to oversee Kayden's training. As much as she wished it were otherwise, the antagonistic relationship she had with the apprentice wasn't conducive to getting the best out of her. It might be necessary to step down as the administrator of Antaris campus—to allow someone else to take on the responsibility.

"I see doubt written all over your face, old friend," said Ari. "I'm not sure I understand why."

"Ari, my relationship with Kayden has never been good. Over the course of the past three years it has grown progressively worse, and I don't see how bringing her here, forcing her to confront her past—with the threat of death hanging over her, no less—hasn't made it worse."

"Fay, you did the right thing bringing Kayden here, even she would acknowledge that, I'm sure." There *was* a surety in Ari's tone; she had heard and trusted it on numerous occasions before. "Your relationship with Kayden can only improve from this point on. I expect she'll be rather eager to mend fences with you."

"How can you be so certain?"

"Like I said, you are a catalyst for her," Ari replied. "You set her on the path to moving past the most painful experience of her life. Now that chapter of her story will shortly come to an end, allowing the next one to commence. A chapter in which you will play a leading role, or so says Idelle. She believes you are going to become the most important person in Kayden's life," Ari smiled at her, "and when is Idelle ever wrong about anything?"

Could it be true? She would certainly love to improve her relationship with Kayden. She had devoted the last three years of her life to the young woman, after all.

Ari gently stroked Fay's upper arm again.

"The quickest way to remove all your doubts is to go and see your apprentice right away. You'll probably be surprised at how happy she is to see you." He adopted an exaggerated frown, adding sarcastically, "She might be a little less happy about missing her classes today, though."

A half smile curled Fay's lips. "Is that your way of dismissing me, dear friend?"

"Well, you do have a campus to run, not to mention one exceptionally gifted young apprentice whose training needs overseeing." Ari held her gaze, affectionately. "You have done everything you came here to do, old friend."

Ari was right. If Kayden had been granted a reprieve there was no reason to remain in Temis Rulan any longer than necessary.

"Where is she now?" she asked. "I guess I should get her back to campus."

"When I saw her last, she was returning to your quarters."

"Then that is where I should be."

Fay gazed at her counterpart, feeling regretful. They had not been in each other's presence in three years, and now they had to part ways, yet again.

"I'm sorry we didn't have the opportunity to spend more time together. I will make it up to you the next time."

"Just make sure I don't have to wait three years for your next visit."

Ari held his arms open, inviting a hug. She stepped into his embrace, wrapping her arms fervently around him.

"You do realise you have the option of visiting me at Antaris?" she said.

"That is correct," replied Ari, "and now I have two reasons for paying a visit to the campus."

The two friends released each other from their farewell embrace. They silently held each other's gaze for a protracted moment; it wasn't necessary for either to say their goodbyes. Eventually, it was Fay who stepped away from Ari, turning on her heels to march purposefully for the exit, vacating the chamber through the south facing double doors, without looking back.

She navigated her way through several corridors. For the duration of the walk back to her quarters, all she could think about was Kayden. How would her next meeting with the apprentice play out? Ari was certainly of the opinion Kayden would be better disposed towards her, henceforth, so she was inclined to believe it to be so. However, his mentioning of Idelle's prediction was much harder to believe. The idea that she was to become the most important person in Kayden's life seemed beyond far-fetched in light of her experience with the young apprentice, thus far.

Stopping outside the door to her quarters, Fay didn't enter right away. Instead, she took a moment to compose herself, wanting to be prepared for every eventuality; there were several different directions the upcoming conversation with Kayden could go in.

Once she felt ready, she pushed the door open and entered her quarters. There was no sign of the apprentice anywhere. She called out to Kayden, and though there was no reply she advanced through the living area towards the open doorway of the bedchamber. As she was passing her tea table she spotted a handwritten note upon it. She stopped to pick it up; it was from Sister Nelda.

Fay,

I have accompanied Kayden to the flower garden. Upon your return you may find us there.

Nelda.

Fay set the note back down on the tea table. She contemplated waiting in her quarters for Kayden to return, but why prolong matters any longer than necessary? It made more sense to go to the flower garden immediately, so she promptly departed.

A short while later she had left Kassani House, and was making her way along the grey brick pathway that led to the flower garden. She couldn't understand why she felt so anxious, the last time she felt this nervous was on her wedding day, three decades ago. And now, as then, her nerves were the by-product of excitement rather than fear. Her gambit with Kayden—bringing her to Temis Rulan to meet Ari—seemed to have paid off, and she was eager to find out just how well.

Upon entering the gardens, she observed several Sanatsai and Jaymidari milling around. Casting her gaze here and there, she saw no sign of Kayden or Nelda in the immediate vicinity—they had to be somewhere further in. She reached out with her senses, courtesy of a ley-line, to pinpoint Kayden's presence. A subtle smile curled her lips. The apprentice was on the far side of the gardens, not too far from her own favourite spot. She set off along the pathway to meet her charge, returning the occasional warm greeting from other visitors to the flower garden along the way.

Finally she came around the corner of a hedgerow then stopped. Further along the path before her, she found what she was looking for, Kayden sitting on a wooden bench on the right hand side of the path. Sitting beside her was Nelda, casually running a comb through Kayden's flowing, raven locks.

Fay resumed her steady approach towards them. As she drew nearer, first Kayden, then Nelda, noticed her approaching. Kayden rose quickly to her feet, staring at her, so again she halted in her tracks. Sister Nelda rose more slowly—the welcoming smile on her face barely registering with Fay. Her eyes were locked on Kayden, just as Kayden's eyes were locked on her. It suddenly dawned on Fay that she had never seen Kayden with her hair down before. Until that moment, she had always taken for granted the notion it wasn't possible for the apprentice to be any more beautiful—an assumption she now realised was incorrect. But that wasn't important. What mattered now was whatever happened next.

Who would make the first move now that she and Kayden were back in each other's orbit?

The moment of truth was at hand.

While Kayden stood, gazing back at Fay, several thoughts flashed through her mind. She had so many things she wanted to say to the woman, but no idea where to begin. Just a day earlier, if anyone had suggested that she would feel as happy to see Fay as she felt at that moment, she would have mocked the suggestion, as well as the person making it. Yet here she was, and she couldn't be happier.

Nelda placed a hand on her shoulder then spoke quietly into her ear. "I think I'm going to leave you alone now," she said. "I have the distinct impression you and your master have things you need to say to each other."

Kayden didn't reply—she couldn't tear her eyes away from Fay.

"Before I go," Nelda continued, "it was very nice to meet you, Kayden. I expect we'll meet again in a few years time. Until then, farewell."

Watching Nelda leave in Fay's direction, Kayden uttered, "Farewell, Sister Nelda."

She then watched her walk up to Fay, stopping just long enough to exchange a few words before leaving. At last, she was alone with Fay in a secluded corner of the flower garden.

After a moment's hesitation, she decided to make the first move but Fay beat her to the punch, advancing towards her, steadily closing the distance between them. While the other woman approached, Kayden tried to read the expression on her face, but it was a futile undertaking—she simply didn't know Fay well enough to read her. Besides, as was usually the case, Fay's face was inscrutable, which told her nothing about how things might play out.

"How are you, Kayden?" asked Fay, halting in front of the apprentice.

"Good, thank you," she replied. "I'm glad you're back, Master Fay. I take it your assignment in Lirantana yesterday was a success?"

There was no immediate response from Fay, which—much to Kayden's surprise—made her feel gutted. Not just because of the lack of response, but also because of the frown that appeared on Fay's face. Apparently, the woman was in no mood for small talk.

"Is something wrong, Master?"

"I don't know, is there?" said Fay, a tinge of uncertainty in her voice. "In the three years I have known you, Kayden, you have never once addressed me as Master. But you've just done so, twice in quick succession."

Without thinking, Kayden retorted, "That can't be right."

She promptly began searching her memories for at least one example that would refute Fay's assertion.

"It's true," Fay insisted. "You usually address me as 'Administrator Annis' or just, 'administrator'."

Kayden stopped trying to recall a time when that wasn't the case; Fay had spoken truthfully.

"And behind my back," continued Fay, "I believe you generally refer to me as, 'That Woman'."

It dawned on Kayden that she had, indeed, pointedly refused to address Fay as Master ever since she arrived at Antaris campus; she'd gone out of her way to avoid doing so, in fact.

"You're right, Master," she conceded reluctantly, "I hope you will accept my apology when I say I'm sorry for all the disrespect I have shown you these past three years."

Fay looked taken aback.

"No apology is necessary, Kayden."

"Well, you have it, nonetheless. And for what it's worth...from this day forward you'll hear the word master from my lips so frequently, you may very well beg me to stop." She flashed a beaming smile at Fay.

Judging from the reappearance of the frown upon Fay's face, Kayden had to assume her attempt at humour was not appreciated. The reunion with her master was not going nearly as well as she wanted, but she was determined not to allow things to become antagonistic.

Still smiling, she added light-heartedly, "What did I do wrong this time, Master?"

"You haven't done anything wrong, Kayden." Fay's expression remained unchanged. "This is the first time I've ever seen you smile.

What a bizarre claim, Kayden thought.

"Don't be ridiculous, Master," she retorted. "You must not have been paying attention. I smile all the time."

"No, you don't," Fay countered. "You smirk. A withering smirk to let the recipients know they are less significant than the dirt beneath your boot."

The smile Kayden had been trying to maintain vanished from her face. Was that really how Fay saw her? If so, what did other people on campus see when they looked at her? She suddenly found she could no longer meet Fay's gaze, so she stared down at her feet, shame-faced.

For the very first time it dawned on her just how poorly she had behaved towards many of her peers on campus. But it wasn't just fellow apprentices who had been wronged by her. What about Sister Daria from the campus infirmary? She had taken advantage of the Sister's attraction to her, for her own ends, for a considerable period of time. Not only had she persuaded Daria to cross several lines for her, she had also toyed with her emotions to the extent that—though she'd never actually said it—the woman was clearly in love with her. For her own part, she had no genuine romantic feelings towards Daria, and never would. Yet only now was she troubled by guilt about the whole affair.

Unexpectedly, she felt Fay's fingertips gently settle beneath her chin. Slowly her head was tilted upward as Fay compelled her to meet her gaze once more. She was surprised by the warm half-smile Fay was wearing.

"You have a beautiful smile, Kayden," said Fay. "I hope you will allow me to see it more often in future."

Kayden's heart skipped a beat; it was the sweetest thing Fay had ever said to her. She smiled, hesitantly, at her.

"I think I can manage that, Master."

Fay slowly drew her hand away from Kayden's face.

"I guess now would be a good time to get you back to Antaris."

"Do we have to go now?" Kayden blurted. It was not a good time to leave as far as she was concerned. "I was hoping we could stay a little while longer."

"The longer you remain here, the more questions will be asked. As it is, you're already the subject of much speculation that I'd like to nip in the bud. We really should leave without delay."

"But I really wanted to talk to you," Kayden lamented. She was bitterly disappointed, and it must have shown on her face judging from the curiosity in Fay's gaze. "There are things I need to tell you, Master—things I want to share with you."

"Is it important?"

It certainly was, from her point of view. Whether Fay would deem it as such remained to be seen.

"Yes, Master. It's important to me that we have an opportunity to talk before returning to Antaris," she said. "If nothing else, I'd like to tell you about my mother. I think it will help you to understand me better. Understand why I am the way that I am."

She paid close attention to Fay's reaction. For a protracted moment the woman's face was the epitome of contemplation; she appeared to be giving much consideration to the request.

"I *would* like to get to know you better, Kayden," Fay conceded, finally, "but we still need to leave Temis Rulan right away. However, there's no reason for us to return to campus immediately. The Sisterhood has a seminary a few miles outside Timaris; we can travel there first. It should take us about an hour and a half to walk back to campus from there—more than enough time for us to talk, don't you think?"

Kayden smiled. "Yes, Master," she agreed. "More than enough."

"Very well, let's get going, our time here has come to an end." Fay turned on her heels to begin the walk back to Kassani House.

"Master Fay!" exclaimed Kayden, halting Fay's departure, and prompting her to peer back over her shoulder. "There's one more thing before we go."

"Yes?"

"Thank you for bringing me here." Her voice had an uncharacteristic solemnity, her words heartfelt. "I'm not accustomed to having anyone other than my mother be genuinely concerned about my wellbeing, but I've come to realise that you've been looking out for me these past three years—not persecuting me. It means a lot that you would care, even though I've given you many reasons not to. I feel like I've been granted a second chance and I'll never forget it. My words cannot convey how truly grateful I am for what you have done. All I can do is promise that from this day forth, I will work my hardest to make you proud of me."

Fay appeared to be scrutinising her very closely.

"I would love to know what Master Ari said to you while the two of you were away. I can see that something within you has changed—it's evident. You no longer appear...burdened. It's as though a great weight has been lifted from your shoulders."

It pleased Kayden that Fay had noticed the fundamental change in her psyche.

"That's an apt way to put it, Master" she replied, "but it isn't so much the result of anything Master Ari said to me. I owe more to what I was shown. My eyes were opened up to something I was blind to before: a struggle within myself, between the person I am meant to be, and the person I don't ever want to become." To her mind the words sounded silly, but it was the only way she could describe it. "But that struggle is finally over. I can now focus on being who I really am—the person I was always meant to be. And I know I have you to thank for that, Master."

Fay said nothing in response. But if Kayden was reading her correctly, there was no need to say anything. The subtle smile, coupled with the emotion in Fay's eyes, told her everything she needed to know. Fay was feeling contentment and relief. She had accomplished what she set out to do, by saving a wayward apprentice in her charge, having doubted it could be done.

Kayden quickly fell into step alongside Fay as they left the flower garden. Somehow, this scenario seemed so surreal. Just a day earlier she would never have believed she would be in Temis Rulan, walking the grounds of the headquarters of the Order with Fay Annis for company. And the notion of she and Fay being on good terms, having mended fences, would have been inconceivable. Yet, unless she was dreaming, this was exactly what was transpiring.

While the pair marched side-by-side in silence, following the grey brick path leading towards the northern entrance of Kassani House, Kayden noticed a young male Sanatsai to her right, rushing to intercept them where his path intersected with the path they were walking.

"Danai Annis!" called out the Sanatsai. "Danai Annis!"

Fay brought the duo to a halt at the intersection to wait for the Sanatsai to reach them. Moments later the excited looking young man stopped before Fay, standing to attention.

"Danai Annis, I'm glad I caught you," said the Sanatsai.

Kayden would have felt slighted by the way the newcomer not only failed to acknowledge her, but also seemed completely oblivious to her presence, had she not noticed the reason why. He was clearly smitten with Fay—it was written all over his face. She could not recall a time when another female overshadowed her when it came to attracting the attention of the opposite gender.

Obviously, it was something she might have to get used to when in Fay's company, she realised. There was no question Fay was a beautiful woman.

"Kai Darbandian, what can I do for you?" said Fay formally.

"Danai Annis, I just wanted to let you know that..." The Sanatsai paused momentarily. It was as though he had just remembered something vitally important. "May I call you Fay?" Perhaps not so important after all.

Kayden almost laughed out loud seeing Fay's reaction. The frown on her face was presumably meant to convey how much she did not appreciate the young man's attempt at over-familiarity.

"No, Kai Darbandian," retorted Fay, "you may not." Her tone of voice seemed to indicate displeasure, but then Kayden realised from the subtle smile that followed the words, Fay was just teasing her subordinate. "At least, not yet," she appended. "Now, what did you want to tell me?"

"When we arrived back this morning, I requested an assignment outside Temis Rulan. My timing couldn't have been any more perfect because—as luck would have it—the Council has sanctioned the deployment of an additional three thousand men to Yaristana, to discourage any intervention by Randissar on behalf of the separatists. I just wanted you to know that I will be among the ranks of those being deployed. We leave this afternoon."

Kayden couldn't work out why Kai Darbandian sounded so excited and pleased with himself. Despite his apparent young age and low rank, this surely couldn't be his first mission for the Order, and even if it was, he'd likely have nothing to do once there. Hostilities in Yaristana's Mattis province had already ceased thanks to intervention by the Order, and the deployment of additional manpower more or less ensured Randissar wouldn't attempt to openly annex the province. Without continued outside support, there was very little chance of the separatist rebels resuming their insurrection.

Fay smiled at her male counterpart.

"Good for you," she declared. "From what I have heard, the situation in Mattis at present probably means you won't see any action—unless the rebels do something stupid. But if the worst should happen, I have no doubt you will acquit yourself admirably." Finally, Kayden's presence was remembered. "While you're still here, allow me to introduce you to one of my young charges from Antaris campus. Kenit, meet Kayden Jayta, the most promising apprentice in the Nine Kingdoms; Kayden, this is Master Kenit Darbandian."

Kenit extended a hand to her. "Greetings, it's a pleasure to meet you Kayden," he said formally.

"It's nice to meet you, Master Kenit," she replied, clasping his forearm in greeting.

"So," drawled Kenit, "you're the apprentice everyone seems to be talking about at the moment. I've heard some...*interesting* things about you."

She could discern from Kenit's tone, and the look upon his face, the nature of the 'interesting' stories he was referring to.

"I wouldn't put much stock in the things you have heard, Master Kenit," she replied, releasing her grip of his forearm. "I'm well aware of the kind of rumours circulating among the gossip-mongers here, and I can assure you they are way off the mark."

She noted, with some amusement, the obvious relief on Kenit's face once she'd said that. Clearly he didn't welcome any competition for Fay's affections.

"Kai Darbandian, if there's nothing else," interjected Fay, "Kayden and I really must be going."

"Oh, yes, of course." There was no concealing Kenit's disappointment at effectively being dismissed. "Please don't let me hold you up, Danai." He stood aside to allow the pair to continue on their way.

Kayden fell into step alongside Fay, once more, as they departed, leaving Kenit behind. She briefly glanced back over her shoulder to see him forlornly staring after them—or more precisely, after Fay. In that moment she felt a twinge of pity for the young Sanatsai. Master Fay was clearly so far out of his league, he could be the last man in the world, and still he would never win her heart.

Once they had moved far enough away from Kenit, not to be

overheard, she turned to Fay. "Master, forgive me for pointing this out," she said, "but Master Kenit likes you, and not just in a 'lay with you all night' kind of way."

"He'll get over it."

Smiling at the matter-of-fact tone she'd become so accustomed to hearing, she realised, then, that Fay was above toying with someone's emotions. It was safe to assume Kenit had already been made aware of where he stood. No one would ever be able to accuse Fay of leading the younger man on.

As they approached the steps leading up to the northern entrance to Kassani House, Fay asked Kayden, "Have you left anything in my quarters?"

"No Master."

A moment later she stopped abruptly at the foot of the stairs. She remembered something she wished she hadn't.

"What's the matter, Kayden?" asked Fay.

Kayden was sure her guilt must be written all over her face. She had no experience covering it up, given that—until very recently—she had never felt truly guilty about anything she'd ever said or done.

"Master Fay," she said, "I have a confession to make." She read Fay's silent gesture to proceed. "Um... Yesterday evening...when you left me alone in your quarters..."

"You went through my belongings," Fay finished for her.

Kayden felt nauseous. "Yes, Master," she confirmed. "I'm sorry."

"Did you find what you were looking?"

She was simultaneously relieved and disappointed that Fay was able to remain calm, rather than fly off the handle at her; the woman certainly had every right to be furious at the invasion of privacy.

"Well I..." An image of the phallic-shaped, marble sculpture she found in one of Fay's drawers flashed briefly in her mind. She shrugged it off just as quickly. "Uh...actually, Master, I wasn't looking for anything in particular, though I did find a box under your bed containing several letters and other writings. I realise now that I shouldn't have done, but I read some of them."

After a fraught silence, Fay said, "I see."

"Is that all you have to say?" Kayden just couldn't keep the exasperation from her voice. "Why aren't you angry? Goodness knows I've given you many reasons to be furious with me on numerous occasions, yet you never get mad. Why won't you yell at me, or punch me in the face? No one would blame, not even me; I deserve it."

Fay looked intently at her before replying.

"Kayden, if experience has taught me anything, it's that nothing good can come from allowing anger to dictate one's actions. Besides, no harm has been done. I accept your apology."

Kayden felt certain she was witnessing the first crack in Fay's normally inscrutable demeanour, so the reassurance did not make her feel better about potentially upsetting Fay, especially in light of the change in their relationship. She couldn't be sure if it was the invasion of privacy or something else that had unsettled Fay, but whatever it was, she knew she wanted to say something to assuage her master before they entered Kassani House.

"Master, I had no idea that you had ever been married," she said, "or that you're now a widow."

"It was a long time ago, Kayden."

"Well, at the risk of further intruding where I have no right to," she continued. "I think I can say—having read the love letters he wrote to you—how very apparent it is just how much your husband loved you."

"More than I deserved."

Kayden suspected her attempt at comforting Fay was failing. Everything she was saying seemed to be stirring heart-rending memories for her master. But she could relate to how Fay was feeling. Maybe the best way to comfort Fay was to convey her understanding of the heartache caused by the loss of a loved one.

"Master, I know what it's like to have the person who means the world to you, snatched away. It's like an open wound that never fully heals. I've recently come to realise, the best way to cope with loss is to be grateful for the time we had with our loved ones. We will always have our memories of those good times, and we can prevent them from being snatched away from us."

A half-smile curled Fay's lips as she gazed at Kayden. "We did have nine good years together," she said, wistfully. "And you're right, no one can ever take that away from me."

Hesitantly, she reached out, placing a hand on Fay's upper arm. It was a gesture she would never have contemplated a day earlier. "Shall we continue on our way, Master?" she said, gently stroking Fay's arm. She couldn't think of anything else to say.

Fay silently patted the back of Kayden's hand, then proceeded to ascend the steps up to the entrance of Kassani House.

Once indoors, Kayden was surprised when Fay led her down to a portal chamber deep beneath the building. If she remembered correctly, during their journey to the city, Fay had said there was no portal in Temis Rulan—which clearly wasn't the case. But unlike the large cavern that was home to the portal chamber she now knew to be hidden beneath the Antaris campus, the chamber underneath the headquarters of the Order was not a natural formation at all; it was clearly man-made. Though not nearly as expansive as the portal chamber back at Antaris—as there was no need to conceal the presence of hundreds of Sanatsai—she could only imagine how long it had taken to excavate.

"Master, I could have sworn you said Temis Rulan has no portal," she said, casting her eyes around the vast chamber brightly lit by a network of illumination orbs, and heavily peopled with scores of Jaymidari, and even more Sanatsai.

Fay led Kayden towards the swirling portal located upon a dais at the centre of the artificial chamber.

"Actually," she said. "I believe what I said was, 'no portals open directly into Temis Rulan'—or anywhere else on the island, for that matter—for security reasons. However, as you can see, there is a portal here that can transport us to any of the dozens of facilities run by the Order and the Sisterhood throughout the Nine Kingdoms."

That made more sense, Kayden realised, taking in the sights and sounds of the portal chamber as she continued to walk at Fay's side. The location was obviously a busy hub, if the number of individuals waiting in line to use the portal was any indication. Evidently, there was a steady flow of people leaving Temis Rulan at any given moment, and it wasn't long before she and Fay were joining the queue of Sanatsai preparing to depart the home of the Order.

"Wait here for me," Fay instructed. "I need to inform the Sisters of our destination." She departed to the right, towards the small group of Jaymidari situated nearby.

While Kayden watched Fay march towards the Sisters, she found herself excited by the prospect of leaving Temis Rulan—not because she was eager to get away from the place as quickly as possible, but because once she emerged on the other side of the portal, she would have Master Fay all to herself as they made their way back to campus. For reasons she could not yet explain, she was anxious to narrate the, hitherto, defining moment of her short life to Fay as she had done for Master Ari, the day before. She felt positive that willingly sharing this with Fay would go a long way to bringing the two of them closer.

But seeking an improvement in her relationship with Fay wasn't the sole reason why she had requested time alone for the two of them to talk. Her experience the night before had left her with a host of unanswered questions. The kind of questions she suspected only Fay could provide answers to.

CHAPTER TWENTY-TWO

The Master And The Apprentice

Kayden walked side-by-side with Fay as they headed due north, through sparse woodlands, en route back to Antaris campus. She was surprised at how natural it felt to be walking alongside the woman she once considered a foe. But there was no longer anything adversarial about their relationship. She felt wholly relaxed with this brand new status quo. It was actually easy being alone in the company of her master—for that was what Fay indisputably was to her now. Her master. And she was unequivocally Fay's apprentice. The rumours circulating around campus that she was the favoured apprentice of Master Fay suddenly seemed entirely plausible.

It had been a quarter of an hour since they departed the Sisterhood seminary together, having arrived there via the portal in Temis Rulan. Kayden used that time to narrate the circumstances that led to her birth in the Kingdom of Astana: how her mother had raised her alone, from the age of two after her father had abandoned them both, to return to Zenosha; and how her mother, later, remarried a man who would eventually kill her in a fit of anger.

For some reason, telling Fay about the death of her beloved mother was significantly easier than telling Master Ari had been. Though still upsetting, she shed no tears—all the while keeping her anger at bay.

"I'm so sorry to hear about your loss, Kayden," commiserated Fay. "I had no idea."

"For a long time it was something I couldn't talk about," she replied. "Not until you brought me to see Master Ari."

"Now I finally understand where the anger and bitterness I could see in you was coming from, though you always did cover it up well." Fay's claimed ability to read her provoked a twinge of envy in Kayden. She hoped one day, soon, she'd be able to read her master just as well. "Your desire to avenge your mother's death was also understandable," continued Fay, "though I'm pleased you've come to realise what a dangerous motive revenge can be."

Fay fell silent for a moment, prompting Kayden to glance at her. She found Fay gazing back at her with a knowing look in her eyes.

"Although you have abandoned your quest for vengeance, Kayden," said Fay, "don't give up on justice for your mother. Maybe you will have it sooner than you think."

Kayden wanted to dismiss out of hand the idea of her stepfather paying the price for killing her mother, but seeing the expression on Fay's face made that impossible. Clearly her master was more than just implying justice was a possibility; Fay was indicating her expectation that justice would be done imminently. Nonetheless, she didn't want to get her hopes up. The Order would never countenance sending an assassin on her behalf to take out her stepfather. But there was no doubt the Order did have the requisite clout with authorities in the Nine Kingdoms to ensure that her mother's death—and the subsequent cover-up—was properly investigated. Only time would tell if Fay was correct in her assertion.

"I hope you're right, Master Fay."

Fay smiled at her then returned her gaze to the trail ahead as she continued to navigate the woodlands.

"It seems to me your mother was a very courageous woman, Kayden," she commented. "She made many sacrifices for you—including the ultimate sacrifice. You should be immensely proud of her, as I assume she would be of you if she could see you now."

"Thank you, Master."

She was gratified to hear such praise for her mother from a woman like Fay Annis. It suddenly made her wonder about the woman who had given birth to someone as extraordinary as her master.

"What was your mother like, Master?"

The instant the words left her mouth, Kayden knew she had made a mistake asking the question. The pained look upon Fay's face made apparent she had touched upon a sore subject for her master. "I'm sorry," she said quickly, "I didn't mean to pry, it's none of my business."

"There's no need to apologise, Kayden," said Fay. "The truth is, I never really knew my mother. I only met the woman twice—very briefly on both occasions—so there is little I can tell you about her."

Kayden picked up on the hurt, anger and regret in Fay's tone. There was obviously more to the story than Master Fay was willing to tell, but she had no intention of digging up that part of her master's past. What she needed to do was change the subject. She certainly had several other questions she wished to broach with Fay, though she suddenly found her thoughts drifting to another aspect of Fay's personal life.

"What is it, Kayden?" queried Fay, glancing at her. "You have that look telling me you're thinking of asking a question you aren't sure you should ask." The words were another demonstration of Fay's ability to read her. "Don't be afraid to ask me anything."

"In that case, Master," she said. "I was just wondering if you are a mother yourself."

The query seemed to catch Fay off guard.

"No," she replied after a brief hesitation. "Ren and I never did have any children."

"Can you even have kids?"

She blurted it out before she could stop herself. If she hadn't instantly realised how incredulous her tone made her sound, she could tell from Fay's facial expression.

"Why did you ask like that?" asked Fay, looking quizzically at her. "It sounds very much as though you find the idea of me having children highly improbable."

"I didn't mean to suggest that, Master. It's just that..." Kayden paused to consider her words carefully; she didn't want to put her foot in it again. "Last night, Master Ari mentioned how old you are, and women your age can't bear children."

She hoped Fay wasn't one of those women who was sensitive about her age.

"But, obviously, you aren't like most women," she added quickly, "you still have the appearance of a thirty-year-old."

"I believe there was a compliment in there somewhere," Fay said in mock indignation, returning her gaze directly ahead. "But in answer to your question, I know of no reason why I cannot have children, someday." She glanced back at Kayden inquiringly. "So, what else has Master Ari been telling you about me," a wry smile curled her lips, "other than my old age?"

Kayden had already decided she wasn't going to let on that she was now aware of Fay's infamous past. There was no obvious reason why Fay needed to know that she knew. But the question was a fortuitous one; it would allow her to bring up matters that might otherwise raise red flags if she broached them without prompting.

"Well, for one thing, Master Ari told me the reason why you look much younger than your actual age," she said. "He informed me of the existence of a fourth grade of Sanatsai—far fewer in number, but more powerful than the three known grades—who possess attributes and abilities not possessed by any of the others. He said both you and he are of this elite group." She looked intently into Fay's eyes. "Master Ari also mentioned your belief that I may also be one of these Elite Sanatsai."

"There is no doubt in my mind about that," declared Fay. "But protocol dictates we cannot seek confirmation before you are inducted into the Order."

Kayden noted the certainty on her master's face and in her voice. Fay was not trying to stroke her ego; she really believed what she was saying. That conviction weighed heavily on her. If true, not only had the manifestation of her *Zarantar* given her power that few men and women would ever wield—even among her peers few, if any, would know the burden of responsibility that being so powerful entailed.

"If you don't mind, Master Fay," said Kayden, "my time in Temis Rulan, especially my experience with Master Ari last night, has left me with numerous questions about the extent of my abilities—assuming you are right about me. Until yesterday, my arrogance convinced me I had little left to learn given what I have already mastered, but now I'm left wondering if I've only tapped into a fraction of the power I possess. I'd love to hear any insights you can give."

"My time is your time, Kayden. Ask your questions."

Things were off to a good start, thought Kayden. She could think of no one better to whom she could address her questions; she was sure to learn a great deal from Fay in the time it would take for them to walk back to Antaris campus.

"My first query is in relation to the abilities I have already mastered as an apprentice. I can't help but wonder if I have yet reached the limits of what is possible for me, or can I still push beyond what I have been taught thus far? To give you an example of what I mean," she held a hand out in front of her, invoking *Sinjaydan* to generate an illumination orb, "whenever I create an orb, by default it takes the form of a sphere. I can increase or decrease its size." She demonstrated to illustrate the point. "But why are we apprentices not taught how to alter the form our orbs take? There's no reason why we shouldn't be able to manipulate an orb into different shapes, is there?"

"For you...? I know of nothing preventing you from altering the form of your orbs," Fay replied. "But none of your instructors are capable of teaching you how to do so, any more than your peers are capable of learning; they will never be as powerful as you." Again, Fay's tone conveyed her certainty about Kayden's status. "However, even if you did master this ability, what purpose would it serve," Fay raised her eyebrows at Kayden, "other than to show off?"

Kayden nonchalantly extinguished her illumination orb.

Showing off was no longer a motivation for her. She was thinking back to the encounter with her black clad doppelgänger

397

in the Forest of Revelation. The rogue version of her had manipulated an incendiary orb to take on the form of a Zu'tayral—a huge, winged creature from Zenoshanese mythology. She recalled how that demonstration of *Zarantar* had caused her to turn on her heels, and run for her life.

"Well, I was thinking more along the lines of intimidation," she said. "Imagine a scenario in which I've been tasked with apprehending a fifty-strong group of bandits who have been raiding the convoys of royal tax collectors in Mirtana. When confronting them, the sight of the Order's uniform may not be enough to discourage them from resisting. But witnessing me transforming an incendiary orb into a giant sized fire phoenix, making it soar above their heads, would more than likely scare them into compliance."

"That's an interesting supposition," said Fay. There was a 'but' coming, Kayden was certain. "But you may find that while such a demonstration is effective at terrorising ordinary people, the same may not be the case when facing adversaries who also wield *Zarantar*.

"Besides, you'll never be tasked with apprehending thieves. It would not be a productive use of your time."

Not to be discouraged, Kayden continued.

"Even so, Master, there is no harm in expanding my repertoire to include the ability manipulate the orbs I create into non-spherical forms," she said. "So, how long would it take me to master if I was to receive instruction?"

"As you have already demonstrated both the requisite skill and control necessary, during the 'capture the box' exercise—when you assaulted Master Zalayna," a look of disapproval appeared on Fay's face, "I imagine you could accomplish it in a day."

Kayden felt a pang of guilt at being reminded of how she had beaten up the female Sanatsai two nights earlier, violating her mind by invoking *Barmityanzak* to erase her memory of the attack as she lay unconscious. But she was more confused by Fay's claim that, during the incident, she had demonstrated the skill and control necessary to shape her orbs into the kind of monstrous form her rogue doppelgänger had unleashed against her.

"Master Fay, I never did inquire about the condition of the Sanatsai I assaulted," began Kayden. "How badly hurt was she?" The contrition in her voice was genuine.

"Zalayna was fortunate not to be more seriously injured, given the ferocity of your assault," said Fay. "But you need not worry, her injuries were quick to heal, although nothing could be done to restore the memory of the attack you took from her mind."

Just when she thought she couldn't feel any worse about the incident, that was the last thing Kayden wanted to hear.

"Master," she said, "if possible, I would like the opportunity to say sorry face-to-face."

"That won't be necessary. But I will convey your apology at the earliest opportunity."

"I'd appreciate that, Master." She didn't wish to dwell on her past transgressions for longer than necessary. She wanted to get the conversation back on track. "Going back to what you said a moment ago, I'm at a loss to understand how I supposedly demonstrated the skill and control that would allow me to alter the form of my orbs, during the 'capture the box' exercise."

"Create another illumination orb for me," Fay instructed.

Doing as ordered without question, she invoked *Sinjaydan*, creating an illumination orb that floated ahead of herself and Fay while they walked—its pale blue glow even more muted in the bright light of day.

"Now," continued Fay, "transform it into a lightning flash orb."

Though she failed to see the point in doing so, Kayden was content to humour Fay. She wielded her *Zarantar* again, invoking *Kiraydan*, and the pale blue orb gradually metamorphosed into a crackling, brilliant white sphere.

"Very good!" exclaimed Fay, sounding suitably impressed. "You did the exact same thing during the assignment the other night."

"Right..." Kayden still wasn't certain what Fay was trying to impart. "But what does that have to do with manipulating the shape of an orb?"

"Well, transforming one type of orb into another is very similar to what you want to accomplish. In fact, it is harder. Yet you have clearly demonstrated your mastery of this ability, though you have received no instruction—not to mention you make it look so easy."

Kayden hadn't realised she had done anything out of the ordinary, but Fay's praise of her power filled her with pride.

"And as trivial as it may seem," continued Fay, "it is not something any of your peers can do. So..." She halted in her tracks, prompting Kayden to do likewise. "If you can do that, you'll have little difficulty learning to do this."

She watched in silent awe as Fay assumed control of her floating lightning flash orb. The brilliant white sphere instantly metamorphosed into a fiery incendiary orb, rising rapidly into the air—increasing in mass as it did so. At about a hundred feet up, the large flaming sphere stopped and swiftly took on the form of a large, mythical fire phoenix.

While she observed the winged creature circling overhead, Kayden was even more impressed by Fay's demonstration than she had been of the similar feat performed by her black clad doppelgänger. Suddenly, the fire phoenix swooped into a steep dive, heading straight for them. It came within twelve feet before it blinked out of existence when Fay extinguished the altered orb. Kayden let out the breath she was holding, then turned to stare at her master. It wasn't until that moment she fully appreciated what a fearsome sight must have confronted all the people who faced the Rogue during The Great War.

"What's the matter, Kayden?" queried Fay.

"I've just realised how grateful I am I will never have to face you across a battlefield, Master," replied Kayden. She found it hard to comprehend how Fay could have been defeated all those years ago.

Fay smiled. "Well, that makes two of us." Her tone was more light-hearted than Kayden was accustomed to hearing, and her demeanour more relaxed. "Let's keep moving."

She kept pace with Fay as they resumed their walk. "I guess it's true what they say about you, Master," she commented. "You really are the most powerful Sanatsai that has ever lived."

"Who says that?" Fay replied with a chuckle.

It was apparently a rhetorical question but Kayden elected to answer it anyway.

"Everyone!" she said, as though it were a self-evident truth. "It's one of those things that is always whispered on campus when people see you." For good measure, she added, "I know Master Ari believes it to be true."

"Nonetheless, I cannot confirm the veracity of what 'everyone' says. And even if it is true...there's no reason to believe this will always be the case. It's inevitable someone more powerful than myself shall emerge, eventually." Fay glanced intently at her. "Maybe that someone has already appeared."

After a fraught silence she returned her gaze to the path ahead. "So, what other questions did you want to ask me?"

Kayden tried not to dwell on Fay's less than subtle insinuation that she might be the 'someone more powerful' who would emerge. She still had several pressing questions to which she wanted answers; indeed, the conversation had just conjured up another one she hadn't previously thought to ask.

"Since you brought up the 'capture the box' exercise, Master," she said, "I do have a question in relation to it."

"Go on," prompted Fay.

"On a number of occasions, now, you have made it clear you know every move I made during the assignment. You haven't said how you know, though my assumption is you invoked *Raytandushay* so you could follow us unseen." There was just one problem with that supposition she could not resolve. "However, my ability to sense *Zarantar* should have allowed me to be aware of your presence irrespective of you being invisible—but that wasn't the case. I have subsequently come to realise how you managed it." She recalled how the rogue doppelgänger had punished her arrogant conviction she could anticipate any attack during their duel. "Somehow, it is possible for you to conceal your *Zarantar* from the senses of those who ordinarily can sense the presence and use of it."

"Perhaps," said Fay, but her tone was non-committal. She

glanced quizzically at Kayden. "How did you reach that conclusion?"

Kayden wanted to tell Fay about her encounter with the black clad assailant she had erroneously assumed was the Rogue, but she was mindful of Master Ari's exhortation not to tell anyone.

"Through painful experience," she replied cryptically. "But I can't really talk about it. Master Ari advised me against speaking about my experience last night. He seemed pretty adamant about it, actually."

"Fair enough," conceded Fay. "And, yes, your assertion is correct. I can mask my *Zarantar* from the senses of others when the need arises, as I did the other night to observe your group during the 'capture the box' exercise." She looked pointedly at Kayden. "You are the only person who knows this about me—not even Master Ari knows—so consider it one more thing you cannot reveal to anyone else."

She might have been perturbed by the exhortation to secrecy, but the reason for concealing this knowledge was a compelling one: the ability to mask the use of one's *Zarantar* was an obvious advantage to have when facing a *Zarantar*-wielding adversary who could sense an imminent attack—even more so if your opponent was unaware that such a feat was possible.

"As you wish, Master," said Kayden. "So, is this an ability that is unique to you, or is it something I can do also?"

Fay was staring straight ahead as she replied, "It is my hope you can and will master it as I have."

It dawned on Kayden that if Fay was the only member of the Order who possessed the power to mask the use of *Zarantar*, then the obvious implication of the reply was that Fay herself intended to teach her how to do it.

"Does that mean you plan to teach me, Master?" she inquired.

"If you keep the promise you made to me, then yes."

What promise had she made? Kayden suddenly wondered. *Oh, that's right! To make Fay proud of me.*

"Once you are inducted into the Order—which may be sooner than you think—you'll be ready to learn all those things your fellow apprentices will never master." Fay glanced sideways, gazing fixedly at her for a silent moment. When she spoke again her voice assumed a wistful cadence. "I have so much I want to teach you."

Kayden wasn't sure how to interpret the look Fay had fixed upon her when uttering those words. Something about it was just so reminiscent of the way her mother used to look at her. It made her heart flutter.

"Thank you, Master," she managed to say. "It would be an honour to be instructed by you."

While holding Fay's gaze, she realised that something had just passed between them—something more than confirmation their relationship would never again be characterised by antagonism. She didn't understand fully what that something was yet, but she felt the need to kick-start the conversation again before the silence became awkward.

She returned her focus to the trail ahead. "I have another question, Master."

"Ask away."

Once again Kayden recalled the duel with her doppelgänger the previous night. Her adversary was able to disappear then instantly reappear somewhere else, at will. She had never read or heard of any Sanatsai utilising *Zarantar* in such a manner before, and mastering such ability wasn't on the syllabus back at Antaris campus. At least, not as far as she was aware. Yet she was certain the things she witnessed in the Forest of Enlightenment were in some way prophetic. That at some unspecified point in the future, she was destined to possess all the powers displayed by her doppelgänger—abilities she strongly suspected Fay already had mastery of.

"Would I be correct in believing your *Zarantar* allows you to disappear from one place then reappear in another, in the time it takes to blink?".

When Fay glanced at her to address the question, Kayden noted the mischievous smile slowly curling the woman's lips. Then, all of a sudden, she felt *Zarantar* just before Fay disappeared from view, reappearing almost instantly, some thirty yards further ahead. She halted in her tracks, awestruck.

Again, Fay disappeared, and again Kayden sensed the tell-tale *Zarantar*—this time behind her back. She spun around quickly to see Fay reappear, standing with a close-lipped smile on her face.

"Like that, you mean?" Fay asked rhetorically.

Nodding her head in admiration, Kayden replied, "Yes, Master. Just like that." She was suitably impressed by the confirmation of what she suspected. "I've never read or heard of any Sanatsai being able to do that. I assume no other members of the Order have mastery of this particular application of *Zarantar*?"

"When I was first admitted into the Order, I was never successfully able to teach it to anyone other than Ari. Eventually, I just stopped trying, and once the network of campuses was established the Council made the decision that only those abilities that can be mastered by every Sanatsai would be taught to the apprentices."

Fay paused for a moment, looking contemplative.

"It wasn't until I discovered you at Antaris, three years ago, that I could entertain the possibility of passing on my knowledge to someone else. Before that moment, I had more or less given up on the idea." She resumed walking. "Come along."

The apprentice diligently continued at her master's side.

On account of Fay's words, Kayden was really beginning to feel the weight of responsibility on her shoulders. She was the only apprentice who could inherit the knowledge that Master Fay had to bestow.

"How did you come to know you could do the things you can do?" she asked.

"My mas—"

The abrupt way in which Fay caught herself told Kayden that the slip of her tongue had just aroused some bad memories. Though the perturbed expression was quickly eliminated from her face, it was obvious Fay would be treading uncomfortable ground if she answered the question.

"A former mentor of mine," said Fay, correcting herself, "was very good at persuading me I was capable of so much more than I thought was possible. His constant encouragement helped me to push beyond what I believed to be my limits."

She had to be referring to Josario, the Usurper King, Kayden realised.

"Having said that, he was not a Sanatsai himself, so he couldn't actually instruct me in expanding my capabilities. Most of my repertoire was self-taught through experimentation."

Sneaking a glimpse at her master, she could tell from the expression on Fay's face that the admission was not a source of pride. In fact, it was easy to discern that unpleasant memories had been dredged up. Kayden took this for confirmation the 'former mentor' referenced was indeed the Usurper King, so she quickly decided to steer the conversation away from areas touching upon Fay's infamous past.

"Can I then assume, Master," she began, "that you have overcome a limitation of our *Zarantar* that seems set in stone on campus, but one I have reason to believe is actually just a limitation of the power of most Sanatsai?" Again, Kayden's mind was thinking back to her encounter with the rogue doppelgänger. When she first entered the clearing where they duelled, she had been assailed by a volley of incendiary orbs that initially seemed to come from nowhere. But it transpired her adversary was invisible, while levitating several feet in the air, meaning her doppelgänger was able to simultaneously invoke *Balatlaydan*, *Raytandushay* and *Makfayshulat*.

"Which would tie-in to what you said about the Council deciding that apprentices only be taught that which every Sanatsai can learn to master."

"And what limitation might that be?" queried Fay.

"On campus, conventional wisdom stipulates that many of the high level applications of *Zarantar* can only be employed one at a time, so it shouldn't be possible to invoke multiple applications simultaneously." Something she now had every reason to believe wasn't entirely true. "But is there some reason why I—or any other apprentice—cannot learn how to invoke *Raytandushay* to become invisible, while at the same time invoking *Naymutandushay* to walk through a wall, for example?"

Fay glanced quizzically at Kayden. "For you...?" She paused briefly then returned her attention to the way ahead. "I see no reason why you cannot learn to do what you just described—and more besides." It was the answer Kayden hoped and expected to hear. "But with regard to your fellow apprentices, the power required to invoke just a single high level application of Zarantar, will always preclude them from being able to concurrently invoke a second. They just aren't strong enough." Fay glanced at her again. "No other apprentice on campus will ever be as powerful as you."

Kayden was sure she could see respect and admiration in her master's gaze, but she remained silent, taking a little time to let Fay's words sink in. That she had already believed this to be the case for a long time was one thing, but to hear confirmation of it from the lips of someone eminently more qualified to make that judgement, was another.

"It's not often I have you at a loss for words, Kayden," said Fay, breaking the silence. "Perhaps I should refrain from voicing my belief that no other apprentice anywhere in the Nine Kingdoms today will ever be your equal—you might never speak again."

Kayden wondered if the smile accompanying Fay's words should be interpreted as teasing. But Fay never struck her as the kind of woman who said things she didn't mean.

"You don't have to stroke my ego, Master Fay."

"That's just as well. Your ego doesn't need stroking, Kayden." Now Fay was teasing her, at least briefly. The mirthful expression on her face swiftly gave way to a more serious look. "I just have high hopes for you."

Not knowing what to say that, she just kept pace at her master's side. They were now emerging from their sparse woodland surroundings, walking out into open fields.

"I'm curious, Master," she said moments later to get the conversation back on track. "How many different applications of Zarantar have you mastered?"

"How many are there?"

Assuming the reply was rhetorical, Kayden didn't try to come up with an answer. Instead, she contemplated how best to broach her next question. It was the one she most wanted an answer to, but it also had the most potential to raise a red flag if she asked it.

And given her awareness of how well things were going with Master Fay, the prospect of jeopardising that, gave her pause for thought. Was alarming Fay really worth the risk?

"Kayden, you have that look again," said Fay, after the silence between the pair had extended. "I've already said you can ask me anything."

"I know, Master. It's just..." she trailed off.

She knew she couldn't inform Fay of the duel against her doppelgänger, but the encounter had raised an obvious question she had never considered beforehand. A realisation she hadn't been able to stop thinking about ever since: the doppelgänger's demonstration of the three expressions of *Zarantar*.

"The truth is, during my excursion with Master Ari I witnessed something that has sent my thoughts to places it probably shouldn't go. I'm now left with a question I'm worried to ask you. Yet, by the same token, you're the only member of the Order I feel I can risk asking."

"Why don't you just get it off your chest so you can stop worrying?"

"I'm concerned you might find it troubling that I would think of such a question."

"Your questions cannot trouble me, Kayden," insisted Fay. "Only what you choose to do with the answers."

That was reassurance enough.

"All right," she said. "My question relates to the three expressions of *Zarantar*. I know that the Jaymidari have mastery of *Zarantar Jist*, the Sanatsai have mastery of *Zarantar Shayd*, and the Saharbashi have mastery of *Zarantar Najist*. But what I want to know is...is it possible for one individual to have mastery of all three expressions of *Zarantar*?"

Fay glanced at her then mused, "Whatever Master Ari showed you last night has certainly made you inquisitive." She scrutinised Kayden with a studious gaze. "Now I understand why you were worried about asking me. It is a dangerous question to ask."

"Because asking," Kayden interjected, "could be interpreted as a desire on my part to learn *Zarantar Najist*."

"Which would be very problematic given the prohibition of

learning the ways of the Saharbashi," continued Fay. "Merely possessing such knowledge, regardless of whether one intends to use it, carries the death penalty."

She was fully aware of the forbidden nature of *Zarantar Najist*. Nonetheless, if her experience the previous night was in any way prophetic, as she suspected it might be, then it was likely that at some point in the future she would have mastery of the three expressions of *Zarantar*. She idly wondered if Fay had already accomplished this specific feat which, given her history, made sense. If anyone could master all three, it would surely be the woman who had been the Rogue. But she decided against putting her master on the spot by asking such a loaded question.

"Still, that doesn't really answer my question, Master," said Kayden, as neutrally as she could. It was probably best not to seem too pushy about this particular matter.

"Theoretically, a single individual could master the three expressions of *Zarantar*," confirmed Fay. "In practice, however, the odds are heavily stacked against anyone doing so—there would be no feasible opportunity to learn all three, especially not in the Nine Kingdoms."

Finally, Kayden had confirmation of what she more or less already knew. Now she could voice her theory on the type of person who could achieve what Fay had confirmed. "Such a person would have to be a female Sanatsai, right?"

The intensity of Fay's scrutinising gaze increased. "How exactly did you reach that conclusion?" The lack of denial implied Kayden was correct.

"It's the only thing that makes sense. There's no plausible way anyone other than a female Sanatsai could wield the three types of *Zarantar*." Kayden now felt versed enough at reading some of Fay's non-verbal cues to recognise the indication to elaborate further.

"Firstly, a woman can choose to join the Sisterhood, thereby learning to master *Zarantar Jist*, an option that will never be open to a man because—for reasons that remain a mystery—men cannot wield this expression of *Zarantar*. Any man who is inclined to do so can pursue the path of the Saharbashi to gain mastery of *Zaranatar Najist*, instead. And while it's highly unlikely any

Jaymidari would ever seek to learn the ways of the Saharbashi, I'm not aware of an actual impediment, other than ideology, that could prevent a Sister from mastering *Zarantar Najist* as well."

She paused briefly to give Fay the chance to contradict the assertion, but no correction came, so she continued.

"Though it is well known that the Jaymidari and the Saharbashi are diametrically opposed to each other, the one attribute they share in common is that neither can ever master the *Zarantar* of the Sanatsai. To wield *Zarantar Shayd* one must be born a Sanatsai. Our calling isn't a choice; it's a birthright."

Master Fay appeared to be following her line of deductive reasoning thus far, so she continued. "So, by default, the Saharbashi will only ever have mastery of a single expression of *Zarantar*, while the Jaymidari, on the other hand, can, in theory, have mastery of two. But the end result is the same: it's not possible for an individual from either group to have mastery of all three expressions of *Zarantar*." Again, she briefly paused to allow Fay to contradict the assertion, but again Fay offered no refutation, so she continued. "As for my conclusion that only female Sanatsai can master each of the three? Well, our male counterparts are in the same boat as the Saharbashi—they can never wield *Zarantar Jist*. But there is nothing preventing you or I, as women, from doing so. Plus, female Sanatsai also have the option to master *Zarantar Najist*...if they were outside the jurisdiction of the Order, that is."

Fay's appraising gaze upon Kayden quickly lost its intensity, and a subtle smile curled her lips as she returned her focus to the trail ahead of her. It reassured Kayden that she hadn't needlessly created trouble for herself.

"You never cease to impress me," mused Fay. "You possess a very sharp mind, Kayden. And you are, of course, correct in your conclusion. I doubt any of your peers would even think about the possibility of mastering the three expressions of *Zarantar*." She fixed her gaze upon Kayden once more. "Having said that, you should refrain from speaking of such things with anyone else, especially the notion of mastering *Zarantar Najist*."

Kayden noted how the look on Fay's face made it abundantly

clear that ignoring her advice on this matter would be unwise.

"I understand, Master."

She was content for their discussion to remain between the two of them. She was also relieved. Her questions had been answered without causing problems between them; now she could simply walk at her master's side and allow Fay to steer their conversation in any direction she wished, for the remainder of the journey.

"You have no more questions?" asked Fay after a prolonged silence.

"No, Master. You've told me everything I wanted to know, thank you."

"Well, I estimate we have an hour, at most, before we make it back to campus," said Fay. "Is there anything else you'd like to discuss with me in the meantime?"

There was nothing in particular Kayden wanted to talk about, but the remainder of her time alone with Fay was a good opportunity to get to know the woman better. "Well," she began hesitantly, "if you don't mind me boring you with small talk, the trip to Temis Rulan has made me realise just what an intriguing woman you are, Master," she hoped her words weren't construed as flattery, "so, I would really appreciate the chance to get to know more about you, assuming it's not inappropriate for an apprentice and her master to get to know each other personally."

"I have no issue making an exception for you, Kayden," admitted Fay. "Nothing would make me happier than for the two of us to get to know each other better. Though, for now, we should probably avoid allowing any small talk to get too personal."

"Oh, don't worry, Master," Kayden said light-heartedly, "I don't want to hear about your sex life any more than you want to hear about mine. Besides..." Her voice lost its mirthful tone as she added, "there are much more interesting things I'd like to learn about you." Again she was able to read Fay's non-verbal cue to elaborate further. "For example, while I was alone in your quarters, back in Temis Rulan, I noticed a number of books written in Zenoshanese sitting on your bookshelf. Does this mean you can speak it?"

"Indeed, I can. Though, regrettably, I get few opportunities to do so," replied Fay in fluent Zenoshanese.

Kayden was both impressed and surprised by Fay's fluency. "Given that we only study other Karlandrian languages on campus, it never occurred to me that a member of the Order would speak any Vaidasovian languages."

Master Fay continued to be full of surprises, she realised—this inevitably led to even more questions.

"When did you learn to speak Zenoshanese? Have you been to Zenosha?"

"I studied the language at Tamarini University, many years ago." Fay had a faraway look on her face as though she was reminiscing. "It was over half a century ago, now that I think about it. And, yes, I have been to Zenosha."

The reminder that Fay was significantly older than her appearance didn't throw Kayden off as much as the revelation she had studied at the renowned university in the Kingdom of Shintana.

"You mean the Order allowed you to attend Tamarini University?" she asked.

"Believe it or not, we are not on duty every waking moment. It is possible to have a life outside of your obligations to the Order." This was news to Kayden. "I have always been fascinated by Zenosha—its people, its culture and history—and my interest eventually led me to enrol at Tamarini University to study Zenoshanese history and learn the language also."

"How were you able to visit Zenosha?" wondered Kayden. "I've always heard the empire forbids entry to members of the Sisterhood and the Order."

"On the two occasions I travelled there I entered covertly on clandestine missions," Fay revealed. "Sadly, this meant I was unable to experience much in the way of what the civilisation has to offer."

It dawned on Kayden for the very first time that the well-known hostility towards *Zarantar*, and those who wield it, prevalent throughout the continent of Vaidasovia, meant she would never be permitted to visit the birthplace of her parents. "I guess once I've been inducted into the Order, I will never have the opportunity to travel to Zenosha," she said ruefully. "At least not openly." Though she had no plans to visit Zenosha, the realisation that the opportunity would likely be denied her, if she did, was a bitter blow.

"I didn't realise you had never been before," said Fay. "Did your mother never take you back when you were a child?"

"No. Mama couldn't face going back."

"If it makes you feel any better, while you are correct about not being able to visit Zenosha openly as a Sanatsai of the Order, the truth is, once you take off the uniform, no one would be able to distinguish you from any ordinary traveller—despite the bogus claims of Zenosha's Border Guard that they are able to detect wielders of *Zarantar*."

The notion of having to hide who and what she is had no appeal for Kayden. If she ever set foot in the motherland, she would do so openly. For now, however, the mention of removing her uniform brought something else to mind. "Master, since you brought up being out of uniform," she said mischievously, "I have to ask you about your wardrobe. Some of the dresses you own are rather risqué. When do you ever get to wear them?"

It was maybe a little impertinent to ask, but by the laws of the Nine Kingdoms all members of the Order were required to be in uniform when in public.

Fay gave her a stern look, eyebrows raised. It would have been easy to interpret the expression as confirmation that Fay did, indeed, regard the question as impertinent, and was displeased by it. But there was something in her eyes telling Kayden that Fay was amused by her front, so she smiled sweetly at her master. Fay's expression immediately softened and she returned the smile. So Kayden was right. Perhaps she was starting to get the hang of reading Fay.

Maybe it wouldn't be long before she was able to read her master just as well, and just as easily, as Fay was able to read her.

CHAPTER TWENTY-THREE

What A Difference A Day Makes

For three quarters of an hour, the master and the apprentice continued their discussion of trivial, mundane matters while they ambled across rolling fields, under the late morning sun. They even shared the odd joke or two, revealing to Kayden that Fay had a decidedly droll sense of humour, with a delivery that was frequently deadpan, as befitting of such a stoic personality.

She was surprised to discover that not only was it easy to converse with Fay, it was also easy to let her guard down for her—in a way she wouldn't have thought possible just a day earlier. The time spent getting to know her master was so engaging, she didn't even realise how much time had elapsed until she and Fay were bypassing Timaris. The town lay a short distance away from Antaris campus, so they were on course to arrive back on campus within the next quarter-hour.

"We will be arriving back at Antaris in a little while," said Fay, "and there is something I must discuss with you before we get there." Her more familiar, formal tone had returned; the campus administrator was back.

"Oh, all right," Kayden replied uncertainly.

"In light of recent events, I think we can both agree there is little point in you continuing your level seven studies." Kayden did agree, though she was immediately concerned about what was being implied. "You are already far in advance of where your colleagues are, and passing the end of level tests will be no trouble for you. That being the case, with the next holiday just over three weeks away, I will arrange for you to take the tests then.

"You are also ahead of the level eight apprentices, but it is too late in the year to join their classes. However, I still want you to take the tests this year, so this is what will happen once the holiday is over and the final term of the year begins. I will condense the level eight syllabus into a single term, and I will personally instruct you so that you may take the end of level tests at the same time as the other apprentices.

"You will commence the new year as a level nine apprentice, and begin your studies along with all the other level nine apprentices. You will complete the full year, like everyone else, and will take the end of level tests at the same time as everyone else. Likewise, come the following year, you will complete the full year of the level ten syllabus before taking the end of level tests.

"Once you have passed all the tests—and I have no concerns about your ability to do so—you will be officially inducted into the Order." Fay paused briefly, looking intently at her. "Only then can I teach you all the things I cannot teach you at Antaris."

Kayden was pleasantly surprised, and gratified. Fay's proposal meant she would complete her ten-year apprenticeship in just seven years. She would be twenty-one years old when she was inducted into the ranks of the Order, making her the youngest ever inductee by two years.

"Thank you, Master," she said earnestly, gazing back at Fay with appreciation.

"Don't thank me yet," Fay cautioned. "It is possible I maybe causing you problems with some of your peers on campus. My plans for you could be interpreted as favouritism."

"It's probably too late to worry about that, now, Master. It was recently brought to my attention that there are already rumours circulating around campus that I am your favoured apprentice."

"I suppose that's not too far from the truth," mused Fay. "And taking you with me to Temis Rulan will no doubt solidify that perception."

"Even so, I won't allow anyone to view me as a teacher's pet,"

Kayden said defiantly, though she felt there was no reason for anybody on campus to regard her as such. There was certainly no justification for doing so, from her point of view.

"Speaking of the trip to Temis Rulan," continued Fay. "I want to remind you, one last time, that you are not permitted to talk about it once we return to campus. No matter how much your friends pester you to tell them, they cannot know the location of Temis Rulan, how you got there, or what you saw and did while you were there."

Well, this is awkward, thought Kayden, neglecting to keep the feeling of awkwardness from her face.

"What is it, Kayden?" Fay inquired.

"I don't actually have any friends, Master," conceded Kayden, "so there's no need to worry about discretion on my part—I don't have anyone to tell." She was surprised by how much it bothered her to have to admit that.

Fay looked at her with disbelieving eyes. "What do you mean you don't have any friends?"

Although she didn't particularly want to elaborate, there seemed little point holding back now.

"When I became an apprentice I had no interest in making friends. I was too focussed on completing my apprenticeship so I could seek revenge for my mother, so I didn't bother."

"It's not too late for you to make some friends," said Fay sympathetically.

"You can't really believe that, Master!" replied Kayden, her incredulity at the suggestion readily apparent. "I'm the most disliked apprentice on campus. You must have noticed all the bridges I've burned over the last few years."

"Then build some new ones." Fay made it sound ridiculously easy in that matter-of-fact tone of hers.

"What about Neryssa Mirandi? I thought the two of you were quite close? She certainly seems to care about you."

Kayden thought about that for a moment. It was true that since being permitted to join the level seven apprentices, Neryssa was the one person who had really gone out of her way to be welcoming and friendly. "I guess Neryssa is the closest thing to a

415

friend I have on campus at the moment," she acknowledged, hesitantly. Unlike several others apprentices she could mention, Neryssa had never expressed any jealousy or hostility towards her.

"Well that's something to build on, wouldn't you say?"

"Maybe."

She didn't want to get her hopes up, though she was now resolved to making the effort to establish a genuine friendship with Neryssa as soon as she returned to Antaris.

"You might even find there are one or two other apprentices you could befriend," appended Fay.

Kayden couldn't understand where Fay's apparent optimism was coming from. Try as she might, she couldn't think of anybody else who was potential friend material. Although... "Well...I suppose Sinton Akasha could feasibly become a friend," she ventured. "I know he respects me, at least."

Fay's response was a smile—she had made her point it seemed.

With Antaris now visible in the distance, Kayden decided to return the conversation back to Fay's plans for the progression of her training. As she was only going to be a level seven apprentice for three more weeks, she questioned the necessity of having to attend all her classes in the interim. Fay immediately nipped in the bud the idea of those classes being skipped; Kayden would have to go to all her remaining classes, as normal.

A short while later, they were within two hundred yards of the south entrance of the campus when Fay stopped in her tracks, prompting Kayden to do the same. She turned to face the apprentice head on.

"Kayden, there's one more thing I want to say to you before we get back," she said earnestly.

"Yes, Master?" replied Kayden, with subtle apprehension in her voice.

"All the people I count as friends call me Fay." Holding her hand out to Kayden, Fay added, "I hope you will do the same."

Staring wide-eyed at her master, she was at a loss for words.

"Of course," Fay continued, "it wouldn't be appropriate for you to do so in the presence of other people while we're on campus, but when we are alone, there's no reason why we cannot interact on a first name basis."

Kayden reached out to clasp Fay by the forearm. "I would be honoured, Mast... I mean... Fay," she said solemnly. For several seconds she maintained her grip on Fay's forearm while holding her gaze. Just a day earlier she wouldn't have believed it possible, but it now seemed she had finally established her first friendship since becoming an apprentice—with Fay Annis, of all people. Yet more surprising than that was her intuitive conviction that Fay would be her greatest friend in life.

It was Fay who released her grip first.

"Let's get going," she said brightly.

The pair resumed walking, side-by-side, the rest of the way to the south entrance of the Antaris campus. The four Sanatsai sentries on duty greeted them with smiles, allowing them to enter the grounds unhindered. The clock tower, in the distance, let them know the time was fast approaching half past Eleventh Hour—Kayden had missed the first class of the morning, as expected, and the second class had begun over an hour ago so it was too late for her to attend that one as well. Fay instructed her to return her weaponry to the armoury then proceed at once to her dorm room, and await the midday bell announcing the commencement of the lunch hour.

Kayden made her way towards the armoury, with Fay remaining at her side since it was on the way to the administration building. While pondering the appropriateness of initiating any further small talk with Fay on campus grounds, her breath caught in her throat when she spotted Sister Daria among a group of five Sisters congregated outside the infirmary, a short distance ahead, on the left. Any hope that she and Fay could walk past the building unnoticed were quickly dashed when, as they drew nearer, Daria's eyes locked on hers. The look on the woman's face was subtle enough to go unnoticed by her colleagues, but apparent enough for Kayden to discern how happy the woman was to see her back.

"Oh no," she murmured.

"What is it, Kayden?" asked Fay.

She glanced at her master.

"What am I supposed to do about Sister Daria?" she implored urgently. "How am I supposed to tell her I've been using her—that we can't continue to see each other any more?"

"You're not going to tell her anything." It was not the answer Kayden was looking for. "Sister Daria is no longer your concern, I will deal with her myself."

Kayden wanted to voice her concern about how Daria might react to the end of their illicit relationship but she refrained, as it seemed rather presumptuous to mention the woman was in love with her, given Daria had never actually said as much.

"Is she going to be in trouble?" The guilt she was feeling seeped into her voice.

"Yes, Sister Daria is in trouble," affirmed Fay, in her matter-of-fact tone. "How much trouble remains to be seen."

Kayden didn't want to think about what that might entail. Though she didn't believe for a moment she was the only apprentice in the history of the Order to embark upon an illicit sexual relationship with a member of campus staff, she certainly wasn't aware of any such liaison being discovered. And with no precedent to look back on, she had little idea of what kind of punishment Sister Daria could expect to receive.

As master and apprentice drew closer to passing by the infirmary, Fay uttered in a low voice, "Do not look at her. Keep your eyes straight ahead and go directly to the armoury."

Before Kayden could respond, Fay veered away towards the gathering of Jaymidari, leaving her to continue on towards the armoury alone. She didn't look back when she heard Fay say, "Sister Daria, I have an urgent matter I need to discuss with you, could you follow me to my office?" but she was relieved there was no hint of rebuke in Fay's voice, nor any indication Daria was in trouble. The last thing she wanted was for the other Sisters to start speculating about what Daria had done. Knowing her luck they would guess correctly and spread the gossip all around the campus.

A short while later Kayden arrived outside the armoury. Only now did she risk peering over her shoulder. She saw Fay and Daria walking side-by-side several yards behind her. The two women appeared to be speaking casually, so she doubted Fay had already mentioned what she wanted to discuss with her counterpart. Certainly the look on Daria's face suggested she had no idea what she was walking into. Kayden quickly entered the armoury to avoid catching Daria's eye; chances were, the guilt and worry on her own face would give the game away.

Inside the armoury, she was greeted warmly by Master Solen who was very surprised to see her back on campus so soon. While she returned her weaponry, the Sanatsai tried to quiz her about the trip to Temis Rulan. She was unsure if the prohibition to speak to her fellow apprentices about her time in Temis Rulan was also applicable to her instructors, but she erred on the side of caution. Fortunately, Master Solen was accepting of her response that she wasn't permitted to talk about any of it.

Once she had finished catching up with Master Solen, she departed the armoury and made her way to the women's dormitory wing. Returning to her dorm room, she found it empty, as expected, and proceeded to one of the windows to catch sight of the clock tower. There was just under quarter of an hour to go until the midday bell sounded. She stepped away from the window then walked to her bed to lay down and wait, trying not to dwell on the conversation no doubt taking place between Master Fay and Sister Daria. Like Fay had said, Daria was no longer her concern. Instead, she thought about what she was going to say to Neryssa when her roommate returned to their dorm. Was she capable of making two friends in one day?

She would find out soon enough.

Fay was seated behind the mahogany desk in her office, looking across at Sister Daria sitting in one of the chairs opposite. It was apparent Daria still hadn't figured out why she was in the administrator's office.

"Sister, let me cut to the chase," she began. "I know all about your illicit relationship with Kayden Jayta."

She noticed the blood draining from Daria's face and the change in her demeanour; the woman was starting to fidget uncomfortably in her seat.

"I know about the clandestine meetings to instruct her in matters you had no business teaching her, including—but not limited to—how to make a siphon cloak, potentially endangering her life."

She waited for some kind of denial of the allegations but none was forthcoming.

"Do you have anything to say for yourself?"

"I... I don't know what you want me to say," said Daria. "There's nothing I can say. I know I have transgressed campus rules and must now pay the price for it." She took a breath that appeared to stiffen her resolve and regain her composure. "So, you needn't drag this out any longer than necessary, just tell me how you intend to proceed."

Fay placed both elbows on her desk, interlocked her fingers, then rested her chin on her hands.

"As tempted as I am to simply report your indiscretion to Sister Idelle, and have you transferred from here, you are a valued member of staff—one I would hate to lose," she said. "So, before making a final decision I'd like to hear your version of events. There are always two sides to every story, and I know Kayden is not entirely blameless in this."

Daria began to squirm in her seat again.

"Fay, what do you want me to tell you?" she said, shamefaced. "Without going into the details...this beautiful creature, young enough to be my daughter, offered herself to me and I was to weak to resist temptation. But, even on the rare occasion I was able to summon the strength to say no to her... Kayden just has a knack for getting me to do whatever she wants."

Fay didn't doubt for a moment the truthfulness of the latter part of that statement. She almost felt sorry for the woman. Once Kayden had set her sights on her, Daria probably had little hope of keeping the apprentice at bay. But that still didn't absolve the Sister of responsibility, especially as she no doubt got what she wanted from Kayden in return.

"I hope you understand that Kayden being young and beautiful, with an uncanny ability to get under people's skin, in no way mitigates the seriousness of what you did?" said Fay. "You know well the rule prohibiting relationships between apprentices and campus staff. And, frankly, you went beyond that." She paused for a moment to allow the rebuke to sink in. "However, I bear some culpability in the predicament you find yourself in."

Daria looked confused, as Fay hoped she would. Technically, she was in no way to blame for the Sister's misconduct, but offering to take some of the responsibility gave her the pretext she needed for not reporting the matter to Idelle...yet.

"I don't understand," confessed Daria.

"As the administrator here, it is my duty to be aware of everything that happens on campus. The fact that you and Kayden have been carrying on under my nose for well over a year means I haven't been paying nearly as much attention as I should." Which was true as far as it went. "But from this moment on, that changes. As a result, I am suspending your punishment...for now. I am placing you on probation until the end of the year. If you can demonstrate to me that not only is the relationship over, but also your willingness and ability to keep your distance from Kayden for the remainder of her apprenticeship, I will not inform Idelle of your egregious indiscretions." Fay could see the uncertainty written on Daria's face; it was necessary to drive the point home.

"You are not to speak to her nor interact with her in any way. If, for any reason, she needs to visit the infirmary, she is to be attended by one of your colleagues while you excuse yourself. Am I making myself clear?"

Seeing the expression on Daria's face caused Fay to suspect, for the first time, that the relationship with Kayden had been more than just physical—for Daria at least. It clearly meant more to the Sister than Kayden had let on.

"Would it make a difference if I said I love her?" asked Daria, meekly.

Fay stared long and hard at the other woman.

"Yes. Yes, it would," she intoned after a drawn-out silence. "It would make things much worse for you." She raised her chin from where it rested on her hands, unlocked her fingers, then placed her palms down on her desk, leaning forward. "So, I suggest you don't say it...and don't even think it. If you are feeling that way, then I'm telling you to stop. And if you're harbouring hopes that once Kayden has completed her apprenticeship you can resume a relationship with her... Well, technically that might be correct, but if I were you, I would abandon such hopes.

"Kayden is a very special young woman—one of a kind, as you are no doubt already aware. And as much as it may hurt you to hear this, I do not see you in her future."

Biting her lower lip, Daria said nothing in response—the pained look on her face said it all.

"That will be all," said Fay, "you may return to your duties." She watched Daria get up from her seat and head for the door. "Sister, one more thing before you leave," she added, before Daria could exit the office. "This matter is to remain between the two of us, I do not want rumours spreading around the campus."

Daria acknowledged the warning with a silent nod of the head, then departed, leaving Fay alone at her desk.

She remained in her chair for a couple of minutes, thinking. Eventually, she stood up having decided the first thing she should do next, having dealt with the Daria situation, is to check in with Isko Nardini, whom she had left in charge of campus, to find out if anything of consequence had occurred while she was away. Once done, she would return to her office to make a call to Ari in Temis Rulan. She had a Kayden-related matter to discuss with him.

Breezing out of her office, she went in search of Isko. As she had mentioned to Daria, she would be paying even closer attention to goings on around campus, though she doubted anything Isko had to report would be half as interesting as her trip to Temis Rulan had been.

Lying on her bed, hands beneath her head, Kayden was staring up at the ceiling when the clock tower bell sounded the arrival of midday. She sat up, and swung her legs around to sit perched on the edge of her bed, facing the door of the dorm room. Her roommates would be returning from their classes shortly, before going to the mess hall for lunch, or maybe even heading into town. She eagerly awaited Neryssa's arrival so she could put her underused friendship-making skills to the test.

When the door swung open for the first time, she was disappointed to see the Malorini Twins—Vida and Aida—stroll into the room, followed by three more of her roommates. The twins looked more than a little surprised to see her perched on her bed.

"What are you doing here?" blurted Aida, as she and her sister advanced into the room. "You've only been gone a day."

"A better question," added Vida, "is why haven't you been expelled yet?"

Kayden had to bite her tongue to avoid delivering a devastating quip at the twins' expense. She was in a good mood and wasn't about to let either of them spoil it.

"And it's so lovely to see you both, too," she said sweetly.

Aida scowled at the sarcasm, but Kayden ignored her.

The other three young women began to quiz her at once about where she really went, as she couldn't possibly have gone to Temis Rulan. According to their logic, for her to have gone there and back in a single day would mean the headquarters of the Order was just half a day's journey away from Antaris campus. If that was true they would surely know about it. Before she could tell them she could neither confirm nor deny their assertions, Kayden's attention was drawn back to the door when Yanina walked in with another roommate.

"Well, look what the cat dragged in," said the tall, swarthy apprentice as she approached Kayden's bed. "I didn't expect to see you back here for at least a week, possibly two, for that matter."

Kayden was about to respond when Aida beat her to it, offering her own explanation for Kayden's, briefer than expected, absence.

"She didn't go anywhere, Yanina," said Aida, a little triumphantly. "She must have aggravated Master Fay so much that she turned around to make the return journey long before they reached Temis Rulan."

Yanina came to a halt at the foot of Kayden's bed.

"Is that true?" she inquired.

"Actually, no it's not," Kayden retorted, as she stared pointedly at Aida. She averted her gaze to Yanina, to add, "But please don't ask me about my time away. Both Master Fay and Master Ari have prohibited me from talking about the trip. I cannot tell you where Temis Rulan is, how I got there, or what I did while I was there."

"Do you seriously expect us to believe you met Master Ari?" said Vida, incredulously.

"Like I said," replied Kayden, switching her focus back to the Malorini Twins, "I cannot talk about my time away."

She couldn't help but feel a twinge of satisfaction knowing her roommates would never know the truth about her recent experience.

"All right, so if we take you at your word that you did go to Temis Rulan," said Yanina, "was it disciplinary action or commendation awaiting you there?"

Kayden had to think about that for a moment. "Maybe a little of both," she answered. "But as I said—"

"You can't talk about it," Yanina interjected.

She nodded in the affirmative then her eyes were drawn to the door once more as someone else entered. Again, it wasn't Neryssa; it was Valeria. So all her roommates were present and accounted for, except the one she wanted to see. But she noticed immediately that Valeria was carrying more books than she should.

"Why isn't Neryssa with you?" she asked the newcomer.

"She had to answer the call of nature, she'll be up shortly," said Valeria, making her way towards Neryssa's bed. "What are you doing back, anyway? Shouldn't you be half way to Temis Rulan right now?"

"Apparently, she's been sworn to secrecy so can't answer any questions about where she went," Yanina answered on Kayden's behalf.

"Really?" said Valeria, before dumping half the books in her arms upon Neryssa's bed.

"I'm afraid so," Kayden confirmed.

"Don't believe a word of it, Valeria," said Vida, dismissively.

"Yeah!" agreed Aida. "Kayden is full of it."

Kayden refrained from responding to the twins. They were making their way towards the door, presumably off to lunch, and she was more than happy for them to leave before they soured her good mood. Their departure sparked a rapid exodus, as the rest of her roommates also headed for the exit, while she remained seated on the edge of her bed.

"Aren't you going to lunch?" said Yanina, standing in the open doorway, looking back at Kayden.

"I'm waiting for Neryssa."

"Suit yourself," Yanina replied. "And for what it's worth...I believe you when you say you went to Temis Rulan. The rumours about you being Master Fay's favourite apprentice are far too numerous not to be true." With that, she departed, leaving Kayden alone in the dorm.

While awaiting Neryssa's arrival, her thoughts drifted as she stared blankly at her booted feet. It wasn't for long, but as she was daydreaming she failed to notice when Neryssa walked into the room.

"I heard you were back."

Neryssa's voice snapped her out of her reverie. She looked up to see her ambling towards her.

"Yes, a short while ago," she stated, rising to her feet to greet her would-be new friend. She positively beamed as Neryssa halted beside the bed.

A frown wrinkled Neryssa's brow.

"What's the matter?" she asked, staring at Kayden with concern in her eyes.

"Nothing!" she replied, confused by the question. "Why?"

"You're smiling," said Neryssa, as though it was the strangest thing she'd ever witnessed. "I've never seen—"

"You've never seen me smiling before," Kayden interrupted. It was the second time that day someone had made this claim. "Oh, don't you start," she added, in mock exasperation. "I am more than capable of smiling when I want to. These lips can do more than just smirk, you know."

"Sorry I spoke," said Neryssa, raising her hands in mock surrender while returning Kayden's smile. "So, what exactly are we smiling about? Shouldn't you be on your way to Temis Rulan?"

"Been there; done that!"

The mirthful look on Neryssa's face gave way to disbelief upon realising Kayden wasn't being flippant. "How is that possible? You've only been gone a day."

"As much as I'd love to tell you, I've been forbidden from talking about my journey to Temis Rulan. However, I can tell you why I'm smiling." She savoured the expectant look on her roommate's face. "I'm smiling because I'm pleased to see you. And, there's something I'd like to discuss with you."

"Well then, why don't we talk about whatever it is over lunch?"

"I was hoping we could talk alone—the mess hall isn't really conducive to that."

The words seemed to pique Neryssa's interest. She raised a single finger at Kayden.

"Hold that thought," she said, then stepped away from Kayden's bed, to cross the room to the trunk at the foot of her own bed. She opened it and reached inside, pulling out a thick blanket. Turning to face Kayden, once more, she said, "How about we grab some food from the mess hall, go to the playing fields, and eat our lunch outdoors? It's a lovely day for it."

"Sounds good to me," replied Kayden, crossing the room to join Neryssa at her trunk.

Closing the trunk, Neryssa slung the blanket upon her shoulder. "So, what is this topic of conversation requiring us to be alone?"

"Well..." Kayden hesitated briefly, trying to think of an appropriate way to broach the matter without sounding desperate. "Um..."

"Well?" Neryssa prompted.

Kayden decided to just go for it—lay her cards on the table.

"Neryssa, I realise you have made many friends on campus during your seven years here," she began, "but I haven't been quite so successful in that regard. As things presently stand, there is only one person on campus whom I can call my friend. I would really like to double that number. So, is it possible that you and I could be friends?"

There was an expectant silence between the pair.

"I would like that," said Neryssa, sounding solemn as she held Kayden's gaze. "Very much."

Kayden held her hand out to her fellow apprentice. "Friends?"

With a smile, Neryssa clasped Kayden's forearm. "Friends!" she replied.

Fay returned to her office after checking in with Isko—letting him know she was back, and hearing his brief account of how he had managed during her absence. As expected, nothing of consequence had transpired so she was back in her office standing in front of the wall-mounted mirror. Her reflection no longer appeared in the glass, having been replaced by swirling lavender mists, indicating she was waiting for her transmission to be answered. The scheduled meeting of the Order's ruling body, to discuss the allegations she had brought against Turan Kodi, should have concluded some time ago, so Ari should be available to respond to her communication.

She didn't have to wait long. The swirling mists in the mirror gradually dissipated to reveal Ari Shinadu standing in the Council chamber.

"Greetings." She was pleasantly surprised it was Ari who answered her call. "I hope I'm not interrupting. Are you able to talk?"

"Yes. The Council meeting concluded a while ago. I've been lounging around the chamber for an hour or so waiting for you to call—Idelle said that you would."

She briefly wondered how Idelle could have known. One of these days she would have to ask the Sister where her awareness of things not yet come to pass came from.

"So, what can I do for you, old friend?" continued Ari.

"Your trip to Astana, tomorrow," she began, "I now know it's the murder of Kayden's mother you wish to bring up with the authorities there."

"Ah, so she told you, did she? I thought she would."

"Yes, she did, the poor thing," Fay sympathised. "Knowing the truth has certainly made her attitude and behaviour more understandable." She shook her head. "What a terrible thing to have witnessed her mother beaten to death, at such a tender age. And if that wasn't bad enough, to subsequently be denied justice."

"Indeed," Ari agreed, before adding. "So, I'm guessing you wish to hear my plans for tomorrow?"

"Unnecessary, I trust your judgement. But I would appreciate being kept abreast of developments. I would love to be able to tell Kayden that justice has been done for her mother."

"Consider it done," said Ari. Then he smiled at her. "So, can I assume your relationship with Kayden has turned a corner?"

"It's early days," she replied cautiously. "But there has been a noticeable change. I am very optimistic about the future, I have high hopes for her." At long last she had someone she could impart all her knowledge and skills to. "I cannot help but wonder how you got through to her last night. Whatever you did seems to have worked."

Ari smiled broadly. "I'm afraid you're going to have to spend the rest of your life wondering about that, old friend," he said mirthfully.

"Fair enough." She looked quizzically at him for a moment. "I have never been truly curious about this before now," she said, "but what exactly is the Sisterhood concealing in the north of the island, Ari?"

"The answer to that question is different for everyone who goes there," replied Ari, cryptically. "What Kayden saw was for her eyes only. I've advised her not to speak of it with anyone else." He was silent for a moment before smiling again. "However, what I can tell you," he continued, "is that anything and everything Kayden goes on to accomplish with her life, henceforth, will be thanks to you."

Fay wasn't sure she could agree with that particular assertion, though she appreciated the sentiment. Nonetheless, she smiled, offering no response.

"Was there anything else you wanted to discuss?" Ari prompted.

She inquired about the outcome of the meeting to discuss Turan Kodi's alleged misconduct. Ari informed her that he was to be recalled from Yaristana to stand before the Council and submit to having his memory examined. If he was found to be guilty of abusing his power to rape numerous women, as Fay suspected, in addition to the attempted assault on Kayden, he would face the full consequences of his actions.

"I'm pleased to hear it. That's everything I needed to know," she replied. "But before I let you return to your duties I just wanted to thank you. I was afraid we would lose Kayden, yet somehow you've managed to set my mind at ease. Now I can focus on helping her to fulfil her undoubted potential. She will be a tremendous asset for the Order; she's surely destined for great things."

Sitting cross-legged upon the thick blanket she and Neryssa had laid out on the grassy playing fields on the eastern outskirts of the campus, Kayden and her roommate sat across from each other with two trays of food from the mess hall placed in between them. Dotted around the playing fields were a smattering of other apprentices who'd had the same idea to have their lunches outdoors—none close enough to eavesdrop or interrupt while they conversed as they ate.

The pair took advantage of the one hour lunch break to solidify their new friendship by getting to know each other better. They agreed to narrate each other's life story prior to arriving at Antaris campus as apprentices of the Order, with Kayden going first. She spent the best part of half an hour chronicling her childhood in Astana, and the circumstances that eventually led her to reside hundreds of miles away in the Kingdom of Mirtana—via the Kingdom of Lirantana. She briefly touched upon her mother dying when she was eleven years old, though she didn't go into detail; she didn't wish to elicit undue sympathy from Neryssa.

"Wow! Kayden, someone could write an adventure novel based on your childhood," Neryssa said when the narration was completed. "My childhood was dreadfully boring by comparison."

Kayden quickly discovered Neryssa wasn't exaggerating in the slightest. As she listened to her friend's story, she couldn't believe just how boring life in a small farming town in the southeast of

Mirtana could be. Yet, inexplicably, she found herself envious of the dull, mundane, uneventful existence Neryssa had lived prior to the manifestation of her *Zarantar*.

"Finally!" she said, in mock exasperation when her roommate's tale came to an end. "I was losing the will to live, here." She immediately flashed a broad grin to make it known she was joking.

"Hey!" Neryssa plucked an olive from her plate and tossed it playfully at her.

She swayed out of the way before invoking *Yuksaydan* to lift an olive from her own plate and send it hurtling at Neryssa, striking her on the nose. Both young women began laughing heartily in response. When their laughter subsided, Kayden noticed Neryssa staring at her curiously.

"Kayden, I hope you don't mind my saying so," began Neryssa. "There's something different about you since you came back. You've changed. I can't exactly put my finger on it but you look less..." She trailed off, clearly searching for the appropriate word.

"Burdened?" Kayden offered. It was the word Master Fay had used.

"I was thinking tortured, but burdened is certainly an apt description," Neryssa agreed. "So, why is that? What's changed?"

"Well, I can't really tell you, except to say the time away did me a world of good."

"So it seems," concurred Neryssa, again. "I'm glad. It's good to see you smiling for a change—you have a beautiful smile."

Kayden looked down at her almost finished lunch, feeling embarrassed. It was the second time that day someone complimented her smile. Glancing back up at Neryssa, she said, "I will always have a smile for my friends."

"Which reminds me!" Neryssa's face made plain that something had just occurred to her. "Earlier, you said there was only one other person on campus you could call a friend."

"That's right."

"Well...?" coaxed Neryssa. "Don't leave me in suspense, who is it?"

"Master Fay."

From the wide-eyed look of disbelief on Neryssa's face, Kayden had to assume her newest friend hadn't anticipated her answer. "Is that really so hard to believe?" she asked.

"Yes...almost as unlikely as you calling her Master," said the incredulous apprentice. "When did this start? I've never heard you refer to her as—"

"Yeah, yeah, yeah!" interrupted Kayden. "You've never heard me call her Master. I call her 'the administrator' or 'Administrator Annis' or 'that woman'. Someone already mentioned that to me today."

While Neryssa silently scrutinised her, she started to wonder if her roommate was deciding whether or not to believe the claim.

"This happened while the two of you were away?" queried Neryssa.

Kayden nodded with a smile.

"Then Master Fay is truly a miracle worker, in that case—to breach your impenetrable defences in just a single day." There was nothing facetious about the way Neryssa spoke. "She is a remarkable woman."

Kayden couldn't argue with that. "More than you know," she replied.

The expression on Neryssa's face shifted again; a half smile slowly curled her lips. "Perhaps I shouldn't be surprised by a friendship between the two of you. It actually makes a lot of sense now I that think about it," she said. "Clearly, Master Fay sees something in you: a kindred spirit maybe. Someone capable of being her equal. She is a legend of the Order, and someday soon, you will join her, by becoming a legend of the Order, too."

She didn't quite know what to say to that, so she quietly resumed eating. It was obvious from Neryssa's tone, she wasn't engaging in flattery; she genuinely believed what she said. As for whether or not her words were true...

Only time would tell.

ABOUT THE AUTHOR

The reclusive Ian Gregoire is a taciturn introvert residing somewhere in London, where he was born and raised. Of all life's diversions, reading and writing are the only ones he ever deemed worthwhile enough to be passionate about. This eventually led to his belated decision to pursue his true calling in life as a fantasy and science fiction author. His debut novel, The Exercise Of Vital Powers, is just the first of many books he intends to inflict upon an unsuspecting world.

On the occasions he steps out of his reading and writing comfort zone, Ian has a fondness for computing, melancholy music, retro gaming, and Asian Cinema. Ian also loves peace and quiet, something that is in frustratingly short supply in his life.

To find out more about Ian Gregoire visit his official website www.iangregoire.co.uk and be sure to sign up to his mailing list to be kept up to date with all his future publishing plans.

REQUEST FROM AUTHOR

I would like to make the following request to those of you who enjoyed The Exercise Of Vital Powers: please help spread the word so more readers may discover it. You can do this, first and foremost, by leaving a review and rating on Amazon, Goodreads or any other online platform you favour. Don't worry if you aren't able to write a detailed, thousand word critique; it's enough to simply state that you enjoyed the book.

In addition to the above, word of mouth remains one of the most effect forms of promotion, so please don't shy away from recommending the book to family, friends and anyone else you who might also enjoy The Exercise Of Vital Powers.

Printed in Great Britain
by Amazon

Microsoft Excel 97

Copyright - Editions ENI - December 1998
ISBN: 2-7460-0055-5
Original edition: ISBN: 2-84072-446-4

Editions ENI

BP 32125
44021 NANTES Cedex 1
Tél : 02.51.80.15.15
Fax : 02.51.80.15.16

e-mail : editions@ediENI.com
http://www.editions-eni.com

On Your Side collection directed by Corinne HERVO

*This book is intended for all users of the spreadsheet **Excel 97**.*

It is designed so that you can find quickly the options you need to activate and the actions you need to perform to reach the end result you require.

The screens illustrated throughout these pages add to the clarity of the explanations provided, by showing the dialog box corresponding to a given command, or by giving a precise example.

This book is made up of 9 parts.

FOREWORD

In the **Appendix** you will find a list of all the available key combinations, along with a full description of each toolbar and a list of integrated functions.

In addition, at the end of this manual you will find an **index** by subject allowing you to look up the information you need and a section on the **menus**.

Typographic conventions

In order to help you find the information you require quickly and easily the following conventions have been adopted.

These typefaces are used for :

bold   showing which menu option or dialog box to use.

italic   giving an explanation of the command you are following, or of any changes on the screen.

Ctrl   showing which keys you should press. When two keys are displayed together they must be pressed simultaneously.

The following symbols indicate :

♦   An action you should perform (activating an option, clicking with the mouse).

❑   A general comment on the command being used.

A useful tip to know and remember.

using the mouse.

using the keyboard.

using the menus.

MICROSOFT EXCEL 97

TABLE OF CONTENTS

MANAGING DOCUMENTS

ENTERING/MODIFYING DATA

TABLE OF CONTENTS

PRESENTATION OF THE DATA

TABLE OF CONTENTS

TABLE OF CONTENTS

TABLE OF CONTENTS

APPENDICES

TABLE OF CONTENTS

Starting Excel 97

♦ Click the **Start** button.

♦ Move the mouse onto the **Programs** option.

♦ Click **Microsoft Excel**.

❑ *If you have a shortcut to Excel on the Desktop, double-click the icon to start the application.*

Leaving Excel 97

♦ **File**
  Exit

Click ☒
in the application window

♦ Alt F4

♦ If you have left any documents unsaved, save them. The **Yes To All** option saves all open documents.

Presenting the workscreen

*All Windows applications run in an **Application window**. Excel opens each document (an Excel document is known as a workbook) in a **Document window**.*

The Application window

OVERVIEW

The title bar (a)

On the left there is the button which opens Excel's **Control** menu (1). Next to it is the name of the application (Microsoft Excel) and the active workbook.
On the right there are the **Minimize** (2), **Maximize** or **Restore** (3) and **Close** (4) buttons.

The menu bar (b)

This bar contains Excel's menus.

Open a menu to see the list of options available.

The Standard toolbar (c) and Formatting toolbar (d)

These tools carry out common commands instantly, and apply formatting. Double-click the move handle (5) to undock the toolbar.

The formula bar (e)

This bar displays the data in the active cell (text, value or formula) so that you can edit it. You can also use the formula bar to enter new data in a cell.

The status bar (f)

The status bar gives information about the current command or task. **Ready** is displayed when there is no task in progress.

The workbook window

The workbook's Control button is on the left of the title bar and the **Minimize, Maximize** and **Close** buttons are on the right (when the window is maximised, the **Restore** button replaces the **Maximize** button):

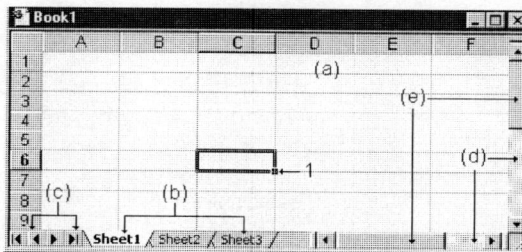

The workspace (a)

The Excel workspace is made up of **cells** ; each cell is the intersection of a row with a column. The **reference** of the cell is the association of its column letter with its row number. For example the cell positioned on row 10 and in column C is referred to as C10.

When you click a particular cell, the cell becomes **active** and its reference appears at the left of the formula bar.

Up to 256 columns and 65536 rows can be used in Excel 97.
The black square at the bottom right corner of the active cell is called the **Fill handle** (1).

Worksheet tabs (b)

A book consists of several **sheets**. Excel identifies them by **tabs** which appear at the bottom of the book window. The name of the active sheet appears in bold type on the tab.

The tab scroll bar (c)

By default each new book contains three sheets. Use the arrows to scroll through them.

The scroll bars (d)

Drag the **scroll box** (e) or click the arrows to move up, down and across the sheet.

Using the menus   The menus on the menu bar

	🖱	⌨
Open a menu	point to the name of the menu with the mouse and click with the left button	press [Alt] and at the same time type the letter which is underlined in the menu's name
Closing a menu	click outside the menu	press [Esc] twice or [Alt] once
Closing an option	click the option	type the underlined letter : do not enter

Shortcut menus

A shortcut menu is a menu containing options relevant to the selected item (cell, sheet tab, chart item...).

♦ To display the shortcut menu, select the item concerned then right-click the selection.

A list of relevant options appears. They can also be found in the menus on the menu bar.

♦ To remove the shortcut menu from the screen, press [Esc].

❏ *The options displayed in grey are not available in that particular context.*

❏ *An ellipsis after an option means that selecting it opens a dialog box. A triangle after an option indicates that it opens a submenu.*

Dialog boxes   *A dialog box usually consists of several different tabs which group together various options. The active tab appears in bold type at the front.*

♦ Choose a tab by clicking it.

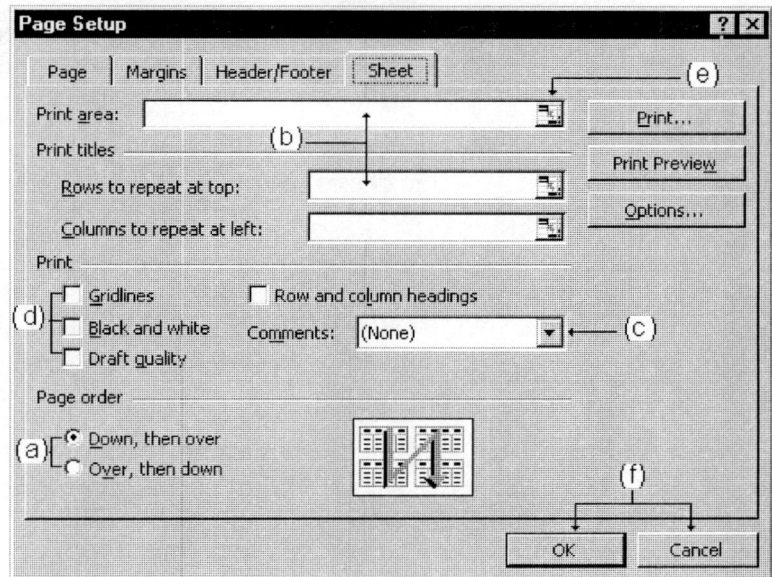

A dialog box contains up to five different elements :

Option buttons (a)

The active option has a black dot in the circle in front of it. Only one option can be chosen from each frame in the window.

Text boxes (b)

When the mouse pointer is in a text box, it looks like an I. Click, and it becomes a flashing vertical bar known as the **Insertion point** : you can now type in your data.
Some text boxes are drop-down list boxes (c) : you can either type the data you want to enter or choose from a list of suitable entries.
Some text boxes include increment buttons : type in the value required, or increase or decrease the value displayed by clicking the arrows.

List boxes (c)

Click the arrow to open and close the list (or press Alt ↓).
To the right of a box used for defining a range of cells, there is a **collapse dialog** button (e) : click it to shrink the dialog box temporarily, leaving only the current text box on the screen. This makes it easier to select cells in the worksheet. Click the button to display the dialog box at its normal size.

Check boxes (d)

A check mark in the corresponding box activates an option. Several options can be active at the same time.

<u>Command buttons (f)</u>

The **OK** button, like the ⌨Enter key, confirms your command and closes the dialog box.
The **Cancel** button negates your command and closes the dialog box (equivalent to pressing ⌨Esc).

❑ *A dialog box is a window like any other : it has a title bar and can be moved around.*

Using help in Excel

<u>Using the contents page or the index</u>

♦ Click **Help** then **Contents and Index**.

♦ In the contents list, double-click a book icon to see the topics in that category. For help with a topic, double-click the question mark icon.

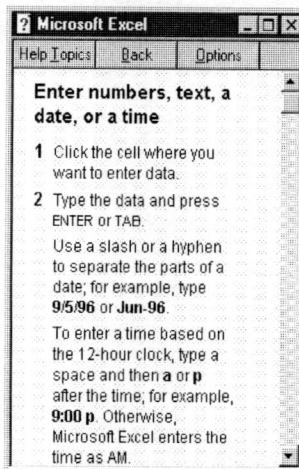

♦ Click one of the following buttons :

Options   displays a menu with options for printing the help text, copying it ...

Back   displays the previous help topic.

Help Topics returns to the contents page.

♦ In the Help Topics window, click the **Index** tab.

♦ Enter the first characters of the topic that interests you, then double-click the topic to see the help text.

Click the ☒ button in the **Help Topics** window to leave Excel's help.

Displaying Screen Tips

♦ Open the **Help** menu, then click **What's This ?**

A question mark attaches itself to the mouse pointer.

♦ Click an item in the window to see a description of it.

A description of the item appears in a Screen Tip.

❏ *In some dialog boxes you can find more information about an option by clicking the* ? *button on the title bar then clicking the option.*

Using the Office Assistant

♦ Display the **Office Assistant** by clicking the 🔲 button.

♦ When you need help with the action in progress, click the Office Assistant.

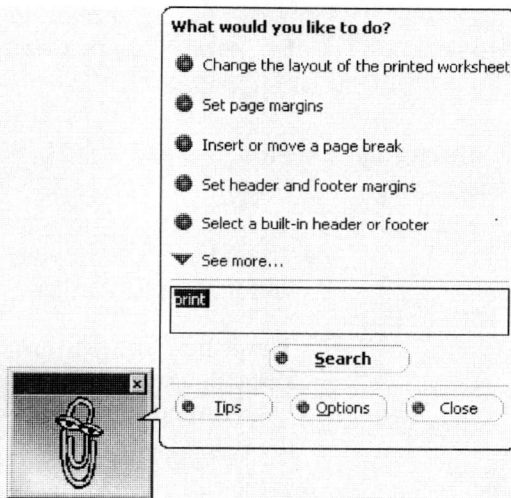

♦ Choose the topic for which you need help, or enter a key word then click **Search**.

Excel displays the help text corresponding to the topic.

Changing the look of the Office Assistant

♦ Click the Office Assistant with the right mouse button, then click **Options**.

♦ Click the **Gallery** tab.

♦ Use the **Next** and/or **Back** buttons to select one of the characters proposed.

♦ Once you have chosen your Office Assistant, click **OK**.

❏ *The Office Assistant displays a light bulb when it has some advice for you. Click the Assistant to see the advice.*

**Repeating
the last actions**

♦ If necessary select the text concerned.

♦ **Edit
Repeat**

♦ Ctrl Y

❑ *When the last command can not be repeated, the* **Repeat** *option is replaced by* **Can't repeat** *(in grey).*

**Undoing
the last action**

♦ **Edit
Undo**

♦ Ctrl Z

♦ To undo several of your last actions, click the arrow on the button to open the list.

The action you performed most recently appears first in the list. Look down the list, and click the earliest of the set of actions you wish to undo (this action, and all those which appear above it in the list, will be undone).

❑ *Excel 97 allows you to cancel up to 16 of your last actions.*

❑ *Certain commands can not be cancelled. In this case the option in the* **Edit** *menu changes to* **Can't Undo** *(in grey).*

❑ *After a command has been cancelled, you can restore it by clicking the button.*

. . . . *Personal notes* . . . .

Moving around on a sheet

There are several ways of moving around a worksheet: some involve the mouse, others make use of the keyboard.

♦ Use the scroll bars to reach the cell you want to activate.

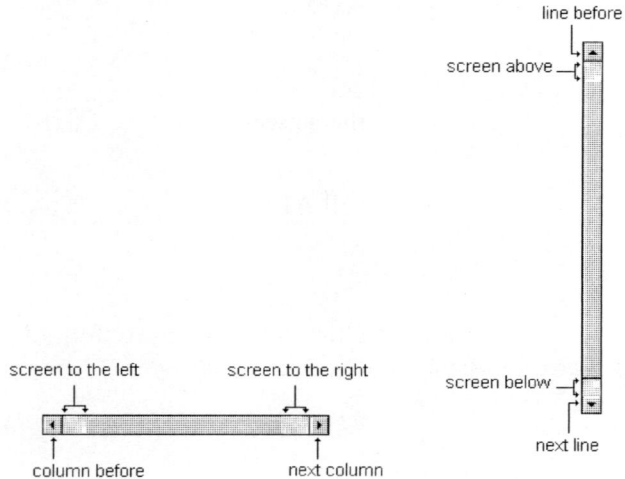

As you drag the scroll box, Excel displays a Screen Tip giving the number of the row you have reached or the letter of the column.

♦ Use the keyboard as follows :

cell to the right	`→` or `⇄`
cell to the left	`←` or `⇧ Shift` `⇄`
cell above	`↑` or `⇧ Shift` `Enter`
cell below	`↓` or `Enter`
screen to the right	`Alt` `Pg Dn`

screen to the left	`Alt` `Pg Up`
screen above	`Pg Up`
screen below	`Pg Dn`
column A in the active row	`Home`
cell A1	`Ctrl` `Home`

Going to a specific cell

♦ Click the box on the formula bar where the reference of the active cell is displayed.

This selects the reference of the active cell.

♦ Type in the reference of the cell required.

♦ Enter.

Finding a cell by its contents

♦ If you want to search the whole sheet, activate cell A1, otherwise select the range of cells concerned.

♦ **Edit**   ♦ `Ctrl` F
Find

♦ Enter the value which you want to find.

♦ Set the options to indicate how you want to search.

♦ Enter.

Moving from one sheet to another

♦ Using the tab scroll buttons, display the tab of the sheet where you want to go.

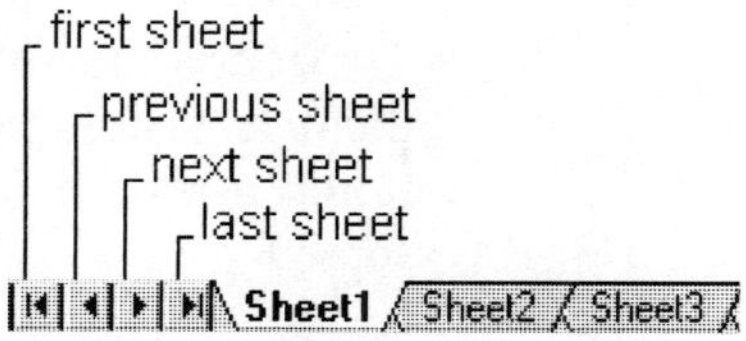

```
                    ┌ first sheet
                    │ ┌ previous sheet
                    │ │ ┌ next sheet
                    │ │ │ ┌ last sheet
                    │�◄│◄│►│►│\ Sheet1 / Sheet2 / Sheet3 /
```

♦ To scroll the tabs quickly, hold down the ⇧ Shift key as you click ◄ or ►.

♦ Click the tab to open the worksheet.

❏ *On the keyboard you can use* Ctrl Pg Dn *to move to the next sheet or* Ctrl Pg Up *for the previous sheet.*

You can increase or decrease the space reserved for sheet tabs by dragging the tab split bar situated to the left of the horizontal scroll bar.

. . . . *Personal notes* . . . .

Freezing and unfreezing titles on the screen

When a table is too big to be visible all at once on the screen, freezing columns or rows is a way of bringing together data at opposite ends of the table.

♦ To freeze the row titles, make sure that the column containing them is visible at the very left of the screen. To freeze the column titles, display the corresponding row at the top of the screen.

♦ To freeze the row titles, select the next column.
Select the next row to freeze the column titles.

	A	B	C	D	E	
1	*In-Service Training Results*					
2						
3	Department	Employee	Marketing	Consumer Law	Tax Law	F Ma
4	Compta.	Ball S.	15	14	14	

In this example, columns A and B and rows 1, 2 and 3 will be frozen, since cell C4 has been selected.

♦ **Window**
  Freeze Panes

❑ *To release the titles you have frozen use **Window** - **Unfreeze Panes**.*

**Changing
the magnification**

♦ **View
Zoom**

```
100%  ▼
```

By default, Excel documents are displayed at 100 % of their actual size.

♦ In the **Zoom** dialog box, choose a factor of magnification or activate **Custom** and enter a value. Otherwise, type the value directly into the zoom box on the Standard toolbar.

♦ Enter.

> The ***View - Full Screen*** command gives over pratically all the space on the screen to displaying the document.

**Hiding/displaying
zeros**

Hiding all the zeros in the worksheet

♦ **Tools
Options
View** tab

♦ Deactivate the **Zero values** option.

♦ Click **OK**.

Hiding zeros in specific cells

♦ Select the cells containing zeros that you do not want to see.

♦ **Format
Cells
Number** tab

♦ ☐Ctrl☐ **1**

♦ Choose **Custom**.

♦ In the **Type** box delete everything and enter **0;0;**.

❏ *To display hidden zeros activate the **Zero Values** option in the **Tools - Options** menu, or apply any other format to the cells concerned.*

Displaying formulas instead of values

♦ **Tools**
  Options
  View tab

♦ Activate the **Formula** option in the **Window Options** frame.

♦ Enter.

❏ *When formulas are displayed, the width of the columns is doubled and their contents are aligned on the left.*

Tracing cells used in formulas

♦ Activate the cell containing the formula.

♦ **Tools**
  Auditing
  Trace Precedents

	A	B	C	D	E	F
1		1st quarter	2nd quarter	3rd quarter	4th quarter	Year
2	WEST	250 000	1 210 000	1 310 000	1 204 000	974 000
3	SOUTH	000 000	990 000	1 100 000	986 000	4 076 000
4	NORTH	600 000	1 420 000	1 545 000	1 375 000	5 940 000
5	CENTRE	210 000	1 208 000	1 320 000	1 199 000	4 937 000
6	EAST	125 000	1 120 000	1 255 000	1 072 000	4 572 000
7	FRANCE (92)	5 185 000	5 948 000	6 530 000	5 836 000	24 499 000
8	AVERAGE (92)	2 061 667	982 667	2 176 667	1 945 333	

The precedent cells are linked to the calculation formula by arrows.

❏ *To delete the tracer arrows use the command **Tools - Auditing - Remove All Arrows**.*

❏ *When you edit a formula, the cells to which the formula refers are marked with a border.*

**Docking
a floating toolbar**

*When a toolbar is displayed as a window it is said to be **floating**.
A toolbar which appears as a bar at the edge of the window, is a
docked toolbar.*

♦ To dock a floating bar double-click its title bar or drag it to one
of the edges of the Excel window.

♦ To undock a toolbar double-click its move handle (at the left of
the bar).

**Displaying/hiding
a specific toolbar**

♦ **View
Toolbars**

♦ To hide or display an individual bar, click its name.
Take the **Customize** option to select all the bars that you want in
the window.

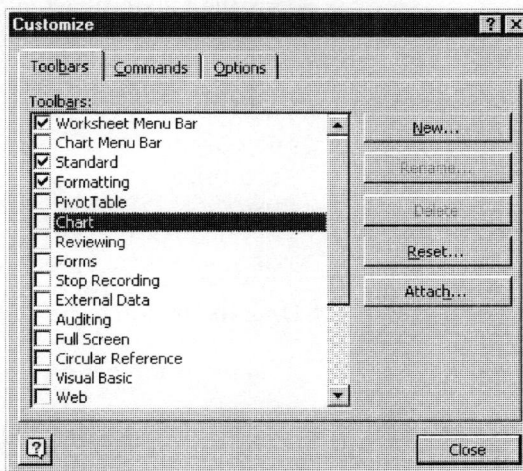

♦ Mark the bars to display and make sure that none of the others
are marked, then click **OK**.

❏ *You can also right-click the move handle of one of the toolbars
then click the name of the bar to display or hide.*

DISPLAY

Click 🔲 to display or hide the Drawing toolbar.

**Creating
a custom toolbar**

♦ **View
Toolbars
Customize**

♦ Click **New**.

♦ Give a name for the toolbar, then enter.

A floating toolbar appears on the worksheet: it has no tools yet.

♦ Add tools to the new bar.

♦ When all the buttons you want have been added to the toolbar, click the **Customize** dialog box's **Close** button.

**Managing tools
in a toolbar
on the screen**

♦ **View
Toolbars
Customize**

Deleting a tool

♦ Drag the button to be deleted off the bar.

As soon as the button is moved away from the bar, it disappears.

♦ Close the **Customize** dialog box.

Adding a tool

♦ Click the **Commands** tab of the **Customize** dialog box.

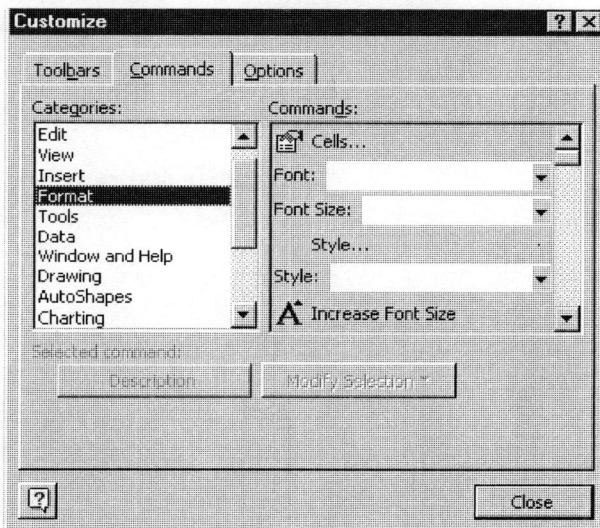

♦ Select the **Category** containing the tool you want to add.

♦ Select a tool from the **Commands** list and drag it onto the bar in the window.

♦ Click the **Customize** dialog box's **Close** button.

❑ *A new tool stays where you positioned it. If you are not satisfied with its position, open* **View - Toolbars**, **Commands** *tab, then drag it to a new location on the toolbar.*

Once a toolbar has been customised, you can retrieve the original version by clicking the **Restore** *button in the* **Customize** *dialog box (***Toolbars** *tab).*

Selecting a range of adjacent cells

♦ There are three ways to select adjacent cells :

♦ Dragging Click the first cell of the selection and drag over the others. When you are satisfied with the selection, release the mouse button.

Be careful not to drag the fill handle (the black square in the bottom right-hand corner of the active cell).

Click and ⇧ Shift Click the first cell to be selected and then point to the last cell concerned. Hold down ⇧ Shift and click; release the mouse button before the shift key.

Keyboard Hold down the ⇧ Shift key while using the arrow keys.

D3	▼		=B3*C3	
	A	**B**	**C**	**D**
1		31-Mar		
2	**Total**	Quantities	Average Price	Total
3	**£12 500**	120	£125	£15 000
4	**£14 016**	610	£32	£19 520
5	**£19 470**	181	£110	£19 910
6	**£14 875**	188	£85	£15 980
7	**£21 105**	126	£201	£25 326
8	**£16 695**	64	£265	£16 960
9	**£98 661**			£112 696

A range of selected cells appears darker on the screen except for the active cell, which appears as usual.

❏ *The status bar automatically displays the sum of the selected cells.*

**Selecting
nonadjacent cells**

♦ Select the first cell or range of cells.

♦ Point to the next cell, or the first cell of the next range.

Do not click at this stage.

♦ Hold down the ⌘Ctrl key and click. Drag if necessary, to select a range of cells.

♦ Release the ⌘Ctrl key.

❏ *In a formula or a dialog box the selected, nonadjacent cells (or ranges) are separated by commas. For example : A5:A10,L5:L10 refers to the ranges of A5 to A10 and L5 to L10.*

**Selecting
rows and columns**

♦ Use the mouse or the keyboard :

	Row	Column
🖱	click the number of a row to select it.	click the letter of a column to select it.
⌨	activate any cell in the row and press ⇧ Shift space	activate any cell in the column and press Ctrl space

A selected row or column appears in inverse video.

❏ *To select several rows (or columns) at a time, you can drag over them, or hold down ⇧ Shift as you click.*

<table>
<tr><td>

**Selecting the
entire worksheet**

</td><td>

♦ Click the button in the top left corner, where the column containing row numbers meets the row containing column letters.
or
press Ctrl ⇧ Shift space .

</td></tr>
</table>

<table>
<tr><td>

**Selecting cells
according
to content**

</td><td>

♦ **Edit**
Go To

</td><td>

♦ F 5 or Ctrl G

</td></tr>
</table>

♦ Click **Special**.

♦ Indicate the type of cells to be selected.

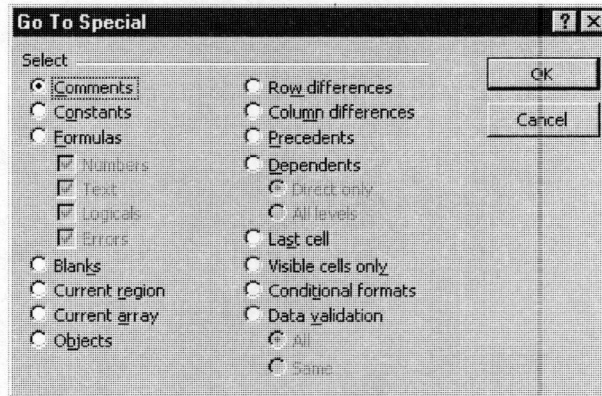

♦ Click **OK**.

Looking at Excel documents

♦ An Excel document is called a **workbook** or book.

♦ A book contains **sheets** : worksheets and chart sheets. Normally 3 sheets are available in each book but you can add and delete sheets as you wish.

Opening documents

♦ **File**　　　　　　　🗁　　　　　　♦ Ctrl O
   Open

♦ Use the **Look in** drop down list to find the document.

This list contains all the disk drives accessible from your computer: floppy drive (A:), hard disk (C:), CD ROM drive and drives in the Network Neighbourhood.

♦ Click the drive in which the document is stored (A:, C:, D:....) if it is on the local computer (**My Computer**), or click **Network Neighborhood**.

♦ Open the folder containing the document by double-clicking its icon.

♦ Click 🔼 to open the folder above.

♦ Click 📋 to see a detailed list.

*The first column displays the **Name** of each document. The **Size** of each document appears in the second column, its **Type** in the third and the date and time it was last **Modified** appear in the fourth column.*

♦ To view the properties of a document, click 📄 then select the document.

*The **Title**, **Subject** and **Author** appear at the right of the dialog box.*

♦ To preview the document, click 📄, then select the document.

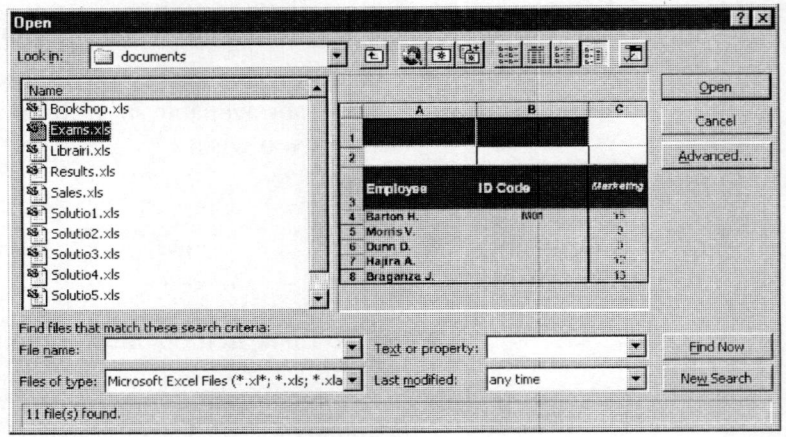

♦ To return to the list, click [⊞].

♦ To open a document double-click its name.

> *The last four documents opened appear at the end of the **File** menu. Click one of them to open it.*

Hiding/displaying an open document

Displaying a hidden document

♦ **Window Unhide**

Excel lists all the open documents which have been hidden.

♦ Double-click the document concerned.

Hiding a document

♦ Activate the document you want to hide.

♦ **Window Hide**

Activating open documents

♦ **Window**

Open workbooks are listed at the bottom of the menu. A check mark indicates the active book.

♦ Click the book you want to activate.

Saving a document

A new document

♦ **File Save** ♦ Ctrl S

♦ In the **Save in** list, choose the disk where you want to save the document.

♦ Open the folder by double-clicking its icon.

♦ Double-click the **File name** box, then give a name for the docu-ment. You can use up to 255 characters, including spaces.

♦ Click **Save.**

The document's new name appears on its title bar. Excel documents have the extension .XLS (this extension may be hidden).

Existing documents

♦ **File**
   Save

♦ ⌨Ctrl⌨ S

*Excel can save your documents automatically at regular intervals you define. For this you need to install the **AutoSave** add-in (**Tools - Add-Ins**). Once this is done, the **AutoSave** option is accessible via the **Tools** menu.*

> *Note that the cell which is active when you save a file and close it will still be active when the file is re-opened.*

Updating a summary

♦ Open the document whose summary needs updating.

♦ **File**
   Properties
   Summary tab

♦ Fill in the summary information then click **OK.**

♦ Remember to save the file.

Choosing the default file location

This folder will be proposed automatically when you are saving or opening a file.

♦ **Tools**
  Options

♦ Activate the **General** tab.

♦ In the **Default File Location** box, give the path of the folder when you save your documents.

♦ Click **OK**.

Closing documents

One document

♦ **File**   Click ☒ in the   ♦ Ctrl F4 or
  Close   workbook window.   Ctrl W

♦ Save the document, if appropriate.

All open documents

♦ Hold down the ⇧Shift key, as you open the **File** menu.

*The **Close** option is replaced by **Close All**.*

♦ Click **Close All**.

♦ If necessary, save any documents which have been modified (the **Yes to All** option saves all the documents).

Creating new documents

♦ **File**   ▯   ♦ Ctrl N
  New
  OK

*A new workbook, called **Bookn**, appears.*

Protecting documents

You can set a password which will be required each time the file is opened or saved.

♦ **File**
  Save As

♦ If necessary, enter the name of the document and its path.

♦ Click **Options**.

♦ To restrict access to a document, type the password in **Password to open**.
  To prevent unauthorised modification of the document, type the password in the **Password to modify** box.

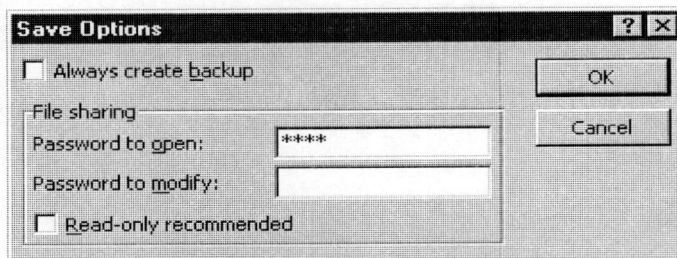

Save Options	? X
☐ Always create backup	OK
File sharing	Cancel
Password to open: ****	
Password to modify:	
☐ Read-only recommended	

Each character of the password is be replaced by an asterisk. Excel registers the difference between capital and lower case letters : be careful which you use.

♦ Click **OK**.

♦ Type the password again, to ensure against error, and enter.

❏ *A password is required as soon as a user tries to open a document. If it is a **Password to modify** that has been set, even a user who cannot give the password can have access to the document by clicking the **Read Only** button ; in this case, if the user attempts to modify the document, Excel refuses to save the modifications.*

❏ *To delete a password, clear the corresponding text box in the **Save Options** dialog box.*

**Establishing
a hyperlink with
another
document**

♦ Select the cell in which you want the link to appear.

♦ **Insert
Hyperlink** ♦ ⌜Ctrl⌝ K

♦ Select the document with which you want to establish the link : it might be a document on one of your computer's disks, or on your network or at an Internet address.

♦ In the **Named location in file** box, you can specify the named range, bookmark, slide number... where you want the insertion point to be when the document opens.

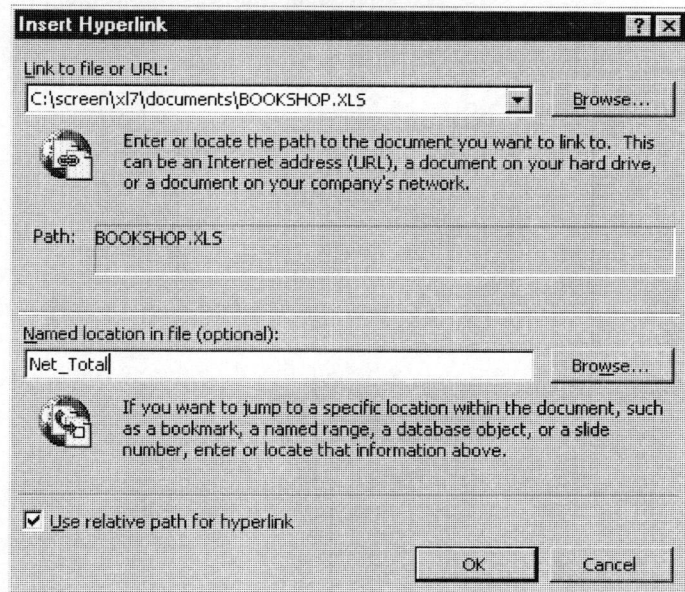

Insert Hyperlink ❓ ✖

Link to file or URL:

C:\screen\xl7\documents\BOOKSHOP.XLS ▾ Browse...

Enter or locate the path to the document you want to link to. This can be an Internet address (URL), a document on your hard drive, or a document on your company's network.

Path: BOOKSHOP.XLS

Named location in file (optional):

Net_Total Browse...

If you want to jump to a specific location within the document, such as a bookmark, a named range, a database object, or a slide number, enter or locate that information above.

☑ Use relative path for hyperlink

OK Cancel

♦ Click **OK** to create the link.

2	January			
3				
4		Quantity	Average Price	
5	Novels	100	12,5	
6	Comic Strips	719	6,2	
7	Anthologies	180	11,0	
8	S.F.	193	8,5	
9	Biographies	104	20,1	
10	Travel		26,5	
11	Total			
12				
13	BOOKSHOP.XLS - Net_Total			

The name of the document appears.

♦ To open the document, just click the hyperlink.

Managing documents

♦ **File Open**

♦ Ctrl O

Using the Favorites folder

*In the **Favorites** folder, you can store shortcuts to the folders and documents which you use most often. The original documents are not moved, but you can access them more quickly.*

♦ Select the documents/folders to be included in **Favorites**, then click .

♦ To add the folder and its contents to **Favorites** select **Add 'documents' to Favorites** or, to add one or more selected documents, choose **Add Selected item to Favorites**.

♦ To use **Favorites**, click then double-click any document to open it.

Finding documents

♦ Activate the drive or folder to search.

♦ To search the subfolders of the current folder or drive, click [image] and activate the option **Search Subfolders**.

♦ Define your search criteria using the four options in the **Find files that match these criteria** frame :

File name	you can use wildcard characters like * and ?.
Files of type	to determine the type of files to look for.
Text or property	to look for a string of characters in the document concerned, or one of its properties.
Last modified	to search for a file by its date.

♦ Click the **Find Now** button.

The result of the search appears in the dialog box.

♦ Click **New search** to clear the search criteria.

. . . . *Personal notes* . . . .

Naming a sheet

The name of a sheet appears on its tab.

♦ Double-click the tab of the sheet you are going to name.

♦ Type the new name over the former one in the **Name** box.

This name can be up to 31 characters long, spaces included. It should not be written inside square brackets nor include the following punctuation marks : colon (:) slash (/) backslash (\) question mark (?) and asterisk (*).

♦ Click **OK**.

Copying/moving a sheet from one workbook to another

♦ Open the book from which you want to copy or move, and also the destination workbook.

♦ Activate the sheet to copy or move.

♦ **Edit**
  Move or Copy Sheet

♦ Open the list entitled **To book** and click the name of the destination workbook.

♦ Indicate the sheet in the destination workbook in front of which you want to insert.

♦ If appropriate, activate **Create a copy**.

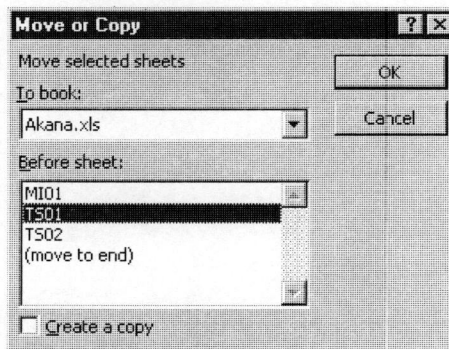

♦ Click **OK**.

❑ *The destination workbook becomes active.*

**Moving
a worksheet**

♦ Click the tab of the sheet to move.

♦ Drag it to its new position.

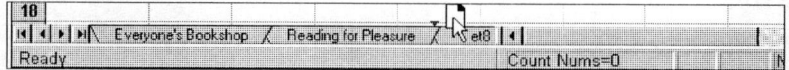

♦ Release the mouse button when you are satisfied with its position.

**Creating
a link between
worksheets**

A sheet can contain a formula referring to cells in another sheet.

♦ Select the destination cells.

♦ Type =.

♦ Select the source cells from the other sheet.

♦ Validate by pressing Ctrl 0 Shift Enter .

*Each cell in column E contains a formula, which displays the
value of the corresponding cell from the "Previous year" sheet.*

Deleting worksheets

♦ Select the worksheets to be deleted. If they are consecutive in the list use the ⬚Shift key to select them ; otherwise use Ctrl.

♦ **Edit**
Delete Sheet

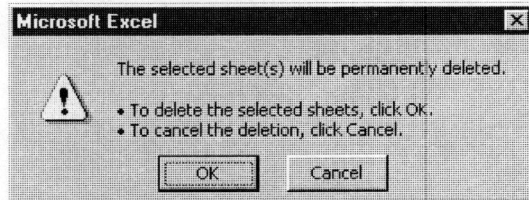

If the Office Assistant is displayed, the request for confirmation appears in a pale yellow balloon.

♦ Click **OK** to confirm.

Protecting worksheets

By protecting the structure of a workbook, you can prevent sheets from being deleted or moved, or new ones from being added...

♦ **Tools**
Protect
Protect Workbook

♦ Check that the **Structure** option is active.

♦ Activate the **Window** option to prevent the workbook window from being moved, resized, hidden or closed.

♦ If you wish, set a password (up to 16 characters long).

♦ Click **OK**.

♦ If you are setting a password, enter it a second time, then click **OK**.

❑ *To remove the protection from the workbook, use the command* ***Tools - Protection - Unprotect Workbook***.

**Using a picture
as background
to a sheet**

♦ **Format
Sheet
Background**

♦ Select the bitmap file which contains the picture to use as the background.

♦ Click **Open**.

The picture is tiled across the sheet's background.

❏ The picture is visible only on the screen and not when the sheet is printed.

❏ To remove the picture, use the command **Format - Sheet - Delete background**.

. . . . Personal notes . . . .

Entering constants (text, values)

♦ Activate the cell where you want the data to appear.

Always check the reference of the active cell on the formula bar.

♦ Type in the data.

A2	▼	✕ ✓ =	31/01/97		
	A	B	C	D	E
1					
2	31/01/97				
3					

As soon as the first character is typed, two buttons appear on the formula bar.

✕   To cancel what you have typed in (equivalent to `Esc`).

✓   To enter what you have typed in (equivalent to `Enter`).

At the same time, the word 'Enter' on the status bar tells you that Excel is in data entry mode.

♦ Activate the next cell that you want to fill in.

Activating a new cell enters what you have typed in the previous cell. As soon as a new cell is activated (with the mouse or direction keys) Excel returns to its Ready mode, and the ✕ and ✓ symbols disappear.
Once entered, text is aligned on the left of the cell while numerical data (or dates) are aligned on the right. Dates are formatted (for example 31/03 becomes 31-Mar).

♦ Type the next set of data.

Until you validate (or cancel) the data you are typing, Excel will not return to Ready mode.

❑ *When entering data keep these observations in mind :*

- *you can type in up 32000 characters in each cell.*
- *with numerical data, be careful to type in the number 0 (zero) and not o (the letter).*
- *negative values can be indicated either by preceding the value with a minus sign (-) or by putting the value between parentheses.*
- *if you enter £10000, Excel will apply the format £10 000 immediately.*
- *type in a % sign after percentages.*

Preventing [Enter] **from activating the next cell**

If this option is deactivated, pressing [Enter] *will not automatically move the pointer to the next cell.*

♦ **Tools**
   Options
   Edit

♦ Deactivate **Move Selection after Enter**.

♦ Click **OK**.

Inserting the PC's date into a cell

♦ Activate the cell where you want to display the date.

♦ There are three ways to insert the computer's control date :

=TODAY()	The control date is updated each time the sheet is opened.
=NOW()	The control date and time are updated when the sheet is opened.
[Ctrl] ;	The control date is not changed automatically.

♦ Enter.

❏ *If the date shown is incorrect, correct the control date of your computer.*

Entering data more quickly

By selecting the range where you are going to enter data, you can work more quickly.

♦ Select the cells that you want to fill in.

♦ When typing in a row of data press ⬚ after each cell to move to the next. When typing in a column of data press ⬚Enter⬚ after each cell.

♦ If you need to return to the previous cell press ⬚⇧ Shift⬚ ⬚ or ⬚⇧ Shift⬚ ⬚Enter⬚ .

❏ *Note : use only these two methods of moving from cell to cell otherwise the selection will be cancelled.*

AutoComplete

AutoComplete enters data semi-automatically.

♦ Type in the first characters.

Excel proposes an existing entry which begins with the same characters (provided that there are no blank cells above the one where you are typing).

♦ If the text proposed is not what you want, type in the correct characters, then press ⬚Enter⬚ or ⬚↓⬚.

♦ To display the list of possible entries, press ⬚Alt⬚⬚↓⬚.

		31-Jan		
1				
2		Total		
3	**Novels**	288		
4	**Comic Strips**	125		
5	**Anthologies**	98		
6	**S.F.**	123		
7	**Biographies**	84		
8	**Travel**	60		
9	**Total**	778		
10	Novels			
11	Anthologies			
12	Biographies			
	Comic Strips			
13	Novels			
14	S.F.			
15	Total			
16	Travel			

*A list of the column's existing entries appears. You can also see this list by right clicking the cell and choosing the option **Pick from List** in the shortcut menu.*

♦ Click the appropriate entry.

❏ *This function only operates if the **Enable AutoComplete for cell values** option is active in the **Options** dialog box (**Tools - Option- Edit** tab).*

Entering the same data in several cells

♦ Select the range of cells concerned.

♦ Enter the formula or text common to all these cells.

If you are entering a formula, enter it as it should appear in the active cell of the selected range.

♦ Validate with Ctrl Enter .

This technique enters and copies the data at once.

ENTERING DATA

Entering several lines of text in the same cell

♦ Activate the cell where you want to type the text.

♦ Enter the text, pressing [Alt] [Enter] when you want to change line.

A1	▾ X ✓ =	Cost
A	B	analysis:
1 Cost		
2 analysis:		

♦ Enter.

❏ *The **Wrap Text** option also uses several lines to display the contents of the cell, but it is Excel which decides where the line breaks occur, to fit the text to the column (cf. the section on wrapping text below).*

Wrapping text

The height of the row is adjusted to accommodate several lines of text. The width of the column is not affected.

♦ Activate the cell where you want to type the text.

♦ **Format**   ♦ [Ctrl] 1
   Cells

♦ If necessary, choose the **Alignment** tab.

♦ Activate **Wrap Text**.

♦ Click **OK**.

**Creating
a data series**

*A data series is a logical progression. An example of a simple data
series :*

4	1st book	Comic Strip	Asterix in Britain
5	2nd book	Comic strip	Tintin in England
6	3rd book	Comic Strip	Father Christmas
7	4th book	Short Stories	Saki
8	5th book	Novels	Jane Eyre
9	6th book	Novels	The Choir
10	7th book	Novels	Hard Times
11	8th book	Novels	Mill on the Floss
12	9th book	Autobiograph	Margaret Thatcher
13	10th book	Autobiograph	Testament of Youth

Simple series

♦ Enter the first value of the series.

♦ Drag the fill handle from the active cell to the cell where you
want to show the last value in the series.

Complex series

♦ Enter the first two values in the series.

♦ Select these two cells.

♦ Drag the fill handle to the cell where you want the last value in
the series to appear.

	January	March	May	July		
PdtA	125 000	135020	124500	128000		
PtdB	132 000	128900	130240	131000		
PtdC	140 000	141200	140790	139800		
Total	397 000	405120	395530	398800		

January and March were selected to create this series.

**Creating
a custom
data series**

♦ **Tools
Options**

♦ Activate the **Custom Lists** tab.

♦ Click **New list** in the **Custom Lists** box, even if this choice has already been selected.

*The insertion point appears in the **List Entries** box.*

♦ Enter the data in the **List Entries** box, pressing ⟦⇧ Shift⟧ ⟦Enter⟧ to separate each entry. For example :

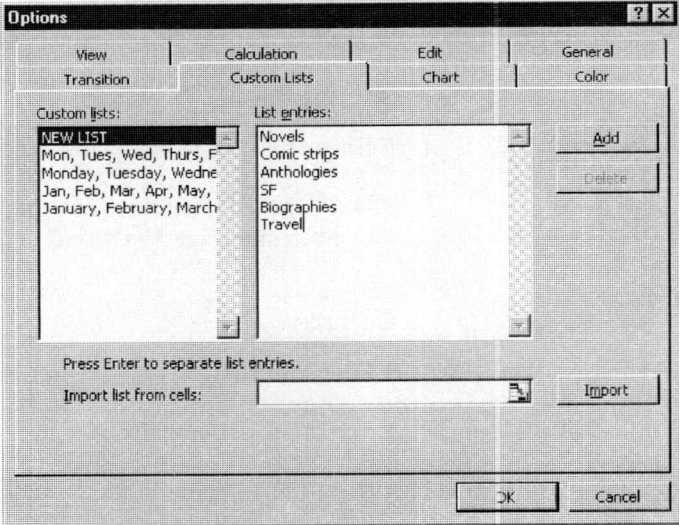

♦ Click the **Add** button.

*The new series appears under **Custom lists**. Each entry is separated from the previous one by a comma.*

♦ Click **OK** to confirm.

Attaching comments to cells

A comment is a means of explaining or expanding on the value in a cell.

Creating a comment

♦ Activate the cell with which you want to associate a comment.

♦ **Insert Comment**   ♦ ⌷Shift⌷ ⌷F2⌷

♦ Enter the text in the **Comment** box.

Use ⌷Enter⌷ *to change lines.*

♦ Press ⌷Esc⌷ or click outside the box.

*A red triangle marks the top right corner of a cell with a comment. This indicator is only visible when the **Note Indicator** option on the **View** tab of the **Tools - Options** menu is activated.*

Displaying a comment

♦ Point the cell with the red triangle.

❏ *If the triangle is not visible, use the buttons from the **Revision** bar :*

                  To scroll through the comments concerning the current worksheet.

                  To show/hide all the comments.

❏ *To edit a comment, select the corresponding cell, then click* .

To delete a comment, select the cell concerned, then click .

Modifying cell contents

♦ Double-click the cell concerned :

	H	I	J	K	L	M
					L1 ▼ ✕ ƒx Global analysses	
1					Global analysses	
2						
3						

An insertion point (flashing vertical bar) appears in the cell and ***Edit*** *is displayed on the status bar.*

♦ Make any necessary changes.

When ***Insert*** *mode is active, the new characters are added to the existing ones. In* ***Overtype*** *mode, the new characters replace the existing ones.*

♦ Press Ins to change from **Insert** to **Overtype** and vice versa.

♦ When you have finished, enter.

❏ *You can also click the cell then edit its contents directly in the formula bar.*

Clearing cell contents

♦ Select the cells to be cleared.

♦ Drag the fill handle backwards over the selected cells to clear their contents.

As you are dragging the cells appear dim, then their contents disappear.

❏ *This technique deletes the contents of the cells without affecting their format.*

Choosing the type of data to clear

♦ Select the cells concerned.

♦ **Edit**
Clear

♦ Choose to delete **Formats, Contents, Notes** or **All** at the same time.

Replacing the contents of cells

In a selected range of cells, you can replace a text which appears in several cells with another one.

♦ Select the cells concerned.

♦ **Edit**   ♦ Ctrl H
Replace

♦ In the **Find What** box, enter the text you wish to replace.

*You can enter letters, numbers, punctuation marks or wildcard characters : ? replaces one character ; * replaces several.*
*Activate **Match Case** to distinguish between capital and lower case characters.*

♦ Press ⇄ and enter the new text in the **Replace with** box.

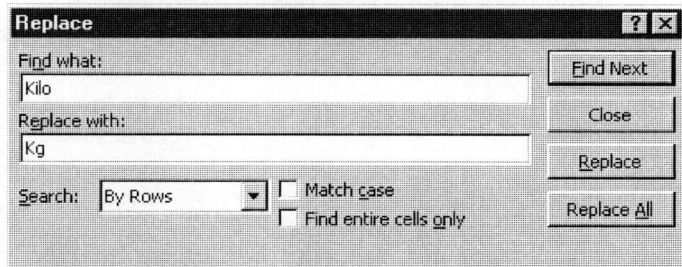

♦ The replacements can be made individually using the **Find Next** and **Replace** buttons, or all at once using **Replace All**.

Sorting data in a table

Simple sorting

♦ Select the table you want to short.

♦ Using ⇄ or ⇧Shift ⇄ activate a cell in the column you want to sort by.

♦ Use :

⤵️A↓Z   to sort in ascending order

⤵️Z↓A   to sort in descending order.

> *Holding the ⇧Shift key down as you click [A↓Z] has the same result as clicking the [Z↓A] button.*

Sorting by several criteria

♦ Select the table to be sorted.

♦ **Data**
  Sort

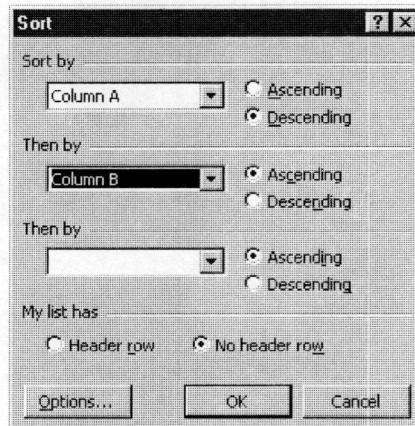

You can sort by up to three columns.

♦ Indicate the columns by which you want to sort.

♦ In a database, select the names of the corresponding fields.

♦ For each column, specify whether to sort in **Ascending** or **Descending** order.

♦ To exclude the first row of the table from sorting, activate **Header Row**.

♦ Click **OK**.

Working on several sheets at once

When sheets are grouped together in a workgroup, anything you do to one of the sheets will be done in all the other sheets of the group.

♦ Select all the sheets concerned by holding down the [Ctrl] key (or the [⇧ Shift] key if they are adjacent) and clicking their tabs. This creates a workgroup.

The tabs of the selected sheets change colour and the word **Group** *appears on the title bar.*

♦ Do the typing, formatting... which will be applied to all the sheets in the group.

♦ To ungroup the sheets, click a tab which is not part of the group.

Checking the spelling in a text

♦ To check the whole worksheet, activate any cell. To check part of the text, select it.

♦ **Tools**
Spelling

♦ [F⁻]

Excel reads the text, stopping at each unrecognised word. This may be :

– one which is absent from Excel's dictionary,

– one which contains an unusual combination of lower case and capital letters,

– one which is typed twice (for example : we know that that is true).

*If the **Always Suggest** option is active, Excel proposes a list of possible corrections.*
Spelling is checked against Excel's main dictionary, and against as many personal dictionaries as you wish (by default, the only existing one is PERSO.DIC).

♦ If the word is correctly spelt, click :

Ignore   to leave the word unchanged and continue the check.

Ignore All   to leave a particular word unchanged each time it occurs in the text.

Add   to add the word to the current dictionary.

♦ If the word contains a mistake, correct it by a double-click on one of the suggestions or enter the correct spelling in the **Change to** box, then click :

Change to replace the incorrect word with the correct one.

Change All to replace the incorrect word with the correct one each time it occurs.

♦ For a word which appears, wrongly, twice in a row, click :

Delete to delete the repeated word.

♦ At the end of the spelling check a dialog box appears.

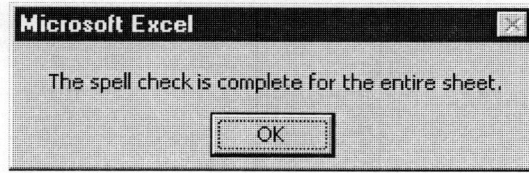

♦ Click **OK**.

❏ *To create a custom dictionary, select the name of the current dictionary in the **Spelling** dialog box, type in the name of the new dictionary, then enter.*

NAMED RANGES

Naming cells   *A range of cells can be refered to by a name.*

First method

♦ Select the range of cells which you want to name.

♦ **Insert**   ♦ Ctrl F3
  Name
  Define

  Excel proposes to take the contents of the top left cell as the name of the range.

♦ If you prefer, enter a different name.

There must be no spaces or hyphens in these names! You can use the ⬚ *button to minimise the dialog box, making it easier to change the selection.*

♦ Click **Add**.

♦ Name any other ranges in the same way.

Second method

This method is useful if the names that you want to apply to the cells are adjacent to them in the worksheet.

♦ Select the cells containing the names to be used <u>and</u> the cells you want to name.

♦ **Insert**   ♦ [Ctrl] [⇧ Shift] [F3]
  Name
  Create

Create Names   [?] [X]

Create names in
☑ Top row
☐ Left column
☐ Bottom row
☐ Right column

[OK]
[Cancel]

♦ Indicate the position of the cells containing the names.

♦ Click **OK**.

❏ *Excel converts any spaces and hyphens into the underscore character (_).*

Deleting names   ♦ Go into the **Define Name** dialog box.

♦ Select the name to be deleted.

♦ Click the **Delete** button.

♦ Click **OK**.

NAMED RANGES

Naming a calculation formula

◆ Go into the **Define Name** dialog box.

◆ Enter the name of the formula in the **Names in Workbook** box.

◆ Enter the formula in the **Refers to** box, remembering to start with the sign =.

◆ Enter.

❏ *To use a named formula, type = followed by the name of the formula, and enter.*

Using a name in a formula

Entering a name

◆ Enter the name instead of the cell references.

Pasting a name

◆ Start entering the formula then stop where the name is required.

◆ **Insert**   ◆ F3
   Name
   Paste

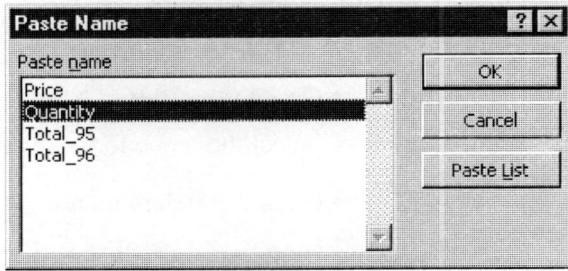

Paste Name	? ✕
Paste name	OK
Price	Cancel
Quantity	
Total_95	Paste List
Total_96	

The dialog box lists all the existing names.

◆ Double-click the name of the range you want.

◆ Complete the formula.

**Replacing
cell references
with their name**

*In a formula, references to named ranges can be replaced by the
corresponding names.*

♦ Select the cells containing the formulas you want to modify.

♦ **Insert
Name
Apply**

♦ Click all the names concerned. If you select a name by mistake,
click it again to deselect it.

♦ Click **OK**.

. . . . *Personal notes* . . . .

Copying data into adjacent cells

♦ Activate the cell you want to copy.

♦ Point to its fill handle.

7 626FF	48 626FF
10 142FF	64 670FF
11 151FF	
8 522FF	
12 786FF	
9 069FF	
59 296FF	

The fill handle is the small dark square in the right-hand corner of the cell. Notice the change in the mouse pointer's shape.

♦ Drag the fill handle to the last destination cell.

The cells over which you drag are enclosed inside a hatched border.

♦ When you reach the last cell, release the mouse button.

Copying and moving cells

These methods are intended for moving data or copying into no-nadjacent cells.

First method

This method is useful when the source cells and the destination cells are visible on the screen at the same time.

♦ Select the source cells.

♦ Point to the edge of the selected range.

	Quar	Av;Price	Total	Quar	Av. P
Novels	100	£12.50		88	
Comic Strips	719	£3.20		531	
Short Stories	180	£11		170	
Sci-Fi	193	£8.50		184	
Autobiographies	104	£20		98	
Travel	60	£26.50		64	
Total					

The mouse pointer takes the form of an arrow. Be careful not to point to the fill handle.

♦ If you are copying, press the Ctrl key and, without releasing it, drag the cells to their destination.

If the cells are being moved, just drag the cells to their new position.

When you are copying, a plus sign appears to the right of the mouse pointer.

♦ Release first the mouse button, then the Ctrl key, if you have been using it.

Second method

♦ Select the source cells.

♦ If you are copying the cells, use :

Edit
Copy   [icon]   ♦ Ctrl C

♦ If you are moving the cells, use :

Edit
Cut   [icon]   ♦ Ctrl X

The selected cells are surrounded by a flashing border.

♦ Activate the first cell of the destination range.

Even when several cells are being copied or moved you should only activate one destination cell.

♦ **Edit**
Paste

♦ Ctrl V

Reproducing a format

All the elements of formatting applied to one range of cells can be copied simultaneously onto another.

♦ Select the cells whose formats you want to copy.

♦ Click .

♦ Select the cells to which you want to apply the format.

Copying formats or the results of calculations

♦ Select the cells containing the results or formats you want to copy.

♦ Go into **Edit - Copy**.

♦ Activate the first cell of the destination.

♦ **Edit**
Paste Special

♦ To copy results only, choose the **Values** option.
To copy formats only, choose the **Formats** option.

♦ Click **OK**.

**Carrying out
simple
calculations
while copying**

*While you are copying data, you can carry out a mathematical
operation (adding, subtracting...) which combines the data being
copied with the destination data.*

♦ Select the data you wish to copy and go into **Edit - Copy**.

♦ Activate the first destination cell (for this type of operation, a
destination cell must contain data).

♦ **Edit
Paste Special**

♦ In **Paste**, indicate what it is that you want to copy.

♦ Under **Operation**, select the mathematical operation to be used.

♦ Click **OK**.

❑ *If there are empty cells included in the selection which should be
left out of the calculation, activate **Skip blanks** before entering.*

Transposing rows and columns while copying

It is possible to change the rows of a table into columns, and vice versa, while the table is being copied.

♦ Select the data to be copied, go into **Edit - Copy** then activate the first destination cell.

♦ **Edit**
Paste Special

♦ In **Paste**, activate the option corresponding to what you are copying.

♦ Choose **Transpose**.

♦ Click **OK**.

The rows selected become columns and the columns become rows.

Creating a link between cells while copying

♦ Select the data to copy.

♦ Go into **Edit - Copy**.

♦ Activate the first destination cell.

♦ **Edit**
Paste Special
Paste Link

This pastes into the destination cells a formula which displays the contents of each source cell.
If you change a value in one of the source cells the content of the corresponding destination cell is updated automatically.

❑ When you use this technique to create a link, the text copied loses its formatting.
If you copy, paste and link an empty cell, Excel displays a zero value.

**Entering
a calculation
formula**

♦ Activate the cell which will display the result.

♦ Type =.

*The word **Enter** appears on the status bar.*

♦ Activate the first cell involved in the calculation.

*This cell is shown with a flashing border and its reference appears in the formula bar. The status bar now says **Point**.*

♦ Type in the mathematical operation to be carried out :

+	for addition
-	for subtraction
/	for division
*	for multiplication
%	for percentage
^	for exponentiation.

♦ Repeat for each of the cells involved in the calculation.

You can follow the development of the formula on the formula bar.

♦ When you reach the last cell, enter.

The result of the calculation appears in the active cell but the cell's true content is the formula, which is displayed in the formula bar.

❑ *Calculation formulas can contain up to 1024 characters.*

If you know the cell references you can type them in rather than using the mouse or arrow keys to activate them.

CALCULATIONS

With the mouse, you can use the formula palette to enter a formula.

♦ Activate the cell in which you want to display the result.

♦ Click the = button on the formula bar.

The formula palette is made up of the formula bar and the grey area containing the OK button and the Cancel button.

♦ Click the first cell to use in the formula.

♦ Enter the mathematical operator you require.

♦ Insert each of the cells that you need in the formula, separating them with the appropriate operators.

♦ The result of the formula appears in the formula palette.

♦ Click the formula palette's **OK** button.

❏ *Using the formula palette makes it easier to insert a function into a calculation formula (cf. the chapter FUNCTIONS).*

❏ *When you are editing a calculation formula, the names of the cells involved are displayed in different colours on the formula bar. In the worksheet, each cell or range of cells involved in the formula has a border of the corresponding colour.*

Adding up a group of cells

♦ Activate the cell which is going to display the result.

♦ Click [Σ] or press [Alt] =.

Excel displays the SUM() function and guesses which cells you want to add up.

♦ If you are not satisfied with this selection, change it.

♦ Enter.

Displaying the results of a calculation

The result of a calculation carried out on selected cells can be displayed on the status bar.

♦ Select the cells involved in the calculation.

♦ By default, the indicator on the status bar says **Sum**. Click the status bar with the <u>right</u> mouse button.

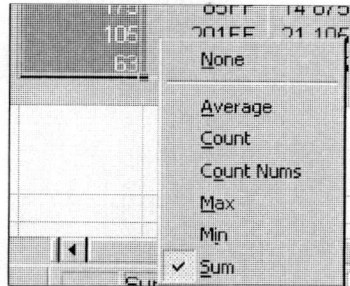

Six functions are proposed.

♦ Click the appropriate function :

Average   to display the average value of the selected cells.

Count Nums to display the number of alphanumerical or numerical values in the cell selection.

Count   to display the number of numerical values in the selection.

Max   to display the greatest value in the selection.

Min   to display the smallest value in the selection.

Sum   to display the total of the values in the cells.

The result appears on the status bar.

CALCULATIONS

**Including
an absolute cell
reference
in a formula**

*Making a cell reference absolute ensures that it does not evolve
when the formula is copied.*

*In the following example the formula in cell E5 is being copied
into cells E6 to E11. When the formula is copied into cell E6, it is
automatically adjusted to D6*D14. This is not what is required :
D14 is empty. To produce the correct result, the formula must read
D6*D13. The reference D13 must be made absolute before the formula is copied :*

	SUM	▾	X √ =	=D5*D13		
	A	B	C	D	E	F
3						
4		Quantity	Average Price	Cost Price	VAT	
5	Novels	£100,00	£12,50	£1 250,00	=D5*D13	
6	Comic Strips	£719,00	£6,20	£4 457,80		
7	Anthologies	£180,00	£11,00	£1 980,00		
8	S.F.	£193,00	£8,50	£1 640,50		
9	Biographies	£104,00	£20,10	£2 090,40		
10	Travel	£82,00	£26,50	£2 173,00		
11	Total			£13 591,70		
12						
13			VAT RATE	17,50%		
14						

♦ Start entering the formula, stopping after the cell reference that
you want to make absolute. If you are editing an existing formula, position the insertion point after the cell reference.

♦ Press F4 .

*The cell reference now contains $ signs before the column letter
and before the row number.*

	A	B	C	D	E	
3						
4		Quantity	Average Price	Cost Price	VAT	
5	Novels	£100,00	£12,50	£1 250,00	=D5*$D$13	
6	Comic Strips	£719,00	£6,20	£4 457,80		
7	Anthologies	£180,00	£11,00	£1 980,00		
8	S.F.	£193,00	£8,50	£1 640,50		
9	Biographies	£104,00	£20,10	£2 090,40		
10	Travel	£82,00	£26,50	£2 173,00		
11	Total			£13 591,70		

♦ Complete the formula if necessary, then enter.

> *When you press* F4 *the cell reference becomes absolute, but press* F4 *a second time and only the row reference remains absolute. Press* F4 *a third time and only the column reference is absolute.*

Adding statistics to a table

By inserting automatic subtotals, you can obtain rows of statistics. This is an easy way to summarise the information in a table.

♦ Sort the table by the column containing the entries you want to group together, as a first step to producing a subtotal for each group.

♦ Select the table.

♦ **Data**
Subtotals

♦ In the **At Each Change in** list, select the column used for grouping.

♦ Next choose the type of statistic you require from the **Use Function** list.

♦ Finally mark the columns containing the values involved in the calculation.

CALCULATIONS

♦ Click **OK**.

Excel calculates subtotals which provide the statistics required, and creates an outline.

Microsoft Excel 9?

Consolidating worksheets

This enables you to carry out an analysis (for example, a sum) of values contained in several tables, possibly on different sheets.

♦ Activate the first cell of the range where you want to display the results.

♦ **Data**
Consolidate

♦ From the **Function** list, choose the calculation you want to perform.

♦ Go into the **Reference** box.

♦ For each sheet to be consolidated :

– Click the button to minimise the dialog box. Activate the worksheet and select the cells concerned.

– click the button to restore the dialog box.

– click the **Add** button.

♦ If you have included data labels in your selection, indicate where they are located by checking one of the boxes under **Use Labels In**.

♦ If you wish to create a permanent link between the source sheets and the destination sheet, activate the **Create Links to Source Data** check box.

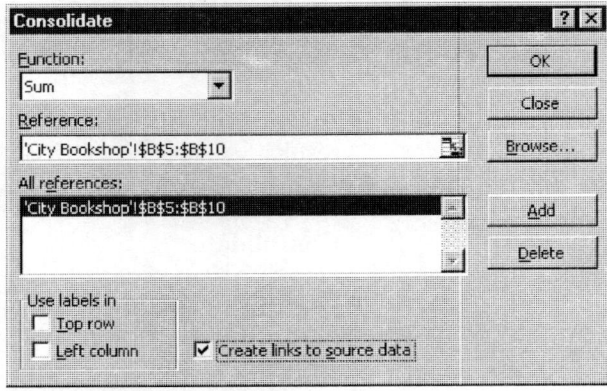

♦ Click **OK**.

After a few seconds the results of the consolidation appear. If you choose to create a link, Excel produces an outline of the table.

Changing the calculation mode

By default, Excel recalculates each time you enter or modify a formula. If this is taking too long, you can deactivate automatic calculation.

♦ **Tools**
Options
Calculation tab

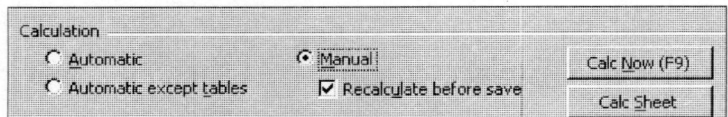

♦ Choose one of the options from the **Calculation** frame : **Automatic, Automatic except tables, Manual.**

♦ Click **OK**.

*If the calculation mode is **Manual**, use the **Calc Now** button in **Tools** - **Options**, **Calculation** tab, or press F9 to calculate.*

**Creating
a two-input table**

The table below shows how the amount paid back monthly on a loan varies according to the number of instalments and the sum borrowed. The interest rate is fixed at 11%. The whole table is based on the formula in cell A5.

♦ In cells located outside the table, enter initial input values for the calculation. Example : Number of instalments = 12, Sum borrowed = £ 10 000.

♦ Enter the variable data, one series in a row, and the other series in a column.

The row should be placed one row above the first variable in a column, and one column further to the right.

♦ At the intersection of the row and the column enter the calculation formula, referring to the input cells outside the table.

♦ Select the range of cells including the formula and all the result cells.

CALCULATIONS

♦ **Data**
  Table

♦ In the **Row input cell** box indicate which of the two input cells referred to in the formula corresponds to the variable data in the row.

♦ In the **Column input cell** box, indicate which input cell referred to in the formula corresponds to the column data.

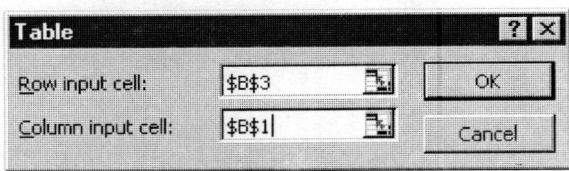

Table	? X
Row input cell: $B$3	OK
Column input cell: $B$1	Cancel

♦ Enter.

Calculating with array formulas

Using an array formula instead of several formulas takes up less memory. Certain functions can only be applied to arrays.

♦ Proceed as for an ordinary calculation but work with cell ranges instead of individual cells and enter with Ctrl ⇧Shift Enter , not Enter or Ctrl Enter .

	B12	▼	= {=(B2:D5-$E2:$E5)/$E2:$E5}				
	A	**B**	**C**	**D**	**E**	**F**	**G**	**H**
1		BRISTOL	BATH	TAUNTON	Average			
2	Accountant	99.75	98.5	98.6	98.95			
3	Secretary	72	73.55	71.9	72.48			
4	Shop Manager	92	94.8	93.83	93.54			
5	Truck-driver	70.35	73.32	69.8	71.16			
6								
7								
8	% difference in relation to the regional average							
9								
10								
11		BRISTOL	BATH	TAUNTON				
12	Accountant	0.81%	-0.45%	-0.35%				
13	Secretary	-0.67%	1.47%	-0.80%				
14	Shop Manager	-1.65%	1.34%	0.31%				
15	Truck-driver	-1.13%	3.04%	-1.91%				
16								
17								

You can recognise an array formula by the braces surrounding it.

Equations containing unknown quantities

Example of a problem : find the quantity of production factors x, y and z required to produce three products in quantities q1, q2 and q3.

Setting out the problem

♦ Enter in the form of an array all the elements of the linear analysis as well as the results you are aiming for.

```
PROBLEM 1 :    Making a calculation involving several unknown quantities


The data

Three types of products (1 2 3)              Linear          2x + 5y + z = q1
Three production factors (x y z)            analysis         x + 2y + 3z = q2
                                                             4x + y + 6z =q3


                                             Aim :           q1 = 36
                                                             q2 = 33
                                                             q3 = 55

State the problem :

               2          5         1              36
               1          2         3              33
               4          1         6              55
```

Calculating the inverse matrix of an array

♦ Select the cells on your worksheet which will contain the array of the inverse matrix.

The new array will be the same size as the one entered as an argument.

♦ Use the =MINVERSE(array) function.

The inverse matrix can only be calculated if the original array is square (if it has an identical number of rows and columns).

♦ Validate with `Ctrl` `⇧ Shift` `Enter` .

Calculating the product of two arrays

♦ Select the destination cells for the result.

♦ Use the function =MMULT(array1, array2)
where <u>array1</u> contains as many columns as <u>array2</u> has rows.

♦ Enter with `Ctrl` `⇧ Shift` `Enter` .

Creation an inverse matrix

0.219512195	-0.70731707	0.3170732
0.146341463	0.19512195	-0.121951
-0.170731707	0.43902439	-0.02439

Number of units for each production factor

2
5
7

In this example, to produce 36 of product 1, 33 of product 2, and 55 of product 3, you will need 2 units of factor x, 5 of factor y and 7 of factor z.

Setting a goal value

This is a technique for working out the value that a given cell must contain if the result of a calculation is to correspond to a goal value.

♦ Activate the cell you wish to set to a certain value and ensure that it contains a calculation formula.

♦ If possible, show the cell containing the variable value in the same screen.

♦ **Tools**
Goal Seek

♦ Set the goal value in the **To value** box and indicate which is the variable cell in **By changing cell**.

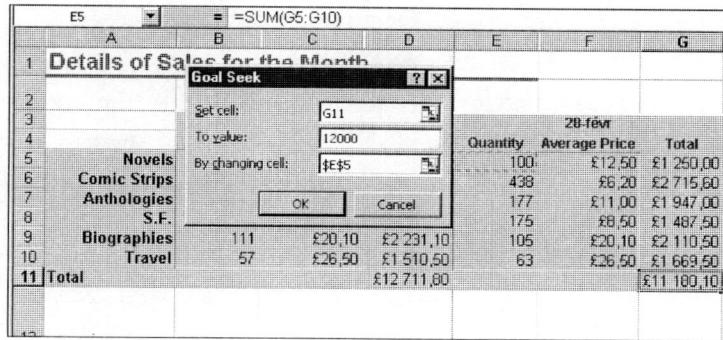

E5		=	=SUM(G5:G10)			
	A	B	C	D	E	F	G

Details of Sales for the Month

Goal Seek

Set cell: G11
To value: 12000
By changing cell: $E$5

OK   Cancel

					Quantity	Average Price	Total
5	Novels				100	£12,50	£1 250,00
6	Comic Strips				438	£6,20	£2 715,60
7	Anthologies				177	£11,00	£1 947,00
8	S.F.				175	£8,50	£1 487,50
9	Biographies	111	£20,10	£2 231,10	105	£20,10	£2 110,50
10	Travel	57	£26,50	£1 510,50	63	£26,50	£1 669,50
11	Total			£12 711,80			£11 180,10

♦ Enter.

As soon as Excel finds a solution, it displays its results on the worksheet.

♦ To accept the result suggested by Excel, click **OK**. The new values are incorporated into the sheet. To return to the original values, click **Cancel**.

Solving problems with Solver

♦ If necessary, install the **Solver** add-in (see the chapter on Macros).

*The **Solver** option is available in the **Tools** menu.*

Entering the basic data

♦ **Tools**
Solver

♦ Enter the reference of the cell for which you are setting a target, in **Set Target Cell**.

♦ In **Equal To** indicate whether the cell is to be maximised (**Max**), minimised (**Min**) or set to a specific **Value**.

♦ Next specify the cells containing the values to vary in the **By Changing Cells** box.

Managing constraints

♦ Enter the constraints one at a time : click **Add**, activate the cell concerned and specify the constraint. When you have finished, click **OK**.

These constraints can be changed or deleted by selecting them in the list then clicking the appropriate button.

Starting the solving process

♦ Click the **Solve** button.

After various messages on the status bar, Excel tells you that a solution has been found, and displays it on the worksheet.

♦ Click **Save Scenario** to save the solution found by Solver. Give the scenario a name then click **OK**.

♦ If the result is satisfactory, keep the solution by clicking **Keep Solver Solution**, otherwise choose the **Restore Original Values** option.

♦ Click **OK**.

❑ *To remove all the elements of a problem go into the **Solver Parameters** dialog box, then click **Reset All** and **OK** to confirm.*

❑ *Once a scenario has been created, it can be used in the same way as those created by the **Scenario Manager**.*

Saving/loading problem parameters

Saving a Solver model

♦ On the sheet, activate the top left cell in the range reserved for the model.

♦ **Tools**
Solver

♦ Set out the problem you want to save.

♦ **Options**
Save Model
OK

❏ *A model is a collection of logical values.*

Loading a model

♦ **Tools**
Solver

♦ **Options**
Load Model

♦ Select the range reserved for the model and click **OK**.

♦ Confirm the request to use the model with **OK**, then use **OK** again to close the options window.

In this way all the elements of the problem are retrieved.

Making scenarios   *A scenario enables you to solve a problem by considering several hypotheses.*

Creating scenarios

♦ **Tools**
  Scenarios

♦ For each scenario to create :

 – Click **Add**.

 – Enter the **Scenario Name**.

 – Delete whatever appears in the **Changing Cells** box and hold down <kbd>Ctrl</kbd> while selecting from the sheet the cells with the values to vary in this scenario.

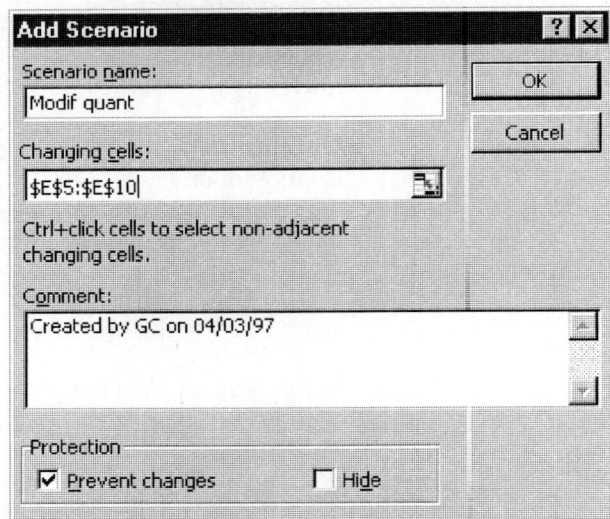

Add Scenario	? X
Scenario name:	OK
Modif quant	Cancel
Changing cells:	
$E$5:$E$10	
Ctrl+click cells to select non-adjacent changing cells.	
Comment:	
Created by GC on 04/03/97	
Protection	
☑ Prevent changes ☐ Hide	

 – Click **OK**.

 – Then enter the values for each changing cell and click **OK**.

Using a scenario

♦ If you only want to run one scenario select it then click **Show**. The result replaces the current values on your worksheet (this is why it is a good idea to start by creating a scenario containing the current values). If you want a summary report of all the scenarios, click **Summary**.

♦ If necessary, select the cells which interest you.

♦ Enter.

The summary is presented as an outline on a separate worksheet.

❏ *Scenarios and views can be associated in a report.*

FUNCTIONS

**Inserting
a function
into a formula**

Excel 97's formula palette makes this much easier.

♦ As you are entering the formula, select the function from the first list in the formula palette. If the function you need does not appear in the list, use **More functions**.

♦ To define each of the function's arguments :

  – Click the appropriate text box then click the ▦ button.

  – Select the cells relevent to the argument from the worksheet.

  – Click ▦ to restore the dialog box.

♦ If necessary, finish the formula, then click **OK**.

❑ *Pressing* ⌴Shift⌴ F3 *opens the **Paste function** dialog box, where you can select a function from one of several categories.*

Calculating simple statistics

♦ Use one of the following common functions :

=**AVERAGE**()   to calculate the average value of a set of cells.

=**MAX**()   to extract the maximum value.

=**MIN**()   to extract the minimum value.

The cells concerned should appear between parentheses in the function.

Setting a condition

♦ Activate the cell where you want to display the result.

♦ Enter your condition, taking care to follow the syntax :
=**IF(condition,action if TRUE,action if FALSE)**

M4	▼	= =IF(L4>=120;"Pass";"")				
	A	B	H	I	J	K
1		Results announced:				
2						
3		Department Employee	Subtotal	Professional Project	Interview	Subtotal O
4	Accounts	Barton H.	55	24	56	80
5	Accounts	Morris V.	37	26	54	80
6	Production	Hajira A.	54	32	48	80
7	Production	Braganza J.	53	34	46	80
8	Sales	Dunn D.	26	32	51	83
9		Average				
10						

If the value in cell L4 is greater than or equal to 120, the text "Pass" appears in that cell ; if it is less, no text appears.

FUNCTIONS

❏ *A variety of actions can be performed in a conditional expression:*

Display a number	enter the number,
Display a text	enter the text between quotation marks,
Display the result of a calculation	enter the calculation formula,
Display the contents of a cell	point to the cell,
Display a zero	enter nothing,
No display	type "".

❏ *For conditions, several operators are available :*

>	greater than
<	less than
<>	different from
>=	greater than or equal to
<=	less than or equal to.

❏ *You can set multiple conditions, linking them with the operators AND and/or OR :*

=IF(AND(cond1,cond2, ... ,condn),action to be carried out if all the conditions are satisfied,action to be carried out if any condition is not satisfied)

=IF(OR(cond1,cond2, ...,condn),action to be carried out if at least one condition is satisfied, action to be carried out if no condition is satisfied)

Calculating with dates

♦ If you are calculating in days, proceed as for other calculations, since any date entered is treated as a number of days.

♦ To add a number of months to a start date, use the following syntax :
=DATE(YEAR(start_date),MONTH(start_date)+
period_in_months, DAY(start_date))

♦ To add a number of years, use
=DATE(YEAR(start_date)+period_in_years,
MONTH(start_date),DAY(start_date))
For example to calculate the date two months from now, use:
=DATE(YEAR(NOW()),MONTH(NOW())+2,DAY(NOW()))

❑ *If the results of your calculations are four years ahead of what they ought to be, deactivate the 1904 Date System (**Tools - Options - Calculation** tab).*

Managing lookup tables

Constructing a table

♦ A lookup table is made up of a row (or column) containing a list of "compare values", and other rows (or columns), which list associated information.

♦ The table should be sorted in ascending order of the compare values.

Searching for values in the table

♦ In the cell where the information is to be displayed, use the following function :
LOOKUP(**lookup_value,lookup_vector,result_vector**)

lookup_value   is the compare value, a value which can be entered in a cell or directly into the formula.

lookup_vector   is the search range for the compare value

result_vector

is the search range for the corresponding data.

Item Code	Category	Title	Author	Price
Cl011	Classics	The Woman...	Collins W.	£ 4.50
Cl108	Classics	Confessions...	De Quincey T.	£ 4.99
Cl401	Classics	Persuasion	Austin J.	£ 4.50
Co150	Contemporary	London Fields	Amis M.	£ 6.79
Co203	Contemporary	Brownout	MO T.	£ 6.79
Hi300	History	Richelieu	Fraser A.	£ 3.99

Sheet1 / Sheet2 / Sheet3 / Sheet4 / Sheet5 / Sheet6

H13 `=IF(G13<>"",LOOKUP(G13,Item_Code,Title&" "&Author),"")`

	E	F	G	H	I
11					
12			Item Code	Category and Title	Price
13			Cl108	Confessions... De Quincey T.	4.99
14			Co150	London Fields Amis M.	6.79
15			Co203	Brownout MO T.	6.79
16			Hi300	Richelieu Fraser A.	3.99
17					
18					

In the example, when the code of a book is entered, the function returns its title and author.

. . . . *Personal notes* . . . .

Inserting rows and columns

♦ Select the row/column before the position where you are going to insert the new row(s)/column(s).

♦ Point to the fill handle.

Check that the mouse pointer has taken the shape of a cross : do not start until it has.

♦ Hold down the ⇧Shift key as you drag the fill handle over as many rows/columns as you wish to insert.

When inserting rows drag downwards, not upwards ; for columns drag to the right, not the left.

♦ Release the mouse button first, then the ⇧Shift key.

While you are dragging, the position where the new columns are going to appear is outlined in grey.

❑ With this method, it is impossible to insert new rows above line 1, or columns before column A.

♦ Select the row or column <u>after</u> the position where you are going to insert.

♦ **Insert**
  Rows or **Columns**

Deleting rows and columns

♦ Select the rows (or columns) to be deleted.

♦ Point to the fill handle (the mouse pointer should change to a cross hair).

♦ Hold down the ⇧Shift key as you drag upwards for rows (to the left for columns) over the rows (or columns) to be deleted.

As the fill handle is moved across the sheet, the selection changes colour.

♦ Release the mouse button, then the ⇧Shift key.

ROWS, COLUMNS, CELLS

**Modifying
the width of
a column/height
of a row**

♦ Select each column to be resized to the same width (or each row to be given the same new height) ; if only one column or row is concerned, do not select it.

♦ Point to the vertical line on the right of one of the selected columns (or to the horizontal line under the row number) :

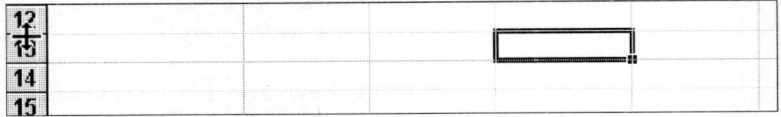

Notice the new appearance of the mouse pointer.

♦ Drag to the size required.

The new width (or height) is represented by a bar on the sheet and displayed in a Screen Tip.

❏ The width of a column is expressed as a number of characters, the height of a row as a number of points.

To save memory, use this method to create space in your sheets rather than inserting more rows and columns.

**Adjusting
the width of
a column/height
of a row**

You can adjust column widths to fit the longest value in the column, and row heights to the tallest value in the row.

♦ For column width, double-click the vertical line to the right of the column letter.
For row height, double-click the horizontal line below the row number.

Inserting blank cells

Cells are inserted below the active cell or to its right.

♦ Select the cell before the position where you are going to insert the new cell(s).

♦ Hold down the ⬜ Shift key and drag the fill handle downwards (or to the right) over as many cells as you wish to insert.

♦ Select as many cells as you wish to insert.

♦ **Insert Cells**

♦ Activate either the first or the second option to indicate what you want to do with the cells already in place.

♦ Click **OK**.

Moving cells then inserting them

This action moves cells and inserts them elsewhere in the sheet : existing cells slide backwards.

♦ Select the cells to be moved.

♦ Point one edge of the selected range.

♦ Holding the ⬜ Shift key down, drag the cells into position.

Deleting cells

♦ Select the cells to be deleted.

♦ Drag the fill handle upwards while keeping the ⬜ Shift key pressed down.

❑ *The gap left by the deleted cells is filled by moving up the cells below. If you prefer to move the cells from right to left, use **Edit - Delete**.*

Limiting the cells where data can be entered

To authorise writing in certain cells only, you should first unlock these cells, then apply protection by password to the whole sheet.

Unlocking selected cells

♦ Select the cells where writing is allowed.

♦ **Format**   ♦ [Ctrl]**1**
  Cells

♦ Deactivate **Locked** under the **Protection** tab.

♦ Enter.

Protecting the sheet

♦ **Tools**
  Protection
  Protect Sheet

♦ Deactivate the first options if the items that they refer to do not need protection.

♦ Enter a password if required, otherwise press [Enter].

The password can be up to 16 characters long. Take care : Excel distinguishes between capital and lower-case letters. These letters never appear on the screen.

♦ Enter the password a second time to confirm.

If you attempt to enter data into a locked cell, the following warning message will appear :

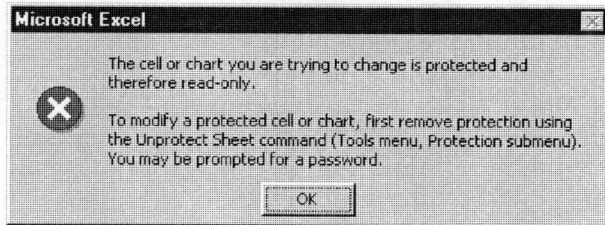

> **Microsoft Excel**
>
> The cell or chart you are trying to change is protected and therefore read-only.
>
> To modify a protected cell or chart, first remove protection using the Unprotect Sheet command (Tools menu, Protection submenu). You may be prompted for a password.
>
> [OK]

♦ Click **OK** to close the dialog box.

❑ *On protected sheets, certain options on the **Format** menu become unavailable (the corresponding buttons appear dim).*

> *To remove the protection from a sheet, use the command **Tools - Protection - Unprotect Sheet**. If necessary give the password which protects the sheet, then enter.*

. . . . *Personal notes* . . . .

FORMATTING

Applying an automatic format to a table

◆ Select the table to be formatted.

◆ **Format**
   AutoFormat

◆ Choose the most suitable format from the **Table format** list.

◆ Enter, then click outside the selection.

Customising an AutoFormat

◆ Select the table to be formatted.

◆ **Format**
   AutoFormat

◆ Choose a format from the **Table format** list.

◆ Activate the **Options** button.

   Excel lists the separate items which make up the AutoFormat.

◆ Deactivate the formats you do not want.

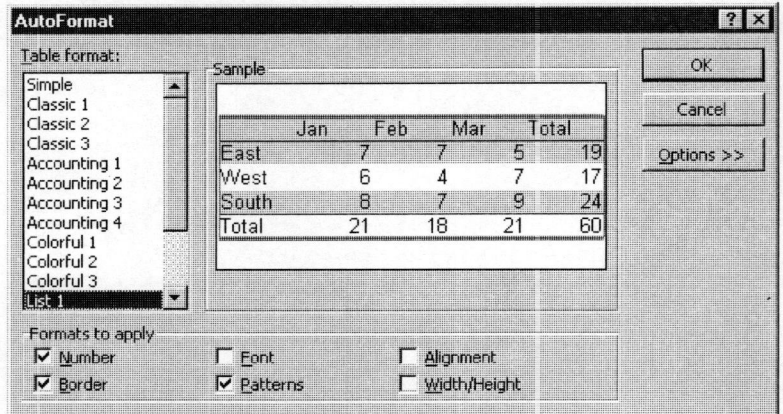

*Look at the **Sample** to see what effect your changes have.*

◆ Enter.

Formatting numerical values

♦ Select the values concerned.

♦ Choose one of the following three formats from the Formatting toolbar :

    🔲   **Currency(£10 000)**

    %   **Percent(100 000%)**

    000   **Comma(10,000)**

❏ *In certain cells number symbols (#) may appear when the column is not wide enough to display the value with the formatting applied to it.*

To show more, or fewer decimal places, select the cells concerned and use the [⁺₀₀] button or the [⁰⁰₀] button.

Creating a custom number format

♦ Select the cells to which you want to apply the new format.

♦ **Format**   ♦ Ctrl 1
Cells

If you use the shortcut key, press the 1 on the main (alphanumeric) keyboard.

♦ If necessary, activate the **Number** tab.

♦ Select **Custom** in the **Category** list.

♦ Choose the format closest to what you need in the **Type** list.

The # ## code separates the thousands from the hundreds with a space.

♦ Enter your own format in the **Type** box.

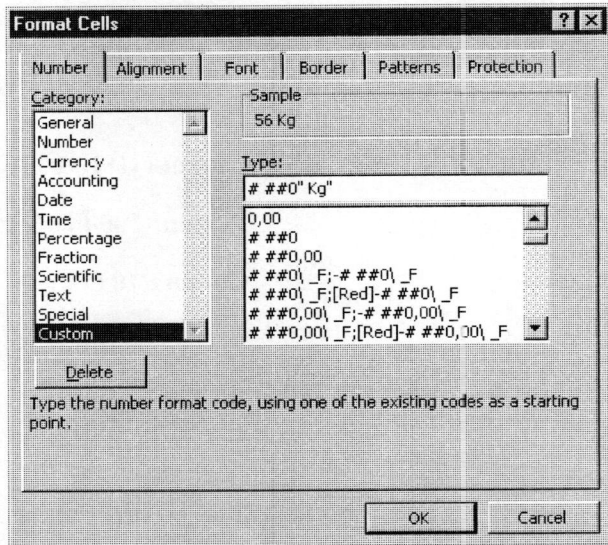

If you want to include text in the format, you should enter it between quotation marks. Take great care when leaving spaces : if you type a space outside the quotation marks Excel will interpret it as a command to divide by 1000 !

♦ Enter.

Formatting dates

♦ Select the dates to be formatted.

♦ **Format**   ♦ [Ctrl] **1**
   Cells

♦ If necessary activate the **Number** tab.

♦ Check that **Date** is active in the **Category** list box.

♦ Select the format in the **Type** list.

♦ Enter.

Creating a custom date format

♦ Select the dates to which you want to apply the new format.

♦ **Format**   ♦ Ctrl 1
Cells
Number tab

♦ Activate the **Custom** category then select the format closest to the one you require.

♦ Enter your own format in the **Type** box. For example :

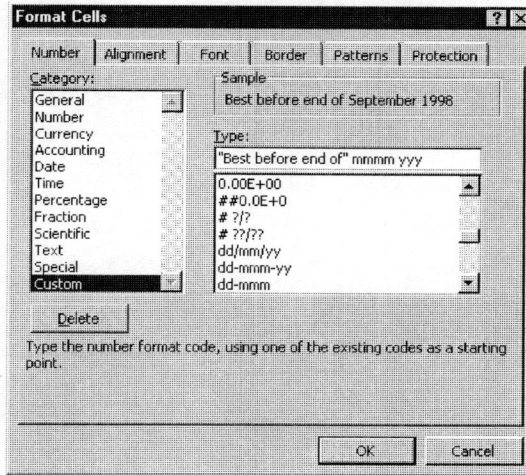

For days use the codes : d (1) - dd (01) - ddd (Mon) - dddd (Monday)
For months, use the codes : m (1) - mm (01) - mmm (Jan) - mmmm (January)
For years, use the codes : yy (96) - yyyy (1996)

Use any character you like as the separator.

When inserting other text, put it inside quotation marks.

♦ Enter.

Creating custom text formats

These formats apply to text contained in cells.

♦ Select the texts concerned.

♦ **Format**   ♦ [Ctrl]**1**
Cells
Number tab.

♦ In **Category** choose **Custom**.

♦ Delete everything in the **Type** box and enter your own custom format. For example :

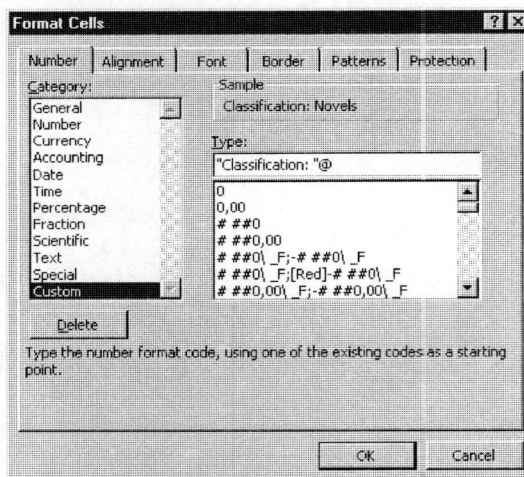

This format adds "Classification" before the contents of each cell.
The text involved in your custom format must be placed between quotation marks. The @ character represents the contents of the cell.

♦ Enter.

Creating conditional formats

For example, in a table, you can use this method to display all the values inferior to 1000 in red.

♦ Select the cells concerned.

♦ **Format**
Conditional Formatting

♦ In the **Condition1** list, select :

Cell Value Is	if the condition refers to a value contained in the selected cells (a constant, or the result of a formula).
Formula Is	if the condition refers to a formula.

♦ In the first case, continue by selecting an operator of comparison and a value.
In the second case, give the formula (one which will return TRUE or FALSE). If the condition refers to a formula, enter an equals sign (=) in front of the formula.

♦ If necessary, click the **Add** button to set further conditions.

♦ Click the **Format** button.

♦ Use the options under the **Font**, **Border** and **Patterns** tabs to define the format which will be applied to the cells if the condition is met.

♦ Click **OK**.

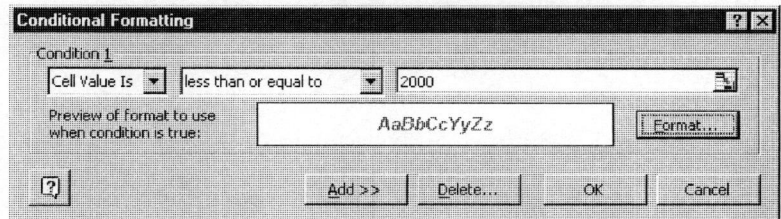

♦ To define a format which will be applied if the condition is not met (or to define different formats connected to other conditions), click the **Add** button and continue as before.

♦ Click **OK**.

The formatting applied to the cells will vary according to whether or not the contents meet the condition.

♦ Enter.

**Hiding
the contents
of a cell**

♦ Select the cell(s).

♦ **Format
Cells
Number** tab

♦ If necessary, activate **Custom** in the **Category** list.

♦ Delete everything in the **Type** box.

♦ Type in **;;;** (three semi-colons).

♦ Enter.

❑ *To display the contents of the cells, apply any other format to them.*

Modifying the orientation of a text

♦ Select the cells concerned.

♦ **Format**   ♦ Ctrl 1
   Cells

♦ If necessary, activate the **Alignment** tab.

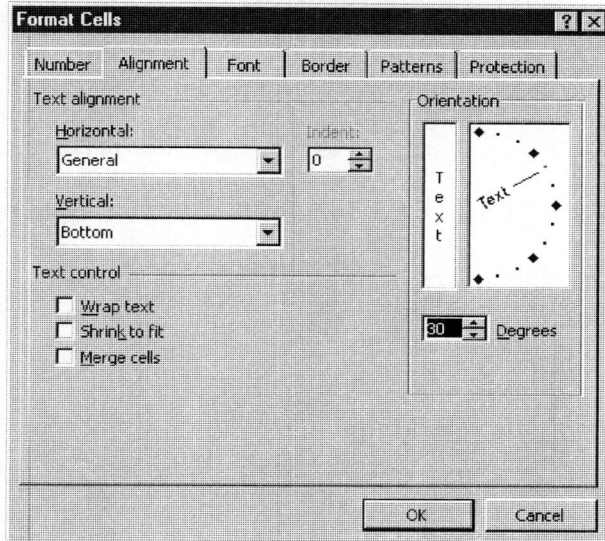

♦ In the **Orientation** frame, point the word **Text** and drag it to the angle you require. You could also enter a value for the angle in the **Degrees** box.

♦ Click **OK**.

> To position characters one underneath the another, click the box, in the **Orientation** frame, where the word **Text** is written vertically.

FORMATTING

Aligning cell contents horizontally

The horizontal alignment of a cell is calculated with reference to the width of the column which contains it.

♦ Select the cells concerned.

♦ Click one of these three buttons.

    left alignment

    centered

    right alignment

♦ To indent the text in a cell, use :

Format   ♦ Ctrl 1
Cells
Alignment tab

♦ In the **Indent** box, give the value of the indent from the left edge of the cell.

♦ Click **OK**.

Aligning cell contents vertically

The vertical alignment of a cell is defined with reference to the height of the row.

♦ Select the cells concerned.

♦ **Format**   ♦ Ctrl 1
  Cells
  Alignment tab

♦ Select an alignment from the **Vertical** list.

♦ Click **OK**.

| **Centering cell contents across several columns** | *This method can be used to centre a title over the width of the whole table.* |

♦ Select the cells across which the text should be centered.

The first cell in the range must contain the text.

♦ Click ▦.

| **Modifying the font and/or size of the characters** | ♦ Select the cells or characters concerned. |

♦ Select the font and the size from the first two list boxes on the formatting bar.

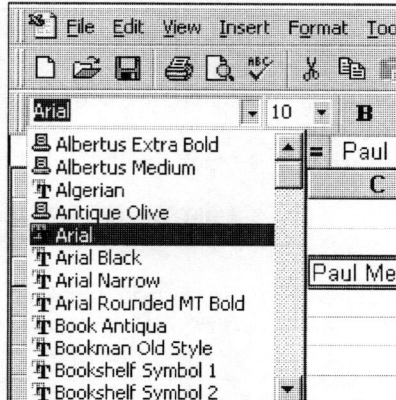

The fonts preceded by TT are TrueType fonts managed by Windows.

❏ *To set a default font and size for all new folders, use* **Tool - Options - General** *tab (***Standard font** *and* **Size** *options). These changes will only take effect the next time you start Excel.*

**Adjusting
the size
of characters
automatically**

If this option is active, Excel reduces the size of the characters automatically when there is not enough space in the cell to display them all.

♦ Select the cells concerned.

♦ **Format**   ♦ [Ctrl] **1**
  Cells
  Alignment tab

♦ Activate the **Shrink to fit** option.

♦ Click **OK**.

❑ *Characters which have been reduced in size return to their original size if you widen the column.*

**Changing
the colour
of the characters**

♦ Select the cells or characters concerned.

♦ Open the [A ▾] list by clicking the down arrow.

♦ Click the colour required.

The button displays the colour you have chosen. To apply the same colour to another text, just click the button again without opening the list.

Formatting characters

♦ Select the cells or characters concerned.

♦ Activate the attributes to apply.

B or [Ctrl] **B** for **bold** characters

I or [Ctrl] **I** for *italic* characters

U or [Ctrl] **U** for underlined characters.

❑ *If you repeat the same action for the same text, you cancel the corresponding attribute.*

❑ *You can apply more than one attribute to the same text.*

♦ Select the cells or characters concerned.

♦ **Format**   ♦ [Ctrl] 1
  Cells
  Font tab

♦ Activate all the formats to be applied to the text.

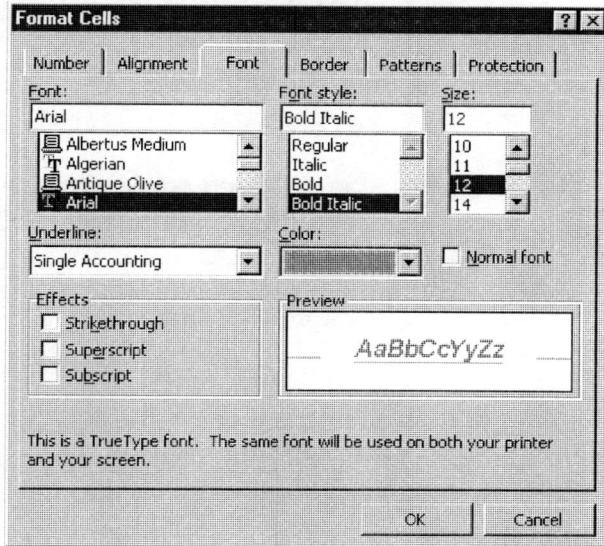

Format Cells		? X
Number	Alignment	Font	Border	Patterns	Protection

Font:
Arial

Albertus Medium
Algerian
Antique Olive
Arial

Font style:
Bold Italic

Regular
Italic
Bold
Bold Italic

Size:
12

10
11
12
14

Underline:
Single Accounting

Color:
☐ Normal font

Effects
☐ Strikethrough
☐ Superscript
☐ Subscript

Preview

AaBbCcYyZz

This is a TrueType font. The same font will be used on both your printer and your screen.

OK   Cancel

*As well as the options available from the toolbar, this dialog box gives you access to the three choices in the **Effects** section and additional options in the **Underline** box.*

♦ Click **OK**.

Drawing borders around cells

♦ Select the cells concerned.

♦ Open the [▢ ▾] list by clicking the down arrow.

| ▾ | **B** | *I* | **U** | ≣ | ≣ | ≣ | ▦ | 🔮 | % | **,** | +.0 .00 | .00 +.0 | ⟸ |

= Anne Berry

C	D	E	F
		Anne Berry	

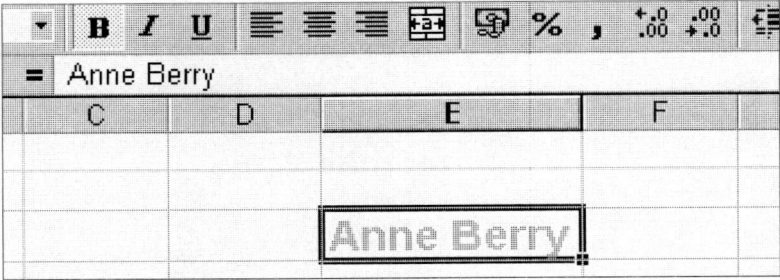

♦ Click the border you want to apply.

The [▢ ▾] tool displays the type of border you have chosen.

♦ Deselect the cells to view the finished result.

❑ *If you need coloured borders or dotted lines, you should use the second method, described below.*

> *To apply the same border to another range of selected cells, simply click the button without opening the list.*

♦ Select the cells concerned.

♦ **Format**   ♦ Ctrl 1
  Cells
  Border tab

♦ To put a border all around the edge of the selection, choose the **Style** and **Color** of the border then click the **Outline** button.

♦ To place a border along one or more edges of the selection, choose a **Style** and **Color**, then click the buttons corresponding to the borders you require.
  Click the **Inside** button to apply the border to the edges of each individual cell in the selection.

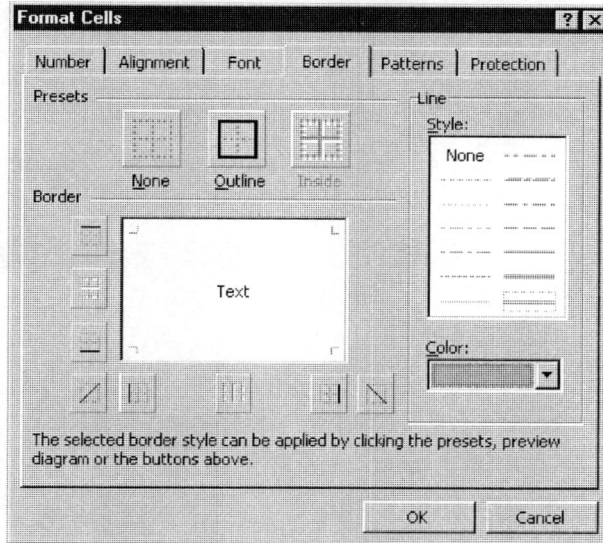

The buttons ▨ and ◩ draw diagonal lines accross individual cells.

♦ Enter by clicking **OK**.

♦ Click outside the selection to view the finished result.

FORMATTING

Colouring cells
- Select the cells that you want to colour.
- Open the [🎨▾] list by clicking the down arrow.
- Choose the colour.

  The [🎨▾] tool displays the last colour chosen. You can apply the same colour to another selection simply by clicking the tool button.

Shading cells
- Select the cells that you want to shade.
- **Format**   ◆ [Ctrl]1
  Cells
  Patterns tab
- In **Color** choose the colour required for the cell background.
- Open the **Pattern** list and choose the type of shading : the pattern and its colour.

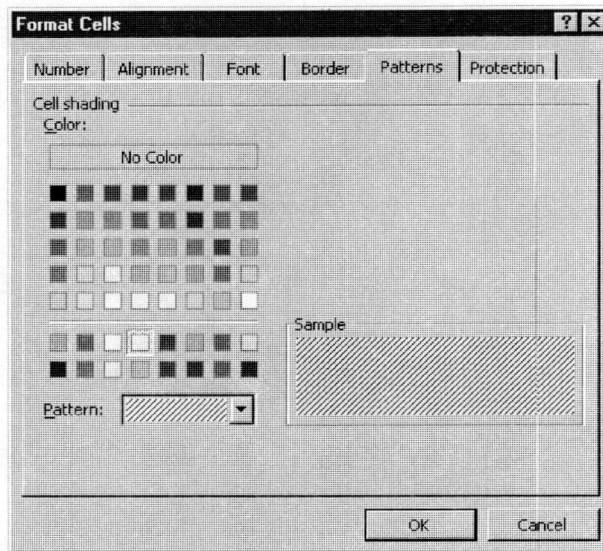

- Click **OK**.

Merging cells   *Cells which have been merged become one cell :*

The text REGIONS is the content of cell C5, but appears accross the merged cells C5, C6, C7 and C8.

♦ Select the cells concerned. Only the data in the first cell of the selection (at the top left of the range of cells) will appear in the merged cells.

♦ **Format**   ♦ Ctrl 1
  Cell
  Alignment tab

♦ Activate the **Merge cells** option.

♦ If necessary, specify the alignment that you wish to apply to the data in the merged cells.

♦ Click **OK**.

> The 🔲 button merges selected cells (provided that they are in the same row) and centres the data in the first cell across the merged cells.

Creating a style

Save a collection of attributes as a style then apply them all at once, as often as you need to.

♦ Activate the cell whose formatting is to be saved as a style.

♦ **Format**   ♦ [Alt] '
   Style

♦ Name the new style.

*A description of the style is displayed in the **Style Includes** frame.*

♦ Deactivate any attributes you do not require.

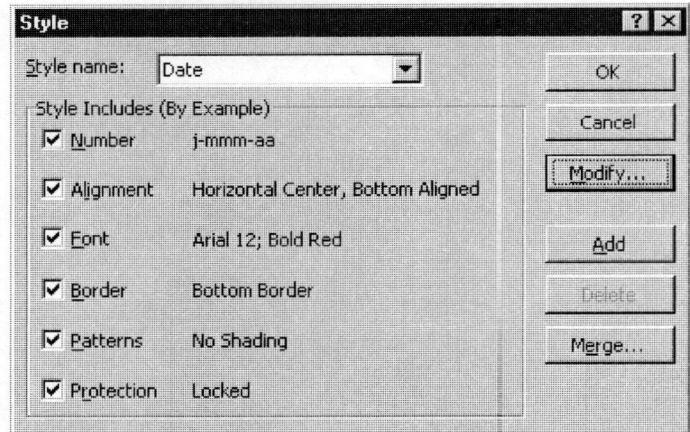

Style		? ✕
Style name:	Date ▾	OK
Style Includes (By Example)		Cancel
☑ Number	j-mmm-aa	
☑ Alignment	Horizontal Center, Bottom Aligned	Modify...
☑ Font	Arial 12; Bold Red	Add
☑ Border	Bottom Border	Delete
☑ Patterns	No Shading	Merge...
☑ Protection	Locked	

♦ Use the **Modify** button if you want to change the style before saving it.

♦ Click **OK** to confirm.

Using a style

♦ Select the cells to be formatted.

♦ **Format**
   Style

♦ ⌊Alt⌋ '

♦ Select the style in the **Style name** list.

♦ Click **OK**.

Using styles from another document

♦ Open the document containing the styles, and the document where you are going to apply them.

♦ Select the cells to be formatted.

♦ **Format**
   Style

♦ Click the **Merge** button.

♦ Excel lists the workbooks which are currently open : double-click the one containing the styles you are going to use.

♦ To apply a style to the cells which you have selected, choose the style then click **OK**.

Managing existing styles

Modifying a style

♦ **Format**
   Style

♦ In the **Style name** list, select the style that you want to modify.

♦ Click the **Modify** button.

♦ Make the necessary changes then click **OK**.

♦ Click **OK** again.

Deleting a style

♦ **Format**
 Style

♦ Select the style from the **Style name** list, then click the **Delete** button.

♦ Click **OK**.

*A **template** is a document containing formatting and maybe data, which you can use to create new workbooks.*

♦ To transform a worksheet into a template, delete from it everything which you do not need to reproduce in other documents, and activate any appropriate protections.

♦ **File**
 Save As

♦ Open the **Save as type** list and click **Template (*.xlt)**.

♦ Give the new template a name.

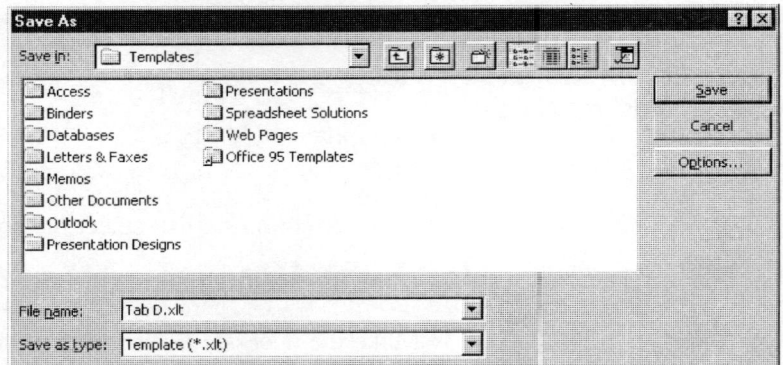

*Excel proposes to save the template in the folder called **Templates**.*

♦ If necessary, select another folder or a sub-folder of **Templates**.

♦ Click **Save**.

❏ *All templates have the extension XLT.*

❏ *A template can be modified just like any other document.*

Using a template ♦ **File**   ♦ Ctrl N
New

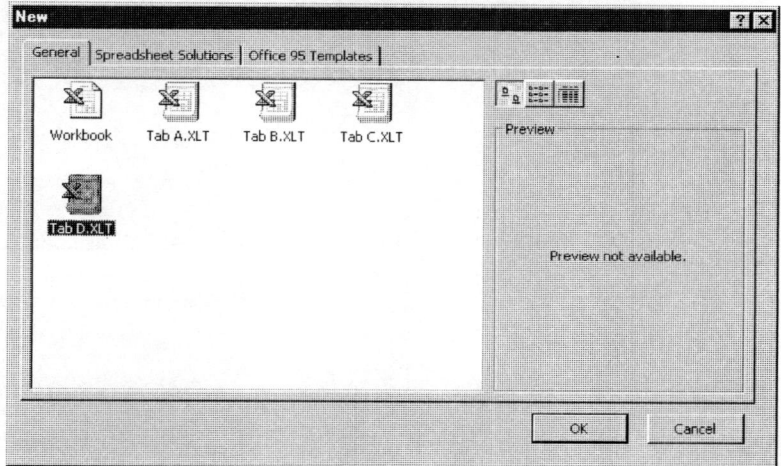

♦ The templates that you have created yourself appear on the **General** page.

♦ Double-click the template's name.

When you open a template, Excel copies its contents into a new worksheet ; this sheet takes the name of the template, followed by a number.

♦ Enter and format the data ...

♦ Save the new workbook, just as you would save any other.

OUTLINES

Creating
an outline

When you are not interested in the details of a calculation, creating an outline allows you to view or print just the results.

Automatically

♦ Select the table concerned.

♦ **Data**
Group and Outline
AutoOutline

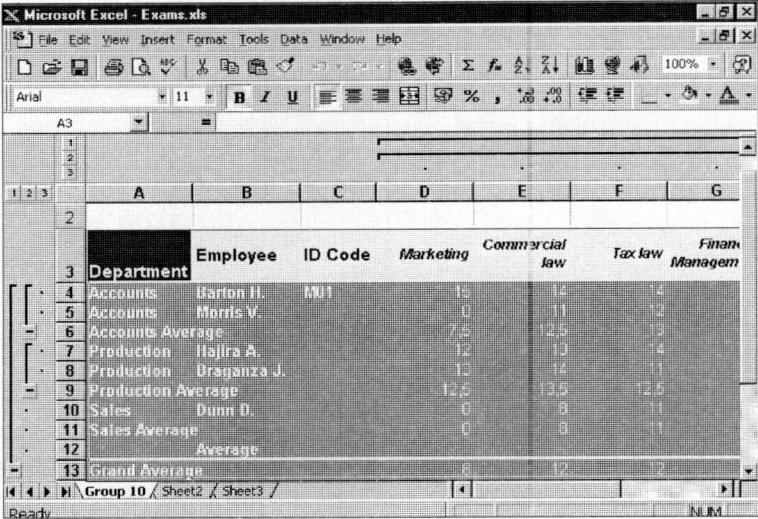

Buttons for managing the various levels in the outline appear to the left of the worksheet and above it.

Manually

♦ Select the rows (or columns) that you do not need to see in the outline.

♦ Display the **Query and Pivot** toolbar, if it is not already on the screen.

♦ Click ⬚.

❑ *If you need to remove a row (or column) from the outline, select it, then click* ⬚. *To add a row/column to the outline, click* ⬚.

Using outlines

♦ To hide lower-level rows or columns, click the ⬚ button.

♦ To hide all the groups of a particular level, click the button with the number corresponding to the level.

The rows belonging to level 2 are no longer visible. The ⬚ *buttons are replaced by* ⬚ *buttons.*

♦ To make the hidden rows/columns visible again, click their ⬚ buttons, or click the button with the number corresponding to the next level ; for example click the **3** button to restore level **2**.

Destroying an outline

♦ Data
  Group and Outline
  Clear Outline

. . . . *Personal notes* . . . .

Printing a sheet ◆ Activate the sheet to be printed.

◆ Click the 🖶 tool.

*Excel gives you a brief opportunity to **Cancel** the print job ; the data is then transmitted to Windows' Print Manager and the pages are printed.*

Printing part of a sheet

Printing particular pages

◆ Go into the sheet concerned.

◆ **File** ◆ Ctrl P
Print

◆ Under **Print Range**, click the **From** box and enter the number of the first page to print, then enter the number of the last page in the **To** box.

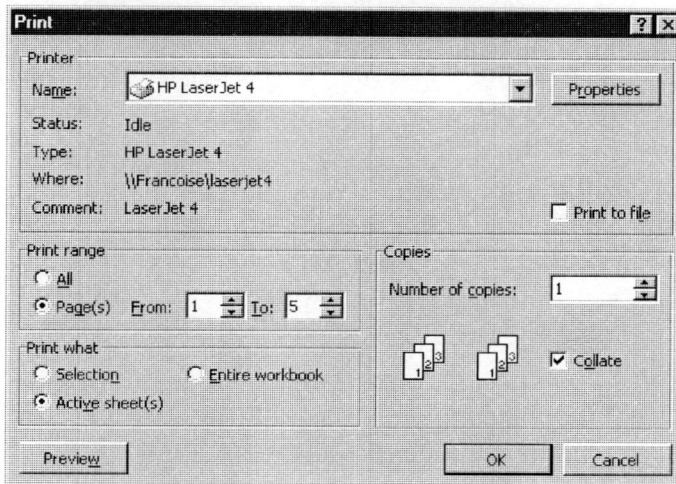

◆ Click **OK**.

Printing selected data

♦ Select the cells to print.

♦ **File**   ♦ Ctrl P
  Print

♦ Choose the **Selection** option under **Print What**.

♦ Click **OK**.

❏ *In Print Preview, the **Print** button also opens the **Print** dialog box.*

Printing several copies

♦ **File**   ♦ Ctrl P
  Print

Indicate the **Number of copies** *to print.*

♦ Click **OK**.

Creating a print area

You can define the part of the sheet you want to print as a print area.

♦ Select the range to be printed.

♦ **File**
  Print Area
  Set Print Area

❏ *To delete the print area use **File - Print Area - Clear Print Area**.*

Managing page breaks

Inserting a page break

♦ Activate the cell which is going to be the first of your new page.

The page break will be inserted above and to the left of the active cell.

♦ **Insert**
Page Break

Almost instantly, a dotted line appears representing the page break.

> To delete the page break, activate a cell in the next row or column and use **Insert - Remove Page Break**.

Managing existing page breaks

♦ **View**
Page break preview

*This option is also available in Print Preview : click the **Page Break Preview** button.*

♦ A dialog box may appear, informing you that you can drag page breaks to move them. If you do not want this dialog box to appear every time you use the **Page Break Preview** option, activate **Do not show this dialog again**, then click **OK**.

Page breaks are represented by blue lines on the worksheet. These lines do not prevent you from working normally (entering and editing data, changing the way it is presented...).

♦ To move a page break, drag the blue line representing it.

♦ To return to the usual view of the page, use the command **View - Normal**.

Repeating titles on each page

You can repeat rows and/or columns, often those containing titles, on each printed page.

♦ **File**
Page Setup
Sheet tab

♦ Activate the **Rows to Repeat at Top** box or activate **Columns to Repeat at Left**.

♦ Click the ⬛ button to minimise the dialog box then, in the worksheet, select a cell from the row(s) or column(s) which you want to repeat.

In this example both the department and the name of the employee will be printed on every page.

♦ Click the ⬚ button to restore the dialog box.

♦ Click **OK**.

**Previewing
a printed sheet**

Going into Print Preview

♦ **File
Print Preview**

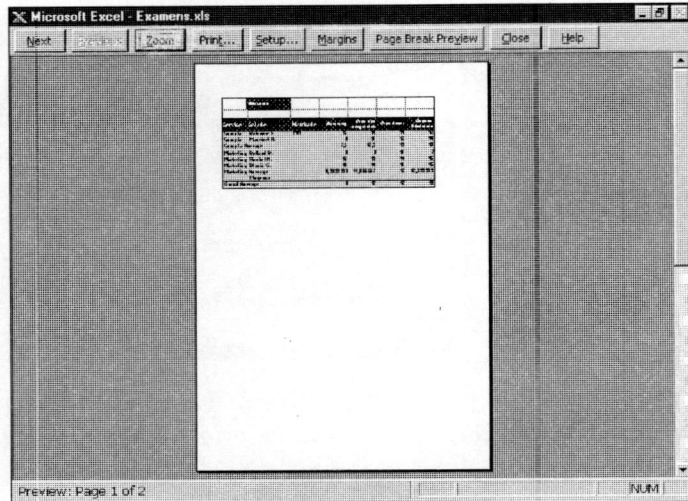

This produces a scaled-down view of the sheet as it will be printed. On the status bar Excel displays the page number and the total number of sheets to be printed.

Magnifying a preview

♦ To zoom in on a preview, place the mouse pointer on the item to be magnified and click.

Before you click, the mouse pointer appears as a magnifying glass ; afterwards it becomes an arrow.

♦ To return to the scaled-down preview, click the page again.

Displaying another page

♦ Use the **Next** and **Previous** buttons.

❑ *In the scaled-down preview, you can also use the vertical scroll bars to change page.*

Modifying margins and column widths

♦ Click the **Margins** button.

Handles appear at various points in the window :

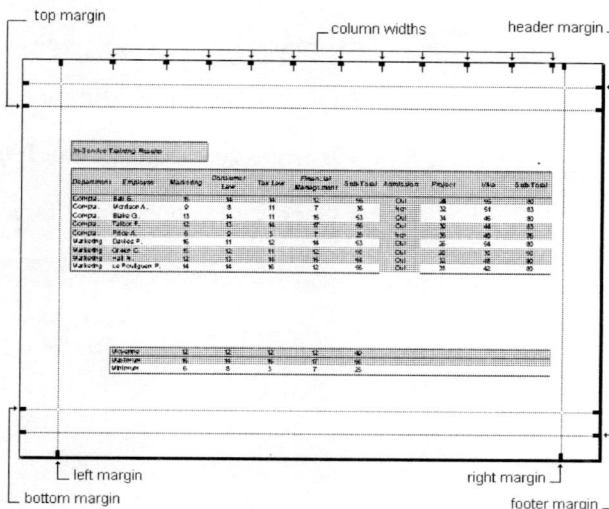

♦ Drag the appropriate handle.

Starting to print

♦ Click the **Print** button.

♦ Check that the printing options are correct, then enter.

Leaving Print Preview

♦ Click the **Close** button.   ♦ [Esc]

❑ *The **Page Break Preview** button makes the page breaks visible, so that you can reposition them.*

Modifying page setup options

♦ If you are in the Print Preview, click the **Setup** button. If you are working in the document, use :

File
Page Setup

Modifying the page orientation

♦ Go into the page setup options.

♦ If necessary, activate the **Page** tab.

♦ Choose the appropriate **Orientation**.

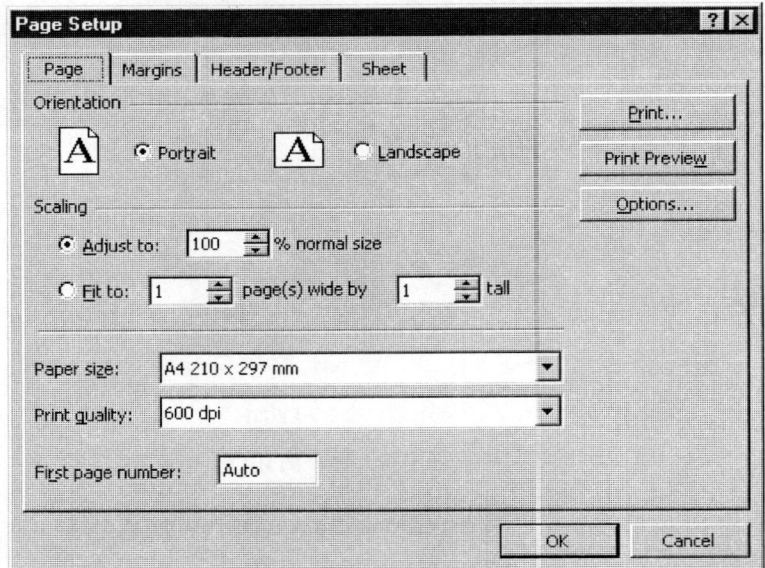

Portrait is also known as "Vertical" or "French". Landscape is also known as "Horizontal" or "Italian".

♦ Enter.

Changing the scale of printed pages

♦ Display the page setup options.

♦ If necessary, activate the **Page** tab.

♦ In the **Adjust to** text box under **Scaling**, give the percentage of the normal scale to apply.

♦ Enter.

> If the **Fit to** option is active under the **Page** tab in the **Page Setup** dialog box, Excel automatically adjusts the scale of printing so that the document fits the number of pages you specify.

Printing a sheet without gridlines

♦ Go into the page setup options.

♦ If necessary, activate the **Sheet** tab.

♦ Deactivate **Gridlines**.

♦ Activate the option Row and Column **headings** to print column letters and row numbers ; deactivate it if you do not want them to print.

♦ Enter.

Defining margins and position on the page

♦ Go into the page setup options.

♦ If necessary, activate the **Margins** tab.

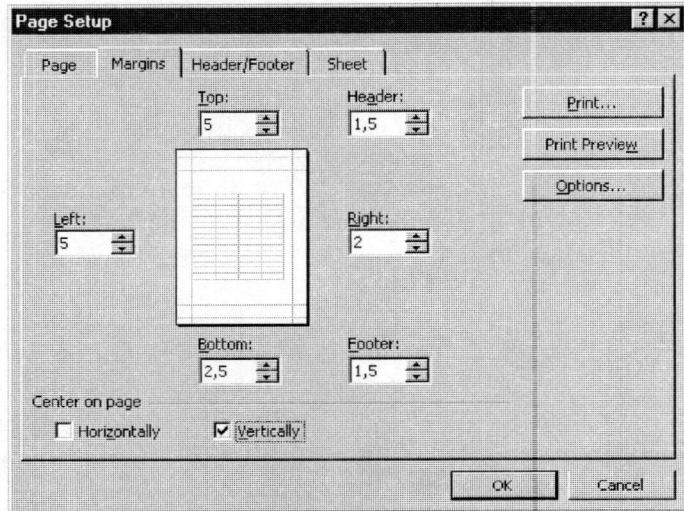

♦ Indicate the width of the various margins in the corresponding text boxes.

*The **Header** and **Footer** options determine the position of the header and footer in the top and bottom margins.*

♦ Centre the table either **Horizontally** or **Vertically** on the page.

♦ Enter.

Creating headers and footers

The header is printed at the top of each page and the footer at the bottom of each page.

♦ Go into the page setup options.

♦ If necessary, activate the **Header/Footer** tab.

♦ If you wish, choose pre-set a **Header** and/or **Footer** from the appropriate list.

Headers and footers chosen from the list are automatically centred at the top/bottom of the page.

♦ If you prefer, create your own header and footer. To do this :

    – click the **Custom Header** or **Custom Footer** button.

    – activate the text box which corresponds to the position on the page were you want the text to appear : **Left section**, **Center section**, or **Right section**.

    – enter the text to be printed.

♦ To create a second (third ...) line of text, press Enter .

♦ To insert variable details click the appropriate buttons.

    Page number

    Total number of pages

    Date of printing

    Time of printing

    File name (name of the workbook)

    Tab name (name of the sheet).

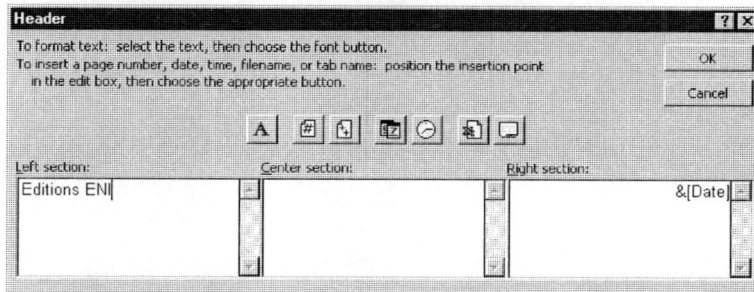

Each of these variables corresponds to a code which appears between square brackets.

♦ To format the text, select it and use the **A** button.

♦ Click **OK**.

Excel displays a preview of the header or footer as it will look in print.

♦ When you have defined your header and footer, click **OK**.

. . . . *Personal notes* . . . .

Using views

In a view you save one of a set of possible print areas and page setup parameters. When you switch to a view these options are automatically activated.

Creating a view

◆ Prepare the sheet for printing (page setup, print area, hiding columns).

◆ **View**
  Custom Views
  Add

◆ Enter the name of the view being created.

◆ Indicate whether the view should include the **Print Settings** and **Hidden rows, columns and filter settings**.

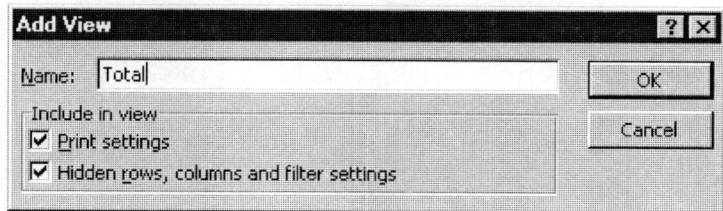

Add View	? X
Name: Total	OK
Include in view ☑ Print settings ☑ Hidden rows, columns and filter settings	Cancel

◆ Enter.

Using a view

♦ **View**
  Custom Views

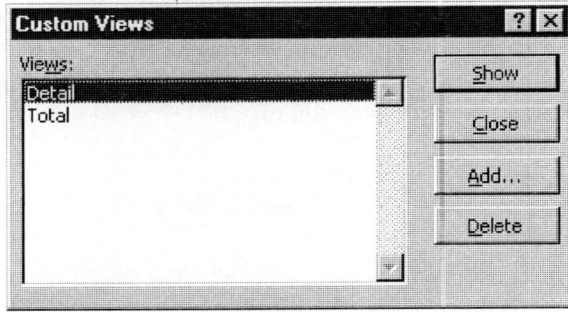

♦ Click the name of the view that you want to activate.

♦ Click **Show**.

Creating a report

A report prints a series of views in succession.

♦ Create all the views that you want to include in the report.

♦ **View**
  Report Manager

♦ Click the **Add** button.

♦ Give the report a name.

♦ For each view to be included in the report :

  – activate its name in the **View** list,

  – click the **Add** button.

Add the views in the order in which you want to print them.

♦ Activate **Use Continuous Page Numbers** to number the pages consecutively.

♦ To change the order in which the views are printed, select one of the views under **Sections in this Report**, then click **Move Up** or **Move Down**.

♦ Click **OK**.

The new report is included in the list of existing reports.

♦ Click the **Close** button to leave the dialog box.

Printing a report   ◆ **View**
Report Manager

◆ Click the name of the report.

◆ Click the **Print** button.

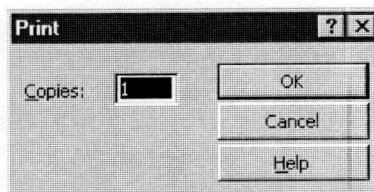

When you are printing a report, the options available in the ***Print*** *dialog box are very limited ...*

◆ Indicate how many copies you want to print then click **OK**.

Managing   ◆ **View**
existing reports   **Report Manager**

◆ Click the name of the report concerned.

◆ Use the **Delete** button to delete it or **Edit** to modify it.

◆ Finish by clicking **Close**.

**Creating a chart
on a sheet**

This technique inserts a chart into a worksheet (for example, next to a table).

♦ **Insert
 Chart**

♦ Select the **Chart Type** and then the **Sub-type**.

♦ Click the **Next** button.

♦ If all the data that you need for the chart is contained in cells adjacent to one another, leave the **Data Range** page active.
Click the [button] button then select the range of cells in the worksheet.
Specify whether the series are in **Rows** or **Columns**.

♦ It the data needed for the chart is contained in cells which are not adjacent to one another, start by indicating whether the series are in **Rows** or **Columns**, then click the **Series** tab.
In the **Series** list, delete any series you wish to remove from the chart, using the **Remove** button.
If necessary, redefine one or more series :

– Select the series and give its name : either enter the name in the appropriate text box, or click the text box then, in the worksheet, select the cell containing the name that you want to use.

– Give the references of the cells containing the values for the series : click the **Values** box to select its contents, click [button], select the values in the worksheet then click [button].

Next use the **Category (X) labels** option to specify the range of cells which contains the text for the labels.
If you need to insert further series, use the **Add** button.

The chart displayed is based on the options which you defined.

♦ Click **Next**.

♦ Give the various titles used in the chart.

♦ Click **Next**.

♦ If you wish to create the chart on its own chart sheet, activate the **As new sheet** option, then give a name for the new sheet ; otherwise leave the **As object in** option active, then select the sheet where you want to insert the chart.

♦ Click **Finish**.

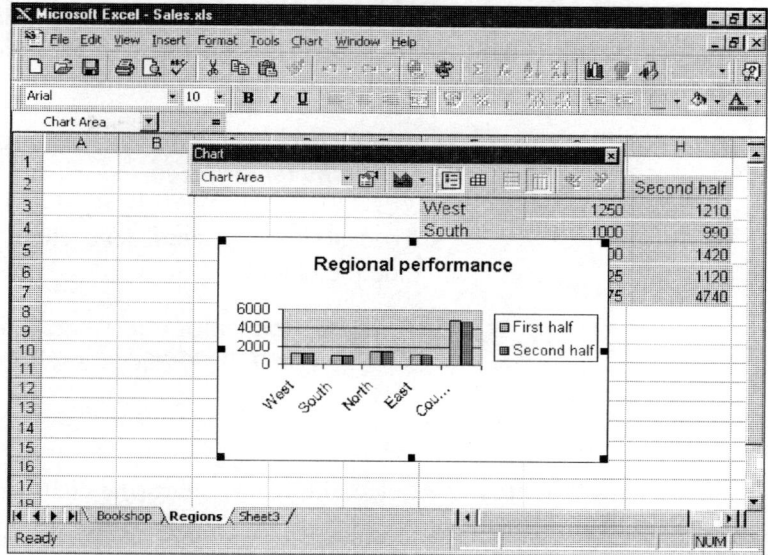

*In you chose to insert the chart into a worksheet, it appears in the workspace. Square black handles show that it is selected. The **Chart** toolbar appears.*

♦ If necessary, move the chart as you would move any other drawing object : point to one of its edges and drag it. You can also resize the chart by dragging one of the handles.

❏*A chart created on a worksheet is known as an **embedded chart** : it belongs to the family of drawing objects.*

❏*In a 2D Chart, each series can contain up to 52000 points.*

❏*By default a chart is linked to its source data : if the source data changes, so will the chart.*

❏*When the chart is active, the **Chart - Chart Options** command opens the corresponding dialog box.*

CHARTS

Activating and deactivating an embedded chart

♦ To activate an embedded chart click it once to select the whole chart object, then click if necessary to select one of the chart items.

*The **Chart** toolbar appears automatically. The **Data** menu is replaced by the **Chart** menu.*

♦ To deactivate an embedded chart, click a cell in the sheet, outside the chart.

❏ *To display an embedded chart in a window, select it then use **View - Chart window**. To deactivate the chart, close the window.*

Copying a chart into a worksheet

♦ Select the whole chart (the chart object called **Chart Area**).

♦ Go into **Edit - Copy**.

♦ Activate the destination worksheet.

♦ Paste the chart (**Edit - Paste**).

❏ *An embedded chart is created.*

Different objects in a chart

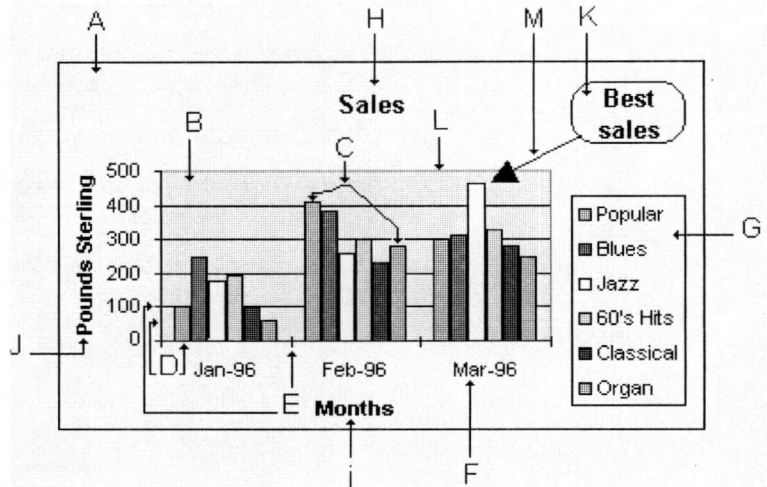

	Object	to select	contents
A	Chart area	click in the chart but not in any object	all the chart object
B	Plot area	click in the plot area but not in any object	axes and data markers
C	Point	click the series then click the point.	each value in a series
	Series	click one of the data markers in the series	all the points which constitute a data series.
D	Value Axis Category axis	click one of the tick mark labels	
E	Tick marks	no selection	lines which divide up the axes
F	Tick mark labels		texts attached to tick marks
G	Legend	click the object	shows the names of the series represented in the chart and identifies the symbol or colour used for the data markers.
H	Chart title		attached text
I	Axis title		attached text
J	Axis title		attached text
K	Text boxes		unattached text
L	Gridlines	click one of the lines	lines crossing the plot area to make it easier to read the chart
M	Arrow	click the item	

❏ *When you point to an object in a chart, its name appears in a Screen Tip, providing that the **Show names** option is active under the **Chart** tab of the **Options** dialog box (**Tools - Options**).*

*To select a chart object, you can also open the list box on the **Chart** bar then click the object's name.*

Setting up the chart for printing

♦ **File**
Page Setup

*The worksheet options are inaccessible for a chart. The **Sheet** tab has disappeared, replaced by a new tab : **Chart**.*

♦ As well as modifying the usual options, you can adjust the **Printed Chart Size** on the **Chart** tab :

Use full page	Distorts the proportions of the chart so that it fills the whole page.
Scale to fit page	Increases the size of the chart as much as the page allows, without distorting its proportions.
Custom	Prints a chart the same size as the chart on the screen.

♦ Click **OK**.

♦ Start printing.

Changing
the chart type

♦ **Chart**
   Chart type

♦ Choose the chart type.

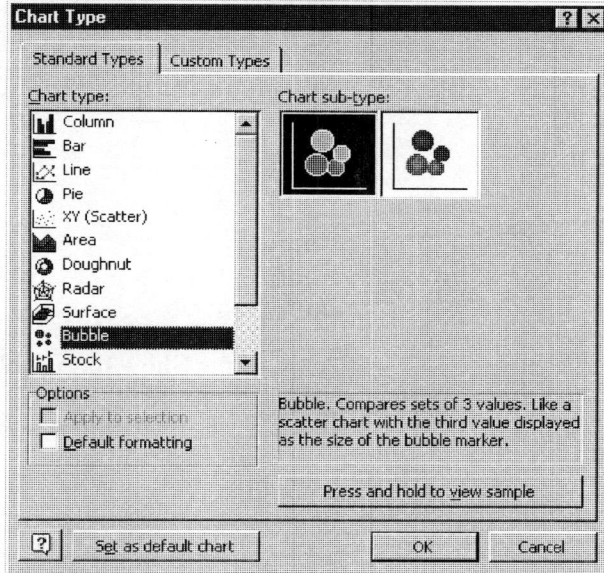

♦ Double-click the sub-type you prefer.

❏ *You can use the* [button icon] *button on the chart toolbar to change the chart type but not to choose from the various sub-types.*

❏ *If you need to redefine one or more of the chart's series, take the* **Source Data** *option in the* **Chart** *menu.*

> *All the options for managing the chart can be found in* **Chart - Chart Options**.

Displaying the data table

Next to the chart, you can display the table of data on which it is based :

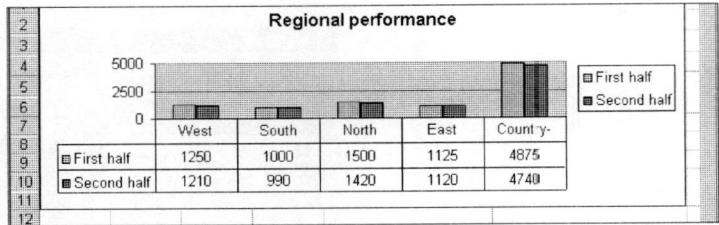

	West	South	North	East	Country-
First half	1250	1000	1500	1125	4875
Second half	1210	990	1420	1120	4740

Regional performance

First half
Second half

♦ **Chart**
Chart options
Data table tab

♦ Activate the **Show data table** option.

♦ If you wish, activate **Show legend keys.**

♦ Click **OK**.

You can also click the ⊞ option on the ***Chart*** *bar.*

Managing pie charts

Rotating a pie chart

♦ Select the series.

♦ **Format**
Selected Data Series

♦ If necessary, activate the **Options** tab.

♦ In the **Angle of first slice** box enter the number of **Degrees** through which you want to rotate the chart.

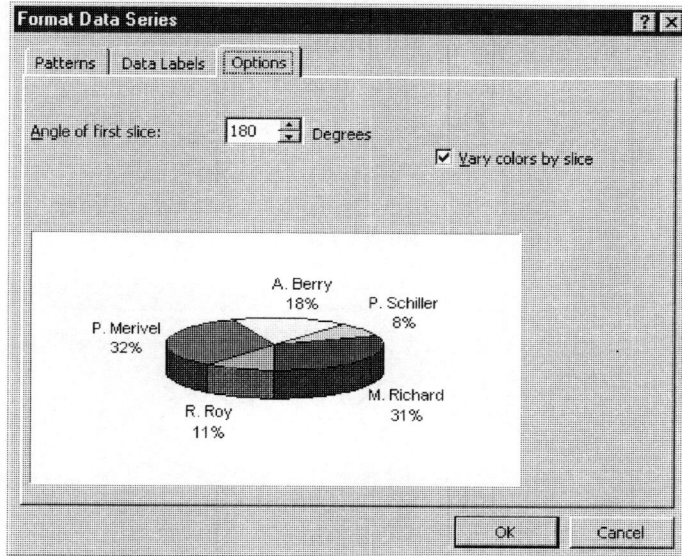

It is always the angle of the first slice that determines the rotation of a chart. Bear in mind that a full-circle rotation is 360°.

♦ Click **OK**.

Exploding a slice

♦ Select the slice you want to explode.

♦ Drag it away from the rest.

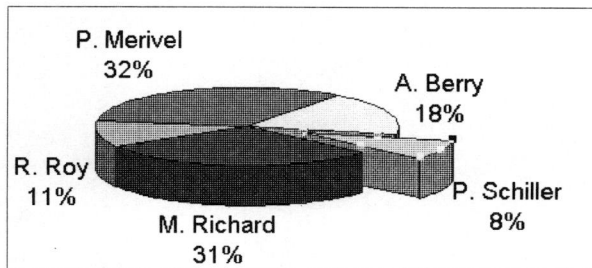

CHART OPTIONS

Inserting gridlines in a chart

♦ **Chart**
Chart Options
Gridlines tab

♦ To add vertical gridlines to the chart, activate the options in the **Category (X) axis** frame.
To add horizontal gridlines, use the options under **Value (Y) axis**.

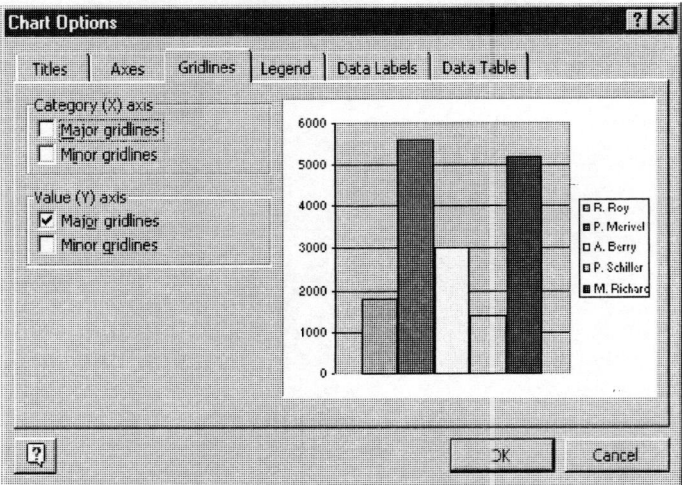

♦ Click **OK**.

Changing the scale of the chart

♦ Select the value axis.

♦ **Format Selected Axis** 🖻 ♦ Ctrl 1

♦ If necessary, activate the **Scale** tab.

♦ Set the scale options.

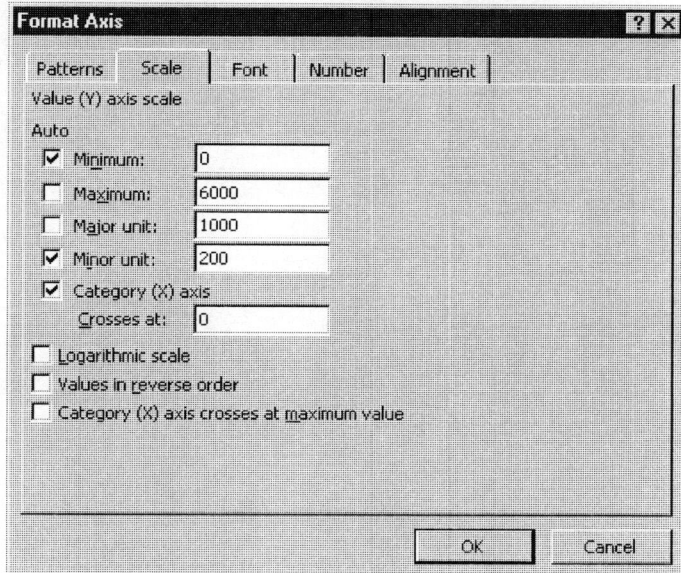

Format Axis ? ✕

| Patterns | Scale | Font | Number | Alignment |

Value (Y) axis scale

Auto

☑ Mi_n_imum: `0`

☐ Ma_x_imum: `6000`

☐ Ma_j_or unit: `1000`

☑ Mi_n_or unit: `200`

☑ Category (X) axis

_C_rosses at: `0`

☐ _L_ogarithmic scale

☐ _V_alues in _r_everse order

☐ Category (X) axis crosses at _m_aximum value

OK   Cancel

♦ Click **OK**.

Modifying the display of tick mark labels

♦ Select the axis on which the tick mark labels need formatting.

♦ **Format Selected Axis** 🖻 ♦ Ctrl 1

♦ Use the **Font** and **Number** tabs to define the format of text and numbers in the labels.

♦ Define the position of the labels relative to the axis, using the options under the **Patterns** tab.

♦ On the **Alignment** page, determine the orientation of the text in the labels.

♦ Click **OK**.

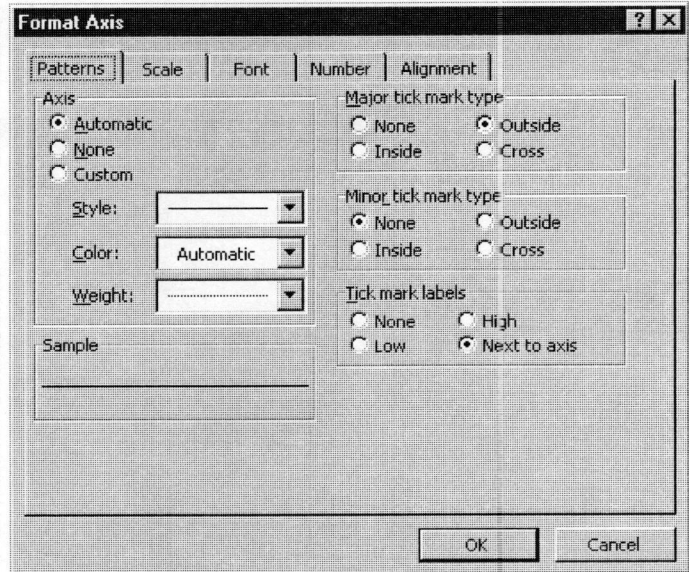

❏ With the [icon] and [icon] buttons on the **Chart** toolbar you can also change the orientation of the text in the labels.

Modifying the content of the category labels

♦ **Chart**
Source Data

♦ Change the contents of the **Category (X) labels** box.

♦ Click **OK**.

❏ You could also select the first series in the chart, then edit the second argument of the SERIES() function, on the formula bar.

Managing tick marks on the axes

♦ Select the axis concerned.

♦ **Format**
  Selected Axis   [icon]   ♦ [Ctrl] 1

♦ If you want to change the appearance of the tick marks use the **Patterns** tab. If you want more or less of them, use the **Scale** tab.

Making bars overlap

♦ Select one of the series in the chart.

♦ **Format**
  Selected Data Series   [icon]
  Options tab

♦ Enter the percentage of **Overlap** you require.

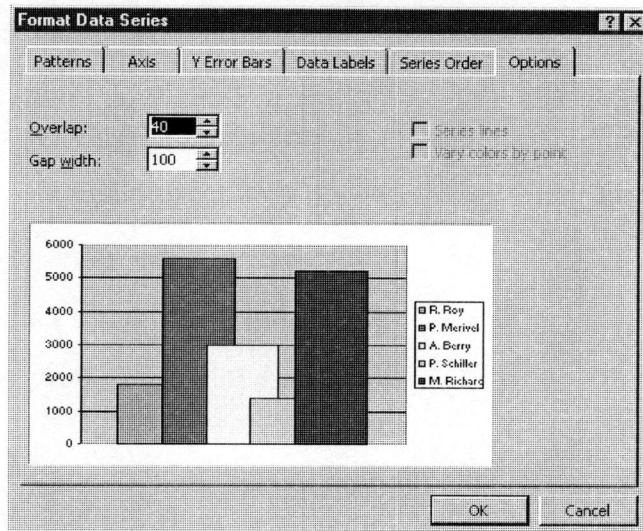

♦ Use the **Gap width** option to reduce or increase the space between the clusters of bars.

♦ Click **OK**.

CHART OPTIONS

**Formatting
an object's
characters**

♦ Select the text concerned.

♦ If possible use the buttons on the formatting toolbar, otherwise click the [button] button to define the new format.

The format of numerical values in the chart is defined in the same way.

**Adding a border/
colour/shading
to a chart**

In this example, the bars of the first series in the chart are filled with a picture. The bars in the second series are shaded.

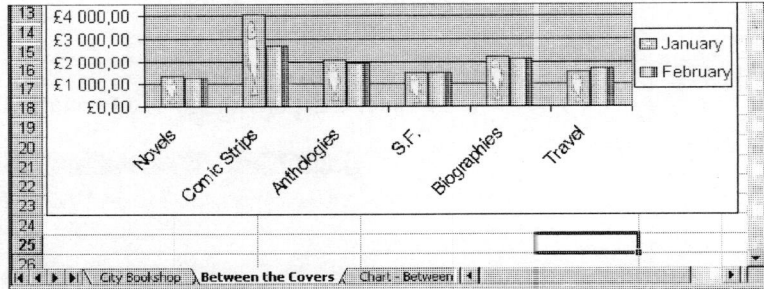

♦ Double-click the object concerned.

For unattached text double-click one of the selection borders.

♦ If necessary, activate the **Patterns** tab.

♦ Choose a **Border** from the various options offered.

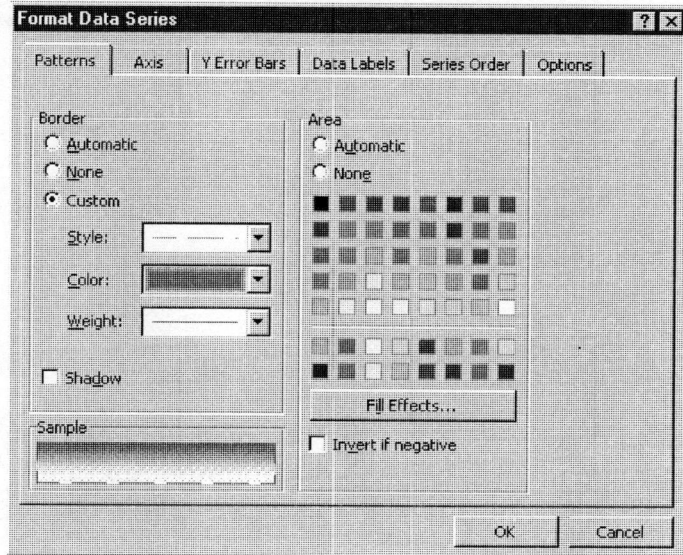

Check the effect in the Sample box.

♦ Select a background colour for the item in the **Area** frame.

To apply shading, a pattern or a texture to the item, click the Fill Effects button.

♦ To apply shading, choose between **One color**, **Two Color** and **Preset** shading (if you choose **Preset**, go on to select one of the named colour combinations). Next select one of the **Shading styles** and one of the **Variants**.

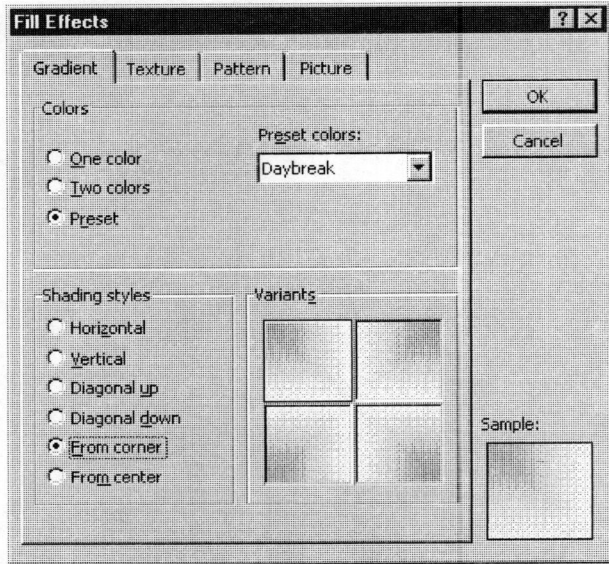

♦ To apply a texture, choose from the options under the **Texture** tab.

❏ *If you prefer to fill the object with a pattern, click the **Pattern** tab then select a **Background** colour and a colour for the pattern (**Foreground**).*

❏ *To fill the object with a picture, click the **Picture** tab then click the **Select Picture** button to select the file which contains the picture.*

♦ Enter.

You can apply colour to an object by selecting it then using the ⬛▾ *list.*

**Deleting
the border from
an object
in a chart**

♦ Double-click one of the borders of the object concerned.

♦ If necessary, activate the **Patterns** tab.

♦ In the **Border** frame, click **None** and check that the **Shadow** option is not active.

♦ Click **OK**.

**Moving/
resizing an object**

♦ Select the object.

♦ Drag one of the selection handles to change its dimensions, or one of the borders to move it.

**Deleting
an object**

♦ Select the object.

Check the name of the item on the formula bar.

♦ **Edit
Clear
All**

♦ [Del]

CHART OPTIONS

Adding text to a chart

A title

♦ **Chart**
   Chart Options
   Titles tab

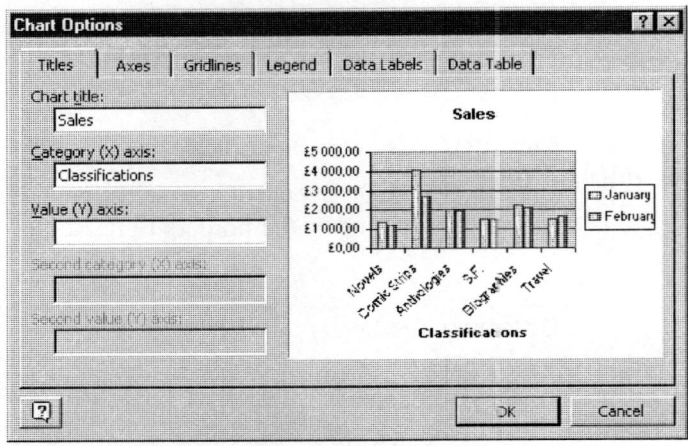

♦ Give the various titles you need in the chart.

♦ Click **OK**.

A text linked to a point in a series

♦ Select the point or series concerned.

♦ **Format**
   Selected Data
   or **Selected Data Series**

♦ [Ctrl] 1

♦ On the **Data Labels** page, select **Show value** or **Show label**.

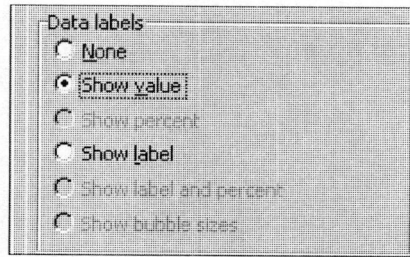

♦ If necessary, activate the **Show legend key next to label** option.

♦ Click **OK**.

Unattached text (text box)

♦ Make sure that you have not selected any text items.

♦ Enter the text required.

The text appears on the formula bar.

♦ Press `Enter`.

The drawing object created is named Text Box. It appears in the middle of the chart. Drag it into position.

To create a second (third ...) line of text, press `Ctrl` `Enter`.

Inserting a text from a sheet

♦ Make sure that you have not selected any object in the chart containing text.

♦ Type =.

♦ Select the cell(s) containing the text to be inserted.

♦ Enter.

♦ Drag the text box to where you want it.

❏*Each time the contents of the cells from the worksheet change, this text will be updated.*

CHART OPTIONS

Modifying an item of text

♦ Select the object to be modified (if it is a text box, you do not need to select it).

♦ Click inside the text.

The selection frame disappears, replaced by the insertion point.

♦ Make the necessary changes.

♦ Finish by pressing Esc.

❏ *While modifying text, use Enter to create a new line.*

Managing legends

♦ To display or hide a legend, click the [icon] button on the **Chart** toolbar.

♦ To determine the legend's position, double-click the legend then activate the **Placement** tab :

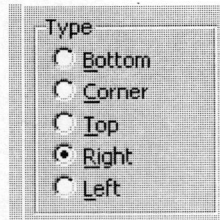

Type
- ○ Bottom
- ○ Corner
- ○ Top
- ◉ Right
- ○ Left

♦ In the **Type** frame, choose the position.

❏ *When moved to the top or the bottom of the chart, the legend is displayed horizontally.*

The legend can also be dragged to its new position.

Linking points
in a chart

This option is only available for line charts.

♦ **Format**   ♦ `Ctrl` **1**
Selected Data Series
Options tab

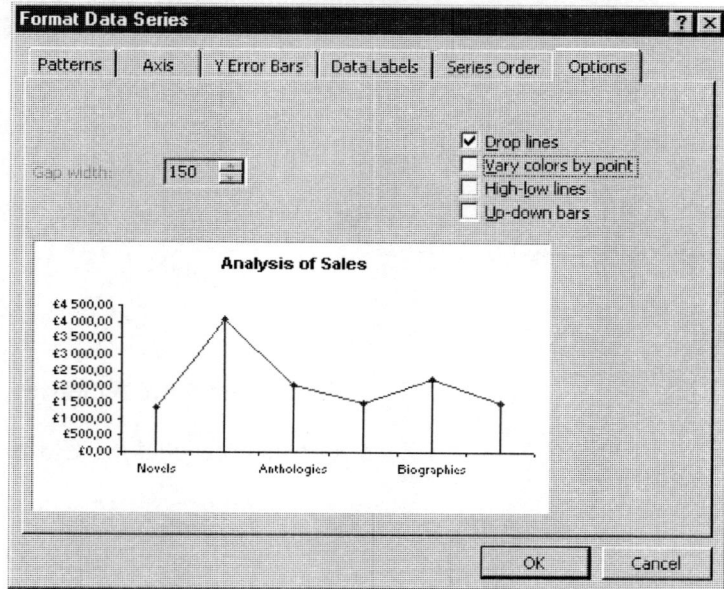

♦ Choose between :

Drop lines   These lines originate from the point and finish on the category axis.

High-low Lines   These lines link point to point.

Up-down bars   The points are linked by bars instead of lines.

♦ Click **OK.**

**Changing
the depth
of a 3D chart**

♦ Select a series in the chart.

♦ **Format
Selected Data Series
Options** tab

♦ Ctrl 1

♦ Activate the **Chart depth** box and enter the percentage of depth in relation to width.

♦ Click **OK**.

**Adjusting
the display of
data in 3D charts**

♦ **Chart
3-D View**

♦ Enter your own values in the **Elevation, Perspective** and **Rotation** boxes or click the arrows to increase/decrease the values given.

♦ Click **Default** to return to the values proposed by Excel.

♦ Enter, or cancel by clicking **Close**.

Drawing an object

♦ Display the **Drawing** toolbar (⊞).

♦ Click the button corresponding to the shape you want to draw or click the AutoShapes button then choose one of the shapes proposed.

*See Appendix B for a description of the **Drawing** toolbar.*

♦ Drag to draw the object. Hold down the ⌐Alt⌐ key as you drag to align the shape with the cell gridlines.

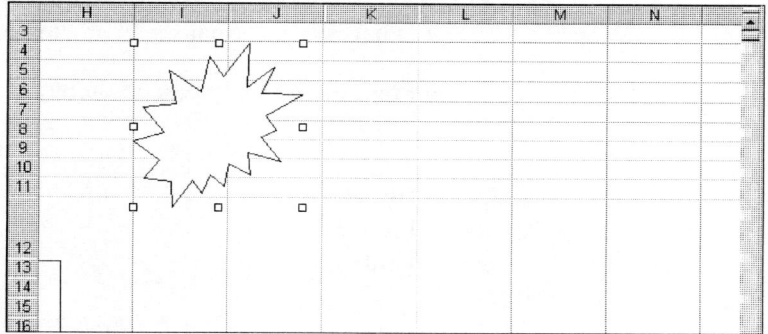

❑ Notice that the name of the object appears on the formula bar.

Hold the ⌐⇧ Shift⌐ key down to draw a perfect circle, square or arc, and for a perfectly straight horizontal, vertical or diagonal line.

Creating a text box

A text box is a drawing object intended to contain text.

♦ Click ⊞.

♦ Drag to draw a text box.

As soon as the box has been created, an insertion point appears inside it.

♦ Enter all the text, using ⌐Enter⌐ to start new paragraphs.

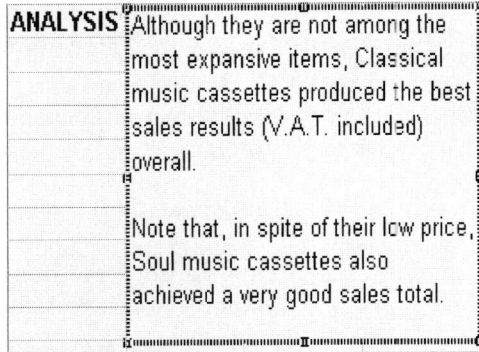

ANALYSIS Although they are not among the most expansive items, Classical music cassettes produced the best sales results (V.A.T. included) overall.

Note that, in spite of their low price, Soul music cassettes also achieved a very good sales total.

♦ If necessary format the characters.

♦ Press the ⟨Esc⟩ key when you have finished.

**Inserting
a picture,
sound or video
object**

♦ **Insert
Picture
Clip Art**

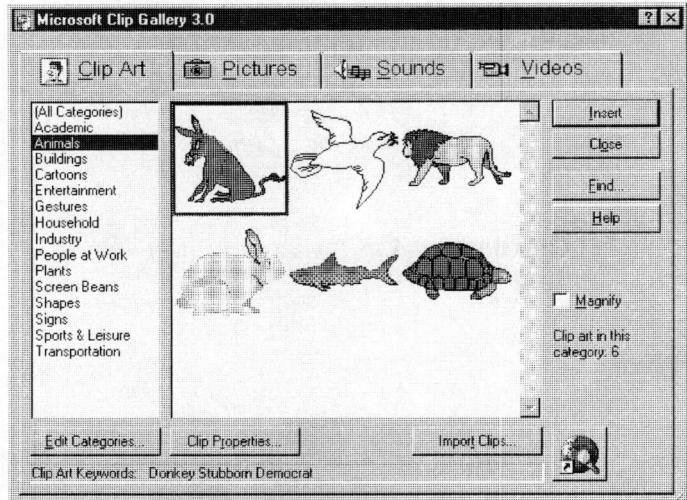

Microsoft Clip Gallery 3.0

Clip Art | Pictures | Sounds | Videos

[All Categories]
Academic
Animals
Buildings
Cartoons
Entertainment
Gestures
Household
Industry
People at Work
Plants
Screen Beans
Shapes
Signs
Sports & Leisure
Transportation

Insert
Close
Find...
Help

☐ Magnify

Clip art in this category: 6

Edit Categories... | Clip Properties... | Import Clips...

Clip Art Keywords: Donkey Stubborn Democrat

♦ Click the tab corresponding to the type of object you wish to insert.

♦ Select the category to which the object belongs.

♦ Double-click the object.

The object is inserted into the worksheet. If it is a picture, you can edit it using the tools of the Picture bar. If it is a sound or video, double-click its icon to play it.

❑ *The* 🖻 *button on the **Picture** bar can be used to import the picture contained in a WMF or JPEG... file.*

Inserting a WordArt object

The WordArt application applies special effects to a text :

♦ Click the 🔲 button on the **Drawing** toolbar.

♦ Select an effect then click **OK**.

♦ Type in the text to which you want to apply the WordArt effect ; use the Enter key to change line.

♦ Use the **Font** and **Font Size** list, as well as the **B** and **I** buttons to format the text.

♦ Click **OK**.

The text appears in the worksheet as a drawing object.

❑ *When the text object is selected, you can edit it using the tools from the **WordArt** bar.*

DRAWING OBJECTS

Selecting several objects at once

♦ Click ⬚.

♦ Click the first object to select it.

♦ Hold down the ⬚Shift key as you click on each of the other objects you want to select.

❏ *When several objects are selected, no name appears on the formula bar.*

> You can also drag to draw an invisible frame around the objects to select.

Resizing/moving an object

♦ Select the object concerned.

The small squares surrounding the selection are called **handles**. *The mouse pointer changes shape when you point to one of these.*

♦ To change the dimensions of the object, drag one of the handles.

♦ To move the object, point to its border (not a handle) and drag it.

> Use the ⬚Alt key to align the object with the cell gridlines.

Changing an object's appearance

A 2D object

♦ Select the object.

♦ Use the buttons on the **Drawing** toolbar :

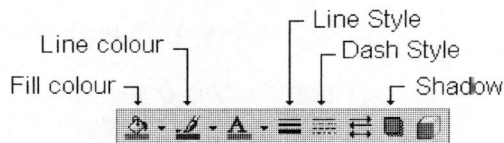

❏ *The* ⊞ *button is used to add arrowheads to line objects.*

A 3D object

◆ Select the object, then click the ▣ button to choose a preset 3D style.

If none of these styles suit you, click the **3D Settings** *button to create a specific 3D effect :*

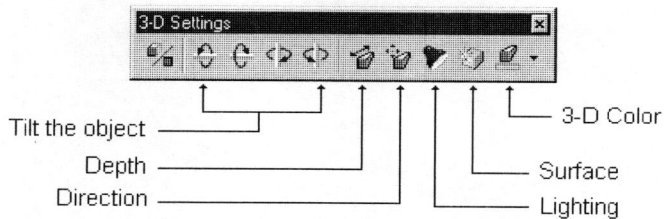

Tilt the object
Depth
Direction
3-D Color
Surface
Lighting

> *Some of these effects can be obtained through the* **Format - AutoShape** *dialog box : double-click the object to display the dialog box.*

Grouping/ ungrouping several objects

◆ Select all the objects that you want to include in the group.

◆ Click the **Draw** button on the **Drawing** toolbar, then click **Group**.

You can check that the item selected is a group : **Group** *should appear on the formula bar.*

❏ *To ungroup objects, select the group then use* **Draw - Ungroup**.

Reorganising overlapping objects

♦ Select the object that you want to bring forward or send further back.

♦ Click the **Draw** button then point the **Order** option.

♦ Choose **Bring to Front, Send to Back, Bring Forward** or **Send Backward**.

Aligning objects with one another

The bottom edges of these objects have been aligned :

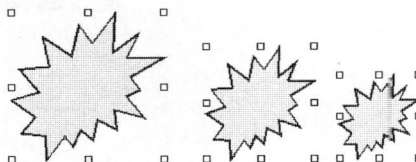

♦ Select the objects concerned.

♦ Click the **Draw** button then choose one of the first six options in the **Align or Distribute** menu.

❑ *The **Distribute horizontally** and **Distribute vertically** options in the same menu equalise the spaces between the selected objects.*

Rotating objects

♦ Select the objects concerned.

♦ Click the **Draw** button and choose one of the options in the **Rotate or Flip** menu.

♦ If you choose **Free Rotate**, point to one of the handles and drag to turn the object.

♦ When you have finished, click [⟳].

**Adding
a data series**

First method

♦ Select the source data corresponding to the series you want to add.

♦ Drag the selection onto the chart by its border.

❏ *This method is very quick but can only be used for embedded charts, when the source data is close by. If the chart is on a chart sheet, copy the data using the clipboard.*

Second method

♦ **Chart
Source Data
Series** tab

♦ Click the **Add** button.

Excel creates a new series, named Series 1.

♦ Select the new series.

♦ Click the **Name** box, and rename the series.

♦ Click the **Values** box, click to work in the sheet, select the cells containing the values for the new series then click to restore the dialog box.

♦ Click **OK**.

❏ *You can also use this command to change the cells associated with a series.*

Changing the position of a series

♦ Select one of the series in the chart.

♦ **Format**   ♦ Ctrl 1
   Selected Data Series
   Series Order tab

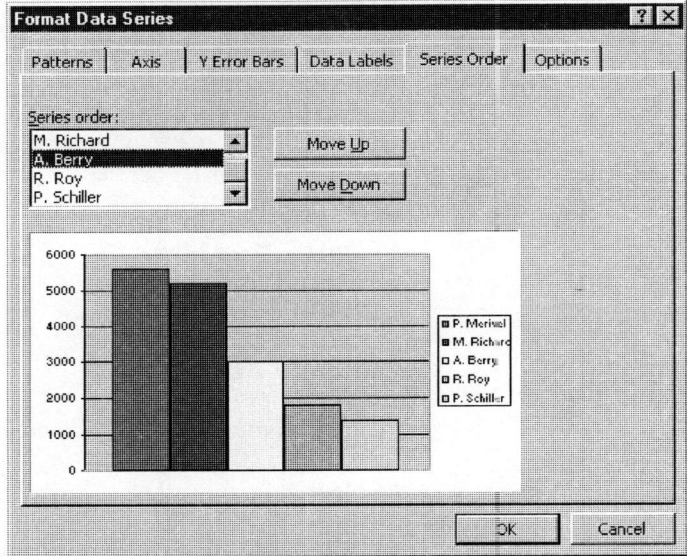

♦ Click the series you wish to move then click either the **Move Up** button or the **Move Down** button.

♦ Click **OK**.

❑ *When the series is selected, the SERIES() function appears on the* ***Formula*** *bar.*
The last argument in this function gives the position of the series in the order.

Cancelling links between the chart and the worksheet

♦ For each data series :
- select the series,
- select all the text in the formula bar,
- press F9 ,
- enter.

❏ The arguments in the SERIES() function no longer refer to cells in a worksheet.

Deleting a data series

♦ **Chart**
Source Data
Series tab

♦ Select the series.

♦ Click the **Remove** button.

♦ Click **OK**.

. . . . Personal notes . . . .

DATABASES

Database vocabulary

♦ Each separate column of data is called a **FIELD**.

	A	B	C	D	E	F	G
1	Team	Salesmen	Region	Dates	Sales		
2	Lloyd	10	Centre	01/10/92	£100 833.00		
3	Carter	10	West	01/10/92	£104 167.00		
4	Dickson	11	North	01/10/92	£152 500.00		
5	Allsopp	7	South	01/10/92	£83 333.00		
6	Harvey	9	Est	01/10/92	£93 750.00		
7	Lloyd	10	West	01/17/92	£10 400.00		
8	Lloyd	10	Centre	01/17/92	£80 837.00		
9	Carter	10	West	01/17/92	£93 764.00		
10	Allsopp	7	Centre	01/17/92	£20 000.00		
11	Allsopp	7	South	01/17/92	£83 337.00		
12	Harvey	9	Est	01/17/92	£46 875.00		
13	Dickson	11	North	01/17/92	£122 500.00		
14	Dickson	11	North	01/24/92	£100 000.00		
15	Dickson	11	Est	01/24/92	£46 875.00		
16	Lloyd	10	Est	01/24/92	£46 875.00		
17	Lloyd	10	Centre	01/24/92	£50 833.00		

Sales

In the above example there are five fields : for the sales manager, the number in his team, the region, dates of the results and total sales for the week.

♦ Each field must have a column heading which is its **NAME**. There are no restrictions on the name you can give, but short, clear field names are easier to manage.

♦ The first row of the database contains the field names and all the other rows are **RECORDS**. In the example above there is a record for each set as results received.

❏ *When you create a database, you can control the type of data authorised for each field by setting validation rules.*

Defining authorised data

♦ Select the cell(s) concerned.

♦ **Data**
Validation
Settings tab

♦ Open the **Allow** list and choose the type of data you wish to authorise.

Any value	No restrictions.
Whole number	The cell must contain an integer.
Decimal	The cell must contain a number or a fraction.
List	This option allows you to list cell references containing authorised data.
Date	The cell must contain a date.
Time	The cell must contain a time.
Text length	This option allows you to specify the number of characters authorised in the cell.
Custom	This option allows you to enter a formula to limit the data which the cell will accept.

♦ If you have selected **Whole number, Decimal, Date** or **Time** from the list, choose an operator of comparison from the **Data** list and give values for comparison.

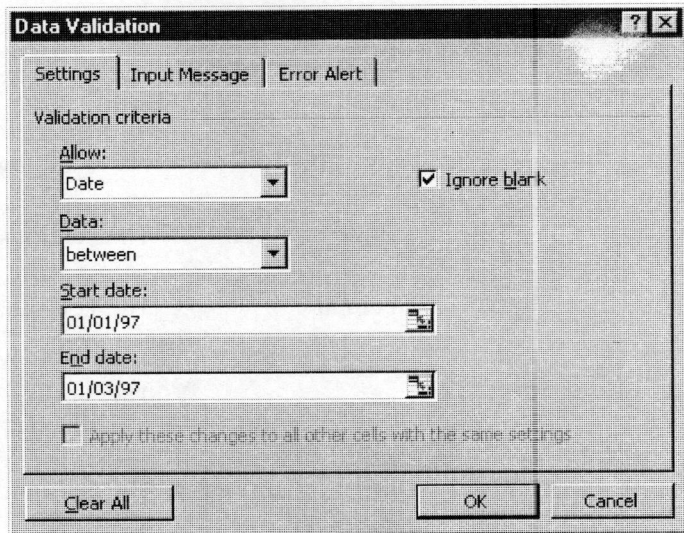

The validation criteria above reject any data entry which does not have a date format, or any date outside the period from 1st January to 1st March.

♦ If you have chosen **Text length**, select the **Equal to** operator, then give the authorised number of characters in the **Length** box.

♦ If you have chosen **List** enter the references of the cells containing authorised data in the **Source** box.
To add a drop down list of authorised data to the cells concerned, activate the **In-cell dropdown** option.

♦ If you have chosen **Custom** enter your **Formula**, starting with an equal sign (=). The formula must be of the type which returns TRUE or FALSE.

♦ Whatever the type of data specified, activate **Ignore blank** if you authorise the cell to remain empty.

♦ Click the **Error Alert** tab to enter a message to display when the data entered do not meet the validation criteria.

♦ Leave the **Show error alert after invalid data is entered** option active and set the following options :

Style	The warning symbol which will appear in the dialog box containing the error message.
Title	The title of the dialog box.
Error message	The text of the message.

♦ Click **OK**.

Any data which do not meet the validation criteria will cause an error message to appear :

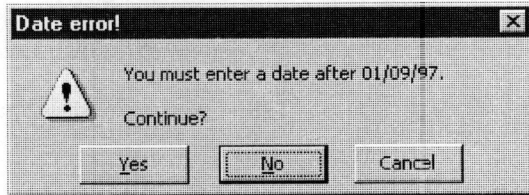

❏ *Data entered before the criteria were set are not tested (there is, however, an option in Excel which will find any data which do not meet the criteria. cf. below : Tracing unauthorised data).*

❏ *The options on the* **Input Message** *page of the* **Data Validation** *dialog box make it possible to display a message in a Screen Tip when the mouse pointer is on the cell.*

Tracing unauthorised data

This is a technique for finding cells containing data which do not meet validation criteria. Any cells found are circled in red.

Team	Region	Dates	Sales
Merchant	Centre	10/01/95	£100 833,00
Carlson	West	10/01/95	£104 167,00
Duffy	North	10/01/95	£152 500,00
Allen	South	10/01/95	£83 333,00
Herman	East	10/01/95	£93 750,00
Merchant	West	17/01/95	£10 400,00
Merchant	Centre	17/01/95	£80 837,00
Carlson	West	17/01/95	£93 764,00
Allen	Centre	17/01/95	£20 000,00
Allen	South	17/01/95	£83 337,00
Herman	East	17/01/95	£46 875,00
Duffy	North	17/01/95	£122 500,00
Duffy	North	24/01/95	£100 000,00
Duffy	East	24/01/95	£46 875,00

These cells should contain dates between the first and the fifteenth of January 1995.

♦ Display the **Auditing** toolbar :

Tools
Auditing
Show Auditing Toolbar

♦ Click [▦] then click the worksheet.

❏ *To remove the red circles, click* [▦].

**Using
the data form**

This form is used for entering records and for locating records in the database.

Going into the data form

♦ Click a cell in a table designed as a database. This table must include the field names and at least the first record :

♦ **Data
Form**

The form contains the following items :

(A)   Field names
(B)   Edit boxes for entering field contents
(C)   Data form fields containing computed fields
(D)   Command buttons

DATABASES

(E)	The number of the current record
(F)	The total number of records
(G)	Title bar
(H)	Vertical scroll bar

Adding records

♦ Start by clicking the **New** button.

♦ Fill in each new record as follows :

– press ⏎ to move to the next box (or press ⇧Shift ⏎ to go back).

– press Enter to confirm the data you have typed and go on to the next record.

Moving from record to record

♦ Use the scroll bar, or the arrow keys :

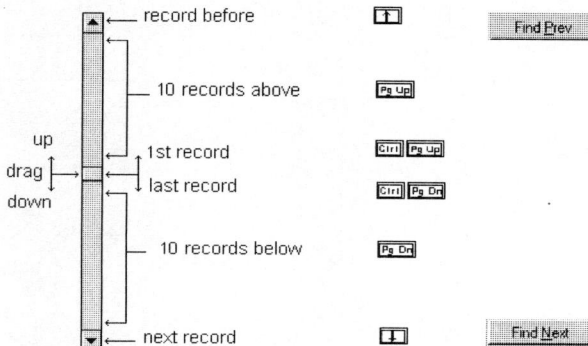

```
        ┌─┐ ←── record before        [↑]        [ Find Prev ]

        │ │ ──── 10 records above     [Pg Up]

  up     │ ├─┐ 1st record             [Ctrl][Pg Up]
drag ├── │ ├─┘ last record            [Ctrl][Pg Dn]
  down   │ │
         │ ──── 10 records below      [Pg Dn]

        └─┘ ←── next record           [↓]        [ Find Next ]
```

The last form displayed is always a new form ready to be filled in.

Going to a particular record

♦ Display either the first or last record.

♦ Click the **Criteria** button.

*The record number indicator is replaced by the word **Criteria**, the fixed data form fields become edit boxes and the **Criteria** button is replaced by a **Form** button.*

♦ Enter the search criteria as if you were filling in a record but without pressing Enter . For example :

♦ If you started from the first record, begin your search with the **Find Next** button. If you started with the last record, use the **Find Prev** button.

♦ Continue your search using the **Find Next** button or the **Find Prev** button.

Modifying a record

♦ Display the record to be modified.

♦ Make your corrections then press Enter .

*If you make a mistake click the **Restore** button, before you press Enter , to retrieve the former values.*

Deleting a record

♦ Display the record to be deleted.

♦ Click the **Delete** button.

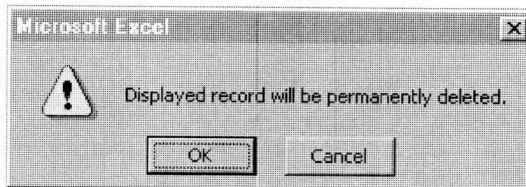

♦ Confirm the deletion with **OK**.

Leaving the data form

♦ Click the **Close** button.

Creating and using a simple filter

Using a filter, you can select records corresponding to a particular criterion.

Activating AutoFilter

♦ **Data**
  Filter
  AutoFilter

Each field becomes a drop-down list which opens when you click the down arrow.

Filtering by one of the values listed

♦ Open the list associated with the field concerned.

Sum of Sales	Dates						
	A	B	C	D	E	F	G	H
Region	10/01/95	17/01/95	24/01/95	31/01/95	07/02/95	14/02/95	21/02/95
Centre	100833	100837	100833	100833	100833	100833	75000
East	93750	46875	93750	75000	126563	126562	92000
North	152500	122500	100000	125000	125000	125000	150000
South	83333	83337	83333	83333	83333	125000	
West	104167	104164	104167	104167	100000	108334	104167
Grand Total	534583	457713	482083	488333	535729	585729	421167

Each list includes all the values in the field.

♦ Click the value that interests you.

All the records that do not concern the selected value are hidden. The number of records meeting your criterion appears on the status bar and the row numbers of the records displayed change colour.

Filtering by a value which is not listed

♦ Open the list associated with the field concerned.

♦ Click **Custom**.

♦ Use the first list box to select the operator of comparison.

♦ Activate the text box next to it and enter the compare value.

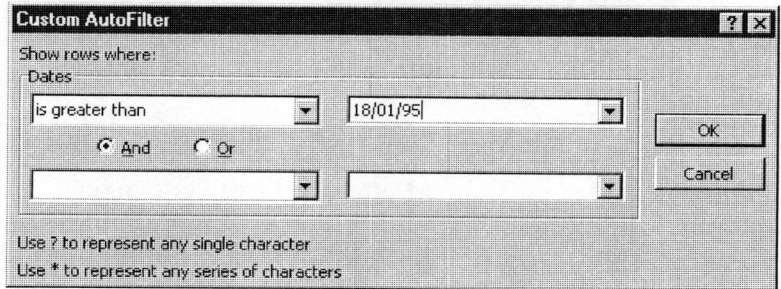

```
Custom AutoFilter                                    ? X
Show rows where:
 Dates
 [is greater than        ▼]  [18/01/95        ▼]        [   OK   ]
        ⦿ And    ○ Or
 [                       ▼]  [                ▼]        [ Cancel ]

 Use ? to represent any single character
 Use * to represent any series of characters
```

♦ Click **OK**.

Filtering the highest and lowest values

♦ Open the field concerned.

♦ Click (**Top 10...**).

♦ Indicate whether you want **Top** values or **Bottom** values.

♦ Specify how many of the top/bottom values you wish to see.

♦ Choose **Items** to filter all the records corresponding to the criteria (top or bottom), or **Percent** to filter a number of rows corresponding to a percentage of the total number of values in the list.

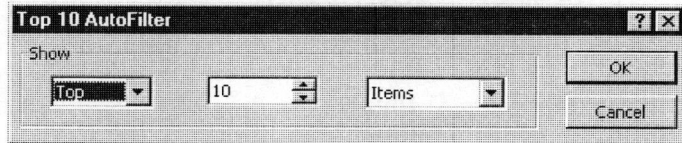

```
Top 10 AutoFilter                                    ? X
 Show                                           [   OK   ]
 [Top     ▼]  [10  ⬍]  [Items    ▼]            [ Cancel ]
```

♦ Click **OK**.

FILTERS

Filtering by several criteria

Two criteria for the same field

♦ Activate **AutoFilter**.

♦ Open the list for the field concerned.

♦ Click **Custom**.

♦ Define the first filter criterion.

♦ Indicate how the two criteria are to be combined :

– if both must be satisfied together choose **And**,

– if either one or the other must be satisfied, choose **Or**.

♦ Enter the second condition.

♦ Enter.

Criteria concerning several fields, combined with "and"

♦ Activate **AutoFilter**.

♦ Enter the conditions in each field concerned.

Displaying all the records again

♦ If just one filter is active, open the list for the field concerned, then click **All**.

♦ If several filters are active, use the command :

Data
Filter
Show All

Filtering by complex criteria

Creating a criteria range

♦ Create the criteria range in a space on the worksheet (typically, next to the database).

♦ Type a first row mode up of the names of the fields to be used in the filter criteria.

♦ Into the rows below, type the criteria paying attention to the following rules :

combination	method
OR AND AND and OR	the criteria are entered in several rows the criteria are entered in several columns the criteria are entered in several rows and several columns

The examples below will help :

Requirements	Criteria ranges	
Records concerning Central, Western and Southern regions : Central region OR Western region OR Southern region	**Region**	
	Centre	
	West	
	South	
Central Region records made by Lloyd : Central Region AND Lloyd's team	**Region**	**Team**
	Centre	Lloyd
Central Region records made by Lloyd or Allsopp or Carter : Central Region AND (Lloyd's team OR Allsopp's team OR Carter's team)	**Region**	**Team**
	Centre	Lloyd
	Centre	Allsopp
	Centre	Carter

Using a criteria range to filter records

♦ Click inside the database.

♦ **Data**
Filter
Advanced Filter

*Notice that the **Filter the List, in-place** option is active by default. For details of the alternative option, cf below : Copying records which meet filter criteria.*

♦ Click the **Criteria Range** box, use the ▨ button to minimise the dialog box and select the criteria range in the worksheet. Click ▨ to restore the dialog box.

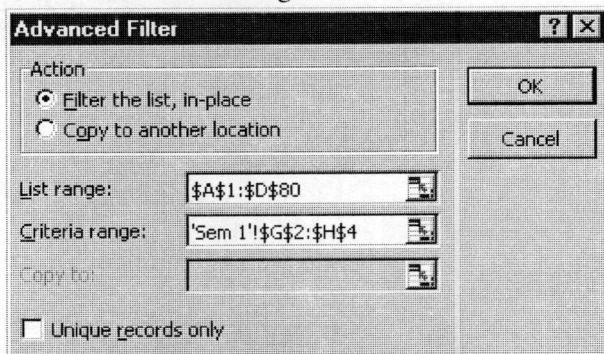

Advanced Filter	? ✕
Action	
⦿ Filter the list, in-place	OK
○ Copy to another location	Cancel
List range: `$A$1:$D$80`	
Criteria range: `'Sem 1'!$G$2:$H$4`	
Copy to:	
☐ Unique records only	

♦ Activate **Unique Records Only** to filter out duplicate records.

♦ Click **OK**.

❏ *The cells in the criteria range are now called **Criteria**.*

❏ *To use an exact text as criteria in a criteria range, enter the text expressed as ="= text".*
For example : To extract MARTIN but not MARTINEZ, MARTINELLI ... , enter the criteria ="= MARTIN".

Copying records which meet filter criteria

♦ In another location on the sheet, enter a row made up of the names of the fields to filter.

♦ Create a criteria range.

♦ **Data**
  Filter
  Advanced Filter

♦ Under **Action**, activate **Copy to another location**.

  The Copy to box becomes available.

♦ If necessary, indicate the location of the criteria range in **Criteria range**.

♦ Activate the **Copy to** box and select the row of names you have just typed in the sheet.

♦ Click **OK**.

❏ *If you change the criteria range, run the filter again.*

Calculating statistics from the records

These functions return statistics based on the records whose values meet the criteria in the criteria range.

♦ Create the appropriate criteria range.

♦ Use the following functions :

Function	Effect
=DCOUNT(database,field,criteria)	counts the cells
=DSUM(database,field,criteria)	totals the values of the field
=DAVERAGE(database,field,criteria)	calculates the average for the field
=DMAX(database,field,criteria)	extracts the maximal value in the field
=DMIN(database,field,criteria)	extracts the minimal value in the field

Replace :

– **database** with the reference of the cells containing the list of records (including column headings).

– **field** with the column heading.

– **criteria** with the references of the cells containing the criteria range. If you have created a complex filter, type the word **criteria**.

❑ *As soon as you change anything in the criteria range, the statistics are automatically updated.*

Making a Pivot table

A pivot table allows you to synthesise and analyse data from a list or an existing table :

	Region	10/01/95	17/01/95	24/01/95	31/01/95	07/02/
2	Region	10/01/95	17/01/95	24/01/95	31/01/95	07/02/
3	Centre	100833	100837	100833	100833	1008
4	East	93750	46875	93750	75000	1265
5	North	152500	122500	100000	125000	1250
6	South	83333	83337	83333	83333	833
7	West	104167	104164	104167	104167	1000
8	Grand Total	534583	457713	482083	488333	5357

This table calculates total sales by region and by date.

Creating a pivot table

♦ **Data**
PivotTable Report

*The **Pivot Table Wizard** takes over.*

♦ Indicate the source of the data for the pivot table. If the source is a database, leave the first option active.

♦ Click **Next >**.

♦ Select the cells containing the data used to fill in the table (this could be the entire database).

♦ Click **Next >**.

♦ Define the table's design by dragging the field buttons from the list into the appropriate areas (**PAGE, ROW, COLUMN, DATA**). For example :

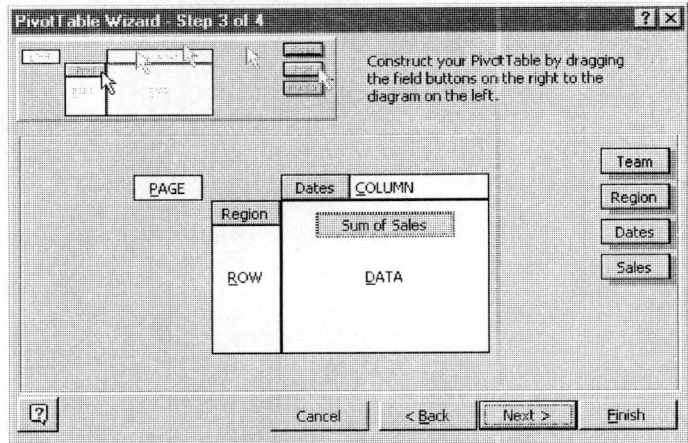

The table being created will calculate total sales by region and by date.

*The **DATA** area can only contain elements that Excel can use in its calculations.*

♦ If necessary, customise the fields included in the table by double-clicking the corresponding field button. For example, to change the function to something other than sum, double-click the sum button in the DATA box then choose another function.

♦ Click **Next >**.

♦ In **Where do you want to put the PivotTable** indicate whether to create it on a new sheet or in an existing sheet.

♦ Click **Finish**.

❏ *Although a Pivot table is linked to the list which is the source of its data, it is not updated automatically.*

**Modifying
a pivot table**

Modifying the contents

♦ Click inside the pivot table.

♦ **Data
PivotTable Report**

♦ Redefine the contents of the table, by giving different values for the options which you defined when you created it.

Updating and recalculating

♦ **Data
Refresh Data**

Changing the presentation

♦ Select the items you wish to format :

click here to select the titles

click here to select the whole column

click here to select the whole table

click here to select the whole row

	A	B	C	D	E	F
1	Sum of Sales	Dates				
2	Region	Mar	Apr	Feb	Jan	Grand Total
3	Centre	178250	192350	161750	200125	732475
4	East	93280	84590	100670	98850	377390
5	North	98850	100670	192350	178250	570120
6	South	178250	192350	161750	200125	732475
7	West	93280	84590	100670	98850	377390
8	Grand Total	641910	654550	717190	776200	2789850
9						

♦ Format the selected cells, in the same way as you would format cells in a worksheet (you can apply an AutoFormat to the whole table).

Grouping rows or columns in the table

♦ Click the name of the field by which you intend to group the data.

♦ Click the ⬜ button on the **Pivot table** toolbar.

```
┌─────────────────────────────────────────────────┐
│ Grouping                                  ? X    │
├─────────────────────────────────────────────────┤
│ ┌─Auto─────────────────────────┐   ┌─────────┐   │
│ │ ☑ Starting at: │10/01/1995│   │   OK    │   │
│ │                               │   └─────────┘   │
│ │ ☑ Ending at:   │10/04/1995│   ┌─────────┐   │
│ │                               │   │ Cancel  │   │
│ │ ┌─By──────────────────────┐  │   └─────────┘   │
│ │ │Seconds              ▲   │  │                 │
│ │ │Minutes                  │  │                 │
│ │ │Hours                    │  │                 │
│ │ │Days                     │  │                 │
│ │ │Months                   │  │                 │
│ │ │Quarters             ▼   │  │                 │
│ │ └─────────────────────────┘  │                 │
│ │      Number of days:  │1│    │                 │
│ └──────────────────────────────┘                 │
└─────────────────────────────────────────────────┘
```

In this example, the dates will be grouped by month.

♦ Indicate how the data is to be grouped.

❑ *To ungroup the data click the field name then click* ⬜.

. . . . *Personal notes* . . . .

Creating a macro

♦ If necessary, open the workbook concerned by the macro.

♦ **Tools**
Macros
Record New Macro

♦ Give the macro a name.

♦ If you wish, specify a shortcut key which will run the macro.

♦ Indicate where the macro is to be stored : in the current workbook or in a new one. If you want the macro to be permanently accessible, choose **Personal Macro Workbook**.

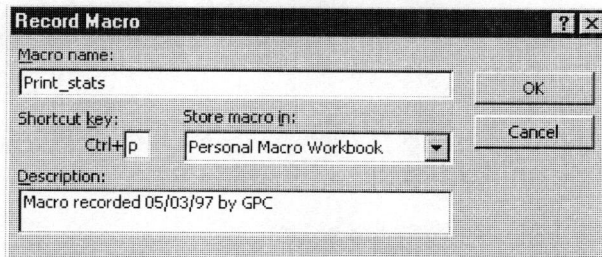

Record Macro	? X
Macro name:	
Print_stats	OK
Shortcut key: Store macro in:	Cancel
Ctrl+p Personal Macro Workbook ▼	
Description:	
Macro recorded 05/03/97 by GPC	

♦ Click **OK**.

*The **Stop Rec.** bar appears, and the word **Recording** appears on the status bar (you should check this).*

♦ Go through all the actions to be automated in the macro.

♦ When all the actions have been recorded, click the [■] button on the **Stop Rec.** bar.

❏ *Macros recorded in this way are created in a file called PERSO-NAL.XLS, where all personal macros are stored.*
This type of macro is always accessible as the PERSONAL workbook is automatically opened when Excel is started.

MACROS

Running a macro

♦ If a macro has been created in a workbook other than PERSO-NAL.XLS, open it.

♦ **Tools**
   Macro
   Macros

♦ [Alt] [F8]

♦ In the **Macros in** list, indicate where the macro you require is stored.

♦ Double-click the macro you want to run.

> *If the macro is stored in a workbook which is open or in PERSO-NAL.XLS, you can also run it by pressing the shortcut key defined when the macro was created.*

Opening an Add-In

These macros are provided with Excel but are not automatically loaded.

♦ **Tools**
   Add-Ins

As this option is also an add-in, allow it time to load.

♦ Activate the add-ins to load.

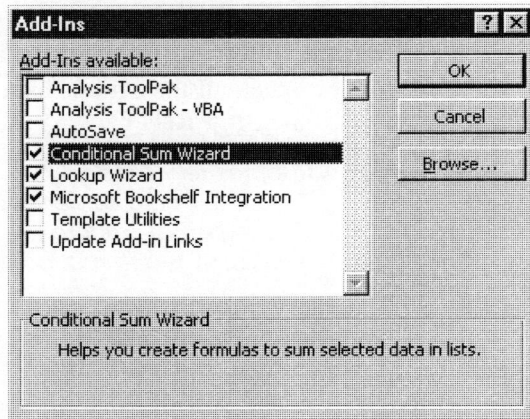

♦ Enter.

The name of the add-in being loaded appears on the status bar.

❏*Add-ins appear as options in different Excel menus.*

**Viewing
the contents of
a macro**

♦ If the macro is stored in PERSONAL.XLS, use the command **Window - Unhide** to display it, as you would for any other hidden workbook.

♦ **Tools**   ♦ [Alt] [F8]
  Macro
  Macros

♦ Select the macro, then click **Edit**.

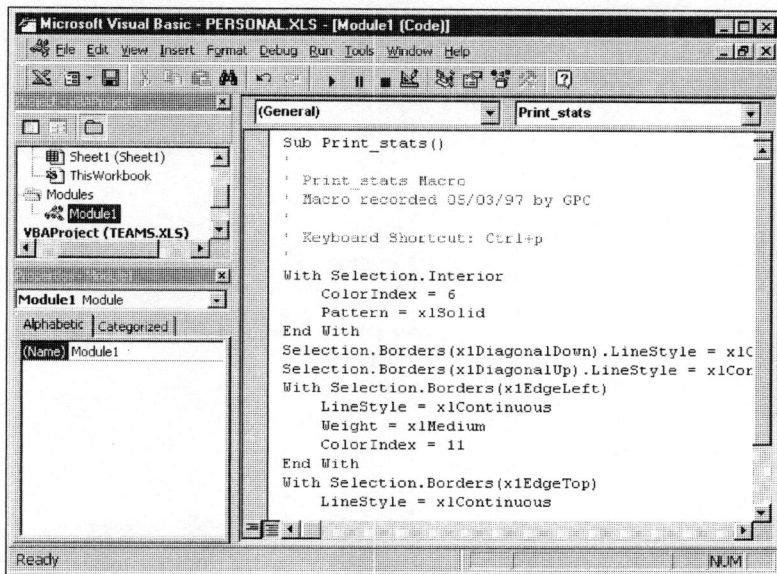

The contents of the macro, written in Visual Basic appear.

♦ When you have finished, close the **Visual Basic** window.

WORKING WITH MENUS

⇧ Shift F10	Display shortcut menu
	Document window Control menu
Ctrl F5	Restore window size
Ctrl F7	Carry out move command
Ctrl F8	Carry out size command
Ctrl F9	Minimize window
Ctrl F10	Maximize window
Ctrl F4 or Ctrl W	Close window
Ctrl ⇄	Switch to next window
	Application window Control menu
Alt F4	Close Window
Ctrl Esc	**Start** menu
	File
Ctrl N	New
Ctrl O	Open
Ctrl S	Save
F12	Save As
Ctrl P	Print
Alt F4	Exit
	Edit
Ctrl Z	Undo
Ctrl Y	Repeat
Ctrl X	Cut
Ctrl C	Copy
Ctrl V	Paste
Ctrl D	Fill down
Ctrl R	Fill right
Suppr	Clear contents
Ctrl -	Delete
Ctrl F	Find
⇧ Shift F4	Next
Ctrl ⇧ Shift F4	Previous
Ctrl H	Replace
F5 or Ctrl G	Go To

Keys	Menu
`Ctrl` `+` `⇧ Shift` `F11`	**Insert**
	Cells, Rows, Columns
	Worksheet
`F11`	Chart
	As New Sheet
`Ctrl` `F3`	Names
`F3`	Define
`Ctrl` `⇧ Shift` `F3`	Paste
`⇧ Shift` `F2`	Create
	Cell comment
`Ctrl` `1`	**Format**
	Cells, Object
`Ctrl` `9`	Row
`Ctrl` `⇧ Shift` `(`	Hide
	Unhide
`Ctrl` `0`	Columns
`Ctrl` `⇧ Shift` `)`	Hide
`Alt` `'`	Unhide
	Style
`F7`	**Tools**
	Spelling
	Macro
`Alt` `F8`	Macros
`Alt` `F11`	Visual Basic Editor
	Calculation
`F9`	Calc. Now
`⇧ Shift` `F9`	Calc. Sheet
	Data
	Group and Outline
`Alt` `⇧ Shift` `→`	Group
`Alt` `⇧ Shift` `←`	Ungroup
	Help
`F1`	Microsoft Excel Help
`⇧ Shift` `F1`	What is it ?

OTHER KEY COMBINATIONS

Individual data

`Ctrl` `;`	Enter the date
`Ctrl` `⇧ Shift` `:`	Enter the time
`Ctrl` `'`	Insert formula in cell above
`Ctrl` `⇧ Shift` `"`	Insert value of cell above
`Alt` `Enter`	Insert a line break
`Alt` `=`	Insert Autosum formula
`Ctrl` `⇧ Shift` `Enter`	Insert matrix formula
`Del`	Clear the selection of formulas and data
`Ctrl` `K`	Insert a hyperlink
`Alt` `↓`	Display list of AutoComplete entries

Working in the Formula Bar

`F2`	Activate a cell and the formula bar
`=`	Start a formula
`Ctrl` `Del`	Delete from insertion point to the end of line
`Esc`	Cancel a cell entry
`Enter`	Validate a cell entry
`Ctrl` `Enter`	Fill selected cell range with the current entry
`F4`	Relative and absolute references
`Ctrl` `A`	Displays the formula palette after a function has been typed in
`Ctrl` `⇧ Shift` `A`	Displays arguments and parentheses after the function is typed in

Formatting cells

`Ctrl` `⇧ Shift` `&`	Apply the outline border
`Ctrl` `⇧ Shift` `-`	Remove all borders
`Ctrl` `B`	Apply or remove bold type
`Ctrl` `I`	Apply or remove italic type
`Ctrl` `U`	Apply or remove an underline
`Ctrl` `⇧ Shift` `F`	Apply or remove strike through
`Ctrl` `⇧ Shift` `P`	Display font list

Formatting numbers and dates

`Ctrl` `⇧ Shift` ~	Standard number format
`Ctrl` `⇧ Shift` !	Thousands separated with commas ; two decimal places (0,00)
`Ctrl` `⇧ Shift` $	Currency format with two decimal places (# ##0,00 F)
`Ctrl` `⇧ Shift` ^	Exponential number format with two decimal places (0,00E + 00)
`Ctrl` `⇧ Shift` #	Date format with the day, month and year (dd/mm/yy)
`Ctrl` `⇧ Shift` @	Time format with the hour and minute and indicate AM or PM

In Outline mode

`Alt` `⇧ Shift` `←`	Ungroup a row or column
`Alt` `⇧ Shift` `→`	Group a row or column
`Ctrl` 8	Unhide/hide the outline symbols

Display

`Ctrl` 7	Unhide/hide the standard toolbar

Selections

`Ctrl` A	Select the entire worksheet
`Ctrl` `space`	Select the entire column
`⇧ Shift` `space`	Select the entire row
`F8`	Extend the selection
`⇧ Shift` `F8`	Add to the selection

Selection of individual cells

`Control` `⇧ Shift` O	Select cells containing comments
`Ctrl` `⇧ Shift` *	Select rectangular array of cells surrounding the active cell
`Ctrl` /	Select the entire array to which the cell belongs
`Ctrl` [	Select only cells to which the formulas in the selection make direct reference
`Ctrl` `⇧ Shift` {	Select all cells to which formulas in the selection make direct or indirect reference
`Ctrl`]	Select only cells with formulas that refer directly or to the active cell
`Ctrl` `⇧ Shift` }	Select all cells with formulas that refer directly or indirectly to the active cell
`Alt` ;	Select only visible cells in the current selection

`Ctrl` \	Select cells whose contents are different from the comparison cell in each row. For each row the comparison cell is in the same column as the active cell
`Ctrl` `⇧ Shift` |	Select cells whose contents are different from the comparison cell in each column. For each column the comparison cell is in the same row as the active cell

Moving from one window to another

`Ctrl` `F 6` or `Ctrl` `⇄`	Display the next window
`Ctrl` `⇧ Shift` `F 6` or `Ctrl` `⇧ Shift` `⇄`	Display the previous window
`Ctrl` `Pg Dn`	Move to the next sheet in the workbook
`Ctrl` `Pg Up`	Move to the previous sheet in the workbook
`F 6`	Go to the next pane
`⇧ Shift` `F 6`	Go to the previous pane

Standard Toolbar

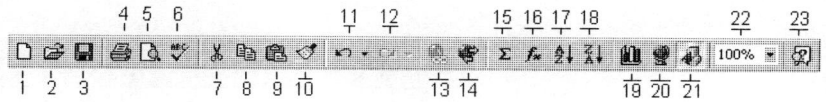

1	New Workbook	12	Redo
2	Open	13	Insert Hyperlink
3	Save	14	Web Toolbar
4	Print	15	AutoSum
5	Print Preview	16	Paste function
6	Spelling	17	Sort Ascending
7	Cut	18	Sort Descending
8	Copy	19	Chart Wizard
9	Paste	20	Map
10	Format Painter	21	Drawing
11	Undo	22	Zoom
		23	Office Assistant

Formatting

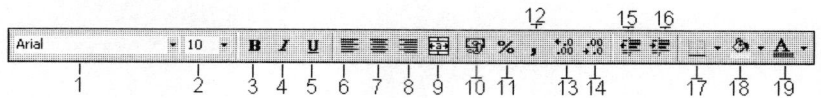

1	Font	10	Currency style
2	Font Size	11	Percentage
3	Bold	12	Comma style
4	Italic	13	Increase Decimal
5	Underline	14	Decrease Decimal
6	Align Left	15	Borders
7	Center	16	Fill Colour
8	Align Right	17	Font Colour
9	Merge and Centre		

Chart

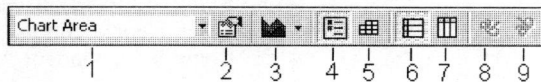

1	Chart Objects list	6	By Row
2	Format Selected Object	7	By column
3	Chart Type	8	Angle Text Downward
4	Legend	9	Angle Text Upward
5	Data Table		

Drawing

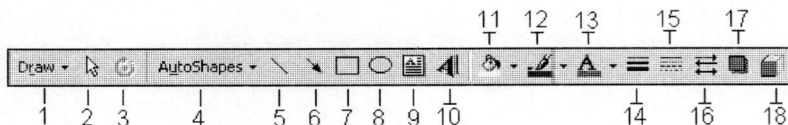

1	Draw menu	10	Insert WordArt
2	Select Objects	11	Fill Colour
3	Free Rotate	12	Line Colour
4	Autoshapes menu	13	Font Colour
5	Line	14	Line Style
6	Arrow	15	Dash Style
7	Rectangle	16	Arrow Style
8	Oval	17	Shadow
9	Text Box	18	3D

Reviewing

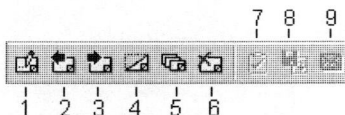

1	New Comment	6	Delete Comments
2	Previous Comment	7	Create Microsoft Outlook Tas
3	Next Comment	8	Update File
4	Show Comment	9	Send to Mail Recipient
5	Show All Comments		

Audit

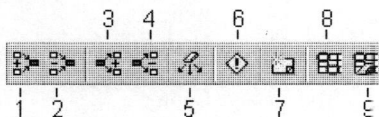

1	Trace Precedents	5	Remove All Arrows
2	Remove Precedent Arrows	6	Trace Error
3	Trace Dependents	7	Attach Notes
4	Remove Dependent Ar-	8	Show Info Window
rows		9	Clear Validation Circles

Picture

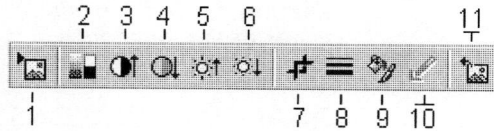

1	Insert Picture from File	7	Crop
2	Image Control	8	Line Style
3	More Contrast	9	Format Object
4	Less Contrast	10	Set Transparent Colour
5	More Brightness	11	Reset Picture
6	Less Brightness		

WordArt

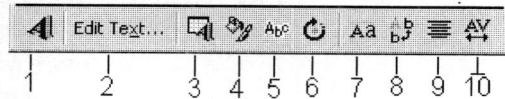

1	Insert WordArt	6	Free Rotate
2	Edit Text	7	WordArt Same Letter Heights
3	WordArt Gallery	8	WordArt Vertical Text
4	Format Object	9	WordArt Alignment
5	WordArt Shape	10	WordArt Character Spacing

PivotTable

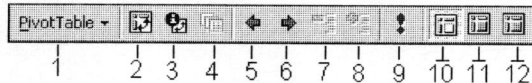

1	PivotTable menu	7	Hide Detail
2	PivotTable Wizard	8	Show Detail
3	PivotTable field	9	Refresh Data
4	Show Pages	10	Select Label
5	Ungroup	11	Select Data
6	Group	12	Select Label and Data

The text in italics to the right of the function represents the arguments of the function.

FINANCIAL FUNCTIONS

cost	the initial cost of the asset
salvage	the value at the end of the depreciation
life	the number of periods over which the asset is being depreciated
pv	present value that a series of futurepayments is worth right now
fv	the future value, or the cash balance obtained after the last payment; if it is omitted, it is assumed to be 0
Type	indicates when payments are due. If it is 0 (or omitted), the payments are due at the end of the period. If 1, they are due at the beginning
rate	the interest rate per period
nper	the number of periods for an investissment based on periodic, constant payments and a constant interest rate
pmt	the payment made each period
period	the period for which you want to calculate the depreciation. This argument must use the same unit as life

ACCRINT

(issue,first_interest,settlement,rate,par,freqency,basis)
Returns the accrued interest for a security that pays periodic interest.

ACCRINTM

(issue,maturity,rate,par,basic)
Returns the accrued interest for a security that pays interest at maturity.

AMORDEGRC

(cost,date_purchased,first_period,salvage,period,rate,basis)
Returns the depreciation for each accounting period.

AMORLINC

(cost,date_purchased,first_period,salvage,period,rate,basis)
Returns the depreciation for each accounting period.

COUPDAYBS	*(settlement, maturity,frequency,basis)* Returns the number of days from the beginning of the coupon period to the settlement date.
COUPDAYS	*(settlement, maturity,frequency,basis)* Returns the number of days in the coupon period that contains the settlement date.
COUPDAYSNC	*(settlement, maturity,frequency,basis)* Returns the number of days from the settlement date to the next coupon date.
COUPNCD	*(settlement, maturity,frequency,basis)* Returns the next coupon date after the settlement date.
COUPNUM	*(settlement, maturity,frequency,basis)* Returns the number of coupons payable between the settlement date and maturity date.
CUMIPMT	*(rate,nper,pv,start_period,end_period,type)* Returns the cumulative interest paid between two periods.
CUMPRINC	*(rate,nper,pv,start_period,end_period,type)* Returns the cumulative principal paid on a loan between two periods.
DB	*(cost,salvage,life,period,month)* Returns the depreciation of an asset for a specified period using the fixed-declining balance method.
DDB	*(cost,salvage,life,period,factor)* Returns the depreciation of an asset for a specified period using the double-declining balance method or some other method you specify.
DISC	*(settlement,maturity,pr,redemption,basis)* Returns the discount rate for a security.
DOLLARDE	*(fractional_dollar,fraction)* Converts a dollar price, expressed as a fraction, into a dollar price, expressed as a fraction.

DOLLARFR	*(decimal_dollar,fraction)* Converts a dollar price, expressed as a decimal number, into a dollar price, expressed as a fraction.
DURATION	*(settlement,maturity,coupon,yld,frequency,basis)* Returns the annual duration of a security with periodic interest payments.
EFFECT	*(nominal_rate_npery)* Returns the effective annual interest rate.
FV	*(rate,nper,pmt,pv,type)* Returns the future value of an investment.
FVSCHEDULE	*(principal,schedule)* Returns the future value of an initial principal after applying a series of compound interest rates.
INTRATE	*(settlement,maturity,investement,redemption,basis)* Returns the interest rate for a fully invested security.
IPMT	*(rate,per,nper,pv,fv,type)* Returns the interest payment for an investment for a given period.
IRR	*(values,guess)* Returns the internal rate of return for a series of cash flows.
MDURATION	*(settlement,maturity,coupon,yld,frequency,basis)* Returns the Macauley modified duration for a security with an assumed par value of $100.
MIRR	*(values,finance_rate,reinvest_rate)* Returns the internal rate of return where positive and negative cash flows are financed at different rates.
NOMINAL	*(efect_rate,npery)* Returns the annual nominal interest rate.
NPER	*(rate,pmt,pv,fv,type)* Returns the number of periods for an investment.

NPV	*(rate,value1,value2...)* Returns the net present value of an investment based on a series of periodic cash flows and a discount rate.
ODDFPRICE	*(settlement,maturity,issue,first_coupon,rate,yld,redemption,frequency,basis)* Returns the price per $100 face value of a security with an odd first period.
ODDFYIELD	*(settlement,maturity,issue,first_coupon,rate,pr,redemption,frequency, basis)* Returns the yield of a security with an odd first period.
ODDLPRICE	*(settlement,maturity,last_interest,rate,yld,redemption,frequency,basis)* Returns the price per $100 face value of a security with an odd last period.
ODDLYIELD	*(settlement,maturity,last_interest,rate,pr,redemption,frequency,basis)* Returns the yield of a security with an odd last period.
PMT	*(rate,nper,pv,fv,type)* Returns the periodic payment for an annuity.
PPMT	*(rate,per,nper,pv,fv,type)* Returns the payment on the principal for an investment for a given period.
PRICE	*(settlement,maturity,rate,yld,redemption,frequency,basis)* Returns the price per $100 face value of a security that pays periodic interest.
PRICEDISC	*(settlement,maturity,discount,redemption,basis)* Returns the price per $100 face value of a discounted security.
PRICEMAT	*(settlement,maturity,issue,rate,yld,basis)* Returns the price per $100 face value of a security that pays interest at maturity.

PV	*(rate,nper,pmt,fv,type)* Returns the present value of an investment.
RATE	*(nper,pmt,pv,fv,type,guess)* Returns the interest rate per period of an annuity.
SLN	*(cost,salvage,life)* Returns the straight-line depreciatioin of an asset for one period.
SYD	*(cost,salvage,life,period)* Returns the sum-of-years' digits depreciation of an asset for a specified period.
TBILLPRICE	*(settlement,maturity,discount)* Returns the price per $100 face value for a Treasury bill.
TBILLYIELD	*(settlement,maturity,pr)* Returns the yield for a Treasury bill.
VDB	*(cost,salvage,life,start_period,end_period,factor,no_switch)* Returns the depreciation of an asset for a specified or partial period using a declining balance method.
XIRR	*(values,dates,guess)* Returns the internal rate of return for a schedule of cash flows that is not necessarily periodic.
XNPV	*(rate,values,date)* Returns the net present value for a schedule of cash flows that is not necessarily periodic.
YIELD	*(settlement,maturity,rate,pr,redemption,frequency,basis)* Returns the yield on a security that pays periodic interest.
YIELDDISK	*(settlement,maturity,pr,redemption,basis)* Returns the annual yield for a discounted security. For example, a treasury bill.
YIELDMAT	*(settlement,maturity,issue,rate,pr,basis)* Returns the annual yield of a security that pays interest at maturity.

DATE AND TIME FUNCTIONS

The digits to the left of a serial_number represent dates, those on the right represent the time. Date serial numbers are between 1 and 65380 : the 1st of January 1900 and the 31th of December 2078.

DATE
(year,month,day)
Returns the serial number of a particular date.

DATEVALUE
(date_text)
Converts a date in the form of text to a serial number.

DAY
(serial_number)
Converts a serial number to a day of the month.

DAY360
(serial_number,end_date,method)
Calculates the number of days between two dates based on a 360-day year.

EDATE
(start_date,months)
Returns the serial number of the date that is the indicated number of months before or after the start date.

EOMONTH
(start_date,months)
Returns the serial number of the last day of the month before or after a specified number of months.

HOUR
(serial_number)
Converts a serial number to an hour.

MINUTE
(serial_number)
Converts a serial number to a minute.

MONTH
(serial_number)
Converts a serial number to a month.

NETWORKDAYS
(start_date,end_date,holidays)
Returns the number of whole workdays between two dates.

NOW
()
Returns the serial number of the current date and time.

SECOND	*(serial_number)* Converts a serial number to a second.
TIME	*(hour,minute,second)* Returns the serial number of a particular time.
TIMEVALUE	*(time_text)* Converts a time in the form of text to a serial number.
TODAY	*()* Returns the serial number of today's date.
WEEKDAY	*(serial_number,return_type)* Converts a serial number to a day of the week.
WORKDAY	*(start_date,days,holidays)* Returns the serial number of the date before or after a specified number of workdays.
YEAR	*(serial_number)* Converts a serial number to a year.
YEARFRAC	*(start_date,end_date,basis)* Returns the year fraction representing the number of whole days between start_date and end_date.

MATH AND TRIGONOMETRY FUNCTIONS

ABS	*(number)* Returns the absolute value of a number.
ACOS	*(number)* Returns the arccosine of a number.
ACOSH	*(number)* Returns the inverse hyperbolic cosine of a number.
ASIN	*(number)* Returns the arcsine of a number.

ASINH	*(number)* Returns the inverse hyperbolic sine of a number.
ATAN	*(number)* Returns the arctangent of a number.
ATAN2	*(x_num,y_num)* Returns the arctangent rom x- and y- coordinates.
ATANH	*(number)* Returns the inverse hyperbolic tangent of a number.
CEILING	*(number,signifiance)* Rounds a number to the nearest integer or to the nearest multiple of significance.
COMBIN	*(number,number_chosen)* Returns the number of combinations for a given number of objects.
COS	*(number)* Returns the cosine of a number.
COSH	*(number)* Returns the hyperbolic cosine of a number.
COUNTBLANK	*(range)* Counts the number of blank cells within a range.
COUNTIF	*(range,criteria)* Counts the number of non-blank cells within a range which meet the given criteria.
DEGREES	*(angle)* Converts radians to degrees.
EVEN	*(number)* Rounds a number up to the nearest even integer.
EXP	*(number)* Returns e raised to the power of a given number.

FACT	*(number)* Returns the factorial of a number.
FACTDOUBLE	*(number)* Returns the double factorial of a number.
FLOOR	*(number,signifiance)* Rounds a number down, toward zero.
GCD	*(number1,number2...)* Returns the greatest common divisor.
INT	*(number)* Rounds a number down to the nearest integer.
LCM	*(number1,number2...)* Returns the least common multiple.
LN	*(number)* Returns the natural logarithm of a number.
LOG	*(number,base)* Returns the logarithm of a number to a specified base.
LOG10	*(number)* Returns the base -10 logarithm of a number.
MDETERM	*(array)* Returns the matrix determinant of an array.
MINVERSE	*(array)* Returns the matrix inverse of an array.
MMULT	*(array1,array2)* Returns the matrix product of two arrays.
MOD	*(number,divisor)* Returns the remainder from division.
MROUND	*(number,multiple)* Returns a number rounded to the desired multiple.

MULTINOMIAL *(number1,number2...)*
Returns the multinomial of a set of numbers.

ODD *(number)*
Rounds a number up to the nearest odd integer.

PI *()*
Returns the value of Pi.

POWER *(number,power)*
Returns the result of a number raised to a power.

PRODUCT *(number1,number2,...)*
Multiplies its arguments.

QUOTIENT
Returns the integer portion of a division.

RADIANS *(angle)*
Converts degrees to radians.

RAND *()*
Returns a random number between 0 and 1.

RANDBETWEEN *(bottom,top)*
Returns a random number between the numbers you specify.

ROMAN *(number,form)*
Converts an Arabic numeral to Roman, as text.

ROUND *(number,number_digits)*
Rounds a number to a specified number of digits.

ROUNDDOWN *(number,num_digits)*
Rounds a number down, toward zero.

ROUNDUP *(number,num_digits)*
Rounds a number up, away from zero.

SERIESSUM *(x,n,m,coefficients)*
Returns the sum of a power series based on the formula.

SIGN   *(number)*
Returns the sign of a number.

SIN   *(number)*
Returns the sine of the given angle.

SINH   *(number)*
Returns the hyperbolic siine of a number.

SQRT   *(number)*
Returns a positive square root.

SQRTPI   *(number)*
Returns the square root of (number * PI).

SUM   *(number1,number2,...)*
Adds its arguments.

SUMIF   *(range,criteria,sum_range)*
Adds the cells specified by a given criteria.

SUMPRODUCT   *(array1,array2)*
Returns the sum of the products of corresponding array components.

SUMSQ   *(number1,number2,...)*
Returns the sum of the squares of the arguments.

SUMX2MY2   *(array_x,array_y)*
Returns the sum of the difference of squares of corresponding values in two arrays.

SUMX2PY2   *(array_x,array_y)*
Returns the sum of the sum of squares of corresponding values in two arrays.

SUMXMY2   *(array_x,array_y)*
Returns the sum of squares of differences of corresponding values in two arrays.

TAN   *(number)*
Returns the tangent of a number.

TANH
(number)
Returns the hyperbolic tangent of a number.

TRUNC
(number,num_digits)
Truncates a number to an integer.

STATISTICAL FUNCTIONS

AVEDEV
(number1,number2,...)
Returns the average of the absolute deviations of data points from their mean.

AVERAGE
(number1,number2,...)
Returns the average of its arguments.

AVERAGEA
(number1,number2...)
Returns the average value of a range of cells, including in the calculation cells which contain text, or the values TRUE or FALSE.

BETADIST
(x,alpha,beta,A,B)
Returns the cumulative beta probability density function.

BETAINV
(probability,alpha,beta,A,B)
Returns the inverse of the cumulative beta probability density function.

BINOMDIST
(number_s,trials,probability_s,cumulative)
Returns the individual term binomial distribution probability.

CHIDIST
(x,degrees_freedom)
Returns the one-tailed probability of the chi-squared distribution.

CHIINV
(probability,degrees_freedom)
Returns the inverse of the one-tailed probability of the chi-squared distribution.

CHITEST
(actual_range,expected_range)
Returns the test for independence.

CONFIDENCE
(alpha,standard_dev,size)
Returns the confidence interval for a population mean.

CORREL	*(array1,array2)* Returns the correlation coefficient between two data sets.
COUNT	*(value1,value2,...)* Counts how many numbers are in the list of arguments.
COUNTA	*(value1,value2,...)* Counts how many values are in the list of arguments.
COVAR	*(array1,array2)* Returns covariance, the average of the products of paired deviations.
CRITBINOM	*(trials,probability_s,alpha)* Returns the smallest value for which the cumulative binomial distribution is less than or equal to a criterion value.
DEVSQ	*(number1,number2...)* Returns the sum of squares of deviations.
EXPONDIST	*(x,lambda,cumulative)* Returns the exponential distribution.
FDIST	*(x,degrees_freedom1,degrees_freedom2)* Returns the F probability distribution.
FINV	*(probability,degrees_freedom1,degrees_freedom2)* Returns the inverse of the F probability distribution.
FISHER	*(x)* Returns the Fisher transformation.
FISHERINV	*(y)* Returns the inverse of the Fisher transformation.
FORECAST	*(x,known_y's,known_x's)* Returns a value along a linear trend.
FREQUENCY	*(data_array,bins_array)* Returns a frequency distribution as a vertical array.

FTEST   *(array1,array2)*
                         Returns the result of an F-test.

GAMMADIST   *(x,alpha,beta,cumulative)*
                         Returns the gamma distribution.

GAMMAINV   *(probability,alpha,beta)*
                         Returns the inverse of the gamma cumulative distribution.

GAMMALN   *(x)*
                         Returns the natural logarithm of the gamma function, Γ or $\diamond$(X).

GEOMEAN   *(number1,number2,...)*
                         Returns the geometric mean.

GROWTH   *(known_y's,known_x's,new_x's,const)*
                         Returns values along an exponential trend.

HARMEAN   *(number1,number2,...)*
                         Returns the harmonic mean.

HYPGEOMDIST   *(sample_s,number_sample,populatoin_s,number_population)*
                         Returns the hypergeometric distribution.

INTERCEPT   *(known_y's,known_x's)*
                         Returns the intercept of the linear regression line.

KURT   *(number1,number2,...)*
                         Returns the kurtosis of a data set.

LARGE   *(array,k)*
                         Returns the k-th largest value in a data set.

LINEST   *(known_y's,known_x's,const,stats)*
                         Returns the parameters of a linear trend.

LOGEST   *(known_y's,known_x's,const,stats)*
                         Returns the parameters of an exponential trend.

LOGINV   *(probability,mean,standard_dev)*
                         Returns the inverse of the lognormal distribution.

LOGNORMDIST	*(x,mean,standard_dev)* Returns the cumulative lognormal distribution.
MAX	*(number1,number2,...)* Returns the maximum value in a list of arguments.
MAXA	*(number1, number2,...)* Returns the maximum value in a range of cells, including in the calculation cells which contain text or the values TRUE or FALSE.
MEDIAN	*(number1,number2,...)* Returns the median of the given numbers.
MIN	*(number1,number2,...)* Returns the minimum value in a list of arguments.
MINA	*(number1,number2,...)* Returns the minimum value in a range of cells, including in the calculation cells which contain text or the values TRUE or FALSE.
MODE	*(number1,number2,...)* Returns the most common value in a data set.
NEGBINOMDIST	*(number_f,number_s,probability_s)* Returns the negative binomial distribution.
NORMDIST	*(x,mean,standard_dev,cumulative)* Returns the standard normal cumulative distribution.
NORMINV	*(probability,mean,standard_dev)* Returns the inverse of the normal cumulative distribution.
NORMSDIST	*(Z)* Returns the standard normal cumulative distribution.
NORMSINV	*(probability)* Returns the inverse of the standard normal cumulative distribution.
PEARSON	*(array1,array2)* Returns the Pearson product moment correlation coefficient.

PERCENTILE *(array,k)*
Returns the k-th percentile of values in a range.

PERCENTRANK *(array,k,signifiance)*
Returns the percentage rank of a value in a data set.

PERMUT *(number,number_chosen)*
Returns the number of permutations for a given number of objects.

POISSON *(x,mean,cumulative)*
Returns the Poisson distribution.

PROB *(x_range,prob_range,lower_limit,upper_limit)*
Returns the probability that values in a range are between two limits.

QUARTILE *(array,quart)*
Returns the quartile of a data set.

RANK *(number,ref,order)*
Returns the rank of a number in a list of numbers.

SKEW *(number1,number2,...)*
Returns the skewness of a distribution.

SLOPE *(known_y's,known_x's)*
Returns the slope of the liner regression line.

SMALL *(array,k)*
Returns the k-th smallest value in a data set.

STANDARDIZE *(x,mean,standard_dev)*
Returns a normalized value.

STDEV *(number1,number2,...)*
Estimates standard deviation based on a sample.

STDEVA *(number1,number2...)*
Estimates standard deviation based on a sample of the population, including in the calculation ...

STDEVP	*(number1,number2,...)* Calculates standard deviation based on the entire population.
STDEVPA	*(number1,number2...)* Calculates standard deviation based on the entire population, including ...
STEYX	*(known_y's,known_x's)* Returns the standard error of the predicted y-value for each x in the regression.
TDIST	*(x,degrees_freedom,tails)* Returns the Studen's t-distribution.
TINV	*(probability,degrees_freedom)* Returns the inverse of the Student's t-distribution.
TREND	*(known_y's,known_x's,new_x's,const)* Returns values along a linear trend.
TRIMMEAN	*(array,percent)* Returns the mean of the interior of a data set.
TTEST	*(array1,array2,tails,type)* Returns the probability associated with a Student's t-Test.
VAR	*(number1,number2,...)* Estimates variance based on a sample.
VARA	*(number1,number2,...)* Estimates variance based on a sample, including ...
VARP	*(number1,number2,...)* Calculates variance based on the entire population.
VARPA	*(number1,number2,...)* Calculates variance based on a sample including ...
WEIBULL	*(x,alpha,beta,cumulative)* Returns the Weibull distribution.

ZTEST *(array,x,sigma)*
Returns the two-tailed P-value of a z-test.

LOOKUP AND REFERENCE FUNCTIONS

ADDRESS *(row_num,column_num,abs_num,a1,sheet_text)*
Returns a reference as text to a single cell in a worksheet.

AREAS *(reference)*
Returns the number of areas in a reference.

CHOOSE *(index_num,value1,value2)*
Chooses a value from a list of values.

COLUMN *(reference)*
Returns the column number of a reference.

COLUMNS *(array)*
Returns the number of columns in a reference.

HLOOKUP *(lookup_value,table_array,row_index_num,range_lookup)*
Looks in the top row of an array and returns the value of the indicated cell.

INDEX *(...)*
Uses an index to choose a value from a reference or array.

INDIRECT *(ref_text,a1)*
Returns a reference indicated by a text value.

HYPERLINK *(link_location,friendly_name)*
Creates a shortcut that opens a document stored on a network server, an intranet or the Internet.

LOOKUP *(...)*
Looks up values in a vector or array.

MATCH *(lookup_value,lookup_array,match_type)*
Looks up values in a reference or array.

OFFSET	*(reference,rows,cols,height,width)* Returns a reference offset from a given reference.
ROW	*(reference)* Returns the number of a reference.
ROWS	*(array)* Returns the number of rows in a reference.
TRANSPOSE	*(array)* Returns the transpose of an array.
VLOOKUP	*(lookup_value,table_array,col_index_num,range_lookup)* Looks in the first column of an array and moves across the row to return the value of a cell.

DATABASE FUNCTIONS

DAVERAGE	*(database,field,criteria)* Returns the average of selected database entries.
DCOUNT	*(database,field,criteria)* Counts the cells containing numbers from a specified database and criteria.
DCOUNTA	*(database,field,criteria)* Counts nonblank cells from a specified database and criteria.
DGET	*(database,field,criteria)* Extracts from a database a single record that matches the specified criteria.
DMAX	*(database,field,criteria)* Returns the maximum value from selected database entries.
DMIN	*(database,field,criteria)* Returns the minimum value from selected database entries.
DPRODUCT	*(database,field,criteria)* Multiplies the values in a particular field of records that match the criteria in a database.

DSTDEV	*(database,field,criteria)* Estimates the standard deviation based on a sample of selected database entries.
DSTDEVP	*(database,field,criteria)* Calculates the standard deviation based on the entire population of selected database entries.
DSUM	*(database,field,criteria)* Adds the numbers in the field column of records in the database that match the criteria.
DVAR	*(database,field,criteria)* Estimates variance based on a sample from selected database entries.
DVARP	*(database,field,criteria)* Calculates variance based on the entire population of selected database entries.
GETPIVOTDATA	*(pivot_table,name)* Returns data stored in a PivotTable.
SQLREQUEST	*(connection_string,output_ref,driver_prompt,query_text,col_names_ logical)* Connects with an external data source and runs a query from a worksheet, then returns the result as an array without the need for macro programming.
SUBTOTAL	*(function_num,ref)* Returns a subtotal in a list or list or database.

TEXT FUNCTIONS

CHAR	*(number)* Returns the character specified by the code number.
CLEAN	*(text)* Removes all nonprintable characters from text.

CODE	*(text)* Returns a numeric code for the first character in a text string.
CONCATENATE	*(text1,text2,...)* Joins several text items into one text item.
DOLLAR	*(number,decimals)* Converts a number to text, using currency format.
EXACT	*(text)* Checks to see if two text values are identical.
FIND	*(find_text,within_text,start_num)* Finds one text value within another (case-sensitive).
FIXED	*(number,decimals,no_commas)* Formats a number as text with a fixed number of decimals.
LEFT	*(text,num_chars)* Returns the leftmost characters from a text value.
LEN	*(text)* Returns the number of characters in a text string.
LOWER	*(text)* Converts text to lowercase.
MID	*(text,start_num,num_chars)* Returns a specific number of characters from a text string starting at the position you specify.
PROPER	*(text)* Capitalizes the first letter in each word of a text value.
REPLACE	*(old_text,start_num,num_chars,new_text)* Replaces characters within text.
REPT	*(text,number_times)* Repeats text a given number of times.

RIGHT	*(text,num_chars)*	

RIGHT   *(text,num_chars)*
Returns the rightmost characters from a text value.

SEARCH   *(find_text,within_text,start_num)*
Finds one text value within another (not case-sensitive).

SUBSTITUTE   *(text,old_text,new_text,instance_num)*
Substitutes new text for old text in a text string.

T   *(value)*
Converts its arguments to text.

TEXT   *(value,format_text)*
Formats a number and converts it to text.

TRIM   *(text)*
Removes spaces from text.

UPPER   *(text)*
Converts text to uppercase.

VALUE   *(text)*
Converts a text argument to a number.

LOGICAL FUNCTIONS

AND   *(logical1,logical2,...)*
Returns TRUE if all its arguments are TRUE.

FALSE   *()*
Returns the logical value FALSE.

IF   *(logical_test,value_if_true,value_if_false)*
Specifies a logical test to perform.

NOT   *(logical)*
Reverses the logic of its argument.

OR   *(logical1,logical2,...)*
Returns TRUE if any argument is TRUE.

TRUE	*()*
	Returns the logical value TRUE.

INFORMATION FUNCTIONS

CELL	*(info_type,reference)*
	Returns information about the formatting, location, or contents of a cell.
COUNTBLANK	*(range)*
	Counts the number of blank cells within a range.
ERRORTYPE	*(value)*
	Returns a number corresponding to an error type.
INFO	*(type_text)*
	Returns information about the current operating environnement.
ISBLANK	*(value)*
	Returns TRUE if the value is blank.
ISERR	*(value)*
	Returns TRUE if the value is any error value except #N/A.
ISERROR	*(value)*
	Returns TRUE if the value is any erro value.
ISEVEN	*(number)*
	Returns TRUE if the number is even.
ISLOGICAL	*(value)*
	Returns TRUE if the value is a logical value.
ISNA	*(value)*
	Returns TRUE if the value is the #N/A error value.
ISNONTEXT	*(value)*
	Returns TRUE if the value is not text.

ISNUMBER   *(value)*
                    Returns TRUE if the value is a number.

ISODD   *(number)*
                    Returns TRUE if the number is odd.

ISREF   *(value)*
                    Returns TRUE if the value is a reference.

ISTEXT   *(value)*
                    Returns TRUE if the value is text.

N   *(value)*
                    Returns a value converted to a number.

NA   *( )*
                    Returns the error value #N/A.

TYPE   *(value)*
                    Returns a number indicating the data type of a value.

INDEX BY SUBJECT

INDEX BY SUBJECT

E

INDEX BY SUBJECT

INDEX BY SUBJECT

INDEX BY SUBJECT

W

Z

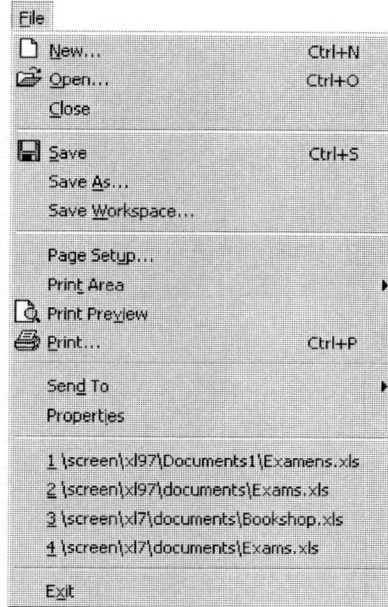

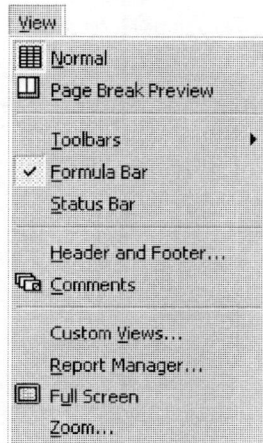

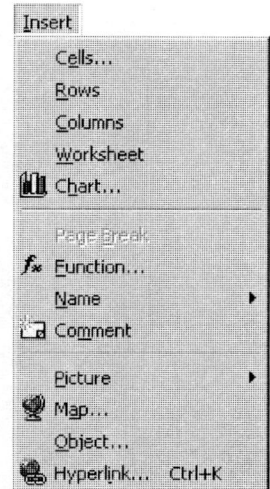

MENUS

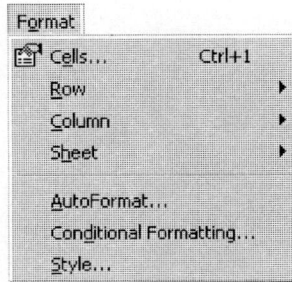

Format

Cells...	Ctrl+1
Row	▶
Column	▶
Sheet	▶
AutoFormat...	
Conditional Formatting...	
Style...	

Tools

Spelling...	F7
AutoCorrect...	
Look Up Reference...	
Share Workbook...	
Track Changes	▶
Merge Workbooks...	
Protection	▶
Goal Seek...	
Scenarios...	
Auditing	▶
Solver...	
Macro	▶
Add-Ins...	
Customize...	
Options...	
Wizard	▶

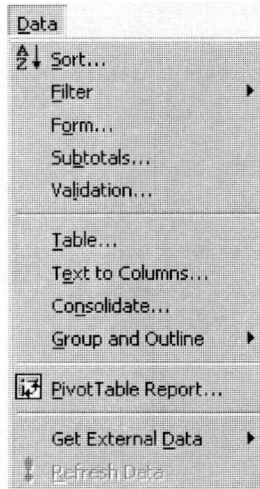

Data

Sort...	
Filter	▶
Form...	
Subtotals...	
Validation...	
Table...	
Text to Columns...	
Consolidate...	
Group and Outline	▶
PivotTable Report...	
Get External Data	▶
Refresh Data	

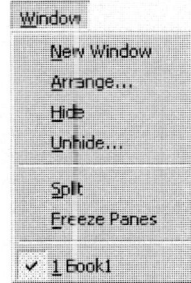

Window

New Window
Arrange...
Hide
Unhide...
Split
Freeze Panes
✓ 1 Book1

Help

Microsoft Excel Help	F1
Contents and Index	
What's This?	Shift+F1
Microsoft on the Web	▶
Lotus 1-2-3 Help...	
About Microsoft Excel	

Microsoft Excel 9